MAN'S BOOK

MILLS

Manning O'Brine

★

DANCE
OF THE DWARFS

Geoffrey Household

★

EAST OF
DESOLATION

Jack Higgins

ODHAMS BOOKS

LONDON

MADE AND PRINTED IN GREAT BRITAIN
BY ODHAMS (WATFORD) LTD.
S.170.SB.
SBN.600359581.

CONTENTS

MILLS

Manning O'Brine

*'Mills' is published by
Herbert Jenkins Ltd.*

The Author

Manning O'Brine has more than 100 TV scripts to his credit. After studying Art and Architecture at Rome University he worked as a scenic designer. During the war he served in France with the Resistance, then in North Africa as a secret agent. In 1943 he was parachuted into Montenegro to join the partisans and finished the war with the Garibaldi partisans in Italy. After the war he fought for Israel in the Arab Wars, managed an opera company, and wrote several thrillers. Still a believer in authentic background, he recently smuggled himself in and out of Albania to get material for *Crambo*, a second novel nearing completion. He now lives at Saltdean in Sussex.

For
SHELAGH
Ti voglio
tanto bene

PROLOGUE

1

THERE WERE no flowers on the coffin. Not even a twist of forget-me-nots. No mourners either, unless one counted the man named Mills.

He sat at the wheel of the Volkswagen following the hearse through the rainswept streets of East Berlin. He wore a dark suit and a black tie and a set purposefulness about his face for a task that had to be done. The rest, it seemed, had no interest in the passing of Ernst Reinecke.

Inside the coffin, Reinecke lay cold, stiff, hands folded on his breast, face waxen. As with death. Only he was not dead. He was very much alive, breathing through holes let cunningly into the woodwork. Uneasily, perhaps, in this macabre environment, but where there was life there was hope . . . and Reinecke was desperate with that.

He was going 'over' the Wall, into West Berlin and the British Zone. The one way it could be achieved without let or hindrance or the risk of a bullet from some trigger-happy Vopo. Or so Mills had told him.

Reinecke had no reason to doubt Mills' word. He was aware that Christmas goodwill was as dead as yesterday that summer, that East-West German relations were in the sourest of moods, and that even the cockroaches wore pro- and anti-labels. Only in death was there unity, the barriers down, both sides clinging to a maudlin obsession for the family grave.

Reinecke understood this. He had lived between the devil and the deep for more than twenty years, since the end of the war. A wanted man in both camps. In the West for the butchering of Jews, in the East for the liquidation of Czechs. His impartiality had helped send both to the gas chambers. And, like so many of his kind, he had escaped retribution, living under a false identity, as Willi Schultz, a small, insignificant cog in the machine of the Democratic Republic.

Time had been on his side. He had made home out of the rubble that was Dresden, had taken up with his landlady's daughter. Now they were married, with three children—a girl of twenty and two boys, sixteen and fourteen . . . What was past was past and except for those awkward moments when he had been asked 'What did you do in the war, Papa?' he had begun to forget he had ever been with the SS.

Then came the Eichmann trial, stirring up the slime once again, dirty ripples spreading outwards, names brought to light, old files seeing the dust blown from their covers. Yet Reinecke had not been unduly worried. Not until the past six months when a chain of arrests of ex-colleagues had grown too close for comfort. With the premonition that his turn was not far away. So he had walked out on his family and moved to East Berlin.

A move that solved nothing. Instead, a cold fear had taken root in his gut. He had sensed a net closing. The Czechs—in common with the Israelis—had a tenacious taste for hunting down former enemies. Lidice was as green in the memory as the grass that now covered the site. If the Czechs got him . . . Reinecke had no illusions that his post-war record as a good Communist would cut much ice in a Prague courtroom.

He had reasoned, therefore, that it might be better to flirt with West German justice if it came to the crunch. There were enough ex-Nazis in high places, including the present Chancellor, and pressure groups urging a general amnesty for all such as he.

He had put out feelers through an organization with contacts in West Berlin. He had let it be known he possessed information—scientific information, in the field of pharmaceutical chemistry.

In truth, no more than a sprat to catch a mackerel. Reinecke had been working in a laboratory back in Dresden, engaged on secret work, but his knowledge was limited—no more than any minor assistant could know about a major product. Yet if it encouraged the Americans or the British to help him over the Wall, that was enough. When they came to realize he knew nothing of value, he figured they would hardly throw him back . . . And his gamble had paid off. It had brought Mills to him.

To many such as Reinecke, meeting Mills for the first time must have been a disappointment. There was nothing of the fictional spy about him; no James Bond; not even one run to seed. A man in his late forties, medium height, stocky, tending to jowl at the face, his only outstanding feature a shock of prematurely white hair. Small hands, hairless, almost womanly, looking much too soft to deliver any kind of karate chop. Eyes a gentle bluish-grey, inclined to water—either from cigarette smoke or flush of emotion. Voice quiet, German hesitant—reluctant might be the better word—as if unhappy speaking the tongue. Dress sober, cut for comfort rather than style; no suspicious bulge at the armpit.

Yet a British agent. Reinecke had never entertained any doubts of that. Not before he entered the coffin, at least . . . and, paradoxically, one of the things that had convinced him was the lack of enthusiasm Mills had shown for helping him; off-hand and distinctly cool.

'What makes you think you have something of strategic value, Herr Schultz?'

Reinecke had come back glibly. He had worked on his story. No blatant lies, no extravagant claims. A blend of fact and clever half-truth. Enough to convince his listener he had knowledge of his subject, to hint that he knew a great deal more.

'If you mean in a military sense, I have no way of knowing. None, I would hope. I'm a man of peace who thinks all scientific knowledge should be shared freely for the benefit of humanity as a whole.'

Mills had smiled thinly.

'Another Klaus Fuchs, eh—only going the other way?'

'I wouldn't know about that, either.' Reinecke had shrugged. 'All I know is that chemists and physicians the world over are searching for treatments of certain mental ailments. They are delving into the chemical reactions involved in the process of thought itself. Drugs are being developed that will change the thinking patterns of the mentally ill and restore them to health.'

'You make it sound highly commendable. But to me it has the sinister smack of brain-washing.'

'You could put it that way. In the wrong hands there is always that danger. Yet the fact remains that in the not too distant future the motivations and emotions of normal daily life may be controlled and maintained in any desired state through the medium of drugs.'

'Perish the possibility! That day we'll all be reduced to zombies, except for those who administer the needle!'

Reinecke had trotted out the standard boffin reply.

'Whether such a state is desirable is not for the chemist to decide. It is a matter for the society we live in. Some, we may hope, will use the knowledge for the betterment of man——'

'—While others will use it to their own advantage . . . which is why you wish to defect, yes?'

Reinecke had nodded slowly.

'Fair enough,' Mills had continued. 'But tell me something about this drug you've been working on.'

Reinecke had shown the right amount of hesitation before answering.

'You have heard of LSD-25?'

'The with-it kick of the 'sixties? If that's all you have to offer, you're wasting my time. Given another year, it'll be old hat!'

Reinecke had ignored the flippancy.

'It stands for D-lysergic acid diethylamide tartrate,' he had said. 'A relative of the ergot fungus. A common disease in the seed of rye-grass. LSD-25 is not new in itself. It was synthesized as long ago as 1943. But since then there have been a number of developments. Two years back, for example, something bordering on a sensational breakthrough was reported from Prague. Security clamped down, dismissed it as an exaggerated rumour. However, they were astute enough to allow certain information to leak, to be scooped up by industrial spies and passed on to a laboratory doing parallel research in California. Information that was genuine in so far as it concerned a development of LSD-25. But it was one that had resulted in failure.'

'Why the leak-out?'

'Twofold. If the Americans had not already experimented on that line, they might do so and waste valuable time. On the other hand, if they were aware of it, they might be lulled into false security, believing that the Communist powers were not so advanced as themselves. Meanwhile, the real development went on in secret—and successfully.'

'So it has military significance?'

'I can only repeat—it could have.'

Mills had probed deeper.

'Chemical warfare? In the form of a gas?'

Reinecke had refused to be drawn.

'And you have been working on this in Leipzig?'

'No. Dresden.'

'Ah, yes, of course . . . where the china comes from!'

'There are other industries,' Reinecke had pointed out with a hint of sarcasm. He had gone on to mention the name of his laboratory and the man at the top. He had not expected this to register with Mills, but felt sure it would impress those who mattered on the other side. And it must have done. Their next meeting was much more promising.

Mills had sailed straight into the question of how best to get

Reinecke out. He had been at pains to stress that it would not be easy. Every day another loophole was being plugged. The underground movement was riddled with Vopo spies, the guards less conducive to bribery. He had come up with the mock funeral. Hearses were a commonplace occurrence going through the Wall, especially since the typhoid outbreak that August. The only formalities required were a death certificate and a written request from a *bona fide* relative in the western sector for the body to be interred in the family plot.

'All we have to do is find a suitable corpse,' Mills had said, 'and file the necessary application. Then we do a switch. You take its place.'

'And the relatives? They won't like that.'

'You should worry!'

Four days later, Mills had brought Reinecke to a house in Weissensee, where a gaunt old man lay stretched in death. Between them, they had removed the body from the coffin and dumped it under a pile of anthracite in the cellar. Reinecke, hands and face waxed white to simulate the skin of a corpse, had taken its place. Finally, he had been given an injection.

'As a chemist, you should know this drug.' Mills had made a mirthless smile. 'It won't harm you. It merely induces a temporary paralysis, giving the necessary rigidity to the limbs and lowering the body temperature. Just in case some officious snooper insists on inspecting the cadaver.'

Reinecke had looked worried.

'Is there any chance it will come to that?'

Mills had shrugged.

'If it does, I've got the necessary papers to prove you are dead. Rest assured, I'll see you through, Ernst Reinecke!'

Reinecke felt a shiver that had nothing to do with the drug.

'My name is Schultz . . . Willi Schultz.'

'Schultz . . . Reinecke . . . what's in a name?'

With that, Mills had screwed down the lid of the coffin.

2

WHAT WAS in a name? thought Mills, as he kept the Volkswagen close on the tail of the hearse. Twenty-odd years of avoiding justice, in the case of Ernst Reinecke. Twenty-odd years of living, breathing, eating, sleeping, knowing a woman. While his victims

were so much bones and dust in countless graves. Twenty-odd
years of fruitless search on Mills' part. Until now, at last, the man
had dropped into his lap like a ripe plum.

And by the merest chance. It could so easily not have happened. If the file had been passed to Glennon, for instance, or to
Zilahy . . .

Glennon might be one of the Bright Young Things in MI6,
with an Honours Degree in modern languages and a three-year
short-service commission in the I Corps behind him. But in truth,
he wouldn't know a war criminal from a wart on his backside.

As for Janos Zilahy . . . a Hungarian is always a Hungarian no
matter the colour of his passport. His interest in any job was
governed by what was in it for him financially, the opportunity
for the black market sidelines that were usually his cover.

But Glennon had been held back, pending a posting to the
School of Arabic Studies at Shemlan in the Lebanon, and Zilahy
had been given a DLB assignment. So it had come to Mills, who
had been sitting around for months on the Ku-damm in Westens
or the Uhlandeck or the Kranzler, taking *Kännchen Mokka*, reading the *Daily Express*, and watching the world go by; or lying on
his back in his bedroom on the Knesebeckstrasse, twiddling his
thumbs and wondering what the hell he was doing there. He
loathed Germany, but Berlin most of all: its brash veneer, its
soggy suet-pudding humour, its crocodile wailing at the Wall—
the biggest tourist attraction since Hitler's bunker. A purgatory of
his own making. For he had requested the posting for a reason
that had not worked out. And he was stuck with it . . . until the
Reinecke file had come his way.

At the beginning, it had contained no more than a vague note.
Some scientist (?) named Schultz had expressed a wish for
political asylum should he reach West Berlin and the British
sector. It might be genuine. Or it might be a HVA job, part of an
elaborate plot by East German Intelligence to infiltrate a key
man; or, alternatively, to blow the cover of a British agent—an
exploitable victory where they were so thin on the ground. But
Mills would know all about that—or should, with his experience.
Anyway, would he investigate and report. A photograph of
Schultz was attached for identification purposes.

The photograph had not been sharp, but something in the face
had rung a bell. Reinecke would have changed in twenty years,
even without the aid of plastic surgery. That was to be expected.
Nevertheless, Mills had had the feeling that this was the same

man. Some discreet digging into records of those on the Wanted list, a comparison of pictures, and he had been more than ever convinced.

There was one source he could turn to for complete confirmation . . . Moshe Singer. When it came to dossiers on ex-Nazis, no security department in the West could match the files of the SIS—Singer Intelligence Service. Operating from a two-room office off the Praterstern in Leopoldstadt, the old Jewish quarter of Vienna, it was world-wide in its tentacles. It had helped put the finger on Eichmann; it had brought a hundred others of lesser notoriety to trial. If anyone could add to what Mills already knew about Reinecke, Moshe Singer was that man. And there was no need to go to Vienna. As chance would have it, Moshe was in Berlin, staying at a small hotel in the Steinplatz.

'You ask me about Ernst Reinecke?' Moshe's initial reaction had been cagey. 'Ayeeeeh! You cannot hang a dead man, gelibter! Reinecke was buried in that train the partisans sealed off in a tunnel in the Dolomites. You should know . . . you blew the bloddy thing up!'

'Same old Moshe, same old answer. He *should* have been on that train. Only he wasn't. You know that and I know that. He was spotted in Villach a month after the war was over, then in Klosterneuburg the following August. And there have been other reports since——'

'And haven't I helped try to verify them? But always they are without foundation——'

'He is still alive!' Mills had made a fist on the table. 'And within a mile of where we're sitting!'

'So? If you know this, why ask me?'

'I want confirmation.'

Mills had passed the photograph. The old Jew's face had remained an impassive mask. He had handed it back without comment. Mills had tried another tack.

'Among your dossiers, you still have Reinecke's original SS file?'

Moshe had nodded.

'Complete with fingerprints?'

'Natürlich.'

'Then you can do me a favour. When you return to Vienna, look them out. I may have a matching set for you in a few days.'

Moshe had smiled, patted Mills' shoulder.

'That's what I like about you, gelibter—you never give up.

You should have been born a Jew! As for fingerprints, they would be nice . . . if they are one and the same. But for this, you will do *me* a favour. You will help me to keep my records up to date?'

'That goes without saying.'

'A dank. Un zol zayn mit mazl!'

Two days later, Mills had met Schultz for the first time. An impression of fingerprints had been a simple task. Moshe's answer had come by telephone. Schultz was Ernst Reinecke.

That same day, Mills had received a second message—from London. *Top secret. Priority. Schultz must be lifted out of East Berlin at all costs.*

From the urgency, he could only imagine that someone was having a baby over the information on LSD-25. A tip-off, maybe, that the MfS had not taken kindly to Schultz's disappearance from Dresden. Possibly, too, the GRU boys from Moscow were after him. The code-word HUGO that signed off the message meant a flap was on in Whitehall.

His own knowledge of Schultz's real identity he decided not to pass on at this stage. Whitehall would do no more than raise an oblique eyebrow. Adept with the long spoon, supping with the Devil was second nature to them. They could argue—in this case —that the Communists had already done so, that the Americans would, given the same opportunity. No occasion to denigrate Greeks bearing gifts, but to accept them—even if such acceptance carried with it a total absolution of Reinecke's past.

So Mills kept quiet, and got on with the job.

3

NOW REINECKE was on his way, sweating inwardly under the wax that masked his face. That Mills had used his real name had been an unpleasant jolt. A thought crowded in upon him . . . what if he had made a mistake? What if Mills was not a British agent, after all, but a Czech? It would mean not through the Wall, but back to Prague—shipped like that double-agent the Egyptians tried to smuggle out of Rome in a trunk! Only would they go to that trouble? He was trapped, screwed down in this casket, unable to raise a finger. . . . They might even bury him alive!

A ridiculous idea . . . claustrophobia was getting the better of him. So Mills knew his true identity; but what did that signify?

The British were not fools. They kept records. His name had been mentioned at the Eichmann trial. But they had a reputation for being fair. At the most they would only hand him over to the authorities in Bonn—a chance he had been prepared to take . . .

He sensed rather than felt the hearse grind to a halt. They must be at the Wall now. At that place they called Checkpoint Charlie. No, not quite; they still had to pass through *this* side, the Friedrichstrasse Kontrollpunkt. *If* they were at the Wall and not at the *bahnhof*, ready for shipment to Prague . . . Christ, no! Shut out *that* idea! Listen, concentrate . . .

Voices came to him in disembodied whispers. Impossible to make out what they were saying. Then the queer sensation of moving, the coffin sliding from the hearse, the uneven jerk and tilt as hands lifted it and shoulders humped it. Followed by a gentle bump as it was set down again.

But where exactly? In the guard-house? If so, why? Or was it the baggage coach of the Berlin–Prague express? He was back with that thought again. He strained for the tell-tale sounds, the clank of pistons, clink of buffers, escape of steam, shrill of a whistle—anything that might confirm his worst fears.

He heard nothing. Nothing at all.

The murmur of voices again, close by now, yet still unintelligible. He thought he caught the alien intonation of Mills' accent, a rustle of papers . . .

Of course. They *must* be at the Wall, going through the usual formalities. Yet why take the coffin from the hearse?

Suddenly, he knew why. A quick, light drum of fingers on the left-hand side of the coffin. The pre-arranged signal from Mills. The alarm. Then something tapped and grated directly over his head, a sound that turned his blood to ice water, gave him the urge to piss . . . a screwdriver, Jesus God!

They were going to unscrew the lid and take a look! We're not going to get away with it! Shut your eyes tight, Ernst Reinecke. But not too tight. Hold your breath, hold your bladder, and pray as you've forgotten to pray these forty years!

A prayer answered. Nothing happened. The screwdriver—or whatever it was—stopped grating. Another silence took its place. A long, drawn-out, toothache of a silence. Then, without warning, he was being jerked upwards again and carried away—left, right, left, right, he felt the lurch and sway—once more to be set down on a firm surface. Another light tap of fingers, on the right-hand side this time, the relax-all's-well signal, and he was ready to weep tears of relief . . . They've changed their minds! Mills—smart, cunning, *lieber* Mills—has talked them out of it . . . Oh, my dear friend, I'll never forget you for this as long as I live!

The coffin was sliding forward, smoothly, as if on runners. Back into the hearse, that was it. Came the distinct, dull thud of a door shutting, the low-pitched hum of a motor turning. They were on their way, through the Wall!

The mind fumbled for a prayer, a dim recollection from childhood catechism . . . Hail Mary, Full of Grace, Blessed Art Thou Amongst——

The first nine words. No more.

For Reinecke was shrieking in a split moment of searing, terrifying, overwhelming agony.

Then oblivion.

'Have you chosen a casket for the ashes?' the man at the crematorium asked of Mills.

PART ONE

4

MILLS LAY ON THE BEACH at Noli, on the Riviera delle Palme, cooking gently under the Mediterranean sun. He had posted three letters that morning. One had been to the Ministry of Justice in Prague, another to Moshe Singer in Vienna. Both told baldly of the demise of Ernst Reinecke. His file could be closed, energies conserved to tracking down some other war criminal.

The third letter had been to a Miss Naomi Pryce in Clapham, London, S.W. Mills had never met Miss Pryce, but one look at the envelope and the alignment of the stamp and she would know what to do with the letter. It would finish up on a desk somewhere in Whitehall, and would read of his resignation.

Whether or not the letters would be taken seriously was a moot point. With MI6, you didn't and couldn't opt out just like that. Once you were in, you were part of it until *they* decided you'd outlived your usefulness. Then, and only then, were you put out to grass—or, in some cases, *under* it.

One thing for sure: Mills knew he wouldn't receive an acknowledgment. Not on paper. It would take the form of someone either walking in on him at the *pensione* or appearing under the beach umbrella beside him, murmuring polite conversation in tones of chill affability . . . Now, then, old chap; what's this I hear? What's it all about, eh?

The letters to Prague and Vienna . . . Well . . . Moshe Singer would click his tongue and smile, pencil an inverted noose about the dead man's picture, thicken it into a question mark until he received confirmation from another source. Not that Moshe wouldn't take his word. He was just careful, that's all.

Prague? Mills hoped they would take notice, but he didn't much care. Reinecke had been sentenced to death *in absentia* as long ago as March, 1945, by a partisan courts-martial at Udine, Northern Italy. His crimes in that country had never reached the proportions of those committed against Czech or Jew. But only because he had not had the time. The war had come to an end. Indeed, the courts-martial had arraigned him on a single charge of murder—one Angelo Vitelli, a youth of sixteen, caught stealing a jerrycan of gasoline from the back of a German truck. Reinecke's punishment had been to pour the stolen gasoline over the boy and put a match to it.

The prosecuting officer at the trial had demanded the death penalty. The court had so decreed, the sentence to be carried out when and if Reinecke could be found. Mills had been appointed executioner. The trial had been correct, fair, legal, no matter what authority might say now. At the time in question there had been no properly constituted government in Italy. Only AMGOT —Allied Military Government for Occupied Territories. And AMGOT could scarcely claim jurisdiction over Udine, then under the Nazis and a puppet Fascist Republic.

When Mills had finally caught up with Reinecke and carried out the sentence, he had not been spitting in the face of justice. His method of execution might offend some sensibilities. Yet he would have argued that after twenty long years of searching he could be excused for showing a touch of bitter humour.

How he came to be in Udine, at the trial, is not pertinent to this story. The crux lies in another act of war: the battle for the *caserma* of San Martino a Montalbino. And the reprisals that followed. The motivation for his subsequent code of behaviour, the pattern for nearly half his life.

Yet he would have been the last to put it forward as an excuse, a justification, a defence of his own ethics or lack of them. He saw no reason to apologize, to justify, to defend. Rather he saw a parrotic misnomer called civilization—more accurately described as The Society We Live In—that was in no position to cast stones, to pontificate in moral judgment on the individual who chose not to go along with the pack.

As Mills saw it—East, West, North, South—the doctrine was fundamentally the same. The Good of the Country must come first, the Power of the State is paramount, let's all swim in the treacle of Togetherness, and Christ help the poor sod with a mind of his own. If being an individualist was anarchy, then Mills was an anarchist; if it was an act of treason, then he was a traitor. That he was subject to no one but his own conscience was a fact.

5

NINETEEN FORTY-FOUR saw Mills parachuted north of the Arno. His task, to co-ordinate partisan activities so that they fell into line with the overall Allied stratagem. He had found the Garibaldi eager enough to fight, but hopelessly under-equipped. One light machine-gun to a thousand men, and only every tenth man possessing a service rifle. For the rest—shotguns, sickles, knives, any weapon that could be fashioned on a blacksmith's forge. Colonel Giongo, who led one particular group, actually carried a longbow and a quiver of arrows. An archery champion, a crack shot at one hundred paces.

But this Tuscan Robin Hood, for all his guts and skill, was a sad anachronism in a world of Stukas and flame-throwers. And his men were far from merry. Each new recruit joining them in the hills did so in the knowledge that his family in the valley was open to reprisals. Being given nothing with which to fight soon raised doubts about the value of it all. Some had departed the way they had come; and who could blame them? Those who did hang on were men of the hills whose kin were close to hand, those on the run from the conscripted labour service, and the eternal optimists.

Mills had set about to change all that. He had signalled for supplies to be dropped, listing the bare necessities that might turn a raggle-taggle-gipsy outfit into something approaching a fighting machine. But he should have known better than to expect so much.

This was Italy. Churchill's soft underbelly. An underbelly with a shark's mouth filled with razor teeth, as was evident as early on as Salerno. Even at Cassino, where the ground gained could be measured by the shadow from a dead man's cross, the 'soft underbelly' idea had stuck limpet-tight in the minds of chairborne warriors. And with the fifth of June and the bells of Rome going ting-a-ling, they saw their strategy vindicated. Next stop Florence; Milan in a fortnight; over the Brenner to Berchtesgaden. Adolf, here we come. As simple as that. And seven divisions pulled out of the campaign and sent to the South of France.

As for partisans . . . Mills' appeal for help was answered. After a fashion. Three parachute drops by the Americans. One reached

the Garibaldi. The other two fell in an adjoining valley. It could
have been a crater on the moon. The Nazis got there first.

The British were more meticulous in their aim, less with content. He had asked for grenades and sten guns. He got mortar
bombs and ·303 ammunition. With neither a mortar nor a rifle
of corresponding calibre, he would have preferred a parcel of
Naafi rock-cakes. They could have stunned the buggers with them.

Colonel Giongo had remained philosophical. It was a beginning. They were not forgotten men. The next drop would bring
the mortars and the rifles. One must not lose heart, one must
retain faith in the Allies.

'Hal-le-lu-*jah* and up my perishing flue!' had been Mills'
comment.

That night he had put out his call-sign, blistered the air with
words not common to morse, together with his requirements for
the next drop.

He waited a week for a signal, for news that his request was
being met. Nothing came. Not so much as a soldier's farewell.

That resolved it. Giongo might go on believing in fairy god-
mothers decked out in red-white-and-blue. Mills had become a
cynical Cinderella. If the partisans were to dance at this ball, they
would have to find their own finery.

Mills made plans to do that very thing.

6

THE *caserma* had been some thirty kilometres south from where
the partisans were holed up. An artillery barracks built into a
scoop of hills, with a firing range above and beyond. Il Duce
himself had laid the foundation stone, returning months later to
cut the tape and unveil the fasces excrescence over the main
entrance. One of his customary flamboyances—the pisspot Caesar
inspecting his troops, gesticulating at the concrete columns, the
marbled mosaic floors, striding through the latrines, sampling the
cookhouse *pasta* with a nod and a flourish of salt, architect, head
chef, and sanitary wallah all rolled into one. A great gas for a
show was our Benito.

But that was in the past. The Germans had taken over the
caserma since—various units, depending on the course of battle.
At the time of the raid, it had been part of a motorized battalion
engaged on convoy guard between the railhead and forward

positions. One hundred and fifty men—according to the grape-
vine—a mixture of green kids fresh out of the Hitler Jugend and
old sweats who had learned to be cagey about dying for the
Fatherland.

Even so, the task had not been that easy. San Martino a
Montalbino was close to the Gothic Line. So close as to be inviting suicide, in Giongo's considered opinion. Mills had argued
that point in its favour. Hope lay in audacity. The last thing the
enemy would expect. Given a modicum of luck, a night assault
would find the bastards feet up, heads down, dreaming of
Gretchen of the Flaxen Hair—or dropping their drawers in the
nearest whorehouse.

And to sway the decision was the fact that one of the partisans—Tomaso Lucarelli, an ex-sergeant of artillery—had spent
eighteen months on the staff of that particular *caserma* and knew
it like the back of his hand. Including the less obvious approaches,
thus ensuring the maximum in surprise.

Surprise would have to make up for lack of weapons. From the
one successful American drop, Mills could equip a task-force of
twenty-five with automatic weapons and grenades. They would
carry out the actual attack. A second group, made up of riflemen,
would set up a road-block between the *caserma* and the village. A
third group—virtually unarmed, these—would stand by, ready to
move in and strip the *caserma* down to the last tripod-mounted
Spandau . . . if things went that well.

They did.

The Garibaldi went in under cover of a fine mist that swept
down from the hills, across the shell-pocked horror of rock and
scrub that was the artillery range—where only a sapling here and
there thrust a defiant finger skywards to make horns at the
stupidity of men—down to the pink-white splash of concrete and
glass that was the *caserma*. The mist carried them to the very
walls, and the sentries never knew what hit them. Cold steel,
mainly, driven hard between the shoulder-blades or ripped up the
gut. Only at one point along the perimeter was one of them wide-
awake enough to loose off a shot. An answering stutter dropped
him in his tracks.

Going over the barrier at the main gate, Mills cursed the
sound. It meant the end of surprise. From now on, it had to be
speed and movement—keep the enemy guessing where the attack
was coming from and its probable strength.

In the nearest barrack-room, sleepy, reluctant men stirred,

querulous at being disturbed. Mills swerved towards it, stove in a window with the butt of his gun, lobbed a grenade through the gap. Further down the block, two of his section did the same thing. All three dropped flat, hugging the wall, waiting for the crunch. It came in an upsurge of flame and shattered glass. The complaining voices changed their pitch to high screams of agony and fear—a signal for the rest of the section to jump forward to the smashed windows and spray the room with lead. Three sharp bursts, then one for luck and away—after Mills and the other two, already heading for the next target.

The officers' quarters. Mills came in upon one clad in pyjamas and a hair-net. He was yammering frantically at the bar of a telephone. A single burst from six feet flung the German bodily across the room. He slid down the wall slowly, clutching his chest, blood spurting crimson between his fingers, incredulity on his face. He was as dead as the telephone before he hit the floor.

This was the pattern of attack throughout the *caserma*—to give the enemy little time to think, beyond imagining they were hit by an overwhelming force. Deceived into that frame of mind, Mills reasoned that the old sweats among them would know when to cry *kaput*. The Jugend might prove more fanatical but much less battle-wise. Sudden terror in the dark, from out of nowhere, was not to be found in the training manuals; in no flight of fancy was this how they anticipated fighting for their Führer . . .

When Giongo and his party had moved in to strip the *caserma*, the only living German there had been a dying one. The parade-ground a bloody shambles, an untidy heap of bodies against the wall, thinning out to a scatter where some had made a break for it. In the barrack-rooms the wounded had been bayoneted or had had their throats cut. The sickly-sweet odour of death mingled with the fumes of cordite and burning oil.

Victory had been complete. The speed and ferocity of the attack had wrought the desired effect. Nothing less than the combined Allied armies had somehow swept through the Gothic Line and converged upon San Martino. Or so it had seemed to the enemy. Those who could still walk had come out shambling, dazed, hands held high, led by a lieutenant who, faced with an untenable situation, had thrown in his hand. The Jugend among them had broken down and begun to blub.

Compassion for the German was alien to Mills. As they were herded on to the parade-ground, he had climbed into a captured half-track, swivelled a machine-gun, trained it upon them. The officer who had surrendered stepped forward. He started to babble about articles of war and the treatment of prisoners. Mills had given him his answer. A short burst in the belly. Then he had raked the line with a methodical sweep of the gun . . .

7

MILLS' STOMACH told him it was lunch time. His watch confirmed it. He yawned, stretched, rose, pulled on a T-shirt, dug his feet into wooden sandals, and left the beach umbrellas behind.

Crossing the promenade and the coast road that ran beside it, he went under a railway arch and turned up the twist of steps that led to the Villa Fiorita.

The Villa Fiorita was modern, bright, airy, each bedroom equipped with wide French windows that slid back on individual balconies. Similarly, the dining room on the first floor gave out on to a patio that stretched the length of the villa. Below this, the main entrance opened on to a garden that was a blaze of late summer blooms, climbing honeysuckle, and lizards that scuttled at the slightest shadow. Beside the entrance, the wall rolled back to reveal a small bar.

At this hour, there were no customers. Only Gianni, the barman, wiping bottles with a damp cloth. Mills ordered a Punt e Mes. Gianni reached for the bottle, but came back with an envelope.

A telegram.

Mills ripped it open.

AUNTIE ASKING AFTER YOU COME HOME BILL BAILEY—JAY

Well, well. They hadn't let the grass grow under their feet. On to his whereabouts before they got his letter . . .

'Auntie' was just another way of saying the Old Man, the Big White Chief. Someone had once dubbed him Aunt Tatiana—the matriarchal Slav figure who dishes out treats and back-handers to unruly children. The Old Man had done most of his field service in the Balkans, so it had seemed apt at the time. It had stuck ever since, had become almost a code-word. Only the treats were rare with this Tatiana—a grudging compliment for a job well done. Do it any other way and there would be hell to pay.

The 'Come home, Bill Bailey' bit was just like Jay—Jay for John Herries, the Co-ordinator, whose main function was that of adjutant-cum-movement control officer. He prided himself in having a light touch with all and sundry, including that red-headed secretary of his with the long legs who looked capable of doing a Mary Rand around the office furniture, and probably had to if Mills knew anything about John Herries . . .

And now what?

He finished his drink, went upstairs to his room. He stripped, showered, put on slacks and a loose shirt, went down to the dining room. He shared a table with three others—an English couple named Sangster and a Miss Odell from Dublin. The proprietor of the *pensione* arranged it that way, putting nationalities of a similar tongue together. He probably thought it made for more sociability and easy conversation.

Mills was not overwhelmed with the idea, but had raised no objection. It could have been worse. He might have been placed with those three battle-axes at the far end of the room. The Walkyrie, he called them. They made more noise over their food than the whole Gottdämmerung. Fortunately for his peace of mind, they were the only Germans in the place. Apart from a pair of Finnish spinsters and a young Dutch couple, the rest of the guests were English, or English-speaking: a block booking from a travel agency in London. And Mairhi Odell was the resident rep who mothered such parties throughout the season.

For some absurd reason he had always equated a 'resident rep' as someone in her forties, ex-WRAF officer or something-in-the-Red-Cross material, with a bias to tweeds and brisk efficiency. He didn't doubt Mairhi Odell's efficiency; but beyond that, she was an anomaly. At least ten years younger than he would have expected, she was good looking, with deep-set grey eyes, thick reddish-chestnut hair, and that soft, unblemished skin characteristic of many Irish women. Her figure and carriage, however, were Latin rather than Celt—high-breasted, full-hipped, with a swing to her walk that had a man looking twice. Her grasp of Italian, too, was good, if not exactly *lingua toscana in bocca romana*—the Tuscan tongue in a Roman mouth—said to be the ideal accent. He guessed she had learned the language in or around Florence, though not from the best teacher, aspirating the letter 'c' . . . *hasa* for *casa*, *hasho* for *cacio*.

She was talking English with the Sangsters as Mills joined the table. Mervyn Sangster was around Mills' age, tall and very thin, an angular frame accentuated in daytime, by khaki shorts, boy scout stockings, and a small haversack perched permanently on his upper vertebrae. Eileen Sangster, by contrast, was a pixie of a woman, an inch over five feet in her brogues. But she possessed a tongue long enough for both of them, running on for ever, like the River Jordan. And before Mills had time to pour his first glass of *vino commune*, she was pecking at him with questions that required no answer.

'Hello there; you're late; where've you been? Mervyn and I walked to Spotorno, the next bay round; not a bad little place, more touristy than Noli; and would you believe it, we bumped into a couple who live not a stone's throw from us in Sussex— well—we live in Rottingdean *proper*, the old village, you know, and they live in Saltdean, over the hill . . .'

'Over the hill' was plainly equivalent to the other side of the tracks.

'Saltdean?' said Mills, as she paused for breath. 'Isn't that the Arab quarter of Brighton?'

He kept it dead-pan. Mairhi Odell choked a giggle over her *pasta*.

'Arabs?' Eileen Sangster stared. 'We've no Arabs in Brighton!' She made it sound like the bubonic plague. 'Some of the Chosen, maybe. But they get in everywhere.'

'Don't they so!' Mills tut-tutted. 'My uncle Israel complains about it all the time!'

He poured *acqua minerale* and passed it to Mairhi Odell, who was going crimson. 'Pellegrino is the best for hiccups,' he said. 'Cyanide is recommended for a non-stop tongue,' he added, in Italian.

Mairhi spluttered. Eileen switched her stare, suspiciously, sensing collusion.

Mervyn smoothed things over. 'Eat your spaghetti, dear, before it gets cold.' He had been surreptitiously chopping his own into short strands instead of twirling it around his fork. His voice was mild and dry, cultivated over years of trying to get a word in edgeways.

A plate of *pasta* appeared in front of Mills. Mairhi passed the *parmesan* dish, avoiding his eye.

'What did you do?' asked Mervyn. 'Have a bathe?'

'Slept, mostly,' said Mills, sprinkling cheese. 'I've a lot to catch up on.'

Mervyn nodded.

'Fairly enervating, the air. Haven't done one-half the walking we planned. Still, we must tackle the old castello before we leave. Started up there yesterday evening, as a matter of fact. Got to a point just past the church, then decided it would be dark before we reached the top, so it was hardly worth it.'

'You wouldn't have reached the castello by that path, I'm afraid,' said Mairhi, her composure recovered. 'It only leads to the cemetery.'

'Surely not——'

Eileen came back into the fray. But Mairhi overrode her firmly.

'The path you want climbs up from the little piazza, this side of the church——'

'Which also leads to the cemetery,' murmured Mills. 'Unless you watch your step! It's no more than a scatter of rubble.'

He caught Mairhi eyeing him oddly.

'Oh . . . you do know it?' she said.

'Yes . . . but not recently, I'll admit. It could have been improved, I suppose.'

'You've been to Noli before, then?' asked Mervyn.

Mills nodded, went on eating.

'When, exactly?' asked Mairhi.

He smiled at her. 'A long time ago. When you were a schoolgirl in plaits, probably. If, indeed, you had started school.'

'Nineteen forty-five, perhaps?'

His smile broadened. 'Either I guessed well . . . or you did.'

'Nineteen forty-five, eh?' mused Mervyn. 'The end of the war. With the forces, I suppose?'

'No. Not with the forces.'

'Of course not. There wasn't much action around here, was there? I mean, the Allies—once they took Genoa—they bashed on up towards Milan, then it was all over——'

'Mervyn was out here, you understand.' Eileen was putting it to Mairhi as if her husband had been an army in himself. 'He knows all about the fighting in Italy——'

'Not really, dear——' Mervyn cut her short for once. He turned back to Mills. 'I was 56 Div. Copped a blighty one at the Garigliano. But you were here in forty-five . . . though not with the forces.'

An unspoken question-mark in the voice showed curiosity he was too polite to put direct.

'I was with the Garibaldi. The partisans,' said Mills.

'I read about them,' said Eileen. 'They killed Mussolini and that woman of his, then hung them upside down for everyone to see.' She pursed her lips in a grimace. 'What a dreadful thing to do! I mean, he may have been awful and all that. But there you are. What can you expect from Communists?' She darted Mills an accusing look.

His answer came quietly.

'Not every partisan was a Communist.'

'All the same'—Eileen was sticking to her guns—'reds or no reds, they still did horrible things when the war was over. I mean, the way they took vengeance on the Fascists.'

'You don't think the Fascists deserved it?'

'Maybe they did, maybe they didn't. But that's no excuse for hunting them down like animals. There's such a thing as proper justice.'

'Justice . . . the old girl with the blindfold.'

Eileen pursed her lips again. 'Naturally you would say that—if you were one of those who hanged Mussolini. Is that what brought you to Noli in nineteen forty-five?'

'Really, dear,' muttered Mervyn. 'There's no need to become personal——'

'I've no objection,' said Mills. 'Mussolini was caught near Como. I came here for another reason——'

He paused. He felt Mairhi Odell's grey eyes upon him. For some reason—he wasn't sure why—he suddenly had no desire to pursue the matter.

8

THE REPUBLICAN FASCIST SECRETARY in San Martino a Montalbino had been Vincenzo Colapassa, a native of Savona, near Noli. The locals had quickly twisted the name into Culopuzza. An epithet only his mistress, Nella Barbiscio, could have answered with certainty. He had been wound in her embrace at the time of the raid on the *caserma* . . .

The sound of gunfire brought his copulative exertions to an abrupt halt. He bounced out of bed and across to the window. He threw back the shutters and peered out. Flames singed the low-lying clouds beyond the trees. The gunfire grew more intense.

Colapassa wasn't the only one aware of it. Down in the street, below his window, people flitted aimlessly, white-moths in their night-attire, this way and that, men shouting, women squealing supplications to the Madonna, children crying. He saw Dom Teodoro, the old priest, his soutane pulled on in such haste it was still rucked up at the back, showing an indecent length of long woollen drawers. Dom Teodoro rapped the cobbles with the stick that gave support to his arthritic leg.

'What is going on?' he demanded loudly of nobody in particular.

The answer came back.

'The liberation! The Allies are coming! Viva Italia!'

'The church, Dom Teodoro!' Another shout. 'Let's ring the bells! The americani will be here any minute!'

Jesu, this is it, thought Colapassa, ducking back inside the room. He turned to Nella, still on the bed, knees drawn up, legs wide and inviting. He flapped a hand at her bare backside.

'Get up, slut! They say the americani have blown up the caserma and are moving down the road!'

'The americani?'

Nella unhitched her nightdress from the bedpost, dropped it over her head. As it slid down her thighs, she moved towards the window. Well, it had to come some time, she consoled herself. And if it had to be the Allies, better it was the americani. She didn't know for sure, but rumour had it they were more generous than the English. She'd have to get her hooks into one before the locals got around to her with scissors and razor and scragged her bald. That was a thought. Not a pleasant one. It had her all of a shiver . . .

'For God's sake, woman!' cut in the voice of Colapassa. 'Can't you see there isn't a moment to lose? I've got to get away fast or it's——' He made a nervous chop with the side of his hand.

'*You've* got to get away? What about me?' Her thoughts were still with the scissors and razor. 'I don't figure in your plans any more. Is that it?' Her voice began to shrill.

He stepped across, fetched her a back-hander across the mouth.

'Get dressed, you stupid cow! Of course you come with me. Did I ever say otherwise?' He paused, listened. 'Hear that?'

The church bells had started their tinny, monotonous jangle. Nella stopped whimpering, rummaged around for underclothes. The very sound put the fear of God into her. As she got one leg in her drawers, she had the sudden urge to make water. She dragged the chamber out from under the bed, squatted over it.

Colapassa glared down at her. 'You choose a bloody fine time for that!' he yelled, impatiently. 'Cut it short and get moving!'

Nella Barbiscio was not the only one disturbed by the church bells. Lieutenant Orti, in command of the road block party, looked at Guglielmo Serato, his second-in-command, with some alarm.

'Porco miseria! Che successo?'

Serato, a grizzled veteran from the Bersaglieri, gave him back a sour smile.

'My guess is they think it's the liberation. They'll have the flags out for us inside the hour!'

'And draped over our coffins!' grunted Orti. 'That's how it'll be if the tedeschi get the message. They'll swarm like bees. Take two men and put a stop to it before it's too late.'

Serato and his comrades went off down the road at a regimental trot. Coming to the outskirts of the village, a ragged cheer went up from windows and doorways—a cheer that sighed away in puzzled disappointment as no others appeared behind them. These three didn't look like americani. Where were the field guns and the tanks?

There was no time to answer shouted questions. The trio ran on, through the main street and up the steps of the church. Dom Teodoro had lit candles and was on his knees at the altar rail, leading a huddle of womenfolk in prayer. 'Holy Mary, Mother of God, pray for us sinners . . .' It rose and fell, a hollow hum against the clamour of the bells. Heads turned, the catechism faltered in its stride at the sight of three ragged, unshaven men strung with bandoliers and gripping rifles.

Dom Teodoro rose, came towards them, limping heavily without the aid of his stick. His eyes fluttered over the red kerchief at Serato's throat. There was a transparent thought in that look that made Serato remove his cap and cross himself. His companions followed suit. Dom Teodoro inclined his head, accepting this belated recognition of the house of God.

'What is it you want, figli miei?' he asked.

'The bells, Father,' said Serato. 'They must stop.'

The old priest's eyes came back again to the red kerchief. 'The bells belong to God,' he said, simply, as if that was the end of the matter.

'È vero,' said Serato, diplomatically. 'But God does not pay out on Saturday. Only the German devils will—if they hear them!'

This twist on an old proverb might have brought the flicker of a smile from Dom Teodoro at any other time. But a more troubled thought set his lips in a thin line.

'This, then, is not the liberation?'

'No, Father, I'm afraid not—yet.'

'That is God's will,' Dom Teodoro flipped his hand in a little gesture. 'And you, I suppose, must do yours.'

'Thank you, Father,' said Serato, and headed for the belfry.

'The bells have stopped,' said Nella, twisting her head to look back over her shoulder. She was beside Colapassa in his Fiat, heading for the highway.

'So what?'

'So it could have been a false alarm.'

Colapassa raised his eyes from the road, peered into the rear mirror. The sky flamed angrily above the trees behind them. An occasional crackle of gunfire came down on the wind.

'The fighting isn't,' he said drily. 'We're well out of that!'

Nella gazed at his profile, a mocking smile on her mouth. Why had she taken up with this pompous jackal? No Fascist, she. Never had been. Politics were a bore. Not the glamour of the uniform. He didn't wear it well—and no chin to thrust out like Mussolini. Some kind of dream, perhaps, of being another Claretta Petachi? That one was an intelligent girl, by all accounts, yet she had fallen for a man twice her age. Still, they did say our Benito was a stag with the women. Took them across his desk in the Palazzo Venezia, on the marbled floor, or up against the wall, without so much as a by-your-leave or the undoing of more than a pair of fly-buttons. Now Vincenzo, here, he wasn't all that marvellous in bed. Always rushing at it, bom, bom, in and out, over and done with, gasping like a stranded fish just when she was whetting her appetite . . .

Her smile developed into a sneer of contempt.

'I thought the Mai Morti were not afraid to die!' She thrust home the barb. 'Or is it a case of Chi si ferma è perduto?'

This sarcastic use of one of Il Duce's slogans brought a snarl to Colapassa's throat.

'Stop or go, I won't be lost!' He flung the words at her as he wrenched at the wheel, skidding the Fiat northwards on to the highway. 'And if, as you say, it is a false alarm, I'll be back! Then God help them!'

9

NINETY MINUTES LATER, Mills had driven into San Martino with
Lucarelli at the wheel of a German staff car. No cheering at the
windows. The doors shut. The only movement on the street the
men of the road-block party, taking up fresh positions, eyes
peeled for Fascist militia or *carabinieri*.

Mills glanced about him. He felt a sense of death more manifest
than all the corpses up at the *caserma*. A brooding disquiet, an
atmosphere of foreboding. One could almost hear the beating
wings of the Dark Angel, see him perched on top of the *campanile*, a vulture, waiting . . .

Lucarelli's eyes met Mills' in troubled understanding. The
elation of victory had gone sour, the honeymoon was over. They
had danced at the wedding, taken the bride's maidenhead. Now
they were calling on the bride's father with the bill for the
reception.

Lucarelli climbed from the car, moved across the *piazza*
towards the one and only inn. What he had to do had to be done
quickly. Mills wanted a meeting with the most influential men of
the village. Lucarelli wasn't sure who they might be, but he knew
one who could be relied upon to help. Battista Tognazzi, the
innkeeper.

Mills climbed out, turned towards the church. Serato came
down the steps to meet him. He had stayed on to ensure the bells
remained silent. He saluted.

'Lieutenant Orti's order——' he started to explain.

'I know,' said Mills. 'You did well, Guglielmo. No trouble, I
hope?'

Serato cocked a horny thumb, grinned.

'At first he took me for a mangiapreti——' He fingered his
kerchief. 'But when I explained, he saw the point.'

Mills smoothed the square of silk about his own throat.

'Let's hope he won't take me for a priest-eater, too!'

He went up the steps . . .

Ten minutes later, he crossed to the Osteria Il Buco with Dom
Teodoro at his side. Lucarelli had gathered a dozen men. They
were joined a few moments later by a man in his shirtsleeves.

Doctor Cifariello had been on his way to the inn at the same time as the partisans struck the *caserma*. The purpose of that visit was plain. The thin wail of a new-born child filtered down from a room above, and the smirk of pride on the face of their host—genial, rotund Tognazzi—gave clue to the paternity and sex of the infant. A *maschio*, the fourth in a row and the sixth boy in a family of eight. Mills apologized—inopportune, under the circumstances. Tognazzi dismissed it with a friendly grin, drew him a glass of wine with which to wet the baby's head.

No further time was wasted on courtesies. Mills had already explained his business to Dom Teodoro. The rest had a shrewd inkling what it was all about. A military operation against the *caserma*, a successful one. But the Garibaldi were not in sufficient strength to hold the area. They had to withdraw. Mills offered no illusions as to the outcome. The fact that the populace of San Martino had taken no part in the affair would cut no ice with the enemy.

With no partisans around on whom to take reprisals, they would almost surely turn on the village. He was sorry, but that was the blunt truth. All he could offer was an escort to those who might wish to move higher into the mountains, where they might find comparative safety until the Allies liberated the area.

The villagers listened to him gravely, without interruption. When he finished, most eyes turned to Dom Teodoro, advancing him the courtesy to speak first. But the old priest showed no such inclination. His lips moved, but only in silent prayer, gnarled fingers slipping the rosary beads.

It was Gianoli, the schoolmaster, a streak of green ribbon in his lapel and an empty left sleeve, who put the first question.

'How soon can we expect the Allies?'

The inevitable one, thought Mills wrily.

'A month—maybe three. I cannot say. I'm not a general.'

'Maybe not until next spring!'

This was Rocca, the humpty-dumpty-shaped cheesemaker. He spoke with a mixture of cynicism and disgust.

Gianoli was quick to support Mills.

'The terrain is difficult, much easier to defend than attack——'

'Florence has been liberated,' countered Rocca. 'That isn't so far away.'

'Bologna is the same distance and still in tedeschi hands,' argued Gianoli. 'As the capitano says, it could be a month or three——'

'Or six! The capitano should have considered that before putting us all in jeopardy!'

'The capitano has shown us courtesy,' jumped in Doctor Cifariello. 'Let us return it. At the best, it may be only a matter of weeks. At worst, a winter in the mountains. The problem is, so many children. Where would they stay?'

'We would move them north,' said Lucarelli. 'To some of the higher villages. And there are any number of huts scattered around . . . and caves.'

'Not for those old bones! Rocca spat emphatically into the fireplace. 'I'll take my chance with the tedeschi. We've only the capitano's word they will turn on us.'

'Your cheese will account for a few if they do,' chuckled Tognazzi. 'Gas warfare!' He gave Bolognini, the postmaster, a nudge.

Bolognini saw no humour in the situation. His thoughts were with his wife, Lucia. A winter seldom passed without bronchitis. She'd not survive a month in the open.

'I will stay,' he said. 'But I will help those who wish to go.'

Mills glanced at his watch.

'The decision will have to be a quick one,' he warned. 'My men must soon be on the move.'

Tognazzi took Mills' glass, refilled it. 'You'll find many anticipating you, capitano. Most of us realized the situation the moment the bells stopped ringing.'

He glanced at Dom Teodoro.

Mills followed the look. Dom Teodoro had finished telling his beads. He was staring blankly at the wall in front of him, as if trying to pierce the veil, to see what future hung over his parish.

Mills spoke to him quietly.

'Your counsel would be welcome, Father.'

'*My* counsel?' Dom Teodoro came out of his reverie. 'What worth is my counsel in a world that has shut its ears to Him who preached forgiveness and brotherly love? You speak of reprisals, signore capitano, of bloodshed to be wrought by our enemies. But who are our enemies? I only see men, fashioned in the manner of God the Father. There is evil in all of us, good in some.' He stretched a thin, white hand in a gesture. 'These—my children— will decide for themselves. Those who have faith in the Almighty's protection will stay. Those who will go, will go. But it is not for me to judge them. I can only answer for myself. While there is one solitary mouse in my church, I will remain.'

'I will go,' said Gianoli, firmly. 'A schoolmaster may be of some use where there are children.'

'For me . . . it depends,' said Cifariello. 'Where the need is most.'

Just about everywhere, thought Mills. He drained his glass, prepared to leave. He shook each man by the hand, including the sceptical Rocca. Tognazzi placed his other hand over the grip, pressed it warmly.

'Come si chiamo?'

Lucarelli nipped in smartly.

'The captain uses a nome di guerra. He is known to us as Irlandese.'

'Bene, bene . . . Irlandese.' Tognazzi nodded approval. 'Alberto Irlandese—that is what we will call the piccolino born this night!'

'You do me a great honour.'

'Not at all. The honour is San Martino's!'

Mills moved on, pausing at last in front of Dom Teodoro. After what the old priest had said, he wasn't sure his hand would be welcome.

'I can only hope I am proven wrong,' he said.

Dom Teodoro rose, leaned on his stick. He looked long and deep into Mills' eyes. Mills looked back. He saw no animosity there, no reproof, no condemnation. Only a flicker of something intangible . . . fear, perhaps; but not fear for personal safety.

The old priest raised his free hand, rested it lightly on Mills' shoulder.

'Pray for me, figlio mio,' he said, simply.

'And you for me, Father,' said Mills.

10

COLAPASSA had kept his word. He had returned to San Martino a Montalbino. But the threats had not been for him to execute. A combined detachment of army and Waffen SS had done it for him.

The carnage had been wholesale.

Tognazzi, Bolognini, Rocca—they had been among the first to die, hauled out and shot down as random hostages. When Dom Teodoro had pleaded sanctuary for those who had taken refuge in his church, a hand-grenade had spattered his remains on the altar steps. The old and infirm had been locked indoors and flame-throwers put to their houses. Babies had been tossed, screaming, into cement-mixers. Women had been cut down by machine-guns as they fled to the chestnut groves. Some who escaped were to be maimed or killed afterwards, returning to booby-trapped homes and a water-supply wilfully polluted with typhoid germs.

Only a handful managed to straggle up into the mountains to join the earlier refugees. Mama Tognazzi had been one of them, carrying with her the infant Alberto Irlandese.

Behind this massacre had been Ernst Reinecke. Mills was not to know it at the time. Nor even later, at the courts-martial in Udine—though it was suspected. It was after the end of the war in Europe that he learned the truth for sure. After he had hunted down to Noli the one man—the one Italian, at least—who could give him the answer . . . Vincenzo Colapassa.

11

MILLS FOUND HIMSELF making the climb up to the old *castello*. He wasn't sure why he had agreed to make up a party with the Sangsters, the last company he would have chosen willingly. It was Mairhi Odell who had allowed herself to be talked into it, and he had sensed a mute appeal from her to come to the rescue.

He had responded with a gallantry that left him wondering. Not since adolescence had he pictured himself as a Galahad. Yet he had agreed to make up a fourth without hesitation. And, to his surprise, was enjoying it.

The steep route up from the Strada del Cimitero was still only a loose scatter of rubble. But this didn't prevent the Sangsters from bounding ahead. Mervyn, festooned as usual with camera and rucksack, climbed with the agility of a mountain goat. Eileen scrambled behind, short legs pumping like clockwork, back bent, rump out-thrust—a tailless baboon in a tweed skirt.

Mairhi and Mills were in no hurry. Both had done the trip before, knew the goal was far less impressive at close quarters than from a distance. Theirs was a leisurely pace, pausing at each twist in the path to ease the strain on calf muscles. They fell further and further behind, so that by the time the Sangsters were traversing the heap of rubble that had been the west wall, they were not much beyond the villa set halfway up.

At this point, the steepness increased. Mills went past Mairhi, clambered up, then turned and gave her a hand. It brought them to an outcrop of rock away from the path. He looked at her, she nodded, and they sat down. The rock made a natural seat, a chair-back of ferns and wild strawberries, with a view out across the Gulf of Genoa to where, on a sharp, haze-free day, one could see the tip of Corsica thrusting over the horizon. This was such a day. The sea sparkled blue, the sky vied with it for colour, marred only by a solitary furrow ploughed by a high-flying jet.

He picked a handkerchief punnet of strawberries—small, sweet, fresh with a flavour only the uncultivated possess. When they had eaten, he produced cigarettes. She rarely smoked, except after a meal; but she accepted, if only because it might prolong this interlude.

This man intrigued her. From the moment he had walked into the *pensione*, four evenings back. Hard to put a finger on why. The attraction was not physical, she told herself, though he had poise and self-assurance. Not tall, dark, or handsome; but the eyes were nice and gentle . . . at least, some of the time. If only they were less pouched with tiredness and he could lose the grey pallor about his face, with that *distingué* shock of white hair he'd be dishy in a mature kind of way.

Nor was it personality. He had been polite and—until lunch the other day—rather muted, withdrawn. Inclined to wait for conversation to come to him rather than make it himself. That had suited Eileen Sangster, soon ferreting out that he had come from Berlin. He had been non-committal until asked whether he had seen 'that awful wall'. Then he had smiled a bitter smile and replied that it was, in fact, quite a useful wall as walls go—from the west, concealing much that was drab in the east; from the east, hiding the garish façade of the west; and in general, a source of masochistic pleasure to Berliners on both sides who were never happier than when feeling sorry for themselves.

Said without heat, never once losing that smile, it had killed the subject of Berlin stone dead. The Sangsters were much too 'refained' to argue with someone they were meeting for the first time. She, herself, had been a little shocked by his answer, but had secretly enjoyed seeing Eileen shot down in flames. In her job she had to deal with all kinds, but it was the Eileen Sangsters who tried her patience to the hilt.

Meal-times apart, she had met him only briefly. In the Piazza Ignoto one morning, sharing coffee at the Caffé Sport. And one day he had bought her an aperitif in the garden-bar at the Villa

Fiorita. She had heard him speak Italian with Rossi, the proprietor, and with Gianni, the barman, and envied him his fluency. It flowed faultlessly, gesture and idiom alike. Never once groping for a word. Anyone who spoke the language that well must truly love the country. In that, at least, they had a common bond.

Yet such a love could be motivated by an entirely different driving force. Her Italy and his could be poles apart. Gianni, who knew all about everybody, had told her that Mills had once been Irlandese, leader of the *famoso* Lugubregigio—the Grey Ghost Brigade of the Garibaldi. To prove it he had unearthed an old copy of *Oggi*, which carried a 'Twenty Years After' illustrated feature.

There was little doubt that the photograph taken in 1945 was of the same man. Slimmer then, face more finely drawn—but he had not altered all that much. The article had told about the exploits of the partisan band—how they had ambushed convoys, derailed trains, fought on and killed Nazis for ten days after the official armistice, even attempting to kidnap General Kesselring from the Allies so that they could hang him for war crimes.

Seeing him now, seated beside her, it was hard to imagine this quietly spoken man doing all those things. And yet, somehow she knew that the violence was still there, underneath. That bitter appraisal of Berlin, the talk about his previous visit to Noli . . . 'I came here for another reason,' he had started to say. Ice-cold hate lay behind those words. They still made her shiver whenever she thought of them.

12

MAIRHI ODELL had had no experience of war with a childhood spent in Dublin, a neutral backwater. Her father had served with the British army but she had never seen him in uniform, outside of a photograph. And never once had there been any anxiety for his safety. Tim Odell had spent his military career at an ITC in County Tyrone, just north of the border. Something to do with his medical grade had kept him from going overseas, and Mother had been grateful for it—until five years after, in 1950, when he had died from the very disability that had kept him out of the firing line.

Within twelve months, Mother had married again. An old flame. Diarmuid MacBride, a widower himself, with three young children. On the Odell side, besides Mairhi there had been a brother, Michael, and a baby, Siobhan. So the amalgamation of the MacBrides and the Odells had been a practical expedient. Diarmuid owned a house at Merrion. He was in a position to support six children. They had not wanted for a thing, materially: though Mairhi missed deeply the affection of her real father, who had doted upon her. Something Diarmuid could never replace.

MacBride's business was import-export, trading almost exclusively with West Germany. A Germanophile, he was openly contemptuous of the sloth of his fellow Irish. As a consequence, Germans alone got the *céad mile fáilte* treatment at the house in Merrion; and in the year Mairhi was twenty, the compliment had been returned. The whole family had taken a holiday in the Rhineland.

They had stayed with the Edthofers, business associates of MacBride, and the hospitality had been lavish. Mama Edthofer had been a darling—plump and homely, ever fussing that one didn't eat or drink enough. There were five children, of much the same age-pattern as the MacBride-Odells. The eldest was Wolfgang—twenty-one, blond, handsome with exquisite manners and infinite charm. And as heir to the Edthofer business empire, it was hardly surprising that Mother had seen him as the perfect match for Mairhi. From the outset, she had been bent on fostering a romance. When she had learned that Papa Edthofer was proposing to send Wolfgang to London to further his English, she had suggested he would be better off in Dublin and welcome to stay at Merrion. With Mairhi on hand to entertain him, Mother reasoned wedding bells the following spring.

It hadn't worked out that way. That same summer, the family were out of Dublin at their seaside cottage at Tramore. She and Wolfgang had stayed behind for the Horse Show. Mother, as usual, had decreed it. The Show was a *must* for their guest, and, on the domestic side, it was a good opportunity for Wolfgang to see how well Mairhi could cope with the duties of a *hausfrau*. To observe the proprieties, Cormac, the eldest stepbrother, had offered to stay on in Dublin too.

It had gone smoothly until Mairhi had met Pat Felaney at the Show. An old friend, he had dated her on and off ever since school. No more to it than a good-night kiss. Pat had been going on to a party—a dance and a giggle out at Bray. He had asked her to go, and on the spur of the moment she had accepted. Why not? Wolfgang and Cormac had drifted off with a stag gang of

Cormac's friends. And whatever Mother might say or think, Wolfgang was as much Cormac's guest as hers.

When Pat had delivered her home around two a.m., Cormac and Wolfgang were there, waiting: Cormac out cold in a drunken stupor, Wolfgang in an ugly, jealous mood. He had called her a whore and God knows what else. There had been no point in arguing. She was tired and headachey. She had walked out of the room and gone to bed. She would sort him out in the morning, make him understand that only when and if they became engaged could he question what she did and who she went with.

Wolfgang hadn't waited until morning. Two hours later, she had been roused from a heavy sleep to find her nightdress up under her chin and he crawling all over her pawing and fumbling. She had screamed and fought until Cormac was finally roused. He had dragged the German off and punched him half-way through the window and into hospital for six stitches in his face.

Looking back on it, Mairhi felt Wolfgang had not been entirely to blame. Her mother and stepfather had encouraged him to believe she was his for the taking, providing the route to her bed was paved with orange-blossom. He had been full of contrition, begging forgiveness—the Irish whiskey had gone to his head, he wasn't used to it . . . For her part, though sick and disgusted, she might have said no more about it and counselled Cormac to do the same. But the evidence of the stitches awaited the family on their return.

That had been more nauseating than any physical shame. She had been roundly blamed for the whole sorry affair. She had led him on, flopping around the house the way she did, bending over and showing her bosom, never bothering to tug her skirt down, in and out of the bathroom with next to nothing on . . . and then, after getting the poor boy all worked up, flirting off with that good-for-nothing Pat Felaney. If that wasn't asking for trouble, what was?

Diarmuid's attitude Mairhi had been able to understand. He was obviously worried sick about the effect it might have on his business relationship with the Edthofers. But that Mother should take the same stand—even more so—was more than she could stomach. Mairhi had packed her bags and left home the same day.

Eight years now, and she had never been back; had not written so much as a postcard. She had met her brother Michael in

London only last year, quite by chance. She had gathered that things went on much the same at Merrion, with everyone just that much older. Wolfgang, it seemed, still kept in touch with them. He had married the daughter of one of his father's partners, a girl named Lisl. Mairhi vaguely remembered her from that holiday at Bad Godesberg—flaxen-haired, heavy-breasted, a bit of a dumpling. All the makings of a timid, pliant *hausfrau*. He had probably made a good choice.

She wished him well, bore him no animosity, though she was aware that there had been—still was—a hangover from that unfortunate experience.

It was in her attitude to men—or rather, to sex. As a Catholic Irish girl, she had been taught nothing. Her mother had always dismissed such questions with, 'You'll know all about it when you are married and that'll be soon enough.' It had been not knowing what to expect that had made it all the worse.

Now, at twenty-eight, she was still a virgin—a phenomenon, she supposed, by modern standards. But she could honestly say she had yet to taste the vinegar of frustration. Far from being spinsterish, on the shelf, she could have had lovers. Particularly here, in Italy. She had even been tempted to toss her cap over the windmill once or twice. Yet something had held her back. Not a religious morality. Roman Catholicism was not her chastity belt. Much of her faith in that had been shed along with the tears at her father's funeral. Once free of it, it had been like the lifting of a suffocating blanket. No, it was the simple, old-fashioned, non-denominational virtue of wanting to save herself for the right man, whoever he might be. She would know him when she met him, she felt sure of that.

13

MAIRHI pressed out her cigarette, flicked it away. She glanced at Mills. He lay back, face upturned, drinking in the warmth of the sun. Already looking better, he had a tan to show for those few days in Noli. Her eyes lingered shyly, not quite sure if he was watching her. Behind those dark glasses, it was hard to tell. Evidently he was, for his lips curled in a smile.

'Penny for them.'

Penny for them! Holy Crippen, she thought, if you knew what had been slipping through my mind these past minutes. The colour mounted in her cheeks. There was nothing she could do to stop it.

His smile broadened. He read his own signs.

'Bad as that, eh?'

'What d'you mean . . . bad as that?'

More confusion than ever. She turned her head away, gazed out at the sea. He shifted his position, removed the sun cheaters. He rubbed his eyelids, cast a sly look at her profile.

A nice profile, he decided. Nose small, tip-tilted; mouth generous; chin determined, with no hint of a companion. The flush remained, adding a ripe-peach quality to her tan. He sensed it would stay for as long as he continued to stare at her or she was conscious of that stare. You should worry, my Irish *alanna*. Blushing becomes you. This was the first time I've taken a good look, and I like what I see. I'd like to kiss you, but the chances are you'd scream blue bloody murder, slap my face, take me for a good-for-nothing lecher . . .

He said: 'This job of yours. Tell me about it.'

'My job?' She looked at him, arching her eyebrows. It was the last thing she had expected. 'It's—just a job. Nothing special.' She felt lame, disappointed. She hadn't wanted to talk about herself. But she went on: 'I quite like it. I like this place. I like meeting people.'

'Such as our two upstairs?' He cocked a thumb in the direction of the *castello*.

She plucked a blade of grass, put it in her mouth, gave a little shrug.

'It takes all sorts. I've met worse. So, I'm sure, have you.'

There was more to it than a casual observation.

'Meaning what exactly?'

'Meaning—if you like—that other time you came to Noli.'

The ball had been dropped neatly into his court. He gave her a long, hard look.

'Do you really want to know about that?'

She pulled a fresh blade of grass. She ran a fingernail along it, creased and split it, then threw it away, looked at her hands.

'I heard a story . . .' It came quietly, almost a whisper. 'It wasn't a nice story. I don't even know that it's true. It concerns a Fascist on the run and a partisan leader . . .' She hesitated.

'Go on.'

'I—well—I got it from one of the boatmen. I know most of them to speak to. This one's usually to be found along by the

Caravella, near the Mole.' She pointed downwards, through the trees, to where the sea dribbled in lazily, splintering into flecks of white on a grey-green tumble of rocks.

'Old Enzo Sgambati,' he said.

She shot him a quick glance. It was confirmation in itself. He smiled.

'Is that old devil still alive? He must be ninety if he's a day! I can imagine his stories grow longer with the years and more bawdy.'

'I don't know him that well.' She was instantly on the defensive. 'Except that he's related to Gianni, the barman back at——'

'I know.' He nodded. 'A great-uncle or third cousin. But then, who isn't, in Noli? Like Jacob, the Sgambati progeny is great. He'd buried two wives and raised eighteen children when I knew him. And I wager he still has an eye for some concubine with whom to beget.'

Mairhi saw an insinuation that didn't amuse her.

'If you don't want to talk about it, let's drop the subject!'

She curled her feet up, made to rise, putting out a hand to steady herself. He caught it—pulled. A mild pull, mischievous. But it was enough. Her feet skidded away on the smooth surface of the stone. She lost her balance, sprawled on top of him.

In that brief moment, she was crushed against him, her hair cascading lightly over his face. He swept an arm about her, pulled her back until her head lay in the crook of his elbow.

She made no attempt to struggle, but she looked up into his face with a flicker of something in her eyes. Not exactly fear; not completely trustful. Not fully accepting, yet not rejecting.

He saw this disquiet, wondered about it. She had been hurt at some time; the shadow was with her still. She needed reassurance.

He offered it by ignoring her mouth. He kissed her eyelids instead, very gently. Then her forehead and her hair. It had the desired effect. Her eyes closed; her lips relaxed, slightly parted. He looked at the mouth, still retaining the blade of grass she had been chewing. His free hand plucked it away, then he kissed the lips softly, almost without pressure. Once, twice, three times—teasing, until her hand came up and about his neck to catch and hold him close, stirring him to show more ardour.

His hand moved from the curve of her throat, slipped beneath her dress, caressing the shoulder, his fingers gently massaging, then tracing their way down, over the soft contour of her breast.

As the nipple came under his touch, her eyes opened. Wide.

That troubled look there again; the tension returning. He withdrew his hand slowly, kissed her once more—teasingly again, smiling a smile of reassurance.

But the spell was broken. She pulled away, without panic yet leaving no doubt that the interlude was over. She sat up, smoothed back her hair with a nervous hand.

He caught it, held it for a moment, brushed it with his lips.

'That was so much better than stories told by Enzo Sgambati,' he murmured.

'You're very sure of yourself—aren't you?'

She retrieved her hand, went back to combing her hair with her fingers.

'Not really.' He took out a cigarette, put it between his lips. 'I've been wanting to do that for some time.' He put a flame to the cigarette, blew smoke. He embroidered his words with a white lie. 'Why d'you think I volunteered for this expedition?'

Her hand paused in its combing.

'So that's why we let the Sangsters go on ahead!'

He grinned. 'I had no adulterous thoughts about our Eileen.'

She misunderstood the remark.

'You are married, then?'

'Me?' His puzzlement was genuine. 'No . . . but she is, surely?'

'Oh, help us, yes . . . I would think so!'

A little giggle. The idea of the Sangsters living in sin was faintly ludicrous. She smoothed her skirt down over her thighs, drew up her knees, clasped her hands about them. A natural, unconscious movement, but it drew his eyes like a magnet. He attempted to cover his interest by pushing his cigarette case towards her.

'No, thanks.'

She went on hugging her knees. There was something akin to smugness in her face—a kitten with a saucer of cream.

He could almost hear the purr. The temptation to tease was strong.

'I had no intention of going any further, of course.'

She rose to the bait.

'Oh? And what makes you think I'd have let you?'

He grinned, pointed upwards.

'I meant to the castle . . . where else?

'Oh, that!'

The blush was back, deeper. She was conscious that he had trapped her into a more intimate interpretation of his remark.

She blurted out, 'No . . . I mean—well—you've been there before, haven't you . . . when . . .'

The words faltered. The purr was silent, the eyes unhappy.

'When . . .' he prompted.

'Nothing.'

Abrupt. Lifeless.

He said, 'So we're back to square one . . . and Vincenzo Colapassa.'

She stared at him. 'Vincenzo——?'

'The man found hanging from the battlements in nineteen forty-five. And I'm here to revisit the scene of the crime. Is that it?'

Harsh and stinging, the words. Like hailstones. She flinched under them, turned her head away.

'I—I don't want to know about it.'

'Not even the truth,' he said, flinging away his cigarette.

She turned back at that, hope flickering. A hand went out towards him, but it was too late.

He was already on his feet and moving away, back down the path they had climbed together.

14

A QUIRK OF FATE had led Mills to Vincenzo Colapassa. The Fascist and his mistress had been scurrying northwards, tagging along under the protection of a retreating German column, vacillating between decisions—to stay as they were and cross into Austria, or leave their Nazi umbrella and make a dash for neutral Switzerland.

Then came the rumour that Il Duce had been caught and shot on the shores of Como. With the rumour came another . . . Claretta Petacci had betrayed him in an attempt to save her own skin.

Wildly untrue, but it had served to make Colapassa look sideways at Nella and wonder if she might not do the same to him. He figured she would, the trollop. She'd open her legs to the first Allied soldier who came to her waving a bar of *cioccolata*. So why go on lumbering himself when he might make it easier on his own?

He had ditched her in a small township up beyond Bolzano, leaving her to the mercy of those who would condemn her for a Fascist whore and collaborator. This had happened, and the things she feared most—the scissors and the razor—were being brandished in her face when Mills came to the rescue.

The partisans had swept into the town close on the heels of the German column. He had seen her being manhandled by a mob and had put a stop to it by firing shots in the air. Nella had been brought to his car—a captured Mercedes tourer—her clothes ripped to her waist, her breasts spilling out and heaving with hysteria. It was Tomaso Lucarelli, still with him and now promoted to a unit commander, who had thought he recognized her as a girl from San Martino a Montalbino. When he suggested as much, she had screamed her denials and grovelled on the floor of the car, away from his gun—a reaction that was proof enough.

Mills had known for some time about the reprisals carried out on San Martino, though he had not been back there since. Only forty-eight hours after the *caserma* raid he had received fresh orders, to move further north and weld together a scatter of partisan units into a brigade . . . the brigade that was to become the Lugubregrigio.

Up there, in the Alto Adige, Mills had continued his attacks on the enemy, but with far less compunction about possible reprisals. The local inhabitants were mostly *sud-tirolese*, German-speaking, a lost tribe of the *Herrenvolk* that had campaigned long and loud to be incorporated into Hitler's Greater Reich.

It was from just such a township that Mills had rescued Nella. The sight of hitherto pro-Hitler louts putting on a show of turncoat patriotism, making a Roman holiday out of some poor bitch, had made his hackles rise. Even when he knew who she was, that she might be implicated in some way with the bloody massacre at San Martino, he still saw no reason for a change of heart. If she deserved the traditional short back-and-sides, it was for her own people to decide—what was left of them. Certainly not this bunch of stein-swilling hypocrites.

He had left Lucarelli and his men to take care of the town and had driven away with Nella beside him in the front seat of the Mercedes. Her large dark eyes never left his face for a moment, watching him fearfully as she endeavoured to arrange the strips of clothing into some modicum of decency. Finally, she plucked up sufficient courage to ask, 'Where are we going?'

The answer was short and crisp. 'San Martino.'

'Oh, no, Madonna mia, no! Please . . .'

She began to quiver with fright again. She put out a hand to touch his sleeve, to implore him to change his mind. It meant losing hold of one side of her tattered dress, and with it some of her carefully gathered dignity. A breast made a jump for freedom, swung towards him.

He gave it a sidelong glance. It was big and firm, full and high-pointed. He had seen nothing like it in months. Only a eunuch could have ignored it. He pulled the car off the road, applied the brakes.

Nella gave a little sigh, a shrug of resignation. She presumed the obvious. She was about to be raped, there and then, on the spot. Ah, well. If it had to be, it had to be. No use making a fuss about it. If I holler blue murder, he'll like as not cut my throat. On the other hand, if I show willing, he might take pity on me afterwards and not return to San Martino. *Maledetto*, it'd be better to submit to a troop of Cossacks *and* their horses than have that happen! Anyway, giving this man what he wanted was infinitely preferable to losing her hair and being tarred and feathered back in that town . . .

She allowed the rest of her dress to fall away, made to clamber over into the back seat. He caught her arm, jerking her back. He removed his tunic, tossed it to her.

'Cover yourself with this, for Crissake! How the hell can I drive with that lot dancing under my nose?'

She stared at the battle-dress tunic, then slid her arms into it, eyes wide with astonishment. What kind of man was this? Not Italian, that was for sure. Catch one of them passing up the opportunity! Was he an *americani*, perhaps? She tried a little smile on him.

'Must we?'

'Must we what?'

'Must we go back to . . . San Martino?'

His look was ice.

'Is the prospect so bad?'

She began to sob loudly, turning her back on him, curling herself in a tight ball. The view was as provocative as before. The skirt had been ripped up the back seam and revealed two rounded buttocks split by a wisp of black lace. He gave them a stinging slap with the flat of his hand, changed her sobs to a sudden gasp.

'Va bene,' he shrugged. 'You'll know soon enough, anyway. It isn't *your* San Martino.'

She twisted round, rubbing her posterior, stared at him through her tears.

'Not *my* San Martino . . . ?'

'Not San Martino a Montalbino. You don't imagine it's the only San Martino in Italy, do you? This one is San Martino di Neve. And it's well-named! We've had snow up there since November, and there's still some hanging around.' He massaged his forearm through his shirtsleeve. 'You'll find it cold without my jacket. And that's how you'll be if you give me any trouble!'

The car was on the move again, climbing and twisting around a series of hairpin bends, before she ventured another word.

'Why do you take me to this San Martino?'

'It happens to be my headquarters.'

'Is it a big place?'

'No luxury hotels—if that's what you're hoping for. This San Martino won't look so different from the other one, the last time you saw it. Burnt-out, deserted, its people scattered . . .' His mouth tightened, his knuckles went white at the wheel. 'Your tedeschi friends paid this place a visit, too!'

'Tedeschi, non è vero!' The words shrieked from her. 'Not *my* friends! I never went with any! Never, never, never!' She made little fists and punched the seat on either side of her. 'Per Bacco, che sciocchezze! I was only ever with that Vincenzo, that—that filthy culopuzza!'

He raised an eyebrow at the final vulgar epithet. A sly grin broke through the tension in his face. He clucked his tongue in mild reproof.

'That's no expression for a lady to use!'

She pouted her lower lip.

'That's what everyone called him. His name is Colapassa.'

'Republican Fascist?'

She nodded, sullenly.

'Your boy friend?'

Hesitation, then again the nod.

'He left you stranded . . . back there?'

She nodded a third time.

'You silly bitches never learn,' he said in English. Then, switching back to Italian, 'Where was he heading for?'

'Austria . . . Switzerland . . . he couldn't make up his mind.'

'He'll be lucky if he makes either—unless he can sprout wings. He'll collect those soon enough . . . when he's caught!'

'Is it true about Mussolini being dead?'

He grinned, ran a finger across his throat.

'And Petacci . . . did they . . . ?'

'I believe so.' The grin faded, the words were sober. He repeated what he had said before. In Italian this time. 'You silly bitches never learn.'

She suddenly looked frightened. Her hand fluttered upwards, began to fiddle with the buttons of the tunic.

'They won't . . . *you* won't . . . kill me?'

He thought: If you undo that tunic, I'll likely roger you to death! Aloud, he said, '*I* won't kill you or take a razor to your head. But I can't answer for San Martino a Montalbino.'

'You are going to send me back there?'

'That depends.'

'On what?'

'Some straight answers to some straight questions.'

'Oh, I will, I promise.'

'We'll see.'

She heaved a sigh of relief, could hardly believe her good fortune. She had to ask a final question, just to be sure.

'Is that all you want from me?'

Is that all I want from you, after all these months without hide or hair of a woman? Jesu Hosanna, give me strength! He punched the horn of the Mercedes in an effort at self-control. Then he saw the funny side of it, began to laugh.

She stared at him.

'I said something?'

'You said something. A bridge we'll have to cross when we come to it!'

The bridge was not a difficult one. Nella met him more than half way. Willingly, anxious to please, touched by his consideration, that he did not take without asking. A novel experience for her, it made her a little shy and awkward at first, not wanting him to see her for a trollop. Yet responding swiftly to his needs, the urgency of his desire, she brought all her voluptuousness, her passion, her skills at love-making into play, finding her own pleasure and gratification in the fulfilment of his.

And when it was over and he lay beside her—spent, supine, relaxed, his tensions gone—she was to lean over and kiss him, tenderly, almost chastely, not a little genuinely in love with him. She knew it could not last, that the day would come when he would drive out of her life just as suddenly as he had driven in. But while he wanted her, needed her, that was enough . . .

Only once did he have to question her about San Martino. He wanted the truth and it was no use lying, even if it told against

her. And he wanted it without rancour towards Colapassa. Just
the bald facts.

She told him how they had fled that night of the *caserma* raid,
how they had come back, with Colapassa breathing vengeance.
How the Germans had taken over, running riot in systematic
terror. She couldn't tell him the name of the SS commander. She
had kept well out of his way, scared that she, too, might be a
victim. As Mills suspected, she was just a village girl who had
slept with the wrong man in the wrong uniform. Not a crime. But
reason enough for her to be scared out of her wits at the prospect
of going back to a small community that had suffered so
grievously.

Afterwards, Nella felt better for the telling; cleaner somehow,
less afraid, even less guilty of her association with Vincenzo. A
spirit of penitence, as if she had been to the confessional. Though
how Mother Church would have viewed her ritual of self-
purgation—naked as she had been, receptive, unashamed, revel-
ling deliriously in the fierce embrace of her father confessor for
the rest of that night—she did not consider.

Her true propitiation was to follow after two weeks, when she
learned Mills was leaving. A decision there could be no going
back on.

The territory that, for a short time, had been his command,
was now swarming with the Allies. Sooner rather than later, the
Garibaldi would be disbanded, the men would return home to
their families. But what of him? This Italy he had made his
home, these partisans had become his family. When they were
gone, he would have nothing. No mother, father, wife, or children
waiting to hug and hold him tight and thank God for his safe
return. All he had was a job to do, a personal debt to settle—the
debt of San Martino a Montalbino. Until he had paid that debt
to the full, he could not be absolved of his own guilt in the affair.

Nothing could make him see otherwise. Lucarelli had tried. So
had his other lieutenant, Serato. Both had counselled and argued
that such things happen in war, he had no cause to take the
blame. But Mills knew differently. His responsibility then, it still
was—and would be, always.

In this he was showing the depth to which he had become
italianizante, ready to risk all to avenge what was to him a family
outrage. In his failure to protect them, he had invited dishonour.
It must be expiated in the only way he knew: *la vendetta*. Out-
moded, barbaric, retrograde it might be. It made no difference.

The courts-martial at Udine had given him the task of executioner. If Reinecke had been—as was suspected—the one responsible for the massacre, there was no more to be said. But first he
must find Colapassa, the man who could confirm it for sure.

15

MILLS had gone first to Milan, taking Serato and Nella with him.
Serato had used the excuse that he had family to look up, to make
sure they had come through the war safely. His real reason had
been his devotion—a protective instinct towards the younger man,
who seemed hell-bent for trouble and disaster. Mills guessed this,
but raised no objection. He knew that Guglielmo would never
attempt to thwart him, only help in whatever way he could. He
might be glad of that help before he had finished.

For Nella, it was the end of the road. He had fitted her out
with fresh clothes, a suitcase, and some money. Plus an official-
looking piece of paper offering evidence that she had worked for
the Garibaldi. It would help her with the authorities; might even
find her a job. He had left her on the doorstep of an 'Uncle' Aldo
with a kiss and a slap on the bottom. And some words of advice:
don't drop your *mutandine* indiscriminately; wait for a man to
put a ring on your finger and a permanent roof over your head.
But after meeting 'Uncle' Aldo, Mills had the distinct feeling
that sexy Nella would be horizontal as soon as he had turned the
corner. Ah, well. That was her business. He had problems of his
own.

The city was still in a state of ferment. Gangs of youths roamed
the streets, wearing the red scarf of the Garibaldi, showing the
clenched fist and mouthing Communist slogans. How many were
entitled to wear the partisan insignia was open to question, but
it brought home to Mills how easily the symbol could fall into
disrepute.

That had been evident at the headquarters of Allied Military
Command. His kerchief had got the fish eye from the first officer
he encountered. An even bleaker eye when he spoke perfect
English. Little interest was shown in the problem he raised—the
need to track down Colapassa; to find out if, indeed, he had been
arrested and in what camp he might be interned. On the other
hand, a great deal of interest was shown in the Mercedes parked
outside. Where had he got it? Was it documented and officially

requisitioned? Could he produce work-tickets and permits to draw petrol—or, for that matter, a movement order for his own person? If not, why not? Mills had bluffed his way out of that one, left in a hurry.

It was then that the wisdom of allowing Serato to accompany him proved itself. Guglielmo had a cousin who had a brother-in-law who had a friend who was a *poliziotto*. The *poliziotto* had held down his job under the Republican Fascist regime. Politically clean, he was nevertheless aware of the dangers of association. He wanted to go on being a policeman, to collect his pension. So anything he could do to help a *capo* in the Garibaldi might stand him in good stead when heads began to roll. He was swift to gain access to Records, and from these Mills gleaned vital information.

Photographs and party history apart, Mills learned that Colapassa's home was in Savona and that he was married to Fulvia Salvatori, only daughter of a wealthy businessman. As well as a luxury apartment, they owned a villa along the coast at Noli. All of which suggested to Mills that, whether he had escaped across the border or not, at the crunch Colapassa would contact his wife. If only because Fulvia had the money.

Fulvia Colapassa was entertaining an American at the villa, a captain in the Service Corps, PBS. She had met him on the Friday morning and now it was Saturday night, and she had been entertaining him all that time. Mostly on her back, with only a break now and then to eat the food and drink the whisky and smoke the cigarettes he had brought with him. It wasn't that she was mad for sex—but it had been a long time. Only twice in the past six months. An Abwehr officer in Genoa and a Luftwaffe pilot in Turin.

When Mills and Serato arrived, she and her PBS captain had been back at the serious business of the weekend, her legs twined about his neck. *Dio mio*, what an appetite! She had never known a stallion like this before. But the sudden banging on the door had her swinging in fright, taking his head with her, off the bed to finish up a fleshy heap on the floor.

'Aw, shit!' said the PBS captain.

'Sta zitto!' whispered Fulvia. 'Whoever it is, maybe they will go away!'

They didn't.

Mills kicked the door in, had them *flagrante delicto*.

One glance at his uniform, the red kerchief, the Luger in his hand, was enough for Fulvia. She backed away, stubbed her heels on the bed, flopped down.

'What goes on?' The captain was trying to resurrect his dignity. Not easy, with his shirt-tail flapping.

'You do,' said Mills. 'If you've got any sense. We're after the lady's husband.'

'Husband? What kind of crap is that? The Krauts got him—when he was with the partisans. He's dead.'

'He's very much alive—and a war criminal,' said Mills. 'Now, do you go—or do I call the Provost Marshal?'

Magic words. The captain was way off his beat, and knew it. He left in a hurry.

'Razza di cani!' Fulvia spat contemptuously after her departing guest. She grabbed a dressing-gown, eyed Mills coldly. 'So you want Vincenzo. Well, you can see for yourself, he's not here.'

'Not yet,' said Mills. 'But he will be. Get some clothes on, signora. We may be in for a long wait!'

Four days, in fact.

Vincenzo Colapassa came down to them from over the mountains, through Calizano and Melogno, taking the widest and most rugged detour possible and looking as if he had walked every inch of the way. He had long since shed his blackshirt uniform, exchanging it gratefully for the garb of a scarecrow. Unshaven, hollow-eyed, filthy, his guts knotted with hunger, his feet blistered and bleeding. He came through the villages of San Clemente and San Michele soon after sunrise, skirted the houses to the north of Noli, stumbled across the Cian da Crava-Voze road and down through the olive groves to the villa. He literally fell over the gate into the garden, kissing the stone terrace and weeping his relief.

He raised his head and there was Fulvia, clad in a filmy negligee, the sleep still in her eyes. He cried out with joy. Then he looked beyond her, saw Mills and Serato, their red kerchieves, the guns in their hands. The cry shrilled to horror, utter disbelief, fear—choking into a sob as he scrambled to his feet and backed away.

He reached the gate, turned once again to the rocky path upwards, tripped, fell, picked himself up, cursing, weeping, heart and lungs pounding.

They caught him before he had covered fifty yards.

'Up there, at the castello . . . if he wants it that way,' said Mills to Serato. 'Move, you bastard!'

He stirred Colapassa with his boot . . .

Up among the ruins, Mills knotted a noose, secured it to the battlements, let it swing free. Colapassa crouched against the wall, pleading his innocence and the mercy of Christ.

'What have I done?' he wailed.

'Ask the dead at San Martino,' was the answer. 'I want names. Everyone you know who took part in the massacre.'

'I can't remember!'

Mills caught him by the throat, twisted him round, smashed his face against the wall.

'Try,' he said. 'Try hard!'

He swung Colapassa round again, face pitted with needles of gravel, seeping blood in a dozen places. A moan, then words came tumbling out: Lutz . . . Sturm . . . Holtzer . . . Fricke . . . Oberdorfer . . . Steibl . . . a score of others dredged up from the slime of memory—and Ernst Reinecke, the man in command.

Mills opened his fingers, allowed the Fascist to slide to the ground sobbing and heaving, a dark stain spreading the man's pants where he had urinated.

Serato looked at Mills, then at the noose dangling above their heads. But Mills shook his head, slowly, contemptuously.

'No, Guglielmo. I wouldn't soil my hands any further on *that*!'

He spat on the prostrate Colapassa, turned away.

When Colapassa finally stirred and raised his head, Mills and Serato were gone. But he was not alone. In their place stood Fulvia, dressed now in skirt and blouse.

'Have they'—he smeared the mingled blood and tears with his sleeve—'gone?'

She nodded.

'Thank God!' He sighed his relief. 'Give me a hand. Help me up.'

'Help you up? Si . . . I'll help you up. On to the wall and into that noose!'

He stared at her, saw a white face pinched with utter loathing and contempt.

'But tesore mi' . . . this is your Pippo . . .'

'Hang yourself, my Pippo,' she said. 'For if you don't, someone else will. So far as I'm concerned, you've been dead for years!'

She turned on her heel, walked away. As she went down the hill, his sobs followed her. But her steps never faltered. She never once looked back.

16

MAIRHI found Mills in the little *piazza* on the Strada del Cimitero. He was slouched on a bench outside the church, staring out at nothing in particular, one hand flapping irritably at a persistent fly. She hesitated, half turning away to continue the downward path, then, changing her mind, approached him.

He saw her coming, out of the corner of his eye. He took out a cigarette, lit it. If it was meant as a cue, she took it gladly.

'I'll have one now, please . . .'

Her glance was shy as she sat down beside him. He passed a cigarette, flicked his lighter.

'I'm sorry——' they both said, together. Then laughed.

'A couple of school-kids.' His grin was one of embarrassment. 'I behaved like a first-grade nit!'

'I wasn't much better,' she said. 'I need my backside slapped.'

'Don't tempt me,' he murmured. 'I might enjoy it!'

'So might I.'

The lighter snapped off, but she retained his hand. Fingers curled together.

'I didn't kill him,' he said quietly.

'It doesn't matter,' she said. 'That's all in the past and none of my business anyway.' Then, suddenly tremulous for the future, 'How long are you staying in Noli?'

He flicked ash from his cigarette.

'I'm booked till the end of the week. But Rossi said I could stay on if I wished.'

She nodded quickly. 'Yes. The season is over. At least, so far as the Bluebird agency is concerned. We've no more parties arriving.'

'So what happens to you?'

'What happens to flies in winter? I go wherever I choose.'

'And that is?'

He threw away his cigarette, looked deep into her eyes. She slipped her hand from his, reached up, touched his cheek.

'Where do you suggest . . . ?'

He made to kiss her, but she moved the hand over his mouth.

'You know Italian law,' she smiled. 'We can be arrested for doing that in public.'

He caught the hand, drew it away.

'I doubt if there is more than one police cell in Noli. I have no objection to sharing it.'

'Then it doesn't matter, does it?'

She lifted her face to his.

PART TWO

17

THAT EVENING they dined at the Giardino, on the Via Defferrari, above the town and close to the *piazza* where they had come together that afternoon. A pleasant little restaurant, quiet and intimate. Perfect for their mood.

Mairhi did most of the talking. Willingly. Not wishing to repeat the near-disaster of that afternoon, the probing into his past. Instead, she talked of her various jobs: *au pair* to a Florentine family; a financial misadventure running an Anglo-Italian bookshop with a middle-aged ex-governess; a spell in Rome at the enquiry desk of BEA; a stint as a tourist courier that had led to her present employment. As a consequence, they reached the coffee stage before she realized how taciturn his mood was, how much she had carried the conversation. Her mind panicked at that.

'Heavens above! You must think I'm a gas, going on like that.'

He reached out, placed a hand over hers, smiled.

'Not at all. It was more interesting than anything I have to tell.'

What else could he say? That he had let twenty years of his life drift away in the dreary, sordid atmosphere of espionage? Glamour? That was strictly for the birds. Birds? Forget the Mata Haris . . . sexual libido usually meant some back-street hotel with a tottie who barely knew what time of day it was. Danger? If ever, the result of one's own stupidity. The rest belonged to the dream-world of the Ian Flemings, and rarely climbed out of fiction into fact. The only highlights he had known were the jobs done for men like Moshe Singer, ensuring that some war criminal got his just desserts.

Could he talk about that? Could he say: Oh, by the way . . . less than a week ago, I cremated a man alive in fulfilment of a task I set myself in nineteen forty-five; and having done it in defiance of my employers in Whitehall, I now await their reaction. But not to worry. They won't put me on trial or anything. Nothing worse than a pat on the rump and a golden handshake —tut-tut, naughty boy, you've gone too far this time; but in view of your valued service in the past, here's a six-month salary cheque in lieu of notice; don't spend it all at once; good luck and goodbye . . . Like bloody hell!

No . . . there was going to be trouble over this. He felt it in his bones; had done from the moment he had embarked on liquidation of Reinecke. But then it had been something involving only himself, no innocent party. It had never crossed his mind that he might meet someone like this girl, this woman across the table from him, with her anxious grey eyes and sensitive nature, so fearful yet so transparently wanting to love and be loved . . . How could he involve her, too?

He could, he supposed, take her, sleep with her, revel in her physically for a night or two. Then disappear, out of her life, hoping she wouldn't think too badly of him. In theory, yes, he could do that. In fact, he knew he couldn't. That didn't mean he was some kind of saint with women. Far from it. But his attitude was always governed by the woman herself. The Nella Barbiscios had been numerous in his life—no strings, women to bed with for orgasmic satisfaction, a peck on the cheek and come again. But *this* one—it just wasn't on; not without the promise of some future. And logic said there was no future, not beyond misery for her and a lasting regret for him. Yet, for only the third time in his life where women were concerned, he felt the urge to toss logic out of the window.

He felt her hand turn under his palm to gently caress his fingers.

'I could put the same question you put to me this afternoon,' he heard her say. 'A penny for them.'

Her face came back into focus. It was a quite beautiful face. She had done things with her hair for this evening, sweeping it back and pinning it high, showing more red in it than he remembered, revealing the graceful curve of her neck and shoulders, tanned and satin-smooth. But it was her eyes that knocked him for a loop—above all else, those eyes, smiling at him now with a reflection of inner happiness.

'You were miles and miles away.'

'Sorry. I didn't mean to be rude.' He added what was, in effect, the truth. 'I was thinking about you.'

'Oh . . .'

Embarrassment obvious, but genuine. His practised eye knew the manufactured article when it saw it—the cultivated coyness that always made him want to throw up.

'You are beautiful,' he said simply. 'And men are plain idiots —particularly Irishmen—ever to let you escape from under their noses.'

'Irishmen prefer to see their women through a glass darkly. Usually a Guinness glass. Didn't you know that?'

'I suppose I did. Maybe that's why half the world's population stakes a claim to an Irish grandmother. The old darlings had to climb upon a bicycle and emigrate to be appreciated!'

'You had one, too?'

'A bean sidhe from Connemara.'

'Bean sidhe!' She laughed. 'You have the Irish?'

He shook his head. 'No more than she taught me. And that wasn't much. But she taught me other things that left a deep impression. I've never forgotten her.'

'Which explains something—why you were known as . . .'

She stopped herself in time. He completed it for her with a grin.

'Irlandese? You needn't be afraid to mention it. I'm far from being ashamed. It represented a grim chapter in my life, but grim chapters have their moments. Great moments, when you're made aware of selfless courage and sacrifice by one man for another. Bonds of loyalty that have nothing to do with flags and patriotism and that crap.'

He paused, hoping he had not made it sound pompous.

'I know what you mean,' she said. 'All the same, you really love this country, don't you?'

'Italy?' He shrugged. 'I suppose I do. But not with a capital "I"; not as a political entity or a freak of geography shaped like a riding boot. But if you mean the country for what it is, its way of life, warmth, beauty, compassion, laughter, tears, earthy smell— yes, I do. I love it for its past, its present, its civilized resistance to complete materialism, its pure anarchy of mind, its virtues and its failings. Even . . . yes, even the amoral lip-service it pays to a religion that few, in honesty, give a fig for. Above all, the thing that is Italy for me is the family and all that word implies. The devotion and love for the young, the reverence and respect for the old, the ties of fidelity, and the strength of purpose. This is the true religion, the law, the politics of the people. It goes back beyond the Popes and pagan gods of Rome, to the oldest faith of all, the Mother Goddess herself. That's why the Madonna springs to the lips in prayer more readily than the Christ. In essence, I suppose, my religion, too—hence the tie.' He climbed down from the rhetoric, grinned self-consciously. 'Some say I talk like a mafioso. They could be right.'

'Are you?'

'Omertà. And all that? Do you mind!'

'I didn't mean in the gangster sense. But the principle, the family concept. You have that. Yet you are not married. This I find very strange.'

His mouth took on a crooked smile.

'Once, nearly . . . if the fates had been kinder. On another occasion, I was too late. Someone else had beaten me to it. Both were a long time ago.'

'I wasn't attempting to pry. Forgive me.'

'Don't keep on apologizing. I'll need to be measured for a halo! Though that, I suppose, is preferable to wearing cornuti!'

He made horns with his fingers.

She laughed.

'No fear of that. Not so long as you stay single.'

'Exactly.'

He lifted his hand, made a gesture for the bill. This conversation, he decided, was getting out of hand.

They walked down slowly, through the old town that had once known the tread of Saracen and Crusader. Noli diffused the same warm odour peculiar to most medieval Italian towns. A mingle of wine vinegar, smouldering charcoal, and left-over sunshine. It rose from the cobbled streets, trickled out from doorways, accosted them from alleys that smudged in an inkwell of blackness.

It was still with them in the Piazza Ignoto, outside the Caffé Sport, where a school of old men played *scopa* in a pool of lamplight and the post-mortems that followed each hand bounced hollow from the ancient clock tower.

Further on, along the Corso, the odour dispersed, only to be taken up by another on the promenade. There the boats were queued in silent rows; with them the fish-tables, scrubbed and bare but redolent with the ghost of the day's catch. On the shadowy beach below, the nets were spread and waiting for tomorrow's trawl. Only the sea moved with them as they paced along, a violet-dark murmuring tongue tipped with phosphorescence where it licked the shore.

Away again, into the town, up the narrow street that led to the Villa Fiorita, hand in hand like young lovers they climbed the steps—she, light-headedly happy, yet tensing somewhat as the villa drew nearer; he, aware of this and not quite sure what she expected him to do, or if she would be disappointed if he didn't . . .

They need not have dwelt upon it. The matter was out of their hands. As they came through the gate and across the garden, a shadow spoke up from a deck-chair spread beside a folded beach umbrella.

'Hello, there. I've been waiting for you.'

Voice male, English. Mills knew it before the shadow divorced itself and rose to meet them. John Herries.

Mills said: 'Hello, Herries,' then went past him, guiding Mairhi by the elbow. He offered no introductions and they were already through the glass-door entrance.

Herries turned, shrugged, sat down again.

Mairhi threw Mills a quick glance.

That taut, hard look was back in the jaw, lips creased thin. This Herries, whoever he was, spelled trouble. She knew it instinctively. The whys and wherefores didn't matter; only the pang that something might take Mills away.

She caught his hand again, pressed it to the curve of her breast. It conveyed more to him than words. He wanted to take her in his arms, there and then, and to hell with Herries, MI6, the lot.

He collected their keys from the board, escorted her up to her door. He unlocked it, opened it, motioned her to enter. Her hand went automatically for the light switch. She felt his fingers cover hers, draw them away.

There was light enough in the room. The French windows were drawn back wide; a brilliant canopy of stars splintered over the balcony. They stood for a moment, just inside the door. Then she turned, crushed herself against him.

'Don't go away,' she whispered. '*Please* . . .'

'Who said anything about going away?'

'That man down there—it's true, isn't it, he wants you for something? I can feel it in my bones.'

His hands moved gently over her back, along her shoulders.

'You have no bones,' he said. 'The good Lord moulded you in one piece, then stuck on a hank of hair. If you turned out to be a *dame de voyage*, I wouldn't be surprised.'

She had no idea what that meant. Nor did she want to know at that particular moment. All she wanted was for him to say, 'I'm

not going. Not now or at any time. That man down there—forget
about him. Forget about everything.'

But he didn't say it. His lips came down on hers—crushed
them, held them, crushed them again. When he finally pulled
away, it was not to shut the door and turn the key on the inside. It
was to utter one short, guillotine of a phrase that cut through her
desire and left her numb with frustration.

'Good night, amore . . . sleep well!'

And he was gone.

18

DOWN IN THE GARDEN, Herries said, 'You're a BF. You know that,
don't you?'

Mills said, 'You came all the way from London just to tell
me?'

'What I want to know is—why?'

'Why not? Twenty years with the service. It's time I quit.'

'Fair enough . . . if that's the only reason. You've been a good
man; the best. But tempus fugit. We all have to pack it in some
time——'

'With handshakes all round—and a gold watch. Plus a D-
notice to stop me writing my memoirs?'

'It's money, I suppose.'

'Money?'

'Come off it, Millsy. I know what you pull in each month. It
wouldn't keep a vice-consul in salted peanuts. True, you've
always managed a bit on the side with Moshe Singer . . .' Herries
flapped a hand. 'We know you never really ceased working for
him. But Auntie was content to give it the Nelson eye. Still,
Moshe didn't pay you to do this one—even though you did meet
up in Berlin!'

Herries smirked his omnipotence. But all he got was a curled
lip in return.

'Big Brother watching, eh? And me brought up to believe that
only the Ivans did that. Or was it Bigger Brother, the one who
wields the stick from Washington, a CIA tip-off? I remember
seeing Berg bumming around the Ku-damm, making out he was
a pretzel. And we know the CIA have had it in for Moshe ever
since Eichmann. Such a godawful embarrassment that trial,

reviving all the atrocity stories, just when the pricks had the people accepting the Hun as a nice, clean, stalwart ally!'

Herries flapped his hand again.

'I'm not here to argue politics. I know you'd have had every German in the gas chambers if you'd had your way. You have your reasons; but with some, anti-Germanism brands you automatically a Commie. We didn't go along with that. We knew you better. We even used you as a double-agent with the cold war on the boil. That's how far we trusted you—allowing you to work for the Ivans. Because we knew you had no time for them, either. And you still haven't . . . so far as we know.'

' "So far as we know" being the operative phrase?'

'You can thank Auntie you've lasted as long as you have. Washington marked you down for a pinko years ago; raised all Cain about it. But he dug his heels in. No Yankee Doodle tells me whom I can employ; they wouldn't know a good agent if they crapped one . . . That kind of thing. He had utter faith in you. But after this little lot . . .' Herries shrugged. 'Knocking off this Schultz in a crematorium, then charging up the department with the coffin and the hearse . . . Christ, you've got a nerve!'

Mills grinned. 'I thought that'd get up your nose. I could have added flowers and a crocodile of professional mourners, but I knew there'd be a squeal about expenses. As it was, I paid for the frying out of my own pocket.'

'It really was Schultz, I suppose . . .?' Herries let a hopeful note creep into his voice. 'I mean, if the Ivans were on to you . . . We know they and the HVA were in a flat spin about his defection. If you had to work a flanker . . .'

Mills shook his head.

'Sorry. It *was* Schultz who went crisp. Or—as I prefer to call him—Reinecke. But I can't hope to make you see it my way— that I could carry a torch for twenty years, waiting for the chance to push it under the bastard's tail. That's too simple. There must be an ulterior motive. And the first thing that comes in to your grubby little mind is money . . . I must have done it for money. And who was the paymaster? Not Moshe Singer. You've ferreted out that much. Neither was it the Salvation Army nor the Pope. So it must have been Moscow. Is that it? They paid me to stop his defection?'

'It isn't what *I* think,' said Herries. 'Or even what Auntie thinks. We don't really believe the Ivans paid you to kill Schultz or Reinecke or whatever you like to call him——'

'What, then?'

Herries shifted in his chair, eyed Mills carefully.

'Look, chum. I was never one for talking round corners. I'll lay it straight down the line. This bird had information. Valuable information. And I mean that. LSD is not just a charge in Technicolor that helps the hippies find God. It has the makings of a sophisticated weapon that could go a long way towards winning an all-out global war. And without reducing us all to gamma rays and radioactive dust.'

'Very considerate of it! It merely makes us into zombies!'

Herries ignored the interruption, went on: 'The Ivans have been stockpiling the stuff for years. So have we. So has our Uncle Samuel. We're all working on it, researching and improving—or trying to. From time to time, there've been rumours of a breakthrough on the other side——'

'Reinecke told me. I put as much in my first report. A phoney leak-out, deliberately piped to confuse the Americans.'

'He also told you there was a genuine new development going on in Dresden.'

'True . . .' Mills nodded. 'But he could have been bluffing. And even if he wasn't, he was certainly bluffing about his own part in it.'

'How can you know that?'

Mills smiled bleakly. 'I wasn't born yesterday. If Reinecke had been a Grade A boffin, he wouldn't have been chewing his arse off in Berlin, fretting he might have to answer for his Nazi past. He would have had nothing to fear on that score. The Russians are as capable at wielding the whitewash brush as the West. Unless you've forgotten, Hitlermen who worked at Peenemunde and Nordhausen, who plastered London and Antwerp with V-2s, now play as happily with space-rockets at Cape Kennedy and Kazakhstan. The more efficient a killer you were for Adolf in the field of technology, the wider the red carpet laid down by the Kremlin and the Pentagon. Reinecke must have known that. But not being the top-secret chemist he pretended to be, he knew he was in dead nick. Particularly with Prague. They'd have had him under the sod in no time flat. That's why he was on the run, why he wanted across the Wall.'

'An interesting theory,' mused Herries. 'And if true, we could have found it out for ourselves . . . if you had obeyed orders and brought him over. But you didn't.'

'And why? Because I knew full well what would have happened. Having been found a fake, he would have been turned over to Bonn. They'd have given him one of *their* trials—for what they're worth—and fifteen years, maybe, with five off for good behaviour!' Mills lifted his hands in disgust. 'Where would that have left me? A doddering sixty by the time I caught up with him again. With just about enough strength to stand him up in a pissoir and shake it for him. Oh, no . . . not for me! I had my dispensation to stick him in that oven . . . and I'm not talking fancy double-o-sevens with licence to kill. My authority goes back to a courts-martial——'

'Don't give me the history. I've seen your dossier. I'm the one who keeps it up to date, remember?' Herries couldn't keep the sarcasm out of his voice. 'I know you're a nutcase when it comes to Nazis. I can sympathise, up to a point. I've seen the secret archive films, and still get nightmares. But that's neither here nor there. Even if I could go along with your theory and why you did for Schultz, even if Auntie could—and, for all I know, he might —it doesn't stop there." He paused for effect.

Mills lifted his eyebrows. 'Go on.'

'I will. This bloody business has been bouncing signals around the globe loud and clear. We know for gospel that both Moscow and Washington have it firmly fixed in their minds that Schultz *was* in possession of vital information. That you hi-jacked it from him, then shut his mouth.' He made something of a rueful smile. 'I need hardly tell you the rest. Moscow sees you flogging it to the Pentagon. The Pentagon sees you flogging it back to Moscow. Both have grounds for such beliefs, or think they have. The KGB know you for a British agent . . . ergo, you're a tool of the White House. The CIA, on the other hand, have it in their pinhead minds that the hammer and sickle is patterned all over your drawers . . .'

'And where do *you* stand? You and Auntie? Officially, that is?'

Herries gave an elaborate shrug.

'Like I said before, you're an old man . . . in this business, at any rate. Don't let's kid ourselves. In a year, maybe two, you're due for the chop. We know your financial position down to the last farthing. We know you can't retire to the sun-soaked Bahamas with a bevy of brown-tittied bibbies. So what faces you? Some kind of security job? Sorting out the fluff for the International Wool Secretariat? Or doing guard duty at a sub-branch of Barclays Bank? In other words, you're up the creek, chum.

Unless, of course, you've managed the one thing every free-lance operator dreams of—pulling off the Big One!'

Mills crooked his mouth at this candid glimpse into his future. He said, 'So that's it? I'm holding you all to ransom—ready to sell to the highest bidder, be he Christ Almighty or the King of Siam.'

Herries nodded curtly.

'That's about the size of it. So long as you squat on your arse in Noli. Face it man, read the signals for yourself! Turn right . . . what is it? A gnat's piss into France and le grande Charles, ready to buy anything if he thinks it'll spite the Americans. Turn left . . . a flea-hop across the Adriatic to Albania and Hodza—friend of the Yellow Peril, who'd buy it for the pleasure of kicking the Cossacks in the teeth. And if you want to play it neutral, all you have to do is back-pedal over the hills to Zurich, where they'll buy for the best reason of all—to turn it into a profit. And you won't have to climb off your backside for Uncles Samuel and Ivan. They'll come to you!'

'You forgot to mention Liechtenstein. They're the coming world power . . . or haven't you heard?'

'I've heard enough—said enough,' said Herries. He opened his mouth in a wide yawn, glanced at his watch. 'Christ, look at the time! I'll see you in the morning, packed and ready to leave. We're booked on a flight from Nice.' He threw it at Mills casually, got to his feet, gave a shiver in the night air. 'By the way,' he added. 'That flossie you had in tow—she looked a cracker. You reckon she'll still be awake and panting?'

Mills made no comment, merely asked, 'Where are you staying?'

'At the Monique. And I was lucky to get in. I thought the season was over, but it seems I'm wrong. I tried here, naturally, but they could only offer me a broom closet.'

'By the end of the week you can have the place to yourself.'

'So I heard. A pity. I think I might like it. Very quiet, very restful. Nothing to do but swim by day and screw by night. If only I'd brought Penelope!'

'Penelope?' echoed Mills, without any real interest.

Herries grinned broadly.

'The latest piece of crumpet, Just eighteen, and all Mary Quant. A wing-dinger in ever-so-mini skirts. And when she sits down, Jesus Chirst—no pants! Dead kinky!' He leered at Mills. 'Has a thing, too, about mature men. Anything under thirty-five is strictly for schoolgirls. You'd be right up her alley. I might even loan her to you for a weekend . . . if you're a good boy.'

The leer snapped off like a flashlight. The banter went on, but with the chill of finality for Mills.

'You *are* going to be a good boy? No pulling a fast one on your Uncle John? I should hate to have to give you the needle in order to get you back nice and quiet. It always makes for problems with the douane, turning up at the airport in an ambulance. The Frogs are suspicious devils. Show an Elastoplast over a split fingernail and they want to dig under it for smuggled diamonds——'

'Good night,' said Mills, abruptly.

19

MILLS let himself into his room, threw the key on the dressing-table. He lit a cigarette, jerked at his tie. He had expected trouble —that went without saying—but he hadn't bargained for this . . . if one could believe all that Herries had said.

Was it the truth? Common sense told him it was. Auntie never sent the Co-ordinator out on a collection job; not unless there was an almighty flap on. It couldn't be that Auntie feared he might defect, pull a Philby on them. What knowledge he had would scarcely fill a vodka glass. The KGB could tell *him* more about the inner workings and set-up of British espionage.

No . . . it had to be this LSD-25 business, the top-secret hog-wash that Reinecke was supposed to have been toting. Had he slipped up there?

Oddly enough, the thought had crossed his mind that something like this might arise . . . at the very moment the coffin had disappeared into limbo. A ludicrous thought, at the time. He had been so intent on seeing the bastard fry, he had dismissed it. Yet if he had given it a second reading, he would have realized its possibility—that whether it was true or not, there would be some who would think so.

With twenty years' experience behind him, Mills knew well enough the complexities of espionage thinking. He had studied all three services—British, American, Russian—at close quarters. He had a fair idea what made them tick.

Fundamentally, there was little to choose between them— though the KGB and the CIA were thicker on the ground and more lavishly supplied with funds. All three—in a sense—could be likened to thoroughbreds: highly trained, and bolstered by a stud-book that guaranteed stamina and ability. Equally, all three were shod with a finely tempered logic to prevent them going lame.

Yet, at times, a plate could be spread. It happened whenever one of them became obsessed with a theory. Then logic found itself on the anvil being hammered into shape to fit that theory. It happened rather more often with the Russians and the Americans, who both carried imbalance and over-weight in the leaden form of ideological bogies—the one with his anti-capitalism, the other with his anti-Communism.

Perfidious Albion hadn't this problem . . . at least, not in the secret service field. The jockeys at the top were all career civil servants, unfettered by politics, aloof from any emotional patriotism. Auntie was a good example of the breed. He gave God Save The Queen and The Red Flag the same icy super-ciliousness; showed a surface politeness to jingoists and left-wing intellectuals alike. Then hoisted two sly fingers at both when their backs were turned.

To the CIA, with their computed zealousness, this show of British phlegm was a complacency bordering on insufferable conceit.

To the dogmatic KGB, it was further proof of a hidebound caste system on the crumble, eventually to decay. And in the same context, Mills could see how easy it must be to equate an agent such as he with moral turpitude. No patriotism, no political conviction, an anarchist to authority . . . he could only be in the spy game for monetary gain. In their twisted logic, neither could accept the truth—that he had killed Reinecke simply because the man was an ex-Nazi. There had to be more to it than that. Reinecke, as Schultz, had worked on something secret. Mills had murdered him for that secret. So when Herries had said both would have agents on his tail, it was a safe bet he wasn't exaggerating.

Which brought him back to MI6 and Auntie. Contrary to American and Russian yardsticks, Auntie was neither complacent nor ready for the rubbish-tip. Auntie, in truth, was a tough, demanding, quite ruthless realist. Not a man to love, or even like. But one held in the highest esteem. Mills had always found him to be a fair man. It was conceivable he might believe the truth about Reinecke's death . . . but it was only a *might,* not a certainty. And Herries had put his finger unerringly on the reason why—his future.

Future? How well that was summed up! He had a few hundred pounds in his London bank account, with precious little hope of increasing the balance over the next two years on his present salary. He could hardly spin that out over his retirement without taking some other employment in whatever field was open to a man of fifty. There was no pension—not for a permanent-temporary. That status earned one a slightly higher rate of pay, a form of compensation for not being on the Establishment. On the other hand, it was true—and, he profoundly hoped, unknown to Whitehall—he had salted away eight thousand pounds here, in Italy, made on the side but strictly legit. Very useful at a time like this, but still far from enabling him to become a lotus-eater.

So what to do? Go back with Herries and maintain his innocence? And what then? They would never be sure of him again, never let him out of their sight. He had heard rumours of what could happen to someone in his position. Certified as mentally unstable, tucked away in some nuthouse—for his own protection, of course. Until, with the years, LSD-25 was old hat and over with cobwebs . . .

A living death. Not for him, that. He must take his chance with the KGB and the CIA and anyone else who tried to strong-arm him . . .

20

'HELLO,' said Mills.

'Hello,' said Mairhi.

The terrace, next morning. She was taking breakfast. Wearing enormous sun cheaters, although the sun was having trouble pushing back a veil of fibrous cloud. She pulled a spare cup towards her, picked up the coffee-pot.

'How do you like it?'

'Black as it comes . . . thanks.'

He took it as an invitation, sat down opposite her. She made a face as the coffee-pot dribbled dry.

'Oh, dear . . .'

She half turned; but Gianni, who served at breakfast, was

already hovering with a fresh pot. He glanced at Mills enquiringly. Breakfast was a casual affair, no strict table arrangements.

'You take breakfast with the signorina, signore?'

Mills cast a quick glance at Mairhi. She did not meet his look, went on filling the coffee cup. The decision was up to him. He nodded.

'Si . . . grazie.'

'Prego.'

Gianni moved away. Mairhi passed the cup across the table.

'Where's your friend?' She made the question casual, light.

'He's staying at the Monique.'

'Oh. He was lucky to find a room.'

'So he said.'

'Is he staying long?'

'Just the one night. He goes back today.'

'Short and sweet.' She sipped her own coffee. 'Still, that's people. They rush about these days.'

'One of the penalties of the world growing smaller.'

He tried a smile. It came gingerly, as if attempting an excursion across a bed of nails. Hell, he thought, what's with me? I've got trouble enough . . .

She gave him the smile back.

'You are going with him?'

'He wants me to.'

'And you'll do as he wants?'

'Not necessarily.'

'That's a peculiar answer.'

'It's a peculiar situation.'

'Oh . . .'

The conversation suffered a seizure. Embarrassment was saved by Gianni, reappearing on the terrace with a tray. He unloaded it in front of Mills, who watched the performance like a man who had never seen a waiter unload a tray before. Mairhi poured herself fresh coffee, unwrapped a cube of sugar, slipped it on to a spoon, held it to the surface so she could watch it dissolve. Like Mills, she studied it as if for the first time.

Gianni picked up his empty tray and left. Mills broke a *brioche*, made a clumsy job of smearing it from a foiled pat of butter. Mairhi watched the last of the sugar crystals froth white from the spoon.

'Mairhi——' he said, suddenly.

Her pulse skipped a beat. The first time he had used her name.

'—Would you mind doing something for me?'

'If I can.'

'You'll be going into town as usual? After breakfast?'

'As usual,' she nodded. It was part of the daily routine to go around the other hotels, checking if her customers had any problems and to take bookings for excursions if they were required.

'I need to hire a car,' he said. 'I thought—well, in your position, you'd know the best one to contact.'

Her heart lurched.

'There's a taxi service to Savona, for the Genoa train that connects with the Rome-Paris express. If you have it pick you up at a quarter to six, you'll have ample time.'

The words tripped off her tongue. A parrot answer, she was called upon to use a thousand times in a holiday season. Mills recognized it for what it was—the efficient Miss Odell at work. He found himself grinning broadly, suddenly at ease with her again.

'Who said anything about the Savona and the Rome-Paris express?'

'I thought . . . you and your friend——'

'He's going the other way. To Nice.'

'A car for Nice, then?' Her mind was still working as a tourist agent. 'It'll cost a pretty penny. You must expect to pay double fare——'

'Jumping the gun again! I'm not interested in Nice. I want the car for myself . . . a self-drive job.'

A ray of hope again.

'Where to?'

He shrugged. 'Does that matter . . . so long as I pay the mileage?'

'Well, how long for, then?'

'I'm not sure. Two or three days, I imagine.'

'H'm. Self-drive in Noli,' she mused. 'I could try Fratelli Rilla. Or the Azienda Autonoma might know . . .' She hesitated, then, 'I have a car myself. A small Fiat. You're welcome to that, if it's only for a few days.' She went on, hurriedly. 'I really have no use for it in Noli, as you can imagine, except to drive around to the Cap Hotel. And anyway, I much prefer to walk.'

'That's kind of you,' he said. 'But I may not be coming back.'

It was like stepping under a cold shower. Just when her hopes were rising.

'Not coming back? But——'

'I was prepared to pay whoever hired me the car for the trouble of collecting it.'

She chewed her lip thoughtfully. 'You could still take mine. I'll be leaving here myself on Monday, once I've seen my last party off. If I knew where you would be leaving it . . . I could. . .'

She removed the sun cheaters, looked at him.

He saw the dark rings under her eyes. She'd had a lousy night —that was evident. And the eyes themselves were worried, perplexed. Their message not hard to read. They said: Please, I want to help; don't be too proud or stubborn; don't make me have to spell it out in words; I've got my pride, too; I can't just throw myself at you so soon a second time . . .

Her hand came down on the table between them. His own dropped over it gently.

'It's all so bloody complicated,' he said.

His eyes drifted away from hers, across the terrace and over the low balcony, down towards the gate and the steps beyond.

She followed his glance. She saw a man approaching. She couldn't be sure—she hadn't seen him by daylight—but it must be Herries.

Her fingers twitched instinctively. Mills felt the movement, turned back to her.

'The fact of the matter is, I have to go along with him at least part of the way. The last thing I wanted was to get you involved. Yet I do need your help.'

'It's yours. You must know that.'

He squeezed her fingers. 'I only wish I could explain what it's all about. Maybe, later—I don't know—but not now.'

She helped him over the hurdle.

'Never mind that. Just tell me what you want me to do.'

'That must wait until I've spoken to *him*.' He jerked his head, glanced out again towards the gate.

Herries looked up, waved a hand in salute.

21

HERRIES had hired a Citroën with a French driver—a squat, pock-faced man named Jean-Pierre. Jean-Pierre drove in the manner of most Frenchmen, shoulders hunched and foot down, pushing the car at a fair lick.

Herries and Mills sat in the back seat, smoking in silence.

Mills was taking it remarkably well, Herries thought. Not a murmur of dissent. His suitcase had been packed and ready to go. Herries had had the chance to see Mills' room on the pretence of giving a hand, and had made a sly check of the clothes-closets. Swept clean; not so much as a collar stiffener in sight. No question of something left behind to come back to.

Except the bird, of course. Herries grinned to himself. Name of Odell, a rep for Bluebird Tours—just in case Auntie wanted her checked. But just a casual hotel acquaintance, this one, he reckoned. Mills hadn't even bothered to say goodbye.

Herries tossed his cigarette out of the window as they sped through Varigotti. The sun was high now, beating warm on the roof. He took out a handkerchief, patted his upper lip. He saw a girl on the promenade ahead, her bikini so brief it showed three inches of buttock cleavage from the base of the spine . . .

He twisted round to get the front elevation as they went past . . . Stacked to perfection *that* side, too . . . 38s or 40s, apple dumplings on the boil . . . Ah—so long, pretty pussy. It's back to bloody Whitehall, grey and pissing with rain, I shouldn't wonder . . . Still, there was always Penelope . . .

Mills read Herries' thoughts without looking at him. It wasn't hard when you knew the man's weakness. He killed his own cigarette, said:

'This Penelope bird of yours—you taking her back a stick of rock?

Herries jerked his head round.

'Thanks for reminding me. She'll expect something besides the usual. Any suggestions?'

'You can always make it perfume at Nice Airport, I suppose.'

'She has enough Chanel to do the butterfly in.' Herries shook his head emphatically. 'It'd better be something Italiano this time. But don't say a cameo brooch, for Gawd's sake! She's got one already, big enough to cover her crotch!'

'How about a handbag?'

'H'm . . . that's an idea. A suede job to go with her pussy pelmet and boots. Where d'you suggest we stop for it? Alassio? San Remo?' Herries was possessed of a sudden, suspicious thought. Mills was making his move, seeking an excuse for them to stop. Alassio or San Remo would suit him nicely—both jam-packed with tourists, tailor-made for giving one the slip.

'You could do worse.'

'Yeah.' And I could do better, thought Herries. He looked ahead, over Jean-Pierre's shoulder. The road curved and rushed through a tunnel, then out and into a second one. Beyond, it stretched straight in a blue-black line—beach to the left, villas terracing upwards to the right. A sign swept by: Finale Ligure.

Herries leaned back in his seat, looked smug. 'We'll try here.'

'Suit yourself.'

Mills sounded disappointed.

That satisfied Herries. He leaned forward again, tapped Jean-Pierre on the shoulder.

'Stop somewhere in the centre. I want to do some shopping.'

Jean-Pierre found a spot to park, slid the car into the kerb. Herries looked about him, made a grimace.

'Not much here,' he muttered.

'Better wait for Alassio,' said Mills. 'Or why not try Loano? It's only a few kilometers further on.' He made it sound as if he couldn't care less.

Loano. So that's it, thought Herries. One place he'd make sure they went through like a dose of salts!

'Sure; we'll try Loano,' he said. 'But we might as well have a look-see here first.' He climbed out of the car. 'You're coming with me?'

Shaded as a question, it implied an order. Mills eased himself across the seat, got out beside Herries. They walked away to a side-road that dipped to the left.

A narrow road, shadowed from the sun, cobbled from wall to wall. It led to an intersection, running at right-angles, also cobbled, but wider, dappled with sunlight and noise. Herries thought it looked promising. He could see a shop ahead, tails of straw hats and raffia baskets hanging down the open front— typical tourist come-on.

'Is it still a handbag?' Mills asked. He nodded along the street. 'There's a likely place.'

The shop had windows and doorway crammed with wares and

a generous overspill racked on shelves outside. A bold-eyed woman with frizzed-up hair offered them a smile as wide as her ample bosom. Mills gave her back the eye and the smile. He had a hunch about her. He clucked his tongue, made a mildly bawdy gesture that was pure Neapolitan. When she opened her mouth he knew he was right.

'Hey, hey! What's all this, you cheeky monkey!'

The Italian that rolled out was *basso* and strident, chewed off at the tail, and cluttered thick with *mms* and *nns* and *zzs*.

Mills answered in the same dialect.

'An English sucker for you, bella; wants a bag for his wife; thinks it'll keep her sweet, stop her making horns at him!'

'I don't see her around. Where is she, then?'

'In bed with the other man—where else?'

'You know too much! Is the other man your father?'

'Right on the button. He's keeping it warm for me!'

'And you fancy me as an encore, I suppose?'

'Who wouldn't! But get this one's money first. I want my percentage.'

The bold-eyed woman slapped her thighs, roared with laughter. Mills did the same. Herries looked from one to the other, ventured an uncertain grin.

'What was that all about? At best, his Italian was limited. When it wandered off into dialect, he was completely lost.

'She thinks you one hell of a good-looker . . . very sexy,' said Mills. 'You have an open invitation to turn over her goods—and you can take that any way you like!'

Herries grinned, eyed the woman. She was smiling at him wickedly and winking at Mills.

Neat, he thought, trying to get me on the lay. By the time I got past her corsets, he'd be on his way. 'Thanks very much,' he muttered. 'But not tonight, Josephine!' He picked up the first handbag in front of him, opened it, and looked inside.

Mills went through the same motions. But his eyes were sliding up and down the street. Just beyond Herries was a fruit stall, heaped in a small alp of ripe, squashy persimmons. A few had slipped and splattered on the cobbles, not six inches from Herries' right heel.

Away past the stall, weaving its way towards them, came a three-wheeled carrier, honking and spluttering a path through the pedestrians. And to the other side of him, Mills saw that Bold Eyes had her attention diverted by other customers. A woman in tight slacks, coolie hat, and braided yellow hair. Her companion had wrinkled skin, freckled like salami. They were talking German.

Herries cocked an ear, grinned maliciously.

'Friends of yours?'

'Bloody Krauts,' said Mills. 'This coastline stinks with 'em! Make up your mind and let's go!'

He dumped the handbag he was holding back on the shelf—clumsily, so that it sent a whole row cascading in Herries' direction. Herries flung out his hands instinctively to save them. Mills did likewise, colliding with Herries, nudging him off-balance. Herries stepped back, put his heel squarely on the squashed persimmons, and began to slide. He wobbled like a beginner on a ski slope, a handbag in each hand, a third looped over a wrist. The next moment, he was splayed over the front wheel of the carrier and down on to the cobbles the other side.

The carrier stopped with a screech of brakes, a shower of curses from the driver. Heads turned and eyes swung. Only Mills looked the other way. He touched Bold Eyes on the sleeve, whispered in her ear.

She stared at him, then across at Herries, now coming to his knees on the far side of the carrier. She bounded over, caught him by the hair, tugged at the handbag looped about his wrist.

'Che ladro!' she belted out, *fortissimo*. 'Che mascalzonn'! Ecco le porcherie pubbliche che fanno gli inglesi!'

With Bold Eyes screaming and pulling at him and the carrier-driver waving fingers in his face, Herries looked dazed and bewildered. He let the handbag go, scrambled to his feet, shook off the pair of them, and made to push his way clear.

Too late. By now he had a crowd to contend with, pressing in upon him, setting up a wall of let-justice-be-done, parting only to permit a *carabiniere* on the scene.

Herries glared around, looking for Mills. He was standing at the fringe of the crowd, wearing a pained expression.

'Hey!' Herries beckoned him to come forward, to interpret and explain.

Mills gave him his answer in a gesture. He extended his fingers, moved them slowly back and forth under a raised chin.

Herries didn't need to know gestures to guess what that meant. The next time he looked, Mills was gone . . .

Mills came down into the octagonal-shaped *piazza* close to the promenade, found the Fiat, and climbed in beside Mairhi. He glanced at his watch.

'Hope I haven't kept you waiting.'

She smiled, shook her head, reversed out of the parking space. A moment later, they were heading back towards Noli.

22

THE *carabiniere* was a wise, experienced man. He knew when to apply the unwritten law regarding tourists: only make an arrest if guilty of indecent exposure or being rude about the Pope. He had ignored Herries' insistence that he find his companion, an Englishman — but whom Bold Eyes had been adamant spoke Napule. An *inglese* speaking *Napule*! A likely story. They'd be saying next he had two heads! The *carabiniere* knew what was wrong with Herries . . . too much of the grape under the noonday sun. He'd better see the *ubbriaccone* back to his car, just to make sure he wasn't driving himself. And satisfied at the sight of Jean-Pierre at the wheel, he had saluted and moved away.

Herries—on his way back to Noli some forty-five minutes after Mills—was far from satisfied. The physical hurt was negligible— a bruise or two, a shin grazed, a sore scalp where his hair had been scragged. His pocket had suffered more . . . the price of a handbag he no longer bloody-well wanted; an on-the-spot settle-ment of the damage done to the carrier's mudguard.

But it was his pride that had taken the real beating. Christ, if he got his hands on Mills he'd skin him alive! If . . . There were no ifs about it. He *had* to get him—and bloody quick. He'd be for the high jump if he didn't. He'd never be able to explain away that fiasco in Finale Ligure!

Mills was smart. Grudgingly, Herries admitted that. Pure opportunism. He could never have planned it—not down to the three-wheeler, the squashed persimmons, the bitch at the bag-shop. Yet it couldn't have been entirely opportunism. He had a hunch that Mills had intended they stop in Finale Ligure all along; that he would have worked some excuse, even if the handbag idea had fallen on deaf ears. He must have laid on some-thing, somewhere, some means of transport. He had to go back to Noli some time, if only to collect his other suitcase. There had to be a second. The one in the boot of the Citroën had been checked: a bundle of dirty laundry, a pair of old slacks and wooden sandals, plus some bloody great stones to give it weight. Who helped Mills? That Bluebird crumpet. But naturally— who else? She must have been waiting for him with a car. In that case—Herries felt a sudden qualm—there would be no need for Mills to go back to Noli. The second suitcase could be in the car, together with her own, and they could be off God-knows-where; maybe in the opposite direction or—or—he snatched a road-map from the glove compartment—inland, for Crissakes; through Borgo and the mountains, to any one of a thousand hide-outs to suit their purpose. He was really up the spout if they'd done that!

Then he had a ray of hope. What about her job? Was she so involved with Mills she would walk out on it? He didn't know much about tourist reps, but he imagined they had to hang on until the last of their charges had departed. And Noli wasn't exactly a graveyard yet; not before the weekend. No. It was more likely she'd join Mills later, when her job was over. In which case, going back to Noli was the right thing to do. With any luck she'd lead him to Mills . . .

Herries let out a sigh, folded the map. He lit a cigarette, sat back in his seat. There was nothing more he could do for the moment.

23

MAIRHI sighed, slipped her hands down from Mills' neck, opened the car door, eased herself out from behind the wheel. As he moved over into her place, she shut the door, leaned on it, gave him a lingering glance.

'Ciao, tesore,' he murmured, letting in the gear lever.

'Ciao.' She put out a hand, rested it upon his shoulder. 'You'll be in touch . . . like you said?'

'Like I said. And in the way I said. You have my promise.' He reached up, squeezed her fingers. 'And you know what to do about Herries? Ten to one he'll be back and pressing hard. You are his only lead.'

'I'll deal with him . . . don't worry.'

'But I do. He's no fool, lover. Please be careful.'

'Careful . . . and good. That's *my* promise!'

She slid her hand away, touched her lips, then laid her fingers on his mouth, lightly. Then she stepped back, away from the car.

He glanced at the mirror, let the clutch rise slowly. The Fiat was on the move again.

'Ciao, bellezza! Non ti scordai dammi!' were the words she heard as the Fiat gathered speed. She watched it away, past the Cap Hotel, taking the long curve to the promenade of Noli.

'Non ti scordai dammi," she murmured back at the spume of dust. As if I ever could forget, no matter what happens later— whether I am your lover, as you called me, or some old boot kicked aside . . .

She wiped away a surreptitious tear. No use crying, you silly bitch. That won't solve anything. In seventy-two hours you'll know where you stand—whether he wants you or not. You'll either be in his arms again . . . or else the entire Italian police force will be humping all over the peninsula looking for your blessed Fiat!

The thought made her giggle out loud, so much so she had a passing motorist throwing her the quick eye. The car slowed perceptibly, the driver's head twisted round to get a better look. Holy Crippen, she panicked, does he really take me for a tottie? That would just make my day—the respectable Signorina Odell, the virgin Mairhi, had up for soliciting on the promenade at Noli!

She turned into the Cap Hotel hurriedly, hoping to God the man wouldn't have the nerve to follow.

24

SOLOMON NARBUCCO was no beauty. Built like Fagin—as Alec Guinness portrayed him—it had been a cross and a half to bear. The other half had been the ghetto where he was born. A ghetto within the Arab casbah of the French colonial town of Constantine.

Raised in the squalor of the *souks*, he had clawed his way out and moved on to Bizerta, to become an acknowledged master of his craft, a Mantegna among engravers.

He had been apprenticed to one Black Moses of Marrakesh, the greatest of them all, who could inscribe the whole Book of Genesis in both Hebrew and Greek on the back of a postage-stamp—or so the story went. Diligent and painstaking, Solomon had found pleasure in the most laborious task. At the same time, he had eyes for things that didn't require a magnifying glass to reveal themselves . . . the temptations and opportunities presented to one of his skill.

Yet he had not turned to forgery until he came to Genoa after the war. Thousands of lost, unhappy survivors were drifting south from DP camps, eyes fixed on the Promised Land, the Jewish National Home in Palestine. Genoa was one of the ports they came to, scrabbling for places aboard overladen ships bound for Haifa. But immigration quotas were severely limited—politics had priority over humanity—and for every ship that ran the blockade successfully, a dozen were turned back to Cyprus, to yet another post-and-wire perimetered camp.

Stubbornly oblivious to the situation, still more refugees poured into Genoa. The Hagana agents were at their wits-end what to do. The pressure had to be filtered off somewhere. But somewhere was always bureaucratic in its demand for papers, passports, proof to rights of citizenship. So Solomon Narbucco's skills had come into their own. Supplied with the necessary tools and equipment for the trade, he had forged many hundreds of passports and documents.

As a direct result, there was a sudden and remarkable increase in apparently British-born Jews who spoke German, Polish, Magyar, Czech, Russian—almost any language other than English. The authorities became sceptical. British Intelligence was given the task of tracing the source of the discrepancy—a source that led back to Genoa and to Solomon Narbucco.

In its turn, his had presented a problem. The obvious answer was to reveal his shortcomings to his hosts, the Italians, and hope that they, in their wisdom, would place him behind bars. However, it was far more likely that the judiciary in Italy would have shown clemency. They couldn't be expected to see his crime through British eyes. All he was doing was helping to off-load from Italian soil a large number of stateless human beings who plagued the Questura from dawn to dusk, pleading for *soggiorno* permits which only inhumanity could refuse them.

The British, therefore, took the alternative course dearly beloved to them—the one of compromise. Narbucco would issue no more forged British passports or visas of entry into Palestine. He could concentrate on South America or the USA, anywhere that was in the opposite direction, providing he was not too obvious with it. And out of gratitude for their munificence, he could also work for MI6.

So a new chapter had been initiated in the life of Solomon

Narbucco. And Mills had been one of the first British agents to be supplied with forged papers to aid his espionage activities: one of the first of many who had reason to be grateful to the superb workmanship of the Jew from Constantine in the years that followed.

Mills came into Genoa late that afternoon, caught in the swirl of commuter traffic, its fumes shimmering in the sunlight. He made straight for the Hotel Narbucco, in the Via Balbi, sure of a room and a welcome from Solomon and his wife, Rachel. A vociferous welcome in a backwash of languages: *medina* Yiddish, Moroccan Arabic, Tunisian French, Genovese Italian, and fractured English, tossed together in a verbal salad impregnated with garlic. It was not until he had showered, changed his shirt, and put a dish of *polla alla contadina* under his belt that he got down to the reason for his visit.

'Solomon, old darling, I want two passports.'

'Eeeeeeeyeh!' The old man raised his hand in front of him in a straight line—the recognized gambit of respectability being asked to do the impossible.

'You can, and you know it, you old villain!'

'But two . . . ? Mama mia! Qu'est-ce que tu veux avec deux, gelibter? Ecco! Vat in the name of Jerusalem!'

'Not in the name of Jerusalem. Let's say Winkler for one . . . and Irlandese for the other.'

'German? Italiano? Impossibile!' Solomon's eyes went into orbit. 'I could let you 'ave a United Arab Republic, si, and a Costa Rican mit lots of permissions to enter Hong Kong. Yoi, yoi . . . vat you ask of me you don't know!' He rubbed his long nose in thought. 'This is your British Foreign Office, oui?'

'British Foreign Official, non. Strictly a personal favour.'

The eyes came down from the ceiling. They flickered at Mills like the tongue of an adder.

'Why for you want two, hein?'

'To cover you, my love. They know I'm here in Genoa. Or thereabouts. They know I'll come to you like a homing pigeon looking for a new flight of tail feathers. And they'll be down on you to find out.'

'You t'ink I gif you away——'

'Of course not. But they could be nasty with it. I wouldn't want that on my conscience. Anyway, it would suit me down to the ground if you did tell them.'

Mills paused. Solomon's eyes darted again. He showed a row of yellow teeth in a wicked grin.

'Ah . . . capeesh! I tell 'em all about the vun, but say noddinks about the odder!' He tapped his nose, drooped an eyelid in a grotesque wink. 'While they for Herr Winkler is looking, Signore Irlandese is arrivederla vavvia presto . . . molto furbo!' He laid one hand stiffly across the wrist of the other and waggled fingers up and down.

'You'll do it for me, then?'

Solomon's answer was to rise, pick up a bottle of Vecchia Romagna and two glasses. He filled these to the brim, passed one to Mills. Then:

'When you want la roba?'

'Yesterday,' said Mills.

'Si, of course, always yesterday . . . your English yoke! I need time, gelibter—molto tempo. I ain't no magical-maker!'

'The one thing I haven't much of.' Mills sipped his cognac. 'Midday tomorrow is my deadline.' He lowered the glass, pulled three passports from his inside pocket. One was British and genuine. The other two were early Narbucco masterpieces. He dropped them on the table. 'You're welcome to cannibalize any or all of those.' He fished out an envelope, put it down on top of the passports. 'Photographs. You can't say I haven't come prepared!'

He didn't mention the money that made up the bulk of the envelope. He knew better than talk prices with Solomon. The sum was ample payment for the work and the urgency. The old man would take it and be satisfied.

'Midday tomorrow.' Solomon muttered the words. 'It will kip me up all the night. Vat do I say to my Rachel ven she screeches for me to come to bed?'

'Tell her she's a shameless hussy. At your age, the pair of you shouldn't be at it every night!'

Solomon croaked happily at this compliment to his virility. He downed his cognac, picked up the passports, began to turn the pages. Mills was quick to notice the gleam of pride in his eyes. The old man would do the job and find pleasure in the doing. He relaxed back in his chair . . .

25

HERRIES was waiting for Mairhi when she got back to the Villa
Fiorita. He had already moved in and taken over Mills' old room.
He was on the terrace with an iced drink when she came into the
garden. He called down to her.

'Could I have a word with you, Miss Odell?'

Mairhi had a panic thought, to turn away hurriedly. In the
same split second, she recovered her poise, smiled and nodded.
'Don't worry, I'll take care of Herries,' she had said. Well, it was
up to her.

She accepted his offer of a drink, picked a deck-chair across
from him, ignoring the one he pulled out beside his own.

'Aren't you surprised to see me back?' he asked.

'I can't say I really thought about it.'

'But you knew Mills and I were leaving.'

'I knew *he* was.'

'I'm sure you did!'

A smutty undertone that made her skin crawl. She gave him a
straight look, bleak and chilly. He read the message. He would
have to play it carefully.

'No offence meant,' he apologized.

'I would hope not.'

Rossi came out with her drink. He handed her an envelope.

'Signore Mills left this for you, signorina. He was sorry he did
not see you to say goodbye.'

'Grazie.'

'Prego.'

Rossi withdrew.

'Would you excuse me?' she said to Herries. She slit the
envelope.

Cunning, thought Herries. The neat touch one might expect
from Mills. As if he knew they would be sitting on the terrace
together when Rossi handed her the note, riveting a doubt in the
mind automatically.

Dear Miss Odell: May I thank you for the kindness shown
me these past few days. You helped to make my short stay very
enjoyable. Perhaps you will allow me to return the compliment
when you are next in London. I will leave a message with the

Bluebird office where you can contact me. Warmest regards—
then the scrawl of his signature.

Mairhi read it with an inward smile. Not exactly a love letter.
She folded it, put it back in the envelope, picked up her drink.
She glanced at Herries.

'You were saying?'

Herries tinkled the ice in his glass.

'Was I? I'm sure it was nothing important.'

'But you wanted to speak with me—ask me something.'

She wanted it out in the open; no cat-and-mouse game.

'Did I?' He smiled lazily. 'Yes. Come to think of it, so I did.
Where is your car?' The last bit had a snap to it.

'My car?'

'A Fiat 600, red in colour, registration number . . .' He snapped
his fingers. 'Let's see now if I can remember.'

The panic thought was back with her. He must have seen the
car in Finale Ligure. And if he knew the registration number, he
could have it traced . . . Mairhi pulled herself up sharply. Mills
had warned her that Herries might bluff. So he knew she owned
a car. He could have got that much from a casual chat with Rossi
or Gianni.

'Go on,' she said. 'What is the number?'

Herries shrugged elaborately. 'Numbers are just numbers to
me.' He thought: A clever bitch. Or else well primed by Mills.

'Why the interest in my car?' she asked.

'Er, yes. I was wondering. I had to send the Citroën back, you
see. Which is a pity, as I'd have liked to take a look at the country
around here. And you having a car—well, you might consider
driving me around. I'd pay the ex's, of course.'

'I'm a tourist rep, not a guide, Mr. Herries.' No more than a
hint of sarcasm in her voice.

He put on a Herries special, a dazzling smile. 'Oh, please, now
—don't let's be stuffy! The name is John. And the truth is, I was
getting around to suggesting we have dinner together.'

'I'm sure we will. The meals here are very good. Signora Rossi
is an excellent cook.'

'I dare say; but I didn't mean here. I was thinking of somewhere fancy, à la carte. You know the kind of thing.'

'In that case, try the Cap Noli. You won't need a car for that.
Just a gentle stroll to give you an appetite.'

'Will you join me?'

She studied her drink for a moment. Why not? Whatever else
Herries might try, she knew this gambit. The old seduction
routine. It happened all the time. Never a holiday season passed
without some would-be Lothario trying his luck. An angle she
understood and could handle. The only tricky thing was the conversation. Well, she'd not done so badly, so far. She would
make out.

'Thank you. I would like that.' She drained her glass, rose. 'I
must go and change. Will you give me an hour?'

'An hour,' said Herries, climbing to his feet. He watched her
go, eyes licking over her. All the makings of a good lay there.
Who said one couldn't mix business with pleasure?

He rang the bell, ordered another drink.

26

THE DINNER wasn't bad. Prawns *cacciatora*, breasts of chicken
with mushrooms, and a good wine.

After the prawns, Herries handed her the envelope. The note
from Mills.

'You left it on the terrace.' He didn't add she had done it
deliberately so that he could read it for himself. They must take
him for a mug!

'Thank you.' She put it away in her handbag. 'But it wasn't
important. Something about seeing him in London when I
return.'

'How did you get on with him?'

'I found him—well, interesting. Especially when I learned his
identity.'

'Oh?' Her answer surprised him.

She smiled. 'Well, he is a bit of a legend, you know. Irlandese,
the partisan leader. A long time ago, perhaps, but memories die
hard in this country.'

Herries felt a sudden pique.

'War records are a bit old hat, aren't they? Not that I'm
decrying the man. Don't think that. I've known Mills a long time;
buddies for years. I've the greatest possible admiration for him.
But he's human, like the rest of us. He can make mistakes. Still,
I've got to hand it to him—he made no mistake in his choice of
partner.' He paused, slit his eyes in a cunning smile.

'Partner?' She looked puzzled.

'Partner for life . . . wife! A real doll is Mafalda—one of the loveliest women I've ever met. Italian, of course. They came together during the war. Though she couldn't have been much more than a child then. There's a good fifteen years between them. And four of the most gorgeous kids imaginable. I was godfather to one of them . . . the second, I think—or was it the third? Anyway, they must be growing up now. The way time flies. I certainly envy him his luck on that score. I dare say that's why I'm still the bachelor gay . . . looking for another Mafalda—the perfect woman!'

Mairhi felt momentarily shattered. Was it true? My God, but Herries made it sound convincing! And it made sense—that was the trouble. She had been left wondering. She had even asked why hadn't he married. He must have known many women. He had mentioned two. Was one of them his Mafalda? A wife and four children! What did that make *her*?

She stared down at her plate as the waiter served the chicken. Mills had warned her Herries would pull every trick in the book. He was making a thorough job of it.

She smiled across at him as the waiter left.

'What is your idea of the perfect woman?'

His answer was smooth. 'The one I happen to be with.'

'Oh, I'm sure!'

'But I mean it. And why shouldn't I? You've got what it takes. Good looks, all the physical attributes. The other ingredients, too—charm, poise, intelligence.' He smiled. 'But not too much of the latter, I hope! I get over-awed in the presence of a bluestocking. That's awfully bad for a man's ego!' He dismissed the waiter and then refilled Mairhi's glass. 'Oh, I know you think I'm shooting a line. I don't deny I've used it in my time. But once in a while, it happens to be the truth.' He finished it with a warm look.

Mairhi thought: Well, well, well. You've overplayed your hand, you chancer! What do you take me for—some eighteen-year-old fresh out of the Bog of Killywilly with the Sign of the Cross on my forehead to protect me from Mortal Sin? And just when you really had me going—sick to the belly-button with all that talk about a wife and four kids!

'I think you are given to rash judgments,' she said. 'Certainly about me.'

'You're being modest.'

'No . . . a perfect woman, in any estimation, should have some understanding of men.' She lifted her knife and fork in a gesture of perplexity. 'That includes me out—I haven't a clue!'

Herries grinned. 'Come, now, men are only boys in long pants. Surely you know that? Take our mutual friend. A lovely wife who adores him, four kids who worship the ground he walks on. A good job, well paid. It takes him around, enables him to travel. He told you where he was before he came here?'

'Something about Berlin.'

'That's right . . . and what does he do there? He gets mixed up with some fraulein on the wrong side of the Wall. Creates what is damn near a diplomatic incident and has to skip the country. But does he go home to face up to his wife, to his boss? Not at all! He comes scuttling down here to Noli. God knows why . . . unless he imagined that by ignoring the situation long enough it would give up and go away. That's a little boy in long pants for you!'

Mairhi made no comment. She went through the motions of eating, but with little appetite. Finally, she laid down her knife and fork, took a long sip of wine. She could plead a headache, she supposed. But that would smack of the Victorian vapours. And it would solve nothing. She had stuck her chin out on this one; she could stick it out a little further. First it was a wife and four children. Now there was a fraulein. If it was all true, then the most she had lost was a Fiat 600 . . . a thought that prompted a wry smile.

Herries caught the smile, took it for a green light.

'You find what I said amusing?'

'Not particularly.' She lowered her glass. 'But it prompts a thought. You came down here to smack his bottom and send him home?'

'Something like that.'

'For the wife? Or the boss?'

'Both, you might say. We do work for the same firm.'

'What line of business? Or shouldn't I ask?'

'Why shouldn't you? D'you imagine we're spies or something?'

She gave a little laugh. 'You'd be surprised the number I meet in this job! Every other man who travels alone is a secret agent—or likes to give that impression. The little boy again, I suppose.'

'Did Mills give you that impression?'

'He might have done,' she replied, impishly. 'Indeed, the pair of you might have done. All this hush-hush coming and going and talks in the dead of night. And I must admit I'm curious about one thing—in view of what you've told me. Why didn't you go back with him? I mean—how can you be sure he hasn't changed his mind again and scuttled off somewhere else?'

Herries pushed away his plate. You cool cow, he thought—jumping the net and playing it in my court! He offered her a cigarette. He tried to hold her eyes while he lit it for her, but she wasn't in the market for that kind of pat-a-cake.

The waiter hovered. They settled for coffee and cognac.

'You didn't answer my question,' she said.

He manoeuvred his chair round slightly, closer to her. He looked at her bare, brown arm resting on the table. He brought his own hand down and patted her wrist. 'That's enough,' he said. 'I didn't invite you out to talk about Mills.'

'You've talked about little else.' She slipped her hand away and transferred the cigarette to it. 'In fact, I got the impression I was being warned off.'

His fingers played piano on the tablecloth.

'It was meant well. I hate seeing a decent girl taken for a ride.'

'Except when you are at the wheel?'

'Touché.' He made a rueful grin, waited until the coffee and cognac were served, then tried another approach—attack again.

'Talking about cars . . .'

'Ye-es.' She had been wondering when he would come back to that.

'Any chance I might borrow yours?' he said. 'Preferably with the owner, of course. But if you're too busy, I'd cut my losses.'

'Sorry. It's out of commission.'

'Oh? What's the trouble? I might be able to put it right. I'm a dab hand at do-it-yourself.'

'What can go wrong with a car?' She shrugged. 'I know when it needs petrol and water. I remember, occasionally, about oil and tyre pressures. But on other things, I'm just a helpless female.'

'Very right and proper. The way a female should be . . . helpless!'

He tried a repeat of the warm look. Her arm was back on the table, the cigarette curling lazy smoke between her fingers. He began to stroke the arm. She crooked the elbow as if to bring the cigarette to her lips. But it slipped from her fingers, cascaded in a shower of sparks on the back of his hand. He jerked his hand away swiftly.

'So sorry.' She snatched up the cigarette, brushed vigorously at the cloth. 'I'm hopeless with cigarettes, too!'

'No damage done.'

'Stupid bitch! He sucked at the back of his hand. His tongue felt the blister rising. He looked around for the waiter, snapped his fingers for the bill.

He was the perfect gentleman all the way back to the *pensione*. Not a false move until they reached the landing outside her room. He waited for her to unlock the door. When she didn't, he slipped the key from her hand and did it for her. He turned the handle, pushed the door wide.

'Thank you for the evening.' She smiled at him. 'Good night.'

'Good night? Just like that?' He put on the hurt look. 'Don't I qualify for the ritual kiss?'

She laughed softly.

'Really! We're not teenagers——'

'Teenagers the devil——'

He crowded her into the room, pulled her close, sought her mouth with his. He felt her go limp, her arm slide about his neck, her body press against him. He raised his foot, made to heel the door shut.

His shoe never made contact. She went backwards, towards the bed, taking him with her. Then, shifting her grip, she jerked hard. He sailed past in as neat a judo throw as ever came out of the text-book. He went clean over the bed, slid across the marble floor, and clappered his head against the woodwork of the French windows.

By the time he was upright and turning towards her, she had the light on. And a look that was pure ice.

'All part of the Bluebird service! Or shall I call Signore Rossi to show you to your room?'

He dabbed at a graze on his forehead, glared at her.

'A bloody teaser! Keeping it pure for Mills, eh——'

'Get out!'

He shambled past her, turned, spat words at her.

'One thing you don't know, my Irish bitch! You're on heat for a murderer!'

Her eyes widened. She slammed the door in his face. She stood there, breasts heaving, perspiration beading her upper lip. She felt it oozing from her pores, along with the fear that flowed from her mind. She squeezed her palms together, tightly, as if to crush it out of existence.

'No . . . no! It can't be! Not you, amore mio!' she whispered to herself.

Her face suddenly crumpled, she dissolved into tears.

27

ART ELISCU of the Central Intelligence Agency was a full-blooded American of Rumanian-Irish-Latvian stock—very bright, very able, still in his thirties. One of the youngest men to hold down a key post abroad. His office was in Rome, in the Via Boncompagni, not a home-run from the Embassy, from where he justly suspected an eagle eye was kept upon him.

He had been there a year, and so far had given the diplomats no cause for alarm or despondency. All reports showed that he could be found there without fail from Mondays to Fridays, mornings and early evenings, behind a walnut desk with an ice-water dispenser at his elbow and his Italian secretary, Paola Barbetti, equally cool and near at hand.

From Friday night until Monday morning, the arrangement was much the same. Only the locale differed. Then it became a villa he had leased at Trevignano, on the Lago di Bracciano, some fifty kilometres north of the city. Up at Trevignano, Eliscu still had his ice-water dispenser. And Paola. But she was no longer cool. At Trevignano it was hair down, everything down, giving and taking full vent of desires bottled up the other four nights of the week.

Paola's Latin temperament hardly approved of the spartan discipline imposed by her lover-boss. It could be awkward when menstruation clashed with amatory duties. At such times she had a feeling of guilt, that she should be able to regulate her cycles in the same manner as Eliscu controlled his own sexual requirements.

Still, this way she was able to stay respectable and live at home with her widowed mother, who was in no position to protest since Paola's money kept the home going. Mama Barbetti's only recourse was to light a candle to the Maddalena every Friday night and pray her daughter wouldn't be *incinta* come Monday morning. So far—ten months and some forty-three candles later—her Paola's belly still showed no signs of swelling. To Mama, either the americano was impotent—all that central-heating dried out a man—or else her prayers were being answered.

But Art Eliscu was far from impotent. Merely goddam careful. He liked his job, he liked Rome, he even liked Paola. But common sense prevailed. His superiors didn't expect celibacy, but they did demand circumspection. Dabbling in the Dolce Vita had brought the hatchet down on his predecessor. And Eliscu was making sure it didn't happen to him. Self-discipline, his anchor, had been learned as a Navy 'plebe' at Annapolis Academy. The Navy had cured him of all his weaknesses except one—seasickness. One look at an ocean wave and he turned pea-green. Which was why he had transferred to CIA. And why, when others sought their leisure on the beaches, he preferred Trevignano on the lake.

It was to Trevignano that Rod Schaeffer, Eliscu's second-in-command, came early that Saturday morning with the coded flash from Foggy Bottom, Washington, to put Operation Slow Grind into action. Slow Grind was a sample of egg-head wit contrived by someone who knew his Longfellow . . . 'the mills of God grind slowly'.

Eliscu had been at his pre-breakfast swim. He towelled himself down, went through his daily routine of press-ups while Shaeffer imparted the news.

'What do we know about him?' Eliscu spoke without pausing from his exercises.

Shaeffer fished out a wad of other data he had decoded. A fairly concise history of Mills from way back. No reaction was offered as Schaeffer read it out. Not until he reached the bit about Schultz. Then Eliscu lowered his stomach to the terrace and didn't come up again.

He lay there, stared up at his visitor.

'Shit and sauerkraut!' he exploded. 'Cremated him alive?'

He got to his feet, flapped grit from his navel, ran fingers across his hairy bath-mat of a chest. 'That's enough, Rod. No more till I've gotten some Java in my gut!' He padded away to the villa, calling out. 'Coffee, honey! Black and strong! Presto, chop, chop!' He picked up a terry-robe, shrugged it on, rejoined Shaeffer. 'You'll stay for breakfast?'

'Thanks.'

'Cremated the poor bastard alive!' Eliscu murmured. 'Holy cow, but that's something. What kind of son-of-a-bitch would do a thing like that?'

'An ex-partisan with hate in his marbles.' Schaeffer thumbed through the sheets of flimsy. 'Ten pages of dope on his war activities alone. It reads like he fought Adolf Hitler single-handed!'

'He's an old guy, then,' said Eliscu. 'Well, comparatively old.'

'Coming up fifty. Plays it by his wits rather than his reflexes, I'd imagine.'

'And his nerve. For Crissakes, you can't pull a trick like that without nerve. But why load it on us? It's Berlin's problem——'

'He's here . . . in spaghetti country. And Berlin is assigning Manny Berg to help.'

'Let me see that crap,' said Eliscu, reaching out for the papers.

Schaeffer passed them over. As he did so, Paola came out with the coffee, put it down. She made to pour, but Eliscu flapped a hand without taking his eyes from what he was reading.

'Rod'll pour, honey. Go fix him some eggs, three or four, sunny side . . . and pancakes. Some for me, too; but no eggs. Okay?'

Paola nodded, moved away. Schaeffer watched her posterior float out of sight, then picked up the coffee-pot.

'You know this Berg?' asked Eliscu.

'Yeah . . . I know him.' Schaeffer didn't sound very enthusiastic.

'But you don't rate him, huh?'

'I don't like him. That's all.'

'Like him or not—you're going to have to work with him.' Eliscu stirred sugar vigorously. 'At least, Berg knows the man we're after. We'll have to use his evaluation until we know the subject first-hand.'

If we ever do, thought Schaeffer, as he sipped his coffee. Don't let's count our chickens. While we're sitting here, Mills could be getting his fat ass out of Italy and through the Iron Curtain . . . a thought that prompted a question.

'One thing I don't get. He chilled this Schultz in *East* Berlin. If he did it for the Kremlin, why come back to this side and risk being picked up? He could have high-tailed it direct to Moscow.'

Eliscu smiled slyly, rubbed thumb and forefinger together.

'How many roubles make five? In Moscow, he'd have no bargaining power. He'd have to take what they offered. But from *here* he can name his own price!'

'Or get a bullet in the back,' argued Schaeffer. 'Aren't we forgetting something? He's not in the market with goods the Commies haven't got. It's their own property he's hoping to sell back . . . if that's what he's really up to.'

'You think he's planning to sell it to *us*?' Eliscu looked thoughtful.

Schaeffer shrugged.

'Like you said . . . how many roubles make five? This is a bum with the skids under. He's washed up as an agent; over the hill.

He has to make a killing somewhere—in every sense of the word.
It's his only hope of social security in his old age.'

'He should live that long.'

'That might be the answer. A job for Peas Piselli.'

'Not quite,' said Eliscu. 'We find first, negotiate, fix a deal. If
Washington approves, we can make it ten, maybe twenty per cent
cash, the balance in a bank deposit wherever he chooses, payable
when the formula or whatever it is has been proved genuine——'

'But——'

'But—and here is the but—who says he will collect?'

'I get it . . .' Shaeffer smiled. 'That's when we move in Piselli.'

'The hell with Piselli! Let the Commies do their own dirty
work! A leak in the right direction is all that is needed. Comrade
Kuznets can do the rest.'

A suspicion of smugness showed in Eliscu's smile as he glanced
towards the villa. Paola was approaching with their breakfast. He
folded the papers, slipped them into the pocket of his robe.

'Yeah, Kuznets . . . of course,' echoed Shaeffer, wishing he had
thought of it first.

28

VASILI KUZNETS, head of Soviet Intelligence in Rome, walked
the high-walled gardens of the Embassy, taking pleasure in the
scent of the roses, watching the lizards basking on the rockery.
One of the lizards he knew by sight—or swore he did. He had
named it Lavrenty Pavlovich, after the late, unlamented, in-
famous Beria. There were so many points of similarity; the grey-
white skin, the basilisk stare, the lightning fork of the tongue
that was sudden death to small fry foolish enough to cross its path.

Kuznets had never been a Beria man. Indeed, only since that
day in December, 1953, when roly-poly Nikita had given Lavrenty
Pavlovich the chop, had he seen any real promotion. Krushchev
had tumbled since, but not Kuznets. At forty-five, he had a
lot in his favour. A good war record, a sound political one, shrewd
enough not to show too much ambition. As a consequence, he
was seen as a reliable man to station in the West. Istanbul had
been his first spell of duty, then Athens, and now Rome—though
his wife, Tamara, and their three children had remained behind
in Borisoglebsk-on-the-Khoper.

Tamara, too, had a job to do—a geneticist, engrossed in her

work on the control of enzymes. As fond as he was of Tamara, as knowledgeable as she might be on biochemical catalysis, she never had been or would be the sex-pot he had found in the nubile Analia. He had shifted Analia from Athens across to the Piazza Dante, half way between the Santa Maria Maggiore and the San Giovanni in Laterano. Analia was half-Greek, half-Spanish—the copulative product of two dialectical Marxists who, for one night in their lives, had run out of words. Their momentary tongue-tiedness had passed with the seed. Conversation was not Analia's strong point in any language. The one phrase in Italian she used most to Kuznets was murmured in bed—*fammi godere a morire*—a demand to which he did his utmost to comply.

In a different context, the same phrase might equally apply to Mills—Kuznets ruminated on the problem that had been tossed into his lap—if any man was pleading to be done to death, he was. Kuznets had read the reports and digested them thoroughly. And out of it all, he felt a sneaking sympathy. Mills had killed a German. That was a good thing. Nazi or non-Nazi, east or west of the Oder-Neisse, Kuznets loathed all Germans. They had butchered his parents, raped his sister and three nieces—the youngest no more than eight years old—bayoneted the bodies and flung them into a well. Kuznets could understand that a man might carry a hate for twenty years and then kill out of revenge.

But that was a personal opinion. The KGB wanted Mills found, and quickly, before he passed on the secrets Schultz was thought to have stolen in Dresden. And Mills was in Italy, which made him Kuznets' headache.

Kuznets sighed, took out a pocket-knife, cut himself a wine-red rose, threaded it into his buttonhole. He retraced his steps to the bench where Sergei Zibrt, his second-in-command, was poring over the papers of Operation Mye'neetsi.

'Well, comrade? What do you make of this one?'

Sergei Zibrt was a much younger man—intense, ambitious, with quick eyes that took cover behind blue-tinted, steel-rimmed spectacles. A brilliant linguist, a brilliant chess-player, a brilliant theorist; brilliant in most things except the one Kuznets evaluated highest—field experience.

Kuznets, moreover, did not trust Zibrt. His devotion to duty was too puritanical. Any slip-up over this Mills business and the word would flash back to Moscow that Kuznets had succumbed to the flesh pots of Western corruption. The association with Analia would be quoted as proof. Kuznets, therefore, could not afford to take chances. If anything went wrong, the fault must not only rest with Zibrt but be seen to rest with Zibrt. On the other hand, he would be quite happy for Zibrt to share any success. It would mean promotion for the younger man to some more vital field of espionage, and Kuznets would have the little bugger out of his hair.

Zibrt shuffled the papers together neatly, replaced the pins, put them away in the brief-case. He snapped it shut, locked it, then rose to his feet. He hated sitting when others were standing. It put him at a disadvantage. He did not look into this superior's face, but fixed his gaze on the rose in the buttonhole of the Via Condotti-tailored gaberdine jacket. There was an unspoken criticism even in that. In the name of Karl Marx, thought Kuznets, what am I expected to wear? A hammer and sickle in a Leningrad serge, with bowler hat and brown boots! He made a mental wager on what Zibrt's opening phrase would be. Even money on 'Moscow is right, of course . . .'

'Moscow is right, of course, comrade Counsellor,' said Zibrt. 'One must expect the laboratory in Dresden to deny that the defector had any access to secret information. That is the natural ploy to cover their lamentable lack of security. It is disturbing, however, that the authority of the Democratic Republic should see fit to support that assertion. Though, of course, one must make allowance for the fact that as a comparatively new nation they have still much to learn . . .' Zibrt allowed himself the faintest wisp of a smile.

Kuznets thought: The Germans have much to learn about security! *Davolnaw,* you untesticled little twit, how far east of the Urals were you born! Did nobody ever mention the *Schutzstaffel* in Sredne Kolymsk? Or the *Allgemeine,* the *Sipo, Orpo, Gestapo,* the *Gauleitung, Kreisleitung, Ortsgruppenleitung*—the forbears of both East and West German Intelligence?

'One can see that Moscow would be dissatisfied with such an explanation,' went on Zibrt. 'Why else would Schultz have wished to defect from the Utopian benefits of world socialism, unless the lure of sordid, materialistic gain had reached out to him? And why should the Western imperialists have bothered to lure him if he had nothing to offer? He was not a key scientist. It had to be for the secrets he had obtained treasonably. And why else would this Mills have disposed of him, unless it was for a similar profit?'

'He gave his reasons to Prague,' said Kuznets. 'In the letter he wrote.'

'Ah, yes, the letter. Do I take it you accept the word of a British agent, comrade Counsellor?'

Zibrt shifted his gaze slightly, rested his eyes on Kuznets' mouth.

'British agent he might be,' said Kuznets warily. 'But he's no fool. His record is that of a clever, experienced operative. Never underestimate an opponent, however much one may deplore his motivation. We, in the Soviets, may be the enlightened, with the destiny of mankind our inevitable glory—but that doesn't necessarily mean the opposition are illiterate morons with the brains of a Czarist flea.'

Put that under your dandruff and let it fester!

'Very true, comrade Counsellor.' Zibrt was swift in his contrition. 'Yet . . . I do find it hard to believe that any Western agent could profess to be that anti-Fascist. If so—then surely he would have been removed from the service a long time ago. As for the letter—could not that have been a devious way of letting us know he possessed the secrets and was in the market to sell them back?'

'Such a thought had occurred to me.' Kuznets was at pains to prevent sarcasm creeping into his voice. 'You may have noticed the question-mark I pencilled in against the paragraph appertaining to the letter.'

Zibrt had noticed. And he didn't approve of documents being disfigured with vague, untidy symbols. Another of those Western habits the comrade Counsellor had acquired, along with his style of dress, his Italian haircut and after-shave lotion. And, of course, that woman of his in the Piazza Dante . . .

'It was that which prompted my attention,' Zibrt said obsequiously.

Kuznets smiled. 'The letter was posted in Noli——'

'—In the province of Liguria, a medieval watering-place approximately fifty kilometres from Genoa——'' Zibrt pulled up sharply, aware of Kuznets' frosty stare.

'I'm well aware where Noli is! I suggest we forget the geography lesson.'

'My apologies, comrade Counsellor.'

'Accepted.' Kuznets smiled once more. 'I know you mean well, Comrade Zibrt. And I have the utmost faith in you to perform the task ahead.'

Zibrt's eyes reached Kuznets' for the first time since they had started talking.

'You mean . . . you want me to handle Operation Mye-'neetsi?'

'I mean,' said Kuznets, resting a hand lightly on his assistant's shoulder, 'I want you to go away into some quiet corner and think—and produce a thorough exposition of the situation and its possibilities as only you can, together with a co-ordinated plan of strategic manoeuvre, bearing in mind the counter-action we can expect from Eliscu of the CIA. And to consider, too, the parallel action that must come from Herries of MI6, resident—or so I am reliably informed—at the pensione Villa Fiorita in Noli. Also, while you are about it, don't forget our allies in HVA—even, possibly, VFK.'

Zibrt's eyes glinted behind the shaded spectacles.

'How soon do you want this, comrade Counsellor?'

'Seven o'clock this evening . . . on my desk.'

Kuznets glanced at his wrist-watch. Eleven forty-five already, and he had promised Analia a picnic on the beach at Fregene . . . He must shed this piece of *seretsni*-Volga crow-bait and get moving.

29

HERRIES made three telephone calls that Saturday morning. The first was to Rome, to a Charles Lister at the Palazzo del Drago, in the Via Quattro Fontane, headquarters of the British Council.

Lister's appointment with the Council deceived few, least of all Art Eliscu and Vasili Kuznets. Any Council work that found its way on to his desk was dealt with promptly and efficiently by an ex-debutante from Kensington with lesbian tendencies. For Lister was an Auntie man—had been for five years, with an unblemished record and a reputation for unflappability. Though Lister himself would have argued modestly that neither his record nor his reputation had been hard to maintain. Rome was a tiddler patch under the willows, these days—far from the broad stream of espionage and counter-espionage.

But it was a great city for crumpet. Which suited Lister down to the ground. If his personal diary had fallen into the wrong hands, it would hardly have divulged secrets vital to the security of Britain. The cipher clerk, instead, would have been drooling enviously over such items as *Didi*** and Rossana* 69 + .

That previous night, Lister had been out with a Didi and a Rossana. A birthday celebration. He wasn't sure who's—but it had zig-zagged its way from party to party right across town. Somewhere on the way he had lost one of the girls—he couldn't rightly remember which—and had seen the dawn in bed with the other—or, maybe it was a third, a quite different pussy-cat . . . anyway, he had finally crawled into the Palazzo del Drago with one thing in mind—the Alka Seltzer and the pep pills in the bottom drawer of his desk.

Herries' voice had only made him want to throw up the more. Herries always spelled trouble, just when he wanted to die nice and gentle. Lister put a clamp on his stomach and listened, lying back in his swivel chair with wet cotton-wool pads over his eyes. But Herries, thank God, liked the sound of his own voice and demanded no more than an occasional yes or no, plus a final 'will do', in response to a list of instructions.

Lister wound back the tape that had recorded the conversation, played it over again, translating the coded nuances that made the chat sound innocuous. My Christ, he thought, what a way to start a weekend! One of our own people on the run . . . Why did he have to pick Italy, when Beirut and Cairo were the 'in' places for defectors? And what did Herries think he, Lister, was—a bloody centipede with three heads? Keep a close eye on Kuznets, watch what he was up to and report every move. Ditto for Eliscu. And then there was Mills himself. If he blew into town he was to be shadowed night and day, never out of sight.

Lister fizzed more Alka Seltzer with a paper-knife, let the bubbles spatter cool in his face. No more birds till this barney was over. Cold baths, plenty of exercise, bromide in his morning cuppa. Whatever happened, *he* mustn't balls it up. What had Herries called it? Operation Pony Race . . . What kind of silly, bloody code-name was that?

Herries' second call had been to Glyn Meredith at the Consulate office in Genoa. Meredith, too, in a loose way, worked for Auntie, dove-tailing his duties as a Consular official with any sudden emergencies that brought his other talents into play. His talents were varied, from having a good baritone larynx that had won him transitory fame in his home-town Welsh choir to a pair of sturdy feet that would have been a credit on any beat police-man. In addition, he had a brain, quick and expansive—rather quicker and more expansive than was the norm in the Consulate division. He had all the right in the world to expect to make the top of the ladder. But enough nous to know he never would. Not with his accent and background, a grammar-school boyo with a mine-shaft winder for a dad. The Rhondda Valley still came

through, d'you see, man, voice lilting upwards at the end like a
moggie's tail—whether he spoke Welsh, English, Italian, or how's-
your-father . . .

Herries' first task for Meredith was a straightforward one. Pay
a visit to Narbucco on the Via Balbi and check if Mills had been
there for a passport, and, if so, collect the details. The second
task was not so easy. Find Mills himself, or get tabs on him as
quickly as possible.

Up your jacksy, Jack, thought Meredith, when Herries had
rung off, want me to save your buttermilk for you? I've heard of
this Mills; in fact, I attended a lecture of his once when I was on
the training course. He's big time, way out of my class. What
have you been up to then, Millsy *bach*? Kicking against the
pricks, is it? Christ help you then, man, no one else will . . . not
in this business, that's for sure!

30

MEREDITH had been wrong. Mills was not destined to be alone.
Not if Rachel and Solomon Narbucco had anything to do about
it. Rachel had come to Solomon just before dawn, when the old
man was still working on the second of the two passports. She had
brought him coffee laced with cognac, and a *zabaglione* whipped
thick in a glass. She planted two fat elbows on the table and
looked her husband square in the eye.

'Our boy is in trouble, Papa . . . bad trouble, è vero?'

To Rachel, Mills had always been 'our boy'—from way back in
his early days as an MI6 man. It had been his unpleasant task
to investigate Solomon over the forged passports for the refugees.
The compromise of having Solomon work for them had been
Mills' idea. And—as Rachel saw it—he had kept her husband out
of jail. Rightly or wrongly, that was how her mind worked, and
Mills to her was the son she had never had.

Solomon pushed his spectacles up to the crown of his head,
spooned the *zabaglione,* savoured it with his tongue.

'Mi pare, Mama,' he nodded. 'Eyeeeeeh! I hope these some
help will gif!' He waved the spoon at the documents.

'It is not enough. We must do more.'

'More? How so we do more? Jesu Christmas, you tell me that,
hein?'

When tired, Solomon was easily swayed to agitation. Agitation took the form of bouncing up and down on his stool. Rachel rescued the coffee before it slopped over the night's work, drained the saucer back into the cup.

'Finish your breakfast, you old sciocco, and listen! Moshe!'

'Moshe?'

'Singer . . . who else?'

'Moshe Singer . . .' Solomon paused, the spoon suspended in mid-air. He stared at Rachel, then popped the gooey mess into his mouth with a loud, sucking noise. 'Moshe Singer, si, of course!' Then he had an afterthought, waggled the spoon at the ceiling. 'But Moshe is miles away . . . in Vienn' or somewheres.'

'So what is Vienn'?' demanded Rachel. 'At the end of a telephone, not the end of the world! And don't say why for he do things for us. We help him so many the times. Now we ask him the little favour. Is that so much? For our boy, who helps Moshe many times himself—we know that. And who helped us, who kept you out of the galera when I think I don't see you no more for years, maybe for life——'

It was Rachel who was getting agitated now, to the point of tears.

Solomon put down the *zabaglione* glass, eased the coffee cup from her trembling fingers, swallowed the contents in a single gulp, then put an arm about her shoulders.

'All right, Mama, all right . . . you gif yourself the blood pressures, going on like that! I telephone Moshe in two, t'ree hours, when he is out of his bed—and he calls Yehudi Perlmeyer or maybe Shmuel Farb to help. E cosi, our boy is away, anywheres you want. Sout' America, Israel—in a kibbutz, maybe, growing the radishes and wearing the prayer shawl . . . ho, ho, ho . . .!'

Solomon gave her a squeeze, and shook with wheezy laughter at the word-picture he had painted. Rachel pressed her face to his, wetting his cheek with hers. A watery smile broke through her tears.

31

HERRIES' third call had been to Chertsey, in the county of Surrey —to Auntie's private residence. A call made with not a little trepidation. And a sense of relief when Jennifer, the sixteen-year-old daughter of the household, answered the phone and said that daddy was out on the golf course and wasn't expected back until after lunch.

This gave Herries breathing space, time to think up some adequate excuse, to explain away the clanger he had dropped.

Meanwhile, he sweated profusely, though it was grey and overcast, with clouds scudding in from the south-east and carrying a damp chill that portended the arrival of autumn. There was scant consolation in the one constructive thing he had accomplished so far—the naming of the operation as Pony Race. In other circumstances, he might have basked in his own brilliance of mind—LSD-25, twisted to read as twenty-five pounds sterling, or—in horse-play parlance—a pony. And the race to see who got Mills first.

But he could almost hear Auntie's dry comment on that . . . 'Very neat, John, but must we always carry an apprentice jockey who doesn't know his arse from his elbow?'

Herries knew only too well that his future was at stake on this one. To make matters worse, he had pressed for the assignment. Auntie—much to his surprise—hadn't demurred, had given him *carte blanche*, which could only be interpreted as a token of faith. But once that faith was shattered . . . well, he might as well ask for a transfer to Passports Division in Petty France or the Immigration Branch at London Airport.

He felt sick and sorry for himself. His head was bruised and still tender from the mistake he'd made with that Odell bitch. She, of course, might still lead him to Mills, unwittingly. But it was a slim chance. No use banking on it. The sly bastard was probably only using her as a delaying tactic.

32

MAIRHI waited in the Loggia della Republica, at the public telephone office. Mills had promised to call her there at eleven. It was now ten minutes past.

She felt awful. Two nights in a row with scarcely a wink of sleep. Would he phone? And if he did, what should she say? A hundred and one questions she wanted to ask, but none over the telephone. You didn't question a man about having a wife and four children, or whether he was wanted for murder . . . not without seeing his face and judging if he was telling the truth or not. Those things would have to wait until they met—*if* they met. She glanced at her watch for the umpteenth time. A quarter past. Oh, come on, come on . . .

She was suddenly aware of being watched. Her mind flashed: Herries. She twisted round. But it wasn't. Just a man in a black slicker-raincoat, a thin cigar between his lips. His eyes dropped, embarrassed, under her frown. He pulled out a copy of *Der Spiegel*, buried his nose in it. Another tourist. She felt sick of the sight of them. Thank God the season was over and she could get away . . . away . . . where?

'Signorina Odell?' It was the voice of the girl at the desk. 'Genova vi chiamo . . . numero due, per favore!'

Mairhi hurried into the second booth, snatched up the receiver, and hurled a 'Pronto, Mairhi Odell!' down the line.

'Hey,' said a cool voice at the other end. 'I'm not in High Street, China. No need to blast my ear-drums.'

'Sorry,' she whispered. 'But you're late. I thought you were never——'

'What's happening? You gone off the line? I can't hear you at all now.'

'I can hear you,' she said, speaking up.

'That's better. Sorry I'm late, but I got held up. How did it go with Herries?'

She caught the slight note of anxiety in his voice. For her, she hoped. She told him about the dinner date and the way Herries had fenced around the question of the car.

'The Don Juan approach,' he commented. 'I rather thought he'd try that. You didn't fall?'

She wanted to say 'Would you care very much if I had?' Instead, she giggled. 'I'm afraid Herries did the falling!' She went on to describe the sequence that had occurred in her room, concluding with the judo-throw.

There followed a long pause at the other end. If she could have seen Mills' face she would have been gratified. It was a study. 'You're joking,' was all he could say.

'I'm not. A girl has to know how to defend herself in this day and age. A rudimentary knowledge of nagewaza is usually enough. One doesn't have to be a yudansha.'

She wasn't joking. She knew her ruddy judo, all right! Mills began to laugh.

'Have I said something funny?' she asked.

'Oh, no . . . that is, yes. I'm not laughing at you, tesore. It's Herries. He puts himself up as a black belt or something.'

'Oh, my God!' she said, shaken to the core.

Her note of panic killed his laughter.

'Don't worry. He won't try that again.'

'I hope not . . .' She hesitated. 'What do you want me to do now?'

'Nothing. Not until Monday—when you join me. If you still want to, that is.'

No thought of a wife now, or of him being a murderer. Her spirits soared.

'Where?'

'I'll phone you Monday. Same place, same time.'

'Why not tomorrow?'

He sensed the plaintive cry.

'Tomorrow, then. But it'll be Monday before I can say where exactly.'

'All right, but—but——' The words dragged out of her. 'If something goes wrong . . . how will I know?'

He spoke slowly. 'If you don't hear from me—go to Genoa. Via Balbi; the Hotel Narbucco. Ask for Solomon or Rachel; tell them who you are. They will give you a letter. That will explain everything. Capito?'

'Capisco.'

'Allora . . . arrivederla!'

'A domani! E non ti scordai dammi.'

'As if I could,' he said, simply.

PART THREE

33

MILLS left Genoa shortly after lunch with seven hundred thousand lire and two passports in his pocket—and Glyn Meredith less than fifty yards behind him in a Cortina.

Mills was aware of the shadow. It didn't perturb him. He had expected Herries to move fast, and Herries hadn't let him down. After the call to Mairhi, he had returned to the hotel to find Rachel hovering near the entrance, nervous, worried . . .

There was an *inglese* with Solomon, asking questions. All Rachel's protective instincts were aroused. He must fly at once, hide in the cellar, anywhere, until their visitor was gone.

Mills patted her bustle affectionately. 'Not even under your ample skirts, bellezza!' Then, with an appreciative sniff: 'Perciatelli rapollese—that gives me an appetite! The biggest plate in the house, with plenty of ricotta, and a mezzo to wash it down!'

A gesture brooked no further argument. He sat down deliberately at a table facing the stairs. Shortly afterwards, Meredith came down and glanced into the restaurant. Mills was engrossed in the *Corriere Sportivo,* apparently unaware of his existence.

Meredith slipped away quickly and across to a bar on the opposite side of the street. A hurried phone call to Herries, then a wait-and-watch, perched on a bar stool.

Solomon joined Mills. He confirmed the reason for the enquiries. And he had passed on what Mills wanted Herries to know—that he had got a passport in the name of Winkler, that he was staying at the Narbucco but planning to leave that day. Enough information to safeguard Solomon from recrimination; not enough to smell of a put-up job.

'He gave his name?' asked Mills.

'I know him,' said Solomon quietly. 'Meredith—from the Consul Office.'

Meredith. Of course. Mills knew him, too. A keen type who wouldn't give up easily. But lacking in experience. Would he have the sense to relax and eat a good meal? He was going to be hungry otherwise. Next stop was Viareggio, a haul of one hundred miles.

Solomon must have read his thoughts.

'Vere it is you hoppa the twig?'

'I hoppa the twig down the Via Aurelia.' Mills poured the old man a glass of wine. 'As with all roads, it leads to Rome——'

'Benissimmo! I t'ink you go to Rome, then—gazoom!—to Tel Aviv!' Solomon rolled his eyes to where Rachel was coming through with a piled plate of *pasta*. 'Jest for to please Mama, hein?'

Mills gave them both a shrewd look. 'Something besides perciatelli has been cooking. Give, give . . . what is it?'

'Ma niente!' Solomon waved fingers. 'I was speaking wit' Moshe, no more. A good boy, Moshe—ver' fond of you. He would like to do the toyve . . . 'ow you say, good turn——'

'A regular boy scout, eh? You're a craftsman with your hands, vecchio mio, but a lousy liar!' He softened the words with a smile. Then his eyes moistened visibly, and his hands went out to the pair of them. 'I love you both . . . very much. I won't forget this.'

'Then you will speak with Moshe?' Rachel pleaded.

'If I need him. I promise. But it may not be necessary. A storm in a tea-cup, this business. It'll blow over. I'm just being cautious.' He could tell by their eyes he hadn't convinced them. He changed tack. 'I'll let you know how things go. I mean to write. There's a letter—or will be—I want you to keep for a girl . . .'

Rachel's face bloomed. Her hands lifted high, then down to give him a hug.

'Finalmente! Una donna! È una belloccia, si? Quando ti sposi——?'

Solomon clucked his tongue, leered approval.

'Hold your horses!' Mills protested. 'I never said anything about getting married.'

'But *she* will,' Rachel beamed. 'And I'll teach her how to make perciatelli just how you like it!'

'Which isn't cold!'

Mills shoo'ed the pair of them away.

As he drove along the coast road, through Rapallo and Sestri Levante, then over the Passo di Bracco, Rachel's words kept coming back to him. Marriage. Was that to be the end? Could he expect the girl to settle for less? Christ Almighty, what was he thinking about?

A quick glance in the mirror. Meredith was still there—two hundred yards between them on the open road, closing a fraction when they passed through a town. There was little traffic. Most of it went past at speed. A Peugeot roared through, raising dust. They passed it farther on, stopped at a wayside café. Three men. His eyes flickered over them, then they were gone. He glanced upwards. The skies had clamped down. There was thunder in the air. A storm would blister the hills before nightfall. He hoped so. A downpour at the right moment would suit his plans.

Through La Spezia; then Sarzana; and Carrara, with its overall film of marble dust; then Massa and Pietrasanta. Thunder rumbled and burped the hills, cow pats of rain spattered the windscreens as both cars veered away from the main highway towards the shoreline of Lido di Camaiore. It tipped down in stair-rods along the sweep of beach, churning the sand into grey sludge, goading the sea to growl angrily at the intruder on its patch.

Desolation everyhere. No nut-brown beauties, languid in tan lotion and little else. The arabs who pitched the sun-tents had folded and stolen away. The only umbrellas a scurry along the Viale Pistelli—natives underneath, not tourists lost for somewhere to go. The tourists had gone, together with the aquacycles, the rubber floats, the gaily coloured flags. The pavilions that had echoed for months with flapping towels and squeals of pleasure now offered a shuttered, sightless, not-again-till-Mardi-Gras look. The ice-cream kiosks tombstones now, in memory of summer departed.

The Viale Pistelli became the Giosue' Carducci and the Fiat left the ghost town of Lido di Camaiore and entered the larger ghost town of Viareggio. The rain bucketed down and bounced high, then fell back to elbow its way like a football crowd, jostling for position in the culverts. The Cortina swished along behind, with Meredith anxious now, wondering: In the name of all that's holy, when is the fellow going to stop? He must have the bladder of an elephant. I've been breaking my neck for the past hour. It wouldn't be so bad if I could cross my legs . . . but how to do that *and* drive a bloody car?

Mills, out in front, grinning slyly in almost telepathic certainty of Meredith's need. His own waterworks had an hour's advantage, at least, over Meredith's. He had used the loo before leaving

Genoa, which was more than Meredith could have done. Unlike English pubs, Italian bars don't always offer toilet facilities; and even if the one in Via Balbi had, Meredith wouldn't have dared break vigilance. Mills had made to leave four times, just to keep him on the hop. And now, after three hours of non-stop driving, with all this rain splashing down like a tap turned on . . .

He drove the whole length of the promenade, then turned left, up past the shipping basin, only to double back along the Michelangelo Buonarroti, into the Pineta di Ponente. At the edge of the trees he saw a *pissoir*. He slowed deliberately, only to accelerate again through a puddle, spraying a fountain upwards with his wheels. The Cortina seemed to hover at the *pissoir* as if reluctant to pass it by.

Now Mills began to weave in and out of a criss-cross of side streets, aware that every turn of the wheel and change of gear meant a similar movement for Meredith, thus adding to his suspected discomfort. Finally, the Fiat slid to a halt at the top of the Via Mazzini, almost opposite the station, parking outside a pair of adjoining hotels. But it wasn't over. Mills sat on for a further ten minutes, smoking and eyeing the mirror with almost fiendish glee, watching the Cortina parked two blocks down. Ah, well! he thought; dark in a few minutes, better let the poor devil off the hook. He opened the door of the Fiat, killed his cigarette, grabbed a suitcase, and made a dash for the Hotel Spagnoli.

A small hotel—eighteen rooms, no private baths. The sort used by travellers with an early train to catch. Mills booked in as Hans Winkler, handed over the passport for registration. He also reserved the room next to his in the name of Mairhi Odell. Then he asked the hotel porter if he would mind parking the Fiat in the *piazzale* around the corner, and placing the second suitcase in the car with Left Luggage at the station. That done, he followed the boy with the first suitcase upstairs.

The room looked out over the street. Mills tipped the boy, half shut the door, crossed to the window—in time to see the Cortina draw up and Meredith climb out. Awkwardly, pressing a sly fist into his abdomen. He moved to the hotel, walking stiltedly, as if a sudden knees-bend might precipitate an accident.

Mills grinned. Then he moved to the door and waited. He had reasoned out what he would do in Meredith's shoes: check that his quarry had booked a room, do the same himself—one on the same floor, if possible, the better for observation—then head for the nearest loo before he ruined himself. And that—Mills had been swift to notice—was on *this* floor, at the end of the corridor.

Meredith kept to form. He came up the stairs and along the corridor at a trot, room-key jingling in his hand. The *gabinetto* door opened and slammed, the bolt was fumbled and shot home.

Mills picked up his raincoat, stepped into the corridor. He cocked an ear, heard the crash of the seat flung up, the deep gasp and groan of a man suffering the pain of a near-stricture. Having held himself so long, Meredith would have a problem starting. When he did, it would seem it would never stop. And when, eventually, it did, he would have to lower the seat and sit down, drained, weak, exhausted, needing time to recover.

Time that was precious to Mills. Five to ten minutes was all he needed. He shut the door of his room, turned the key softly, crept away to the stairs, and went down.

34

MILLS didn't go far. No more than the few steps that took him across to the station—to Left Luggage, where he collected the second suitcase put there by the hall porter. Then back to the Brunello this time, the hotel next door. There he booked in as Irlandese; a room on the first floor, overlooking the street, identical to the one he had just left.

He stayed long enough to unpack pyjamas, toilet bag and razor, remove the pins from a shirt, and hang up a suit. From the window, he watched Meredith come out from next door, climb into the Cortina, and drive it away around the corner. A few moments later, Meredith came back on foot. Walking normally now.

Mills left the Brunello and crossed the *piazzale* once more. Quite dark now; the rain settled in for a steady drizzle. The Fiat was there. And the Cortina, about six parking slots away. And one other car—on the far side. A Peugeot. Was it the same one that had leapfrogged them down the Via Aurelia? He thought about that as he picked up a cab from the station rank. Possibly. The classic method of tailing, being more often than not out in front. He drove to the public telephone office of the Giardini d'Azeglio.

He made two calls. Both to Rome: to the American and Russian Embassies. The calls had the same content. Hans

Winkler from Berlin was staying at the Spagnoli in Viareggio. He
had vital information concerning a dead man named Schultz and
a very quick one named Mills. Information worth twenty-five
pounds sterling. No less, and no more.

With the first call, he asked that the message be conveyed to
Mr. Eliscu of the American Students' Aid Center in the Via
Boncompagni. With the second, the message was for Kuznets,
Press Counsellor to the Embassy. To both calls, the voices at the
other end were polite but non-commital, as if used to receiving
calls from cranks all the time. Mills was not disappointed. He
had expected no other reaction. Not over the telephone. It would
follow—he hoped—in a more visible form.

He mooted a third call to Auntie, at his home in Chertsey.
Sorely tempted, he decided against it. It would only ram home
the incompetence of Herries and prompt Auntie to set a more
skilled operative on his tail. A thought that brought a sobering
one . . . Auntie may have done that already. Herries used
deliberately as a red herring, while someone else unbeknown to
him was on the job. The Peugeot, for instance. Three of them in
that. Quite a thought . . .

No, it would never do to play chicken-across-the-road with
Auntie. He was much too fly a bird. Whatever else you do, don't
get cocky, mate . . . the first and last universal rule, the *alpha* and
omega of espionage.

Back once more at the Spagnoli, Mills caught a glimpse of
Meredith in the phone booth in the foyer. No need for a wire-tap
to guess who he was talking to. Mills collected his key, stopped
long enough to order sandwiches and coffee to be sent up and ask
for a late late-call in the morning; a bath and to bed was his
programme. While he was talking, the door to the phone booth
opened a fraction. Mills smiled slyly. He hoped it had registered
with Meredith, too.

Upstairs, he opened the other suitcase and unpacked. He
stripped, shrugged on a bathrobe, picked up a toilet bag and
towel.

He waited by the door, then went out into the corridor as
Meredith came up the stairs, padding ahead, bare-footed, the
towel lumped in his hands.

The bathroom adjoined the *gabinetto*. Mills had a thorough
soak, then sprayed himself with the hand-shower. When he came
out, twenty minutes later, he was singing quietly to himself and

giving his hair a friction-rub. Meredith's door was slightly ajar, as he had expected it would be.

The sandwiches and coffee were waiting in his room, but a swift check told Mills he had had another visitor—someone decidedly nosey.

He had left his trousers folded, hung over the chair, a fraction out of crease. Now they were lying *on* the crease. The zipper to his suitcase had been shut to within seven ratchets off the end ... now it was eight. A Bank of England note topmost in his wallet had shown only the *17S* of the serial number ... now it showed *17S26*—. There had been fifteen pounds sterling in the wallet; plus Deutschmarks and lire that made up to the equivalent of a further thirty pounds. It was all there. If just one of those folded ten-thousand-lire bills had been missing, he might have suspected the search as the work of a clever, light-fingered waiter on the look-out for spare pocket money. As it was, it had to be Meredith.

Mills grinned. Herries could now be informed of the finer details ... the full extent of his quarry's wardrobe, the exact state of his finances. He wouldn't be too upset that Meredith had failed to unearth the precious LSD formula. If he had found such a thing it would have been suspect immediately, nothing more than a plant. The real thing Mills would be expected to keep on a micro-dot in a plastic capsule stuffed up his anus. No, the thing that would cheer Herries would be the impecuniosity of Mills. Forty-five pounds *in toto* wouldn't get him very far—and they would have already made sure it was bloody nigh impossible for him to draw on his British bank account ... Mills put a hand into the pocket of his bathrobe, pulled out the wad of money he had withdrawn that morning from the Banco di Napoli, and put it away with the rest.

He drank and ate, relaxed on the bed and smoked awhile. When the chambermaid knocked and came in to turn down the covers, he told her what he had told the desk clerk: he was *molto stanco* and wanted no rattling of his door before eleven-thirty the next morning. He pressed a five-hundred-lire piece into her hand. And he had bought himself a female Peter-at-the-Gate.

All that was needed now was the final touch—the shoes outside the door. He timed it nicely as Meredith appeared in the corridor. Going in search of food, without a doubt. The man must be bloody ravenous if he had missed his lunch.

He shut the door, flicked off the light, crossed to the window. Ten minutes passed, but Meredith didn't emerge on to the street.

He was obviously relying on the hotel dining room rather than
risk going farther afield. But that in itself presented no problem.
Trained to observe, Mills had checked automatically where the
dining room was . . . along a narrow passage, out of sight of the
foyer.

He switched on the light again, dressed quickly. He pulled on
a second pair of shoes—the pair he had carried with him wrapped
in the towel when he had taken his bath. He wasn't sure that
Meredith was so well trained as to notice and remember whether
there had been more than one pair, but he had taken no chances.
If the one pair had been noted, so much the better. That pair
stood outside the room . . .

He shrugged on his raincoat, looked at his watch. It was time
enough—time when the desk clerk and the hall porter should
both be off duty and replaced by the night man. The night man at
a small hotel out of season might be anyone from the youngest
waiter to the inevitable old odd-job man out in the backyard
brooming away the flood water. Mills switched off the light,
locked the door, pocketed the key.

His surmise proved correct. He met no one at all on his way
down and out into the street.

35

THE RAIN had lifted. But the pavements were treacherous.
Puddles everywhere, and sudden cascades from overworked gut-
ters.

But Mills felt the urge to stretch his legs. And anyway, he
needed cigarettes. He started across the *piazzale*, towards the
station. The Cortina and the Fiat were still there. But not the
Peugeot. Something prompted him to go to the Fiat and check it,
a hunch, no more than that.

It had been got at. The leads severed clean with a penknife. As
dead as a dodo.

Mills lowered the bonnet, said a four-lettered word. It was not
something that could be repaired in a hurry. The only consolation
lay in the fact that he had checked it now, instead of finding out
when he came to use it again. He forgot about the cigarettes,
started back towards the Brunello.

Two men slid out of a doorway near the corner. One was short,
thick-set, built like a bulldozer. The other was taller, thinner,

with a herring-bone scar on his left cheek. The short man crowded forward, lipping a cigarette. Unlighted.

He said: 'Have you a match, signore?'

The words were Italian, but not Italian Italian. Neither the idiom nor the accent. That came out thick, guttural.

'I don't smoke,' said Mills.

He brought a knee up, sharply, caught the short man square in the groin. The short man gasped, doubled up. The cigarette spat from his mouth.

'Unnecessary,' said the man with the herring-bone scar. 'So unnecessary.' He brought his hand from his pocket, pointed a 9-mm. Browning at Mills' navel. 'I would much rather we avoided violence.'

He raised his other hand, made a gesture. The Peugeot purred out of the darkness coming into the kerb beside them.

Mills raised a laconic eyebrow.

'I should have stayed in bed,' he said.

The Peugeot made a U-turn, headed south to the Cavalcavia. Then right, towards the yacht basin. It crossed over and down the Michele Coppino, came to a halt among the fish barrels.

'Out,' said Herring Bone. The pistol was back in his pocket again. But so was his hand. Mills did as he was told. Herring Bone nodded towards the dark hulk of a motor-launch tied up to the quay.

'You have a boat, too?' said Mills. 'That's what I call anticipation.'

'We are just borrowing it. For an hour or two. Maybe less.'

'Depending on what?'

'Depending on you. And whether you are co-operative.'

'Ah,' said Mills.

He went aboard. Herring Bone followed. And the driver of the Peugeot. The short man took up the rear, holding himself the way Meredith had done earlier. But for a different reason.

The Peugeot driver took the wheel. Mills sat to starboard. Herring Bone opposite him. The short man lowered himself into the stern, feet resting on a coil of rope, hands nursing his guts. They cast off and began to chug out through the channel, towards the Porto and the open sea. Nobody raised a shout of protest or a finger to stop them. There was nobody around to do so. Only other boats—dark, silent, slapping gently with the water.

The launch bucked a little as it met the open sea. The Peugeot driver was not so much at home with marine craft. He swung the wheel too hard. They yawed badly and shipped water. Some of it splashed over Mill's feet, slopped around.

'Not British,' said Mills, to no one in particular. 'Not CIA. Not KGB. BND, perhaps . . . or HVA?'

'Does it really matter?' said Herring Bone, his hand still in his pocket.

'It does to whoever it isn't,' said Mills. 'If you get my meaning.'

Herring Bone ghosted a smile. 'I get your meaning. But it's of little importance to you.'

'On the contrary. I like to know who is on the ball and who isn't.'

Again the ghost of a smile. 'You're not, obviously. Or you wouldn't be here.'

The boat lurched again under the erratic skill of the Peugeot driver, shipping more water.

'We all make mistakes,' said Mills.

He went forward, suddenly, on the pitch. He reached and caught Herring Bone's wrist as it came out with the pistol, turned it. The pistol coughed twice. The second time must have been involuntary—a post-mortem twitch. For Herring Bone was already dead, shot through the heart.

The Peugeot driver snatched up an axe clipped above the wheelhouse, turned. But Mills had the Browning now. He fired upwards, under the rib cage, the shot ploughing through and shattering the spine. The Peugeot driver spun and fell, still clutching the axe. It thudded blade foremost into the bottom of the launch.

In the stern, the short man was struggling to his feet, hands still low on his belly. Mills aimed, squeezed the trigger. The pistol jammed. Mills hurled it.

The short man took it on the cheek-bone. His hands flew up from his belly to his face. His feet trod wildly, snaking the rope about them. He swayed, lost balance, went overboard. The rope went with him, paying out to its full length and jerking taut.

The short man surfaced, kicking frantically to free his ankles. 'I c-can't swim,' he gurgled, then went under again.

'Your chance to learn,' said Mills. And ignored him. His own feet were awash. The fallen axe had stove in a rotten plank. The launch was taking water fast.

Mills went over the side and struck out for shore. They had been closer in than he had imagined. A few strokes and he was

touching bottom. He waded out, flopped down on the beach, lay
there, chest heaving.

'I'm too old for this lark,' he said aloud. 'It really is time I
retired.'

36

THE COW BELLS that herd good Catholics to Mass awakened Mills.
His watch told him it was a quarter to seven. The skies told
him that rain was likely to take over Viareggio again. Low,
grey, and scudding fast, rolling up from the direction of Elba.

He had breakfast in his room, wrote four letters. To Eliscu,
Kuznets, Solomon, and Mairhi. The one to Mairhi was the
difficult one. Whatever he said, it would sound trite. And it did.
He tore it up and chose the easy way out in the end. If she wanted
to know more about him, she could ask Solomon.

The letters to Eliscu and Kuznets were almost identical. He
regretted to say he had been forced to leave Viareggio for his own
safety. He now offered a change in plan; a meeting at the top of
the Leaning Tower of Pisa at three-thirty that afternoon. The
recognition would be effected by producing a 1/10th-litre
miniature *Vecchia Romagna* from which he would take a drink.
He would keep the appointment unless further harassed by other
agents—in which case, he would try the next day, Monday . . .
this time under the fresco of the Last Judgment by Francesco da
Volterra in the Campo Santo. If this, in turn, was forestalled, the
meeting would be on Tuesday at ten a.m. at the mineral baths of
San Giuliano or at four-fifteen p.m. outside the biscuit factory at
Navacchio. Both letters he signed Hans Winkler.

He sealed the envelopes, washed, shaved, and dressed. At five
minutes to nine, he left the Brunello and crossed to the station.
There were three new cars in the *piazzale*—a Bianchina; a coupé
Millespecial; and a Ferrari sports, the kind of car Herries would
fancy. Fancy, perhaps, but not readily obtainable. Ferraris didn't
come easy in the self-drive hire market; and besides, this one had
a Lombardy registration. Mills didn't reckon the other two,
either. A fat woman with a fat cocker spaniel was squeezing out
of the Bianchina. And a blonde in tight slacks with an interesting
behind was busy feeding luggage into the boot of the coupé.

In the station, he bought cigarettes, posted the letter to
Solomon, then telephoned Mairhi at the Villa Fiorita. The call

came as a surprise—it was earlier than she had expected. But she understood why with his first question: had Herries left?

He had, it seemed. Around eight that morning. He had tried to hire a car the previous evening, but without success. And the one that had come for him had been an hour late, and he was in a flaming temper.

All this she passed on from Rossi, the proprietor. Now she brought the subject round to them.

'Where are you speaking from?' she asked.

'Viareggio.'

'Viaregg—is that where you want me to meet you?'

'God help us, no. Have you ever been here out of season? I wouldn't wish it on a maiden aunt!'

'I'm glad you don't see me that way. Where, then?'

'I'll phone tomorrow, early. At the pensione. No need to worry now that Herries has gone.'

'But I do,' she said. 'Very much.'

'Then don't,' he said bluntly. 'I'm not worth it.'

There was a silence at the other end.

'Ciao, amore,' he added, more gently.

He hung up quickly before she could reply, left the station and went to the Spagnoli. The lobby was empty save for an old man in a baize apron teasing sawdust with a broom.

Mills rang the bell. The desk clerk appeared, dabbing breakfast from his lips. Mills handed him the letters for Eliscu and Kuznets, together with a thousand-lire note . . . he was expecting visitors, a business deal, very confidential—he laid a finger along his nose—he'd rather one didn't know about the other; so if the desk clerk would check the name first, then pass on the right letter . . . ?

The desk clerk smiled, nodded, pocketed the money. Leave it to him, signore. He'd be discreet . . .

Mills left, went back to the Brunello.

He sat in his room and waited. A few minutes to eleven, and no sign of Herries. He shouldn't be long now. He'd make it fast . . . unless he had a breakdown. Mills shrugged at the thought. Herries didn't matter that much. It was the other two—Eliscu and Kuznets—he was hoping to see. If only one of them took the bait, his plan could still work in part. Eliscu versus Herries, or Kuznets versus Herries. If they both turned up, he would really have them going.

He had thought it out carefully. It would prove beyond doubt that the CIA and the KGB *were* after him. If they were, he wasn't going to be the stag with a pack of hounds at his heels. He had witnessed that kind of savagery, with the terror-stricken animal reaching a point of no return.

If one had to go, that was no way for it to happen. His way, he would still be the hunted—but the chase would be on his terms. He'd lay the trail and watch them follow it, from the sidelines. Three separate packs sniffing each other out, wasting time and energy trying to shake the other two, unaware that it was the quarry giving them the run-around. Before they figured that out, they could be venting their spleen on each other, maybe to the point of violence.

That didn't bother Mills one little bit. If Kuznets, Eliscu and Herries finished side by side on a mortuary slab, he wouldn't turn a hair. Three secret services chasing their own tails in ever-decreasing circles might conjure up an amusing picture, but Mills didn't see it as fun and games. Underneath, it was for deadly earnest. Last night's little episode put the stamp on that.

True, Herring Bone and his friends hadn't been the big league. He reckoned them for BND—Federal German Intelligence, Bonn brand—born of the *Sicherheitsdienst* and the *Abwehr*, financed by the USA dollar, Nazis without the swastika, excrement that needed the chain pulling on it . . . he had flushed three, but would it stop there? He didn't think so. And for the first time in three years, he had a loaded gun tucked in his trouser top and a spare clip in his pocket.

He had no desire to use them, hoped profoundly he wouldn't have to. He couldn't kill them all. His ultimate hope of survival lay in wearing the opposition down, bringing it to its senses, settling for the truth . . . *that he had no formula.* But that would mean a final confrontation somewhere, some time, after which they might pack up and go home and leave him in peace. But that day wasn't today, and Viareggio wasn't the place . . .

Mills ordered fresh coffee to be brought to the room. While he waited, he saw Herries arrive, looking as mad as hell—a mood shared by his driver, whose gestures were plain. *Chi sanno frega,* he wanted payment and away, Herries could find another car from there on. Herries paid up and went into the Spagnoli.

A moment or so later, Eliscu arrived. Mills didn't know him by sight, but the Pontiac was a fair clue. Confirmed when Manny Berg of CIA, Berlin, came strolling down from the station entrance. The two men stood by the Pontiac, shaking hands and talking. Then they, too, entered the Spagnoli.

Five minutes passed. Herries came out again, Meredith with him. Herries was madder than ever now. And Meredith was shaking his head, plainly perplexed. He gestured towards the *piazzale*, as if inviting Herries to see for himself what had been done to the Fiat. Herries, in turn, gestured first at the Pontiac, then at the Cortina, which, earlier on, Meredith himself had brought round and parked up the street. Herries won. They both moved to the Cortina, climbed in, and waited.

Eliscu and Berg came out. They got into the Pontiac. Mills saw Eliscu hand his letter to Berg, who read it. They sat there discussing the matter; then Berg suddenly jerked his head back, as if to indicate the Cortina. Eliscu glanced at it through his mirror, and then the Pontiac was away with a squeal of tyres. The Cortina kicked and took off after it.

Mills finished his coffee, lit a fresh cigarette. Now for Kuznets . . . No sooner the thought than there was a Rolls-Royce, gliding up and stopping outside the Spagnoli. Two men stepped out. One could have been any nationality by the cut of his clothes. But the other was as unmistakably Russian as his Leningrad serge suit.

Close behind the Rolls came a Mini-Cooper. It went straight past and parked a hundred yards down. As soon as the two men went out of sight into the Spagnoli, a fair-haired young man clambered from the Mini and stretched his legs. He passed under Mills' window, as British as the packet of Player's Gold Leaf he pulled from his pocket. Shades of a brave, new world and a balance-of-payments situation, Mills grinned to himself: the Soviets swan it in a Rolls while Perfidious Albion tags behind in a Mini!

The two men reappeared on the pavement. The taller one in the Italian-cut suit had the letter in his hand. He must be Kuznets. He had the look of authority.

They got back into the Rolls, and it purred away as smoothly as it had arrived. The young man hustled back to his Mini and went after them.

Mills shrugged on his jacket. His suitcase was already packed. He left the room, paid his bill, and collected his Irlandese passport. He took the suitcase across to the station, checked it in with Left Luggage.

The Ferrari sports had gone from the *piazzale*, as had the Bianchina and the Millespecial. Only the Fiat remained—

deserted, rather forlorn. He gave the bonnet an affectionate pat. He would arrange for a garage to do the necessary repairs, pay for the damage in advance, and leave instructions for delivery back to Noli in case he was unable to collect it himself. It was much too early to know that for certain. His plan was off to a good start. But that was all it was—a start.

He went now to the Spagnoli, checked with the desk clerk: Ah, *signore*, your friends, you have just missed them. First the Signore Eliscu, then the Signore Kuznets . . . No, he had not mentioned a word to the third *signore*, the one with Signore Meredith . . .

Mills thanked him, asked for his bill to be made up. He was sorry. A change of plans. He wouldn't need the room a further two nights, after all; or the one reserved for the lady. He collected the Winkler passport, went upstairs, packed the second suitcase. He smiled at the chambermaid tidying the room. The clouds were breaking, he said; maybe it was going to be fine after all; he might drive over to Pisa and look at the tower.

'È bella la Torre di Pisa,' she nodded.

'Evviva la Torre di Pisa,' he chanted. 'Che pende, che pende, che pende . . .'

'. . . E mai non va giù . . . bravo!' She clapped her hands in simple delight.

He crossed to the station with the second suitcase, still chanting the old song under his breath: 'Viva the tower of Pisa which leans and leans and leans . . . yet never, but never, falls down . . .'

With a bit of luck, he thought, the same might apply to him.

37

THREE TWENTY-FIVE.

Mills stood back in the gloom, just beyond one of the bronze doors of the cathedral. He looked out over the lush green turf that spanned to the entrance of the tower. He had been in Pisa since three o'clock. After a leisurely lunch, a taxi had carried him the fourteen miles from Viareggio. It had dropped him off in the centre and he had strolled around, keeping a weather eye open. He had spotted the Pontiac and the Cortina, both parked on one of the wide quays of the Arno. The Rolls he had found opposite the University, the Mini-Cooper in a street close by.

Of their occupants, no sign. Busy trying to shake one another,

he guessed, and getting hot and sweaty in the shaking. It had
turned out to be that kind of afternoon. Heavy, sultry, with the
sun coming out every so often just as a reminder it was still up
there, doing its job.

Three twenty-six.

A motor-coach disgorged a chatter of American tourists.
Panama hats and crew cuts, 8-mm. cine-cameras at the ready.
Mommas with fleshy arms in sleeveless frocks, daughters with
shortish skirts swirling about pretty legs, juniors in long pants
and bow ties.

They streamed away in a ragged crocodile towards the tower—
ten minutes up, ten minutes down, ten minutes to buy souvenirs,
then away . . . Mills caught sight of Eliscu.

He had appeared from nowhere and was tagging along with the
tourists—dark glasses, camera slung, the inevitable clutch of
postcards in his hand. Rather neat of him, thought Mills.

He ranged the rest of the group, but no sign of Manny Berg.
He hadn't really expected to see him. Berg would have been
detailed to lead Herries and Meredith astray. And he had made
his usual lousy job of it—for there was Herries, standing outside
one of the gift-shops across the street, getting a reflection of the
group in the plate-glass window.

Eliscu went down the steps and into the turnstiled entrance to
the tower. Then Herries turned and hurried across in the same
direction. But his eyes ranged this way and that, no doubt on the
look-out for Mills.

Three twenty-seven.

Kuznets' turn. He came buzzing out of the beehive Baptistery,
winging his way, dapper and casual, across the wide sweep of
lawn. He hovered for a moment by a bunch of Swedish roses
sprawled on the grass, their student caps at rakish angles. Mills
saw him smile at them, savouring their nectar. But the eyes were
flicking around, wary for British and American thorns.

The Swedish girls were posing for a group photograph.
Kuznets gestured to the one with the camera to join the group, he
would take it for her. The job done, he handed back the camera
and said something that provoked a laugh. Then some of the
party strolled with him towards the tower—captivated, no doubt,
by one they took to be a native charmer.

Of Kuznets' serge-suited assistant there was no sign. But the fair-haired young man who smoked Player's Gold Leaf was suddenly no more than a few feet from where Mills himself was standing . . . on the steps of the cathedral. And as Kuznets and the Swedish *fröken* moved in on the tower, the young man stepped back sharply into the shadow of the doorway, almost treading on Mills' toes.

'You want postcards, signore?' Mills breathed hoarsely into Lister's ear, gestured at the stand by his elbow.

'No—no, thanks,' said Lister. His eyes searched beyond Kuznets, hoping to spot Mills. He had no time to glance at the man beside him.

Three twenty-eight.

All inside the tower now . . . Eliscu, Kuznets, Herries. Seven galleries to climb, one hundred and seventy-nine feet of spiralling stone steps to the top—and the best of luck to all who sail in her.

Mills craned his neck and looked up at the drunken *campanile*. A patch of white, broken cloud drifted past and the effect was eerie. The cloud became the fixture, it was the tower that moved . . . It seemed to yaw dangerously, swinging downwards.

Three twenty-nine.

Herries would be prowling the spiral towards the top. Eliscu must be there already. The blue shirt and tight pants had appeared for a brief moment at the gallery rail, just below the final ascent to the bell tower. Kuznets would be climbing more leisurely, one eye casting about for his contact, the other dwelling on the neat *derrieres* of his Swedish flock. But he would get there in the end. And all three would meet face to face.

They could not avoid it. Up at the top, there was only room to swing a bell. Would they look past one another with a gargoyle glare, or exchange polite conversation? Eliscu must know Kuznets; Kuznets must know Eliscu. Herries would know them both. Mills didn't denigrate the Co-ordinator entirely . . . He might not be the brightest boy in the field, but he had an astonishing gift for logging facts, figures, and faces. Not for nothing was he known as Auntie's Human Card-Index and Rogues' Gallery. Yes, Herries would know Eliscu and Kuznets, all right . . . But would they know *him*? What a gas if they took him for their contact, Winkler!

Mills' next move was to join a straggle of sightseers emerging from the cathedral and heading for the gift-shops across the street. He mingled with them and went past the fair-haired young man now sitting broodily on an egg-shaped stone bollard with his eyes clamped on the tower entrance.

Crossing between two parked coaches, Mills paused at the nearest shop. He stared into a window that was a ragbag of Holy Church and classical paganism—saints and satyrs side by side, plaster madonnas rubbing powder-blue shoulders with naked aphrodites; and Leaning Towers galore, in bronze, alabaster, and porcelain, varying in size from a paperweight to a hitching post . . .

Three-thirty precisely.

'Hello, Dad!'

The voice came from behind him. Mills didn't turn, or even peer at the shadow reflected in the plate-glass. The voice and the greeting he knew only too well . . . Ray Pavane. The one man he should have guessed Auntie would use.

Mills smiled sourly. He fished into a pocket, came out with cigarettes. He took one, then offered them over his shoulder. A hand waved them aside, flicked a lighter. Mills used the flame, said, 'Are you the Ferrari sports?'

'How did you guess?'

'Who else but Raymond Pavane!'

'Shall we take a spin? Or do you want to stay for Act Three?' Pavane nodded at the tower.

Mills shook his head, blew a stream of smoke.

'I know it by heart,' he said.

They walked away.

38

THE FERRARI gobbled up the miles, swishing past sentinels of cypress, down Route 206 to Cecina and on south along the Via Aurelia.

'Don't tell me I'm being banished to Elba,' said Mills.

'What makes you think that?'

'Piombino, just ahead.'

'Not quite,' said Pavane, swerving the car away at San Vincenzo. 'Just a ride.'

Just a ride. Mills glanced at the younger man. Thirty-five, lean, hard, tough. Ray Pavane might well measure up to the fictional spy. He measured up well with women, too. Fifteen to fifty, they all flipped over him. But Pavane had always played that side of his life cool . . .

Pavane cut into his thoughts.

'Nice play you made back there,' he grinned. 'I enjoyed every minute of it.'

'You didn't do so bad yourself,' said Mills. 'I had a fleeting thought when I saw the Ferrari in Viareggio, but no more. And the way you finally jumped me was bloody near perfect.'

'Thanks, Dad. But the credit's all yours. Hell, you trained me. I should be good.'

The Ferrari swung right, away from the Grosseto road, bearing towards the coastal strip between Follónica and Portiglione. The scenery was flat; the sand-dunes sweeping in among a belt of pines.

Pavane changed down sharply, swung the car off the road, bouncing it smoothly to a halt in a deserted glade. He switched off the engine, offered Mills a cigarette.

'Gitanoes!' Mills shook his head. 'You still smoke those things? I'll stick to my own.' He took a light from Pavane, had a casual thought. 'I ringed most of the crew back there,' he said. 'Kuznets, Eliscu, Berg . . . but who is the fair-haired lad with the Mini-Cooper?'

'Lister. Charles. Rome office. Very young, not much experience. But he might do well enough under your coaching.'

'Is that the deal Auntie is offering? Potty-training the new kids?'

'We all have to start. I was one once, remember?'

'Let's skip the small talk. Herries has made a balls up and you've been brought in. Is it to take me out?'

Pavane shook his head.

'Not you, Dad. Only your information. And for that you can name your price . . . within reason. The Rome office, if you want it. I mean, if you're planning to take it nice and peaceful in your old age. Though, personally, I can't see it myself. Woodworm and Wordsworth in the Palazzo del Drago isn't exactly *you*, somehow.'

'Thanks for that, anyway.'

'On the other hand, if you still want to remain active, I dare say you could have Herries' job as Co-ordinator. I'd say he'll get the chop when Auntie gets a full report on this one . . . and damn good riddance! You're a ringer for the job, for my money. And

Auntie'll think the same when I tell him how you've manoeuvred this little lot today.'

'Why not put me up for a knighthood while you're about it? For Christ's sake, Ray. There is no information, no formula, nothing! If you know me at all, you must know that!'

'I know, Dad.' Pavane looked apologetic. 'I know the gutsache you get whenever you hear two bars of Wagner. A good deal of that same hate has rubbed off on me. I'd accept your reason for frying the bastard, but I'm not the CIA or the KGB. Nor am I Auntie. Everyone else, it seems, thinks you've something to sell. Why else the jamboree at Viareggio and Pisa?'

'Because I invited them,' said Mills.

'You did . . . ? Well, that explains a lot! I've been trying to figure out how you made it work so well. But if you've nothing to offer, why do it?'

'Something else you can figure out,' said Mills. He climbed out of the Ferrari, walked away slowly through the trees, towards the shore.

Pavane caught up with him at a point where grass and sand merged thick. 'I hear you've got a girl,' he said, casually.

'So?'

'Herries passed it on to Auntie.'

Mills paused in his stride. He didn't look at Pavane. He stared out over the beach to where the waves slopped in idly.

'You plan to get at me through her—if everything else fails?' he asked quietly.

'She does matter, then?' said Pavane.

'Leave her out of it!'

Mills went down on his haunches, gathered up a handful of flat pebbles. Pavane looked down at him, gave a slow smile.

'Don't let's go melodramatic, Dad. If I was planning a trick like that, would I have mentioned her?'

Pavane watched him skate pebbles expertly, skipping the surface three, four, five times before sinking. He tried a hand at it himself, but only one in three came off. He hadn't the knack. He went back to the talk.

'If you're planning to marry this Mairhi Odell, I, for one, am delighted. If you need a best man——'

'Cut it out!'

Mills lowered himself on to a dune and began to pull at the grass.

'Okay—keep your hair on!' Pavane squatted beside him. 'But

I'm dead serious, if you are. You told me a couple of years back you wouldn't be sorry to kiss the job goodbye. And I know how you are on the family kick. Well . . . now you have the girl, why get involved in trouble? Once it's clear you've passed the dope on to us, the other parties will accept the situation and fade out of your life. That's the way the game goes. You know that.'

'There is no formula,' said Mills. 'So there can be no deal. Not with Auntie, nor with anyone else. Right?'

'If you say so . . .'

'I do. So what's the answer? Tell me that!'

Pavane shook out another Gitano, gave a shrug. 'You know the rules, Dad,' he said, soberly.

I know the rules . . . Mills went on pulling at the grass, watching out of the corner of his eye as Pavane put flame to his cigarette. Then he brought up his hand, sharply. Sand flew from it, straight into Pavane's eyes. The hand flattened out and went on, the edge taking the younger man across the windpipe. As Pavane clutched at his face, swayed, lost balance, Mills was up on his knees with the gun in his other hand.

'I know the rules, son,' he said. He brought the barrel down, catching Pavane behind the left ear. Pavane slumped on the dune. A thin trickle of blood oozed up through the broken skin and started to dribble towards his jaw-line.

Mills rose, stepped back, eyes wary, not ready to accept that the younger man was without fight. When it became evident even to him, a wry smile came to his mouth.

'I trained you, son,' he murmured. 'But not well enough, obviously. You were prepared to trust me!'

He stirred Pavane gently with his foot. Pavane gave a slight groan.

'You'll live . . . and learn,' said Mills.

He walked back to the Ferrari, climbed in, and drove away.

39

MONDAY EVENING. Viareggio.

Pavane lay on a hotel bed, better in health and temper than he had been twenty-four hours before. He had got back to the *piazzale,* sore of head and foot—a seven-mile walk before hitching a lift hadn't improved matters—to find the Ferrari parked with a note wedged under the dashboard.

Sorry, Ray—but I can't take chances. If you must talk sense into someone, try Auntie. Signed: Dad.

P.S. Thanks for the loan of the car. You'll find the keys at the desk of the Brunello.

Pavane stroked his windpipe gingerly. An expert karate chop, that blow—delivered with just enough force to incapacitate. That much harder and it would have fractured the hyoid and he'd have been corpsed. And the smack on the head . . . Pavane grimaced wrily, swallowed cognac.

He should have reasoned out that Dad would be armed. Yet the thought had never crossed his mind. Six, seven years he had known Mills. In all that time he had never seen him carry a gun, let alone use one. One of the first maxims Dad had taught him: a gun to a spy is morphine to an addict, Jesus Christ to a convert. A crutch to lean on when your wits are gone. But like morphine and Christ, a gun can be salvation in a crisis. That is the time to use it. Sparingly. And the moral: don't let a situation reach a crisis.

Espionage—Dad used to say—is like a Rotary. Choosey whom it elects. From the moment you're in, the eyes are upon you, watching if you measure up to standard. If you don't, you may be asked to leave. Rotarians do it politely. Espionage is less polite. Develop a reputation as a gun-slinger and it won't be polite at all.

Spies are people. As people they like to live. And—unless the alternative is forced upon them—let live. Spies are fluent linguists —if they are true professionals they certainly are. A gun, on the other hand, has a limited vocabulary and a boring one. Bore spies and they will call in another bore, one quicker on the draw —and that's *you* where no gun, no morphine, maybe only Jesus Christ can help you.

Dad had said much the same about karate. Excellent for chopping wood with the bare hands, useful if you planned to be a tycoon in the kindling business. By all means take up karate if you wanted violence. But not espionage. The same went for knives, cyanide pellets, booby traps in french letters—all the paraphernalia of the fictional agent. In real life they were no substitute for wits.

Yet did he practice what he preached? Yes and no, thought Pavane ruefully. No—in so far as he used both a gun and karate on *him*. Yes—because he knew I wouldn't expect it . . . That act of his, too, looking sour when I picked him up, congratulating me on my skill. When all the time he was waiting for me to show, because he wanted confirmation, to know for certain the identity of *all* his hunters, and where they were. That is what he had meant by 'Something else you can figure out' in reply to the question 'Why bring them all together?' 'You'll live and learn' the sly old bastard had muttered when I was wondering what hit me . . .

Pavane bore no grudge. Any soreness of mind was with himself for being too cocky. But he still had a job to do—to pin down Mills before the others.

That afternoon, he had gone back to Pisa. The gang were still there, chasing around. Shaeffer had joined Eliscu and Berg; a pair of baggy-trousered Ivans had augmented Kuznets and Zibrt. Herries, Meredith, and Lister he had found drowning their sorrows in the cocktail bar at the Nettuno.

Herries had blown his top at the sight of Pavane, and had called Whitehall, full of protest and indignation. Only to subside into a 'yes, sir! no, sir; three bags full, sir'. Which just about summed it up. Bags full, and home, John. Don't spare Alitalia. And Pavane left in charge.

He had decided to keep Meredith and Lister. They would do at a pinch, until he could rustle up someone better. But he had switched them around—Lister to watch Eliscu, Meredith to tail the KGB. Auntie had given him a blank cheque, so he had summoned Brinati from Milan and Vessel from Trieste—both of them Mills-trained operatives. Levine figured that once he was on to the quarry again, they could 'ghost' it . . . a line of bluff that might lull Dad into believing they needed his full attention. It probably wouldn't work, but it was worth a try.

Meanwhile, he had Janni on stand-by in Bologna and Crambo rushed down to Noli. Noli, of course, meant Mairhi Odell.

Pavane found himself thinking about her. One thing he did know about Dad . . . he didn't play fast and loose with women. Oh, he liked his crumpet—Pavane knew some of them—Lucille in Paris, Barbro in Stockholm, Maruja in Madrid, Sasha in Belgrade, and that piece built like Sophia Loren in Amalfi . . . nice, warm-hearted women with bodies to match. But you could scramble all their brains together and not cover a sixpence. To them all he was a *galanthomme,* a *caballero, trevlig, simpatico,* the old flame that lit them up when their husbands were away . . .

So, this Mairhi Odell . . . What about her? Irish; a travel agency rep; twenty-eight; good looking, by all accounts. Pavane had the dope on her but not a photograph as yet, though Auntie had promised to get one. Not known to MI6 as a foreign agent. At the same time, she didn't appear to qualify as another Lucille or Barbro. So what did that make her? Was she really *the* one—the settling-down-wife-and-kids bit? Or was she being used to outwit his pursuers?

Pavane found this a poser. It wasn't in the Gospel according to St. Dad. He didn't get his women involved, he didn't make use of them. Certainly if this girl meant anything to him he would never allow it. He would have to be desperate to let such a thing happen. And there were no signs of that as yet. The only thing was, he might be pulling something akin to the gun and karate trick: they knew him, knew his pattern—cardinal principles stuck to for twenty years—why should he break them now? . . . which was precisely why he did.

So—find Mairhi Odell . . . and maybe you'll find Mills. It was so obvious, one would automatically dismiss it for what it was worth. Herries had fallen for it. But Herries was meant to be taken for the chop, to be utterly discredited. Out would go Herries and with him his theories, including the one that the Odell girl was the lead to follow. The old double-bluff. Forget her, then find yourself wrong.

Or it could be a treble-bluff—so obvious you are expected to ignore her; but you're so damned smart you don't; only you'd have been smarter if you'd stuck to the obvious in the first place.

Pavane had groaned aloud, conscious of the lengths to which Mills' Machiavellian mind could go. He had tried logic; had thought and thought again. In the end, he had spun a coin. Tails he'd pin his hopes on the girl, heads he'd give her a miss. It had come down tails.

Now he poured himself another cognac, drank to Crambo and Mairhi Odell.

40

MONDAY EVENING. Póggio alla Malva.

Mairhi sat watching the rain splash down the windows of the train. Some journey, so far . . .

The Ventimiglia—Roma semi-express had come into Savona jam-packed. It had been as much as she could do to find room for her suitcases in the corridor. She had guessed why. No tourist train, not this one Monday of the year, but the *cameriere*-cum-chambermaid caravan, the autumnal exodus of holiday help from the French Riviera—Neapolitans, Calabrese, men and women from the Marches, Abruzzi, Apulia—leaving the dream-world *ricchezza* of the vodka-martini set for the reality, the sharp contrast of the Mezzogiorno. They had reached Sestri Levante before she was able to get a seat, and then facing a man who had brought his eyes out of their sockets and laid them on her knees all the way to Pisa.

She had changed at Pisa, choosing the luxury of first-class for the rest of the trip—to sit alone and relax, to be at her best when she met Mills.

Well, not quite alone. She had deliberately chosen this compartment occupied by a dowager and a lap-dog, instead of the one next door that was empty. It wouldn't have been empty for long. That man she had caught eyeing her on the platform, he had boarded the train. Ten to one, he'd have got in with her and tried his luck. One of the recognized hazards of travelling alone on the Continent. Here, it was less likely. The dowager looked the epitome of a formidable chaperone. She might have proven garrulous, of course, but that was the luck of the draw. As it was, before they had reached Pontedera, the old girl had followed the example of her dog and gone to sleep.

Yet relaxation had not come to Mairhi. As the train sped through the flat, fertile country that made up the valley of the Arno, the tension had built up within her. Empoli had come and gone.

Soon they would be crossing to the north side of the river. Then it would be Signa . . .

She had spent two years there with the Pessarelli family. Nice people. She had adored the children, and her job had not been hard—mostly improving the English of the eldest two. Signore Pessarelli was an industrialist, wealthy, ambitious. Signora Pessarelli was equally ambitious socially, and had always referred to Mairhi as the *precettrice inglese*—there was such snob value in claiming an English governess for the children. Mairhi hadn't minded the deception. The only thing she now regretted was that, in her innocence, she had moulded her Italian on the *signora* and had picked up that unfortunate aspiration of the lesser-educated Florentines.

Mills had teased her about it that night they had dined at the Giardino . . . Four days ago, that's all; but it had turned her life topsy-turvy. Crazy, really. What did she know about him? Come to that, what did she know about men?

A hissing of brakes made her peer out in a mild panic. Lights, a platform, the familiar shape of a station remembered . . . Signa. The train jerked to a halt. Both dowager and dog opened their eyes with a start. The dowager blinked at the window, read the sign, stroked the dog's head, and both closed their eyes again.

Now is the time to leave, if I'm going to, thought Mairhi; to seek sanctuary and take the veil with the Pessarellis. She remembered an old paraphrase of a typing exercise she had learnt during one brief term at commercial college: now is the time for all good girls to keep their drawers on at the party. She giggled aloud at the thought. The dowager and the dog opened their eyes again and stared at her.

Mairhi rose under the four-eyed gaze, picked up her small travel bag, went along to the toilet. The hot-eyed character from the platform was standing in the corridor. Damn! she thought. But he moved aside to let her pass, gave her no more than a glance. Maybe she had him wrong, after all . . .

As she locked herself in, the train gave a hollow toot and started to move. Next stop Florence. Now she was committed. She eyed herself in the mirror, applied a little make-up. Thank goodness she didn't need much of that. And her eyes looked better, thanks to a decent night's sleep last night. But what of tonight?

The colour came flooding up her neck and into her cheeks . . . My God! How that betrays me for a foolish virgin! She straightened her suit, smoothed it down over her hips. A green wool-jersey, it went well with her hair and he hadn't seen her in it before. She tucked her blouse in tidily around the waist-band. Only her hair to do now. She glanced at her finger-nails . . . oh, no! One of them was chipped, it must have happened getting her luggage down at Pisa.

Out came the polish and the brush. She made a patch, but with the train swaying it was a horror. She blew on it, waved it in the air, took a second look. But it was still a botched-up job. There was only one thing for it, if there was time, and she supposed there was . . . off with the lot! ,

Polish-remover, cotton-wool, wipe, wipe, wipe; eight fingers, two thumbs, get moving. No time to do them over; and even if there had been, a train-toilet that jerks like a dodgem-car was no place to try . . .

The train rattled over points, brakes hissing, slowing down again. Only time to pack up the bits and bobs, no time to do my hair or even spend a penny . . . Blast! There go my nice white gloves, down on the dirty floor, utterly ruined. Did I wash the spare pair? A quick check. Thank goodness, yes—and out!

Down the corridor and into the compartment—but it isn't Florence yet, only a signal set against the train. But no time to go back there again, the red turns to green and we're moving once more. He'll just have to put up with you as you are, like it or lump it. Whatever you do, don't get into a flap. Play it cool, girl . . .

A porter's face glided past the window. She raised her hand and hoped he saw it. His tread along the corridor told her he had. Just the two cases; she'd carry the travel bag herself. Take it nice and easy down the platform, and remember—play it cool!

Her eyes searched the barrier ahead. Was he there? Can't see him. What'll I do if he isn't there? Some of her poise went. She felt her shoulders sag. Then a voice whispered in her ear, 'Carry your bag, miss?'

Old Hot Eyes off the train . . . She quickened her pace. Then the voice again, 'Hoity-toity, contrary Mairhi!'

She whirled around. It was Mills. A rush and she was in his arms, clinging, hugging him tight.

Play it cool, girl? What a load of old cobblers, that was!

41

MONDAY EVENING. Livorno.

A three-man conference at the US Officers' Club. Over Collins Specials, Eliscu made a resumé of the past forty-eight hours—an appreciation of the situation delivered Navy style. The other two listened without interruption—Berg nodding wisely to show he was all ears, Shaeffer more interested in the prospect of a second drink than the drone of Eliscu's voice.

'That's it, gentlemen,' Eliscu concluded. 'Where do we go from here?'

'You're the boss.' Shaeffer shrugged. 'You tell us.'

'Some constructive ideas,' Eliscu snapped back. 'You're not employed to sit around on your can!'

Shaeffer boiled inwardly at the reprimand. 'Let's hear what the maestro from Berlin has to say,' he countered.

'Permission to speak, sir,' said Berg. Then, with Eliscu's nod, 'Winkler is Mills, of course. There can be little doubt about that——'

'Why not?' Shaeffer jumped him, determined to harass all the way.

'I know something about the man,' retorted Berg. 'He would never use a German as a go-between——'

'Horseshit!' sneered Shaeffer. 'The more I think about it, the more I see this for a bum steer. The whole thing was cooked up in the Kremlin—making it appear he's hard to get. Then when we do get him, we congratulate ourselves on being smart!'

'And the purpose of that?' said Eliscu.

'To con us into paying good dollars for a load of shmoo. Money that goes straight to Moscow, to come out again through the KGB to pay traitors back home! Like I've said all along, this is a job for Peas Piselli . . . find the son-of-a-bee and rub him out!'

'We haven't found him yet.'

'You're telling me!'

'You think you could have done better?'

The red light in Eliscu's voice made Shaeffer apply the brakes. He jinked ice in the bottom of his glass. 'I didn't say that, Art,' he answered, smoothly, 'I was merely outlining a course of action.'

'First things first. Let's find him. Have you any suggestions?'

'Isn't that why Berg is here?' Shaeffer deliberately ignored the man's presence. 'He knows him . . . or says. He's the one to read the crystal ball.'

Eliscu looked at Berg. 'Well?'

'Well . . .' said Berg. 'He chose Italy for a reason. This is home ground for him——'

'I've read his record.' Eliscu made it curt.

'What I was going to say was, there's the ex-partisan set-up. Mills was a big wheel with them in the old days. I think they would cover him, hide him out, if he asked them to. The man he killed was wanted by them for war crimes, or so it's said. If he went to them claiming he had carried out a justifiable vendetta——'

'We're back on that kick, eh?' This from Shaeffer.

Berg swung round on him. 'Truth or not, Mills could use the line and get away with it. The ex-partisans are not interested in secret formulae!'

'That makes sense,' nodded Eliscu. 'So they hide him. But where?'

Berg shrugged. 'Just about any place. But if we have to start somewhere, I'd plump for Bologna. He worked that area for part of the war. If not the town itself, there are places around—any one of them with easy access to Florence, Pisa, Viareggio. How far is it from one side to the other . . . a couple of hundred kilometres?'

'A little more, I'd say . . . but not much.' Eliscu looked thoughtful. 'Near enough for easy access, far enough not to reveal his base.'

'Why the hell should he need a base?' argued Shaeffer. 'All he has to do is scuttle into the Russian Embassy for safety.'

'Because we're still working on the theory we discussed at Trevignano—that he's playing this one for himself, to cut a slice of gravy to retire on.' The words snarled. Eliscu was fed to the gills with Shaeffer. He decided to get Berg out of the way for a minute or two. He turned to him. 'Do something for me, Manny. You'll find a set of road maps in my car. Touring Club Italiano, numbers twelve and, I think, thirteen. They cover the area we're talking about. Get them, will you?'

Berg was out of his chair in a flash and moving through the door.

Eliscu turned cold, steely eyes on Shaeffer.

'Now,' he said. 'Let's get one thing straight. I'm running this outfit. In my book, you're just the office-boy——'

'Wait a minute——' Shaeffer started to protest.

'You wait . . . and listen! You either take orders or get off your ass and out! And I mean *out*—back to Washington, with a misconduct report on your sheet! Maybe you can plead your case through some anti-Eliscu senator—okay, go ahead! Hang my scalp on your belt! That's what it's all about, isn't it?'

Shaeffer opened his mouth to answer, but Eliscu jumped down his throat.

'But it won't do you much good, Shaeffer. No matter how this business is balled up, *you* won't get the Rome assignment in my place. There's a bigger boy than you, with three years seniority, just itching for the chance. Hate my guts you may, but you won't relish working under Toni Taramelli!'

Shaeffer's jaw dropped. 'Taramelli?'

Eliscu smiled sourly. 'You'd find it hard to twist the knife in Toni. Not with his connections. His wife is Mamie O'Hara—the Houston O'Haras, close enough neighbours to hang their Monday wash on Lady Bird's line!' He paused. 'You want out or in?'

'Jesus, Art . . .' Shaeffer began to mumble, 'I didn't mean . . .'

'Out or in?' Eliscu barked the words.

'In . . . I guess.'

'Okay. But keep your lip buttoned unless you've something constructive to say. We'll find this egg, whether he's Kremlin-laid or free range. And when we do, we'll decide how he's to be served —sunny side or scrambled!' Eliscu glanced up to see Berg showing at the door, maps in hand. He lowered his voice. 'And stop riding Berg. If it gives you any satisfaction, I think he's a creep, too. But he has ideas. And we can use them.'

42

MONDAY EVENING. Florence.

Mills said: 'I chose Fiésole. A small hotel. One not on the Bluebird list—so we're not likely to run into the Sangsters!'

They were in a taxi, climbing away from the centre of the city. Mairhi glanced at her watch.

'I know where *they*'ll be. On the platform at Genoa, waiting for the Paris train, with Eileen fussing over the couchette reservations!'

He pulled a face. 'Couchettes! My friend Giongo can offer us something better than that.'

His hand pressed hers. She felt a mild panic, hoped she wouldn't make a fool of herself. It was on the tip of her tongue to ask what accommodation he had arranged. Instead, she asked why the taxi and not the Fiat.

He grimaced again. 'I had to leave it in Viareggio. Nothing serious, but it'll take a few days to put right.'

'Oh, dear. Did it let you down?'

'Not a bit.'

'And everything else is all right?'

'So far, so good.'

'And Herries . . . where is he?'

'Going round in tight circles last time I saw him.' Mills grinned. 'He won't disturb us again. Certainly not at the Tiro dell' Arco.'

'Tiro dell' Arco?' She wrinkled her brow.

'The Archery. Its owner was a one-time champion at toxi-cology——'

'Toxophily, you mean . . . I think.'

'Do I?' He shrugged. 'You're probably right. Anyway, let's say he's a dab hand with a bow and arrow. There's a range, or whatever they call it, in the garden. He'll sign you up when he sees that suit of Lincoln green——'

'Forest green, actually——'

'Whatever green, it's very smart. My compliments.'

'Glad you like it,' she said, on top of the world that he had noticed.

'I like everything about you,' he said. 'And don't spoil it by saying I must be easy to please. Nothing could be further from the truth.'

He lifted her hand, kissed it. The taxi chose that moment to take one of the several sharp curves of the road, throwing her against him.

His arm went about her, held her. His lips found hers. She lay back, gave a little sigh.

'I'm glad you came,' he whispered.

'Did you ever think I might not?'

'Most of the time, if I'm to be honest.'

'I said I would, didn't I?'

'Yes, I know, but——'

'No buts. Not now . . .'

She lifted her mouth to his. The rest of the journey was completed in silence.

43

MONDAY EVENING. The Via Aurelia.

Kuznets sat alone in the rear of the hired Rolls as it sped south towards Rome. Like Eliscu, Kuznets was having trouble with his second-in-command. And like Shaeffer, Zibrt was cock-a-hoop over the failure of the Pisa business. Not so blatant in his gloating; but it was there, behind the blue-tinted spectacles. Kuznets had been aware of it, and he had made his decision.

Zibrt would stay behind to try to contact this Winkler, who was probably Mills, at the baths of San Giuliano or at the biscuit factory at Navacchio, aided by the baggy-trousered duo—Donostchenk and Boyarov. And if that failed, he had permission to open up his brief-case containing the thirty-five neatly typed sheets of foolscap and go ahead with his master plan.

It was a complex idea, the way everything was that crawled out of his assistant's mind. It had more convolutions than a millipede and needed just as many legs on the ground to make it work.

This was no problem to Zibrt. He had pointed out with party fervour that Italy had no less than one million eight hundred thousand registered Communists—more than Czechoslovakia or Poland or the Balkan trinity of satellites put together. On Zibrt's brand of logic, it meant eighteen hundred thousand eager and willing agents all panting to get their proletarian paws on Mills. And providing they would do it for Karl Marx and not for money, Zibrt was prepared to use them, even to dig up Palmiero Togliatti from his six feet of final rest and put him to work.

Kuznets had pointed out tartly that with Italian Communists the operative word was *Italian*, which was all the difference between caviar and *scamozza affumigata*—both went well on triangles of toast, but you couldn't make sturgeon's eggs out of smoked cow's-milk cheese.

Nevertheless, in principle, he had given Zibrt verbal permission to use his plan, subject to certain limitations. Zibrt could only use local agents marked in the Confidential file as Good Security Risk.

With the flat, monotonous smudge of the Maremma landscape sliding past, Kuznets had to admit that the plan might work. Mills could be Almighty God, but not He—nor yet the Pope—could finger every Communist agent in Italy. And it needed only one clue—a solitary lead from a comprehensive hotel check spreading outwards from Pisa—to find him.

If the plan worked—fine. A glowing report on Zibrt, and the little runt would be promoted and away. And Kuznets would be commended for his shrewdness in utilizing such a brain while showing a self-modesty befitting a good Communist.

If the plan failed, he was covered against repercussion. The top copy of the plan, marked *Personal—for the attention of Counsellor Kuznets*, now reclined in the Embassy safe—sealed in an envelope together with his own criticisms. Criticisms that detailed every possible error of judgment and, in general, giving it the sniff of pork-on-the-turn. If questioned why, in view of these opinions, he had allowed Zibrt his head, he had the ready answer: a directive from the new chief of KGB, urging that all junior intelligence men be given practical opportunity in the field. Espionage failures in Holland, Norway, Sweden, and Belgium—as well as allowing the defecting Svetlana to outwit them—had prompted that. Very well; the buck would be passed back. And as a further cover, a second copy of Kuznets' criticisms would find their way into Zibrt's desk, implying that Zibrt had been warned—though, in fact, he hadn't—and had chosen to ignore his superior's advice.

All of which didn't leave the Counsellor free to forget Mills and rush back to the open arms of Analia. He knew he must continue the search independently.

A vague plan of his own was formulating, a plan that needed a microscopic study of Mills' dossier, a check and counter-check of the minutest fact, a shrewd reading between the lines. The dossier was back at the Embassy. Hence Kuznets' sudden impatience to get to it . . .

44

MONDAY EVENING. Fiésole.

Mairhi entered the Tiro dell' Arco. Mild panic was back with her again as the suitcases were brought in and Mills spoke to the porter.

'Room Thirteen.' Then, to Mairhi, 'You're not superstitious . . . ?'

'Er . . . no,' she said. The question that had been on the tip of her tongue in the taxi now reared its head again. But before she could summon up courage to ask it, it was answered—by a friendly looking face at the reception desk.

'Buona sera, signora!'

Signora, thought Mairhi . . . well, that's it, the bridal suite; the *fait accompli!* But what happens when I hand over my passport for registration? Or has he taken care of that, too?

Mills must have been mind-reading. 'The formalities can wait,' he said. 'If you want to freshen up, the room is just up the stairs, turn right, and straight ahead. It has its own bathroom, French windows, and breakfast balcony. I hope you like it.'

'I'm sure I shall.' She hesitated. 'But I don't think . . . not at the moment.'

His smile faded. 'Is something wrong?'

'No—yes—' She blushed. 'The plain fact is, I'm hungry. It was a very early lunch at Noli.'

'Of course. How stupid of me!'

The smile was back as he led her across the vestibule and into a low-ceilinged room with windows that ran the length of one wall. The *maître* appeared, bowed.

'Buona sera, signora,' he said, and led the way to the far corner of the room.

That *signora* bit again. That clinches it, thought Mairhi. Not that she really minded. She wouldn't be here otherwise. All the same, it was a bit calculated on his part, taking her for granted . . .

Then she saw the spray of lemon roses on the table beside her plate, and the card attached—*Non ti scordai, alanna*—and her heart melted on the spot.

She really was hungry and the meal was superb. Melon and *prosciutto,* baked fish Florentine, marinated steak grilled with *manteca,* side plates of *pomodori* and *fagiolini* sliced in oil, with fresh peaches in wine to finish off. The wine, itself, Castelli di Jesi, was new to her, but suiting her palate. She thought it must be something local. But he said no, not quite, but he did know the vineyard in a personal way.

'Another one of your Colonel Giongos?'

'You might say that.'

'Well, they've both done you proud. The meal was delicious. My compliments to the chef.'

'The colonel himself, no less—next to archery, his second love.'

'A cupid and a cook. What a combination!' She laughed. Then thought: Holy Crippen, what am I saying?

'You can tell him yourself . . . in the morning.'

A perfectly innocuous remark, but it had her blushing. He beckoned the waiter, ordered coffee and cognac. 'Shall we have it here?' he asked her. 'Or upstairs?'

'I—I'm very comfortable here.' Her fingers fumbled at the cigarette he offered. Oh, my darling, she felt like saying, can't you see you've got a ripe one here? Don't ask *me* what to do. Grab me by the hair and drag me off—the only way you'll get a firm decision!

'Tell me about Herries,' he said quietly. He had kept away from the subject until now.

'What about him?'

'What did he tell you . . . about me?'

'You'd be surprised!'

Her eyes watched the *maître* pour the cognac. When he had finished he looked at Mills, who gave a nod. The bottle was left on the table.

'Such as?' Mills prompted.

'Such as, well—a great gas of nonsense that was intended to be off-putting, naturally . . .' She hesitated until the *maître* was out of earshot, then went on, 'Something about you having a wife and four children.'

'Only four?' He grinned. 'I made it eight at the last count.'

'Eight? Oh, then you've been a dark horse.' She was keeping it light, but her smile was a shade over-bright. 'He really made it most convincing; even gave your wife a name.'

'Did he, indeed!'

'Yes. Mafalda. Isn't that ridiculous!'

It's out now, she thought. All he has to do is give it the lie, once and for all.

The next seconds were an agony of suspense. His answer did nothing to alleviate it. 'The bastard!' he muttered. 'The utter bastard!'

She watched his hand tremble as he picked up his glass, tossed back the cognac in a single gulp, then poured himself a fresh one.

'There is . . . a Mafalda?' The words choked in her throat.

He gazed at her without seeing. He lowered the bottle, brought out a wallet. He took something from it, passed it across the table. She stared at it for a long moment, then slowly picked it up.

It was a photograph—head and shoulders. An exquisitely beautiful girl, with large dark eyes and a sweet, gentle smile. The photograph was mounted on a card and there was a name: Mafalda De Matteis. Below the name, in smaller print: . . . *venti anni . . . vittima della guerra . . . i tedeschi hanno ammazzato tutta la famiglia . . . il papa . . . la mama . . . la sorella Angelina . . . e tre fratelli Mario, Ettore, Cesare . . . anche lo zio Ubaldo . . . la zio Felicita . . . cugini——* The words blurred with the tears that had started in her eyes. Even had she not understood a word of Italian, the heavy black border that edged the card would have told her enough. She heard herself saying, 'And she was . . .'

'The girl I would have married. And that bastard had the gall to say . . .' His hand tightened about the stem of his glass as if it was Herries' neck.

'Why did I have to mention it?' she whispered. 'If only I'd known. You're right. He *is* a bastard to say that if he knew . . .'

'He knew, all right. It's on my record sheet.'

Her eyes went back to the photograph, the picture of a dead girl.

'The whole family massacred . . . Why, in the name of reason? I don't understand.' She looked up at him, saw the tell-tale harshness gathering at the corners of his mouth. She thrust the picture back across the table. 'No, no. I shouldn't ask. I'm sorry.'

He gazed at the picture for a long moment. The lines about his mouth softened as he picked it up and returned it to his wallet.

'I can talk about it now,' he said, slowly. 'It isn't a sweet story, that's all. It happened not twenty-five miles from here—down south towards Arezzo. Two villages; Meleto and Castelnuova dei Sabbioni. Two hundred and twenty people butchered and burnt alive by German soldiers. The army, not the SS, you understand. And for no valid reason other than an excuse that the local baker was thought to be supplying the partisans with bread.'

He stubbed his cigarette savagely, still only half-smoked. He found and lit up a fresh one immediately.

'Mafalda and her family didn't even live there,' he went on. 'They were visiting the aunt and uncle; had come down from Florence for a christening—her baby cousin . . . also murdered.'

His fingers were turning the lighter over and over ceaselessly. She put out her own hand, caught them, held them still.

'No more, darling. Please . . . You're only torturing yourself.'

'I'm okay.' He brushed his eyes with the back of his hand holding the cigarette. 'Damn cigarette smoke . . . I should give it up.' He tried to smile. 'How about some more coffee?'

She nodded quickly, drained her cup. He beckoned the waiter. As he did so, she brought her chair round closer. An instinctive, spur-of-the-moment move. As was her next when the waiter came forward.

'I wonder . . .' she said. 'Could we have more coffee served upstairs?'

'Ma certo, signora.'

'Room Thirteen.'

The waiter nodded, moved away.

She didn't look at Mills, but went on caressing his fingers. Then she took a sip of her cognac, poured the rest into his glass.

'Give me ten minutes,' she said. 'While I unpack.'

45

ROOM THIRTEEN. It was all that he had said it was: spacious, airy, French windows opening on to a balcony, a luxury bathroom, built-in wardrobes, two easy chairs, a coffee-table, an *escritoire* . . . and an enormous double-bed.

Mairhi's eyes lingered on the bed. Then she went to the webbed stand that held her two suitcases. She began to unpack methodically. But her mind was elsewhere.

I've made a real langers of it, she thought. If only I hadn't mentioned the name. If I had left it at being married with four kids and laughed it off as a joke . . . Damn you, Herries—damn, damn, damn . . .

A tap on the door—but it was only the waiter. He put the coffee down, went away. She removed her jacket, hung it in the wardrobe. Without being consciously aware, she checked the second wardrobe. Empty. She carried toilet things into the bathroom, laid them out. No signs there, either, of sharing. But even then it didn't register. Her thoughts were still walking a tightrope . . . What could she do?

Comfort him, of course. Pour out her own love and hope that please God he might reciprocate in time. That was unselfish love. Could she measure up to that? She had her doubts, quite honestly. Saintly love—for want of a better word—was all right for the hour, the day, a week or two, maybe even a month. But not a lifetime. In a lifetime, a saint can become a martyr. And the stigmata would show. That would be the beginning of the end. She wanted him for a lifetime. She was sure of that. Married or unmarried wasn't the point; but the terms mustn't be his entirely. Did he want her for keeps? Or merely for the hour, the day, the week or two that it might work if she could shut out the grief that must surely follow . . . ?

She sighed. It was easy to argue it out in the mind, when she was alone. But when he was there, close, beside her, emotions took over; she couldn't think straight . . .

The unpacking was finished. She picked up her nightdress, slipped it under a pillow. Again, subconsciously, she lifted the pillow beside it . . . no pyjamas. Now, a little wrinkle of puzzlement appeared on her face.

A tap on the door. She let the pillow drop as if it was a hot cinder, was away from the bed swiftly. She was snapping the locks of her suitcases as he came in.

'Let me put them away.' He took them from her hands. 'You like the room?'

'Perfect.' She wanted to put her arms about him, ask his forgiveness for raking up the past. But common sense prevailed. 'What is the view like?'

He pulled back the curtains a fraction.

'Bloody awful! Rain pelting down enough to float an ark. All we need is Shem, Ham and Japhet under the bed, a couple of camels in the bathroom, and we can cast off!'

She giggled, poured coffee. 'What about doves? We can't sail without them.'

'Doves—shmoves,' he dropped the curtain, turned back into the room with a smile. 'One bird at a time . . . that's my motto!'

'I'm a bird, am I?'

'In the nicest possible sense.'

He leaned over her chair and brushed her cheek with his lips. He perched on the arm, offered her a cigarette. She shook her head, watched him as he lit up. He smokes too much, she thought. She sipped her coffee, wishing she could find something to say, not necessarily witty or clever—just something that might recapture the mood as it had been before.

His free hand stroked the nape of her neck.

'What else did Herries say?'

'Just a load of rubbish.'

'What kind of rubbish?'

'Nothing, really. The usual small talk.'

She leaned forward, away from his hand, put her cup down on the tray. She gestured at his cup, still untouched. He chose to ignore it.

'About me?' he persisted.

'About you?' She looked up at him, raised an eyebrow. 'You don't flatter yourself much! If you imagine he spent the whole evening——'

His hand came forward, caught her chin, lifted it slightly. 'No need to flip your bustle,' he said. 'You've put me in my place.'

She pushed the hand away, refilled her cup.

'If you really must know—he said you'd been fooling around with some fraulein in Berlin, that you were in trouble and wouldn't face up to it. There!'

'You didn't believe him?'

'Would I be here if I had?'

'I suppose not.'

'Then let's drop the subject of Herries, please. I don't know much about him, but what I do know is loathsome.'

'I'm sorry,' he said. 'I was forgetting the nuisance he made of himself.' He rose, moved to the other chair, sat down. He looked so contrite, her momentary annoyance fled.

'Don't look so glum. That kind of thing doesn't upset me

nearly so much now I've learned to cope.' She smiled. 'The only thing about it—for one awful moment, I thought he was going to skate right through the French windows and finish up on the terrace below!'

'A pity he didn't.'

'And break his neck? Thank you, no. I wouldn't want that on my conscience. Not mur——'

She killed the word hastily. But it was too late. Or too early. If she had finished it, it might have passed for a casual observation. But her attempt to choke it only threw it into relief. She saw his eyes turn to gimlets. She swallowed her coffee quickly, rose and went to her handbag on the *escritoire*. She fished out a handkerchief, went through the motions of dabbing the corners of her mouth.

She pulled back the curtain, peered out at the rain.

'What is it like in the daylight?' She spoke over her shoulder, without looking round.

'A green lawn, a grove of lemon trees, a line of cypress. Then, below and beyond, the amphitheatre,' he said quietly.

'Lovely. I hope it's nice tomorrow. I'd like to explore.' She waited for him to say something, but he didn't. She turned. 'All those two years I spent at Signa—while I often visited Florence, I never did get up here to Fiésole. Wasn't that dreadful of me?'

You're making a brave show, he thought; you deserve to get away with it. I don't know how much the rat told you about Berlin, but obviously he said something about murder. Yet you haven't asked—have no intention of doing so, apparently . . . not now, at any rate. Understandable, that. Learning about Mafalda is grimness enough for one night. But it points up one thing: it matters more to know for certain whether or not I'm married than whatever else I might be.

He said, 'We'll go wherever you want—see everything—make an early start. By the time we're finished, you'll know Fiésole the way you do Noli. But first I want your promise.'

'What's that?'

'Not to bring your Bluebird tribe here.'

She laughed, more out of relief for what he had not said than anything he had.

'I promise. Cross my heart!'

She traced her finger on her blouse.

The gesture made him wince inwardly. Don't do things like that, girl. It's tough enough for me as it is. Now isn't the time to make love to you. I'd regret it afterwards. Even worse, you might regret it: the last thing I want to happen.

He got to his feet, winced again—showing it this time, as if in pain.

She couldn't miss it.

'Is something wrong?'

He rubbed a hand across his solar plexus, looking rueful. 'Indigestion. Too much manteca on the steak. I made a hog of myself.'

'Some Alka Seltzer——'

She made to move to the bathroom, but he caught her hand, drew her back.

'No . . . I'll try a good night's sleep. I need it. And so, I imagine, do you, after that journey.' He kissed her gently, without passion. 'Buona notte, love. Dormi bene'

She looked at him, eyes wide, anxious, bewildered. He realized what she was thinking, gave her the answer obliquely.

'No Herries to bother you here,' he said. 'But if by chance there should be, don't use judo. Call me. I'm in Fourteen, just along the balcony.'

'I see . . .'

What else could she say? A first thought told her it was for the best, under the circumstances. A second thought made her feel affronted.

It prompted her to say something else as he moved to the door, anything rather than see him go like this.

'My roses . . . I left them downstairs.'

'I know,' he said. 'I told the *maître* to put them in water and have them sent up on the breakfast tray. Is that okay?'

'Ye-es . . . that's okay.'

She nodded numbly as he closed the door behind him.

46

OUTSIDE, in the tipping rain, a man in a dark slicker mackintosh watched the lights of the Tiro dell' Arco go out, one by one. He stifled a sneeze, cursed the weather under his breath.

He was up to the neck with it . . . That long, bloody journey from Noli, for a start; corridor-standing most of the way. Then a mad scramble for a taxi at Florence to keep them in sight . . . Well, he had found Mills. And Mills was up there, in one of those

rooms, warm and dry—well fed, no doubt, and now hitting the
bed with as lush a piece as a man could wish for . . .

The sneeze came again, not to be thwarted—once, twice—
sounding off like the clappers of hell.

He turned, squelched away into the darkness. Tomorrow was
another day. It could wait till then.

47

A BEAUTIFUL MORNING. One that showed Fiésole off to advantage.
A warm sun, without the brassiness of high summer blurring the
tints and shades. Washed-peach walls bloomed rich in the golden
light, and the countryside around had slaked its thirst at the oasis
of three days' rain. Everywhere the look of resurgent vitality, a
greenness of new awakening. Only the leaves, russet-brittle with
the dried blood of dying, betrayed the mood. Where they had
fallen, they whispered the truth underfoot: this was no second
spring, but a prelude to winter.

They walked for a while, following paths alongside the Bosconi, through cypress and pine, as far as the Vincigliata. As they
walked, Mills talked. Mostly about a childhood spent in these
parts.

His father had been an English teacher in Florence, his mother
Italian. An only child, happy in a tight-knit world of three until
he was ten. Then tragedy. They were taken from him suddenly,
and were buried together in the Cimitero degli Allori, just south
of the city. After which, apart from occasional visits to his
grandmother in Ireland, he had been shuttled back and forth
between foster-parents . . . Years of unadulterated misery.

Then Florence again, as a student . . . the happy days. Not a
little due to lodging with the De Matteis family—and Mafalda.
They had become engaged on her seventeenth birthday, a month
or so before Italy came into the war.

He had gone to Ireland, to make a last visit to a dying grandmother, when that had happened. Getting back was out of the
question, except by joining the British Army. He had hoped they
would realize his potential and parachute him into the country he
knew so well. But it had taken them nearly four years to get
around to it. Then he had learned what had happened at
Meleto . . .

The route back brought them to the tiers of the Roman amphitheatre. They paused and sat down among stones that had witnessed Sulla and Claudius and Septimus Severus. The stones were warm in the sun, but the scent of damp earth rose about them. Blue sky and white cotton clouds reflected upwards from pools of rain not yet siphoned away.

His eyes made a long sweep of the arena, then came back to her. One hand still clasped hers, squeezed her fingers.

'I must tell you about Berlin,' he said. 'The trouble I'm in——'

'You don't have to——'

'Yes, I do. You have a right to know.'

'A right? Are you sure?' Her eyes searched his for the reason.

'I love you, Mairhi,' he said, simply. 'There is your right.'

She opened her mouth to speak, but he put his hand to her lips.

'No . . . hear me first. Then you decide. I don't ask approval of what I'm about to tell you. Only that you might understand, or try to. It's something that goes back to Meleto, and a hate ever since that can never die . . .'

He told her about the *caserma* raid and his vengeance unleashed on the garrison of San Martino. How the SS had matched the massacre with one of their own. How he had traced Colapassa to Noli and got the name of Reinecke. How he had searched for more than twenty years to find the man until, at last, it had happened.

'You killed him?' she whispered.

'I executed him . . . yes.'

'Execute . . . kill—isn't that playing with words?'

Her eyes came back to his face. Her hand still lay in his. She had made no move to withdraw it. If she had done so, at any time, he would have taken it as a sign to stop, that maybe there was no point in going on. But she hadn't, not even now. That gave him hope.

'Playing with words?' He lifted his shoulders. 'But who defines what is murder and what isn't? With some Hindus it's murder to kill a fly that carries disease. While pilots drop napalm bombs on children in the name of duty. Authority decides what is justifiable and what is not. And who is Authority? A president, a politician, someone who has jockeyed himself into the seat of God. A someone I cannot accept as having more right to decide than myself when it comes to matters of personal conscience.'

'There is the sixth Commandment——'

'And all the laws of the Prophets,' he said, quickly. 'And who were the Prophets but men? Men who interpreted a clap of thunder as the voice of Jehovah to the ignorant, the better to secure their own positions of power. And when it suited their book they came with the "eye for an eye" bit.'

'Then you maintain you are a law unto yourself,' she argued quietly. 'That amounts to anarchy.'

'Possibly.'

'But anarchy—the rule of oneself—is idealism, a dream. In reality it is chaos.'

'It is only chaos when other seek to impose it,' he said. 'I'm no crusader for anarchy. I don't seek to impose it on society. I choose it for myself and am content with that. It is my right as an individual. What others do with their right is up to them. If they wish to herd together, that's their privilege. Their laws, their rules, their leaders are theirs. But they are not mine. Only at those points where we can agree am I prepared to conform. Beyond that, I cannot go.'

'But the will of the majority—isn't that what democracy is all about?'

'A pretty phrase; but what does it really mean? It means, for example, that if the will of the majority were to put the Ku Klux Klan into office with powers to exterminate all Negroes, Jews, Catholics . . . that would be acceptable?'

'You're being wildly hypothetical,' she said. 'It would never happen. You know that.'

'Perhaps not. But there was nothing hypothetical about the majority of Germans supporting Hitler. Nothing hypothetical about a will that imposed yellow badges and Juden geraus on a hapless minority. A will that condoned the rubber truncheon and the gas-chamber, the slaughter of ten thousand a day, every day—Sundays and Christmas included, sing Silent Night, Holy Night! And don't tell me it couldn't happen again!'

'What you are saying is—the war isn't over for you.'

'How can it be? It didn't start one Sunday morning with Chamberlain's declaration. The British may think so, but the villagers of Guernica will tell you differently. Nor was the cancer destroyed by a stroke of the pen on an Armistice treaty. Don't give me that forgive and forget routine, it's twenty years on, a new and innocent generation, blah-blah! Neither the red rag of Communism nor the wax-polish aerosol of Western democracy has done more than put a different sheen on the surface. Under- neath, the woodworm is still there; nationalism, anti-semitism come as natural to Germans as eating and sleeping. The spirit of Adolf Hitler doesn't need a medium to reveal it to those who care to look!'

Mairhi shivered at the words. She found herself thinking of Wolfgang. Not what he had tried to do to her, but his arrogance about the future of the new Germany. Reunification; masters of Europe again. His admiration for Ireland because—as he put it —it was not tainted with Jews. Yet the Edthofers had not been Nazis, according to them. Mama Edthofer had talked only of the bombing they'd been subjected to in Cologne; the camps were so much evil propaganda; Germans didn't do things like that . . .

And this man beside her, with his undying hatred—he hadn't asked her to approve his action, merely to try to understand. This she could do. Not because she wanted to, because she loved him, but because she could see the motivation that drove him on and on. But where to? Where would it end, she asked herself?

'You are on the run because you killed this man?' She voiced her thoughts aloud.

'Not quite.'

He told her about the suspected formula and the events that had followed.

'And there is no formula?' she asked.

'Not that I'm aware of.'

'Why can't they believe you?'

He explained briefly.

'What will they do?' She sounded anxious now. 'For that matter, what will you do?'

'The only thing I can . . . for the moment.' He smiled thinly. 'Play scopa.'

'Scopa? The card game? I don't understand——'

'It's a game with one cardinal rule. Find out—by fair means or foul—what hand your opponent is holding. Then, and not before, do you attempt to play.'

She looked at him searchingly. 'You don't seem all that worried about it.'

'I dare not be. Worry clouds the mind, impairs thought. Only one thing nags me—that I have involved you in this.'

'You mean my presence is—could be—a hindrance?'

'Heavens, no! Without your help, I couldn't have got this far. That's the truth.' He pressed her hand.

'I might be in some danger, then. Is that it?' She added swiftly, 'Not that I'm scared . . . just curious.'

He shook his head. 'No; not really. You see, these people know me—or think they do. They reckon me as someone with ice-water in his veins—unlikely to expose myself to an obvious weakness such as having a woman around. Then, when they find there is one, they cannot accept she is there because she means something. She must be some kind of bait—a bluff to be ignored.'

'Is that what I am?' She wrinkled her nose.

He looked pained. 'D'you really think so?'

She didn't answer the question, but posed one of her own. 'Would you have told me all this in Noli—I mean, if Herries hadn't turned up?'

'Yes. I would have had to eventually, the way things were going. But Herries *was* there, and there was no time. It wasn't something I could explain over the telephone.' He hesitated. 'If you walked out of my life now . . . I would understand.'

'You want me to do that?'

'I said I would understand—not that I wanted it.' Then, 'Just as I would understand if you said addio, so I would understand if you said arrivederla.'

'Go away and wait until this was all over . . . and then think about you—us—again?'

'Something like that.'

She took her hand from his slowly. He felt his stomach lurch. But it wasn't meant that way. She said:

'You have that picture of Mafalda with you?'

He nodded, produced the wallet.

'Show it to me, please.'

He took it out, passed it to her. She gazed at it for a long moment, then handed it back.

'I think I know what she would have done,' she said, quietly. 'I want to do the same.'

He looked at her long and hard, as if not really believing it.

'You are going to stay?'

She smiled sweetly. 'I'm going to stay . . . but not here!'

She rose to her feet. He followed suit, looking perplexed.

'Not *here*? But where, then?'

'I don't mean Fiésole. I love it, you dote!' She gave him a sudden, quick peck on the cheek, then brushed her dress. 'I'm talking about this monument to Caesar. The Romans must have had cast-iron sit-upons!' She stroked her own ruefully. 'Where to now?'

He glanced at his watch.

'Back to the hotel. It's nearly lunch time.'

He slid an arm about her waist and hugged her. She swung round to face him. They kissed. It was a long kiss.

When they came up for air, she murmured: 'Really, mister . . . what would old Claudius have said!'

'Let's write and ask Robert Graves!' he grinned.

'Let's. But not before lunch. I'm starving!'

She caught his hand. They climbed back towards the hotel.

48

LUNCH WAS EATEN in near-silence. For them both, talk was super-fluous. She had committed herself to him, whatever the future might hold. He, in his turn, knew this as surely as if he had put a ring on her finger.

Looking at her across the table, he felt his self-control slipping. He wanted her so much, he couldn't keep the desire from his eyes. She read the message and had the butterflies, not only because it was so obvious in his look but also because she could feel it mounting within herself.

She forked her way through a plate of *lasagne* in a daze, aware that he, too, was merely toying with his food. She found herself saying, without giving it thought, 'This is very nice, but very rich. I hope it won't give you indigestion.'

Words no sooner out than the truth dawned upon her. The previous evening . . . it had been his excuse to leave her, no more. She giggled and blushed. Unwittingly, she had put a *double-entendre* into her remark.

He got it first time. He laid down his fork, pushed back his chair. 'Let's not risk it,' he said. He rose, picked up her handbag from the window-ledge.

She gave him no argument. Her heart was pounding.

'If you say so . . .'

They left the dining room.

Upstairs, Room Thirteen was dark and cool, shuttered against the sunlight. She kicked off her shoes, turned, and was in his arms.

He kissed her, held her close. She felt his fingers reach for the zipper of her dress and run it down her spine. Her dress fell away to the floor. She closed her eyes, whispered, 'Be gentle with me.' Her own fingers helped him with the bra. Her pants joined the dress.

He stroked her back, gave her bottom a little pat, let her go. She was a blur of white about the buttocks, where the sun had been denied the privilege. He caught a brief glimpse of a full, white breast; then she was between the sheets. He shed his own things swiftly, joined her. He reached out and drew her to him— kissing, caressing her gently, easing away the tension that was with her. His own desire was apparent, but he knew it must be tempered with patience. Above all else, this must be her moment . . .

Just as suddenly, the tension was gone, her body no longer rigid, but receptive, alive, reaching for his. Only for another brief moment was there reluctance, the last resistance of virginity assailed. She moaned a mingle of pain and fear of an experience unknown. 'No . . . no . . .' Her eyes tight shut, her body wriggled from his, seeking to disengage. He silenced her lips with his, hands holding her firmly, reassuringly, quelling her panic. Then the last barrier was down and her eyes opened wide with wonder-ment at the depth and ease of penetration. Her arms swept up and about him, hugging him tight. 'Oh, I *do* love you! I do love *you*!

The flame within her was incandescent, consuming, melting her every fibre, until her whole being diffused in a molten glow. Nothing mattered any more except to give and to receive, to love and be loved, to go on and on and on . . . until, finally, all strength ebbed away.

She lay there passive, silent, conscious only that they were one flesh. And from there, a drift into sleep . . .

When she awoke, he was sitting on the side of the bed, about to slip on his shirt. He looked down at her and smiled.

'How do you feel?'

Her reply was to lift up her arms, reach out for him. He raised an eyebrow, twitched back the sheet, revealed her nakedness. He looked at the soft, curved beauty of her body, accentuated by the tanned shoulders and legs.

No coy squeals, no flurry of hands to cover herself. She just reached out the more.

'I can see I've got myself a shameless hussy,' he teased, conscious that this was the challenge he had known would come after—the reward for being a gentle, understanding lover. And he was in her arms again, this time fiercely demanding. The murmurs that came from her now were not fear, not pain, but cries of pleasure as the miracle of love was experienced to the full.

Later, as they lay side by side, sharing a mutual cigarette, she suddenly had the giggles.

'What's the joke?' he asked.

'I had a sudden thought,' she said. 'I wonder if they're still waiting down there to serve the second course!'

He grinned.

'Isn't that what you've just had?'

'Oh, darling'—she buried his shoulder with her hair—'was it greedy of me to want you again so soon?'

He stubbed out the cigarette, brushed back her hair.

'Let's call it a healthy appetite.'

'You know what I mean . . .' She dropped her eyes shyly. 'I—well—I don't know about these things. I am—was——'

'A virgin,' he murmured, kissing her nose.

'You could tell?'

'If I was a Greek, I'd hang a towel out of the window for all to know.'

'You wouldn't dare!'

'Want to bet? Old Giongo would fire an arrow through it and send us up a bottle of champagne!'

'Stop teasing! How did you know?'

'I suspected all along, from the moment I met you. And I was very conscious of the proof.'

'I suppose it's a silly thing to say in this day and age, but I'm glad you had that proof.'

'And I'm old-fashioned enough to say I'm honoured. Not that it would have made any difference——'

'It was yours, by divine right,' she whispered. 'As I am . . . For as long as you want me.'

'That may be for a long time—if I'm spared my health and strength.'

'I can vouch for that. Mama mia!'

Her lips sought his and passion took over as she pulled him down upon her yet again . . .

That night, after dinner, when they went upstairs again, she caught his hand at the door of Room Thirteen.

'Are you . . . are we . . .'

'Going to sleep together?'

He gave the answer by shutting the door behind them and

dropping the catch. She leaned against him, rested her head on his shoulder.

'As I said this afternoon—I don't know about—well—how many times a man . . . and you never answered my question.'

'Didn't I? Was it someone else made love to you three times?'

'It really can go on and on like that?'

'It depends on the woman, too. How much he loves her, how much she feeds his desire.'

'And you do love me?'

'I love you, tesore.'

'Then show me again . . . please!'

'Just try and stop me,' he said.

PART FOUR

49

CRAMBO had missed Mairhi by a matter of hours. He had gone to the Villa Fiorita with the story that he was from the Irish Consulate and had to contact her urgently. Rossi had come up with a forwarding address—the Pensione Delle Rose, Via Bartolomeo Eustacchio, Rome. The same address as the previous winter, when she had taken a job as a part-time translator. Rossi thought she was doing the same this year, after her usual three weeks' vacation in the south. Where? He couldn't answer that, beyond the fact she had left by train from Savona.

Crambo had struck lucky at Savona. Mairhi was well known at the station by virtue of her job. She had left on the Ventimiglia-Rome express, booked—the clerk remembered—to Florence.

Pavane had taken the information with caution. Crambo could have been *too* lucky at Savona: Mills could have primed her to drop the clue, then met her at Genoa or Rome or even Pisa, for that matter. It would be like his nerve to be under everyone's nose.

Nevertheless, Pavane had gone to Florence. The trail had ended at the station cab-rank. Mairhi's photo had received *fischi* of admiration from the cabbies, a tongue-cluck of commiseration for Pavane . . . another poor devil made a subject of horns by a beautiful but erring wife, *culo di angelo* . . . but, they regretted, she had not been their passenger. The only answer Pavane had expected. If Dad had met her in Florence, he would never have used a cab from the rank outside. He'd have brought one with him and told it to wait.

Pavane had set up headquarters in the Lungarno Corsini. It had to be somewhere, and Florence was more central than Viareggio. While he was about it, he had made a systematic check of every hotel, *pensione,* and private lodging-house in the city. But no Mairhi, no Dad. That didn't mean they weren't there. Mills could have friends willing to give him sanctuary.

He had been collating a list of possibilities when the first surprise came in from Brinati, up in Milan. Brinati had a lead on Mills, away north at Vercelli, in Piedmonte—a man answering the description with a red-head in tow. Crambo was put in to help cover the ground.

Then, two days later, Vessel—working from Trieste—reported something similar at Padua. A middle-aged man and a young woman had rented a self-drive car in the name of Winkler. They were thought to be south-bound, travelling to the hill-top republic of San Marino. Janni had been despatched from Bologna to cover that.

Another forty-eight hours—and the first couple were no longer in Vercelli but up in the Lago Maggiore, heading for the Swiss border. Pavane had contacted Pohl in Berne, got him down there post-haste. Sure enough, a silver-haired Herr Winkler and his wife had stayed the night in Lugano and had re-crossed the frontier in the direction of Como. But just when there seemed credence in the possibility, news had come from the other side of the Apennines . . . their Winkler had moved on to Senigallia, on the Adriatic coast.

And so it had gone on. With the one couple it had been Brescia, Cremona, then Venice—always one jump ahead. With the other, Bologna, Rapallo, Tortona, Casale Monferrato . . . A tantalizing search-and-find that drifted into four weeks. At which point, a new menace entered into it . . . the ex-Garibaldi, in the shapes of Serato and Lucarelli.

Brinati had finally caught up with one pair of elusive Winklers at Serato's place at Novara. They had turned out to be Shmuel Farb—a Moshe Singer operative—and his lovely wife, Becky. Shmuel had dyed his hair silver, Becky wore a titian wig. Pavane was not surprised, therefore, to learn the next day that the couple staying at Castelfranco with Lucarelli were none other than Yehudi Perlmeyer and his current girl friend.

This realization that Mills was no longer one against many but had the Moshe Singer boys aiding him, as well as a probable network of ex-Garibaldi, deepened Pavane's growing depression. It didn't finish with the unmasking of the impersonators. Novara and Castelfranco must still be kept under surveillance, just in case the exposures were red herrings to confuse and persuade the hunters to drop the scent—for Pavane wasn't the only one with four operatives tied up in knots. Wherever they had gone they had reported signs of KGB and CIA leg-men. Evidence that all three secret services were on a piece of string.

Yet Pavane couldn't believe Mills intended to play this game for ever and a day on the premise that all three would eventually retire from the field licking their wounded pride. For one thing —how could he afford it? Someone had to foot the bill for Farb and Perlmeyer, if only to cover their expenses. Mills probably had some money tucked up his sleeve but he couldn't be a rich man. Unless, of course, he had promised them a percentage of the take once he disposed of the LSD formula. But he had insisted there was no formula. And the longer this business went on, the more likely that seemed.

On the other hand Mills knew MI6 better than that. There would have to be more to it before Auntie gave up. The same went for the Russians and the Americans. This, therefore, could only be Phase Two in the game—but an important one, with an obvious purpose: to soften up the opposition; to bring their claws out prematurely so that they scratched at each other instead of at the quarry.

It was working, too. Pavane only had to look at his own associates. Herries had been the first victim. Meredith and Lister were cheesed off. And one didn't need to be a radio-doctor to hear the four men in the field spitting blood. If it was happening with *his* lot, one could bet Eliscu and Kuznets were having the same kind of trouble.

Psychologically, of course, it shouldn't be. All three organizations were trained to measure up to this kind of thing, the divide-and-conquer technique that thrived on internal suspicion, criticism, and contempt between subordinates and superiors. But the fact remained that suspicion, criticism, contempt did mature over long periods of negative result. The KGB and the CIA were no better mentally equipped than MI6. If Auntie was showing impatience—and Pavane was getting his ear bruised daily—then it was dollars to roubles Washington and Moscow were doing the same.

It was the entry of the ex-Garibaldi into it that gave Pavane the idea. Under which wing was Mills hiding . . . Serato or Lucarelli? Or could there be a third party, as yet to show his hand? The link was there. Both men had been at the *caserma* raid. Who else had been with that group of partisans?

Not the easiest task to check. Most of them had used a string of aliases to confuse the enemy. But it had turned up in the end . . . a Colonel Giongo, a Florentine. And Giongo, Pavane discovered, owned a small hotel up at Fiésole.

Five weeks of search, and it had been under his nose the whole bloody time!

50

PAVANE had been right about Eliscu and Kuznets. Both were wrestling with private contortions of mind, both had trouble with superiors and subordinates. Both had watched their agents get the run-around. And both had developed respect for the man responsible.

Kuznets had suffered most. Thanks to the misplaced enthusiasm of Zibrt and his master plan, reports had not been confined to two areas of activity. Mills, it seemed, was everywhere at once —even as far south as Sicily.

In all this, one crumb of comfort for the Counsellor. His mealy-mouthed assistant had as good as planned himself all the way to Outer Mongolia. There he would only have to match his wits with the yaks. And Kuznets would have put his roubles on the yaks.

Unfortunately, *he*, too, might just be around to do so . . . a prospect that filled Kuznets with abysmal gloom. He didn't much fancy the idea of a tallow-fat-plaited, almond-eyed Analia, even if she was—as the sailors used to tell—cut on the cross. His only hope was to find Mills himself.

He had gone over the dossier a score of times, seeking some minute clue. Reinecke, the *raison d'être*—a massacre and counter-massacre. And with the reports of ex-Garibaldi comrades being drawn into it, Kuznets had finally come—by the same process as Pavane—to Giongo . . . and Fiésole.

Eliscu, too, had returned to the Via Boncompagni, there to figure it out for himself. And like Kuznets, he had dug beneath the surface, the better to know how Mills ticked. By his own process of deduction, he had begun to come up with the same answer . . . this had been a revenge-killing—no more, no less. Look at the number of ex-Nazis the guy had chilled—or was reckoned to have chilled. A screwball, nuts, the complete fruit-cake . . . but Jesus, clever with it. All too easy for Foggy Bottom to beat the drum and demand action; they weren't here to cope. And they weren't ready to take the truth—if he was right and it was the truth—not yet. Which meant he still had to find the s.o.b. before Kuznets and that new man the British had put in. And by concentrating on the Garibaldi association, he had come to Giongo.

Eliscu decided he would play this one on his own, without Berg and Shaeffer to louse it up. He would do it casually, to avoid Kuznets and Levine latching on. He would go east to Pescara, then up the coast to Ravenna, and come into Fiésole by the back door. He might even take Paola with him, give it the air of vacation.

His mood brightened at the prospect: get Mills off his own bat. That would show Shaeffer and Berg how to operate, and—more important—vindicate himself with Washington.

51

IT HAD BEEN nearly five weeks of bliss for Mairhi—in everything but name, a honeymoon. Only the first few days had carried a shadow of unease, a fear that something would happen to bring it to an abrupt end. Her heart would skip a beat every time she heard the telephone ring or saw a strange car in the driveway, a new face in the hotel lobby. And on those occasions when he said, 'I must leave you for an hour or two; but I'll be back. Don't worry . . .'

But she did worry.

That first time he had left her, she had taken a walk in the Bosconi, alone, listening to the bird-song, scuffing the leaves with her shoes. Then suddenly in front of her, on the path, that man . . . She had recognized him at once . . . the train from Pisa, in the corridor. And in the same flash remembered him before, in Noli, at the telephone office, reading *Der Spiegel* . . . Oh, God! She had turned to run.

And there was another of them, coming from the opposite direction, between the trees, lost in shadow for a moment—but there, menacing. Only the next minute it wasn't. It was Mills, back earlier than he had said, out looking for her.

'Go back to the hotel,' he had said quietly. But so firmly, brooking no argument. And she had done what he had asked, not looking back for fear of what she might see. She had sat in the lobby, waiting, waiting—a bundle of nerves, sick with apprehension, eyes switching from door to clock and back again.

Thirty minutes had passed, snail-crawling each second. Then he had walked in and handed her a posy of wild flowers, with a smile and a kiss on the cheek.

'That man——' she had started to say.

'Forget him.'

'But who—what . . .'

'Forget him, I said.'

And that night they had made love as if the separation had been for a year.

With the weeks, she had forgotten. Such had their relationship gathered momentum, she found herself with a solitary regret—in itself a tribute to him. Never again would she experience the awe and wonderment of that very first fusion between them. So different from the old wives' tales, the veiled hints by her own mother of gory ugliness, of sex being a cross for women to bear, a distasteful duty rather than a pleasure. Pleasure in sex—as her church had striven to teach her—was a sin of the flesh. If that was so, then she was the all-time sinner!

But their compatibility went beyond the bedroom. She loved music, had learned to play the piano, but not very well. One afternoon, in the upstairs lounge, when the world outside the windows was shrouded in a mist of rain, he had sat down and started to play, quite brilliantly by her standards, Chopin, Ruben-stein, Granados . . . Then he had slipped into a number popular in Italy some years before . . . *Amorevole . . . resta qui con me, adorabilemente cosi, voglio te* . . . a favourite with her. She had flung her arms about his neck and hugged him with delight. The words were no longer those of a sentimental ballad; they had a deeper meaning for her. She found herself repeating them over and over again to him. And when she was alone, soaping in the bath or brushing her hair—with the added plea—please, God in your heaven, let this go on, don't let anything happen to spoil it!

The days went by and it went on. Some of their excursions took them to Florence, with visits to the Uffizi and Pitti galleries. Once again, their likes and dislikes were on the same plane and they played a little game of what pictures they would choose if they had to decorate a villa such as the Tiro dell' Arco, with one extra painting as a personal choice. He had plumped for Titian's *Venus of Urbino*, for his private bedroom. She had pulled a face at that.

'Why should you want a private bedroom?'

'For when I'm in the doghouse!' He had pointed at the red-haired nude on the bed. 'That's you all over—and that's me——'

He had gestured at the little dog curled up at the nude's feet.

'Am I really built like that?' she had asked.

'Well—not quite such a pot around the navel, and a little more above.'

'Thanks for something! But look where her left hand is—you could never accuse me of covering up like that!'

'You would if I was in the doghouse. That would teach me a lesson.'

'Me, too—for letting the sun set on my wrath!'

The thought had stayed with her on the way back to Fiésole.

'If we must quarrel—as I suppose we must some time—let it be over and done quickly.'

'No private bedrooms?'

'Not unless I snore.'

'I'm afraid you do.' His expression was dead-pan. 'Like an elephant. And while we're on the subject, you hog the bed and dig your rump into my spine.'

'Oh, no! Do I really?' Then she had seen the sly grin at the corner of his mouth. 'I've a good mind to pay you out for that!'

'Banish me back to Room Fourteen, d'you mean?'

'Only if the bed is bigger than mine!'

Later, she had had another thought on Titian's pneumatic Aphrodite. It prompted a question she had been meaning to ask since Noli—that she had no bones and was fashioned like a dame de voyage . . .

'Oh, dear,' he murmured. 'Did I say that?'

'You certainly did. Is it a polite way of saying I'm fat? Or does it mean what it says literally—a woman for the journey?'

'Yes and no. I mean, you're not fat. The yes and no answer the second question.'

'You make it as clear as mud.'

'You really want to know?'

'If it's to do with the facts of life,' she nodded. 'I'm old enough.'

'Be it on your head, then. A dame de voyage is a piece of French erotica exotica, sometimes called a ventre de la femme. The product of an enterprising rubber company, it's an inflated travelling companion that brings douce consolation de l'amour——'

Her eyes widened as he went on: 'In other words, elastic ladies that can be blown up to life-size, authentic in shape and minutest detail, even to hair in the right places.'

'Holy Crippen—you're joking!'

'Perfectly serious.'

'But men *don't*—surely? Do they?'

'Why else would they manufacture them? They had a large mail-order sale with the Navy and the Foreign Legion, so I'm told. And they must be a boon in monasteries.'

'But *you* never——'

'Do you mind?' He looked pained. 'Though I can see the advantages they offer. Money saved in hotel bills. They don't answer back. Just pull out the stopper, fold her up, and stick her in a suitcase.'

'That last bit might almost apply to me,' she murmured. Then: 'Heavens! What am I saying?'

'I'm not sure—but it sounds interesting!'

'No. I couldn't . . .'

'Go on, lover—be a devil! Something about pulling out the stopper, was it?'

She giggled, buried her face in his shoulder. Then it came in a whisper.

'Only that when you do, I'm usually so limp you could easily fold me up and put me away!'

'Want me to try?'

'Not *that* part, darling.' Her arms went about him. 'Just keep this dame de voyage permanently inflated!'

52

FOR MILLS, the time spent at Fiésole had been a revelation. Not so much of Mairhi—from the start he had sensed her love meant all the way or not at all—but of himself.

Logic had been his mistress from puberty, the guideline of his life for so long. Only once since Mafalda had he let go and grasped at emotion—Marisa, a diplomat's wife, a bitter-sweet experience that had ended in disaster.

Now he had allowed it to happen again . . . *Allowed* it? No, it had happened because he had wanted it to happen, and with no regrets—except, maybe, in its timing. Logic seized on that and argued it was sheer lunacy. A lunacy pointed up by that episode in the Bosconi . . .

He had returned from Florence that afternoon to find Mairhi had gone for a walk, alone. Nothing to that; but a sixth sense had taken a knife to his guts. He had hurried into the woods, looking for her. And she had come running, a man at her heels.

One glance had been enough. The fedora, the black slicker coat. It put the clock back—so reminiscent of the Gestapo. No taking flight at the sight of Mills. Merely stopping and leaning against a tree some fifty yards away, smoking a cigarette, waiting . . .

'HVA this time, I suppose,' said Mills in German, after Mairhi was out of sight.

'*This* time, Herr Mills?' A flicker of a smile. 'Oh, yes, of course . . .' The man pulled a newspaper from his pocket, flapped it. 'Those three washed up at Viareggio. Very careless of them. Very inefficient. But what one would expect of neo-Nazis.' The voice was thick with a heavy cold.

'Your lot wear a different label,' said Mills. 'But the same rats under the skin.'

'How you do hate us!' The man threw away his cigarette. 'A pure racialist. Born a German, you'd have made an excellent Heydrich!'

'Born a German, I'd have cut my mother's throat!'

'Instead of which, you would like to cut mine, nicht wahr?'

'Give me the chance.'

'Sorry . . .' The man let the newspaper fall. His hand clutched a gun. Just like a bad spy movie.

Mills shrugged. 'Where to?'

'Anywhere. Just a walk. And a talk.'

'Of ships—and shoes—and sealing wax . . .'

' ''Twas brillig and the slithy toves did gyre and gimble in the wabe!' The man in the fedora showed his teeth. 'I've read my Lewis Carroll, too.'

'Congratulations.'

'I don't pretend to understand it.' He pulled out a handkerchief, wiped a dewdrop from his nose. 'English humour is verrückt——'

'For Allah created the English mad—the maddest of all mankind,' quoted Mills.

'Did Carroll say that?'

The man stifled a sneeze.

'No. Kipling.'

Mills fired from his pocket at three feet. The man whirled like a top into a scatter of pine cones. His last breath was a sneeze. Then he was dead.

Mills looked down at him.

'You'd best be getting home, the nights are very damp. Carroll said that, also.'

He caught up the body by the heels, dragged it deeper into the woods.

Sheer lunacy, logic argued. Well, that remained to be seen. There was the other side of the coin. In Mairhi he had found an anchorage, a *raison d'être* beyond personal survival. He hadn't discussed the future with her—as things were it would have been pointless—but he had given it thought. A Villa Fiorita of their own, perhaps? He had the capital, she had the knowledge and the connections. They might make a go of a *pensione*. But first things first. He was not—the Bosconi apart—out of the wood yet . . .

So far as he could tell, Phase Two had gone well. Thanks to Lucarelli and Serato, both of whom he had kept in touch with over the years. When he had telephoned them, said he might need their assistance, neither had shown the slightest hesitation.

And Moshe Singer. Moshe had been willing to do most anything except fall in with Solomon Narbucco's idea of getting Mills to Israel. It was not hard to see why. He wanted no part in turning Israel into a hunting ground for three secret services. Israel had problems of its own. But once it was understood that Mills had no intention of leaving Italy except in a crate, there had been no objection—and in had come Yehudi Perlmeyer and Shmuel Farb. The one word—Reinecke—had been enough to co-opt their services.

Last, but not least, the gallant Giongo. Mills had a stalwart ally in the proprietor of the Tiro dell' Arco, who clearly regarded Mairhi as a dish beyond his culinary skills. And his chance to help would come with Phase Three.

It had been Phase Three that had taken Mills away from Mairhi on those unexplained trips. Not fraught with danger, as she imagined. Mostly they had been spent in Florence, at the Accademia di Scienze and, later, at the Istituto Per Le Lingue Estere. Between them they had supplied him with the material that, he hoped, would add the finishing touch to his plan.

All that remained now, so far as Fiésole was concerned, was the decision to leave. A reluctant decision; but sooner rather than later he knew he would be traced there. The HVA man had done it. Levine would find it for sure. So would Eliscu and Kuznets. But the hardest part of his decision was telling it to Mairhi.

He told her the morning after the night they had joked about the dame de voyage. She had been so passionate, so hungry for love, it was as if she sensed the 'honeymoon' was coming to an end. It had been nearly three a.m. before she finally slipped into an exhausted sleep . . . 'sunk with all guns firing' was her way of putting it. But he had lain beside her, wide awake—physically relaxed, yet mentally on edge.

In the end, he had crept from the bed, pulled on his dressing-gown, and gone out on to the terrace with a cigarette. He had sat there watching the stars arc away and the eastern sky turn pale with the approaching light. As he shivered in the first breath of morning air, he had felt the touch of her hand caressing his cheek.

She had turned in her sleep and missed him and awakened immediately. For one awful moment it had been a nightmare—he wasn't there, he never had been . . . Then she had seen his silhouette out on the terrace and had gone straight to him. Naked.

She hadn't worn a nightdress since that first night together. This was the new Mairhi Odell—the voluptuous, unashamed mistress . . . that other virgin Mairhi was light-years behind her. He caught her wrist, pulled her round and down into his arms. He kissed her again and again, crushing her breasts, his hands moving restlessly over her back.

There was a brooding violence about him that had her bewildered. 'What is it, darling? What is it?' she kept whispering between kisses. Then, for answer, he gathered her up, carried her back into the room, and made love to her with an intensity, almost a savagery, such as she had not known before. She was gasping aloud with pain, but that only seemed to drive him on the more. Then, just as suddenly, it was over in a shudder of convulsions. In the half-light, she saw he was weeping silent tears.

Instinct gave her the answer. The dream was over, before them the harsh reality. She held him tight, gripping his buttocks with her hands, entwining her legs about him, holding him within her, as if this way they might postpone the truth. And by her action, he knew that she knew. So he stayed with her while he told her the crueller fact of life: the job had to be finished, settled once and for all—and that meant leaving.

'Not without me,' she whispered.

'I must do this alone, lover. On my terms.'

'And I am here on *my* terms,' she murmured, firmly. 'Remember what I said in the amphitheatre? I would see it through with you, no matter where or how.' She lifted one hand from his back, brought it up and stroked his hair. 'Amorevole,' she whispered, soothingly. 'Abbandonate . . . rest' ancor' vicino me, cosi . . . I love you, you dote. And if you love me, you must understand.'

'I do love you. You know I do.'

'Then get this into your thick skull'—she knuckled his head— 'you're not leaving me behind!'

'But——'

'A hump on the buts! I'm in no danger—you said that. And if I was, I'd be in more danger without you around. Unless, of course, it's a case of "out of sight, out of mind".'

'You know that could never be so.'

'Maybe. But I'm not taking the chance.'

She gave his ear a sudden nip with her teeth.

'Ouch! What was that for?'

'For raping me without warning—I hadn't time to enjoy it!'

With that she released him from her hold and he keeled over on to his back. The tension was gone. He rubbed at his lumbar regions, grinned up at her ruefully as she propped herself on one elbow and ran a fingernail down his chest.

'That was the Indian death-lock you had on me,' he grunted. 'You didn't learn that at judo school, I hope?'

'Really!' She dug sharply with her fingernail, making him squirm. 'I was taught by a woman—and I'm not that kind of girl! It was something that came naturally and it'll teach you a lesson—calling me a dame de voyage!'

'You could fold *me* up and stuff me in a suitcase,' he muttered. 'My back is broken.'

'Roll over and I'll kiss it better.'

'A woman's panacea for all ills.'

'There are worse.' She prodded him. 'Go on, take your medicine like a good boy, and you'll grow up to be strong.'

He turned over on to his front.

'I'll need to be . . . with you around.'

She kissed his spine, then began to massage with her fingers. 'That's where I'm going to be—around. Capito?'

'Capisco,' he said.

He never suggested again that he leave her behind.

53

THREE LETTERS awaited collection at the Tiro dell' Arco.

Ray Pavane.
You are here. I am not. Nevertheless, we should meet up in
48 hours. But if Auntie wants the dope on LSD-25, he will
have to collect it himself. I leave you to tell him in your own
inimitable way.
                                                          Dad.
P.S. I nearly called on you at the Lungarno Corsini, but
thought it might embarrass you.

Counsellor Kuznets.
Zdrasste! Sorry to miss you but will see you on Tuesday,
with luck. And providing none of your KGB gorillas are
around. In which case, no deal. A room is booked for you at the
Villa San Michele. You will be contacted there. Dasfedanya!
                                                        Mills.

Commander Eliscu, USN.
Welcome aboard! The information is yours if you play it
solo. Tuesday suit you? A double-bed is in your name at the
Aurora. Make good use of it and await contact. Over and out.
                                                        Mills.

The letters were dated Sunday. If they were not collected by
four p.m. Monday, Giongo had instructions to make contact. The
instructions were unnecessary, as it happened.

Pavane was first, shortly after eleven on Monday morning. His
reaction was to wince at the P.S. It was below the belt. Mills had
known where he was yet again. But where was Mills?

A bland shrug out of Giongo. He would pass on further instructions as he received them.

Pavane went back to Florence and telephoned London. To his
relief, even more his surprise, fire and brimstone did not pour
down the receiver. A moment of hush, then a mild announcement
from Auntie that he would be there the same evening. Pavane
could meet him at the airport.

Pavane was left with the distinct impression that Auntie had
intended all along to be in at the kill. But who would do the
killing? Dad had said he had no formula. Now he talked of

handing over 'the dope on LSD-25'. The answer? Whatever it was, let it be soon. Then they could all go home.

Kuznets arrived at lunch time. 'The damn nerve' was his reaction, and a move to climb back into the Moskvich and return to Rome. Then common sense took over. He had come so far, sticking his neck out a further inch made no difference. He went instead to the Villa San Michele and worked on a plan to double-cross Mills.

Eliscu turned up at three forty-five. His reaction was: 'A double-bed! How could he possibly know I'd have Paola with me!'

He, too, felt like calling the whole thing off, but reason prevailed in the end. To do so was an admission of failure. And all those years of training at Annapolis would not countenance that. It had resolved itself into a personal issue, a challenge, a duel of wits. Okay, he wouldn't chicken out now, give Shaeffer the last sneer.

There was also the factor that Mills now admitted, in writing, that he had the LSD-25 information. Washington's orders were to obtain it, come what may. He'd just have to find a way that didn't leave Mills holding all the cards.

As for the accommodation . . . they had to sleep somewhere and the Aurora was as good as any. He'd just go round the room with a toothcomb—check for 'bugs', spike mike 4255s, keyhole acoustic tubes . . . He had his pen scrambler to jam any audio surveillance, if that was Mills' game . . .

Paola needed no such complicated manoeuvres to settle *her* mind. It was a nice room, with private bath and a southern aspect. The whole trip made a pleasant change. Four weekends of celibacy had had her wondering, was she losing her grip? This king-size, well-sprung mattress must surely give her the answer one way or the other . . .

She was undressed and between the sheets before Eliscu had unknotted his tie.

54

MILLS turned off Highway 65 in the direction of San Martino a Montalbino. Whatever else, this return after more than twenty years was no haphazard decision. He had reached it back in Genoa, at the Hotel Narbucco, when he had formulated his plan. San Martino was where it had started. At San Martino it would finish—always supposing the intermediary phases were successful.

He felt they had been. His pursuers had been chasing a mirage for five weeks—endeavouring, at the same time, to outwit one another. He had made fools of them. Not for its own sake, but to convince them beyond doubt they had been wasting their time, that he had nothing to offer, that revenge alone had been his motive. If he couldn't convince them at San Martino, he never would.

He glanced at Mairhi out of the corner of his eye. She had been strangely quiet throughout the journey. A mood he could understand. He had felt the pang of leaving the Tiro dell' Arco.

She lay back against the upholstery of the drop-head coupé he had hired for the trip. She wore dark glasses and a silk scarf wound turban-fashion about her hair, her face up-tilted to allow the sun and wind play upon it.

He slipped a hand from the wheel, touched hers.

'Asleep, tesore?'

'No.'

'Happy?'

'Of course.'

'But very quiet—like a dame de voyage.'

She turned her head fractionally at that, smiled. But a little smile, as if out of politeness. As she did so, she shivered.

He pulled the car over to the side of the road and braked. He twisted round, picked up a cardigan, motioned her to sit up.

'I'm not cold,' she said.

'Don't let the sunshine fool you.' He slipped the cardigan about her shoulders. 'It's November and we're three thousand feet up. I don't want you catching a chill.'

He latched the buttons over her breasts. It reminded him of Nella Barbiscio, all those years ago, only the circumstances had been very different.

Mairhi caught his smile. 'What are you grinning about?'

'Just a thought.'

'About me?'

'No-o, I must confess.'

'Oh. Some other woman?'

'As a matter of fact . . . yes.'

'Mafalda, I suppose.' It was out before she could stop it. The faint shadow came into his eyes, the smile faded.

'No. Not Mafalda.'

'Someone connected with this San Martino place?'

'In a way.'

'Will she be there?'

The smile came back at that. 'I shouldn't imagine so.'

'Does that mean you hope she isn't?'

'It doesn't mean anything. I've never thought about it either way.'

'But you thought about her just now!'

The smile went again. The joke had gone sour. 'A thought crossed my mind.' His tone was curt. 'It meant nothing. She meant nothing. Whether she'll be there or not I don't know. Nor do I bloody well care!'

He turned back to the wheel, released the brake, set the car in motion. She sat very still, eyes on his profile.

'For one who doesn't bloody well care you're most vehement about it.'

'Annoyed, if you must know.'

'With me?'

He made no answer, kept his eyes on the road. He was aware she had removed her sunglasses. He felt her hand rest lightly on his knee.

'I'm sorry . . . I didn't mean to be a bitch. I don't know what came over me.'

'Blame it on the altitude.' He let his own mouth relax. 'It takes people that way sometimes. But you'll get acclimatized.'

'I hope so. I can't bear to think of us quarrelling.'

'There's a first time for everything.'

'But this is the second time. There was Noli . . . remember? Just after you kissed me?'

'True.' He grinned. 'But look where that led!'

'You've no regrets?'

He caught the anxious note in her voice. He stopped the car, switched off the engine. He slipped an arm about her, kissed her.

'Will that do for an answer?'

'For the time being.' Her fingers squeezed his thigh. He slapped her hand gently, caught it.

'Maybe I have one regret,' he said.

'And that?'

'That we didn't meet ten years earlier.'

'No,' she said. 'I don't agree. At eighteen I was prissy and precious.'

'Precious you still are. Prissy—I'd have lathered that out of you!'

'Slapping my behonkey, I suppose?'

'Why not? It's a nice behonkey, tailor-made for slapping. A bit on the big side,' he teased. 'But I'm not complaining. Nor have you as I recall.'

'Nor did this other girl, I bet!'

'*Other* girl?' He looked puzzled.

'The one at San Martino. Tell me about her.'

'There's nothing to tell.'

'Please, darling——'

'I don't see the point.'

'There is no point,' she persisted. 'I know there must have been others, lots of others, before me. I'm not jealous—not really. Just curious, this once.'

'Alice down the rabbit hole. Very well, if you insist.' He told her about Nella and the circumstances. She listened without interruption. When he had finished, she asked a single question.

'Have you seen her since?'

'Once . . . about ten years ago, oddly enough. In the Galleria in Milan.'

'She remembered you, of course.'

'Remembered me? She was pushing a twin pram, with two more toddlers beside her and a husband close behind . . . at least, I presume he was the husband.'

'It seems she took your advice!'

'I like to think so,' he smiled.

'And do you always advise your old girl friends to marry someone else and raise a large family?'

That pulled him up with a jerk.

'Subject closed,' he said, abruptly. 'San Martino is around the next bend.'

He started up the car again.

55

SAN MARTINO was larger than he remembered it. Not due to modern development, but rather to a previous false impression. He had seen it in 1944 at close quarters for a brief hour or so, and at night—a single main street and a small *piazza* in front of the church. The black smudges in the darkness he now saw as narrow, cobbled streets stepped up and down from the Corso d'Italia, as it was called.

It sat astride a hill in its own right, with vineyards and olive groves cascading away to narrow gorges thick with trees and tangled undergrowth. And the approach road curved along a ridge, passing through the village and up to the *caserma*. The *caserma* was still in use. There were military road-signs along the way, and an army truck had passed them going down.

San Martino was walled, too, with an imposing entrance gateway—Roman, probably, built on early Etruscan. That was the pattern in these parts. The outer side of the wall appeared to be crumbling, but as they drew close he could see it was pitted with scars. Mortar shrapnel, at a guess. He didn't know for sure, but he could imagine . . . San Martino had suffered a second terror a few months after Reinecke—barrage and counter-barrage when the Allies finally broke through the Gothic Line.

Of the first terror there was a poignant reminder just within the gateway. The inner wall was a mass of little plaques and glass frames with faded photographs, each with its own wire holder and pot of flowers.

Mills stopped the car, climbed out. He posed an unspoken question at Mairhi. But she made no attempt to join him.

'You go alone, darling . . .'

She said it quietly. This was something very private, and she had no wish to intrude. She added, 'Just leave me a cigarette and a light.'

He dropped case and lighter beside her, walked back to the wall. An old man with a bin on wheels was sweeping brittle leaves from the cobbles. A woman was busy splashing out and refilling fresh water into the pots. Both looked at him, both murmured a polite 'Buon' giorno', both went on with their work.

His eyes ranged over the tablets cemented to the wall. A few of the names he remembered: Battista Tognazzi, Bolognini, Rocca, the old priest Dom Teodoro . . . a number of the others at that fateful meeting. Only two, so far as he knew, had escaped—Gianoli, the schoolmaster, who had gone higher into the mountains with the children; and the doctor, Cifariello. For the rest on the wall, they were names only. He had never met them.

At the base, a larger plaque told the accumulative price that San Martino had paid for that raid on the *caserma*: one thousand four hundred and eighty-seven men, women and children murdered by the Waffen SS and the Wehrmacht. As he stood there, reading the inscription, the woman glanced at him, caught the grave expression on his face. She lifted a hand in a helpless gesture.

'La guerra, signore!'

'Si, signora,' he answered. 'La guerra. Una causa brutta.'

'E già!'

This from the old man, now leaning on his broom. He had pushed back his peaked cap and was looking hard at Mills, as if trying to place the face.

'Always the war,' he went on. 'If not here, then somewhere else!' He hawked and spat on the cobbles. 'The politicians and the generals, they forget so easily. Only the people remember!'

And San Martino, it seemed, had not forgotten. Mills took some money from his pocket, gestured at the flower-stall close by the gateway. He pressed the money into the woman's hand.

'Some flowers from me.'

She misunderstood, thinking he wanted them for his lady in the car. She waved a deprecating hand. She had so little to offer today. It was Monday—the best had gone. Just a few chrysanthemums, some gladioli, and the inevitable violets.

He took a bunch of violets for Mairhi, but gestured at the empty communal container beside the main plaque. The rest of her stock to go there. She stared at him, surprised, then touched by his action.

As he turned away, he heard her stirring the old man to give her a hand.

'Hai visto! Un gentiluomo quello. Molto buono!'

A good, kind gentleman. Was that how the rest of San Martino would see him? Mills wondered about that.

Back at the car, the cigarette case and lighter were still on the seat where he had left them. Mairhi had not moved. She had that languid, pooped look that often comes with a change of altitude. He handed her the violets. She smiled her thanks. He climbed in behind the wheel, sat looking up the main street.

'We'd better find a place to stay,' he said; adding, almost apologetically, 'No Tiro dell' Arco, I'm afraid. We'll be lucky to find even a pensione. I should have thought of that before we started.'

'I don't need to be pampered,' she muttered. 'If that's what's worrying you.'

That something again in her voice—a tetchiness that kept coming through for no apparent reason. The thought repeated itself: it could be the altitude. It did play tricks, shorten tempers. He must watch his own tongue, not bite back.

'I'll pamper you as much as I like,' he smiled.

The obvious place to try was the *osteria* . . . Tognazzi's old place. Was it still in the family? he wondered. He knew Mama Tognazzi had survived the massacre, and there had been a host of kids . . .

Then the shrill sounds of children caught his ear and his eyes saw a river of black smocks with white collars and blue looped ribbons come spilling out of a gateway some thirty yards ahead. The school-house. Was Gianoli still alive and running it?

He eased the car forward, stopped just short of the gate. The river swirled around them—bright-eyed, brown-limbed, inquisitive. The little girls gazed at Mairhi, whispering, giggling; the boys stared boldly at Mills, tapping the radiator grille and wings, one coming close enough to lean over the door and peer cheekily at the dashboard. Mills made a pass with his hand, as if aiming to catch the nose between his fingers. The boy was too quick. He pulled back with a wide grin.

Children, another generation, the same yet so very different. Not the horror of war for them, the hungry look and the parrot cry of *cioccolata, caramello* that ghosts of countless soldiers knew so well.

Mills was crooking his finger at the boy to come nearer so that he could ask a question when there was a sharp word of command from the gate. At the sound, the river surged away in all directions, voices raised and smocks flying in a wind of their own making. Mills turned his head. A young woman in the neat black of a teacher stood at the gate. She smiled shyly, apologetically. He climbed out, went over to her.

'Forgive me, signorina . . . is Professor Gianoli still head of the school?'

She nodded. 'Si, signore.'

'Would it be possible to see him?'

'I suppose so, yes . . .' She was too polite to show her own curiosity. But she threw a second glance at the car and Mairhi before turning back across the playground.

'You know my father well?' she asked.

'Your father? I must confess I didn't know that. No, not very well. It was many years ago. But he may remember me.'

'Your name?'

'Irlandese.'

'Irlandese. Grazie.' There was a slight hesitancy as she repeated the name, as if it rang a faint bell. 'If you will excuse me for a moment . . .'

She went inside the cool dark of the school entrance. He waited at the door, eyes wandering across the dusty, flagstoned playground. How many who had played here during those autumn days of '44 had survived? Gianoli had pied-pipered some of them into the mountains; but there could have been little refuge in the heights that winter—a winter when the elements and the murderous intent of man had vied with each other in cruelty.

'Signore Irlandese?'

Mills turned. He could recall two things about the schoolmaster. The war ribbons in his lapel and the empty left sleeve. The man facing him wore both. And, like Mills, he was searching his memory.

'We met the night of the raid on the caserma,' Mills prompted.

'The partisan captain?'

Mills nodded. This was the moment of truth. Would Gianoli turn on his heel and walk away?

Gianoli did not. His face creased in a warm smile, his hand came out. A firm, strong grip.

'At last . . . finalemente! I have often wondered and hoped you might return. Your sergeant——'

'Lucarelli?'

'Si, Lucarelli. He was here some two, three—perhaps it was five—years ago. Time passes so quickly.'

Of course, Tomaso Lucarelli would have been back. If I had asked him, I could have saved myself a lot of heartburn, wondering if I would be welcome . . .

'It is good to see you, capitano!' Gianoli was still pumping his hand. 'Capitano! Just listen to me. What am I saying? Generale they tell me you were at the end!'

'Just plain mister now.'

The daughter was hovering in the passage. Gianoli released his hand, beckoned to her.

'Carmella . . . come here. Meet my old friend, Signore Irlandese. You've heard me talk about him many times.'

A polite subterfuge. The welcome was genuine, but somehow Mills didn't imagine his name had cropped up that much. He shook hands with the girl, who smiled gravely. Gianoli continued, 'My daughter was only a baby then . . . four years old.'

She would be Mairhi's age. The sudden realization that Mairhi had been no more than four when he had been fighting at San Martino made Mills pause for reflection. At the same time, he was aware that the girl was exchanging a glance with her father—a glance that Gianoli interpreted into a question.

'You will lunch with us?'

'It's kind of you. But I really can't intrude.' Mills gestured back across the playground. 'My wife is waiting.'

The first time he had used those words . . . 'my wife'. At Fiésole, Mairhi had been referred to as *la signora* by all the staff, from Giongo downwards. Polite as well as ambiguous, he had slipped into the habit himself when talking about her to others. But now he had called her *mia moglie* . . . and he liked the sound of it.

'But, of course. Your wife . . . Then you both must. Please!' Gianoli put the matter beyond argument by turning to his daughter. 'Fetch the signora to the house. What are we thinking of, keeping her waiting out there!'

He took Mills by the arm, turned towards the house that adjoined the school. 'My own wife is dead, alas . . . but Carmella is a good daughter. She won't leave her old father. We have a housekeeper, a good cook, but always complaining we don't entertain so she can show off her culinary talents. Now we give her the chance, eh?' He chuckled, changed the subject. 'Just a passing visit, I suppose. No one stays in San Martino but the military.'

'I noticed that. The caserma is still in use?'

Gianoli nodded. 'Italians only now—thanks be to God. I don't think even NATO would dare suggest bringing the tedeschi back here.'

'I stopped at the wall,' said Mills. 'I saw the plaque. One thousand four hundred and eighty-seven. That's an awful reminder.'

Gianoli caught the tone of his voice, gave him a quick glance. But he said nothing until they were inside and he had produced vermouth and glasses. Then, shrewdly, 'You must not carry the cross for what happened after that night's work, old friend.'

'What makes you think——?'

'I know. Lucarelli told me how you felt—of your wish to avenge.'

'It has been done,' said Mills. 'Reinecke is dead.'

'Reinecke?' A slight tremor of the hand caused the bottle to clink against the glass.

'The man responsible.'

Gianoli looked at him, handed over a glass.

'And until then you could not come back?'

'Something like that.'

Gianoli's eyes moistened. He reached out, squeezed Mills' shoulder. 'You have come back. That is the important thing. Let us drink to that.'

He picked up his own glass, then put it down again at the sound of voices outside. Carmella and Mairhi. But they went past the room and up the stairs.

Gianoli shrugged, picked up his glass again, smiled. 'The ladies must pretty themselves up before making an appearance. Drink up and have another.'

Refilling the glasses, he said gravely, 'I repeat, you had no need to carry that cross. San Martino was living on borrowed time anyway.'

'Borrowed time?'

'You have not heard what followed?'

'Only what the SS did in revenge.'

'You and your friends risked your lives to warn us of that—ah, yes.' As Mills shook his head, Gianoli patted his empty sleeve. 'I was a soldier, too—though not a very good one. I can appreciate what you did. There was no strategic purpose in coming down from the caserma after the raid, other than to lose valuable time in which you could have made good your own escape.'

'But we did escape——'

'Maybe; but you weren't to know that. No. When I said borrowed time, I was referring to months after.'

'The Allied push for Bologna?'

The schoolmaster nodded. 'First it was the Turkomens—the Ukrainians in German uniform. They retreated through here, pillaging, booby-trapping. Then came the Americans with their big guns and their strategy—if it moves, shoot at it. And finally, the liberation'—a wry smile at the word—'at the hands of the Indians. Liberation to them meant a licence to rape.'

He said it without heat or anger, just a shrug of the shoulders. A fatalist acceptance of something that had happened long ago.

'I didn't know,' said Mills quietly.

'I'm sure you didn't . . . and I am only telling you now for one reason. If you came here expecting animosity from San Martino for what you may think you were responsible, then forget it. You won't find animosity. You'll find——'

But he never did say. Carmella chose that moment to enter with Mairhi.

56

ALBERTO IRLANDESE TOGNAZZI was a lean, handsome youth in his early twenties. His dark eyes flickered from Mills to Mairhi and back again. There was accommodation, yes—a double-room overlooking the *piazza*, if the *signore* would fill out the registration form at his convenience. He handed Mills the printed slip, picked up a key and their luggage, led the way upstairs.

Alberto was ambitious, full of ideas. Of his five brothers and two sisters, only Ginetta—the next to him in age—was still in San Martino. Two brothers and a sister had died in the massacre along with his father. Then Carlo had been killed by a mine buried in the vineyards as late as 1949. The other two brothers were working in Milan. Alberto had been left to manage the *osteria* with Ginetta and her husband and, of course, Mama Tognazzi. But all three were stick-in-the-mud about change, though change must surely come. The *caserma* had outlived its usefulness. The range was inadequate for modern guns. There was talk of shutting it down. When that happened, the military would go and the tourists would come. San Martino would be a winter sports resort like Lioana or Monghidero, across the hills. The Osteria Il Buco could be developed into a good second-class hotel by converting the properties on either side. Then they would have more than a mere three rooms and a bath. Alberto had had to work hard on Mama to dip into the family purse to provide even that facility, her attitude being that what was good enough for Papa and eight children was good enough for them today.

Alberto couldn't argue that he had never known his Papa. That only brought on a floor of tears. But for God's sake, all that was twenty-odd years ago. One couldn't go on living in the past. The future was the thing. Maybe these unexpected guests were an augury of things to come. He hoped so.

Alberto lowered the bags, turned the key, opened the door, stood aside for them to inspect the room. His personal pride and joy, he had chosen the *mobili* himself, purchased it in Bologna— very chic, very modern, twin single divans. His eyes flickered from Mills to Mairhi. Would this oldish man and his young wife approve of the innovation? After all, it wasn't much of a barrier if they still fancied one another.

Mills was thinking much on the same lines. He glanced at Mairhi with a somewhat rueful smile. If there was one thing he hadn't expected to find in San Martino it was twin beds. But for once their telepathy didn't click. Mairhi merely nodded and said, 'Very nice.'

She flopped down on the nearest bed the moment Alberto was gone. Mills moved to her, slipped off her shoes.

'You don't look at all well,' he said anxiously.

'Only tired . . . out of breath. I think you're right about this altitude business.' She stretched out, closed her eyes.

'Take it easy,' he said. 'I'll do the unpacking.' He picked up one of her two suitcases, snapped back the locks.

She opened her eyes, sat up. 'No . . . leave it alone!' Her tone was sharp. 'I'll do it myself, in my own time!'

'As you wish,' he said equably. 'It was only an idea——' He made to shut the case; but she was off the bed and beside him, touching his arm.

'I'm sorry, darling. I didn't mean to snap. Forgive me.'

Her lip was quivering, a hint of tears in her eyes. He put his arms about her.

'Nothing to forgive,' he said. 'If you feel like bawling me out, or just plain bawling, go ahead. I understand.'

'I wish *I* did. It's stupid, I know. But I would like to be left alone, for a little while.'

'Fair enough. I'll take a stroll, look around.'

'Do that, darling,' she murmured. 'There must be other people you want to meet, things to do. I'm sure you can do them much better without me tagging along all the time.'

'I could see Doctor Cifariello now instead of later, I suppose.'

'Doctor Cifariello?'

'Yes . . . surely you remember? Gianoli phoned him just before we sat down to lunch, and then I spoke to him. He asked us all up to dinner this evening.'

'If you say so. It must have gone in one ear and out the other.'

'I can cancel it, if you don't feel up to it.' He regarded her with concern. 'Or maybe I should call him in to see you . . . professionally, I mean.'

'No, no,' she said hastily. 'You don't have to do that. I'm pretty sure I know what the trouble is—apart from this altitude business, that is.' She lowered her eyes. 'Feeling low, tetchy. It happens like that with me always—just before . . .'

He saved her the embarrassment.

'I'm a grown man, tesore. I've heard about the visits from the marchesa.'

She leaned her head on his shoulder, gave a little smile.

'Where I come from they call it the fairies,' she murmured. 'Anyway, you just leave me to do the unpacking and maybe take a nap. I'll be as right as rain afterwards.'

'You are sure . . . ?' He hesitated.

'Quite, quite sure. Please.' She gave him a push.

'Anything you say.'

He kissed her on the cheek, left the room.

57

AFTERNOON SIESTA in November was a circumstance of habit rather than a necessity in San Martino. As Mills walked up the Corso in the direction of the *caserma*, he saw few people about. A broad-hipped woman in the eternal black came clacking down from one of the side alleys, her feet shod in wooden sandals, a tin bath perched on her head, piled high with washing. She crossed his path towards the communal laundry with its stone-hollowed basins and rows of taps on the far side of the street.

He glanced up the alley she had left. It was knifed with sharp shadows, yellow sunlight, and a litter of lean cats. From behind doors and shuttered windows came an occasional sound. A baby, fretful, teething. The rumble and shrill of a man and woman arguing. The sharp clatter of a bucket. The bray of a donkey.

Familiar enough, this leaden peace of a Tuscan siesta—as timeless as the hills around, where a falling leaf or a trickle of water exaggerates against the stillness, a stillness that makes even a November sun seem warmer than it is.

Then it happened . . .

A pair of bicycles free-wheeled down from the *caserma*. They slewed to a halt in the *piazza*, deposited two young soldiers from the saddles. The soldiers walked into the only bar that was chromium and formica and Gaggia-countered. And San Martino climbed out of the past at the feather-touch of a pick-up. A juke-box stirred out of hibernation and *A Ticket To Ride* belted out across the square. The sound spewed over the cobbles, assaulting the walls like a battery of guns. And the walls threw it back, contemptuously. They had survived a host of armies in centuries of

wars: electric guitars and the Mersey beat were not the trumpets
of Jericho.

Mills studied these walls along the Corso. Stone, weathered
and mellow, patchy with plaster smears, pitted in places by shell
and machine-gun bullet. The façade might show the same face.
But what of the people it sheltered?

The schoolmaster had said they bore no animosity. Yet the
memorial plaques showed they had not forgotten. But the plaques
were not entirely for the victims of Reinecke. Here and there had
been the mute anguish for a son or husband who had died in the
desert or the snows of Stalingrad. Animosity, if any, was not for
him, the ex-partisan, nor yet for Reinecke; nor for Ukrainian
mercenary, American, Indian . . . but for war itself.

And the younger generation . . . Young Alberto at the *osteria*—
what did he feel? The pointer had been there in the pride for the
modern bedroom suite: *A Ticket To Ride* out of nostalgia and
bitter memories, on to a new way of life.

Mills reached the end of the Corso, where the walls faltered
and gave way to chestnut and pine. Beyond that point, the road
curved away, climbing through the trees to the *caserma*.

He paused.

To go on was not to go forward. It was to go back. In that lay
the crux—and the answer Gianoli had left in the air.

Indifference.

San Martino a Montalbino remembered its martyrs as a mother
remembers her sons. With the passing years, the pangs of child-
birth are sweeter to the memory than the more recent pain that
took them from her. And she finds her solace and compensation
in the bright eyes of the grandchildren who have taken their place.

Need he, then, have killed Reinecke?

Yes, yes, yes! he told himself fiercely. It was necessary and
right. And even now, knowing what he did, he would do it again.
It had only been wrong to come back here to San Martino, to
project his own conscience upon them, to use their past suffering
as a lever in his plan.

But he was committed now. The wheels were in motion.
Tomorrow or the next day the vultures would gather. And unless
he could find some other way, he must still offer them the bleached
bones of one thousand four hundred and eighty-seven San
Martinese as collateral for the truth behind Reinecke's death.

Would they accept it? Or would they still want *his* flesh? For
his old self—the Mills of a few weeks ago—it would not much

matter. That Mills had a past, a day-to-day present . . . but no future beyond mere survival. But the Mills now retracing his steps down the Corso had something more than a bleak horizon— thanks to a girl back there at the *osteria*.

He saw the irony. He had come back to San Martino, seeking confirmation in the past. Instead, he had found a finger-post to the future. It now remained to make sure he had one . . .

58

MAIRHI was asleep when he got back to the room. She had removed her dress and her bra and lay with the coverlet thrown across her. Her face showed a pallor through her tan. There was a bead of perspiration on her upper lip.

He rested a hand lightly on her forehead. No burning, no apparent sign of a temperature. But her sleep was shallow. She stirred at his touch, coughed. A harsh cough, as if the mountain air had taken a rasp to her throat and lungs. It probably had, he had seen it before with those not accustomed to it. Even at this height—three-and-a-half thousand feet—strong men could be bowled over for a day or so, to the point of nausea and vomiting. Mountain air wasn't everyone's cup of tea. And if—as she had put it—she was due for a visit from the fairies, that would only aggravate the moodiness and depression.

The coverlet had slipped in her restlessness. Her right breast had come adrift from the slip she was wearing . . . firm, full, ripe, the nipple hard yet tender-looking . . . *his* Venus of Urbino. Old Titian's tottie wasn't in the same class! He adjusted the coverlet up to her shoulders, then moved away and lay down on the other bed.

He must have slept, for the next thing he knew it was gathering dark outside. He looked across at the other bed. Mairhi wasn't there. The coverlet was thrown back, her underclothes a frilly heap upon it. Then the door opened quietly and she came in. She was wearing a robe and carrying a toilet bag and towel. She came straight to him, sat down on the bed beside him, put her arms about him, gave him a hug. He pretended to protest.

'What's all that in aid of?'

'You're an old dote, and I love you!'

'Old dote? You're for ever calling me that. What is it—a cross between a dope and a goat?'

'You must know the expression—to dote on someone?' Her voice was gravel-husky. 'Well, I dote on you . . . so that makes you a dote!'

'Maybe. But not so much of the old!' He glanced at his watch. 'We'd better get a move on. We're due at Cifariello's in the hour.'

He made to rise, but she held him firm.

'Not before you tell me you love me.'

'I love you.'

'How wildly enthusiastic.'

'Ti amo . . . sempre.'

'A bit better. It'll have to do, I suppose . . . for the time being.' She released him, lay back on the bed, gave a little sigh. 'We do *have* to visit this doctor of yours?'

No crystal ball was necessary to read the invitation. And the temptation was strong. He bent over her, unlatched her robe, threw it back.

She wore nothing underneath. As he gazed at her, the passion rose. 'Amore mi', ti voglio bene . . . tanto, tanto bene!' He buried his face between her breasts, then kissed them each in turn. Not roughly, but he felt her wince.

'Careful, darling,' she whispered. 'They are a little sore.'

He raised his head, ran a hand gently up to her throat. 'So are your tonsils!' He slapped her lightly under the chin, left the bed. 'A reason why we must call on Cifariello—if only to get you a gargle!'

59

Doctor Cifariello lived at the top end of the village, above the Corso, virtually in retirement now, leaving the bulk of the practice to his son-in-law.

The dinner party was small—Gianoli and Carmella the only other guests. While his daughter entertained them, the old doctor showed Mairhi and Mills around his conservatory, to admire his hobby—orchids.

He cut a bloom for Mairhi, a *triana cattleya*. 'It goes well with your colouring, signora,' he said, gallantly. Then, to Mills, 'I am delighted you came back to see us . . . if only that we might gaze upon your beautiful wife!' He winked, motioned them towards the dining room. 'We'd better go, before I get my daughter's tongue for ruining the dinner! You like la cucina Toscana, signora?'

'Very much,' said Mairhi. 'I lived near Florence for almost two years.'

'Ah, yes.' He gave a condescending nod. 'They cook well enough there for city folk. But here, in the mountains, we have our own specialities. A superb cheese, for example—a kind of cacciocavallo. Whatever else goes before, this is a must with us.'

He led the way to join the others. Mairhi looked at Mills, drooped an eyelid.

'No cacciocavallo for you, darling—remember your indigestion!'

But it wasn't he who let the side down. One sniff of the sharp, pungent aroma of the cheese and Mairhi went the same yellowish colour, pushed back her chair, and bolted from the room. Mills rose quickly, but the old doctor was quicker.

'My province,' he said calmly, and followed her out.

Mills crept about the bedroom, undressing in the dark, careful not to disturb her. Cifariello had said not to worry, he was sure it was nothing serious, and that he would look in and see her in the morning.

Mills was about to climb into his own bed when he heard her murmur, 'Darling . . .'

He crossed to her.

'How is it, lover?'

'God, I'm so miserable. The humiliation—having a thing like that happen, in the house of complete strangers——'

'Old Cifariello is no stranger.'

'To me he was. You were right all along. I shouldn't have come with you. I'm only a burden. You've got enough on your plate as it is, without me being sick.'

'Rubbish.'

'It isn't rubbish. I am a burden. And a bore.'

'Who said you were a bore?'

'You don't have to—I know.'

'I'm not going to argue with you,' he said patiently. 'That could go on all night and not be resolved. The doc said you need sleep and rest. Didn't he give you a sedative?'

'It hasn't worked.'

'What can I do, then?'

'Nothing,' she said flatly. Then, 'Those people . . . they are coming tomorrow?'

'I hope so. It has to be settled, one way or the other.'

'Then you go to bed and get some sleep. You'll need it.'

'Yes, I suppose so. Good night, tesore.'

He kissed her gently, moved away.

She heard the other bed creak as he climbed in. Then she turned on her side, her back to him, and began to cry quietly to herself.

60

MILLS looked at his watch. Eleven-thirty. They would be on their way now . . . well on their way. It was thirty-five miles from Fiésole—an hour's drive.

Kuznets would be first. Eliscu close behind. Pavane and Auntie making up the rear. Short of breakdowns or acts of God, it should go smoothly. Up to the point of arrival, anyway. After that, it was up to him.

Serato would be travelling with Kuznets. Guglielmo's one concession to age—he didn't drive himself; so a hired car had been laid on. Mills didn't want the Russian turning up in a Moskvich or a Rolls. San Martino was a small place—even on a Tuesday, market day. Eyebrows would be raised at the sight of a foreign car.

The local *carabs* might get curious. He didn't want that.

The same went for Eliscu. No Pontiac. Lucarelli would be driving him in his own modest Lancia. And Lucarelli would stand no nonsense. If Eliscu showed any inclination to play it tough, Lucarelli would be tougher.

Giongo would be bringing Pavane and Auntie . . . if Auntie deigned to come. That was a fair possibility. At the crunch, Auntie was not one to stand on dignity or think in terms of his exalted position.

The meeting-place was by grace of Gianoli. The schoolmaster had not wanted to know the ins and outs of the business, but had come up with both an admirable and diplomatic suggestion. Above and behind the school-house was the *campo sportivo*. It boasted a compact little grandstand, with dressing rooms for football teams to change in. An Italian tricolour fluttered from one pole, a blue-and-yellow flag—colours of the Sanmartinese

Juventas—from the other. Only the game would be a different one today. Mills crooked his mouth in a thin smile.

From where he was perched, he could not see the *osteria*. The roof of another building obscured his vision. But his thoughts kept straying there. Had Cifariello seen Mairhi yet and what was his verdict?

He had wanted to wait on with her until the doctor arrived. She had been sick again—her pallor ghastly, her voice huskier than ever. But for all her misery, she had been adamant. He must go about his business and leave her to hers.

He glanced at his watch again. Eleven thirty-five. How the time dragged!

The hired Fiat started the climb from Highway 65. Kuznets looked at the signpost, then at Serato.

'San Martino a Montalbino?' he murmured. 'Isn't that where this business began?'

Serato made no reply.

'A partisan raid on the caserma . . .' Kuznets pursued the point. 'You would have been with him, of course?'

Serato nodded at that.

'Quite a battle, from what I've heard. Did you kill many Germans?'

'As many as there were,' replied Serato phlegmatically. 'But never enough.'

Kuznets smiled.

'My own sentiments entirely. We were on the same side, then.' He added, with a sigh, 'Fighting for a common cause. Great days!'

'For some of us,' said Serato, meaningly. 'Not for those at the mercy of a butcher like Reinecke!'

Kuznets eyed him obliquely.

'Point taken, my friend.'

Lucarelli brought the Lancia through the gateway and parked it beside the hired Fiat, not more than a few feet from the Martyrs' Wall. He motioned politely for Eliscu to get out. He made a casually slow but deliberate business of locking the car and checking the doors. As he did so, he noted with satisfaction that the American had moved closer to the wall and was studying the plaques.

'Not very pretty, is it?' he said, joining him.

'I guess not. One thousand four hundred and eighty-seven. That's a few people from a place this size.'

'Four-fifths of the population at the time,' said Lucarelli. 'The price demanded by one SS bastard!'

Eliscu looked thoughtful as he followed towards the narrow street that led upwards past the school-house.

Pavane walked behind Giongo and Auntie as they crossed the campo towards the grandstand. He was in no way surprised, so far—that the ex-Garibaldi colonel should be leading them, that the place should be San Martino, that the car had been parked so near to the wall that offered its mute protest to the inhumanity of the Germans. It all tied in with Dad's leaning towards the dramatic but reasoned attempt to drive more nails into the coffin of speculation—that he had killed Reinecke for personal profit. He would have held this meeting at the *caserma* itself, no doubt, if the place wasn't already occupied.

Under the grandstand, they came to a door. It was marked *Dressing Room—Visitors*. Giongo ushered them in. The room was strictly utilitarian: a concrete floor, a row of wall benches, pegs for clothes, an injury couch, a toilet, two hand-basins, a triple shower with sprinklers; a strong, pervading odour of embrocation, a linger of stale sweat. And one of the sprinklers dripped monotonously.

But Pavane's attention was riveted on a table. A tray of tumblers, a water carafe, and four bottles. The labels read Vecchia Romagna cognac, Haig whisky, Kentucky Bourbon, Smirnoff Blue Label vodka . . .

Giongo offered drinks. Auntie shook his head, crossed to one of the frosted windows, let in fresh air. Pavane took a stiff whisky, threw his chief a quick glance. Unflappability still registered. It only needed the bowler hat and rolled umbrella to be Situation Normal on any Whitehall Tuesday. Maybe the buttoned-up mouth was a shade tighter, the steel-blue eyes a glint steelier. Nothing more.

Serato came in with Kuznets. The Russian's step only faltered slightly as he caught sight of the company. A Mona Lisa smile froze on his face. It said, I'm damned if I'm going to show surprise. He passed over the vodka, settled for whisky.

Eliscu, now, with Lucarelli behind him. Nothing suave about his reaction. He exploded, 'What the flaming hell!' and rounded on Lucarelli. Lucarelli heeled the door shut, stood against it.

'Let me pass,' said Eliscu.

'Sit down,' said Lucarelli.

Eliscu made to thrust him aside. Lucarelli pushed him back. He was giving away ten years, but he was still lean and hard. And he had a gun. He produced it casually, pointed it at Eliscu's stomach.

Eliscu was just mad enough to take that on, too. Pavane moved swiftly, stepped between them. 'For Christ's sake,' he said to Eliscu. 'You so dumb you didn't see this coming?'

Eliscu took a deep breath through his nostrils, dropped his hands. Kuznets murmured commiseration. 'It's not half as bad as the Tower of Pisa,' he said. 'Have a drink and relax.'

The door at the opposite end opened. Mills came in.

'No need for introductions,' he said. 'Shall we begin?'

61

'I'M PREGNANT . . . am I not?'

The old doctor flicked his hands over the wash-basin, picked up a towel, nodded.

'Si, signora. No doubt about that.'

'But isn't it—just a—a little early to be sure?'

'For some, perhaps . . . ma . . .'

That ma was as positive as a urine test. She began to button up her blouse with trembling fingers.

'You knew last night.'

He smiled gently. 'I think we both did.'

'You—won't tell him, will you?'

'Him?'

'My . . . husband.'

'I'm sure he would rather hear it from you.' Cifariello gave her a shrewd glance. 'But take an old man's advice—don't keep him in suspense. The father has a right to know.'

'Of course.'

'And when you do, add my congratulations. You can tell him from me, he has a wife as sound as a bell. Once you are over the sickness you should have no trouble. And for your man—speaking as his friend—I can only say it's the best possible thing that could have happened to him!'

Best possible thing that could have happened to *him*, she thought,

after Cifariello left. Holy Mother of God! What about me? I'm
the one who's pregnant!

If she had been mortified the previous evening, she was utterly
shattered now. She groped for her handbag, pulled out her diary.
A little calendar at the back with pencil-ringed dates told it in
black and white. Twenty-four days on the dot, like clockwork as
a rule. She'd missed out at Fiésole, but she had tried to shrug that
one miss aside as something to do with the sudden change in her
way of life. And the moodiness and depression of the past twenty-
four hours had seemed symptomatic of a return to norm. But that
had been grasping at straws, she knew that now . . .

She sat on the edge of the bed, the diary clutched in her hand,
her mind a squirrel in a cage. It must have happened the very
first time, on the fourth of October. What did that make it? The
fourth of June—no—July . . . some kind of festival . . . Independence Day. *Independence!* Holy Crippen!

In a flash, she saw the cradle and the baby. In another flash it
was gone, rejected, her mind not yet attuned to accept. It just
couldn't be; only six weeks since she met him; before that he
didn't exist. If he hadn't come to Noli, she would have had her
holiday and now be in Rome, working—until April, then back to
Noli for another season. April! Six months gone, and hideous by
then! And where will we be? *We? I,* more like it . . . after all,
we've always by-passed any talk of marriage. How could he, with
the future so uncertain? But I was content; all that talk about
family life had me in a fool's paradise . . . God, what a silly bitch
I've been!

Her inward rage and frustration brought on the nausea. Not
only physical, but mental. Her head keeled back on to the pillow.
The sobs came deep and rending.

62

'EACH ONE OF YOU may regard the presence of the other two as a
cheat and an embarrassment.' Mills' eyes ranged from Auntie to
Eliscu to Kuznets. 'Too bad. But see it from my point of view.
Any other way would imply preference. And preference I've
never had. Not for the KGB, the CIA, nor, as my erstwhile
employers can vouch'—he came back to Auntie with an oblique
glance—'for MI6. When I joined them, back in 1946, it was
simply an expediency—to carry on the work I was doing: the

hunting down of war criminals . . . and one, in particular—Ernst Reinecke.'

Eliscu made to rise. Lucarelli gave him a sharp dig with the gun, prodded him back into his seat.

Mills' expression was sardonic.

'Sorry you find it a bore, but you'll have to listen whether you like it or not. My future's at stake. And if you think that's no concern of yours—think again. In this business, one can always learn.'

Eliscu glared. Kuznets ghosted a look of approval. Auntie held his poker face. Pavane lit a cigarette, eyed all three. Then he glanced at Lucarelli—poised, gun rock-steady in his hand. Serato, too, had taken out a gun and was casually checking it. Giongo moved light-footed to the door, went outside. A key grated in the lock. Clearly, nobody was going to leave the room till teacher had finished. Pavane grinned, blew smoke, turned his eyes back to the speaker.

'I won't go into why I wanted Reinecke. That much is self-evident if your eyes were open when you entered San Martino. But way back in '45 he was only one on a long list. A list, for me, that started with Kesselring, the man who issued the order for the Ardeatine massacre. Ten civilians for every Nazi killed by the resistance. A system of bloody murder that prevailed to the end. For this—a partisan court had sentenced him to death. But Kesselring was no fool. He made a smart surrender to the Allies, gained protective custody; even got a British field-marshal to testify at his trial that his conduct of the war had been soldierly, impeccable.'

Mills looked cynical.

'A myth created by the trade union of professional soldiers, and one the British are peculiarly prone to. They did the same with Rommel, wrote books, even made a film about him . . . the military genius who was never a Nazi. When, in truth, he might never have commanded a latrine squad if he hadn't been Adolf's blue-eyed boy!'

A sly grin began to play on Kuznets' lips. Mills pounced on it. 'Moscow, of course, never dished out haloes to the generals. They reserved those for the scientists, the missile experts, the Willi Brauns—as did Washington!' he added, wiping a similar smirk from Eliscu's face. He went on:

'Kesselring slipped the noose. But not before the Garibaldi came damn close to kidnapping him on the way to his trial. An incident that brought the focus to bear on individuals such as myself. Authority was affronted at the idea. At the same time, it was magnanimous. It didn't throw us in jail. It suggested instead we might work *with* the Establishment, rather than against it. A situation that left me one recourse. I couldn't beat 'em, I must join 'em.

'I did the job assigned to me. I flushed out SS, Gestapo, Republican Fascists—up and down Italy. I even stumbled upon a group planning to make anti-Semite capital out of the Palestine troubles. A group that blew the front out of the old British Embassy at Porta Pia and channelled the blame on Jewish terrorists. But my masters wouldn't buy the truth on that one. They gave me fresh orders. Drop the Nazis and go chase Stern and Irgun Zwei Leumi. I told them to go stuff it. The Jews had spent twelve years under the German jackboot. I had no intention of helping perpetuate the misery just because a new model was being fashioned on the last of British foreign policy!

'It's news to no one that a spy cannot go on strike. Suspended from duty, yes, with a lynx eye kept on his future activities. I couldn't go free-lance, but I was allowed to join the Singer Agency. There was method in that apparent madness. Moshe was a Jew, but clean. No tie-up with terrorism—on the surface, anyway. But if he was involved deep down with the Stern or the Irgun, my joining him would reveal it. I'd be set up as a British double-agent planted among them. If I got the chop, that would be the proof. A sacrificial goat staked out to bait an MI6 trap.'

Mills grinned.

'Moshe and I had a chuckle over that one. Sure, he was prepared to help the Hagana, but not terrorism. His prime purpose then was the same as today—to bring Nazis to book. He took me in, gave me wider territory. Spain, Tangiers, for a start. Then Cairo and the Middle East. I searched and found the bastards . . . even handed them over, when I had to.'

He paused, lit a cigarette. It had not been his original intention to give them a Sunday supplement of his life. Eliscu and Kuznets probably knew the bones of it, anyway—as Auntie did for sure. Nevertheless, he felt he had to put flesh on those bones, to bring it home what made him tick. How were they taking it? Hard to say. A captive audience. He smiled inwardly, went on with his story.

'By now, we were into the fifties. The hunt for Nazis was becoming old hat. The big boys had more fashionable vermin to contend with. Uncle Sam saw hairy great Cossacks in the larder, about to raid the cookie-jar. In Moscow, the bed-bugs swarming behind the wallpaper were capitalist-imperialist agents. The Germans suddenly became clean overnight, martyrs of the Cold War, the sign of the cross waggled over them by the Pope, proclaiming them the new centurions of Christian civilisation.

'For my part, so long as the Iron Curtain kept Germany divided in saecula saeculorum it had my approval. But it had its disadvantages. I had had a tip-off about a man who might be Reinecke hiding behind a Communist party card in Budapest. I wanted after him, but saw it wouldn't be easy. It was then that MI6 turned up trumps. I was back in favour at the time. Only a month before, I'd got a British agent off the hook at Yerevan, on the Turko-Armenian border. He had been picked up by a GRU man named Nikolov'—Mills' gaze rested on Kuznets—'but what MI6 didn't know and, maybe, *your* people didn't know either— Nikolov was Puetz, a Sipo man who had worked for Eichmann, liquidating five thousand Jews in the Ukraine in 1942.'

'May I ask what happened to Nikolov ?' said Kuznets. 'Just for the record, you understand.'

'My pleasure, Counsellor,' said Mills. 'You'll find him mixed with concrete in the foundations of the University extension in Yerevan.'

'Very tidy,' said Kuznets, with a nod that might have been approval.

'With MI6's blessing I went into Eastern Europe,' Mills continued. 'It was worked to appear as if I was a defector. With luck, the KGB might take me on and I could become a double-agent. They did, too. But I had to maintain my anti-Nazi kick. If I had played a Philby, they would have smelled rotten fish.

'They put me to the test, a stiff work-out. I was set to find an SS goon thought to be in the pay of CIA. He might be Reinecke. The Budapest lead proved a dead end. The man I was after might be anywhere between Prague and Warsaw. The idea was to give me plenty of rein . . . and plenty to report back to the British if I was still their man. Tit-bits of espionage planted deliberately; items MI6 would gobble up; but which the KGB could easily trace as having been passed on.

'I ignored the bait, went straight for my man, found him. But he was not Reinecke. He was a Polish Jew, a double-agent named——'

'Wladyslaw Burgraf,' said Eliscu. 'You chilled him!'

Mills gave Eliscu a sorrowful look.

'Don't wear black for the passing of Burgraf,' he said. 'He was double-crossing the CIA every bit as much as the KGB. Just as he had double-crossed his own people in the ghetto from '42 to '44, betraying them to the Sipo.

'So I killed him. It was in the KGB's book that I should. To have dodged the issue would have been an admission that I was still working for the West. If I was, the elimination of Burgraf would damn me for ever with the CIA, who would pass it on to the British that I was a traitor.'

'Which so right they did!' snapped Eliscu.

'So wrong, as it happened . . .' Mills made a patient smile. 'What I had done suited MI6 fine. I was now what they wanted me to be. An operative in the confidence of the KGB. By no means a big wheel—they knew I wouldn't be given that kind of trust—but a useful cog ratchetting around. I did what I was asked to do. No more, no less. And all the time I went on searching for Reinecke. Right up until 1958, when my cover was blown.

'That exposure is no secret. There isn't a spy drawing breath who hasn't heard of George Blake, the double-agent who put the finger on a whole network of MI6 operatives until he, in his turn, was marked down by a defector from the Polish secret service. But his arrest was no comfort to those he had betrayed. Most of us had been allowed to go on working, unaware that our true colours were known. But once KGB knew that MI6 knew that KGB knew—our value for passing on false information was gone. And for most it was a case of "Where have all the flowers gone, long time, no see".'

He shrugged.

'I was lucky. I slipped the net. Not—as the CIA fondly believe —by grace and favour of the Kremlin, to use me on the other side. Not—as the KGB may think—because Whitehall rated me a top man to be helped regardless of cost. Quite the contrary. To them I was a write-off. A file marked Tough Luck, a cancellation of pay slip to the Treasury. That I got out from under was thanks to—well, none of your business . . .'

He smiled cynically, killed his cigarette.

'My erstwhile employers gave me the big hello, of course. Damn good show, old boy, you deserve a break. How's about training younger men to be suckers like yourself?' Mills' eyes flickered for a moment over Ray Pavane. 'I stuck that job until the day I learned that ex-Gestapo Diederichs was being released from prison. Diederichs was the sweet bastard who used a blow-lamp on his victims in the Via Tasso. Like Kesselring, the Allies had saved his neck from the noose. Their tribunal had given him what amounted to a pardon—a mere thirty years. Now he was getting out after serving no more than twenty.

'There was a vacancy going in Berlin. I applied for a transfer. I wanted back to fieldwork was my excuse. What I planned to do was execute Diederichs the moment he stepped outside the prison gate. Then I discovered why he was getting his release. A cancer of the bowel—the kind of agony that drugs never quite alleviate. To have killed him, under the circumstances, would have been doing him a favour. And the day I do a German a favour, cow-shit will grow on trees!

'It left me stuck in Berlin. And if hell, as they say, is the place we know on earth—well, I knew mine . . . until I met up with Reinecke. Then, by Christ, it was suddenly worth every minute of it! This man I had wanted more than all the others put together, whom I had spent twenty years of my life searching for . . . *there*, in the palm of my hand!'

Mills stretched out his hand, slowly closed his fingers.

'What was I expected to do with him? Only deliver him to London, wrapped up in cotton-wool—a fragile defecting chemist with so-called valuable information! Just what did you take me for?' He looked hard at Auntie. 'If he had had Yuri Andropov's whole KGB filing system on a micro-dot transcribed by a laser beam, he would still have gone in that oven!'

He paused, took a flat, wooden box from his pocket, tossed it on the table.

'Whitehall was upset when I didn't deliver. I'm rectifying that omission now—in part. In that box, you'll find some of his ashes. About the equivalent to his brain—the part you all believe was carrying some precious formula. The British paid for the funeral; they are entitled to that much.'

He turned to Eliscu and Kuznets.

'But having brought you this far, I won't send you away empty-handed. You have superiors to satisfy, politicians and top brass to keep sweet—pinheads who see LSD-25 as some kind of magical abracadabra to win wars by sophistication.'

He set a small transistor tape-recorder on the table while he spoke, along with three sealed envelopes. He removed his wrist-watch, unscrewed the back, and pulled out a hairspring of wire which he spooled on to the machine.

'Maybe it can, maybe it can't. I wouldn't know. What I do know is that you—and others like you—are apparently prepared to pay the earth for it; to rob, cheat, even kill me for it. Well, I am giving it to you—for what it's worth—free, gratis, and for nothing!' He waved a hand at the envelopes. 'A transcript for each of you of what is on this wire . . . the German original, plus English and Russian translations. The recording of a conversation piece between Reinecke and myself.'

A chipmunk gabble came as the wire wound back to the starting position. Mills raised his voice above the sound.

'I'm not a gadget man, in the ordinary way. But for once I succumbed. I bugged Reinecke from the word go, on this wrist-watch mike.' He held up the watch, smiled. 'A souvenir of Wladyslaw Burgraf. Though which of you—CIA or KGB—supplied it to him, I wouldn't know. It was made in Hong Kong, so maybe it rightfully belongs to MI6.'

His finger brought the wire to a standstill, hovered over the button marked *Play*.

'The recording is in three parts . . . our three meetings. Part three is short and, to me, sweet. The pay-off line will tell you why.'

He pressed the button. The wire began its journey back. The quality was only fair, here and there the voices distorted. But it was intelligible . . .

'What makes you think you have something of strategic value, Herr Schultz?'

'If you mean in a military sense, I have no way of knowing. None, I would hope. I'm a man of peace who——'

The door behind Mills opened. Two men stepped in. One was swarthy, doing a vintage George Raft. The other was Shaeffer. Both held guns. And pointed them.

Lucarelli brought his round. Mills killed the tape-recorder, said, 'No, Tomaso.' Lucarelli lowered his hand. Eliscu, now on his feet, caught the wrist, twisted it, fielded the gun before it hit the floor. He turned and waved it at Serato. Serato hesitated, then slid his gun across the concrete to fetch up against the leg of the table.

No one else moved. Eliscu smiled a taut smile, went forward to the table. He reached out for the tape-recorder.

'I'll take care of that,' he said.

63

THE PILLOW was damp, but her eyes were dry. She was calm again. She even found a twisted smile for what the old doctor had said . . . 'the best thing that could have happened to him'.

But was it? How could she tell him with this other business hanging over his head? He would feel trapped—the last thing she wanted. Yet—face it, girl—*you* are trapped.

She saw herself as a mother, cuddling the child. A boy, a girl, it didn't matter. The image wasn't rejected this time. Only the thought of insecurity cast a shadow. If she had to, could she cope alone?

The dark thought of abortion was dismissed before it even formulated in her mind; the same went for adoption. This child was her child, *their* child, born out of love.

She put her feet to the floor, rose. Her legs were no longer jelly, her mind and body more on an even keel. She crossed to the wash-basin, splashed cold water on her face, took Optrex to her eyes. She couldn't take refuge behind sunglasses any longer. And come what may, she mustn't look a fright.

She eyed herself in the mirror, looking at her face critically. She felt a subtle change, as if a mantle had fallen about her. That was it: a mantle of motherhood. She should be looking radiant. But all she saw was a pale face and two pinky eyes . . .

Thank God for Elizabeth Arden. If I can't have nature's mantle, I'll settle for the next best thing. Keep the 'honeymoon' look going for as long as I can!

As she worked on her face, she pondered on what to wear. The green suit, she decided; it did something for her figure. She'd better make the most of *that* while she still had it.

How long had she got before he came back was the next thought. Then panic—*if* he came back! She hurried to the window, peered out. All those market stalls and people—it was difficult to see. A whole bunch of men milling around a coach in front of the school-house. Were *they*—No . . . just a hunting-party with dogs and shot-guns; no one she could identify. He was up above, behind the school, out of sight. How was he getting on?

Had he managed to convince them? Or would they do something dreadful—arrest or kidnap him, or even . . . no, girl, for God's sake, no morbid ideas or you'll be bawling again. And it'd be just your luck for him to walk in and find you a mess of blotched mascara and eye-pencil.

No sign of him as yet. She'd look again in five minutes; better make it ten. Just concentrate on girding on your armour . . . and remember—you are still his Venus of Urbino, not the Madonna with Child . . .

64

IT ALL HAPPENED so fast . . .

Eliscu said, 'I'll take care of that.'

Then the other door splintered open and in came the baggy-trousered Donostchenk, waving a machine-pistol. The swarthy Piselli, at the other end, swung up his gun, then crumpled from a belt behind the ear. And Boyarov was digging a Mauser into Shaeffer's spine.

'Checkmate, I think,' said Kuznets.

'Your move,' said Mills to Auntie.

Auntie slid his eyes at Pavane.

Pavane grinned.

'I've got four outside, cock,' he said, to no one in particular.

'Is that all, cock?' said Mills, clucking his tongue. He turned to the open window. 'How many have you got, colonello?'

Giongo's face appeared over the sill.

'A dozen, maybe. And a coach-load coming up the hill. Shot-guns *and* dogs,' he added.

Mills shrugged at those in the room.

'Old comrades,' he explained. 'We like to get together on the Fourth of November. Reunion is a little late this year.' He motioned Eliscu to sit down, fingered the tape-recorder. 'Shall we continue where we left off?'

The recording had ground its way through the first two meetings: Reinecke's first revelations on the properties of LSD-25; Mills' plan to get him through the wall.

'The next conversation,' Mills said, 'took place in the Volkeswagen on the way to Weissensee.'

'One thing I'd like to know, Herr Schultz. Between ourselves —this Dresden formula—is it the genuine article?'

'Naturlich.'

'How did you come by it?'

'How? I told you before. I was working on it.'

'You told me, sure. You told me a string of lies. You're no top-grade chemist. At the most, you were only a bench worker with elementary qualifications.'

'That is not true——'

'It's true. Admit it! Maybe you can kid my superiors, but you can't kid me.'

'Why do you help me to escape, then?'

'Because I'm paid to do so.'

'Good pay . . . yes?'

'Good pay my arse! That's for the free-lance boys who do the Wall run. They can pick up anything between eight and ten thousand Westmarks a trip. At times like these, they could demand twenty thousand and get it without a murmur. You're probably worth five thousand, at least, in reward money if I handed you over to the Vopos.'

'If it's money you want . . . I haven't any.'

'Not at the moment, perhaps. But when you've flogged your precious formula . . .'

'You want a cut—is that it?'

'Ten per cent. A fair business arrangement.'

'Very well . . . I will pay. You have my word.'

'I want more than your word, Schultz. I want something tangible, some proof you're not stringing us along. I mean, you had to get this secret out. How did you manage it? On film? A micro-dot, maybe?'

'No, my friend, nothing so obvious. I am sorry. It is here, in my head. No more than that.'

'Tell me about it.'

'What would be the point? How could you hope to remember? You are not a scientist.'

'That's my problem. But I'd like to hear. Go on—give!'

'This is ridiculous——'

'I could change my mind.' Mills' voice was harsh. 'I could say it wasn't possible to get you out—that there was a last-minute hitch. My people know it can be tricky. They wouldn't doubt my word. And you'd be in no position to contradict—not in the hands of the MfS!'

'Very well . . .' A heavy sigh. 'LSD-25 is D-lysergic acid dieth——'

'Skip that bit and get to the part that's new. And make it nice and clear so I don't miss out!'

A mumbo-jumbo of psycho-pharmacological data followed, a liberal sprinkling of words and symbols—mysticomimetic, hallucinogenic, psycheletic, psychedelic, JB 239, IT 290—all strung together in a manner that sounded both impressive and convincing, at the end of which Reinecke was heard to say, 'Now you know as much as I do.'

'As much . . . and, perhaps, a little more.'

'What does that mean?'

'I'll tell you later.'

The recording cut dead at that point. When it took up again, it was brief . . .

'I'll see you through, Ernst Reinecke!'

'My name is Schultz . . . Willi Schultz.'

'Schultz . . . Reinecke . . . what's in a name?'

Then, finally, a new voice . . .

'Have you chosen a casket for the ashes?'

Mills switched off the recorder. 'Your precious formula,' he said. 'Get your laboratories to check it, if you will. But I can tell you that the Academy of Science in Florence has already done so. Their findings say it contains no more than anyone could obtain by mugging up the latest Pharmacopoeia Codex.' He switched the recorder to wipe clean, smiled a thin smile. 'I've no further use for it. You have the original text, as well as the best translation the Instituto Per Le Lingue Estere could produce. It will provide you with something to read on the way back to wherever you are going. All I ask is—when you are gone, stay gone. Addio!'

He turned to the door. Boyarov still barred the way. But at a gesture from Kuznets he stepped aside.

Mills left the room.

65

PAVANE watched the cars pull out and drive through the gateway of San Martino. The Russians first—Kuznets and his two henchmen. Kuznets, he thought, had taken it very well. Poised throughout, smiling faintly most of the time—as he was at this moment. He knew from their own dossier on the man that Kuznets had personal reasons enough for hating the Germans, reasons that made it easier for him to appraise the single-mindedness of Mills. His final gesture back at the grandstand had spoken volumes. He had allowed Lucarelli to refill his glass, then he had raised it to the door through which Mills had vanished. If there were inner feelings of rancour or hurt pride, Kuznets was much too much of a professional, too old a hand to show them.

Eliscu left next, with Shaeffer and Piselli. The American had been let down by his own lack of experience, finding it hard to swallow that he could be pushed around. That ugly moment, for example, when Lucarelli had produced the gun. Pavane doubted that the ex-partisan would have used it, but the idea behind it was plain enough. Cut the VIPs down to size; show them it was just four men against four. And when, in the end, it had come to a show of strength, Mills had had the edge.

Pavane's own reinforcements took off after Eliscu. Brinati, Janni, and Lister. The fourth man—Crambo—sat at the wheel of the final car, Auntie beside him. Auntie made a gesture of impatience and Pavane climbed in the rear.

Auntie? All Pavane could see was the back of his neck and part of his profile. It told him nothing. But no less than he'd have got facing Auntie full on. A complete dead-pan throughout. What went on behind those bleak eyes and rat-trap of a mouth? Some emotion, surely. Vindictiveness? No. That would be the reaction of a small-minded man, and Auntie certainly wasn't that. Anger? Some, possibly, but not necessarily towards Mills. Disapproval, then? With the dramatic touch, the tossing of Reinecke's ashes on the table . . . but that apart, Auntie never denigrated the unorthodox if it paid off. Regret, perhaps? That might be nearer the truth. Regret at losing a man who, for all his faults, was one of the best agents the department had ever known, and at a time when, God knows, the service was scraping the barrel.

Finally, there was Mills himself. Dad. Pulling the bunnies out of the hat—the wire-recorder bit . . . Was it the genuine article? Pavane had his doubts, strong doubts . . . but did that matter? If it was genuine, the answer was there in the text. If it was phoney, the answer was there in the work that had gone to prepare it: *there was no formula* . . . at any rate, not in Dad's possession. Which was precisely all he was out to show.

Had he succeeded? Only the future could answer that, if all three could prevail upon their superiors to accept the obvious and leave well alone.

No problem for Auntie. Virtual master of his own house, his

recommendation—one way or the other—would be enough. With Eliscu and Kuznets it was different. They could only report their findings to Washington and Moscow and hope they would be accepted.

Pavane thought about Dad's final words ... 'all I ask is—when you are gone, stay gone.'

Polite enough. Almost an appeal. But no appeal for clemency. More an appeal to reason, with a hint of a warning. Next time— if there was a next time—they'd have a tiger by the tail. A tiger, apparently, who had at long last found a mate—who in due time, maybe, would raise a litter of cubs. That would bring the claws out quick ...

Pavane wanted no part of *that* fight. Not that he really believed it would come to that. Unless he was wildly mistaken, Dad had won ...

66

SHE SAW HIM crossing the piazza. Surrounded by a group of men. The hunters from the coach. For a moment, she knew fear. Then she saw Giongo, Serato, Lucarelli. She had met the last two on Sunday at Fiésole. Even at a distance, the joy of his companions was self-evident.

Her heart fluttered. Success. His troubles were over. Then, as they came closer, she saw his face. Flat, subdued, even depressed. A thought wormed into her mind. He had his freedom, but he didn't want it. He wanted to go on doing the same job, regardless ... regardless of her and their love for each other. If that was so, she had a fight on her hands.

She moved back to the dressing-table mirror. Her eyes looked a bit over-bright, but that was better than the other way. Just another touch of lipstick, perhaps, and she would be ready to face him.

She smoothed her skirt over her hips, went back to the window. No sign of him. He must be inside with his friends, drinking, celebrating ... Holy Crippen, what a nerve! Her sitting up here, chewing her fingernails for all he knew or cared ...

The door opened. She spun round. He came in, shut the door. She waited for him to come to her. But he just stood there at the door, shoulders slumped, grave, unsmiling.

What was she supposed to say? Had a hard day, darling, some

problem at the office? She felt a giggle rising killed it; then wished she hadn't—it might have done the trick. Instead, she went on standing there, waiting for him to speak.

He gave a little sigh, loosened his tie, shrugged off his jacket, threw it on the bed. Then he slumped down beside it, found a cigarette, turned it over between his fingers without lighting it.

He looked at her, made a tired smile. I've made a booboo, he thought. I should have gone straight over and kissed her. He said, 'You're looking better.'

'Yes.'

'Did Cifariello come?'

'Yes.'

'What did he say?'

'He said . . . he said I—I was as sound as a bub-bell.' Once committed beyond monosyllables it was impossible to keep the wobble out of her voice.

He peered up at her. She turned her head away, looked out on to the *piazza*. He rose, moved to her, slipped his arms about her.

'Something is wrong . . .' he began. He raised a hand, turned her face towards him, then frowned. 'What on earth have you done to your face?'

'What d'you mean—done to my face?'

'All that mascara and stuff. It doesn't suit you.'

That had her over the ropes, gasping. Just two sentences and her defences were knocked for a loop. All she could do was retreat in a sudden rush of anger. She jerked herself free, went back to the dressing-table.

He gave a shrug. 'I'm sorry. But I don't like it. I never have. Not on any girl.'

The match to the touch-paper.

'Bully for you!' she blasted off. 'But we can't all be as beautiful as your Mafalda! We have to do the best we can!' She picked up a brush, started banging away at her hair.

'We . . . ?'

'All the rest of your women! And just how do you rate us? Give us stars like a Michelin guide? Or do we have to make the Top Twenty?'

He stayed well back, against the window. Christ, he thought, if this is how it is every time she has a visit from the fairies, there was only one of two things to be done . . . join the Athenaeum for five days a month, or put a bun in the oven. He couldn't help it, the idea made him grin.

She caught the grin in the mirror. If she had been looking for fuel, here was the final faggot on the fire.

'And what's the fatuous grin for? Drooling over past conquests —or contemplating who might be next? Why not try the school-master's daughter? Her eyes were all over you yesterday!'

'Lover, please . . . This is ridiculous.' He made a conciliatory move.

'Ridiculous, am I? What else can you expect from a tarted-up Irish tottie! Not brains, that's for sure! Little Carmella has those, you'll find, and other things . . .'

He stopped half way, threw up his hands in despair. She caught that, too, in the mirror, and knew she had gone too far. She lowered the brush and turned to him, ready to make amends.

It was too late. He had turned, also—back to the window, hands thrust deep into pockets.

She thought: If I went to him now and said, darling, I'm sorry, this isn't me making this gas but a daft, distraught female who finds herself up the spout, how d'you fancy being a papa . . .

She heard herself say: 'Well, what are you waiting for? Why don't you go and find out? Take *her* for a walk in the woods. Does it really matter that San Martino hasn't got a castello?'

He turned again, picked up his jacket, shrugged it on. 'I'll do that thing,' he said. 'I'll take a walk.'

As he reached the door and turned the handle, she brought the brush up to her mouth.

'No, darling—please. I didn't mean it——'

'Yes,' he said, quietly. 'It's better that I go.'

'Then go!' she flared. 'Go, go, go! Go to bleddy hell and don't come back!'

He was half way out of the door when she threw the brush. It missed by a mile, hit the light fitting, plopped down on his bed.

She couldn't even do that properly, she thought, as her face crumpled.

67

HE GOT TO WITHIN a few yards of the pole-barrier that straddled the final strip of road to the *caserma*, then turned to walk back again. He was not angry, just bewildered. She had a real Irish paddy, that one, when she let herself go. And deep down, he knew it was good for him . . . so long as she never learned to aim straight.

He had seen the brush fly, heard it clobber the light fitting, before he shut the door.

The blame was his. No excuse to say he had been through one hell of a strain, not knowing which way the cat would jump. It had been an equal strain for her—more so, probably, sitting up there waiting; not knowing whether he'd come back singing glory hallelujah or to kiss her a last goodbye.

I mean, put yourself in her size fives, cocky. Think what she has had to contend with in six short weeks. There she was, sitting in Noli, minding her own business. You come bouncing into her life, out of the blue. One peck and she settles for you, old enough to be her father. One spark and instant combustion, who can say what makes a woman tick, don't try to analyse, be content with your good fortune . . .

And what had you to offer? Sweet bugger-all when it came to the crunch. A past that stalked in the shadows. An Old Man of the Sea astride your shoulders with a cartload of hate. The murder of Reinecke in your lapel like it was a Boy Scout badge. You could hardly expect her to see it as anything other than murder, whatever high flown yak you might put up about lawful execution, retribution, justice.

Yet she had taken it; no matter the misgivings, hurts to her sensitivity, horror that may have assailed her. She had taken it on the chin and come up for more. Not because she was some silly tottie whose mind doesn't rise above the navel, but because she is in love with you.

And you? How d'you shape up against that?

Today you've had your first real bust-up in six weeks of knowing her—in five weeks of intimacy. And just because the poor bitch gets worked up over the fairies, you walk out instead of showing a little patience and understanding . . .

He stopped dead, in the middle of the Corso, at the top end of the village. *Five* weeks of intimacy . . . And *now* the fairies . . . ? Jesus God, it didn't make menstruation mathematics!

He found a cigarette, lit it, saw that his hands were trembling. They had got the message . . .

Other thoughts came crowding into his mind: the sickness last night and again this morning . . . old Cifariello giving him a knowing look and asking how long they'd been married. He had known immediately, of course. This morning he'd given her a thorough examination. She had said as much. He'd hardly go to that for a touch of the altitude willies . . . oh, Christ, no wonder

she was upset! That load on her mind, and not sure how he
would take it. No surprise she'd flipped her wig!

He made to move on, changed his mind. It was but a few steps
to Cifariello's villa. In five minutes he could check and be certain.
It would never do to go off half-cock and find it was all a
mistake . . .

Cifariello was with his orchids. Mills didn't have to open his
mouth. The question was written on his face.

'You are seeking confirmation?'

'You could call it that.'

'You're a lucky man. She'll build you a fine, strong bambino
. . . and many more, if you've the mind to it!' The old doctor
chuckled, slapped his shoulder. 'Now you'd like a drink to
celebrate?'

He hesitated, but could hardly refuse.

'Just one. Then I must get back.'

He ran the last hundred and fifty yards—past the stalls and the
salesmen packing up their wares; past Lucarelli and Serato and
Giongo and the drink lined up for him; past young Alberto
Tognazzi who gave him an odd look; on up the stairs and along
to the room, to fling open the door.

'Tesore, for God's sake—why didn't you tell me?'

There was no answer.

There couldn't be.

She was gone.

68

GONE. Bags packed. Only the hair brush, left where it had fallen,
to remind him she had even been there at all. No note. Nothing.
He didn't need to ask how she had gone. Their car was missing
from where he had parked it.

He flung his own things into the third suitcase, paid the bill,
made excuses to Serato and Lucarelli, thanked them for all they
had done, then grabbed Giongo and was away.

Giongo sat beside him, let him take the wheel. He took the
curves of the mountain road as if he was competing in the Mille
Miglia, all the way down to Highway 65.

'Fiésole, then?' said Giongo, as they turned south.

'Where else would she go?'

'Wherever it is, caro mio, you'll find her. Especially as she wants to be found!'

'I wish I had your confidence.'

'Irlandese, without confidence? Impossible!'

'Irlandese, without Mairhi. It amounts to the same thing from now on. You are sitting beside a lost man!'

'For another thirty-five kilometres, perhaps,' said Giongo, as they flashed through Covigliaio. 'No more.'

'I hope you're right. Heaven help me, I hope so!'

Giongo was right.

She was waiting in Room Thirteen. He came in hesitant, all the things he had thought he would say dying on his lips the moment he had seen the car parked outside. She ignored the entreaty in his eyes, stayed over by the balcony.

'How did you know I would be here?' she said, over her shoulder.

'I just knew.'

'Still very sure of yourself?' For once, she was managing to play it cool. 'If you want to know, I had no choice.'

'No choice?'

'My passport—remember? You took it from me on the third or fourth day . . .' Her voice trembled for a fraction, then she regained control. 'I thought it might be with reception. But they haven't seen it. Where is it, please?'

'Is that all you want?'

'What else?'

He put a hand inside his jacket, came out with the green passport, gave it to her. She glanced at it, saw the folded slip of paper sticking out.

'What's this?'

'See for yourself.'

'Not if it doesn't concern me.'

'It does.'

She unfolded the paper, read the printed words, stared, read again, then looked up at him.

'A notice of marriage?' she whispered.

'In some places they call it a special licence.'

'But when did you——'

'The first time I had some business to attend to.'

'But why—why didn't you tell me, you dote?'

'How could I when I didn't know for certain how things would work out?'

'And now . . . you still want to?'

He looked at his watch, then put his hand back in his pocket again. 'Too late for today, I'm afraid. But tomorrow, the day after, next week . . . whenever you wish.' He brought out a ring, slipped it on her finger. An emerald, set in diamonds. She stared at it in a daze. He went on. 'For myself, I make only one stipulation. No long engagement.' He started to count off his fingers. 'October, November, December . . . not later, say, than the first week in July.'

She let out a squeal. 'You know!'

She was in his arms, not knowing whether to laugh or cry. 'You don't mind?' she whispered.

'Mind? That's the understatement of all time. I'm delirious! What about you?'

'It's ours. What more could I want?'

'The papa, I hope!'

'That, too . . . if he is really sure he wants a new way of life.'

'Quite, quite sure, lover. Of that there isn't the slightest doubt.'

DANCE
OF THE DWARFS

Geoffrey Household

'Dance of the Dwarfs' is published
by Michael Joseph Ltd.

The Author

Geoffrey Household's three most famous books are *Rogue Male*, *A Rough Shoot* and *Watcher in the Shadows*. His new novel, *Dance of the Dwarfs*, is right in that tradition. For the first twenty-five years of his adult life he lived abroad: a banker in Bucharest; an importer in Spain; a foreign representative travelling throughout Europe and Latin America; and then, for nearly six years, of war, a military intelligence officer in the Balkans and the Middle East. Apart from his most famous books with their English setting, he has written *Thing to Love*, a brilliant study of South American politics, *Arabesque*, a romance of Arab and Zionist intrigue, and a Basque novel *Olura*, which tells the story of a dangerous and passionate love affair from three different angles. He is married with three children and now lives in Buckinghamshire.

PREFACE

It will be remembered that the death of Dr. Owen Dawnay was attributed to partisans of the Colombian National Liberation Army. The evidence of his only neighbours, a few families of squatters and masterless cattlemen, appeared conclusive. They had been terrorized into supplying cattle to Guerrilla Headquarters in the foothills of the Cordillera. Two of them had been brutally murdered. The headman of their village had disappeared. Dawnay himself was known to have been threatened.

That a guerrilla detachment did indeed visit Dawnay's experimental station about the time of his death is certain. His arms, his official Journal and all his papers were stolen. The main gate had been forced, and the tracks of a jeep were plainly to be seen in the compound. The Colombian Government and the Ministry of Overseas Development had every reason to suppose that he had been executed for refusing to collaborate with the revolutionaries.

Dawnay's choice of an agricultural station in that remote corner where the great grasslands at last disappear under tropical forest, largely untravelled, was scientifically sound but may have owed still more to his personal tastes. Born and bred in the south of Argentina, he was a superb horseman and an excellent shot with gun or rifle. Undoubtedly he enjoyed the primitive conditions of his life and the still more primitive society in which he found himself.

His supreme self-confidence often inclined him to be impatient with what he considered unnecessary anxiety. His silence therefore aroused little concern, especially since the pilot of the Government Canoe which had called at Santa Eulalia on May 2nd, 1966, reported that he was in the best of health and spirits. Another month was allowed to go by before a light aircraft was despatched to his station with mail, supplies and two administrators of the Intendencia.

His house was a scene of utter desolation. Fungi were growing in the rooms and wasps building under the eaves. Shut in a large inner room were the carcases of two horses which had died from starvation and lack of water. Dawnay's two servants had vanished, perhaps liquidated as the only witnesses to the murder, perhaps panic-stricken.

The compound, which had been intensively cultivated, was turned into rank jungle by the rains. Hidden by the vegetation were the skeletons of Dr. Dawnay and a young female. Birds and insects had picked them clean. Poinsettia and a twisted citrus sapling were growing through the bones. Both appeared to have been shot. The position of the bodies suggested that the executioners, with macabre sentimentality, had permitted the pair to die in each other's arms.

Though Dawnay was only thirty-three, his great promise in his own field of research was internationally recognized. As a man, he was known and loved by a host of Latin-American friends in Colombia and Argentina. His death therefore aroused a storm of indignation against Cuban-financed revolutionaries. This bitterly hostile publicity may have accounted for the mysterious reappearance of his papers.

In November, 1966, a black, insect-proof, metal box bearing Dawnay's initials was delivered to the publishers of his fascinating monograph *Fodder Plants of the New World*. It contained the missing Journal as well as this unexpected personal diary, which was in his handwriting and undoubtedly genuine.

The motive of the anonymous senders may be inferred. Unable to clear themselves of the brutal murder of a man whom in fact they seem to have admired, they realized that the diary supplied a complete answer to the accusation against them. It seems probable that, after examining his correspondence, they found no other trustworthy address—such as that of a firm of solicitors or a learned body—and therefore chose to return the box to Dawnay's publishers, rejecting the Agricultural Mission itself as insufficiently neutral.

The unfinished entry of May 18th, which must have remained on his desk until the partisans recovered it, was discoloured and spotted by damp, but still decipherable. A note in Spanish had been added: *We found no weapon by their bodies. It is to be supposed that he rushed to the door to confirm that his anxiety was needless, and saw what was behind her. There was no time to go back for steel or gun, so he went on bare-handed; and whether she was alive or dead when he took her in his arms we do not know.*

THE DIARY

March 9th, Wednesday

I have recently noticed a tendency to talk to myself. One-sided conversation is humiliating and settles nothing. It is exclamatory. It points at things which are worth remembering, but does not commit them to memory. That is my reason for starting a diary. I want to marshal the facts of my relationship to my environment and compel myself to think about them.

I also need to be able to turn back time and feel what sort of person I was two or three months before. In that way I shall spot any inclination to become a work hermit or to exaggerate this background sense of insecurity—well, not exactly of insecurity but of something unfinished—which I am unable to analyse. I suppose all missionaries suffer from the same questioning of the self.

It amuses Santa Eulalia when I describe myself as a missionary. They have nicknamed me El Misionero. But a field agronomist of the British Tropical Agricultural Mission is surely a missionary. My bishop and archdeacon sit in Bogotá, their chapel being an air-conditioned office and their altar a laboratory. I, since I am a fair horseman and bilingual in Spanish and English, was sent abroad to preach the gospel—or rather practise it—between the rivers Guaviare and Vichada.

I chose the site myself. The others didn't know enough to argue. I thought at first that my chief objective should be testing the right varieties of cereals. I now see that the primaeval problem of agriculture—when to plant—is far more important. The dry season normally begins at the end of December. This year we have had no rain at all since Dec. 3rd. But provided God is a good man, as they say, one can grow practically anything in half the time it takes anywhere else. This is the No Man's Land between savannah and forest: the last, forgotten, blind alley of grass. To the west and south it is bounded by darkness. To the north the llanos spread out towards Venezuela, empty under the blazing sun.

A perfect experimental station. It was never my intention nor that of the Mission that I should be alone on it; but in practice I found that assistants only increased my responsibilities. I settled in four months ago accompanied by a most friendly Colombian and a young Swede from the Peace Corps. I am not sure what qualities he was supposed to have, but it was only too clear that training by a War Corps would have been more to the point. Estrellera threw him into the creek. He missed deliberately when shooting for the pot. Then he broke out in boils and was absurdly horrified when I wanted him to try Joaquin's efficacious herbal remedies. I admit that Joaquin produces his pastes by chewing rather than pestle and mortar, but saliva is a disinfectant.

So I had him flown out. My other young friend went along to look after him, promising a swift return. I shall not see him again, which is a pity, for he was a qualified botanist and I am not. But he preferred the problems of classification and the pleasure of dictating his results to an obliging secretary after hours. The girl either wore no bra at all or had some compensating device of elastic hitherto unknown to me. I regret that I was always too busy for detailed investigation. When I return to Bogotá, I shall make a point of satisfying curiosity.

March 10th, Thursday

I don't seem to have got very far yesterday evening. I rode straight at my blank page and then began to passage sideways like Tesoro when he mistakes a barred shadow for a snake. I started off to analyse the sense of the unfinished, dabbled in the bras of Bogotá and then strolled out to the corral to see the horses. Because I wanted company or because I have recently become uneasy about them?

Certainly Tesoro and Estrellera were very glad to see me. They always are. The horse's capacity for affection never fails to surprise me. A rather stupid, nervous creature, full of love. Like some primitive, laborious Roman slave taking to Christianity when it first appeared.

During the last ten days or so they have had fits of restlessness at night; they are near enough—physically and telepathically— to be able to communicate it. They need not worry. The adobe walls of the corral are still fairly perpendicular, and jaguar on the open llano is most unlikely. Still, one must not assume that two trusted friends are liars.

Leaving out mere nuisances, such as insects and occasional slight fevers, there is less here to be afraid of than in London. On the edge of the forest one could conceivably be in trouble with a very rash or very hungry jaguar, but the risk is less than that of being charged by a drunken driver whom unfortunately one is not allowed to shoot. You could be caught on foot by wild cattle, but you take the same care not to be as you take crossing Oxford Street in the rush hour. You could be bitten by a snake, but that is hardly more likely than electrocuting yourself among the infinite dangers of a modern flat, a paralysis for which there is no serum. I have two phials. Alternatively, I could do worse than put my trust in Joaquin whose concoction of dried venom sacs and gall bladders is reinforced by his confident bedside manner. No, the greatest danger is man just as anywhere else. A band of poor, half-starved devils of the National Liberation Army occupies the wild foothills of the Cordillera, some four days hard riding to the north-west. These guerrilleros must know of my existence, and so I presume they think me harmless. As for my other neighbours, the llaneros of Santa Eulalia, we are on most cordial terms drunk or sober.

Thus physical danger may be ruled out in my search for an influence to fill what I call the blank spot. A too imaginative curiosity due to loneliness? Well, I am not all that lonely and I am neither superstitious nor sceptical. If duendes exist, as Joaquin insists they do, I am eager to meet a specimen illusion, for one cannot begin to explain until one has experienced. I play with the speculation that, just as the collective hysteria of a crowd can persuade it to see angels or flying saucers, so the rampant, hourly visible growth of the forest might produce a communal spirit, a vegetable emanation which could be detected by animal senses. Harness the green power and what green fingers it could give to an agronomist! Duende is a more comprehensive name than our ghost or elemental.

Then the house itself? But I enjoy its solidity in so much emptiness. It is a deserted estancia dating from colonial days, built square and defensible like a legionary fort. I find in it the peace of some forgotten patio where others walked and were content. On the south side are a few still habitable, dilapidated rooms of the boss's house in which I camp. On the north are the peons' quarters: a row of ruinous shacks hung with the black combs of wasps' nests where the shade of wall and roof has encouraged a rank growth of weak lianas. These two sides of the square are joined by adobe walls a couple of hundred yards long, so that a space of some two and a half acres is enclosed. This was originally intended to provide food for the small community and is irrigated by tiled channels barred where they pass under the walls, drawing water from the marshes to the north.

The marshes? Well, all marshes are mysterious in the half light of dawn or dusk when the wild fowl chuckle and the canes and rushes, disturbed at their roots by some eel or amphibian, seem to swing away from the passage of the invisible. The creek which takes the overflow passes close to the estancia and runs south to an unknown confluence with the Guaviare. Two miles beyond the creek is the blue wall of the forest which I find neither friendly nor unfriendly. It is simply an overpowering fact of the planet: a barrier-like sea with its own specialized life and methods of travel.

It seems to be either forest or creek which upsets the horses. Last week I walked as far as the water's edge to see if I could spot puma on the llano or an anaconda watching the shallows where peccary or tapir might be drinking—though I believe they never come so far from the trees. I was only aware of star-lit silence, emphasized by the whine of the mosquitoes. This silence itself sometimes produces a feeling of awe, a prickling of the scalp. So I cannot definitely say that I was uneasy. I did perhaps feel that I was observed. Hostile? No. For the moment a neutral observer like myself.

March 12th, Saturday

I have come to the conclusion that the blank spot is due neither to me nor to this essentially welcoming country which waits to be inhabited. The thing which is unfinished is in the collective mind of my companions. So I will try to dissect them as individuals and see if description forces me into clear thinking.

Our isolation is sufficiently complete to eliminate all outside influences. Now that a man can take a package tour to Antarctica and cross the Sahara in his own car, the immense plains of Colombia and Venezuela and the tropical forest which forms their southern boundary must be the last expanse of world to be left as it was. In the llanos there is nothing unknown or unexplored. They are merely empty and their life has hardly changed in four hundred years. The forest, too, is known in the sense that all navigable rivers are navigated and that here and there some prospector, rubber collector or deliberate explorer has crossed by land from one river to another; but what he could see on low ground was limited to a hundred yards on either side, and on high ground to the world of the tree tops. One assumes that the fauna, the flora and the floor of leaf mould are always the same. It is, I think, a very large assumption. I have plenty of evidence pointing to rapid differentiation of species. But that is for my journal, not this diary.

I have found the Intendencia, which administers this territory, vaguely benevolent, but it does not greatly affect our lives. There are regular air services to Puerto Ayacucho and to San José del Guaviare; but one is five hundred miles away and the other a mere clump of huts to be reached eventually by canoe if a canoe is available. There is also the occasional plane to Colombia's Amazon province. It will come down on the Guaviare at Santa Eulalia if I can advise the Mission that I need it.

A big 'if'. When I decided on my station, the Government —after trying its best to convince me that it was too isolated for what they called a cultured European—told me that at least I should have excellent communications with Bogotá, and like a fool I believed both Pedro and them.

This excellent communication is a transmitter upon which Pedro, by violently pedalling a generator, can painfully tap out a message in Morse. He gets it three-quarters right when sober but invariably transcribes the reply wrong. One can also send a letter or telegram by any launch going up river to the edge of civilization and be assured that it will reach a Post Office in a week or two.

I suppose I ought to have a radio station of my own, but I do not want to make too many demands when both the Mission and the Government have been generous already. And I really cannot spare the time to take a short course and learn to handle the thing.

Entirely responsible for my presence here are Mario and his wife Teresa. In my tentative botanical exploration of the meeting of forest and llano I came upon this estancia and observed that Mario, then living in a solid shack built into the debris of the peons' cabins, had created a kitchen garden and was not only growing melons, beans and pimientos but selling them. Bartering would better describe his complicated half-and-half transactions. I was instantly impressed by this proud agriculturalist among carnivorous llaneros who only dismount to eat and sleep and Indians who scratch the soil for subsistence. I had found my assistant and adviser who at the same time was a caretaker of empty rooms and had a wife to cook and clean.

And for my purposes the place was perfect, allowing me to experiment with wheats and fodders, and with rice around the outlet of the marshes. Most of the known food plants of tropical America can easily be cultivated, as well as a number of unknown collected from the edge of the forest—which I shall find disappointingly catalogued when I return to London in a couple of years.

Mario has the thick, smooth body of the Indian and the mobile, furrowed face of a Spanish peasant. A throw-back. He can have little Spanish blood. He understands what I am doing and talks of remaking the Garden of Eden. On the strength of half a dozen bible stories for children he considers himself a gallant catholic. There is no church within a hundred miles, but I hear that a priest has been known to visit Santa Eulalia to solemnize marriages and baptise children.

Teresa—well, what is Teresa? Gentle, brown, with deep sagging wrinkles and dirty, pendulous breasts. A caricature of the female body, though she cannot yet be forty. She bore three boys in her teens and accepts that she is unlikely to see any of them again: simple labourers vanished into the continent. Every man to her is a son. My clothes are crudely mended. My tastes are studied so far as raw material permits. There is plenty of room for culinary experiment even if most food is grilled over the ashes or stewed in a black pot.

She came up as a girl from Brazil and speaks a mixture of Portuguese and Spanish. She cannot describe how she came or why. None of the forest people has much idea of geography. Any long journey is up and down rivers, and by the time you reach your destination you may have travelled to every point of the compass. Thus the mental map of anyone who cannot read a printed map is very odd indeed. If the sense of locality belonging to a million fishes could be compounded into one brain, it would be somewhere near Teresa's picture of her world. The llaneros of course have a normal picture. Their horizon may be bounded by the precipice of the forest, by high stands of rushes or by a flickering of palms in the haze, but it is usually circular. The sun moves unclouded. East and West are fixed. Few llaneros can read, but all can understand a map—since their world is flat—and can mark accurately vegetation which might be of interest to me.

The next individual in order of importance is Pedro, the headman of Santa Eulalia, who represents government in that he has stamps to sell to anyone who can write a letter. He has authority to arrest—though he has no prison—and to commandeer river transport which means an Indian and a canoe. He also keeps the village store and some pigs. When he kills one, I have to buy pork for the sake of his goodwill but often bury it as unfit to eat. It is unnecessary to swear Teresa to silence. Her manners are courtly by nature.

Pedro was a corporal in the army, and perhaps a quarter of his blood is Spanish. He would be better with less, being too inclined to pointless eloquence. He is short, dark, with a wide, slack mouth and a sprinkling of hairs on the upper lip. He gains face from his intimacy with the Misionero and is pleasant enough when I swallow his abominable spirits in his company.

Santa Eulalia itself consists of some twenty mud-and-bamboo huts on a track which leads up from the river crossed by one short, dusty street with the infinity of the llanos at each end of it. We call the intersection the Plaza because it has a tree, the remains of a seat and Pedro's store. The majority of the inhabitants are llaneros who once worked for the estancia. Others are just nomads who drifted in. There are also a few families of pure Indians permanently camped in the woodland along the river and gathering more food than they grow. There is so little money in circulation that three times the same unmistakable coin has been given to me in change.

Now, what is there in this primitive and friendly society which does not make sense? I will start with the simple fact —there are others less simple—that I can never be sure why the estancia was deserted. Mario, Pedro and the rest vary the reasons they give me and forget what they have said.

Ownership is of the vaguest. Mario has a bit of paper, signed by one Manuel Cisneros, giving him the right to the house and its enclosed garden for as long as he likes. Cisneros, he tells me, was a Venezuelan who undoubtedly possessed the deeds and brought down his men and cattle across the plains. He had a sun-crazed dream of driving herds up to Bogotá on the hoof. When he found he couldn't he deserted the place, vanished into the rivers and has never been heard of since. His capital investment was small and probably never registered. I think he merely added some adobe and timber to the ruins of the ancient house and branded a lot more cattle which belonged to nobody. God knows where and from whom he bought the place! I tried to find some record of him in Bogotá, but there was nothing.

This ghostly ownership is in itself slightly disturbing to modern man. We all live like Indians without any title but custom, floating upon a sea of grass which does not lend itself to precise boundaries of social relationship. We and our horses have just enough to eat. We keep our mouths shut if we see what we are not supposed to see, and we are rather too ready to imagine what we don't see. We tend to die young from violence or accident, but general health is good, far better than in the forest. Our medicine man, Joaquin, is a specialist in tropical diseases. His remedies are more effective and his incantations more impressive than those of, say, eighteenth century doctors. He and I are at present conducting a series of experiments—a leisure activity marked for amusement only—to see whether rhythmic prayer has any measurable effect on growth. Our preliminary results seem to show an increase of 11% in germination, but I must devise a more refined technique for ruling out coincidence.

That is by the way. An example just to remind me that I can and do enjoy myself. I find no lack of personal solidity in this dream life. What I want is to define the other men who share it with me. Difficult, of course. Even Freud could not analyse the motives of one's companions in a dream, only of the dreamer. These people are courteous, trusting and quite intelligent enough to understand my objectives; so there should be no mysteries. Yet they are haunted by a something which they never talk about to me and rarely, I suspect, among themselves. For want of a better theory I shall assume they collectively murdered Manuel Cisneros for good reasons of their own, but put it out that he had taken to the other darkness and might some day return, unobtrusively as he had come, by way of the Orinoco or the Amazon.

March 15th, Tuesday

On Sunday one of the Intendencia's light aircraft came in with mail, some hormone weed-killer which I badly needed, sacks of phosphate, a new microscope and a dozen bottles of Scotch with the compliments of the Administration. A civil, kindly lot they are! It would be so easy to forget about me and leave me to be supplied by pack horse or the Government Canoe. Yet if I have any urgent needs and a plane can reasonably be diverted, down it comes within a mile of the estancia. At the end of the wet season when the grass was long I was limited to rare landings on the river.

The plane also brought me a guitar. It seems incredible that in Santa Eulalia there is not a single guitar. Our remoteness does not account for it. The reason, I think, is that at bottom we are still primitive, horse-riding Indians. Although we speak Castillian and call ourselves Christians the music of the Conquerors is not essential to us. So Santa Eulalia's one guitar was allowed to rot away some years ago. That shows how marginal is our Spanish-American culture. A guitar ought to be one of the simple necessaries of life along with salt, pimientos and alcohol.

Yesterday I slung it on my back like a travelling minstrel and rode Tesoro over to Santa Eulalia in the cool of the evening. I play with more emotion than accuracy and can easily improvise words and accompaniment when memory fails. It is astonishing that the English ever accepted the fashion of writing poetry in rhyme. To find rhymes in a Latin language is effortless and spontaneous, and so laborious a task in ours.

The males of Santa Eulalia collected immediately around Pedro's store crammed on his two benches or squatting more comfortably in the dust. Inevitably he sold more of his rotgut than the public could easily afford. Upon me, too, it was forced, as if Spanish music compelled an exaggerated imitation of Spanish hospitality. I had to drink more than I wanted, but by shifting my position so that I was outside the circle of the single paraffin lamp I was able to spill a glass or two on the ground.

When I slipped off to have a pee against the back of Pedro's store—if they held firmly to one culture or the other they would clean it up—Joaquin spoke to me from the darkness. We have great confidence in each other. Natural enough. The shaman and I are the only two people for hundreds of miles who are professionals.

'I have something hard to speak,' he remarked.

'Between friends nothing is hard.'

'Look! They will all be in debt to Pedro.'

That had not occurred to me. Perhaps it should have. Of

course my amateur, pseudo-Argentine performance on the guitar was as if a fair had come to town, unprecedented, unprepared for, destructive of the local economy.

Joaquin knew that my percipience was sharpened by alcohol. His own people react more brutally to the drug. With llanero or Indian he would never have embarked on the subject so abruptly. It shows what a close observer of human nature he is, even when foreign to him.

I thanked him warmly and said that I would ride home after giving two more songs for the sake of the party.

'No. I have spread a new hammock for you.'

It was pointless to sleep in his hut. I should not be allowed to go to bed for hours, if it were known that I was staying the night in Santa Eulalia. I told him that I was honoured by his invitation, but that the only way to put an end to the drinking was to ride off.

'Alone?'

'There is a good moon.'

'Wait!'

I knew what Joaquin was up to. He was going to arrange an escort of two or three llaneros which in the genial atmosphere would increase to half a dozen.

I would spend more evenings in Santa Eulalia if only I could avoid this ridiculous, noisy cavalcade which always has to accompany me home and then ride the twelve miles back to the settlement, refusing to stay under my hospitable roof—where there is any—till dawn.

They dislike this, however many of them there are. They won't admit it, but they are afraid of night—at any rate in the utterly empty llano between Santa Eulalia and the estancia. In Argentina I found reasonable caution, but not this childish fear. It is due, I suppose, to the proximity of the forest, although the creek and the marshes cut them off from it. These people belong to the open, blazing savannah and are not so familiar with trees as the Brazilians.

So after another song or two I mounted Tesoro without warning, shouted goodnight and was away before anyone could follow. It was hardly polite, but eccentricity in the otherwise entertaining Misionero will be forgiven.

I rode home without incident wondering about the relations between what one might call Church and State in Santa Eulalia. I came to the conclusion that Joaquin's intervention was odd and exceptional—as if in England the village parson had broken up a session in the village pub—and that he must have had some other reason besides that he gave me. But all one can tell is that Joaquin, in spite of the squalor of his house and person, has an older wisdom and more authority than the traditionless, semi-official storekeeper.

This morning, during our desultory conversation while collecting grass seeds, I told Mario what had happened. I suspect that he distrusts Pedro, or rather would distrust him if he could bring himself to do so. It is essential to feel on good terms with the only man who buys and sells. What would you do without him?

'He has a good heart,' Mario said. 'But thinks he knows everything.'

'And Joaquin?'

'This is his country.'

I saw what he meant. Joaquin and a few families of pure Indian blood were here or hereabouts before Santa Eulalia existed. The other inhabitants just drifted together like random particles collecting in a void to form a raindrop.

'He should not have let you ride alone.'

'I gave him no time. One moment there, the next in the darkness. And everyone knows there is not a horse in the village to catch Tesoro.'

As if to excuse Joaquin, he mumbled something about there being little danger on the way to the estancia.

'And what danger is there here?' I asked immediately.

He gave the vague answer that a man should never travel without arms. I replied that my rifle would have been useless, that I couldn't have hit the house after all I had been forced to drink.

'Better the guitar!' I added to amuse him. 'If the jaguars don't like the tune, they'll run. And if they do, they can dance.'

This casual remark had the most surprising effect. He stared at me with his copper face turning yellow.

'Do not even think of it!' he said.

So Mario is afraid of the guitar as well as the dark! Could this be Joaquin's other reason, that he instinctively distrusts so small a tinkle in so much empty silence? I must be more mysterious to them than I have ever guessed, if they think of me as a possible Pied Piper for jaguars.

March 17th, Thursday

When I decided to make this place my field station I was officially warned of possible danger from bandits. There aren't any. They joined the guerrillas in the hope of more regular hours for rations and murder. They will not appreciate Marxist discipline and the leadership of intellectuals; but once in, a man cannot easily get out.

These partisans of the National Liberation Army normally avoid the llanos since any considerable body of men would find no cover from air reconnaissance and attack. All the same, they keep a close watch on this flank from which their strongholds in the Eastern Cordillera might be threatened. It stands to reason that all activities in this emptiness, including my own, must be of interest.

I have at last had a visit from them. In the late afternoon of yesterday two men rode up to the estancia, dressed as forest travellers rather than llaneros and speaking cultivated Spanish. Following the custom of the country, I told them that my house was theirs for as long as they cared to honour it and I laid on drinks in the shade.

One was much taller than the other and, I should say, a Colombian of pure Spanish descent. I did not recognize the accent of his companion. He had some negro blood and may have been a Cuban. Neither of them had the proper air of being born on horseback. They could ride all right, but might have borrowed their two weary beasts for a week's holiday.

Before darkness set in I showed them over our extensions to Mario's garden, the new experimental plots and my field laboratory, explaining the purely advisory role of the Mission. I told them that some day the Government would undertake—or have the pious intention of undertaking—vast schemes of education and colonization, but that for many years to come the only farmers would be experts like myself.

The Cuban—if he was one—seemed to me somewhat naïve, as Spanish-American idealists often are. I could almost hear him thinking whether it was possible that tropical agriculture could be cover for some operation of the C.I.A. A pitiless, malignant bunch they are by all accounts, and no less credulous when it comes to politics!

When we had settled down again indoors, this smaller fellow started to cross-examine me. Where had I learned Spanish? I told him that I was born and bred in Argentina where my father had been a railway manager until we were thrown out. All my university education had been in England and I had opted for British nationality; but I had never lost my liking for the Americas.

Some of the subsequent conversation I shall try to give verbatim, for I might want to refer to it.

'Is it American or British capital behind you?' he asked.

I explained that there was no private capital whatever behind the Mission and that we were simply putting our technical expertise at the disposal of the Colombian Government.

'To prevent revolution?'

I replied that I didn't give a damn about revolution, that Communist dictatorship was a crude, sure way of developing virgin territory, but that I thought it an unnecessary discipline for viable economies.

'Good enough for the peon, but not for the British?'

Brash irony! It was time to put him in his place.

'Exactly. Like that plough you saw out there. A British farmer would have no use for it whatever. But it's cheap, and a vast improvement on anything the Indian villagers ever had.'

The Colombian was, I think, inclined to enjoy this confrontation between his opinionated companion and myself, but did not wish it to go far. I wonder which of them will eventually bump the other off.

'You are not afraid to be alone here?' he asked.

'No. My interest is in agriculture, not politics. And I keep my mouth shut.'

'What would you have to open it about?'

I thought it wise that all our cards should be on the table.

'Gentlemen, would I be right to assume that you have called on me in order to decide whether my throat is worth cutting or not?'

They protested most politely against the thought of such brutality towards a generous and sympathetic host, but admitted that up in the Cordillera my doings had attracted curiosity.

'Do believe me, my distinguished friend, this talk of throat-cutting is quite fantastic,' the Colombian said. 'I recognize that you are giving highly valuable, essential service to my country.'

I was not going to be side-tracked by civility. I wanted to be certain, once and for all, that there would be no interference with my work. So I lectured them bluntly. It went against the grain, but I knew they would expect frankness from an Englishman. One must sometimes live up to a false reputation in order to be trusted.

I emphasized that agitated speculation about what I knew and what I didn't could be dangerous to us all and a waste of time; and I went on in some such words as these:

'Using plain common sense—for I have no military knowledge —it has occurred to me that your partisans must eat and that the llaneros have for the moment a market. I am not asking you to tell me whether I am right. I only want you to feel secure if I have visitors from the Army or the Intendencia, as any time I might. I offer you silence on condition that I am left in peace to get on with my work.'

The Cuban listened to all this as if he were longing to slice me open and search for truth in my bowels. The Colombian's eyes were flickering with amusement.

'What an excellent intelligence officer you would make!' he said. 'But do you think you would notice this supposed movement to market?'

'No. The only route would be north of the marshes. And they don't like grazing cattle even there.'

'So the presence of cattle would be exceptional and worth reporting,' the Cuban declared.

Pedro must have put them on to this. If he could persuade the llaneros to drive a herd round the marshes, they could then continue on, through parkland providing easy going and patches of cover, right to the foot of the Cordillera.

I asked the Cuban with some contempt whether he thought I was prepared to spend weeks on horseback with a pair of field glasses for the sake of political convictions or a hundred pesos reward.

The Colombian waved him down—in fact, back into his chair.

'This is all conjecture,' he said. 'But I observe, doctor, that you are not accustomed to control your curiosity. Please do so! You might find yourself involved in reprisals against Santa Eulalia, and then it would be hard to guarantee your life. Or you might have to jump on the first boat back to Liverpool.'

I replied that I was not going to be scared out of work which I enjoyed.

'Forcibly deported was what I meant,' he answered. 'It would be easy to convince the Government that you are on our side. You're an intellectual, you see. And policemen always consider that the sympathies of an intellectual must be far to the left. Very odd, but there it is!'

He was still amused and cordial. We might have been at a café table with an old waiter hovering around and smiling discreetly at the talk. I don't see how these fellows can mix a sense of comedy with a cold disregard of human life. That comes naturally to the gaucho or llanero, but their disregard is not cold; it is hot and passionate.

'Then may I assume that my life, my guns and my horses will remain with me?'

'Of course! Why not? And we shall hope some day to employ so sympathetic a character.'

'I can't speak Chinese.'

'You revolt me, brother! What's for dinner?'

'Stuffed pimientos and a roast.'

'By God, you're lucky round here!' the Cuban exclaimed, greed or hunger breaking his startled silence. 'Well, no more politics—and be at ease!'

Thereafter their relaxation was genuine. We did not, however, arrive at any convivial relationship. It stands to reason that they were not so eager for companionship as I. They probably longed for privacy and for freedom from the unending duty to their troops. Still, I could sleep soundly and I hope they did.

They were off at dawn after a cup of coffee. The Colombian, before he left, took me to the corral on the excuse that his horse's pastern was cut. On examination I found little or no damage. It was clear that he wanted to talk confidentially.

'I don't understand the llaneros,' he said. 'Few of us do. Are they much influenced by superstition?'

Every llanero would declare himself a good Catholic devoted to the Virgin and the Saints. But since he rarely rides so far as a church and there are few missionaries to correct his errors, what he really worships and fears is a Mother Goddess with her attendant spirits. Even so he is less influenced by superstition than the settled Indians who know just enough Christianity to have lost respect for their own myths. The human longing for faith goes unfulfilled in both, leaving a void through which writhe the misty fears of spirits, the dead and magic. Joaquin at least hangs on to his old traditions, but is unable to explain what he really does believe.

Even Mario and Teresa are afraid of duendes. When I settled in, they moved from their cabin over to the main building. Their excuse was that they could serve me better if they lived alongside. It sounded reasonable; but I am certain, now that I know them better, that the true reason was reluctance to walk the couple of hundred yards across the garden after sunset.

So I told the Colombian that, whatever the superstitions, they were not Christian and would still be alive even if he and his party succeeded in closing every church in the country.

'Why are there no cattle between Santa Eulalia and your estancia?' he asked.

'I wish I knew. They think the grazing unlucky rather than unhealthy.'

'And Pedro? Does he share this belief?'

'Pedro either thinks he knows or is content to be ignorant. An old soldier with no imagination at all.'

'It seems useless to ask why in this country,' he said.

'It isn't useless, but there is hardly ever any answer. That's what I wanted to explain to your companion last night. To whom should I talk and what evidence would I have? He didn't realize the emptiness. All one notices is a speck on the horizon or a dance of the dust which might be haze, perhaps a horseman.'

'You wrote something like that when the Mission questioned your choice of this station,' he said. 'You insisted that the first object of study should be the ecology of fertile soil uncontaminated by man.'

I exclaimed that surely he couldn't get hold of copies of the Mission's reports to the Department of Agriculture.

'Only the first,' he replied. 'I was much impressed by your contribution. Indeed I thought this visit to you quite unnecessary. But my companion is not accustomed to judge by internal evidence. He has not that sort of education.'

Well, I suppose it is not surprising that these able and misguided fellows who take to the mountains should keep a line open to former colleagues in the Administration. Evidently he has no great respect for his lieutenant. It's my guess that the Cuban is their chief of security. All chiefs of security are, inevitably and by profession, bastards. I had better control my curiosity and go on minding my own business whether in Santa Eulalia or Bogotá.

March 20th, Sunday

The heat is windless and silent, illimitable as daylight on the moon. Nothing moves until an hour before sunset when again one hears the birds on the marshes and the monkeys howling at the edge of the forest.

The herds, split up into small languid bunches, are far out in the llano or in the shade of the woodland close to Santa Eulalia along the Guaviare. The llaneros are weary of their half-starved, tireless horses and ride no more than they must to see what casualties, if any, there are among the resting cattle. Losses are few. Puma in the open or jaguar on the edge of cover must be bold and hungry to tackle these formidable, half-wild beasts and are likely to be trampled into a bag of empty skin. Near water the anaconda is the worst enemy. These giant constrictors kill seldom, but a young animal has no chance against them. The llaneros swear that an anaconda can pulp the life out of a full-grown bull but is unable to swallow it.

Among my other reasons for the choice of the estancia was its unfailing water supply. According to Mario, Pedro and Joaquin the chain of marshes and the nameless creek which drains them never dry. I hope not, but the rains ended a month too soon. The creek is a necklace of pools linked by shallows and the level of the marshes has sunk.

The *acequias* which irrigate our garden have little water in them. They must be deepened and extended, but Mario and I alone cannot do it. Labour is unobtainable. The few available Indians of Santa Eulalia, suspended in almost complete idleness, will not work through the heat of the day—for which I don't blame them—cannot be induced to leave their wretched huts to live here, will not ride the twelve miles and return.

Nor can I get llaneros, whatever pay I offer. They are the last of the world's horsemen, now that the Mongols have taken to cities and the Bedouin to oil and education. It would be beneath their dignity to work in a field. I never even see a solitary rider on the skyline who might welcome a change from his futile life of producing valueless, ownerless beef.

So there we are! In this exceptional drought a lot of my work is going for nothing, since I cannot get enough water to the parched crops. I have tried the primitive device of a balanced pole, leather bucket and counterweight. It works and my carpentry was fun, but the labour of raising and tipping water is endless and intolerable. Thank God the horses and ourselves have an inexhaustible supply from the deep well in the courtyard!

I could not persuade Mario to show interest in my hydraulics. Unless I keep him working in my sight he insists on stopping holes and breaches in our ruinous adobe wall. It is good enough to keep out cattle, which don't come here anyway, but it will not, he says, keep out deer. That's true enough, and it might be wise, before the rains, to have some wire flown in to top the wall. Mario has never seen a wire fence and could not understand it until I drew a picture for him. He then assured me it would be useless. He is obsessed by a vision of deer crawling underneath the wire, which is preposterous. To listen to Mario, one might think this country was swarming with game, all eager to eat up experimental crops and not in the least afraid of human settlement. I think I am again faced by the blank—evasive and at present unmeaning.

March 22nd, Tuesday

Alarums and Excursions! Santa Eulalia has been reminded that it is governed.

Normally we have no government, unless one counts Pedro. We have neither education nor police nor public works on which to spend money, and no property or income on which to raise it. Since there is nothing worth stealing, there is no crime but manslaughter. One cannot call it murder, for there is no intent to kill. One gentleman decides that the words or eyes of another are offensive. As they may have one-eighth of Spaniard between them and an ancient tradition of violence while in liquor, they slash at one another with their knives. A pint or two of blood is mopped up. Its former owner quickly replaces it or dies. First Aid is administered by Joaquin. The affair is recorded by Pedro. That is all.

Well, as I say, Government has intruded upon our peace. The first I knew of it was a yellow haze which resolved itself into half a dozen men riding up to the estancia—on borrowed horses since they had arrived at Santa Eulalia by a military launch.

The cavalcade consisted of a captain, a sergeant, three men and an unwilling guide. It never occurred to me before that strangers might need one. The tracks are little used and deceptive. Neither I nor my few visitors follow the same path except in the wet season. We may come in from any point on a semicircle of nothing.

That evening we had little but our homegrown vegetables and canned meat—of which they would all be heartily sick. So as soon as Mario and the guide had seen to the horses and I had exaggeratedly welcomed the party I told their Captain that it was not too late for some duck if we hurried.

He jumped at the opportunity, and I sent him up the marsh with instructions to show himself on the shore of an inlet where the birds were just beginning to settle. They did what I expected, changing direction and circling low over the pools and rushes at the mouth of the creek. The light had nearly gone, but the flighting duck were black against the vivid green of the western sky and it was one of those memorable evenings when I was shooting like the angel of death. Fifteen duck with sixteen cartridges and all dropped where I could get at them!

Meanwhile the sergeant and his men had gathered in the kitchen and their horses were tethered to the old hitching posts outside. Mario and the guide were obstinately reluctant to leave them there, but I would not have them in the corral with my own. I am prepared to put up one or, at a pinch, two when passers-by stay the night, but I drew the line at crowding six into the small enclosure with possible damage to Tesoro, Estrellera and the sun shelters.

'And if they break loose into the garden?' Mario asked.

'Well, hobble them and turn them out on to the llano. They can come to no harm,' I said.

But perhaps I should not be as free and easy here as in Argentina. Pumas do range over the llanos, though I have never seen one. And a horse unaccustomed to marshes might go unwarily into the water over his knees and land himself in trouble with electric eel or sting ray. No shortage of those sods!

'For the honour of the house a horse must not be lost,' Mario insisted. 'I shall put them, if the master permits, in the hall.'

I shrugged my shoulders and told him to go ahead. The hall is a ruin with hardly any roof, but it has four stout walls, a solid door and shuttered windows.

While the rest of the party were drinking rot-gut and helping Teresa to pluck the duck, Captain Valera and I opened up the whisky which the Administration had sent me—presumably knowing that I might have visitors and wishing to reinforce my goodwill. I found Valera a delightful and intelligent companion. He had chosen to serve in the vast wastelands of Colombia and was supported in discomfort and hardship by a vision of what his country could become. He was the type of idealist who might well have joined the revolutionaries in the Cordillera, but he loathed them and their methods. They might, he admitted, bring more social justice to the Indian and the labourer, but then would stick fast in the mess of their doctrinaire economics, and take fifty years, like the Russians, to arrive at the same point that western democracies had reached in thirty.

He knew all about the Mission and was enthusiastic over what he called my self-sacrifice. I explained that I hadn't any, that in me scientific curiosity took the place of patriotism in him. We were both doing what we most wanted to do.

'And what about women?' he asked. 'Forgive me—but I don't see one.'

I replied that I was not too sure of government regulations. Laws for the protection of the Indians did exist, though they were somewhat starry-eyed and unenforceable. So I preferred to avoid illegalities which could be used against me if anyone wanted to stop my work. I may have sounded prim, and he smiled at what he thought typical Englishness.

'I wonder Mario and Teresa haven't shoved something in your bed already,' he said.

'It would have to be pitch dark,' I answered. 'The only possible candidate has not much nose left.'

He said that he might be able to do better for me than that. If I didn't like it, I could return it by Government Canoe. He would let me know.

I hope he does nothing of the sort. The casual way in which Latin-Americans pass second-hand females to each other is inclined to inhibit desire. As soon as the rains come, I shall fly up to Bogotá and fornicate more artistically.

Teresa was using her longest spit for the duck and needed wood as well as charcoal, so we had to wait some time for our meal. Meanwhile Valera opened up the subject of his visit.

It appeared that guerrilla activity had been spotted from the air before the commando could disperse and vanish into the foothills. The General Staff was not in the least bothered about an advance south-eastwards in our direction which could get nowhere and occupy nothing. The guerrilleros might as well put out to sea. But since they had never come down to the llanos before Military Intelligence was curious.

So Valera had been ordered to ask questions wherever there was any articulate soul along the banks of the Guaviare to answer them.

He had called at Santa Eulalia and talked to Pedro, who had denied any knowledge of guerrilleros but had spoken of the mysterious doings of the Englishman at the estancia and his unknown visitors.

I said that I did very occasionally give hospitality to travellers who might be Marxists or horse thieves or Venezuelans on the run for all I knew. It was the custom in Argentina to keep open house and ask no questions, and I presumed that Colombian courtesies were the same.

That satisfied Valera. After all, no one could talk to me for long without realizing that I have no politics. I was determined not to mention my suspicions of the llaneros' cattle market. I shall not give away Valera's secrets either.

While we ate he told me plenty. His second task was to report on whether a small, airborne force could attack from this side and startle the revolutionaries into retiring further north where troops from Bogotá could get at them. After returning to his temporary headquarters he intended to do some mapping with this operation in mind. I advised him to leave his mapping for another month when the rains would reveal unexpected lakes and creeks. I could imagine his handful of troops boldly attacking some guerrilla outpost and finding too late that there was a sluggish river hidden in a fold of the ground.

He asked why I suspected that there was any guerrilla activity so far east. I could only answer that Pedro and the llaneros had told me so.

'That's a lot more than they ever told me,' he said.

I was saved from what might have been awkward interrogation by Mario and Teresa coming in to clear away and to report that the troops had gone over to their former cabin for the night.

Across the garden I could hear singing and general jollity. A red glow suspended in blackness showed that the five men had started to grill a second supper in the chimney. I knew that they had a plentiful supply of rum to go with it. It seemed a pity that Mario and Teresa, whose life was so lonely, should not join the party.

'Can any of your fellows play a guitar?' I asked Valera.

'My sergeant. Like an angel.'

I told Mario to drop everything and take Teresa and my guitar

over to the other side of the garden, leaving us to look after
ourselves.

He would not, though I could see he longed to. I was exasperated by his fear of the dark.

'Look, friend Mario, there are no duendes who can stand an
electric torch!' I exclaimed. 'It is as good as the Sign of the
Cross. I will see you both over to your old house.'

He sulked but had to agree. Valera came as well, assuring him
that duendes invariably respected his rank and uniform.

We stayed long enough to listen to a song and then relieved
them of our presence so that they would be less inhibited. Teresa,
as befitted a respectable matron, had withdrawn to the doorway
of the next room—a shawl-shrouded figure with a black grin.
Mario was becoming noisy. It was clear that I had done the
right thing.

'Why wouldn't they go?' Valera asked when we had settled
down for a last whisky before turning in. 'Snakes? Or is this
place haunted?'

I was surprised that he should accept the possibility so
naturally. But he had an open mind and he probably knew
deserted plantations on the river banks where there is something
one might call an aura of despair and death.

'Not in the least. Thoroughly cheerful,' I said. 'It must be the
result of their loneliness before I came in. In the forest I should
not blame Mario. If a man is superstitious and cannot put a name
to the night sounds, there is no place which is not haunted.'

'But here—' he made a magnificent Latin gesture to describe
emptiness and knocked his glass over '—we have no companions
but the stars.'

'That's what I feel myself,' I answered. 'The forest is on our
doorstep but we are not of it. Like a cinema screen. So near, so
different a life, such limited values. And we observe it all from
our seats.'

I was pleased with that. I usually approach truth through wine,
not whisky.

This morning they rode back to Santa Eulalia. Valera intends
to return to his headquarters and then run up to Bogotá to report.
I think his party should travel in civilian dress, but they will all
flaunt their uniforms. I know nothing of the military art, but
personally I should never employ a Latin-American on any secret
mission. I wonder if the National Liberation Army can do better.
Perhaps that is one of the ingredients of such success as they have.

March 23rd, Wednesday

Today I rode Estrellera over to Santa Eulalia and spent an hour or two with Pedro—ostensibly to buy rice and cans of sardines of which Mario and Teresa are very fond. Shortage of fats, probably. I have seen Teresa with an oily sardine in one hand and a sticky sweet in the other, quivering with delight at the sensation in her pot belly and regardless of the mess on her face.

Pedro is a curious character, fairly honest and utterly unimaginative—the typical corporal. One could not wish for a more useful companion in forest or on the llano; if there was anything edible about, he would climb for it, shoot it or dig it out. But it would be hard to stand his continual chatter. I should get so tired of the rise and fall of his scanty moustache that I should be tempted to pay him to shave it off. He would, too—on condition that everyone believed he had done it to please me and not for money.

Money. He'll need two crates to carry it to the bank when he retires: filthy little bits of paper and packets of small change. As a favour to him I took a sack of the stuff with me the last time I flew to Bogotá. He is not a miser. He knows what interest is, but wouldn't dream of charging it on debts at the store and small loans.

He has not the aimlessness of his fellow citizens. He intends to buy a bar in some poor but honest quarter of Bogotá.

His wife looks after his capital and hides it away in small flour bags, reciting a spell over every cache. She is a pure Indian who never says much. She wouldn't have a chance anyway, since Pedro uses her as an audience when he can't find a better. All their children died young. On these over-violent llanos, death in one's twenties is more common.

The store was empty. It always is till evening. Over the second rot-gut Pedro said to me dramatically:

'One of these days I shall pop a shot in my head.'

He never will, but the fact that he can say it separates him from Indians and llaneros. For them suicide is just as impossible as for an animal. Their business is to live. They have no other.

'And why is that, friend?' I asked.

'Politics.'

'They don't concern us here. Did Captain Valera want you to go along with him?'

No, no, he insisted. As the agent of Government he was too

valuable where he was. A gallant officer such as Captain Valera knew the worth of a reliable ex-corporal at his post.

I think it likely that Valera was taken in. Pedro can play the old soldier very well. But I know that he is at least on speaking terms with guerrilla leaders, and that he tried to suggest the estancia as the cause of any rumours that Valera might have heard.

In view of what goes on in his store, his nerves ought to be proof against anything. But he is never in personal danger. He *is* Santa Eulalia. Without him it would have no official existence. Put it this way. Footballers assault each other, but not the referee. They are aware that if they had no referee, they would be left with only a field: a small, dull, flat llano.

So Pedro's courage—unquestionable in matters of survival and sheer endurance—has never been tested by worries. With one hand he performed his minimal duties to the State; with the other he took a small subvention from the guerrillas. It looked as if that could go on for ever in his apathetic world. Valera's appearance was unexpected and alarming.

'What do you think?' he asked. 'Who is going to win?'

'The Government, of course. There are only a hundred of the others.'

'But more can come from Cuba. Where is this Cuba exactly?'

'An island twelve hundred miles away.'

'It is said that everyone is equal there.'

'So we are here.'

'But in the cities, too, over there. Think of it, friend! If the guerrillas capture Bogotá they will give money to the poor so that everyone is equal.'

He was off. He drew an eloquent picture of Utopia which I swear must have been influenced by some army chaplain's description of the joys of heaven. He left out harps and glassy sea, but gave me a clear impression of a smiling population sitting around listening to brass bands while shining Pedros marched up and down the main street. This stuff could certainly tickle the imaginations of the submerged Indian peons, release from hell in this life being a more substantial promise than release from hell in the next. By giving food to the partisans as well as money to the priests one could take out real comprehensive insurance.

'But do you believe it, Pedro?' I asked.

'I? Not I! There will always be rich and poor, officers and men.'

That was not put on to impress me with his loyalty to the Government. It was his sincere common-sense opinion. The world's middle class of corporals distrust revolution.

'Then what are you worrying about?'

'Such cruelty! They take no prisoners, shooting them in the back and cutting their throats. And worse! Crucifying them with their toes in an ant's nest! Making them sit on sharp bamboos till at last the end comes out of their mouths!'

He was away again—more ants, alligators, skinning with blunt machetes, anything he could think of.

I knew very well that while he was talking about prisoners he was thinking of traitors. So I reinforced his neutrality by assuring him that the Army was just as cruel. I doubt if it is, except in rare cases of revenge. I also suspect that most of the rumours of guerrilla atrocities are set going by themselves. More borrowings from the Church. Threaten the opposition with devils, fire and pitchforks, and they'll behave!

'Thank God I do not mix myself in their quarrels!' he said.

'And I advise you not to. I Pedro, advise you.'

'Me? I'm a government servant! With the friends I have in high places in Bogotá it would be quite impossible.'

So it is. But I reserve the right to talk to guerrilleros if I want to until such time as they are deservedly wiped out. In a village —a true, tiled village—of the Cordillera that might be irresponsible. But here any humanity is welcome. Neither politics nor religion can override the claims of hospitality.

'You will tell your friends when you go to Bogotá?' Pedro asked anxiously. 'You will tell them that I think only of my duty?'

Poor Pedro! Being questioned by Valera has let in the blank. I wonder how far he has committed himself. My guess is that he merely told a few of the wilder llaneros that if they were to drive cattle to some known landmark they wouldn't be the worse for it.

The llaneros live as best they can. The right way to look at them is not as cattlemen at all, but as hunters and conservers of semiwild beasts. Since they have not received any wages for years they keep going by eating beef and rather reluctantly supplying—over vast distances—small herds to anyone who will pay cash. The identity of the customer does not interest them. Pedro could plead absolute ignorance that the cattle were being sold to guerrillas. The trouble is that nobody would believe him for long.

I took my siesta in one of his filthy basket chairs. It was twice as hot under his tiled roof—the only one in Santa Eulalia—as under the usual thick thatch. At last I left him sleeping to go and see Joaquin. I wanted to ask him when he thought the rains would come.

Joaquin was peacefully smoking a home-made cigar. His perfectly expressionless eyes were fixed on the water lapping against the jetty of rotten piles where goods are landed—if they don't fall through. By looking closely one could just tell that life flowed in the river and the man.

I laid down on the floor of his hut a few presents from Pedro's store which were very properly ignored. We chatted about neighbours until it was permissible to come to the point. Then he told me that the drought would get worse before it got better, and that he had never known anything like it for twelve years.

'That would be when the estancia was abandoned?' I asked.

'Yes. Twelve years ago.'

'And before that?'

'The rains always came in time.'

'Can you make them come?'

'Can you?'

He did not understand what I meant. Tropical rains are normally so regular that rainmakers have no market. To set up in business one needs a less reliable climate where a witch-doctor can make a reasonable forecast on the strength of weather experience handed down from father to son. Presumably there is nothing more to it.

'There is more I want to ask you, Joaquin,' I said. 'I must have hands to help me, but no one will come out from Santa Eulalia. Are there any Indians west of the estancia who would work for me?'

'The forest has no men in it.'

'And on the other bank of the Guaviare?'

'Too far. They would not come.'

Well, that was that. No offer will persuade a tribal Indian to do what he doesn't want to do, or to admit that he won't. He will reply that of course he is coming and that he will send his brother and cousin at once. But none of them ever turns up.

Joaquin's flat statement that the forest beyond the estancia is uninhabited lets in the blank. I used the phrase just now of Pedro. It's obsessive. We are able, when in good spirits, to preserve the self in a solid piece; but if anything disturbs this integrity we expand into nothingness. Alcohol is a cure, and the llaneros give themselves to it as I suspect they do to a woman:

very quickly and then to sleep. Myself, when the drought or the absurd fencing or my sheer inability to extract straight answers to straight questions, gets me down, I feel that the gift of speech is useless and wish that I could revel in the nothingness like my ancestor, the running ape, when he first broke out from the crowded darkness of the trees.

Mario and Teresa must have been living the most lonely life imaginable before I came. No wonder he needs a wall around him. A wall drives man and wife back on themselves, giving an illusion of solidarity and safety. So night, when no wall can be seen, is a sort of deprivation. Night forces him into unity with his environment, whereas his life is only tolerable if he can keep his environment at bay.

Amateur psychology, but I can't be far off the truth. Obviously it was a drought twelve years ago that finally finished Manuel Cisneros, the enterprising Venezuelan. I never quite grasped that before. Mario ought to have told me. Naturally he did not. He might have frightened off the boss-companion who had dropped from heaven to make his life more normal. Or am I unjust? He always had enough water for his own surprisingly sophisticated garden and had no reason to suppose there would not be enough for me.

Joaquin and I strolled back to the store to collect Estrellera. She does not care for Pedro, who is too noisy and military, but she always touches muzzles with Joaquin though he never brings her anything to eat. He would make a good vet, if anyone here ever bothered with more than centuries-old bleedings, dosings and cauterization. Such practice as he has is confined to Indian pets: monkeys, agoutis and a variety of small creatures and large birds. His diagnosis is absurd but his sympathy is genuine. For him we are all spirits confined in flesh.

So I rode home, night falling when I was half way. Estrellera has no nerves. She will give a snort of indignation at the unfamiliar like any conservative female, but she never shies, stops dead or trembles. If I were a guerrillero I think I would prefer to ride the too alert Tesoro, but for a journey on which dangers are, I hope, only imagined, give me Estrellera every time!

March 25th, Friday

A day of paperwork. It was about time that I made a précis of my journal and sent up a report to Bogotá, if only to show that I have zealously obeyed my instructions. All experiments of any importance I have initiated myself, disguising such undepartmental enterprise under a respectful amount of paper in triplicate —very necessary when the termites may get it if only in duplicate.

The Director is most reasonable, partly because I'm his showpiece. When politicians suggest that we and our like merely sit on our backsides, with an iced drink in one hand while the other explores the frilly intimacies of Latin-American womanhood, all at the expense of the Ministry of Overseas Development, he can always point to his field officer slapping mosquitoes in the dark heart of the continent.

In fact the habitable rooms are often free of insects and at times cool. When I took possession I repaired all fly screens on the barred north windows facing the courtyard and left the south windows as they were, permanently closed by heavy wooden shutters. Mario advised this on the grounds of keeping out the sun when he really meant the night.

No doubt I sound a much more romantic figure than I am. I have comfortable and modern camp equipment, a sufficiency of medical supplies, a well-stocked bar, all the apparatus I require and a mini-tractor which is the wonder of the district and in the drought is used for giving rides to visitors.

I have even a refrigerator, powered by a small petrol-engined dynamo which supplies enough voltage for half a dozen light bulbs as well.

I prefer living on the country to tinned food. That's where the Americans go wrong. They stock up with cans of rations as tasteless as they are luxurious. You can never really get the feel of an agricultural economy unless you surrender to it. Satisfying my own wants is an essential, additional experiment. Besides the eternal bananas and rice, I have vegetables, eggs, fresh beef and unlimited game. My dear Eibar-made 16 bore keeps me supplied with any size of wild fowl I fancy from snipe to geese, and I picked up in Barranquilla an old British Army Lee Enfield in excellent condition which produces the occasional deer or peccary for the pot.

No, I do myself pretty well. Admittedly the tropical evenings are long, but I pass them reading or playing records (I never can do both simultaneously) or devising a few experiments so unlikely to succeed that they count as amusement rather than work. This diary helps.

March 27th, Sunday

Tesoro has had a touch of colic. Now that the cracked conduits under the wall are delivering such a wretched flow, he is getting too much sediment in his water. I shall have to draw it from the well.

I was possibly unwise to buy him, for he could not be expected to have the resistance of the native criollos. But I have been amply rewarded. The story goes that some singularly vain captain of Venezuelan cavalry—lousy with oil money—imported a Palomino stallion from Mexico which he used as a ceremonial charger to impress the girls. As likely as not it impressed his squadron too. We can none of us resist a touch of lunatic flamboyance.

Tesoro was by this beauty out of a criollo mare. He turned out more gold than dun with the chestnut mane and tail of his dam. I got him cheap, 15 hands being too big for a cow pony. For polo he wouldn't have a fault, being neat on his legs and of quick intelligence. Indeed I cannot see any faults in him at all, beyond those of youth and very sketchy breaking. When I am on his back he expects severity and does not hold it against me; when I am off it, he follows me about like a dog.

I am always entertained by the marked difference of character between my nervous, affectionate gelding and Estrellera. She got her name from being a star-gazer as a filly. It now fits her temperament rather than her conformation. She is inclined to be dreamy with strong likes and dislikes, but all that remains of star-gazing is a slight suggestion of a ewe neck. The llaneros think more highly of her than I do, for she is a typical criollo skewbald of 14.2, well ribbed up and staying for ever.

I would not change either of them. With those two horses I would back myself to reach the Orinoco—and that is more than one could do by canoe and still arrive all in one piece.

March 31st, Thursday

I have always assumed that promises will come to nothing—and not only in Latin-America. Here, however, the promises have such an air of generous enthusiasm that they are a pleasure in themselves. Fulfilment stuns as a devastating and sometimes embarrassing surprise.

On the 28th the Government Canoe—more like a barge with an outboard motor—was expected at Santa Eulalia. Since one can never be sure of the exact date of arrival, especially when the Guaviare is low, I did not want to waste time hanging about and sent Mario over to deliver and collect my mail.

He returned next day, accompanied by a pack horse loaded with hardware which we needed and, on top of it, an unexpected piece of soft ware. She greeted me very shyly and escaped to Teresa. Mario then presented to me a letter which he had received from an immensely fat and dignified negress who had insisted on establishing both his identity and mine in the manner of an obstinate sergeant of police. It was from Captain Valera.

My Very Good Friend,

You will have a few weeks in which to get over your surprise before the Canoe calls at Santa Eulalia on the way back. Put her on board if she does not suit, and accept the excuses of a friend who only wished to be of service to you.

First, this is not a whore, merely an unfortunate. My girl, who has a good heart, found it like a stranded fish upon the river bank. She did not immediately inform me, since it was a good-looking little creature which might have caused some dissension in the family. So she boarded it out for some days until she could settle its future.

When I was about to leave on the little expedition which by good fortune brought me to your house, my girl confessed what she had done. She had to get rid of her find and was afraid that any arrangements made in my absence would come to my ears—as they surely would—and that I should suspect her of commerce rather than charity. Her past, I may say, would justify such suspicion. But her present is in every way loyal and obliging. Her fears that I might change horses if I set eyes on Chucha were entirely unfounded.

Chucha's history is deplorably vague and unsatisfactory. What else can one expect? A woman is lost among the insects and the trees. The soul clings to its name in nameless places and there is no rest for the body.

She was given by her mother to a merchant called Samuel. That regrettable transaction must have taken place in the Eastern

Cordillera of Bolivia or Peru, for her native language is Aymara. Samuel took her down to the Amazon basin. After a stay in a large city where they did not speak Spanish—probably Manaos—Samuel wandered with her up another river—probably the Rio Negro. He seems to have been an irrepressible traveller, but he was kind to her. He was drowned somewhere high up the Orinoco. How the devil he got there from the Rio Negro I don't know, so I can't expect her to.

Chucha, abandoned in the merciless nowhere of our continent, very reasonably presented her undoubted charms to the first man who had a boat with an engine in it—a guarantee that, whatever his appearance, he was not a forest Indian. His name was Pepe and he traded in knives, beads and whistles. He was continually drunk and treated her brutally, whereas Samuel offered her no less affection than he gave to his pet monkey.

When Pepe threatened to open her up with a machete she ran away from him. My girl says that the spirit of her great aunt had locked up Chucha's womb. Her own deceased great aunt is, I am glad to say, more reasonable. I must admit that I had no idea that the plateau Indians could suffer from the muscular effects of a neurosis which one believed confined to the women of Northern Europe. She must have been sufficiently exposed to civilization to have acquired taste.

I do not like allowing the poor little thing to die of damp rot complicated by syphilis, and I send her to you with confidence that you will save her from this otherwise inevitable destiny. In the course of various small medical attentions which she badly needed I have had her intimately examined. Indian modesty was appalled, but my girl held her hand and assured her that such was the custom among the rich.

I can certify that when she left here she had no venereal disease, and that during the undoubted hazards of the journey up river she was under the care of a respectable matron whose husband depends on me for promotion.

All I fear is your British sense of responsibility. I beg you to ignore it. You know as well as I do that her relationship with you will greatly enhance her value and that a dowry—tiny to you, wealth to some young llanero—would persuade him to wear out two horses in his immediate search for a priest.

Sentimental cynicism! And barely redeemed by that warmth of friendship which a generous Latin-American will allow to blaze on the strength of a single meeting! I re-read Valera's letter over a couple of stiff drinks which merely turned one half of me into a rampant stallion while the other half argued. Suppose, I asked myself, this female had been a scientist, or some enterprising young woman come from Bogotá to inspect my valuable services to her country? Well, she'd have to resist attempted rape three times a day, the afternoon attack being marked by the highest fever. Suppose Joaquin had supplied me with something not too jungly from one of the river tribes? I should probably have accepted, since the girl would have a home to which she could return with her presents and be welcome. Chucha had no home. I came to the conclusion that my conscience was bothering me just because she was so helpless. She had no more choice than a mare passed from one llanero to another.

Was all this compunction insincere and did I in fact object to her colour? Certainly not! My first inspection of the consignment had been casual, since I had not then read the accompanying Operational Manual. I thought she was possibly some niece of Teresa's. But I found her colour delightful—like a new penny set in black, straight hair rather more luxuriant than that of our river Indians.

She looked neat and clean, except for the stains of the journey, and no doubt Teresa would delouse her if necessary.

Or did I resent being given no choice? No, she would do very well. I was prepared to put Samuel's little cutie through the hoops within five minutes and go on till next Sunday week. So, after all, compunction did appear to be the true motive for hesitation and quite sincere.

I went to Mario's quarters to see her. Mario and Teresa had no doubt what she had come for. They reminded me of a couple of hopeful parents determined to clear out of the room as soon as possible and leave future son-in-law to get on with it. They had evidently been assuring her that I was a nice chap, a master mind and so forth. I told Teresa that Chucha would eat with me and took her along to my living room.

She was very gentle and submissive like most Indian women, but I preferred to assume that she might have some elementary pride. So I decided to put off the moment of truth as long as I could without going crazy, gave her some sweets to suck, showed her round the habitable rooms and told her a bit about myself and my work.

She followed me around with blank brown eyes, wide open. After a while she began to murmur a little chatter. Her Spanish was soft and passable. The white blouse and skirt that Valera or his girl had dressed her in were damn near transparent when she had the setting sun behind her. It was time for Sir Galahad to have another drink just to keep the conversation going.

When I produced bottle and glass she gave her first sign of being more than a pet monkey with the power of speech—a little involuntary movement as if she were shrinking from an outsize spider. I said I never drank more than a finger—the length of it, not the breadth—and waggled it at her. I showed her the proportion of rum and fresh lime juice that I liked and let her play with the tinkling ice and soda. Confidence was established. She told me that she was about fifteen, that she was born in Peru but couldn't remember it clearly.

She was very hungry and stuffed herself with beef and corn as soon as Teresa brought in our meal. She then was far more talkative. Her father had come down from the Central Cordillera to the lowlands, having been selected for one of the Peruvian Government's resettlement schemes. That, of course, is my own interpretation of her disconnected bits and pieces. He died of TB, as far too many of them do when they leave the winds of the altiplano for the damp and heat, and her mother carried on working in the plantations. When she was twelve Samuel and the rivers gathered her up.

'Why didn't you tell all this to the captain and his señora?' I asked.

'I was afraid.'

'What of, child?'

'Of the señora.'

'But why?'

'Because she hid me.'

I suppose there is some logic in that. Valera's girl created an atmosphere of guilt. Chucha's reaction to it was not unlike that of some city teenager running away from home. To admit exactly where she came from could mean that she would be handed over to the police. She didn't see the Establishment as safety, in which she was instinctively right. The Establishment—if any member of it with a pair of white trousers could be found—would simply have put her on board a canoe in the pious hope that she might reach some nuns and the near certainty that she would not.

Her matt copper had taken on a patina of green. Being fascinated by the quivering of the bell-shaped breasts, I did not notice it until we were near disaster. All those sweets she had eaten were no foundation for an Argentine-sized grill of beef. She was overcome by shame and looked round frantically for somewhere to be sick. Natural good taste or are the Children of the Sun brought up to consider it a disgrace? I don't know. Here we use the open grass or the back of Pedro's store. We also pride ourselves in shooting the contents of our stomachs as far away as possible, regardless of where they land. I suppose she was overwhelmed by a tiled floor, four walls and a table with plates, knives and forks on it. To me it was an indoor camp, but to her the high splendour of a Lord Mayor's banquet.

She made a rush for the nearest window on the outside wall and flung open the wooden shutters. She was very obviously near collapse due to the long weariness of her journey and, perhaps, relief. Relief will often make one more wobbly than the original cause of the strain. She was also in trouble with her hair. So I held her head till she was empty.

I fetched Teresa and explained that Chucha was ill and tired. No doubt Teresa had spotted it much earlier, but had not thought that the master would pay attention. She bedded Chucha down on my spare mattress in an alcove between the kitchen and laboratory and gave her a hot, aromatic tea, possibly more effective than remedies from my medicine chest. Chucha thanked me with great gravity and said she was sorry. So was I.

But I had been rewarded by my first sight of a puma. It must have been crouching very close to the house. However, my eyes had not had time to adjust to the darkness and I only had a vague glimpse of it as it cantered away.

April 2nd, Saturday

The next morning she hardly lifted her eyes, but had put a scrap of ribbon in her hair. She was very attentive to Teresa, learning about a house with walls and how to clean it—all very foreign to her after years of bamboo huts and canoes. She took a little lunch with me and was all 'Si, señor' and 'No, señor' as if she had just come out of a convent.

When the house was closed and silent in the heat of the afternoon I gathered her up. She took it very naturally. Well, one would expect that. But I mean a little more by 'naturally'. There was no immediate, pretended response, nor any of those artificialities which so delightfully disguise a too eager response. She merely hid her face and dissolved into a softness.

I spent a little time and trouble on her. She was nearly passive, except for a slight tremor of muscles which showed that she was not uninterested. There was no trouble due to great aunts. I found her peculiar softness stimulating. It may be due to the fact that like most Indians she has hardly any waist. The little darling had to put up with me from the siesta till dinner time, and soon after that we had the two air mattresses side by side and were off again. For God's sake, what I have been suppressing for the sake of tropical agriculture!

Today I noticed that she was not walking with quite her usual grace. I can't help it. It's going to get sorer before it gets better, like the drought. Her very simple sweetness intoxicates me. She doesn't—or rather didn't—know how to kiss properly. Her minor erotic response is a caress of arms, legs or hands. She ought to have a tail like a cat.

That reminds my one-track mind that she also saw the puma. She was frightened out of her wits and insists that it would have got her if I had not held her. That is nonsense. She would have to be unconscious and lying still for a longish time before the puma would have dared to investigate. I told her it was certainly a dog. I don't want her to catch the jitters from Mario and Teresa. If she is to be happy here, she must have absolute confidence that the llano is just as empty under the stars as under the sun.

Anyway she has never before set eyes on a puma—jaguar, yes. One cannot judge accurately the size of the big felines. I am told that they seem of immense length and impossible narrowness when they spring. Yet the same fellow rolled up asleep is just a furry ball and could easily be a dog, and not a very large one at that. I suspect that I saw what I wanted to see and that it was in fact a stray dog. Santa Eulalia crawls with them, all too bloated with beef offal to travel far from home. But the guerrilleros may well take along a few dogs for hunting. Alternatively it could have been put ashore to earn its own living by some Indian who was tired of its demands for a more dog-like diet than bananas.

April 3rd, Sunday

I like Chucha's smell—an undefinable blend of young animal and fresh vegetable. But I don't like my own. At dawn this morning I felt remarkably clean inside and filthy with stale sweat outside. So I got up, had a shower, climbed the wall so as not to wake up Mario by opening the gate and strolled out over the cool, grey llano.

For the first time I saw cattle between the creek and the forest. What is left of the grazing there seems to me exceptionally good, but beasts are never allowed to stray round the north end of the marshes and down into the corridor. If they do, the llaneros give them up as lost. They say it is because there is no intervening strip of parkland where the cattle could easily be rounded up. Certainly the forest is dense and begins abruptly. On my explorations of it I have found that after cutting a first passage through the green wall one has little further need of the machete and can even ride at a walk under the big timber. The llaneros may be right in holding that if a man tries to follow the cattle he merely drives them deeper into the forest and loses himself into the bargain. But they give up too easily. It's their distaste for the forest which counts.

As soon as the sun began to bite—which it does within twenty minutes of clearing the horizon—the cattle drifted into the shade and disappeared. To get on the wrong side of the creek they must have broken away from a bunch up north. It seems unlikely that they could not have been rounded up in the open. Was a small herd being driven towards the Cordillera through parkland unfamiliar to the llaneros?

I also searched for tracks of our visitor, but could find none—not surprising since the ground is as hard as a city pavement. Dead grass showed an impression where something had lain down about twenty yards from the house. I also found a dropping, but it looked more human than animal.

April 4th, Monday

For civilized man—if I still am—it is a refreshing experience to be sexually and aesthetically satisfied, yet not emotionally involved. Love, no. Tenderness, yes. No concern for the future beyond a firm intention to preserve her as she is. No concern for her past except gratitude that it has led to so satisfactory a present.

I must admit that I am curious to know at what age she ceased to be Samuel's pet monkey and became his mistress. There does

seem to have been a transition. But I lay off the subject, and with
natural good taste she rarely mentions him. She is nearly as neat
and hairless as an infant. Obviously she has never had a child.
I suppose that problem is bound to crop up. I shouldn't be
surprised if Joaquin has some earth-shaking remedies for it.

I find to my amazement that she can very slowly read. Samuel
taught her. While I am working in the laboratory she respectfully
ferrets about among books, papers and written scraps, watching
me to see if all is permitted. Her curiosity is unceasing, and I
try never to show impatience.

The patterns of mathematical formulae fascinated her.

'How do they tell a story, Ojen?' she insisted.

Ojen is the nearest she can get to Owen. With the help of a box
of matches she easily grasped the principle of algebra. Either she
has exceptional intelligence or I should make a very good father.

I should not like her to find Valera's letter. I doubt if she would
understand its complexities, but no woman could miss the tone
of contempt. So I have torn it up after translating it and rewritten
the diary entry of March 31st to include my English version of it.

I do not know whether she is happy, or merely ecstatic at so
miraculous a change in her life. Perhaps the difference between
the two can no more be analyzed for Chucha than for a child.
I am disconcerted by her innocence. An odd word to use. I wrote
it without thinking, but it's true. She has the innocence and
goodness of the savage. Well, more the animal than the savage.
The complicated mind of the savage is repulsive to anyone but
an anthropologist. Chucha is all simplicity. I suppose that's what
I mean.

Her religious beliefs are on a par with those of the llaneros.
Jesus was kind and hangs on a cross in churches. God is very far
away and of dubious importance. But the Virgin is all love and
answers prayers. I gather that Chucha and Teresa are pooling
their knowledge of the subject. It would be blasphemy to add any
commentary of my own. I feel that those two and the Mother of
God all understand each other very well.

April 6th, Wednesday

I really must stop rogering Chucha afternoon and night and get
on with my work. She is setting an example. She remembers

nothing of the cereals and tubers of the altiplano but has picked up some knowledge of nursery gardening while trotting along behind mother in the plantations of the Montaña. With Mario's permission she has taken over the care and watering of his few peaches, lemons and oranges and is trying to raise a lime cutting in the shade. I just managed to prevent myself giving a lecture and telling her that she was doing it all wrong. But she must have green fingers. Not a leaf has flagged or dropped.

I shall give up this diary altogether. There is no need for it. I haven't the time in the evenings and I am no longer interested in fortifying myself against a blank spot which isn't there.

April 7th, Thursday

No need for it? The devil must have been looking over my shoulder if he ever comes as far afield as the llanos of Colombia. Put it this way: I do not need a personal diary, but it looks as if I might need a record of facts. So, having got into the habit, I will keep it up.

This morning I thought Chucha was asleep, but she suddenly raised her head from the odd position where it had collapsed and said: 'Ojen, there is a horse coming.'

I couldn't hear a thing myself. There was absolute silence. I have noticed that she seems to be able to hear sound waves through the ground as well as through air. They arrive, of course, much quicker.

As soon as I too heard it, I slipped on shirt and trousers and put a clip into the Lee Enfield. I doubt if I should have bothered if I had been alone. It was papa being over-protective. All the same, the incident was more than unusual. The rider had come from Santa Eulalia in the dark, which the llaneros will not, and he was travelling at a much faster pace than they ever do.

Mario had recognized the visitor and opened the gate by the time I got there. It was Pedro, riding his grey gelding bareback with only a halter. He had been using his spurs in good earnest. The beast was bleeding, fighting for breath and full of alarm.

He did not dismount and for once wasted no time in empty speech.

'They are going to cut my throat, friend! I have no hope but you.'

He begged me to give him quickly as much food as he could carry and to ride with him to the edge of the forest. He had nothing at all with him but his machete and an old revolver tucked in his belt.

He was not a man to miss a chance of explaining himself dramatically and at length, so I knew that the affair was urgent and that he had good reason to be afraid. I told Mario to throw into a sack rice, dried and canned meat, matches and whatever he could lay his hands on instantly while I saddled up my reliable Estrellera. The disk of the sun was half above the horizon as we galloped across the creek. In another five minutes we were skirting the edge of the forest towards the only possible passage for a horse which I myself had cut. It would take a lot of finding for anyone who did not know it was there.

As soon as we were clear of the undergrowth and into the trees I dismounted and asked him what the devil was the matter.

He told me that four llaneros had been driving a small herd towards the foothills. Where they were going he, Pedro, did not know. But when they were two days out, nearing the rendezvous where the herd would be taken over, they had been machine-gunned from the air, the cattle scattered and two llaneros killed.

The other two, panicked by the discovery that aircraft could shoot, had ridden back to Santa Eulalia. A mere hour ago they had routed Pedro out of bed, told him to get dressed and firmly shut the door on his wife. They then said that they were going to cut his beautiful brown throat and that, as he had once been a friend, they would stretch it tight and do a neat job. He was a traitor who had sent them off on this errand and then told the Government about it on his tac-tap machine.

To me Pedro protested that it was all a mistake and that, as I knew, he never mixed himself up in politics. To them he had said that they might as well have a last drink together—a proposal which appealed to the llaneros' curious sense of humour.

Keeping the bar counter between himself and the naked knives, he picked up a bottle and hurled it at the lantern which one of them was carrying. That of course set the store on fire. Pedro's rot-gut was every bit as inflammable as spilled paraffin. In the confusion he yelled to his wife to get out, jumped on his horse and took off across the llano. How he came to have spurs on I can't imagine. I suppose they were always attached to his boots, though his normal pursuits were sedentary.

'They are close behind you?' I asked.

'Not very close. But now that it is day they will ride harder.'

'How can they tell where you went?'

Not an intelligent question. It seemed to me that he could take off into space and not see another human being for days. But of course they knew that he had not even saddle and bridle. He would have to eat raw beef unless he lit a tell-tale fire. He dared not let his horse rest and graze unless he kept hold of the halter, for no South American horse—except rarities like my Tesoro—can easily be caught. Water he could only find at well-known points, giving his presence away by disturbing the cattle. The forest was his only hope, and the estancia his only source of supply.

His intention was to make his way south-west to the banks of the Guaviare and wait there until he could hail a passing canoe. The crossing of the forest would not take him more than two days or perhaps three, but he might have to wait much longer before seeing any movement on the river.

I asked him if he had a compass.

'Pedro needs no compass, friend. I am accustomed.'

'Suppose they follow you?'

'Have you ever seen any of them between the estancia and the trees? No! Since they are determined to kill me, there will be several of them together. When they have given each other courage, they will ride along the edge of the forest but they will not enter it.'

That was certain. They never went where they could not ride.

Thinking of the days of waiting on the river bank, I wished I had provided him with books and a line. I asked him if he was likely to find game. Even an armadillo might just make the difference between hardship and starvation.

'Nobody knows for sure. But there must be hunting.'

'Joaquin told me there are no Indians there.'

'Joaquin is a fool. There are. But they stay in the deep forest and I shall never be far from the edge of the llano. It is said they are very small. The less reason to be afraid of them! Now go with God before the fools come galloping up to the estancia and frighten your girl! Take my horse and keep it till we meet again!'

'What shall I tell them?'

'They will not hold it against you. Any of them would help a friend without asking questions. Say that you gave me food and know nothing!'

Well, I do not. I am certain that it was Pedro who organized the meat supply and fairly certain that he never informed the Government. The interception of the herd was probably due to some clever work by Valera and his colleagues.

I have little fear for Pedro. The forest, almost impenetrable where it meets the llano, soon becomes as open as, say, a ruined church in which the pillars are still upright but a lot of the roof has fallen on the floor. With luck he should be near the river bank some time to-morrow. Cutting his way through the last half mile will be long and arduous, and then he may emerge into one of those vile tangles where water, land and vegetation are indistinguishable; but with the river as low as it is a shore of sand or gravel can never be far off.

Lord knows where this story of pygmies comes from! I have never heard it before. Provided they have always kept to the shelter of the trees it is no more or less possible than traveller's tales of hundred-foot anacondas.

Leading his grey gelding, I cantered Estrellera back to the estancia and noticed at least three places where the creek was quite dry between shallow pools. Chucha and Mario seemed ridiculously anxious about me. I had hardly unsaddled and turned both horses into the corral when five of the Santa Eulalia toughs galloped up, loudly demanding entry. I received them as if they were the sixteenth century caballeros whose manners and cruelty they have inherited, and they were compelled to respond with due measure of courtesies before coming to the point.

I gave them my word that Pedro was not in the estancia. He had asked for food, which I had given, and then I had ridden with him to the forest and taken his horse. He had told me only that some gentlemen had tried to cut his throat and set fire to his store, but did not say why. Could they enlighten me?

'A private affair,' one of them replied, showing no disapproval at all of my behaviour. 'I need tell you only that he has well deserved it.'

I watched them through field glasses vaguely searching the frontier between trees and llano, and saw no more of them till they called in for a drink, two hours before sunset, on their way back to Santa Eulalia.

April 9th, Saturday

I found Chucha crying this morning. She was comforting her lime sapling, or else it was comforting her. It is a totem, like a vegetable and living Teddy Bear, with which she takes refuge in trouble. She would not tell me what the matter was. I hope the loneliness is not getting on her nerves. She is a creature of closed horizons, of mountain valleys and rivers. This vast emptiness may oppress her. One needs to travel over it on a horse, not to look at it hopelessly from our oasis.

At first she was as frightened of the horses as her ancestors in Peru. For her they were alarming and self-willed animals with ferocious sets of teeth, only to be handled by the Conquerors and certainly not by humble women. Neither Tesoro nor Estrellera were helpful. Tesoro is only half broken—by European standards—and Estrellera was very well aware that at last she had a human being in front of her who could be bullied.

But Chucha's ancestral inferiority complex is now on the way to be cured. Partly this is due to the presence of the llaneros the other evening. They were showing off in front of a pretty girl how magnificently they ride, yet they were all much darker skinned than she is. And partly it is due to Pedro's Pichón who has gone out of his way to be polite to her ever since she nervously offered him the first carrot he had ever tasted. He likes women anyway. Pedro's wife used to treat him as a pet. He is a proper corporal's horse, quiet and unintelligent, willing to carry a pack or a rider. I think I can persuade Chucha to sit on his back.

But what can she wear? That's a problem which Teresa, who dresses in a single shapeless garment with one of my old shirts underneath, would be unable to solve. Nothing at all is the right answer. It would be less indecent than a skirt rucked up round her waist; but both Chucha and Teresa would certainly be shocked at the thought of an Indian Lady Godiva. I should also fear for the pale primrose skin on the inner part of her thighs. The *chiripá* of the Argentine pampas would look very well on her. I must try to remember how the length of cloth used to be folded and fixed in position.

April 10th, Sunday

I made a dashing job of the *chiripá* by cutting up a green nylon pup-tent which it is unlikely I shall ever want. The little darling thought the whole business of fitting the square around and between her legs most improper. In an obscure way I can understand the taboo. The business of a male is to undress, not to take a too intimate delight in dressing. Naturally enough I was entranced by this unexpected modesty. She responded, but still seemed disturbed. Enjoyment without joy. I must be more considerate and stop behaving like an archduke in a high-class brothel.

In the first cool of the evening I mounted her on Pichón—who fortunately approved of the *chiripá*—and suggested that we ride to the edge of the forest. She wouldn't hear of crossing the creek; so we walked our horses up the east side of the marshes where she became more cheerful and exclaimed at the colours of the birds. I should like to dress her in flamingo feathers. A vulgar thought! It offends against her simplicity. In any case I have to be content to set off her prettiness with things folded and belted like the *chiripá*. It would be reasonable to ask the Mission to fly in a sewing machine.

It has just occurred to me that Pedro's tac-tap is out of action, so that it will take anything from three weeks to a month to make a request and get a reply. Well, we are remarkably self-sufficient.

April 11th, Monday

This is the devil! I promised myself that nothing should hurt her while she was in my care, and now she is heading straight for tragedy.

There were tears again during the siesta; so I petted and encouraged her until the reason came out.

'*Porque te quiero, Ojen.*'

I do not know how far the Indian of the Altiplano shares our conception of love. Did the Conquerors import romantic love along with their music, speech and religion? I think I must assume they did, though all the evidence I have is that she looked straight into my eyes when she said she loved me and foresaw that there could be no happy ending.

I replied of course that I loved her too, but she knew very well that my *te quiero* did not mean the same as hers. What am I to do about this when the time comes? Love is a quite unnecessary serpent in our Eden. Valera would laugh and ask me what the hell I expected. Yet I didn't expect it. I could shrug my shoulders if Chucha had been a whore responding desperately to kindness and admiration. But what she feels and cries about is not, I think, that fairly predictable response. It is far nearer a child's unthinking, whole-hearted love. I can't reject it and I don't want to. There is a father/daughter relationship between us. I cannot act as my own psychiatrist, but I suspect that if I had not been using her body with immense physical and aesthetic satisfaction I could have answered with absolute sincerity and in a quite different sense that I loved her. Am I suffering from the stupid contempt of the male for the woman he has bought? But I didn't buy her. She was a present.

I told her that I thought she had been crying because she was lonely. She replied that she could never be lonely any more because she would remember me even if I was not there. I wonder if she read that slowly in some ragged page torn from a magazine or if it came from the heart. Does it matter? Words must have a source. Then for no reason at all she suddenly saw the comic side of the *chiripá* and started to giggle. Her moods travel like the flickering of wind over the rushes.

'Now that we understand each other. . . .' she began.

That, too, was spoken out of a child's instinct. There was a peace and confidence between us which, I see, I had hardly given a chance to grow.

'Now that we understand each other, promise me you will never go to the trees!'

I assumed in some way she did not wish me to be associated with her past. I am always creating complexities where there aren't any.

I explained that it was my trade to go to the trees: that anything which grew on the llano in partial shade was of interest to me and that we knew far too little of conditions of soil and geology at the border. That was beyond her. I put it more simply. Why does the forest stop where it does and not somewhere else?

'And I do not go at night,' I added.

Nor I do. Like the llaneros, I have no exaggerated respect for predators, but it is obviously unwise to ride in the dusk where close cover overhangs the grass.

'Not in the day either,' she insisted. 'Never!'

This smelt of the blank spot again. She had talked to the llaneros only in my presence, so the bad influence had to be Mario.

'Listen, love! Mario has told me a dozen times what I must do and what I must not. Except in the matter of growing pimientos, I pay no attention.'

'But he has not told you about the dwarfs.'

I took this very seriously in order to get it all out of her. I pretended annoyance with Mario and demanded why he had not warned me.

'It is not right to speak of them.'

I told her that they enjoyed being talked about, that Mario was trying to frighten little girls. There was a dwarf who rode on the necks of horses and plaited the manes. The llaneros and I not only spoke of him but cursed him to hell.

'Was Mario afraid that I would leave the estancia?'

'At first, yes. But not now. He says that if you believed they were there, you would go and talk to them.'

What a compliment! To the scientific spirit of enquiry? Or to the essential humanity of Christian culture? But it left the main question of whether they were duendes or pygmies unsettled.

'What else did Mario say?'

'I told him about the dog. He said it belonged to them and that we must take good care when dogs can cross the creek. That is all.'

Odder and odder. That a race of forest pygmies could exist is possible. Between the Cordillera and the llanos they would have more than thirty thousand square miles to play in—a primordial, uninteresting area the size of Scotland and just as unexplored as Scotland would be if travellers were confined to the Great Glen, the Forth and the Clyde.

Against their reality and in favour of myth or a folk memory is this nonsense of dogs. If they have dogs they must have been exposed at some time to Spanish influence. Then there would be some written record of them, perhaps two or three hundred years old. Even if lost, it would be alive as a rumour and I should surely have heard it among a dozen other yarns of man-eating trees and Eldorados. I cannot believe that the memory should be entirely confined to Santa Eulalia.

I shall ride over to-morrow and see what I can extract from Joaquin.

April 12th, Tuesday

Pedro's store is burnt to the ground. No doubt the Government will give him some compensation when the news gets through, which could be several weeks unless Pedro himself quickly finds river transport. Meanwhile his poor wife is living wretchedly in an abandoned hut. She must in fact be far from destitute, but is naturally unwilling to dig up her flour bags from the ashes in the sight of all. Loyalty to Pedro. She must not lose the money which is to buy that tavern in Bogotá, however much she suffers meanwhile. I shall send some food, and I have told her that if she needs petty cash she can borrow from me. Marvellous generosity! She couldn't use more than sixpence a day if she tried.

Joaquin was drying fish in the sun. They stink to high heaven and then become sweet. I find them quite edible if stewed like salt cod with plenty of garlic and tomatoes. So I bought a few from stock in order to vary our diet and encourage so exacting a craft.

'I have a question, Joaquin,' I said at last, 'for your wisdom in such matters is greater than mine. What should a man do if he meets a dwarf?'

He did not answer, busying himself with the fish, and finally spoke more to himself than to me.

'They will not cross water.'

'Can they climb?'

'It is said they cannot.'

That ruled out monkeys, which anyway are one of the staple foods of forest Indians and so familiar that they could not be feared. As for ground-living apes, it is certain that there are not and never were any in the Americas.

'Have you ever seen one?'

'Never. My father did.'

'What did it look like?'

'Who knows what he has seen in the dusk?'

'They don't come out in the day?'

'All such things dread the sun.'

'They are duendes?'

'It could be.'

'What else is said about them?'

'They dance.'

I let that go. Conversation with Joaquin has the advantage that neither party is necessarily expected to say anything for minutes on end. Whether he spends the intervals thinking or merely sitting I do not know. I myself find them useful for chewing over what he has said and working out the next move. This time I had an inspiration worthy of an anthropologist.

'Is that why there was no guitar in Santa Eulalia?'

'That is why.'

'But have the dwarfs ever come so far to dance?'

'Who knows?'

'And at the estancia?'

'It is said that Manuel Cisneros saw them.'

'Have you ever heard that they hunt with dogs?'

'What need would they have of dogs?'

That was all I could get out of him. For Pedro they were real and neither more nor less to be feared than any other unapproachable tribe. For Geronimo they are clearly duendes.

Yet his treatment of the subject differed from the matter-of-fact way in which he usually describes the various spirits which surround us. The llaneros too seem to feel a distinction. They believe, of course, in duendes but will not normally allow them to interfere with their daily life. The dwarfs do interfere. They are responsible for the llaneros' reluctance to travel at night between Santa Eulalia and the estancia, and also for the fact that the grazing west of the marshes and the creek is never used.

I wish Tesoro could speak. There may be some scent from the forest or some trick of the light which alarms horses. That would be enough to create a legend and to cause the abandonment of the estancia through lack of labour. If one's only method of transport proves unreliable without any explanation, one falls back on gremlins like aircraft pilots in the last war. A pity that I cannot materialize some arms and legs on these forest fairies and put them to work on irrigation channels!

April 13th, Wednesday

I have tackled Mario and laid down the law that he is not to frighten Chucha with a lot of nonsense. I got little of interest out of him except confirmation that dwarfs don't climb. That is why he is always mending walls and stopping up holes which a little chap could squeeze through.

He admitted that low morale was the reason for the estancia

being deserted. Cattle grazing in the corridor between creek and forest had been lost. In the llano beyond the marshes, where the line of the trees sweeps away to the north-west, horses had vanished into the darkness and once a man. Why not, I asked, an increase in the number of jaguars following a favourable year for the game? No, the llaneros ruled out jaguars. But why in God's name dwarfs? Because they had been seen dancing. How far away and how much light? Close to the estancia and dark. Any moon? Don't know.

It was all worthless evidence, with a slight bias in favour of actual, physical hunters from the forest. On a starlit night one's eyes pick up movement at, say, seventy yards, and can vaguely recognize size and gait. That is to say, I could not distinguish with certainty a cow from a horse or a puma from a big dog, but I could distinguish a man from any of them.

'So the llaneros killed Manuel Cisneros,' I said in the hope that he would be surprised into confessing it. I could then be sure that they had made up the whole story.

'No, Don Ojen, no! He went away when he could get no one to herd the cattle.'

'Why didn't you go too?'

'What should I do? I am not a llanero. We must eat, Teresa and I and the boys who were then at her skirts. And he gave me the paper saying that I might stay as long as I liked.'

'But all the time you were afraid?'

'Not much. In the day, as you know, what could be more peaceful? At night one must stay indoors. Then there is no danger.'

'How do you know there isn't?'

'Because there never has been.'

Not a satisfying answer on the face of it. But knowledge can only be founded on experience. How do I know there isn't a blue orange? Because there never has been.

My summing up has to be—with a mass of reservations—in favour of pygmies. Here is a picture of them:

1. They are hunters and food-gatherers like the most primitive of the forest Indians. They only leave the shelter of the trees after sunset or before sunrise. Sound enough. That is when the deer, peccary and small game are to be found browsing at the edge of the llano.

2. They will come as far as the estancia in rare and exceptional years when the creek can be crossed.

3. They won't wade (? fear of alligators or eel) and they clearly have no canoes or their presence would have been reported on the river. This is hard to believe. They must have seen canoes and their culture cannot be so primitive that they are unable to build one.

4. They are very timid and won't face a wall. Won't, I think, not can't. Presumably they have observed this place for years and know that it is inhabited by very large men on very strange animals.

5. Tribal dances take place at night on the llano. A forest glade seems a more natural choice; but one must not underrate the power of religious tradition. Perhaps they lived in the open some thousands of years ago.

Having put this down on paper, I feel it adds up to beings as improbable as duendes. You pays your moneey and you takes your choice. But I am determined to know. To be the discoverer of Homo Dawnayensis really would be something!

April 15th, Friday

Teresa tells me that we are shortly going to run out of coffee. That is where Pedro's store was useful. He could always keep us going with staples if I forgot to order in time or the Government Canoe failed to deliver. One would expect some enquiries about him, but it is not surprising that the Intendencia shows no curiosity. I doubt if Pedro transmitted a message a month before I came here. He sent off his reports and did his ordering by the canoe.

Perhaps it is my duty to let somebody know what has happened, since I am the only citizen for miles around who can write. But what with pygmies, fornication and fatherliness I have hardly given a thought to Pedro. I don't know the movements of the Government Canoe—Pedro was the only person who could make a reasonable guess—and I refuse to spend days in Santa Eulalia waiting for the chance to send off a letter. Mañana! One of these days the Intendencia or the Mission will send somebody to see how I am getting on.

We may have had a visit. I woke up at five to hear Tesoro neighing, and some plunging in the corral. So I went out, suspecting that my pair of beauties might have set about Pichón. They do not see why he should have carrots while they get stale bread. Answer: carrots are too precious to be used for wholesale bribery.

I found all the horses sweating. Tesoro had stamped an agouti into the dust. Was the agouti responsible for the excitement, or was there anything else which panicked the horses? My only reason for suspecting there might be is the improbability of an agouti entering our compound at all and then taking refuge in the corral. Mario of course showed no sign of life. He hears nothing and sees nothing, safe from duendes and disturbances behind his closed doors.

I searched the llano with my torch from various points of vantage but saw nothing. When I returned to the house I threw open the shutters on the south side to see if the first grey of morning showed any movements between estancia and forest. It did not. One might as well be out to sea in an absolute calm.

April 16th, Saturday

On the other shore of that sea are a bunch of frightened and murderous outlaws. Should I have foreseen what was on the way to me? I prefer duendes with no politics to men with them.

This afternoon the Cuban and two other fellows, all bristling with automatic weapons, arrived in a jeep—the first motor vehicle I have ever seen in this vast corner of the llanos. They put a lot of trust in their weather man. If the rains caught them in the middle of nowhere, they would have to get back to the Cordillera on foot.

In Santa Eulalia they had found nobody to bully except women and children who did not even understand their questions. Futility and the searing heat had not improved their tempers. Chucha took one look at the party and dashed into the kitchen where she deliberately dirtied her face and hair to give the impression of some sort of half-witted slut working for her food. She instinctively felt that these three sullen revolutionaries had appeared from a traditionless world and might not even have the dubious, vestigial chivalry of the llaneros.

I received them as caballeros, for which they did not give a damn. Marxism is too mannerless a creed for Latin America.

The Cuban wanted to know if Pedro had been killed or not. He had no evidence one way or the other but a pile of ashes.

I said that I had every reason to believe Pedro was alive, failing very bad luck, and explained what he had told me and how he had escaped. 'He was much too frightened of you to give your plans away,' I added.

'How do you know he was?'

'Because any fool could read his thoughts. He never could keep his mouth shut.'

'So it was you who informed the Government?'

I replied that I knew no details. Even if I had, how could I have passed them on?'

'There are aircraft which come down here.'

'Not since your last visit.'

'You expect me to believe that?'

'Go back to Santa Eulalia tonight and ask. At least one horse-man would have seen the plane and by the time it comes down there are always two or three of them on the spot, like ants.'

'Have your servants in!'

He could not let them off without a homily. Mario, Teresa and Chucha were lectured on the joys of a society in which ruthless capitalists would no longer own the land and exploit their labour. I did not point out that Mario was the only land-owner present.

Mario was quite calm and unaffected. He said that not a soul had visited the estancia but Pedro and the llaneros who were after him.

'When did your master last go to Santa Eulalia?'

'On Tuesday.'

'And before that?'

Mario genuinely could not remember. Owing to anxiety over the lack of water and then the arrival of Chucha, I had not been in Santa Eulalia since the guitar-playing evening. He said that the last time the Government Canoe called he had gone himself to meet it.

'What for?'

I was relieved that Mario offered no unnecessary information. He just said that he had gone to fetch our stores.

'Did you send off any letters?'

'Yes, many.'

I interrupted to point out that it was unlikely any of them could have reached Bogotá yet. I was poked in the belly with a machine-pistol and told to shut up.

Teresa came next. Since she never left the estancia, she merely confirmed what Mario had said. If he had claimed to have visited the sun, she would have backed him up. The Cuban disregarded her mumblings and tried Chucha.

'Where do you come from?'

'I am Peruvian.'

'And what do you do here?'

'I am a servant.'

'Do you sleep with the master?'

'Of course.'

'Why of course?'

'Because I like to.'

This reply was too simple for the Cuban. I translated his snort of disapproval to mean that any little Indian would feel affection for any capitalist lecher who was kind to her.

'How did you get here?'

'By the Canoe.'

'Who paid your passage?'

'Captain Valera,' she answered proudly.

She thought all these chaps with guns must belong to the same incomprehensible, ungentle society and that Valera's name would command respect. Her entire conception of politics is that one should avoid policemen. They shut you in gaol until you consent to pull your skirts up.

The Cuban dismissed them all to the kitchen and started to undo his pistol holster. I was not impressed—or managed to persuade myself that I was not. The fellow was irresponsible, but presumably part of a chain of command. I thought it wise to remind him of it.

'I admit that Valera is a friend of mine,' I said. 'But so, I hope, is the gentleman who accompanied you on your last visit.'

'You knew what was planned.'

'I guessed it and told you so frankly, but I could not know time and place. A little logic, friend! Pedro said nothing, but let us assume he did. Then what is the only way I could pass the information on? Through Pedro! So why bring me in at all?'

'It would do me good to shoot you,' he said.

I replied that it was quite safe to shoot me, that my servants would run away and my body would not be found for weeks. He should not be selfish, however. Someone else might like to interrogate me and have the pleasure of shooting me afterwards.

'I shall report to my headquarters,' he said, 'and then come back to fetch you.'

To that I could only answer that I should be delighted to see him at any time, and would he and his party like a few vegetables for their journey?

To my astonishment he accepted them, saying that I was very different to other Anglo-Saxons.

'On the contrary, I am a typical Anglo-Saxon,' I said. 'The Americans are not. They are no more Anglo-Saxon than Filipinos are Spanish. A revolutionary should not confound national origins with language.'

When they had driven away I was left gasping at myself. Insolence combined with extreme courtesy is just the sort of quality which in the French Revolution would have sent an aristocrat to the guillotine next morning. But I am neither aristocrat, landowner or capitalist, and my courtesy is only a flower upon the normal, up-country manners of Argentina. It makes them stop and scratch their heads. Also it emphasizes the superiority of the classless scientist, and that is what they want to believe. Marching together under the Workers' Flag we shall reform society. Balls from the Thoughts of Mao, or vice versa. I shall go and give Chucha a bath.

April 18th, Monday

I am fully occupied by Chucha who wants to be taught to ride and to write. Writing is just a matter of practice. She recognizes the letters and their phonetic values, but cannot imitate them. I can find an exact parallel from personal experience. I know the difference between Estrellera's forearm and Tesoro's, but I'm damned if I can draw it.

Samuel's system of primary education was to teach her words or syllables, not individual letters. The reason seems to have been that they had a couple of books—half a Don Quixote and a Handbook of Butterflies—but seldom any paper. I do not wish to discuss Samuel more than I must. I salute him from a distance. One of his sources of income was the capture and mounting of butterflies. But Chucha, to his credit, was not for sale.

I am getting her used to Pichón before we start on the element-ary aids. Today I took her over the creek, up the west side of the marshes and then across to the forest at a gentle canter. She was so occupied by staying on—or rather by her own pride in staying on without difficulty—that we were only half a mile from the trees before she realized it and squeaked.

I dismounted at once in the shade of a palm—partly because I had already decoyed her nearer to the forest than I thought possible, partly because her blowing hair and the green *chiripá* were sending me crazy. When I lifted her down from Pichón, I found that she was just as impatient. After that first mutual explosion I took the sheep-skin off Tesoro and made her more comfortable while the horses grazed.

It was a good moment to reinforce her growing confidence. I asked her as she lay in my arms why she was so afraid of Mario's ridiculous duendes.

'I am not afraid of anything with you,' she said.

She is not. I wonder what her mental picture of me really is. That remark from a civilized woman would mean nothing. A charming, trivial erotic response. But Chucha means it as sincerely as a child of five. I am No. 2 to God. Fortunately I cannot disillusion her. I write 'fortunately' because I do not know whether I should or I shouldn't.

When we had remounted I took her at her word, and we rode back along the forest; a motionless face of brilliant, light green until the sun disappeared behind the cloud of the tree tops and the continual death of plants became as obvious as the abounding life. It was the same forest that she knew and no more remarkable when seen from a horse than from her rivers. Monotony after monotony, and always safe so long as a man can carry his food and find enough water.

She promised that she would not worry so long as I took Tesoro with me on my explorations of the botanical frontier. It is curious that she should realize his watch-dog qualities when she does not yet recognize exactly how he shows anxiety. He was on edge all the time and fighting my hands, but I was able to pass off his nervousness as greed. I said that he wanted to go closer and see what was edible among such a luscious variety of green stuff. In fact he was set on bolting for the brown llano. He strongly dislikes the forest and is inclined to shy at nothing—which makes him as poor a guardian as a watch-dog which barks at everything.

This evening's ride has cleared the way. I have two objects in wanting to spend whole days in the forest. One is to see if there is any evidence at all of the little hunters. Since I have little field-craft, it would have to be obvious enough for any boy scout—the ashes of a fire, an arrowhead, a blazed tree, something of that sort. The other object is to find a place of refuge for Chucha and myself. I am confident that I can deal with any ordinary bandit and talk him out of unnecessary violence; but political idealists on the run are new to me. It is possible that this obstinate Cuban might return to the estancia with orders to snatch me up to the Cordillera or shut my mouth for good. In that case—assuming I could reach the horses—I should have to try Pedro's trick and find safety for us both in the forest.

April 19th, Tuesday

I must make this a long and exact entry: a record of facts to which I may some day have to refer in public. What public? There is no public. I wish Valera would return or that a plane would come in out of the blue or that some wireless operator would notice that there are never any messages from Pedro. I am here to conduct experiments in tropical agriculture. I am not the secret agent of the C.I.A. or any other bunch of prejudiced whore-cum-spymasters. And I am not to be lied to and double-crossed by a damned mulatto murderer who happens to have read a handbook on the interrogation of suspects—if he can read.

At dawn I saddled Tesoro, who could carry me farther into the forest than I had penetrated by any of my cursory explorations on foot. I knew that, once in the tall timber, the trunks were far enough apart for man and horse, provided always that the rider was not aiming for any particular point and was content to go where he could.

My excuse to Chucha was hunting. We are short of fresh meat. So I took the Lee Enfield on the off chance of meeting deer or peccary. I also took a small bundle of coloured beads, iron nails and dried fish wrapped in a length of the bright green pup-tent. I felt slightly absurd playing at Robinson Crusoe, but it seemed the best method. If I laid out a present in some prominent place and it subsequently disappeared, I could rule out duendes.

I would far rather have taken the mare, but, since Chucha found some special magic in Tesoro, I had to ride him. He began to play up as soon as we had crossed the creek and had to be shown who was boss. The cut passage, through which I had taken Pedro, was already closed by fern and off-shoots from the fallen scrub. I had to use the machete and lead Tesoro with the other hand. After that we had leaf mould under foot and could move generally westwards though never in a straight line. Silence was absolute, proving that two hundred feet above my head the sun was blazing on tree tops and already inhibiting all activity. At dawn and in the cool of the evening I have known the forest as noisy as an ill-organized public meeting.

I was riding more or less parallel to the Guaviare, never turning towards it since the only certain thing about Homo Dawnayensis was that he had never been seen on the banks. Conditions were surprisingly favourable for game, though I saw none. I passed through two glades with good grazing—the first small and entirely open, like a green well in the surrounding forest; the second fairly open, without definite boundaries and gently sloping upwards towards the west. In both I expected to find that game had fed, but there were no droppings except a pat of cow dung —almost certainly from the lost beasts which I had seen on April 3rd and now knew to be stragglers from the guerrilla's herd.

I rode at a good pace up the second glade until I was stopped by a low, overgrown cliff. That was what, sooner or later, I expected to see, for the stretch of grass and parkland could only mean that there was not enough soil for tree roots. When I had followed the outcrop of rock for half a mile to the north, it disappeared and the canopy of the forest closed overhead. It was big timber through which I could easily continue a westerly course.

Here and there to my left I could catch a glimpse of rising ground and thick vegetation, showing that I was travelling along the side of a low ridge where trees were confined to pockets and cracks in the rock, leaving enough light for secondary growth of shrubs. The place was uncannily silent except for Tesoro's hooves. The only sound I heard was unfamiliar—something between a whistle and a sea gull's call. It seemed to come from far away on the other side of the ridge: but among trees it is difficult—for me, at any rate—to tell whether a sound is weak and close or distant and strong. This, I thought, had too much power behind it for a bird. A primitive, man-made instrument?

Soon I could see a confused mass of rocks above me, with grey pinnacles rising out of the jungle which crept and climbed over the lower stuff. These crags looked high enough to give me a view across the tree tops—a rare experience of ethereal beauty. The dark green flows on as solidly as a garden, and eyes insist that one could walk from every dome of blazing flowers to another.

Since Tesoro could easily have broken a leg I tethered him to a tree and left him plunging and protesting. The ridge was a tangle of fallen, rotting trees, of roots, ravines and hollows. Patches of blue sky, red and orange macaws sailing in it with the ease of hawks, tempted me on, but I did not like it at all. Anything —especially snakes—might be living in the dark holes where one could hardly distinguish plant from mineral. I unslung my rifle, which left me only one hand to climb with—and that got fiercely bitten by ants. However, they seemed to be the only inhabitants.

The top was just too low to allow me my view over the trees, but was open, desolate and no doubt a landmark which could be glimpsed from many points in the forest. Facing east was a great sloping slab of rock which I should probably have seen if I had climbed the low cliff at the upper end of the glade. I stripped off moss and cleared the cracks, leaving a whitish patch the size of a billiard table. There I laid out and firmly anchored my square of green nylon, spreading the presents on it. The patch of colour could, of course, attract monkeys who would scatter the lot; but I had neither heard nor seen any monkeys since entering the forest when a band out on an egg-stealing expedition was raising hell among the birds.

The whole place was singularly lifeless, with not even a lizard. The only animal material at all was the point of an antler which I found when scraping earth from the slab. It was worn very smooth. Polished by man? Weather-worn? Or passed through the stomach of scavenger or jaguar?

I am used to desolation and normally excited by it, but there on the rocks I was not. That low plateau was somehow menacing. I felt that I was watched. Any of Joaquin's duendes could have had it all his own way if he had stuck up his sabre-toothed head from a hole or hidden behind a pinnacle. I do not think that human beings would choose to live in such a tangle of primaeval litter when there is shelter on the forest floor, less risk of basking snakes and less annoyance of ants. All the same I have to return to explore further and to see what, if anything, I have attracted. The ridge continues to the south-west, and must be the only landmark between the llano and the Guaviare.

It was now after two and time to turn back. By following the contours I found the head of the long glade without difficulty, and was able to make for the smaller, well-like glade on a compass course. There I allowed Tesoro to graze a little—though he seemed more interested in staying close to me—while I searched on foot for the gap we must have made on our outward journey. I could not find it. We had pushed through giant ferns for the last few yards and the fronds had sprung back into position.

However, it did not matter where we left the glade; so when I spotted a break on the southern side—more a marked difference of foliage than a gap—I decided to try it. A fallen tree had brought the lianas down with it, and a palisade of saplings was growing through the debris. I knew that this mess was not as formidable as it looked, that it would not continue far and that I could easily cut a passage through which to lead Tesoro back into the darkness of the trees.

Once across the fallen trunk I saw to my right the clean cut stalk of a cedar sapling and then a dozen other neat cuts which could only have been made by a machete in experienced hands. It was a thousand to one that I was on the track of Pedro. No one else could have been there so recently.

For a moment I could not believe in the coincidence, but then I saw that there wasn't any. He had entered the forest where I had, and both of us had then taken the easiest route, always going round obstructions rather than over or through them—he, because he wanted to put distance quickly between himself and the llaneros: I, because I wanted to ride as far as possible in a day without much caring where. He had observed the change of vegetation which promised sunlight and more open country and somewhere had forced his way into the glade, no doubt hoping that he was going to find parkland as far as the Guaviare.

When he was at last in the well of grass, he had looked for a possible path to the south and had seen, just as I had, the hopeful break. He cut his way out on a more professional track, round the upturned roots of the tree, so I missed the marks of his machete altogether—visibility being down to about four feet—until I was over the tree and nearly out.

The temptation to see how truly he had headed south ('Pedro needs no compass') was overwhelming, although there could be no trace of his passage until I came to some other barrier. I doubt if even an Indian could discover very much from the forest floor itself. However, I had time in hand and no fear of losing myself. I had only to turn east to arrive at the dividing wall of forest and llano.

There could be little doubt of Pedro's choice of a route once he was clear of the glade. An aisle as straight as that of a cathedral ran south-west for more than three hundred yards until it dissolved into randomly placed trunks. Crossing the end of it, I found a slight suggestion of a narrow path. Since the prevailing gloom of the forest showed no light and shade I could not tell for certain where the leaves had been beaten down and where they had not.

I may have imagined it. If the path existed, it ran fairly straight between the unexplored south side of the ridge and the llano. There were no slots of deer, peccary or tapir and no hoof marks; so bare feet were an attractive possibility. Pedro would have recognized at once whether or not it was a game trail, but would not as yet have gone out of his way to hunt. He was intent on the river, or so I thought, and the going in front of him was open and easy.

I came upon his body at the foot of a tree some distance to my left. The gleam of white caught my eye and I rode towards it, believing it to be a growth of fungus or epiphytes or possibly Loranthaceae. Bits of his clothing lay about on the ground, and the bones had been stripped clean of flesh by black ants which were still at work on it. He was holding his old revolver. An eerie sight it looked when grasped in a skeleton hand. The cause of death was immediately apparent. He had been shot twice at the base of the skull.

I broke open his gun. One round had gone off and the next had misfired. Dwarfs and llaneros were at once eliminated. The former had presumably no fire-arms; the latter, if they had followed up and killed Pedro, would have boasted about it on their return to the estancia. This was plainly a deliberate execution by the guerrillas. Since they could not have found him once he was in the forest, both he and the Cuban had lied to me. When I left Pedro at the cut passage he had been not only escaping from the llaneros but bound for a definite rendezvous.

The more I think of it, the angrier I am. I am too familiar with Latin-America to be horrified by an armed struggle for political power. If men are willing to risk their lives, the strength of discontent is shown more accurately than by the public opinion polls which corrupt and distort our democracies. But cold-blooded execution of a harmless, babbling ex-corporal is another matter. It disgusts me that any human being should be so sure that he has a right to kill.

I examined Pedro's body as closely as I could without disarticulating the bones. No doubt it would have told some sort of story to an expert in forensic medicine; but I could deduce very little from the two bullet holes at the base of the skull, one on each side of the foramen magnum. One could guess at a small calibre weapon. The absence of any severe shattering of the bone was proof that it had been fired at some little distance, probably when Pedro saw a chance to run and took it.

I had the impression that the body, lying in an awkward position with the head slumped against a tree root and both arms flung out, had been left exactly where it fell. In that case the actual bullets ought to be in the skull or on the ground, for there was no exit wound. I could not find them. It was not surprising. The soil around the skeleton had been disturbed by kites and lizards feeding on the flesh. None of the larger carnivores had found the body and cracked the bones, which suggested that there were few of them about.

I had nothing to bury him with, and it was of course impossible to carry back the dry bones on Tesoro. So I had to turn away and leave him under the protection of the little cross which he carried on a thin gold chain round his neck. I blazed trees at intervals on the random route I took back to the llano and made notes of compass bearings wherever obstructions compelled me to diverge from an easterly course. I could not record distances accurately, but I think I shall be able to lead an official enquirer—if there ever is one—to the body.

I hit the llano some two or three miles south of my point of entry and had no exceptional difficulty in getting myself and Tesoro out to the light. Till it was close on sunset I worked away with the machete, cutting and widening a new passage which should be easily recognizable even after a month.

At the estancia all was quiet and there was a rich smell of stew. Chucha admitted that she and Mario had been anxious until they saw me crossing the creek with no shadows following. I told them that nothing could be emptier than this last, lost tail-end of the forests of the Amazon Basin—no game, no dwarfs and no duendes.

I did not mention Pedro, for fear of starting up the oppression of the blank spot. I should have had Mario building walls as fast as a Roman infantryman and Chucha putting on a face like the Mater Dolorosa every time I visited the trees. Teresa is the only matter-of-fact one of the lot. She assumes that my learning is so profound and mysterious that I must know what I am doing.

I wish I did know. I have a strong presentiment that I ought to take the three horses and Chucha and cross the llanos to the River Vichada. But I cannot leave Mario and Teresa without some protection—if only pseudo-aristocratic insolence—against these brutes of guerrilleros. They might come back and cut the throats of the family as pointlessly as they blew Pedro's brains out.

What a curious thing presentiment is! I felt no fear whatever, only pity and anger, when I found Pedro's body although in the gloom of the trees it should have had the crude effect of some dangling oddment in a ghost train. Yet on the rocky plateau, where there was sunlight and not a damn thing to be afraid of, it was an effort to control imagination. In both cases Tesoro's reaction was the same as my own.

April 20th, Wednesday

Today I rode to Santa Eulalia to buy beef. It is not always easy to find unless some llanero has driven home a beast on the previous night for local consumption. The only refrigerator for many hundreds of miles is mine, and meat will not keep in this climate. It is well hung, to say the least, by the time I unload it at the estancia.

I was lucky and got the sirloin and ribs of a heifer. But what a waste! I shall have to throw half of it away, for my refrigerator is small. Those pygmies could have meat for the asking if only there were some way of communicating with them.

I did nothing about Pedro's wife. God knows if I am right! I have two reasons for allowing her to go on hoping. I feel that the body should not be disturbed until someone in an official position turns up to view it. And if I say that I found him murdered I shall start a flaming argument among the llaneros, very likely to make another widow.

Perhaps my real objection is cowardly and selfish. Since nothing would induce the valiants of Santa Eulalia to fetch that body out of the forest—they dread touching the defunct anyway—I should have to do it myself. I don't mind tumbling poor Pedro into a sack, but my life and work could then become complicated if the National Liberation Army suspected that I had killed him and all the llaneros were convinced that the duendes did.

I called on Joaquin and showed him the antler point which I had picked up, asking him if it was any sort of Indian artefact. He was certain that it was not. He thought it might have worked its way out through the skin of boa or anaconda and been smoothed by the digestive juices.

'Do you think Pedro has reached the Guaviare?' I asked.

'No.'

'What could have stopped him?'

'You know very well.'

'What sort of weapons do they have?'

'None. What meets them dies of fright.'

'Animals, too?'

'Yes.'

I maintained the long silence demanded by Indian manners. I suppose it is not polite to make anyone think. Therefore speech should be confined to essentials. The European believes the opposite. He babbles to conceal the absence of thought.

'Neither you nor I have ever picked up an animal which died of fright,' I said.

'If it is eaten, how do we know whether it died of fright or arrow or bullet or claws or teeth?'

He almost chanted this as if it were the beginning of an epic.

'Did Pedro die of fright?'

'No. He was a brave man. But it is no use to shoot.'

Since Joaquin was inexplicably sure of Pedro's death, I tested him a bit further.

'How many times did he shoot?'

'Once,' he replied with utter, calm certainty. 'Once only.'

I didn't go into that. His explanations, when he can be persuaded to give any, are not intelligible.

'If I were killed,' I asked, 'would you see who did it?'

'No. But it could be I should hear you.'

Some kind of rapport between Joaquin and any of his close friends in their moment of agony seems to me conceivable. It is odd that I should accept this more readily than the obvious solution: that the guerrilleros told, say, some woman who in turn told Joaquin.

I just don't believe it. The news would be all over Santa Eulalia. Pedro's wife would have received a formal visit of condolence, and somebody, hand on heart, would have loosed off some antique oratory. Joaquin's character must also be considered. Though his mind is a rag-bag of superstitions and absurdities—some of them not to be dismissed out of hand—he never makes mystery where there is none.

Certainly Pedro was the most unlikely person to die of fright. It is possible among animals. I have seen a rabbit chased by a stoat until it cowered in terror, incapable of movement. That or something like it is as near as a living creature can get to dying of fright from a natural cause.

I leave out the supernatural. I think one must admit that men have died of fright (Shock? Hypothermia?) because of something they saw. But that begs the question: what is seeing? The eye is only a camera; the picture has to be interpreted by the brain. When the brain has no experience of the object photographed, it interprets the message of the eye as it pleases. So what you think you are recording has far more relation to your beliefs than to the facts. That goes for politicians and policemen on one plane, and for Joaquins on the other. It rarely goes for Pedros.

So home to find Chucha menstruating, damn it! She is far more sensitive on the point than civilized women. One would think that the closer a girl is to nature, the more she would understand that this is the period when she most urgently requires the male. But Chucha's propriety is positively Victorian. Gentlemen do not ask questions. Gentlemen do not kiss whatever may be available. And above all gentlemen do not cuddle and comfort in case the unspeakable should happen. What a lot of nonsense— the most universal and powerful taboo without a single fact to support it.

What astonishes me is that she isn't pregnant. I know that I myself am not sterile, for there is a bitter memory of a doctor's bill which had to be paid in cash when I could least afford it. The sudden change of environment and diet might have affected Chucha's ovulation like that of an animal which cannot breed in captivity.

But how day by day I begin to admire the child! She is not in the least the submissive little person of three weeks ago. She is a proud person. Has love done that for her or have I? The first, of course. I never set out to make a companion of her or suspected that her adolescent, eager intelligence could become as irresistible as her body. I wonder if a gentleman would be permitted to say goodnight provided he made it sufficiently fatherly.

April 21st, Thursday

In the dog-house. All my fault. Not even writing lessons permitted, let alone any other kind. I endeavour to meet Teresa's eyes with an expression of absolute innocence.

April 23rd, Saturday

Again an entry which is put down as a vital record of fact, omitting all thoughts of Mao and self-analysis. It has all turned out better than I dared hope, though if the Colombian had not come along I doubt whether I should be here now.

When I saw the jeep bouncing down from the north over the llano I loaded my rifle and the 16-bore and hid them under the fodder alongside the corral. I knew that in the house I had not a hope of defending myself but if Chucha and I were ever given a chance to run for the horses I might be able to hold off pursuit.

There were three of them—the boss, a driver and that detestable tough I called the Cuban. In fact he turns out to be a Dominican. Why is it that these fearless fellows who dare to resist a dictator cannot resist his methods? Three was quite enough to deal with us. Besides their personal weapons they had a light machine-gun mounted on the jeep.

It was close on sunset when they arrived, so I had to feed them and put them up for the night. I was reasonably polite but cold. If I had been certain that they intended to liquidate me I should probably have been greasily companionable in the hope of arousing some sympathy.

This time I insisted that Chucha should receive my so-called friends. She put on the white outfit in which she had arrived—with a shirt of mine underneath—and took the head of the table. I would not even have her hanging around in the provincial manner and serving the men while they ate. If the Dominican had come alone, I should never have risked this display of my pride in her, knowing that after my death she would be raped and abandoned. But the Colombian was a man of taste—so far as his political creed allowed—and I felt sure that he would take her along to the Cordillera where at least she would belong to him or one of his more decent officers. That was better than dying of disease or starvation in or out of a brothel.

She was too embarrassed to do any talking, but I think she found a secret pleasure in the compliments of the Colombian who gallantly took his cue from me and treated her as the daughter of the house. The driver, a pure Indian, could not take his eyes off her. That also made her feel a bit of a native princess. The situation could easily have fallen into ironic comedy. That it never did was due to her simplicity and her unaffected use of my Christian name.

After our supper I kissed her hand and told her to go to bed. She was quite delightful, giving a little bow to each of the guests. Even the Dominican had to smile and bow back.

'I see that Captain Valera was indeed a friend,' the Colombian said.

'It is a pity that I have not yet been able to say thank you to him.'

He got the point. So did his No 2 about twenty seconds later.

'You must understand, Doctor, that we are always in danger of our lives,' he said. 'We think they matter not only to us but to all America.'

I replied that I did understand, but that it was no reason for interrogating me as if I were a spy for the Government or the Yankees and accusing me of being responsible for Pedro's death when they both knew very well that Pedro had been executed.

'He is dead?'

'When men are shot in the back of the head they usually are.'

'Will you believe me when I swear that I know nothing at all of this?'

'I am not accustomed to doubt a man's word when he is armed and I am not.'

'I wish you would not carry on like someone out of the last century,' he said. 'It must be the influence of the llaneros. None of my friends shot Pedro. I am telling you so. Where is his body?'

'In the forest.'

'Can we go there in the morning?'

'Not in the jeep. But I can mount you both.'

'Then there is no need for more discussion at present. One other demand, and afterwards I trust we can just be guests of a generous host. May we see your generator?'

'It's about enough to keep the beer cold and your beef from going rotten,' I told him, 'plus six electric bulbs.'

I showed my neat little 12-volt generator. He seemed satisfied that it could not be used for a radio transmitter—and probably saw as well that I had no notion whether it could or not. Thereafter our relations were much less formal, but I was far from sure of the Dominican thug.

I told Mario and Chucha that I should leave at dawn for the forest with my friends. Mario did not question my description of them. He was used to the violent quarrels in Santa Eulalia, after which the participants became quite amicable. He showed none of his usual distrust of the forest. He must have reckoned that the three of us together could shoot the teeth out of any number of dwarfs.

The two guerrilleros stood by casually while I lifted fodder to give the horses a bite before starting. I observed with pleasure a tightening of their faces when I picked up my rifle with the muzzle on a level with their bellies. They hadn't a chance of drawing their pistols in time and their driver was far away under the jeep. I pretended to notice nothing and they relaxed.

As soon as we had ridden through my new passage I could see that neither of them had ever before travelled in the forests of the Amazon and Orinoco basins. They only knew the steaming slopes beneath the Cordillera where cliffs, ravines and all the rampant growth make it impossible to leave the track. You can't cut a way up and you can't fall down, and if you stand still long enough you can nearly watch the stuff growing over you.

The monotonous ride through the gloom, where only at intervals did we have to dismount and lead our horses, disturbed them. Life in the tree-tops was just dying down when we left the llano behind. Then came the silence, broken only by an occasional shriek. The Dominican wanted to know whether birds or monkeys were responsible. Neither, I said shortly, and shut up. It was of course a bird.

I did not draw their attention to the blazing of trees which marked the route and never rode close enough to make it obvious what tree I was looking at. They thought I was navigating by compass only and were impressed by my frequent halts to check bearings. I was far from confident that I could find Pedro's body again until I had a glimpse of ferns and knew that I was approaching the well glade.

My sharp turn to the left without any apparent reason made the Dominican suspicious.

'I should like your instructions for the return journey,' he said.

'In case anything happened to me? Just go east!'

It was the edge on his voice which first made me realize that I held all the cards. I don't suggest that they were not brave men. They were. I should never have the courage to fight as an outlaw with a merciless army looking for me. But since they lived on their nerves uncertainty affected them.

When I picked up the natural avenue which led in the direction of Pedro's body I immediately turned away from it and rode through the trees along its line. From that angle it was impossible for them to notice that the avenue was there at all.

This was too daring. I went badly off course, and the avenue was irrecoverable. I was so bushed that I refused to trust the compass. Normally I ignored the slight deviation caused by my rifle and machete, since it was a constant, but I wondered if the weapons of my companions, riding as close to me as they were, could have thrown the reading out too far. So I dismounted, laid my machete on the ground and went off a few yards to take a bearing.

The Dominican picked my rifle out of Tesoro's saddle holster and said with pretended politeness that he would carry it for me. So I, equally politely, smashed our only compass against my right spur. That ensured that I should come out of the forest alive, whatever their reaction might be when faced with the remains of Pedro.

'From each according to his abilities; to each according to his needs,' I said. 'And I need my rifle.'

The Colombian ordered his friend to give it back and reproached me for my lack of trust. I think he was sincere, but he had shown no sign of disapproval. A commander, I suppose, hesitates to overrule his security officer.

As the compass, before I destroyed it, had proved to me that I had managed to turn myself inside out, I rode on slowly until we crossed the avenue. It was then simple to pick up and follow my former route until I caught sight of the gleam of bone.

They examined the corpse like the experts they were. It fell in a heap away from the tree. The last insects left the joints.

'How do you know this is Pedro?' the Colombian asked.

'Because I recognize his revolver and belt. Because the skeleton has only been stripped bare very recently. Because no one else has entered the forest.'

'The llaneros of Santa Eulalia?'

'They do not dare.'

'Why not?'

I was not going to tell him about the pygmies, so I elaborated one or two of Joaquin's cautionary stories. Among his better duendes were ghost jaguars. Since their roar had been left behind in this world, all they could manage was to whistle and mew. Shortly afterwards we heard the piercing wail of an agouti. It was far away, possibly as far as the edge of the glade, but the tenuous sound cut the haunted silence at a most convenient moment.

I was interested to see that the Dominican forgot he was a

Marxist and involuntarily crossed himself. Likely enough poor Pedro, looking a traditional ghost in the half light, had carried him back to childhood fears of voodoo and zombies. Atheism is all right for the white-collared technicians of an urban society, but religion tends to reappear when threatened by ghost jaguars.

'Indians?' the Colombian asked.

'There are none.'

The two wounds at the back of the skull puzzled them. They agreed that Pedro would instantly have crumpled up at the first shot, so why the second? If it was fired to finish him while he was on the ground, the shattering of the bone would be markedly greater around one hole than the other; if it was fired from the same distance as the first, Pedro must have turned his head while falling.

'Machine gun?' I suggested.

They thought that must be the answer, but who the hell could have automatic weapons except I or my unknown friends?

They still, I think, wanted to believe that I had killed Pedro; but nothing made sense. Instead of blaming it on the llaneros I had insisted that they were innocent. Besides, I had shown them the body when I could have denied any knowledge of Pedro's fate. And my firm belief that they had done the deed themselves must have appeared sincere.

'If you two didn't execute him,' I said, 'you had better consider some of your friends.'

'Have any of them been seen here?'

'Never.'

That started an argument between the pair. They agreed that the air attack on the herd was probably due to some big-mouthed partisan talking in the villages and a government spy passing on the good news. As regards Pedro, they grew heated.

'Not even in Dominica would Pedro be considered worthy of death on no evidence!' the Colombian exclaimed.

The other retorted that in Dominica they were not accustomed to have time for mercy. That was how I learned what his nationality was. But neither of them ever gave me their names or nicknames.

Whatever it was all about, I was at last in the clear. So I was prepared to lead them out. If it had seemed to me that Chucha and I were in any danger, I should not have hesitated to gain valuable time by losing them in the forest, even though it meant losing Estrellera and Pichón as well. They might or might not have found out which was east. Even if they did, the chances were that they would have borne away to the right and ridden in circles or perhaps—if they had the sense to give the horses their heads—arrived at the Guaviare and water.

In spite of having no compass I found the way back to the llano in three hours with hardly a check. It was, after all, my fourth journey. I discovered that I could now navigate by the contours and appearance of the roof above me as well as by trees which I recognized.

When we had crossed the creek I asked them if they were now satisfied and would leave me in peace to get on with agricultural development.

'We have no proof one way or the other,' the Dominican answered.

I pointed out that I certainly was not a friend, but that he did have proof I was not an enemy.

'If I were a government agent I could have got rid of you twice today,' I said.

'Twice?'

'I was brought up never to point a gun at anyone—even when extracting it from a haystack.'

The Colombian laughed and remarked that the only thing he was sure of was that in any circumstances I should do exactly what I pleased.

'Well, if you know that, we can understand each other,' I said. 'Some time soon I shall be asked what happened to Pedro. Both the Intendencia and his wife have to know. I shall report precisely what happened, including your last two visits. The first visit is our own business, for you were my guests. I shall also say that I believe neither of you were responsible for Pedro's death.'

The Dominican pointed out that Bogotá would know their identities from my description.

'They will know which two we are,' the Colombian corrected him, 'but not our identities—unless they have them on the file already.'

They went straight off in the jeep in order to put as much distance as possible between themselves and Santa Eulalia before nightfall. The Dominican still distrusted me. If ever he comes here without his boss I should be wise to shoot him first and think afterwards. But I know I cannot do it.

Mario and Teresa hate the pair of them. They are instinctive individualists. If they could express their politics—which they can't because they haven't any—they would be anarchists. Chucha, however, is entirely reconciled to my two so-called friends, having listened to their conversation while I thought she was deaf and dumb with self-consciousness. She said they were good men who were persecuted. How could it be wrong to risk one's life in order that everyone should be equal?

I did not attempt to answer that. She might have understood if I had preached that the end did not always justify the means; but to explain why the end could never be reached at all was too difficult. Her simplicity is utterly different from that of Pedro and almost religious in its anxiety for the helpless. I wonder what would have happened if Karl Marx had founded his fantasies on primitive Christianity. Hippies in place of Political Economists?

This is all to the good because I can now allow her to think that my absences are due to close collaboration with these heavily armed saviours of mankind. I hope she never tells Valera so, or I shall be in trouble with the Government as well.

April 24th, Sunday

Today I set out on Estrellera taking my only other compass which is hardly more than a toy; but since I am not surveying, merely searching at random for signs of unknown pygmies, it is good enough.

When we reached the end of the long glade I hobbled the mare and turned her loose to graze while I scrambled up the low barrier cliff. From the top I could identify the sloping rock where I had laid out my presents, but it was far away and the green square of nylon was invisible.

Progress along the length of the ridge was out of the question. Thick scrub and badly eroded ground. Since nobody knew where I was or ever would, any accident such as a broken ankle could be deadly. So I remounted Estrellera and explored new ground, following the southern escarpment of the ridge.

There at last was game. I heard the distant rustling and clicking of a herd of peccary and caught a glimpse of a great ant-eater. Then, when I was searching on foot for a route to the ridge I put up a swamp deer and dropped it with a fluke of a snapshot right behind the shoulder.

This proved that there must be marsh or a small tributary of the Guaviare somewhere near and probably more breaks in the forest cover. A vegetarian tribe of dwarfs, living on roots and whatever fruit the monkeys dropped from the trees, always seemed to me most improbable. That hypothesis might now be rejected. If they existed, they were hunters. A game warden or zoologist could probably gain some clue to their movements from the presence or absence of the peccary, but I have no experience.

After lashing my deer on Estrellera, I found a ravine up which I could lead her as far as a patch of dappled sunlight. The going was easier than on the northern side, but I was floundering about for over an hour before I reached the flat rock. The nails and beads were undisturbed. The dried fish had gone, which was not surprising. Vulture or tyra or any of the forest rats could have taken it.

The silence on the top of the ridge still brooded, but I was not at all afraid as I had been on my first visit. Then the loneliness of the place possibly affected me. Now, the presence of abundant life in the forest below and the exhilaration of killing my deer stone dead without conscious sighting of the rifle gave a saner self-confidence. One must obviously be cautious among all these holes and boulders, especially when confined in a narrow cleft between rocks, but I have not seen or heard anything bigger than a beetle.

Home without incident. I must have travelled nearly thirty difficult miles. I asked Chucha if she minded being left alone all day. She looked blank. She had never conceived any other possibility. Men work and women stay at home. So they do, for that matter, in London. My question reveals a slight sense of personal guilt, as if I *ought* to remain with her when I have nothing to do instead of dashing out to play golf with dwarfs.

She is not idle. She helps Mario to carry water, and she is cleverer than he is at digging and closing little irrigation channels with the hoe. Her lime sapling, which she treats as her personal baby, is doing miraculously well. The fruit is to be for me. I should be worried if I really believed she was thinking that far ahead. But she doesn't. The fruit is a child's dream gift, and has nothing to do with time.

Within the walls our personal food crops flourish, but all my experimental plots have had it. Grasses, wheats and leguminosae are dead except those which live under controlled conditions (See Journal P. 87 & notes). So my professional work is limited to an hour a day, and the only restriction on my explorations is that I refuse to be too tired at night. She is more desirable than ever as her confidence is freed and her youth dances. She will never be a sensualist. Too loving. Her sexual excitement, which becomes more frequent, shakes her but is quiet. A profound giving rather than a desperation.

Where the devil are the rains? With reasonable luck we should have had the first storms. My prospective little labourers can be of no immediate use now. But next year?

April 25th, Monday

Today I took Chucha into the forest. I shall not take her there again until I clearly understand what danger, if any, it holds.

During last week I was not able to give enough time to her riding. If we ever had to get out of here in a hurry, it would be on Tesoro and Pichón with Estrellera for a pack-horse. That would be a lot safer than a canoe out of Santa Eulalia. I don't know the shoals and rapids, nor how long it would take us to reach any sort of settlement.

She has a good seat and is getting on well. Pichón, like an old soldier, is inclined to take advantage of her gentleness. Today he nearly bucked her off just to see what would happen. What did happen was a beauty from me on his fat quarters. Chucha must learn to use the quirt herself when required.

After a few exercises we cantered straight across to the forest, entered through my first passage and then struck north-west. I had not intended to go far from the grass, but a fearsome tangle of lianas forced us away into the big timber. As a result of her travels she was able to put a Spanish or Portuguese name to birds I did not know and to identify several small noises in the tree tops. She also spotted rubber.

When we had ridden four or five miles through the darkness, the big timber opened out gradually into beautiful parkland without any definite wall of low, impenetrable growth. Here was a deep bay of the llano with what will be splendid grazing after the rains. Some small deer were over on the far side, extremely alert so that we only got a glimpse of them.

The going was safe, so I let her canter straight across the bay. She pulled up—or Pichón did—where the trees began to thicken again. I was tempted to show her what my intelligent Tesoro could do: gymkhana stuff which both he and I enjoy. Given his head he will go through timber, zig-zagging like a startled snipe, seldom needing a touch and obeying it instantly. This time I was paid out for exhibitionism. He shied so violently that I nearly went over his withers.

What alarmed him was the carcase of a big bullock, lying half in and half out of a clump of thorn. There at last was certain evidence of jaguar. The neck was dislocated, the ribs were broken and one hind quarter had been completely torn off. The skin, where it was exposed to the sun, was dried and hard. Back and rump showed the stripes of the claws where the jaguar landed. The fore part of the beast was picked nearly clean.

Rats and a largish lizard—of some species which I do not know—were worrying at the remaining flesh under the safety of the thorns.

There was still a noticeable furrow in the grass along which I assumed the jaguar had dragged the haunch. I told Chucha to wait for me well out in the open and followed up the trail with some vague hope of getting a shot, though the jaguar must have finished his meal days earlier and would now be far away looking for another.

What I actually reached was the scene of the crime, showing that I do not yet know enough to be sure which way an animal went, towards me or away from me. The bullock had charged into the thickest stuff he could find, going through it like a bull-dozer in the hope of scraping the jaguar off his back. Further on, a patch of shrubby growth twenty yards across was beaten down in evidence of the fight. The jaguar must have been hungry to tackle the bullock at all, a much heavier and more powerful beast than the peccary and deer which were his usual prey. He had at last killed it, eaten what he wanted and then dragged the whole beast into the thorns.

I returned to the kill to see what more I could discover. Since he had not left the remains of the haunch at either spot, he must have taken it with him. It looked as if he had been disturbed while in the middle of breakfast.

Unless he had taken to the open llano, which was unlikely, there was only one way he could have gone: through a marked tunnel in the forest wall, which on that side of the bay was thick. I could not tell whether he made the tunnel or merely used it. It led me on hands and knees back into the forest. And there, not more than fifty yards from the outside world, were the haunch and the jaguar.

The accident which caused his death seemed obvious. He had jumped for a branch some twenty feet above his head, using the trunk of the tree to get there as the slashes made by his claws revealed. The branch had broken and was hanging down. It was an odd way for any cat to die; they do not misjudge the strength of branches, and even a heavy jaguar, powerful enough to drag a bullock, would surely only be winded by a fall on to softish ground.

He might have intended to store the haunch in an upstairs larder, but its position some little distance away suggested that he had dropped it before he jumped.

Birds had torn open throat and belly, but had by no means finished their job of clearing up. Curiosity compelled me to brave the stench. When I examined the back to see if it had been broken by the fall I felt a sudden revulsion as if an agile centipede had threatened my hand. It was overwhelming surprise rather than nervousness. The jaguar's death was similar to Pedro's, though not an exact parallel. The beast had been shot from a flank, either on the ground or in the act of springing. The bullet had pierced the spine at the top vertebra rather than the base of the skull, and there were two neat wounds. This could be meaningless coincidence. I think it was. The projectile had probably been deflected by the skull and emerged nearly opposite to the wound of entry.

Two possibilities presented themselves: (1) that the pygmies had developed a far more efficient bow than other Indians—a weapon at least equivalent to the old English longbow and war arrow—or that they had a heavy spear and spear-thrower. Alternatively they netted their game or entangled the legs with bolas, then despatching even such dangerous enemies as the jaguar and Pedro with dagger blows at the base of the skull: (2) that somebody in fear of his life from government or guerrillas was living in the forest and competing with the other carnivores for food. He was evidently a first-class shot and would not go hungry. He may well have wanted a steak of that fresh-killed beef.

The latter hypothesis seems the more likely. Pedro mistook him for one of the llaneros, took a shot at him and was instantly killed in return. On the other hand Mario, Pedro and Joaquin have all talked of dancing dwarfs. If I reject this story entirely, I fall into the common scientific error of postulating a complicated cause when the available facts point to a more simple and elegant solution.

I went back for Tesoro and then joined Chucha on the llano. She had not been at all alarmed by the carcase of the bullock, which was as it should be. She was familiar enough with the remains of beasts stranded on the river sand-banks along with other flotsam. When I told her of the dead jaguar, she was eager to see it. There may have been a purely Indian touch of triumph over the dreaded enemy.

To avoid the labour of cutting a way for the horses we rode through the border of parkland on the south side of the bay and then made the circuit through the trees. When at last I found the animal, nose helping where eyes failed, I asked her if she thought it could have been killed by Indians—on the off chance that she might have heard how the river tribes tackled a jaguar. She did not know, but believed they would have cut out the claws for personal decoration. She made the intelligent suggestion that the holes might have been made by a vulture hammering with its beak to get at brains or marrow. Not a bad theory for the jaguar, but I won't have it for Pedro. His wounds were too neat.

She never questioned my explanation, backed up by the broken branch, that the jaguar had been killed by its fall. She took the episode as a mere casual curiosity. It looked as if I had cured her of any obsession with dwarfs and duendes.

On our way home I noticed that the merciless, lunar heat of yesterday and today had put an end to the creek. It was a chequerboard of cracked, dried mud as hard as a brick pavement. Even the horses left no recognizable hoof-marks. I wish now that I had regularly ridden up and down the banks while there was still enough mud to show tracks. That would have been more sensible than searching the forest at random. Perhaps I have accepted too readily this won't-cross-water stuff. One is hypnotized by the desolation of the llano in the searing sunlight. Even at night I have seen no animal life but one agouti and one puma/dog.

Early tomorrow I shall ride to Santa Eulalia, leading Pichón, and see if I can persuade Joaquin to come out. He has not been here for weeks. There are untranslatable scufflings in the dust which may mean something to him.

April 26th, Tuesday

A more or less successful day—though Joaquin is firmly set against any suggestion of small, bare feet and will not discuss the unmentionable. The trees are too near to talk indiscreetly about duendes, which do not, anyway, leave visible tracks.

Chucha was far from impressed by him. Joaquin is the last ragged remnant of the shamans of primitive food-gatherers whereas she descends from the Children of the Sun. She does not herself express the difference like that, since in fact she knows far less than I do of her Peruvian ancestors. She merely says that Joaquin is a filthy old pig who is too fond of the demon rum. He is a pig, but a most interesting one. I suppose one must be secure upon the heights of civilization before one can start stirring up the bottom levels with profit and pleasure.

As soon as Joaquin arrived I had to feed and mildly intoxicate him. What he wanted was to eat food from cans, especially the more colourful and tasteless American emergency rations. With such luxuries about, it was no use to offer him a steak of swamp deer, lovingly tended by Teresa over a charcoal fire and brushed with chilli sauce from an old tobacco tin. I was compelled to wait patiently until he had stuffed himself and slept, so we had not time to go far up or down the creek.

His examination was impressively professional. He translated the scuffles in the dust as rats and a capybara—which had been lying in the rushes for some time until it finally decided to get the hell out into the damper forest. I gathered that I was a disgrace for not shooting and eating it. I have never even seen it.

No deer. No peccary. Remains of a porcupine which had been turned over on its back by somebody's quick and daring paw and eaten out. Joaquin thought one of the smaller felines was probably responsible. He showed me a snake track which had ruffled the surface of the creek more plainly than feet, and told me how I could distinguish between the venomous snakes and the constrictors. The slow wriggles of the former made a wider path than the fast, hunting wriggles of the latter.

He also found the light imprint of a biggish clawed foot in what had been mud a few days before. Not puma, he said; it was an animal which chased its prey rather than stalked it, because it had five digits. It could be the track of the giant Brazilian otter, he thought, and the web might not show. I again talked around the question of dogs, not mentioning duendes but knowing that

Joaquin would remember my inquisitiveness of two weeks earlier.
He refused to be drawn, only saying sententiously that dogs could
live tame or wild.

When we got back to the estancia he distinguished himself
by asking if I would give him Chucha when I left. He reminded
us that his wife was dead and proudly patted his pants, assuring
us that he had an excellent erection as well as a house. He was
prepared, he said (being now full of rum) to fertilize any of my
laboratory plants which needed such intimate magic. Before
Chucha's arrival I should probably have encouraged him to go
ahead and measured results, if any. But simplicity in the male is
not so attractive as in the female. I may be wrong in calling it
simplicity. Joaquin's ritual mating with food plants is religious
and therefore essentially complicated.

I had to get him away in good time. No estancia after dusk
for Joaquin! He fell off twice on the way back, quickly remounting
in case he should go to sleep where he was. Then I rode Pichón
home through the early night, leading Estrellera. That's forty-
eight miles in the day, and they are only healthily tired. Mario
is at his old tricks again and insists that I must not travel after
sunset. He gave me the impression that there is still some part
of the Manuel Cisneros story which I have not heard.

April 27th, Wednesday

A statement of intention to be compared with what actually
happens—generally a source of amusement and disillusion!

It is obviously useless to spend a night in the pitch blackness
of the forest, and explorations by day very possibly frighten
away whatever I am trying to find. If I want to catch Homo
Dawnayensis going about his business I must watch the border
of forest and llano at dusk or dawn when its abounding life is
active.

My choice would be the bay of parkland where Chucha and
I found the dead bullock, somewhere within sight of that tunnel.
But it would mean starting improbably early without any good
excuse. Nearer home, just inside my first cut passage, there is a
half dead caju tree choked by lianas and easy to climb. From
the top I shall have a fair view of the llano and of patches of the
forest floor between the trunks. Meanwhile Estrellera can graze

in peace. She has no nerves and will reach up and munch any tall tuft of grass instead of shying at the rattle of the seeds like Tesoro.

I wish it was not necessary to lie, but for the time being it is. I have announced that I shall be off in the dark tomorrow morning to catch a morning flight of geese far up the marshes. Mario considers the east side safe. Actually—if one wades—it is the only dangerous place for miles. Electric eel and sting ray must be in a filthy temper, assuming they have tempers, at the shrinking level of the water.

Walking to the caju tree is too slow, so I must take Estrellera though I would rather not. There's a risk of her fetching up in a cooking pot if hunting dwarfs exist. Alternatively, if they don't, my hypothetical outlaw has an excellent chance of riding off to Venezuela. A corollary to that. If he wants to escape, why doesn't he sneak over the wall and steal a horse? Or is he a tropical Herne the Hunter who enjoys living where he is? Nothing makes sense.

April 28th, Thursday

What you think your eye is recording has more relation to your beliefs than to facts. I had in mind, when I wrote that, the forest duendes compounded of one half vegetable and one half fear. So I must be very careful. I think that what I have seen is conclusive, but the light was bad, the foliage thick, and my excitement was so mixed with cowardliness that I could not separate them. Probably psychic researchers feel the same, and therefore cold, material evidence is harder to come by than it need be.

I started at 3.30 a.m., taking the 16-bore, chiefly because I had to be seen carrying it when I returned to the estancia. It is also a fast and deadly weapon for self-protection at close quarters when loaded with No 2 shot. I wanted No 4 for geese, but could find none in Bogotá. No 2 turns out to be right for medium-sized ground game.

A half moon was setting which made it unnecessary to use a torch until I was beneath the caju tree. There darkness was absolute, and I had to show light in order to see exactly where I was and what was inhabiting the tree. I disturbed three or four marmosets which cleared off with faint squeaks of protest. The only other sound was of Estrellera crunching dead stalks a safe hundred yards away.

It was still dark when I settled myself in a triple fork of the tree some thirty feet above ground. There was a very light breeze blowing from the forest, so that nothing could scent me or see me. I would of course have been heard—but that was as likely to attract as to repel any creature which lived by hunting. The first chorus of birds began. Before the howler monkeys drowned out all other sounds I heard the very distant call of a jaguar and again that full volumed, tenor whistle which had puzzled me the first day on the ridge.

Life was all in the tree tops except for doves and finches working along the edge of the llano. There was no ground game about at all. This should be significant, but I know too little of the reasons why sometimes there should be plenty and sometimes none. From what I have read of Africa, a lion's kill does not frighten the herds into running far; on the other hand hunting by man can clear the district.

But I doubt if any parallel can be drawn. There are no herds under and just outside the trees but peccary.

Behind me to the east the grey light was growing. I could not help suffering from a compulsive instinct that I had been seen and that eyes were looking at me. I reminded myself that a dozen creatures were probably looking down at me from the roof of the forest and wondering whether the very large monkey was harmful.

I did not feel affected by loneliness as I had on the north side of the ridge, and I can rule that out as a cause of possible hallucination. If there was loneliness it was nearer to the anxiety neurosis of a man in a fairground, unamused by the racket going on around him and resentful of a crowd safe and completely unconcerned with him. Eyes were certainly unsettled by the impact on ears, so that, instead of quiet, thorough observation, I was continually glancing upwards and at the same time trying not to move my head.

To my left I could see a lot of the forest floor before the tree trunks closed the view. To my right front was a nightmare of lianas, which could have passed as an abstract painter's impression of dying forest. No one who did not know the reality would guess that the bare streaks radiating down from the top left hand corner to fill the whole canvas were photographically exact. The lianas, black, grey and dark green against a background of grey and blacks, fell straight as storm rain, then curving away from the trees to their own roots. Seen from my height the pattern was as complicated as that of a vast rush basket.

Beyond and through this tangle I twice thought I saw movement. Distance could not be estimated, for thin ropes and thick ropes were so intermingled that perspective was unreliable. When I spotted the duende, it was not less than thirty yards away. I could not have seen it at all unless at the same time it had been trying to get a clearer view of me. I was reassured by our common motive of curiosity. It was really there.

It was not a monkey. It was dancing up and down to look at me from behind liana stems which approached the horizontal. No American monkey would have done that, but would have pulled itself up by arms or tail. It was not the butt of a rotten liana in an inexplicable state of instability, for it had a face. It was a dwarf all right, but unfortunately I could never see the face in profile which would have helped me to decide whether he was as human as myself or somewhat lower down the family tree.

His ears were not prominent. He seemed to have a small beard, but the light was so bad that I could not tell its colour or the colour of skin. Height was impossible to judge with any precision. Assuming he was standing on the ground and that the rest of him was proportionate to head and shoulders I reckon height as not less than forty-two inches, not more than fifty. The eyes were indistinguishable but the straightforward stare seemed to make binocular vision quite certain. The jack-in-the-box jumps were rather like those of a stoat or weasel popping up to get a view over intervening undergrowth. If that is the dwarf's technique of hunting, one might easily get the impression of a dance. I may have been looking at two of them. I think now that I was.

It was my usually quiet Estrellera who demoralized me. There was a hardly perceptible freshening of the dawn wind. At once she neighed in alarm and was off across the llano with the painful, clumsy rabbit hops of a hobbled horse. Up till then I had been fascinated and half sceptical—still ready to accept one of the startling freaks of radical leaves which account for most deundes —but now I remembered that I was a sitting target against the grey gold of dawn and that, as Estrellera's behaviour proved the dwarfs to be real, the missile which stopped a jaguar could be real too. Leaving that out, one of the normal weapons of the forest Indian is a curare-tipped dart shot from a blow-pipe. A deep scratch, and that—at any rate for birds and monkeys—is it.

However, I had undoubtedly been seen, so nothing would be lost if I could summon up enough guts to show myself openly and emphasize my peaceful intentions. In case they knew what a gun was, I laid it across two branches behind me and stood up with hands spread out and down, which I hoped was an inter-human gesture that they would understand. I then beckoned to him or them to approach. I also threw down my machete and made faces to indicate that it was a present.

Nothing happened. I was aware of the utter inadequacy of my attempts to communicate, yet I suppose the Conquerors when meeting potentially hostile Indians could do little better. I kept telling myself that if anyone got up from behind the lianas to shoot at me I should have time to swing round the trunk into cover. It then occurred to me that any hunter, having once attracted attention to the lianas, would make a circuit into the open woodland and shoot from behind a tree. I had no possible cover from that side; so I forced myself to wave a hand and smile a sickly smile like royalty from a glass coach, shinned down the tree into the bushes and got out fast by the cut passage.

Estrellera was still legging it across the llano, which gave me an excuse to run after her. When I caught her she was damp with sweat and needed a lot of gentling before I dared untie the hobbles. Why on earth should she have been so terrified? For her anything vaguely human is a possible friend carrying possible nourishment. I have known her extend her lips towards a large tame monkey in the hope of getting half his sweet potato. It was the monkey which was alarmed by her greedy and affectionate approach.

Do the dwarfs anoint themselves with jaguar fat or glands? An ingenious theory which would account for her instinctive dash away from the edge of the cover. My own sense of smell— invaluable for detecting fine botanical distinctions—is exceptionally well trained, but the richness of the forest border at dawn drowns all individual scents. I think that I did pick up a faint, musky effluvium, though I cannot be quite sure.

I did not ride home immediately since Mario and Chucha would have noticed that I came from the forest, not from the east side of the marshes. So I walked Estrellera along the wall of trees—well out of range—with the red ball of the sun now hurling its first heat at us. When we were south of the estancia and out of sight I crossed the creek. It is possible that the dancers were moving on a parallel course. The monkeys were certainly hurling abuse at something below.

Teresa's scrawny and hideous hens had been doing their duty while I was away, so there was an excellent and very welcome breakfast. My violent prejudice against canned foods admits one exception. American bacon is superb. Chucha wanted to know why I had no geese and why I came from the south. That was easy. I told her that I had slipped the wrong cartridges into my pocket and found it out too late; so I had gone down the creek in the hope of putting up a capybara in the rushes.

I had to open up a couple of cartridges and show her the difference between No 2 and No 5. She was not suspicious. The little love is always eager to understand what I am doing and why I do it, and I am as eager to satisfy her curiosity. Chuchas taught to university standard might be a greater gift to the world than wheats which resisted our extremes of drought and tropical rain. But one dream is as fantastic as the other. I doubt I shall live to see the day when there are sheets of water above the dams and mile after mile of crops and homesteads on the llanos. And I wonder if the hunting ape which is me would not then be homesick for the remembered heat and emptiness.

It occurred to me while conducting on the breakfast table our elementary demonstration of the weight and diameter of lead shot that there was an explanation of Pedro's wounds which neither I nor the two guerrilleros had ever thought of. If the weapon which killed him was a shot gun fired at fairly close range there would be nothing out of the ordinary in two pellets striking him simultaneously and side by side while the rest of the pattern missed. The same goes for the jaguar; but one must assume much heavier ball than that of any normal cartridge. This theory suggests an old muzzle-loader—just the sort of thing which pygmies would be expected to have. But how do they trade for powder and ball when nobody has ever recorded their existence? It won't do.

In the cool of the evening, some four hours ago, I rode out to see what had happened to the machete. I did not think that the dwarfs would still be in the neighbourhood but, if they were, I should have plenty of warning from Tesoro. I should not get him anywhere near the edge of the forest without a major conflict of wills.

He showed no more nervousness than usual at leaving the llano. Beneath the caju tree my machete lay where I had dropped it. I put it back in its sheath and then explored on foot, leading Tesoro. The rush basket of lianas seemed to be the apex of a very rough triangle, stretching away to the north-west. Chucha and I had ridden along the inner side of it.

I found and closely examined the spot where the pair of little people had been. I could clearly see the top of the caju and the fork in which I had been sitting, but anyone eighteen inches shorter could not and would have to jump up and down unless he climbed on to the prostrate lianas and exposed himself fully. Nothing was to be seen, no tracks, no trace of cutting, no small possession dropped. The tangle was so thick that only a bird or an arrow could have reached me in a straight line. To arrive at the caju tree the dwarfs would have had to make a circuit through clean, close timber. I suspect that they were doing so—with what intentions one cannot guess—when my nerve broke and I took quickly to sunrise and the open llano.

More precautions for my own safety as well as more tact will be needed. I must assume that the pygmies have for centuries observed white men on their horses and Indians in their canoes and that contact, when there was any, proved abrupt and bloody. Take, for example, the melancholy experience of gorillas in Central Africa ever since du Chaillu shot the first of them little more than a hundred years ago. Their opinion must be that we are barbarous apes who pay no attention to the civilized gestures of a decent and respectable paterfamilias. Has anyone ever been killed by a gorilla? Certainly not, provided he obeyed gorilla convention and retired when requested to do so.

I should try to encourage Homo Dawnayensis to visit us and then open communications while remaining in the shelter of the walls. I wonder if prime, fat duck would not tempt him.

April 29th, Friday

I took the beginning of the evening flight and got a fair bag in time to lay out the gifts before it was completely dark. I spread out half a dozen duck on our side of the creek just at the point where I always cross, now beaten hard by hooves. Nearer to the estancia I put a brace of geese and fresh bread; and then, at about a hundred yards from the gate, some bits of pup tent with teal. If any of this should go, I shall soon have them round clamouring

for rations like robins on a window sill. Obviously a rifle must
be close to my hand until I know more of their weapons, but it
should never be necessary to use it.

I am now going to sit up and watch with Chucha. I have let
her into the secret and explained that the absurd duendes of
Mario and Joaquin are as human as ourselves, that I have seen
two of them with my own eyes and that once they come to trust
us they will turn out to be as harmless as other Indians.

April 30th, Saturday

A little after eleven we opened the heavy shutters of one of the
windows which give directly on to the llano. The night was
silent with the stars singing. Insects, which become a bearable
nuisance by the end of the dry season, left us in peace. We had
an oblique view to the south of the estancia: an expanse of low,
dead grass with no cover of any kind except the old rubbish tip
beyond and to the right of the gate. There was no moon. The
brilliant starlight enabled us to detect movement up to at least
two hundred feet.

Sitting so still and so close, we came near to absorption into
the silence. Whether it was a mystic peace or an animal peace I
do not know, and it is possible that they are the same. I will call
it a peace of Eden from which we could advance to the still wider
unity of llano, forest and our neighbour, the Andromeda nebula,
in that clear air shaped rather than misty to the naked eyes.

Our mating was inevitable without definite approach from
either side, then still, intense, utterly motionless. Why is there
no word in English but the wretched "Orgasm" which smells
about equally of the medical school and the brothel. I have never
known that a physical sensation so pure and immeasurable could
exist, as if the spirit were using the body for its own purpose
rather than the normality which is the other way round. Our
reason for being part of the night was all forgotten since we were
the young night itself.

A fine pair of nature watchers Chucha and I would make!
When we returned to our bench as silently as we had fallen from
it, they were there for us, but at the very limit of vision. The
black outline of the rubbish tip was broken. We both saw the
two torsos—though with no more detail than logs of wood—

jumping up and down with the curious movement which could be a hunting technique or a primitive form of the dance.

I did not dare use a torch for fear of frightening them away. When they vanished behind the mound and did not reappear, I was about to attempt speech. Chucha actually did so, in a few musical syllables which I could not understand. She told me afterwards that it was Aymara and that she was appealing to them not to be afraid. They were more likely to recognize Spanish than Aymara, but the gentle voice made her meaning plain whatever she spoke.

The scent had its usual effect on the horses, and I dashed out to restore confidence. Pichón was the craziest, trying to break out of the corral, a rail of which he had already smashed. The other two hate and fear the smell of the forest people, but by now must be more accustomed to it. I partly calmed them and then looked over the wall to see if our visitors were near. They were not, but I again glimpsed an indefinable patch of night cantering away from the direction of the rubbish tip. Cantering best describes the motion. The back of the shadow, so far as it had any outline at all, seemed to be rising and falling more than that of a dog which stays fairly level. The felines come nearer to this flexible, concertina action and I should vote for puma rather than dog if I were not sure that this animal belongs to the pygmies.

May 1st, Sunday

I have left Chucha to take her siesta alone. I wonder if she, too, feels that we have reached a summit of perfection which we shall never approach again. In God's name, why wouldn't she? But she would not leap to masculine immoderation as I do or ever admit, being a woman, that the future cannot equal the past.

That, however, is not the only reason why I have been sitting at the laboratory desk through the hours of heat. It is conducive to thought, and I must think urgently.

When the sun rose, Chucha and I went out to see what had happened to the peace offerings. The feathers of some of the birds were slightly disturbed, but that was all. Though birds are a major item in the diet of all forest peoples, there could be several explanations of why they did not take them. The wild fowl of the llano might be unfamiliar. Or they might consider them carrion, possibly poisoned. How were they to know that the birds were fresh shot and a purposeful gift?

But that was not my problem. What has been occupying my thoughts is the dog/puma. It could have no objection whatever to fat duck killed that evening. Yet the dog did nothing à la Sherlock Holmes. Like a trained spaniel? Nonsense! The solution in the end stuck out a mile. There never was any dog/puma. What I saw on both occasions was a "dwarf" running. He must be an anthropoid which goes on four legs when in a hurry, or else an animal which stands up on two when looking over obstacles.

Once that is accepted, everything falls into place. But I have decided to say nothing until I am quite clear in my own mind. Meanwhile this diary alone will be the inventory of conjectures and material evidence.

Now that the creek is completely dry our friends can stroll over any night to inspect us and leave no tracks. If only I had realized earlier that my dwarfs were nearer duendes—though solid enough—and that even two weeks ago there were muddy patches to reveal where they were crossing, I could have settled all doubts. This may be a nightmare, but I am going to assume that when Chucha leaned out of the window after that first dinner she was spotted and stalked, and that the scent of the horses has attracted duendes on several occasions to a likely source of meat.

I deduce considerable speed and courage, for the jaguar did not stand, preferring to leave its kill and snarl from the safety of a branch. It may have been momentarily winded when the branch broke or it may have been hurt in the struggle with the bullock; but still it was a full-grown jaguar and it was killed by a bite through the spinal column.

It is now so obvious—and always should have been—that the two holes at the base of Pedro's skull were not made by any bullets but by two slender and powerful canine teeth.

May 2nd, Monday

Yesterday before sunset I ordered Mario to stable the horses in the hall at night as he had done when Valera's party were here. Chucha has already announced that we saw small Indians. She is more excited than afraid. From her point of view they are nervous, pitiable little creatures who screw up their courage to look at the estancia and then run. I have let it stand at that.

Mario asked no questions, merely saying that he had heard the horses plunging and heard me go out to them. I suppose he and Teresa checked doors and windows and pulled the common blanket over their heads. It is plain that I can never call on him for help if needed. He is right. A machete would be a useless weapon in the dark, even if one forced attack from the front by keeping one's back against a wall.

Having admitted that precautions should be taken for the safety of the horses, I could talk more frankly than when I pooh-poohed all his dwarfs and duendes. It was essential to find out whether he knew any solid facts at all.

'Have you ever lost so much as a hen?' I asked.

'No, Don Ojen.'

'Then why do you shut yourself up at night?'

'Because the master told me always to do so.'

'What did he know?'

'It was just that the llaneros would not go into the woods after the cattle.'

'Did they ever see what was taking the cattle?'

'It is said that Don Manuel did.'

Always this exasperating 'it is said'! I asked him what the llaneros themselves thought. He replied that they would not talk about it after one of them had been lost, horse and all.

'That bit of paper of yours—when did Don Manuel give it to you?'

'Before he rode away for the last time.'

'He had ridden often into the forest?'

'Just as you do.'

'The llaneros had left already?'

'You know it is hard to say if a llanero has gone or has not gone. Some stayed on the east side of the marshes and rode in for their food and money so long as we had some to give them.'

'So Don Manuel tried to kill the dwarfs?'

'He never said they were dwarfs.'

'Then who did say it?'

'Perhaps those who saw them. Perhaps Joaquin.'

'Was Don Manuel's body ever found?'

'Who would go and look for it?'

'Yet apart from the cattle and one llanero who may have

ridden off to find himself a woman, the dwarfs have never done any harm to anyone.'

'Who knows?'

'Then why did Don Manuel tell you to shut yourself up at night?' I asked, returning to the only solid ground.

'Well, look! I will tell you his words. He said to me: Mario, my valued gardener, take this paper which says that if I do not return you may stay here. And if you do not cross the creek and shut your door tight at night, you and Teresa and the boys will never have anything to fear.'

'How much of this have you told to the señorita Chucha?'

'I? Nothing! A wise man does not mention such things. But she is often with Teresa, and how should I know what women speak of?'

That means, of course, that all along Chucha has known much more of the disappearance of Cisneros than I ever did. When she told me that with me she was afraid of nothing, she was already convinced that there was a nasty something to be afraid of. I wish I were not her god. What have I ever done except to show a lost child that her individuality is as precious to me as her body?

Cisneros. Yes. He had to protect his livelihood and get his llaneros back. I don't know if he too had anything particularly valued in the estancia itself. At any rate he was confident that stout doors and shuttered windows were enough.

Since the rains and a full, roaring creek cannot be much more than a week away, I should perhaps be content to leave the forest to itself and to accept that blank spot which haunted me for so long. But I am not content. Damn it, I am a scientist of a sort! It is my business to add to knowledge.

I rule out any form of anthropoid ape and any Lost World stuff. I do not yet rule out pygmies, remembering stories of Leopard Men. I think they went on all fours to kill. Even if I am wrong in that, there is no form of ritual killing which human beings haven't indulged in. War, after all, is at bottom a ritual with ever more obscene ways of giving death.

Nor do I entirely rule out a whole series of coincidences: that Pedro was in fact executed by guerrilleros; that the jaguar was killed by a combination of a fall and a bullock horn which had nearly but not quite severed the spinal cord; that among the score of species of monkeys there is one which will come down from the trees and on to the llano at night. Time in this emptiness is still geological. No Colombian or Brazilian who has travelled the forests would lay it down dogmatically that the giant sloth no longer exists. And what about the mastodon, thought to be extinct before man crossed from Asia? Yet there is now some evidence that it was in fact tamed and used by the Mayas.

So I shall go ahead with an open mind. At the moment research in tropical agriculture is about as useful as it would be in the middle of the Sahara; amateur research in zoology might as well take its place. I am convinced that the ridge holds the key. It is far from a unique formation, but reasonably rare. The cover and shelter of those overgrown rocks with long glade below, parkland to the north and more parkland lower down the creek, all supporting game, make an excellent base for a carnivore.

May 3rd, Tuesday

I had to take a horse—since my little world would have asked too many questions if I started out on foot—so I rode Pichón till I was near the edge of the forest and out of sight of the estancia. Then I hobbled him and left him well out on the llano where he would be safe till evening.

My original passage under the caju tree offered a much quicker route to the glades and the ridge than the blazed trail further south leading to Pedro's body. I forced a new way into the well glade without much difficulty and slashed down the ferns so that I should be able to recognize it on my return. Once I had passed from the well glade into the long glade I was much slower on foot than riding, but I lost less than half an hour in all and avoided the responsibility of looking after a horse as well as myself.

I made myself comfortable on top of the low cliff at the western end of the glade. Since I had learned that anything white catches the eye in the forest, I kept my face well under cover of leaves, picking off enough to give me a view of most of the glade on one side and the flat rock on the other. I did not expect to see a 'dwarf'. I might have to wait weeks for a clue to how and where they can be observed in daylight. But I did hope that the movements of game would give me a line, although I know far more about the trees themselves than what lives in or under them.

I had the Lee Enfield with me—only as a precaution, for I did not want to shoot at all if it could be helped. Since range and accuracy were not of much value among trees, I loaded with a clip of dum-dums. What I might need was stopping power at close quarters. The .303 bullet has little, unless perfectly placed. So I filed off the points of a whole clip, trusting that a dum-dum would hit harder than a jaguar. I believe I must be right, but am still astonished at my train of thought.

The forest was very still: a few isolated bird calls, some small rustlings at the foot of my cliff, an old tree rumbling like a distant train as it crashed to the ground miles away. At 12.40, when I had been in position a couple of hours, I heard the call which puzzled me the first time I was on the ridge, bearing S.S.W. It still sounded to me like sea gull or hawk, but of greater volume. It could be a jaguar cub's mew—I haven't the faintest notion what noise they make, if any—or just possibly a thin blast from a man-made instrument.

Half an hour later I had a fleeting glimpse of the black back of a tapir crossing the glade. Tapir do not move much during the day and hardly ever into sunlight, so it was a fair bet that he had been disturbed. But nothing followed him.

I gave up nature watching and came down from my perch. Then I worked round the end of the cliff and made my way along the north-west slope of the escarpment on much the same line that I had taken with Tesoro. I admitted to myself that if I felt the same incipient panic as the first time on that desolate, ant-ridden, overgrown tumble of rocks I was not going on.

In fact I felt nothing but growing curiosity. When I was on the north side before, I was always looking ahead of and around me. This time I had my eyes on the ground and soon spotted that the ridge was not entirely lifeless. There were narrow, beaten strips which, with a bit of imagination, one could call paths, but so often they led to bare rock or lost themselves among holes, pinnacles and thorny scrub that I was not dead certain until I came across a dried dropping. It closely resembled the puma dog dropping on the llano. All I could tell from it was that the animal was carnivorous and that it ate little or no bone. It could be human. Tracking was hopeless over leaves and rock. The sharp slot of deer or peccary would have been distinguishable, but not a spread foot or paw—at least not to me. Joaquin, I am sure, could have told how his duendes walked and on what.

I made a circuit in the general direction of the flat rock, picking my way among the creeper-covered holes and clefts where I ought to have put up or at least heard some small creatures— armadillo, rabbit, lizards. But there was no sign of life except the skeleton of some kind of viper, of course picked clean by ants. Well rooted in the silt at the end of a shallow ravine were a few dwarf trees, among them a very fine flowering mimosa. While I was working out a possible route to it I came upon the remains of another snake—this time a biggish boa about sixteen feet long. The back of the skull was pierced and partly crushed.

So that was the reason why there were no reptiles among rocks which ought to have been swarming with them. How difficult is it to kill a boa by clamping the jaws on the back of the neck and hanging on? I think any fast little carnivore could do it and that there is no need to postulate a heavy and powerful beast. This suggests that the killer could belong to the family of the viverridae. Some of them do sit up on their haunches. But I don't see any sort of mongoose or civet cat tackling Pedro.

The rock was far away. I could make out my pitiable nylon still on top of it, plus a long, solid streak of bird dropping. One of the carrion hawks had probably come down in the hope of more dried fish and expressed his opinion when there wasn't any. Time was now running short and I had found out all I could; so I scrambled down to the forest, still seeing nothing but insect life. It is obvious that any creature unwise enough to live on the home ground of the duendes does not live very long.

I had left myself three hours to return to the llano before dusk, which was cutting it fine. Round the edge of the ridge and down the long glade was all plain sailing, but when I was under the big timber on my way to the well glade I walked fast and carelessly and bore a little too far to the right. Finding that the borderline vegetation did not appear where it should, I checked my course by compass and discovered that I was heading east all right, but that I had missed the well glade entirely. I should have been wiser to make a sharp turn to the north and pick it up. That, however, would have meant cutting still another way in— since I could not expect to hit upon the fallen tree where both Pedro and I had crossed from glade to forest—or making a difficult detour without any certainty that I would recover my quick route to the llano. So I kept going.

I must have passed fairly close to Pedro's body. At any rate I was somewhere to the south of the cathedral aisle, for I was looking out for it and never saw it. I did not for a moment feel lost, but unless I arrived at one of the holes in the wall—a needle-in-a-haystack chance—I could still be cutting my way out to the llano long after dark. I had little fear for myself either in the thick stuff or in the open, and it is significant that at this point I had confidence.

But to leave Pichón, hobbled and helpless, out on the llano was asking for trouble—let alone little Chucha's anxiety when I did not return before dusk—so I hurried on, bearing half left in the hope of catching sight of one of my blazed trees or any other familiar landmark. All I recognized was the narrow path, a bit of which I had crossed on the day I found Pedro. Then I was not sure that it was a path. Now, after trying to trace the same, vague beaten lines on the ridge, I had no doubt. It seemed to choose a winding but purposeful route between the trunks. A compass bearing showed that it was running more or less in the direction of the estancia and that it could well lead to the liana thicket. Once up against that impassable rush basket I could easily follow the edge of it to the caju tree and so out to catch Pichón.

I was soon sure what had made this faint ribbon of a track. Twice I came on the familiar dropping among the leaves. It then occurred to me vividly that this was the path which Pedro had crossed just before he was killed. I must now try to analyse my odd and disgraceful behaviour.

When I was up in the fork of the caju tree and found myself under observation I was afraid of a missile—more apprehensive, I think, of curare than that improbably powerful arrow. It was a sane and logical caution exactly equivalent to that of some infantryman who finds his cover not so good as he thought it was and makes a dash for dead ground.

There was nothing logical, however, in my reaction to the mewing call when I heard it not very far away—possibly from near the edge of the well glade. It broke my nerve and I started to run. I put it that way because running was what the subconscious commanded. Physically, I did not do more than a jog trot. I told myself that I must be getting along, that the sun would set in half an hour. And I said out loud and firmly that the call was a bird's.

The jog trot was quite enough to lose the faint path, which could only be followed by keeping the eyes steadily ahead and on the ground. If the forest had been completely open, I might be trotting still. As it was, I was halted by a dense stand of second-growth and thorn. Covered with sweat, I took out the compass and had to put it on the ground because I could not hold it steady. I found to my horror that I had run in a half circle.

The shame of this—thank God for the higher centres!—pulled me together and I started off north-east: a course which had to bring me up against the rush basket, whether or not I ever recovered the game track. I hurried on, sometimes involuntarily running but always succeeding in checking and disciplining myself by a glance at the wretchedly wavering compass needle.

The only thing upon which I could congratulate myself was that I worked the bolt of the Lee Enfield, ejected two rounds, examined them and reloaded. And I suspect that even that was not the cool precaution of a big-game hunter but merely another manifestation of panic. I had decided that the filing of the points might upset the spring and cause a jam. God only knows how it could!

There was no definite sign at all that I was being followed, beyond an imagined pattering over leaves which seemed to keep level with me far out to the left. So I started walking backwards until I perceived that it would not do me the hell of a lot of good. If I were going to be attacked from behind, my behind was wherever I chose to put it. Thereafter I made myself walk on normally, jumping round from time to time, until at last I came up against the wall of lianas.

I hit this at least a quarter of a mile further north than I should have done, but it was now easy to retrace my steps. My left flank was safe. Something might conceivably crawl under the rush basket, but nothing could charge or spring from it; so I had only a half circle to my right which had to be watched. I was still hearing soft paws, still pouring sweat, still stumbling about with the safety catch off and my left hand at the point of balance when the caju tree came into sight and I woke up from the nightmare. It was really like that. *Woke* is what I felt when I came out on to the blessed llano still lit, beyond the formidably long shadow of the forest, by the red light of sunset. Pichón was browsing peacefully on leaves not far away. He was listening with his great donkey ears, which meant little. His nose did not confirm my alarm. There was not even a ghost of a breeze to carry scent.

Now, what am I to make of this? If I were an Indian who had lost his head in this way, I should not only accept Joaquin's duendes but be certain I had seen them. Here in the green darkness, green whiskers. Among the myrtles of Greece, goat hooves and shaggy legs. Pan. Panic. Grendel in the Hall of the Sleepers. Which reminds me that I must double check the hall of the horses.

As regards zoological research, am I now salted or am I unfit to be left alone in the forest without someone to hold my hand? Salted, I believe. Let's not forget the snapshot which brought down the swamp deer. If I can keep my wits about me and have fifty feet of warning I am the quickest and surest giver of death in the forest. Singing in the dark? Well, my woodcraft may be lousy but I do know that my shooting is good.

Chucha has been communing with her sapling again. She notices everything. She might have seen Pichón out on the llano. It is possible that her curiosity about No 2 shot was not wholly disinterested.

She accepts, of course, that there must be mysteries. My past, my work, my relations with the outer world are byond her sharing. But I think it likely that she knows from my eyes and expression when she has taken second place—momentarily—in my present life. Then, since she has nothing else but me, the sapling-teddy-bear has to be implored.

Never mind! Tomorrow I shall spend all day with my golden child. After that we'll see. I might ride into Santa Eulalia and buy a bullock.

May 5th, Thursday

I spent a profitable day at Santa Eulalia—if it works out. I found that the Government Canoe had come and gone days before, and that there were letters for me with the blacksmith. Pedro would have sent someone out to warn me that the canoe was expected. Not that it matters. I have no urgent wants.

The smith, Arnoldo—what names they have, going right back to mediaeval Spain!—has taken Pedro's place by tacit consent as head of the community. He is slow and of dull intelligence. He cannot send out orders by the canoe because he can't write, has never more than a week's money and anyway is appalled by the thought of shopkeeping. He has an immense store of old and rusty iron, some of which may have been on the spot since the first smith of the Conquerors crossed the plains and could go no farther. So he can keep our horses shod indefinitely. Saddlery and ropes, however, will run short. Pedro kept a small stock, together with bits, straps, buckles and silver decorations for the headstalls; and two or three of the llaneros who were clever with

their hands could make up whatever simple tack was required—
usually of raw hide, and often with some individual touch of
craftsmanship.

Tesoro's hind shoes had worn paper thin in the last weeks of
drought, so I left him with Arnoldo while I read my letters. He
is a very vain horse, always holding up his head as if he carried
a king, and Arnoldo tells him that it is an honour to shoe him.
So they get on well.

It is still difficult to adjust myself to the erratic mail. The
Director was acknowledging and commenting on reports which
I sent up to Bogotá with Valera over six weeks ago. Valera had,
I gather, delivered my stuff in person and given a somewhat too
romantic picture of my life as a llaneroagronomist. He had
promised all the help that the army could give. That must have
sounded as if the sky was going to be full of helicopters. What
he meant—for his private amusement—was Chucha.

Another letter was only fifteen days old. The Director was
anxious because nobody could communicate with Santa Eulalia.
Remembering Pedro's unintelligible messages, he told me that
if I merely transmitted the word AVION he would arrange for
a plane to call and fly me up to Bogotá. Well, the canoe will
have reported that Pedro's store has been burned down and that
I, according to Santa Eulalia gossip, was in the best of health
and very satisfied.

The Director also mentioned a mysterious and complimentary
letter from headquarters of the National Liberation Army
informing the Mission that I had nothing to fear and could
continue my work in peace. Military Intelligence had confirmed
that the letter was genuine and was furious at such impertinence.
I was warned that the insurgents were killers first, foremost and
all the time, and that I should trust them no more than mad dogs.

Bogotá! I am glad that I have no way of summoning that
plane. I cannot leave Chucha here alone, and if I took her
along what would she make of a Bogotá hotel? And what would
friends and colleagues make of her? Not that I give a damn!
Valera or some other dissolute scamp would undoubtedly advise
me how to handle a situation which cannot be unfamiliar. But,
whatever I did, the coarse and the comic or the degradingly secret
would be emphasized at the cost of all our delicious simplicity.
The only pretence which could come close to our real relationship would be to pass her off as an adopted daughter. But that
would mean laying off the child—which I can't.

No, I shall not go up to Bogotá till I have to. It occurs to me that I am very happy. Is the secret of happiness a mixture of passionate fornication and somewhat chancy hunting? If so, we human beings have been continually frustrated by urban life ever since we were fools enough to invent it. It's little wonder that some of us rush off to war with a sense of relief.

I slipped all this unimportant bumf in my pocket and strolled down to the river to see Joaquin. A medical consultation. Going through the fern and tall grasses into the forest and in and out of the glades I am showered with ticks and have to get them off when I arrive home with a cigarette end or tobacco juice. Chucha's attentions to my back are charming and efficient, but waste a lot of time which could be better spent. Insect repellent is useless.

Joaquin greeted me with his usual impassivity and said that it gave him great pleasure to see me. This was exceptionally polite; indeed his tone was not conventional at all. So I asked him how I could be at his service.

'If you had been here, you would have bought me rum from the canoe,' he replied. 'But I speak of the day before yesterday when you were so afraid.'

I asked him how he knew I was, and he answered that he had felt my fear.

'As for Pedro?' These shots in the dark were so often effective.

'No, not as for Pedro. For Pedro it came quickly.'

'Could you know whether I had died or not?'

'Not yet.'

I think he meant that only when my spirit had recovered from the shock and was wandering about looking for something recognizable would it be prepared to enter his revolting haze of ritual smokes and incantations. But I respectfully record the shaman without trying to explain him. I doubt if the Archbishop of Canterbury's comments on a Mass for the Dead would be any more helpful.

I told him that I had seen his duendes and that they were solid as ourselves, though I could not yet put a name to them.

'How do we know what we are, we men? So how can we tell if duendes are the same?'

He kicked a log, exactly like Dr. Johnson refuting Berkeley, but drawing a different conclusion.

'Is my foot? Is the log? I only know what my toe feels. When we are afraid, that is the duende. That is what a duende is.'

His Spanish is even worse and less intelligible than my translation makes it sound. Understanding of him is due to our deep curiosity about each other rather than to his actual words. But I think I am safe in putting his meaning this way. Panic always has a cause. Whether the cause has green teeth and whiskers or goes on four feet is irrelevant. The only reality is the fear.

Even now I have not got it right. I have made him too sceptical. He believes profoundly in an immaterial duende which lives on fear as we live on meat. Fear gives it an existence and a shape which is material enough to kill.

I did manage to mention the ticks. He gave me a dried gourd with some whitish goo in it which, he assured me, would make any tick let go and wither. He said it was also good for wasp stings and would restore virility in the aged if taken internally. He proposed to manufacture a new batch when I was ready to hand over Chucha.

When I went back to recover Tesoro I shared Arnoldo's dish of beans—having forgotten that one can no longer buy food in Santa Eulalia—and waited in the smithy on the off chance that one of the llaneros might ride in. And what a good and ancient scent it was under the thatch—the charcoal, the sweat of men and horses, the sizzling of a generation of patient hooves! This is rich country for the nose: llano after rain, forest at dawn, sweet cattle, breath of Tesoro when we blow at each other muzzle to muzzle. And that is to say nothing of the musk of Chucha's damp body. It is a melancholy thought that the more successful I am, the more I help to drown the lot with the petrol and hot oil of the machine age.

I was still reluctant to say all I knew of Pedro. I shall report his death to the first official who comes along and I hope tomorrow or the day after to know the cause of it. So I switched conversation to Pichón and said what good care he took of my girl. Arnoldo told me he was nearly twenty—I had thought about fourteen—and sound as a bell. He had been left to Pedro by a llanero who owed the store money and was dying before he could repay it. They are either bandits or punctiliously honest. There seems to be nothing in between.

Alvar, one of the gentlemen who had chased Pedro to his doom, rode in when the heat of the day was fading. He had lost the silver rowel of a spur and wanted a new one. Arnoldo could only offer to file it from mild steel and said it would look like silver if regularly oiled. That didn't suit Alvar at all. Fortunately I was able to produce a silver dollar which Arnoldo could bore and file to shape. He was even going to line the hole with a bush to prevent wear.

Alvar insisted on paying me. Both of us knew that he had nothing looking remotely like money, but neither would ever have mentioned it. However, here was the chance I had been waiting for. I told him that a silver dollar was a trifle among gentlemen such as ourselves and that I had far more important business. Would he sell me a steer and deliver it north of the marshes?

He was suspicious, not knowing whose side I was on and afraid of getting a plane and machine-gun all to himself. I swore that I was not reselling to anybody, and explained that I wanted to follow the steer about, see what it ate and find out if there was anything wrong with the grasses of the unused grazing between the marshes and the forest. He looked at me oddly, but evidently decided that it was not his business to mention dwarfs.

Tomorrow, two hours before sunset, the beast is to be delivered at a tall, solitary palm with an aloe growing alongside it, known to everyone as the Mother and Child.

On my return to the estancia I told Chucha and Mario that the canoe was expected daily in Santa Eulalia and that I should spend a night or two there so as not to miss it. Tomorrow morning I shall pack up rations for myself and Tesoro, though I hope I can persuade Alvar to lead him away before dark and bring him back when the sun is up. I don't expect any trouble and I am determined to take no risks, but I have left a note in my official journal that everything I possess on this side of the Atlantic—there isn't much but books on the other—belongs to Chucha.

May 7th, Saturday

At four o'clock yesterday I found Alva already waiting with a bullock in the shade of the palm. Though its horns were short for our local breed of cattle, white blotches on the flanks showed a not too distant Hereford ancestry. It would be easy, I thought, to see the beast at night.

The Mother and Child were all of five miles from the bay of parkland, about as near to the forest as the llaneros will ever graze their cattle. The horizon was a vast, unbroken circle, looking emptier than I had ever seen it. There was no haze over the marshes which were hidden by the slight folding of the ground. The line of the forest under the low sun could have been a streak of cloud.

I paid Alvar a small sum for the ownerless beast and he asked me, with much circumlocution, what I intended to do with it.

"We think you know already what is wrong with the grazing," he said, "since you have passed so many moments with Joaquin."

I told him frankly that I did know and that I intended to present the bullock to the dwarfs.

'They have had enough already,' he answered sullenly.

'Perhaps this time they will have a surprise."

'You are as mad as Cisneros!'

'Did he go in with a bullock?'

'No, man! He was alone, they say. I tell you that neither you nor your beast will be alive by morning.'

'If we are, you will also find a dead dwarf alongside us.'

He was not impressed by this Castilian magnificence.

'I shall not go and see. Nor any of us,' he said and turned his horse.

I started to drive my beast westwards. It preferred to go home to its herd. When I headed it off, it charged Tesoro who swung his hindquarters professionally—though he knew no more about the business than I did—and then put out for Santa Eulalia himself. While we settled our differences the bullock pretended to be grazing, and I had a chance to catch its fat rump a heavy cut with the quirt which shot it off towards the forest. It then trotted around, not knowing what to make of us, while I tried to get a rope around its horns. I couldn't handle the fellow at all. I remembered too late that the animals which they tie out in Africa and India are tame village goats and buffaloes—not an unmanageable, Colombian steer.

Meanwhile, Alvar was lying on his horse's neck, insane with nervous laughter. It had never occurred to him that a good horseman, as he knew me to be, could not drive cattle. He took pity on me, and we set off for the bay of parkland at such a pace that I thought the bullock would die of heart failure before it got there.

It was now nearly dusk. He was far from laughter while he helped to tether my present for the dwarfs to the bole of a thorn. He took Tesoro and said that he would wait for me all the morning at the Mother and Child, refusing to come nearer.

He did not even wish me luck. I was finished for him. The nearest I got to a goodbye was a whinny from Tesoro.

Since not a one of the present llaneros of Santa Eulalia has, so far as I know, ever seen dwarf or duende, the power of superstition is extraordinary. Long before Cisneros made his rash purchase of the estancia rumours or reports must have been lurking in the grassland like ticks, fastening on to the men as soon as they began to lose beasts between the forest and the water.

Alvar was in such a hurry to be off that I could spend no time searching for a better place to tether the bullock. The tunnel which I particularly wanted to watch was farther on at the bottom of the bay. Since all the trees which overlooked the bait had smooth, unclimbable trunks, I had to be content with a conical termite hill, seven feet high and hard as concrete. I reckoned that if I sat still I could pass as an extra story on top. My back felt naked, but was partly sheltered by thorn and cactus. The breeze was uncertain but seemed to be settling to its usual pattern of forest to llano.

When darkness fell I soon grew impatient, and began to realize how hopelessly inexperienced I was. Starshine among trees was not sufficient to see more than a flicker of white—and that only by straining the eyes—where the bait was quietly chewing the cud. I had tied a pencil torch beneath the barrel of the rifle, but it was not much use. My left hand either had to move to switch on, probably losing the vital half second of opportunity, or it got in the way of the beam. As for sitting still on my termite heap, I could not do it. I envied the hunters of more imperial forests who could summon up natives to build a machan.

The local herd of peccary came out to feed on the edge of the forest, some of them passing close to my spire, which proved that my scent was not disturbing them. I could only just see them and they certainly could not see me. They must have heard me, for my thigh went to sleep and I had to change position. It may be that they put me down as a monkey or that they had never been hunted by man. I think the latter likely. I am on virgin soil, and the game is as ignorantly trustful as I am.

A half moon came up about two and enabled me at last to see the bullock. He had eaten the dry grass stalks in a beaten circle around his thorn bush and was now lying down. I could have shot him neatly behind the ear. There was no need to use the clumsy torch.

The peccary moved off towards the middle of the bay, the

nearest of them still in sight. A pair of owls flitted to and fro, passing low over me and the bait until they decided we were too large to be of interest. After half an hour the bullock got to his feet and started pawing the ground, with his head pointing across the bay.

What I now saw or half saw was out of pattern, for peccary are among the bravest and most formidable of any herbivorous animals. When in danger the whole herd will attack, and lord help the dog which cannot run faster or the man on foot who finds no handy tree! A shot in the air will usually turn aggressive cattle, but will not, I am told, turn a herd of peccary. If the intruder does not get off the premises, he will be under those razor-shaped little hooves.

A single peccary on the outskirts of the herd broke away and took off for the llano, squealing as if the devil was after it. The herd neither attacked in its defence nor crossed its line. Indeed I had an impression—in which I put no faith although I could make out their backs in the long grass—that they actually moved off the line, leaving a space for the pursuer. It was behaviour clean against the norm.

The following shadow appeared for a fleeting second as two loops. By the time I had decided that there could not possibly be a boa constrictor of that size and that no snake heaved middle sections of its body off the ground, the bullock had torn the inadequate thorn bush out by the roots and was off to the llano as well.

I swung round to cover it and never had a second glimpse of the loops. I was pretty sure that what I had seen were the backs of two duendes in line chasing the peccary with their curious loping gait—in fact the sea serpent effect of two porpoises, one behind another, leaping simultaneously.

There was not another movement till birds and monkeys began their racket at dawn. I got down from my perch, stiff, bored, cold, hungry and not much wiser. Still, the duendes had only won the first round on points. The peccary gave away some of their habits. Its carcase was four hundred yards out on the llano with the vultures just settling on it. I drove them off before they could tear away the evidence.

The peccary had been killed by the usual bite. Two canines had met just below the skull. The other two had passed under the spine. That explained why both I and the guerrilleros, seeing only clean perforations in bone, had jumped at bullet wounds.

There was not enough soft tissue left on either Pedro or the jaguar to show the damage done by the canines on the other side of the jaw.

The belly had been clawed open and the soft parts eaten. Teeth had torn open the jugular vein, yet there was no crusted pool of blood. I have a strong feeling that duendes not only draw their life from panic, as Joaquin suggested, but from the blood of the kill, sucked or lapped.

The bullock was a mile farther on, still attached to its bush. It appeared to welcome my arrival, though not to the extent of standing to be patted. I left it to look after itself and walked on wearily over the llano to the Mother and Child.

Alvar turned up at ten with Tesoro and was surprised to see me. I wouldn't say he was pleased. Men are not when beliefs as well as caution are shown up to be exaggerated. No doubt he also expected to be able to keep Tesoro, who would never be much use as a cow pony but at least would win him some silver in bets if he cared to ride as far as Venezuela.

I said that the dwarfs had so frightened the bullock that he had torn out his bush and was now ranging the llano. Alvar asked if I had seen them, to which I replied that I had even seen them dancing and that I hoped to persuade them to work on my irrigation channels. I shall not give it out that they are animals until I am dead certain what they are. Meanwhile let it be dwarfs with whom the learned doctor is nearly on speaking terms! That cuts them down to size and might enable me to get some active help if I need it.

I told him to take the bullock back to the herd and keep it for me. I do not think I shall want it again. This sitting up over a beast is a romantic idea borrowed from books. To be successful one would have to know far more about the habits of the creature one is observing. I had amazing luck in making contact at all, due to my hunch that the bay was regularly hunted and that the tunnel was their way in and out of the forest wall.

The next move must be to try to get a sight of this pair on their home ground in daylight, and I must not play their game when I "feel" their presence. I believe that Joaquin is on to an actual fact related to their method of hunting and general ecology. They produce what one might call a Declaration of Intent which is detectable by horse, man and even jaguar, to say nothing of peccary. So does man himself. His murderous presence signals a warning to all his four-footed cousins, and nothing but a tired, old man-eater will call his bluff. So I hope I can safely assume some timidity in the duendes, or at least the normal strong objection to starting trouble. Pedro's death does not prove that he was deliberately chased and killed. More probably he took them by surprise on a track which they considered their own territory and did not retreat when told unmistakably to do so.

May 8th, Sunday

When I rode in yesterday afternoon, supposedly coming from Santa Eulalia, I had no need to invent a story and truthfully said that the canoe had called. I could not pretend it had not, thus leaving myself free to be absent from the estancia for more nights, since Chucha saw all the new letters I was carrying. I keep her out of nowhere and out of nothing she can understand. Love and youth are privileged.

I noticed a flicker of disquiet at the arrival of so much evidence that I had another, more permanent life. She can only guess at it, but of course she fears it. Some time I have to go, and to what does she return then? I presume she thinks it inconceivable that I would hand her over to Joaquin, for that is a standing joke between us. But she must anticipate an end not far off Valera's solution: that she will be passed with a kiss and a dowry to some fellow like Alvar. I cannot bring myself to tell her that we shall never be separated. I wish I could.

There is no limit to the oddities of the sort of human thinking which isn't thinking. Mario, Chucha and Teresa now take the dwarfs as fact. Mario begs me to be very careful and gives me tips on how to approach untamed Indians. I am never to surprise them, he says. That goes for more than dwarfs.

He has been digesting the question I asked him: whether in fact the dwarfs had ever killed so much as a hen in or around the estancia. The answer is No. He even points out to me that all we know of Cisneros is that he was ruined and rode away. He may not have been killed by the dwarfs. He and his horse may be anywhere in the Americas. Everything is turned a little too much upside down. It is now I who have to impress it on Mario that at night all doors and windows have to be kept shut and that the horses must never be left in the corral.

I have been right round the perimeter with him and insisted

that adobe rubble on the outside must be dug away and piled on top of the wall. To avoid alarm I play up the new legend of the pitiable pygmy. Suppose the poor little sods, I suggested, came in to steal or kill horses and were surprised at the job. Then we might not be able to avoid mutual bloodshed and enmity. So keep them out till they know us better! He never asked why, if they are men, they cannot climb a half-ruined wall like ours. All the traditions of the duende remain in force, though the duende itself is exploded.

The mystery has grown up because—at any rate in the open —the duende is nocturnal, and the secret presence of a nocturnal animal can only be detected by its kill. The llaneros, since they stayed clear of the forest edge, very seldom saw a kill. When they did, it was unfamiliar and inexplicable, probably the work of man. Combine this with the rare glimpse of an upright figure in deep dusk and the terror of horses communicated to their riders, and there you have the origin of the dancing dwarfs.

My next problem is to find out where they drink. When the creek had water in it, they did occasionally come as far. The horses knew it if the wind was the right way. But they do not hunt on the open llano. That is certain. I think that they move out from the ridge in the late afternoon when I was stalked— or merely investigated—and that they watch the forest border when the game moves out to graze on what is left of the grass or to browse on leaves which the sun has packed with nourishment. Whether they kill within the gloom of the forest during the day I do not yet know. It looks as if they do, when tempted or disturbed. But they must have water on their home ground. Blood alone is, I imagine, too salty to quench thirst. The big felines lap it as it flows, but appear to need water in large quantities. Obviously I have not been far enough into the forest. Somewhere below the south-west slope of the ridge must be a pool or spring. The presence of that swamp deer proved it. And the tapir which I saw crossing the long glade must have cool forest water in which to drink and wallow.

Chucha and Pichón are now so sure of each other that she can ride with me to the new southern passage to-morrow and lead Estrellera home while I explore the swamp deer country on foot. She does not object so much as I expected to my wandering in the forest without a horse. She is conditioned by her whole life not to interfere with men's business. And Samuel of course always walked.

May 9th, Monday

That has settled classification, though not much more. Without a doubt they belong to the family of the mustelidae, not the viverridae.

Through the leaves I watched Chucha ride away. She showed some signs of agitation—which she never does when I am with her—and took it out on Estrellera when the mare tried to get her head down to eat. There was no further question who was boss.

Starting from this now familiar entry into the forest navigation was easy. The blazed trees led me straight to Pedro's body. I was very reluctant to look at it again, but forced myself to do so.

The forest was beginning to clean up in its own way. The bones were already greenish in colour. A Desmoncus liana growing in the well fertilized soil had actually disarticulated and picked up the pelvis on its hooked spines, lifting it a foot clear of the ground. If the growth had been through the eye sockets of the skull, the macabre effect would have terrified anyone, Indian or not. I wonder if many of the duende stories may not be due to the fact that there are no wild dogs or hyaenas in this country to destroy what the birds cannot crack or carry.

Since I knew that by walking due west I must somewhere pick up the escarpment of the ridge, I did not bother to take the long glade. The timber was big and well-spaced and the going easy, though melancholy, monotonous and oppressively silent. It was hard to believe—it always is—that a hundred and fifty feet above my head was sunshine so merciless that the domes of leaf and blossom were wilting and the tree-dwellers asleep in the perfumed shade.

When I met rising ground I followed the contours, leaving on my right the ridge itself and the many ravines up one of which I had climbed with Estrellera. Eventually I was stopped by thickening ground vegetation, a sure sign that somewhere ahead the sun penetrated the canopy. I began to climb directly upwards in the hope that I should be able to see into the clearing from the top of the ridge and find an easier route to it.

The tangle of ground creepers and stone was the worst I had hit yet, especially difficult because I thought it wise to take the rifle off my back and carry it. I was moving across the herring-bone of erosion, climbing down and out of one cleft after another. After three hundred yards of this—which took me nearly an hour—I saw a gleam of water below me between the leaves. Cutting a way to it over the flat was going to be quicker than scrambling across rock to the head of the pool or stream, so I took the first practicable ravine down to the forest and then continued westwards.

The ground became spongy and the vegetation mostly soft. One satisfying swipe with the machete was enough to bring down stems as thick as one's calf. I came out at last into the no-man's land of swampy forest, where what you tread on may be a root, may be floating or may be mud.

I have never seen such a concentration of brightly coloured life, animal and vegetable. The branches which hung out over the still water were loaded with epiphytes. There were yellow-flowering cassia, orange bignonia, several species of short-stemmed nymphaeaceae and a very fine purple ranuncula which may be unknown. Humming birds and green-and-blue tree creepers were everywhere, and there were enough butterflies to keep old Samuel busy for a month. Nature's passionate exhibitionism, always repressed under the trees, had been hurled on stage by the sun.

It was impossible to follow the shore of the swamp or to make out its general shape. However, a fallen tree offered a sort of pier running out a hundred feet into clear water. I tested it cautiously and found that it was not yet rotten enough to let me through or to be frequented by the varied and sometimes unpleasant creatures which make their homes in hollow trees. There was only a nest of hornets towards the top of a branch, which I was careful not to disturb.

From the end of the tree I had a view up and down the pool. I could see the stream which fed it and hear a fall tumbling down the lower slope of the ridge. In the rainy season the stream evidently burst out with sufficient force to clear all soil from a shallow rock basin just above the point where it entered the swamp. On one side was a beach of sand or mud which I intended to examine for tracks, but for the moment I was content to sit at the end of my pier and watch, reckoning that if I kept still I could pass as a thick dead branch. The only animal life in sight —beyond insects—was a small and enterprising alligator. After all the noise I had made in cutting my way to the bank it was unlikely that I should see anything else for hours.

There was a very slight current, showing that the swamp

drained into the Guaviare or a tributary. In the rainy season the width of the lower stream must be enough to stop the duendes crossing. That they do not in fact cross water has been pretty well proved by the creek. It follows that their permanent habitat ought to be on a watershed from which they can move in any direction.

The ridge meets their requirements. The faint runways bear this out; so do all those clefts and holes without even a guinea pig or reptile—snapped up for a snack in passing, with enough fragments left to encourage the ants. Additional evidence, for what it is worth, is my instinctive aversion to the ridge when I first visited the north side.

I had started from the estancia at dawn. It was now eleven. Since there was little cutting and no climbing to be done, I counted on getting back to the llano in three hours' hard marching. So I had four hours to play with. I ate my sandwiches and afterwards kept as motionless as I could in spite of the sharp plague of insects.

The afternoon wore on and the place returned to normal. A small brocket deer flashed in and out of sight as it jumped the stream at the head of the swamp without stopping to drink. A green tree snake moved cleverly from branch to branch looking for birds and small monkeys. When my ears had become accustomed to the background of buzzing and humming, the place seemed as silent as the forest. The steaming, lovely pool, under a blazing sun reflected back again from peacock-turquoise water, gave me a quite reasonable day dream that I was drowsily living in the Carboniferous and should be laid down among the leaves in a coal measure.

The duende called clearly from the ridge. It was close, not more than a hundred yards away, and did not sound in the least like a sea gull or any man-made pipe. It resembled the full-throated mew of an otter, though higher in pitch. I remembered Joaquin's doubtful identification of the faint print in the dried mud of the creek. He said it could be that of the giant otter, Pteronura Brasiliensis.

I watched the ragged skyline of the ridge wherever I could see it, but there was no movement. When my eyes at last returned to the swamp and its banks, the dance was in full progress, this time with only one dancer. It must have hunted my line through the bamboos.

It was inspecting me from behind the upturned roots of the

tree, bobbing up and down. I saw how I could have mistaken
the head for human, though it now seemed incredible. The eyes
were round and set well forward, the ears hardly perceptible,
the head held well up so that in bad light one could create for
oneself the illusion of a man's neck. The muzzle was as pointed
as that of a feline, but no more so. When seen full face, as a vague
outline without any scale of reference, it had been easy to
imagine something like a human nose and mouth and to mistake
the slope of thickish fur on the broad, heavy skull for a forehead.

Dancing behind the root it made as easy a target as the head
and shoulders which bob up and down on a rifle range. Naturally
I never dreamed of firing on so handsome and presumably rare
a creature. The round eyes also gave a disarming impression of
innocent curiosity, as much as to say: what the devil are you?

This curiosity was not, I think, a purely anthropomorphic
interpretation. Since all their usual prey is four-legged, they
could well be puzzled by a tall, slender upright-animal with an
outline closely resembling their own—making a false identification exactly like the Indians or llaneros who first saw them in
dusk or darkness. This could account for the fact that I was
undoubtedly hunted on May 3rd, but not attacked.

I saw a slight waving of the tops of the bamboos which
indicated that it had moved out of the cover of the tree root
and a little downstream. It then launched itself from what must
have been a crouching position clear on to the fallen trunk with
the peculiar loping leap which I had seen at night. It was a
magnificent creature, pale fawn with a paler belly, standing
about twenty inches at the shoulder. Length from head to root
of tail approximately four and a half feet. Tail apparently short,
but I never got a leisurely side view. Weight very difficult to
judge because of the markedly lithe and slender build. For a
loose comparison I should say it was longer than a jaguar (not
counting the tail of either) but stood lower and was much lighter.
It did not appear at all out of proportion or dachshund-like. It
was as dangerously graceful as leopard or jaguar when they move
with body close to the ground, but had shorter legs without the
muscular striking power of the felines.

I record all this while the picture is still vivid in my mind,
but at the moment my observations were more of character than
measurements and were urgent. Another long bound took it out
along the tree. When we faced each other with a mere forty
feet between us, its curiosity did not seem all that innocent. It

plainly had no idea of what a firearm was and no fear of man. That cut both ways. I had no way of quickly distinguishing whether it was a beast which could easily be tamed and domesticated (like the ferret) or whether it saw me as helpless meat.

I myself was tense but not afraid. Its Declaration of Intent had no chance to work when I had only to press the trigger and rake it from stem to stern. It did occur to me, however, that the head shot, which was the best that offered, might not be effective. The tremendous jaw muscles, which could drive the canines through the base of a skull, were attached to a formidable ridge of bone.

It had the extraordinary impertinence to pop up for a better look. I could now see at close quarters how the dwarf effect was produced. It sat upright, hind paws and base of tail giving support at three points, fore paws held close to the body and dangling. That made quite a considerable pygmy. I had already formed the opinion that it was one of the mustelidae, and this trick confirmed the classification. Otter, stoat, badger, tayra— they all do it.

Now undoubtedly gathering itself for the spring, it crouched again. I was aiming straight between the eyes when the hornets took a hand. The mustelid had put some weight on their private dead branch, which I had been most careful not to do. The swarm could make no impression on the fur but went for the nose and the belly, which suggested that this was the female of the pair with vulnerable teats, possibly nursing cubs. At any rate he or she was off to the bamboos again in two curving leaps with a cloud of hornets following.

It left behind a strong, not unpleasant whiff of musk: another proof that it was a mustelid. All of them, so far as I know, emit scent when at play or when alarmed, varying in power from the appalling stench of the skunk to the woodland smell of badger. It was evident that the hornets caused more alarm than I did. If jaguars will not tackle this fellow, the only other possible enemies are wasps, hornets and Eciton ants.

My guess—worthless until proved or disproved by anatomy— is that the duende and the giant otter had, a few million years ago, a common ancestor. One genus developed on the great rivers very successfully; the other not so successfully on land—perhaps because it grew too heavy to catch easy prey in the trees and so developed speed and killing power as a rare but formidable land predator.

It was now fully time to start my return home. Whether to go while the duende was close but occupied by hornets, or to wait on the chance that it was moving clear away was a toss-up. I decided to go.

The edge of the swamp, the bamboos and the close thicket behind them were hard on the nerves. I could see nothing. The rifle was so useless that I was tempted to sling it and trust to the machete to deal with any sudden attack; but of course I could not bring myself to do so. I examined every clump before passing it and tried always to face the long grass and looser undergrowth in which an animal could hide, and to keep at my back the impenetrable stuff from which a charge was unlikely.

This meant a wretchedly slow journey. I did not want to climb to the ridge again, where the going would be slower still, so when I came to the beginning of my own path to the water I cut my way straight on. At last I came out into the big timber at the foot of the ridge and felt more confident, though the trees were set too close together for my liking.

When I had covered rather more than a mile—it is difficult to be exact about distance unless one can see well ahead—I turned north and made straight for the long glade. This sudden turn is interesting. I can remember no reason whatever for my decision. I knew where I was. I knew that by making for the glade I should add to my journey. Yet the change of direction was sharp, imperative, unarguable.

In another ten minutes or so I began to run. I did not even make any determined effort to stop myself; the most that my superior human brain could do for me was to insist that I go straight. Even that was difficult. The hair on the back of my neck was bristling. I was panting. I was inclined to run into obstructions or to lose direction when I went round them. The circling must have partly begun, for when I trotted into the long glade I was closer to the cliff than to the middle.

It was perhaps as well. I could burst out into the sun with hardly any delay.

Open space reminded me that I had once claimed to be salted against peccary panic. Thirty yards out from the edge of the glade I dropped to the ground under cover of dead tufts of grass and turned round to face the forest. I was having no more nonsense about rare animals. If I saw what I was dead certain I was going to see, I meant to kill.

Twenty seconds later the mustelid appeared low down in the

ferns. It was not much of a target and I should not have spotted
it at all if I had not been concentrating on my own track. I fired
and was sure that I had put the bullet behind the right shoulder
—a shot which should have raked the lungs on its way to more
damage; but when I got up and walked to the spot—the smell of
cordite having restored my courage like a tot of rum—there was
no sign of blood, only a powerful patch of scent. At least I had
now handed out some alarm myself. I had no intention of being
a proper sahib and following my wounded beast into the jungle
—the main object being, I gather, to prevent disablement turning
it into a man-eater. That seemed unnecessary when all the
evidence suggested that the duende found human flesh as edible
as any other.

This has taught me a lot more of its habits. First: it is a forest
dweller which does not kill in the open except at night; it was
hot on my trail but obviously hesitated to enter the glade.
Second: it does not stalk its prey. Joaquin said as much after
examining the print which he thought might be of otter. The
movement of the bamboos by the swamp and the swaying of fern
tops prove that it is an inefficient stalker. Game would be alerted
and away like a shot. The mustelid chases, not very fast but
relentlessly.

It may also lie up in ambush after foreseeing by instinct or
experience, like any other carnivore, the probable track of the
oncoming game. That is what I think happened. My change of
direction was a wholly unconscious warning—very difficult to be
understood by any townsman with all his natural instincts
degenerated—that if I walked straight on I should run into
certain trouble.

I am becoming a connoisseur and analyst of fear. There is a
definite distinction between that unconscious warning and the
Declaration of Intent; the latter produces a conscious terror in
every way equivalent to that caused by the classical ghost, whether
or not the ghost is an illusion.

It may be that the fear is the reality, which itself causes the
illusion, rather than the other way round. I am reminded of:
*and turns no more his head because he knows a frightful fiend
doth close behind him tread.* Coleridge must have guessed that
by instinct. It's a fact. One runs and does not turn one's head. Or
would not turn it if one hadn't a rifle. But I have still to clarify
my thinking on this whole subject. It is difficult without a library;
and even among books one would probably be muddled by the

psychologists who invent one phobia after another but don't know the first damned thing about real, justified, animal fear.

To return to the journey. All of it must be recorded for future reference. My mind is inclined to suppress and forget incidents which are disgraceful or temporarily unacceptable. If I had not been able to look up what I wrote on May 3rd, I should have sublimated the memory and been unable to compare my two experiences of sheer cowardice or to draw conclusions from them.

I trotted down the long glade—making up time, not running away—and headed straight for the point of easiest access to the forest where any game in a hurry would crash through into the trees. I hoped the duende was dead or dying but, if it wasn't, that was where it would wait for me.

I could not tell how good its long sight was. Available evidence suggested that the round eyes were as good as a cat's in darkness but not designed for daylight. So I dropped down, vanished into the grass again and crawled off to the south-east at right angles to my former course. I had not far to go before I could safely stand up. Then I skirted the well glade, and just in time picked up the cathedral aisle. The light was beginning to fail and the racket in the tree tops was at full blast. The duende certainly could not hear my progress any more than I could hear his. I reckoned that I was quite safe, always provided that I could reach the llano before dark, for the timber was so well spaced that I had time to use the rifle and space to swing it. I did consider spending the night in a tree on the rare occasions when I saw one that was climbable, but the thought of Chucha's anxiety was just enough to prevent it.

I longed for a horse, especially Tesoro, who would have used his gift for dodging fast through woodland to get us out of there in ten minutes. As it was, ten minutes merely brought deeper dusk and slower progress. The just visible compass gave me direction but could not tell me where the passage was. It was really my little howling cousins, the monkeys, who led me out. They were holding a students' demonstration at their usual playground on the edge of the llano, and ears were a quicker guide to it than eyes. I marched on straight for the excitement, when a little casting about revealed starshine and the gap.

I thought that somewhere I heard the slow beat of horses' hooves and supposed they had broken away through the open gate while Mario was moving them from the corral to the hall. I cursed his carelessness, for the llano in darkness so close to the

forest could be thoroughly dangerous. I did not much care for it
myself in spite of the stars. Then I heard Chucha's voice calling
for Ojen and I let out a yell in answer. She was up in a moment,
riding Pichón and leading Tesoro—which always takes some
doing. When dusk fell and still I was not home, she had forced
Mario to help her to saddle up, choosing Tesoro because of her
belief that he looks after me, and ridden straight across the creek
and down to the gap. Courage beyond belief! I wonder if she
would be proof against the Declaration of Intent. Perhaps. I know
that I should be if I thought her in danger. But I have a rifle, and
she has nothing much but an amateur *chiripá*. However, she
must never do this again.

May 10th, Tuesday

The scent of her body reminds me of that other. One would think
that by association I ought to find it repulsive. Far from it!
Many lovers must know what I mean. Our own females also
possess a musk gland—unless the whole thing is an illusion and
comparable to the sweet odours recorded by saints and mystics. It
is emitted in moments of profound and passionate emotion and
has nothing whatever to do with perfume or the normal
excretions of the female.

Life and death combine in that supersensual fragrance, for in
the act of creation I sometimes think that we ought, like the male
spider, to die. And what is death itself but coalescence with the
unknown? So much for the intrusion into my bed of unity with my
fellow animals! A more unpleasant unity was very close yesterday.
This morning, now knowing what to look for, I found clear tracks
in the adobe dust beneath the wall where Mario had built it up.
The pair followed us home.

May 11th, Wednesday

They have got Tesoro. Why did I ever come here? Why don't I
get out now? This is intolerable. I wish I had some man of my
own kind to talk to—Valera, the two guerrilleros, anybody. I
cannot make up my mind. I am neither a zoologist nor a sports-
man nor any kind of blasted hero. I have been a fool not to tell

Mario and Chucha the truth and I cannot do so now. At least
I think I can't. It is better that they should go on believing in
dwarfs and keep everything shut at night until the rains come
and cut these slender devils off from the llano for another twelve
years or more. What is my duty? Have I any duty? I must not
clear out till I have persuaded Mario and Teresa to settle in
Santa Eulalia. They won't, I know.

We may now be left in peace. What is certain is that the
mustelids are keenly aware of a new source of food. The drought
brought them over the creek for the first time in one of their
generations. They then learned that horses were harmless and
and that men ran as well as peccary and deer. I am now sure that
at first I was to them an animal of their own kind and therefore
had to be cautiously observed before it was classed irrevocably
as game. Remembering the musk and the plunging of Tesoro, it
is clear to me that on the occasion of our first visit to the ridge
we were watched but allowed to go.

This morning I had no intention of collecting mustelids. I
wanted to give Tesoro some needed exercise and to clear up my
own mind which had been forced by more than duendes into
too much introspection, too many impossible designs for our
future. Valera and the guerrilleros could not help in that personal
problem, unless it would do me good to be laughed at. I told
Chucha quite truthfully that I was not going to enter the forest and
that I intended to ride fast as far south as I could go—a distance
which would be beyond her and make her painfully saddle-sore.
We might, I said, take out Pichón and Estrellera in the evening.

I carried the 16-bore in the saddle holster with the usual No 5
cartridges in my belt and a few No 2s in my pocket. I also took
a grain feed for Tesoro and a good lunch for myself since this
was a sort of holiday outing in spirit. We crossed the creek and
cantered along it until the tall timber began to close the horizon
and the forest swung to the east to form a deep, dense belt along
the Guaviare. I had not been down at the bottom of the funnel,
where the creek enters the trees, since early days at the estancia.
I was then considering a canoe with an outboard motor and
direct communication with the Guaviare. It was out of the
question. The creek was not navigable—a wild wilderness of
fallen trees, swamps and floating grasses.

There were a few stagnant pools on our route which became
more frequent as we approached the Guaviare forest belt. I
looked in the mud for tracks and found them. A duende had

stopped to drink. Further upstream, the estancia is, I think, the extreme limit of their range; if it were not for the horses, they would never go so far from the forest. But down there to the south they could leave the trees, cross the dry creek and slink back into cover. They could then approach Santa Eulalia without ever taking to open llano at all. They may have done so in some long forgotten drought. What it was that danced (when a guitar was playing?) remained a rumour in the grass. Even in settled territory a nocturnal animal is rarely seen. Here where rivers are the only roads and the forest is neither explored nor worth exploring there is not even anyone to see it.

The country was thickish parkland—say, three or four trees to the acre, all noticeably suffering from drought. Even a single horseman left behind eddies of powdery soil hanging in the windless air. I should say that in the unending war between trees and grassland the forest had recently advanced and was now in course of being thrown back from occupied territory. After the rains this no man's land had been an Eden of astonishing beauty, part sun, part shade, with game always to be seen. Yesterday it was almost leafless, for our only winter is the winter of drought.

Tesoro was at his most affectionate. He was determined to eat my lunch as well as his own and snorted with disgust at the smell of animal fat when he found that Teresa's appetizing crusts hid half a pullet. He had to be content with an onion and to the taste of my ear. God rest his velvet soul, if he has one!

We turned for home at a steady walk through the blazing afternoon. There was little shade, only brown grass striped with black bars as clearly defined as the branches themselves under a nearly vertical sun. The patterns were so confusing to the eye that once Tesoro cat-jumped a shadow, so I made for the deeper shade to the west where the tops of the trees touched. It was the green half-light of temperate woodland rather than the gloom of tropical.

To the south, beyond the Guaviare, huge cumulus clouds hung over the forest. They were the first I had seen for months and showed that the rains drowning the impenetrable country between the Orinoco and the Amazon were on their way to us. There was a puff of wind which blew down dead leaves and settled into a hardly perceptible breeze from the south. It was unsteady in that angle of two forests and blew half way round the compass. When it settled in the west Tesoro took to the air and bolted in the direction of Santa Eulalia.

That's all I can write tonight. I want more whisky and Chucha.

May 12th, Thursday

I could not sleep, so I have got up early to finish the entry before I forget.

I gathered Tesoro up, turned and gentled him, but it was too long a dispute between us. All the while I kept as sharp a lookout to the west as he allowed. I did not want to turn my back on the thickening forest and edged away towards the bed of the creek. The wind veered again to the south. He was then sweating and unhappy but quite amenable. I hoped that the scent he had picked up was jaguar. I was pretty sure it was not.

We were nearing the open parkland and in ten minutes more would have been a mere point in the empty semi-circle of the llano when again he bolted. His skill among trees seemed to have deserted him. A low branch which his head had only just cleared nearly had me off. Just as soon as I had taken my face out of his mane he was into another. Fortunately for me it was only an overhanging mass of twigs, but it was solid enough to sweep me out of the saddle and leave me clinging and struggling to disentangle myself.

Tesoro was still going at full gallop through the tall timber and bearing far too much to the right. I ran after him but it was hopeless. Though the trees were well spaced, visibility at best was limited to a quarter of a mile.

The mustelid passed quite close, loping along with its leisurely, high-arched canter. It must have seen me but paid no attention at all. I was not chosen. I was like the herd of peccary which had left an open space. It seemed to be picking up the scent at the end of each leap. The nose close to the ground exaggerated the looping effect. It had of course nothing like the speed of Tesoro, but kept steadily on until it too vanished among trees.

I shouted to Tesoro aloud to run to the llano, for God's sake straight to the llano, hardly realizing what I was doing until I became conscious of the hoarseness of my throat. Wherever he had gone, it was far away, for there was no sound anywhere except the scraping of dry leaves in the light breeze.

I climbed a tree in the hope of seeing him, but found that I had a longer view on the ground. When I came down again I heard the drum of his hooves approaching and ran towards him, trying to keep my voice calm as well as loud. He passed across my front a hundred yards away, curving towards the gloom, the gold of his coat darkened by sweat and streaked with foam, the gun in its holster bouncing against his flank. He did not turn, never heard or saw me probably. He was near the end of his endurance. The mustelid appeared on his trail two or three minutes later, unhurried, still loping effortlessly along.

I never expected to see Tesoro again, but I underrated the utter cruelty, the hypnosis of the Declaration of Intent. He passed out of sight and hearing but it was not long before again I glimpsed what was left of his gold dodging through the black trunks. He was going at a slow canter now. Once he pecked and was down on his knees, then off again using the last of his breath for a despairing neigh. This second circle in which he ran was so much smaller than the first that I raced frantically across the diagonal in the hope of intercepting him. It could not be done. I only got near enough to be in at the death.

The mustelid bounded into sight ten lengths behind him, never quickening pace, trusting to the exhaustion and terror of the prey. The final attack was a short spurt and a tremendous leap which landed it on Tesoro's back. It bit him straight through the axis, twisting its head to bring the fangs to bear on each side of the spine, and Tesoro went down head over heels, the mustelid jumping clear and then slinking to the throat which it tore open.

Its eyes were just above the level of Tesoro's prostrate neck and closed in ecstasy as it lapped. When it opened them it saw me. There was no handy tree, and even if there had been I do not think I would have turned my back when two long springs could reach me. It crouched down with fore-paws on Tesoro. Face and whiskers were dabbled with blood which dripped from the points of the white, bared canines.

I was not prey. I was a creature, like the jaguar, which had dared to interfere with a meal. I expected a fierce but harmless demonstration warning me to clear off or be killed; but there was none. It meant business from the start, crawling towards me with belly nearly touching the ground. It looked more like some kind of thick, furry snake than a mammal.

I could only stand my ground and hope that the shining machete would be taken as my own demonstration—a better proof than growls and open mouth that I too meant business. I remember thinking that I was the heavier of the two beasts and that cold steel was better than teeth. I felt anger rather than fear. Adrenalin and high blood pressure, I suppose. My life force was aware that fear could not save it.

There must have been some transference, for the mustelid hesitated. It probably did not care for a frontal attack, which was unfamiliar; its prey always turned tail. Hesitation was very short. Like all its kin, even those which are not aggressive, its courage was without limits. The challenger might be behaving in a manner outside its experience, but the end would be that which always happened.

A full spring must have had me down, but it came on with leisurely crawl till it was not more than two yards from me. When it exposed its throat and before it could get fairly launched I lunged forward. The point of the machete, too wide for an effective stab, got caught in the loose, tough skin, pushing a thick fold of it sideways. The force with which we met was enough to roll both of us over. Any feline could then have finished me with a stroke of the paw, but the mustelid had to get its jaws to bear. As it turned head and shoulders I struck out back-handed with the machete and slammed it full on the nose. To my amazement it toppled over as suddenly as Tesoro. I ran to the saddle holster, recovered the gun and blew the back of its head in just as it was getting up from the count.

How long did this take from the time the beast looked over the neck and saw me? I simply do not know. Seconds, not minutes. One's own body clock is speeded up so fast that it is impossible to tell. I am sure that the elapsed time was much less than I felt it to be because the other mustelid who must have taken part in the hunting—not chasing but moving position, I believe, to reinforce panic by a whiff of scent—had only just come to the kill.

I saw her dancing behind a cactus to sum up the unprecedented situation. That gave me time to slip a No 2 cartridge into the choke barrel. She charged directly from her cover and I took her on the second bound at something less than eight yards. I could see that the right ear was perforated and partly torn away from the head; but the main blast of heavy shot which must have hit her between the eyes seemed to have little effect except that she turned and ran. Evidently courage was not quite unlimited. I was right in predicting the strength of the frontal bone of the skull.

It was the male which I had stunned with the machete. Hornets could have done it no harm except on that vulnerable nose and the corners of the mouth where there was an exposed bit of hairless lower lip—possibly an individual deformity, possibly connected with the sockets in which the long fangs fitted while at rest.

I started to skin it, but found the tough hide defeated an amateur. I was also exhausted, impatient and had copiously shat myself. Cleaning up, sobbing over Tesoro and pulling the machete in and out of its sheath seemed occupation enough. I am inefficient at both cleaning and skinning. Mario deals with any game which I bring home.

The mustelid was smaller and lighter than I had thought, weighing perhaps a hundred and twenty pounds, less rather than more. Its true size was exaggerated by the length of the body when fully extended and the loose skin when relaxed. All the other dwarf legends could be as true as that of the dance. Claws were weak. Though the beast could jump to a considerable height, it could not hang on, let alone climb. That it could not swim also seemed possible; it might well have difficulty in keeping the heavy skull above water. But I am too ignorant of comparative anatomy to be sure. An alternative explanation could be that on land this mustelid has no experience of enemies. Even the jaguar, though dead certain to be the winner if not disabled, feels the 'superstitious' fear and does not stop to argue. Alligators, however, could deal very easily with that slender body, and on the edge of the water, ray and electric eel would be more dangerous still.

I confirmed that my shot from the long glade had hit exactly where I thought it did; but there was no shoulder in the way, not even flesh, only the badly fitting overcoat of the crouching animal. The dum-dum might as well have hit a sandbag. I found a neat point of entry. The bullet had then passed under the belly and out, leaving a ragged wound which did not appear to have bled much or to have caused the beast any inconvenience.

The carcase was of course too heavy to carry, so I covered it with brushwood and left it. Tesoro's saddle and tack I piled at some distance from his body to avoid damage by the vultures. He too seemed very small in death. I have noticed that before, when my first ponies in Argentina died, though never with such love and pity. How do they carry us so easily and gallantly while life is still in them?

The walk home tired and exasperated me more than any of the distances I had covered going to and from the ridge. If I kept to the cool darkness I was continually zig-zagging through trees; if I took to the open llano I was baked by that intolerable ball of fire. No wonder the llaneros never dismount! All the way there was something bothering memory, connected with my observation of this unique mustelid; yet I could not pull it up to the surface. It was simply a difference of size which was preventing instant association. I got at it by way of the badger. I had not missed the parallel of the tremendous jaw, the supporting crest of bone and the vulnerable nose. The badger took me back to cold, green England: to Rendcomb where their habits have been closely studied and thus to Rendcomb Agricultural College where I was invited to give a couple of lectures on soil survey in the tropics. In the senior common room after dinner I settled down with a zoologist whose name I forget. He was an authority on small mammals, particularly European mammals, and he gave it as his opinion that of all the carnivores—with the possible exception of man—the most courageous, the most savage, the most tenacious in the chase was the stoat; and like the weasel and the polecat it killed for the sake of killing.

He was full of stories of the stoat. Cornered, it would un-hesitatingly attack and spring to the height of the waist. One would be wise to grab it quickly off one's coat, at the expense of a badly bitten hand, before it reached the throat. He was doubtful if it ever hunted in pack—the smaller weasel undoubtedly did—but farm hands and even reliable gamekeepers had stories of meeting half a dozen stoats in sunk lanes or on woodland paths and getting out of there quick with the little bodies—another point of resemblance—looping along behind.

Both stoat and weasel live in thick cover and use it cunningly. They come out only to hunt or for curiosity. To satisfy curiosity they all sit up to see over obstacles. They kill by seizing the prey at the back of the skull, the teeth penetrating the brain.

This mustelid appears to be on the least specialized line of descent, from which the badgers and the otters have branched off. I wish I knew whether the stoat also hunts down wind. I believe the lion is the only carnivore which does. One animal gives its scent and so drives the prey straight into an ambush laid by another. The killing of Tesoro shows that the mustelids use this trick, but with an important difference. The prey is selected and then relentlessly followed till it drops. The second animal, if not chasing, moves about and gives its scent from various angles to reinforce panic and to ensure that the game does not run straight.

Scent, however, is only an auxiliary. When the wind veered to the west and Tesoro bolted, I am certain there was no mustelid to the east to send him off in a circle. For one thing, the country was becoming too open for them in daylight; for another the wind was too changeable for any planning. Tesoro could have bolted for the llano. He did not. I could have taken the line I knew in the forest. I did not. No, there is more to it than scent. One must remember that in thick forest there is rarely any wind at all.

This singling out of the chosen quarry, the refusal to go off on the trail of any other and the uncontrollable panic of the hunted together add up to what I have called the Declaration of Intent. It is possible that the musk glands release molecules which act directly on the nervous system. That sounds decently material and scientific, but begs too many questions. A more promising line of investigation is the 'superstitious' fear. I have experienced it. I know how it inhibits the inborn mechanism of self-preservation as well as the sense of direction. At that level of consciousness I am not an expert in tropical agriculture; I am a hunted mammal.

The rabbit resembles me sufficiently for it to be a primitive working model in the laboratories. The rabbit which the stoat selects runs straight to start with, then in a circle. Finally it squats down and squeals. Whether it takes to burrow or cover or the open it cannot escape and gives the impression of knowing it. Only long observation of this Colombian mustelid and its tiny relatives could confirm my tentative theory: that a certain quality of fear can operate at a distance, and that this enables the mustelid to hunt in the way it does.

That brought me, while I plodded on through the heat, to the question: what *is* fear? It is not fear of death. The rabbit and Tesoro can have no knowledge of death. Fear is nothing but a chemical change in the organism directed towards keeping itself in a fit state to breed other organisms. But that may be putting the cart before the horse. The adrenalin is secreted after the fear. Leave it at this—fear is an unreasoning, instinctive order to run.

Panic so overwhelming that the animal does not run but sits trembling and takes what is coming is as familiar to man as the rabbit. He cowers before the man-eater, the earthquake and unendurable shelling. Although so powerful, ingenious and bloodthirsty an ape is never helpless, the instincts of self-preservation are inhibited. He sits. He turns no more his head. He pulls the blanket over it.

Somewhere there is the key to the behaviour of stoat and rabbit. I still think the adjective 'superstitious' helps. Fear of the unseen is the most inhibiting of all. But how are we aware of the unseen, unheard, unscented? Pure imagination. I disagree, but accept it for the sake of argument with myself. However, it gets us no farther towards knowledge of the receiving mechanism.

I got in, dead tired, just before dusk. Chucha rode down the creek to meet me, leading Estrellera. She said that she knew I needed another horse to carry a deer. A rationalisation of her awareness that I did indeed want a horse. How close we are!

I told her that Tesoro had been killed by a puma, that I had shot it but too late. Somehow I had to account for my distress. She cried. Indians are very fond of pets, and to her Tesoro was the prize pet. Then she comforted me like—like what? A dear daughter, perhaps, who understands every elemental emotion and does not look beyond.

Evening

She set her heart on coming with me to see Tesoro, and I could not refuse. I felt reasonably sure that the wounded mustelid would have deserted the open woodland and taken refuge in deep cover. So I mounted her on Estrellera and myself rode the broader Pichón. He's a good, solid, old stick, but he too tried to tear down the corral.

Since I had got up early this morning, urgently written up the record of yesterday and then dozed off, it was nearly eleven when we started instead of the regulation hour of six. I badly wanted the skin or at least the head of the mustelid intact, but it couldn't be helped. I haven't a bloody great gang of coolies to carve up my specimen, preserving the bones for a museum and the hide for my living room—where the lizards, the rats and the ants would get it however much Mario and I salted it. In the rainy season I should probably find a couple of trees growing through it as well.

As we rode south, much more slowly than yesterday, Chucha began to search for the truth of my daylong absences. At home she was too dutiful to reveal her fears, but now we were on a joint expedition and bound together by sorrow for Tesoro. Dutiful. Well, not quite that. She is so free to ask questions and be answered that she lays off the subjects such as our future and dwarf-hunting which are exclusive to me. Tactful, perhaps. Or is she afraid of the answers?

'You are always thinking of them, Ojen,' she said.

'It could be that there are five minutes in the day when I do not think of you.'

'Last night in your sleep you were calling for your machete. I got up and gave it to you, but your hand did not want it.'

'I suppose I had cut down what I was dreaming about.'

'Did they kill Tesoro? You must swear to me.'

'I swear to you that a beast killed Tesoro. You will see it.'

I hoped to be able to pass off the mustelid as a puma, though it was remarkably uncatlike except for the fangs. After all, she had never seen a puma, wild or in a zoo, and Indian legend makes it a far more formidable animal than it really is.

I need not have been anxious. When we arrived, the vultures were competing with the ants. Tesoro was a red ruin. Chucha still wanted to touch him but I would not let her. There was such a phalanx of red predator ants spread over him that the exposed muscles of loins and back seemed to be moving. If she went too close the little devils would be all over her arms and legs in a second.

The ants had not found the other carcase, but the birds had. When I came up, two tayras who had been making a meal of their larger cousin gave me a dirty look and slowly removed themselves. They are omnivorous and harmless and have the same air of independence as the badger. They had scratched away my covering of brushwood and let in the vultures.

The mustelid was much the worse for wear and could pass as a light-coloured puma. Even so Chucha was puzzled. She thought that a puma had longer legs, she said, and she was sure that it had a longer tail. I replied that my first shot had hit the tail and cut it off. An incredibly unlikely fluke, but a good enough story for anyone who had never handled a gun. What was left of the tip of the tail was red and raw.

There was no trophy, nothing worth carrying home except Tesoro's saddle and tack. We rode back lazily, keeping to the scattered shade on the edge of the llano while Chucha babbled happily but not altogether at random. She managed to bring the conversation back to dwarfs again.

What islands we are! I doubt if any woman understands the deep loneliness to which men condemn themselves. They think it a moroseness and that our silence in some way disparages them as inferior creatures. We are merely away. The business of the island is briskly proceeding, but all around it is sea and no boat.

Women cannot ever accept that there is no boat. Chucha does accept it as a rule, thereby making our relations so deliciously easy.

'Ojen, have you talked to the dwarfs yet?'

'Not yet.'

'Are they afraid of you?'

'Probably.'

She thought over that unsatisfactory answer and then asked me what weapons they had.

'Only magic.'

'What can they do?'

'Nothing, if one feels no fear.'

'They will never work for you,' she said. 'The rains are coming and we shall all be busy again. We do not need them, Ojen, so let us leave them alone.'

It was the first time I ever heard her use that proprietary 'we.' I love the confidence it shows. Which of us am I going to betray?

I agreed to leave them alone and I shall keep my word. Now that I know what it is that dances, there is no more point in exposing myself on that abominable ridge. If the remaining mustelid recovers, the flowing creek will limit its movements. I have read somewhere that it takes a thousand years to establish an instinctive fear of man, but I think the lesson should be sufficient to instil caution, so long as there are enough peccary and tapir on its home ground to satisfy the hunger of a duende.

This evening clouds are drifting past the moon for the first time since early December.

May 14th, Saturday

Sun again. One greets it as an old friend whose energy is intolerable but whose absence leaves one irresolute. The first great blobs of rain splashed down at dawn yesterday, puffing the dust like charges of shot. One solid silver-edged cloud was being chased to the north-west by the main fleet, with only two hands' breadths of blue sky between them. Then our closed, black world boiled over and rolled with thunder, hit after hit landing on the infinite target of the llano and one on the main building, which fortunately did no damage.

A terrifying storm. I expected a more gradual onslaught of the

rains. We have had nine inches in twenty-four hours. At one time
the garden was a lake between walls and we all paddled about
trying to close the inlets of the irrigation channels.

The marshes overflowed suddenly when the natural dam of
mud and decayed vegetation disintegrated. I was in time to see
the bore, three or four feet high, tear up the underlying silt and
go roaring down the bed of the creek at the speed of a galloping
horse—a tremendous skewbald of brown and white. Behind it the
creek spread out till it was nearly up to the rubbish dump, and
I began to wonder what we should use for a boat if the stream
reached the estancia. It didn't. It settled into a great river half
the size of the Guaviare and is now going down, leaving behind
a band of alluvium where in three days I shall see a flicker of
green and in a week a carpet of grass as thick as English turf.

Our adobe walls have collapsed in a dozen places and would
not keep out an agouti, let alone duendes. But the mustelids will
never visit us again, assuming that such a drought as this occurs
only once in a dozen or more years. Then their cubs might. But,
walls or no walls, the experimental station will be secure so long
as my successors—if there are any—keep up the rules which Mario
has always obeyed and never understood. How right he was never
to cross the garden at night and to see that windows were barred
or shuttered, and all doors locked!

I have a new Chucha. She has done her best to be a Child of
the Sun, but I suspect she is more at ease in the downpour of the
Upper Amazon where she was brought up, and takes it for
granted that human beings should live in a hot bath, decently
wet between the blasts of sunshine. Indecently wet would be
more like it. She ought to go stark naked. Her combination of
provocative, soaked garment and pathetic drowned-kitten relaxation invites immediate attention. I noticed that even old Mario
was affected. So did Teresa—and told him to come in and mend
the roof.

At the same time Chucha has developed a wild gaiety. She
reminds me of a child on its first visit to the seaside. Bucket and
spade and impulsive kisses. It could be that she feels not only the
joy of the rains but also the glorious freedom of her lover from
all these weeks of idiocy. My job is to make a ton of wheat grow
where now there is only one palatable tuft of grass for a bullock,
not to dispute the forest with animals to which the Lord gave
such outstanding power and beauty—though I can't say as much
for their habits.

Somehow one expects the sun to be less fiery after the rain, but of course it is not. The llano steams. Chucha's garment dries to comparative respectability in twenty minutes. The mud crusts very quickly and can be treacherous as thin ice. I must ride up and see how far the marshes now extend to the north and what temporary streams are running into them. Seen from the Mother and Child I expect to find the llano all striped with blue and silver, for the water level must be too high to be hidden by the shallow folds.

The floods will soon go down and then be stationary for four months, fed by daily rains. I ought to make a swimming pool for Chucha on one of the minor soak-aways of the marsh. Or it could easily be done by damming the creek when the level is stabilised. Now, how on earth could I have written that? Proof of how swiftly one can throw off an obsession when the environment changes! To dam the creek is something which never must be allowed.

May 15th, Sunday

It is time the Government replaced Pedro. The Intendencia must know by now that he has vanished and ought to have sent some-one along who could take my evidence. But, to be fair, why should they give a damn for a back end of beyond with ownerless cattle and ownerless men? Apart from the incalculable results of rot-gut working on a horseman's pride—much as it did in 16th century Europe—our life is peaceful, hostility between human beings being pointless when we are all isolated in a hostile environment. The Intendencia knows very well that we govern ourselves by mutual consent with a minimum of murder, and that any emergency will have settled itself long before uniforms and the law arrive.

Chucha and I set out early and rode up the east side of the marshes. The ground was too soft for her to come to any harm, so I let her have her first all-out gallop. Estrellera easily beat Pichón over five furlongs and showed a ladylike pride. Chucha, the darling was ecstatic.

The marshes have not broadened as much as I expected, but the water has inundated three or four miles along the line of a slight depression which was hardly perceptible in the drought. From the Mother and Child we saw four llaneros riding round the head of the flood, their course marked by white flecks of water from the pools instead of eddies of dust. As soon as they sighted us, they galloped towards us. They were Alvar, Arnoldo—in his capacity of temporary headman—a fellow called Vicente who was a particular friend of Pedro's and a fourth who rides the country far beyond Santa Eulalia and is only known to me by sight.

They greeted us with proper solemnity and were particularly formal with Chucha who has acquired my social status. These indispensable ceremonies over, they were eager to know if I had seen any other riders and burst into their story. Vicente told it; Arnoldo threw in a few proverbs from time to time; and Alvar cursed.

On Friday morning at the height of the storm three guerrilleros in the usual jeep bristling with arms, had splashed into Santa Eulalia and taken refuge under the first solid thatch they came to. The men were all out on the llano, weather or no weather, riding round the frightened herds, and there was hardly anybody in the settlement but the women and Arnoldo. Arnoldo made the unwelcome visitors as comfortable as he could and continued his work—a marked discourtesy—pretending that he did not know who they were.

When the men and horses, sodden and cold, began to drift in at dusk, they did not dismount and surrounded the jeep. I suppose there were about a dozen of them, upright in the saddle, patient as Indians, watching with the veiled eyes of ceremonious killers. The partisans demanded cattle. According to Vicente, none of the llaneros had replied, either refusing or accepting. It must have been obvious to the jeep party that these were men of a different breed from their submissive mountain peasants, and that bloodshed meant nothing to them.

The guerrilleros quickly regained the jeep. With all that fire power concentrated on their semi-circle, the llaneros had at least to produce some words. They agreed to drive another bunch of cattle to the foothills of the Cordillera, though they had no intention whatever of doing so. Machine-gunning from the air had put more fear of God and the Government into them than a hundred men on the ground.

Moreover, Alvar said, these fatherless bandits were men of education, well spoken. That puzzled him. It doesn't puzzle me. The bastards, as he rightly called them, are enjoying themselves. They think the eyes of history are on them. Many are law students or unemployable lawyers; so they like playing at soldiers. I hope to live to see the day when soldiers like playing at being lawyers.

They must have eaten the villagers out of house and home and become very short of rations, for they were taking big risks besides gambling against the meteorological reports. They may have thought that open llano was always open llano and they could of course be confident—after their punitive expeditions against remote villages in the Cordillera—that knives and the odd lance were not much use against machine-pistols.

They dossed down, two sleeping and one on guard, in front of the ashes of Pedro's place—a position from which they could cover all four tracks of Santa Eulalia. At dawn on Saturday there was still no sign of a break in the downpour, and it looked as if the whole settlement was about to slide down the gentle slope into the Guaviare. They were in a filthy temper and decided to get out quick. They swore to return and burn the place down if the cattle were not delivered on time.

Two miles out they tried to ford a yellow torrent and stuck fast. They hauled out the jeep backwards, found a likelier crossing and stuck again. God wished the jeep to remain there, Arnoldo said, and remain there it did. All that could be seen of it was one wheel cocked up in a slope of mud.

But God had failed to foresee the consequences. The three, furious and with mud running off them in streams, had marched back and demanded horses. This would have been perfectly acceptable in any large estancia, but not in Santa Eulalia where a man had no possessions but his horse and saddle. Cattle, all right. Women, well, there might be one or two who would consider it an honour. But horses, no!

They took what they wanted, three horses and three remounts. It turned out that they actually needed less, for their leader was neatly spitted on a long lance. The gallant llanero at the butt end was turned into a fountain. They wrote a cross on him with their guns, Alcar said. After that, resistance was hopeless.

The sun was now out again and steaming the mud. The guerrilleros coolly dried themselves, commandeered what food they could lay their hands on and rode off leading their two spare horses in the late afternoon. Before dusk five llaneros followed hard on their tracks, careful to stay out of sight. They hoped to be able to close in with the twilight when their steel would have a chance against automatic weapons. Alternative tactics would be to creep up when the two men camped for the night, cut the horses loose and round them up at leisure. A number of unpleasant things could happen to the pursued if they had to make their way back to the Cordillera on foot.

The two guerrilleros followed the forest belt along the Guaviare. Since the more open space they had for their weapons, the more unassailable they would be, this route was unexpected. The llaneros, cleverly using the folds and skylines which only they could recognize, watched them unsaddle and tether the horses. When darkness came down, they closed in on foot. They found the temporary camp all right, and nothing on the ground but horse dung.

They were innocent, of course. They seemed to have assumed that no men were as valiant and cunning as themselves. They did not realize that these veterans, though knowing comparatively little of horses and the lie of the land, had been hunted for years by experienced, well-armed enemies and were fully capable of foreseeing what the llaneros were likely to do before the honest souls thought of it themselves.

The pursuers had wasted a lot of time but still had a trick in hand. Hoof prints were distinguished with fingers and matches and established that the four horses had quietly moved on westwards. That meant that sooner or later the guerrilleros would be stopped by the lower reaches of the creek. They could not possibly cross it, so they would have to follow it up and go round the north of the marshes.

Four of the llaneros then struck straight across the grass through the night in order to intercept them. The fifth stayed on the edge of the forest as his horse was finished. A shameful failure in their ordinary daily life. Their horses, though they always look thin and ungroomed and are often saddle-sore, can endure anything. But this one, which its owner had had to grab in a hurry, had been weakened by vampire bat the night before.

The four, when we met them, had found no hoof prints north of the marsh and were sure that the guerrilleros were still in the Guaviare forest belt. I said that I doubted it. They knew of the existence of creek and marshes as well as the llaneros did. If they wanted to break contact, they could have followed the forest for a mile or two and then ridden off into the blue. It did not much matter where they found themselves at sunrise. They had only to put it at their backs and go on.

Alvar, who had lost his own reliable mount to them, would

not have it. If they had got that far ahead they would kill their horses, he said furiously, at the pace they were going. I don't suppose they cared. Assuming their jeep was the same as I saw at the estancia, it had a two-way radio in it. Before they abandoned the vehicle they would have called up guerrilla headquarters and reported their intention. Thus, if they could only keep their lead for another day, a party might come out to pick them up.

The four swept off their hats, thanking us for our sympathy and help—though we could give none—and paced on to the west.

Chucha has revised her opinion of revolutionaries. Why do idealists have to kill people, she wants to know. I forget the exact words she used. Idealist is not in her vocabulary. It is extraordinary how we can communicate in depth on any subject, even mildly technical subjects, with language which is really only fit to ask for a banana.

May 16th, Monday

We tried to plough too soon and broke a tine of the cultivator on new ground outside the walls. The water had poured off, soaking in a mere three inches and leaving the soil rock hard beneath. I must remember that if I am here next year.

If I am here. I long to be. That would solve so many problems. But it is highly improbable. Both my Director and the Government, when they know everything, will insist that this is a lunatic choice for an experimental station. If only I had someone to talk to! This goes round and round in circles. I am obsessed with Chucha. It isn't only our exquisite incontinence. I swear I should still cherish her simplicity and grace and youth if she or I were impotent. There is only one word to describe what I feel for her, and I cannot and will not face it.

Oh God! Back to broken ironmongery and mustelids. They may settle the issue yet.

I rode into Santa Eulalia with the two halves of the tine knowing that if Arnoldo had them for a model he could laboriously forge another. I found the men, dark-faced, standing by their horses in the plaza. They told me there had been another murder by the partisans, who had brutally cut the throat of that unfortunate llanero left behind with his exhausted horse.

The other four had returned home early this morning, having

given up the chase as hopeless. They found that their companion
—Jacinto, his name was—had not come in, though he could easily
have walked the distance in three hours. They rode out to meet
him, and caught his hobbled horse far out on the llano. Jacinto
was where they had left him, lying on a bed of dry leaves with his
throat cut.

I had to go to his house, view the body they had brought in and
speak the nothings of convention to his weeping Indian wife.
What happens to the widows? Where do they go and how do they
live? I glanced at the unpleasant sight and then looked more
carefully. I asked Alvar—sure to be experienced in such matters
—whether he had seen many men before with gaping throats.

'Two, or it could be three. It is not,' he added apologetically,
'a very rare occurrence.'

'Didn't the killer usually do a neater job?'

'I believe it! But what can you expect of these sons of whores?
They cannot even handle a knife like a gentleman.'

'Was there much blood?'

'It seemed to me little. But leaves are more thirsty than the
ground. And there had been rain in the night.'

I embarked cautiously on the forbidden subject.

'Have you always grazed cattle along the belt of the Guaviare?'

'Without a care!'

'Jaguar?'

'None! There is no game left for them to eat. We had not
always such a lack of powder and shot as there is now.'

'Could there be other hunters?'

'Not a thought! You know where those live better than any of
us.'

I asked him what tracks they had seen. Unfortunately they had
taken murder for granted and had pretty well ignored tracks.
Jacinto had been sleeping just inside a grove of ceibas, on the
same spot where the two fugitives with their four horses had
pretended to be about to camp. Naturally there were prints of
feet and hooves all over the place. It was difficult to judge which
had been made before the killing and which afterwards, especially
as there had been a short, violent storm in the night, turning the
grove into an island. What was clear was the indentation of two
knees on the leaves where the supposed murderer had knelt to
cut Jacinto's throat while he was sleeping.

I asked if there were nothing else. Vicente said he had noticed
tracks of a big otter.

'Webbed feet?'

Vicente, trying hard to sound more polite than ironical, remarked that it was known otters had webbed feet.

'But with your permission, did you notice the web?'

Alvar broke in impatiently to say that on leaves, especially where they stuck to whatever touch them, you couldn't tell if the Virgin herself had webbed feet. As for otters, wherever there was new water, they journey to look at it. They were bored like the rest of us.

All these excuses were nonsense. They had not examined anything closely, but were not going to admit it. However, they put the identity of the assassin beyond a doubt, and this was the time to tell them what I myself had known for a week past.

'Look, friends! I have seen the animal which made the tracks and I have killed one,' I said. 'It is, if you like, a sort of big otter. It is also the dwarf. And it crouched by Jacinto while he was sleeping and tore his throat open.'

They would not believe it. I may have been too sudden and dramatic. They could neither give me the lie nor laugh at me, which would have ended the conversation; but their general attitude was that I, a mere man of book learning—though, yes, I recognized one end of a horse from the other—could not know more of forest creatures than they who lived in Santa Eulalia. The dwarf could not be an animal, for who ever heard of an animal which could dance or one that drank the blood without eating the flesh?

They trotted out the lot. Live on the other side of the creek. Never go far from the edge of their forest. Do not cross water.

'Well, if all this is so, why would none of you ride alone to the estancia after dark even when there was water in the creek? And why does Joaquin dislike a guitar in Santa Eulalia?'

My obstinacy roused them out of their usual reluctance to talk. It was not true, they said, that none of them would ride alone to the estancia. They were all valiant. It was just that a man on a long ride at night, with no cattle to claim his attention, liked a companion to talk with. It could be there were dwarfs on the other side of the creek, or it could not. But the place was unhealthy. That was known. One had only to observe old Mario who made himself a prisoner every night. As for the guitar, who the devil believed that it could attract dwarfs all the way to Santa Eulalia? Only Joaquin! Good! That did not mean they thought it was true.

'When a priest comes here,' Arnoldo explained, 'we do not believe all he says. There is much that is very improbable. But he is a man who might speak with the Most Holy Virgin tomorrow or the next day. So a wise man will show some faith. The same with Joaquin.'

I replied that I understood all that very well. The beast, however, was so real that it had killed my golden Tesoro before I shot it. I hesitated to say that I had hit it on the nose with a machete.

I now had their instant, warm sympathy. Poor Tesoro! What a loss! Perhaps it had been a jaguar of a strange colour. Men had seen such which had more yellow than black in their skins. There was even a story of a white jaguar. Or it could have been a puma, bolder and stronger than usual. They would ride out to see what left of the carcase and tell me which it was.

'And besides,' Alvar pronounced in the true spirit of science, 'why look for dwarfs and duendes when we all know that these communists, as they call themselves, killed Jacinto?'

It was no use. Even if they saw the bones of the mustelid, they would swear it was a jaguar with short legs, seeing what they were determined to see and anyway having little knowledge of anatomy beyond that of cattle and horses. If the flooded creek were passable, curiosity might lead one or two of them to the scene; but, as it is, the journey round the marshes, down to the south and back, could not be completed in a day—and, valiant or cautious, not one of them would spend a night in that haunted country.

I had in my saddle-bag a couple of bottles of rum for Joaquin and hoped to get some sense out of him before they took effect. He had had to put up with Indian cassava beer for some time and was sure to pass off into the spirit world—a pun which to him would not be one at all—an hour after the corks were pulled.

I told him the story from the time I watched the mustelid at the pool below the ridge up to the death of Tesoro. I told it very slowly with long pauses and invited his comments on the Declaration of Intent. It was difficult to illustrate my meaning by the parallel of the stoat. Small animals in this immensity are ignored, and there is no reliable, intimate natural history. I think it likely that the hunting methods of our *hurón* resemble those of the stoats and weasels, but Indians are only interested in food animals and pets. Joaquin at least did not doubt the facts. I had seen the duende and was none the worse. His father, who also saw the duende, had been sick for days.

'So I have always known it was a duende, not a dwarf,' he said.

I continued to insist that it was a flesh-and-blood animal, less powerful than the jaguar but ferocious and without respect for man.

'That is the shape which the fear takes.'

'But duendes don't die when one blows their brains out, and they don't kill horses.'

'If they did not, horses would never die.'

We had some more rum while I worked out that fantastic statement. I translated it as meaning that whatever the cause of death—time, worms, the misfortune of breaking a leg—there is always a duende behind it. One cannot prove it isn't so, for we have no machine which will detect the presence or absence of the malevolent duende of ill luck. The virus, that little devil of all devils, was hardly more than a word till the electron microscope revealed its material existence. This, of course, is afterthought. At the time I was more exasperated than analytical.

'But this duende died,' I repeated.

'Why not?'

He whispered in my ear, lest invisible listeners under the thatch should hear him, that he too had killed duendes.

I had another shot at it.

'Friend Joaquin, imagine that a jaguar is tearing open your belly with its claws! Do you say that your fear is real and the jaguar is not?'

'Man, what foolishness!'—rum was taking over from politeness—'I should feel no more fear.'

He may be right. Fear is over, leaving only submission to death.

'Then anything a man is afraid of is a duende?'

'If you came at me with a knife, I should be afraid of you. But you are not a duende.'

So there! Logic demands that the moment he fears me I *am* a duende. However, he won't have it. The fact is that he makes no clear distinction between imagined fear and fear of material danger. Thus, when it comes to the mustelid/duende which produces what I call 'superstitious' fear, it would take a theologian to define the difference between us.

The power of myth is vaster than I ever imagined. The llaneros will not have it that Jacinto was killed by an animal because they won't admit there could be an animal which they do not know. For Joaquin we are all spirits and the physical shape of the fiend is unimportant. In maintaining that all is illusion he has a better case than the fundamentalist llaneros who are emotionally bound to the old facts and refuse to accept new ones. To fill up the measure of human oddities I can add the Dominican who would at once and sanely accept the mustelids but shuddered at Pedro's corpse.

Now that I am here in silence, except for the patter of the rain and the bird-song of Teresa and Chucha in the kitchen, I begin to suspect that I too may be making myths for myself. I could be wrong in assuming that it was a fang, not a knife, which ripped open Jacinto's throat. Those fanatics of the National Liberation Army do not shrink from terrorism. They could have found Jacinto sleeping soundly in the ceiba grove and decided that a further lesson would be good for Santa Eulalia. My suggestion that they did not spend the night in the trees but rode straight off over the llano is, after all, mere guesswork.

I must go and see for myself.

May 17th, Tuesday

Today I took Pichón down the east side of the creek. The turbulent yellow river was impassable all the way. I rode Pichón into it at several likely points and we were both very glad to turn tail as soon as he was up to the cinch. Neither man nor beast could have swum across, though it was narrower than it had been at the time of the flood. Acres of mud, smooth and desolate as a sandbank at low tide, stretched along the creek without even the flotsam and jetsam of a beach. There is so little on the llano which can be carried away except dead grass and topsoil.

Where the creek entered the Guaviare jungle the water had torn down everything in its way, piling up trunks and debris, roaring over and round the obstruction, clearing an avenue through the forest like a troop of bulldozers in line abreast. No accidental bridge or causeway could ever have existed for a minute.

This side of the creek was very different from the dark but open forest to the west through which the mustelids had chased Tesoro. There were only a few outlying trees and groves before one came right up against the green wall. In the shattered woodland the area of mud showed no tracks but those of birds, proving than the llaneros were right and that the belt between Santa Eulalia and the creek was empty of ground life.

I thought of following the forest edge eastwards to inspect the scene of Jacinto's death, but decided against it. I did not know the country and might spend hours looking for the ceiba grove without any certainty that I had found the right one even if it fitted the description of Alvar and Vicente. I suspect also that my worrying sense of guilt had a subconscious effect. I did not want to know. So I turned for home following the highest flood mark.

I had been riding along the tracks for quarter of a mile before I noticed and at once recognized them. All five claws clearly imprinted, which excluded felines. No web, which ruled out otter. There could be no doubt. After I wounded it, the mustelid crossed the creek. My failure to follow up cost Jacinto his life.

I dismounted and tethered Pichón to a stranded tree in a good open position where I could keep him covered if he began to show signs of alarm. Then I explored on foot to see if the spoor— a fine, professional word, that!—could be persuaded to tell any kind of story. My first impression was that the mustelid had come out of the forest to drink. But why take to the open llano when there were plenty of pools and rivulets in cover?

It had followed the edge of the flood plain and three times turned to the water. The level of the creek was now lower, proving that the tracks were made yesterday night or the night before. Twice the animal had chosen spits of land curving out into the torrent, and there was some evidence that it had cautiously paddled. It had then bounded off into the llano where I quickly lost the spoor. Both its gait, the walk and the high canter, were distinguishable.

Its movements appeared aimless. Repeated drinking was unlikely, so what about a search for carrion brought down by the flood. All the evidence of diet suggested that it touched nothing which was not freshly killed, and only the blood and delicacies of that. Could it have been trying to panic cattle knee-deep in the water? There were no hoof-marks and indeed no sign that cattle had been in this corner for months. The drought had devastated the grazing on this side of the creek as on the other.

I started home, having made no useful deductions at all. We jog-trotted along in the steaming, sleepy heat until we came to a loop of the creek. On my way down I had cut straight across the base, but I now decided to follow the course of the stream. At the height of the flood the loop had been wiped out, leaving a layer of silt, now dried to powder, which showed indefinite tracks. They were worth following, for the peninsula pointing westwards resembled the configuration of the two spits which the mustelid had visited.

The spoor was there—straight down to the edge of the water and straight back again. I still could not find the answer to what the mustelid was doing out on the open llano when even at night it never moved far from the trees. So it seemed worthwhile to return to the forest and ride slowly along the edge to see if the damp ground in the shade showed anything of interest. This was a productive move. I discovered a clear set of prints where the beast had re-entered the trees. It had chosen the same way in that I would myself—a thicket of low, soft growth through which a body could push fairly easily.

Since the mustelid had done what I would do on this occasion, I thought the principle might hold. Suppose I wanted to return to the forest from the creek and did not feel like going back over the desolate mud where there was no hope of bagging even a duck, what would I do? Obviously I would choose a line through high grass which would hide my movements. But there was none. The only cover I could find was a depression about deep enough to keep me off the skyline if I crawled. I rode back to have a look at it. The bottom was boggy, and the prints were there, even the mark of a tail touching the ground. After this triumph of teach-yourself-tracking I was able to pick up occasional paw marks between depression and peninsula.

The vast clouds which had been towering in the south broke open. Once the lightning had moved away, the downpour was refreshing—a cold shower after a Turkish bath. It allowed my brain to short-cut a little and to appreciate that there were too many tracks. If there had been fewer, I could make a neater story. But nature—to the ignorant—is never neat.

The truth, or part of the truth, seems to be this. After I wounded it, the mustelid crossed the creek, which was then a chain of disconnected pools, and lay up in the Guaviare forest. It started to wander east, possibly attracted by the presence of men and horses. After killing Jacinto and finding no other prey it turned back to the familiar territory of the ridge and the unfailing supply of deer and peccary. But it could not get there. The sudden spate had cut it off from home. Those movements down to the water were exploratory. It was looking for a crossing, a route to the west.

No further evidence turned up on my way home, but I am sure I am right. To predict the mustelid's future movements is nearly impossible, for this is a unique event in the history of this particular animal. Only in this damnable year could it have reached the wrong side of the creek and been caught there.

Since its natural habitat is the deep shade, it must have tried to cross the creek in the forest reaches before ever attempting the open llano. A reasonable guess is that it made a circuit under the trees, reached the Guaviare wherever the creek enters the river and then worked up the impassable barrier. There are now two courses open to it.

One is to raid Santa Eulalia. I hope to God that is not likely. There is no hunting to lead it in that direction and it cannot know that at the end of a long, hungry prowl to the east it would come to horses, and huts with flimsy fences of cane.

The other is that it will range the llano, hunting a little further up the creek every night until it reaches the head of the marshes. There it will find cattle to kill—will the llaneros put that down to dwarfs?—and a quick route home to the ridge.

Meanwhile I must observe the strictest precautions here in the estancia. The animal is in fact a lot more vulnerable than we are. During the heat of the day it can only lie up in clumps of palm or cactus. The choice is very limited. If I cannot detect the right clump, a horse will. It has little chance in the open and full daylight unless it breaks cover before it is within easy range. Even then I can run it down, provided Estrellera is willing to avenge Tesoro. That rather depends on whether we receive the Declaration of Intent, or turn the tables and hand it out.

May 18th, Wednesday

Somewhat light-hearted yesterday, weren't you, Ojen? This fellow whom I observe must, in the dubious jargon of psychologists, be a manic-depressive character. Ups and downs. Well, but I seldom have downs. I should say that I am a man who lives on a steady level of mild enjoyment, whose chart would, I admit, show peaks —Chucha, the forest domes, the green flash which follows sunset on the llano—but few depressions.

Indecision. That is always the cause. But time is short. This record must be completed. The afternoon is sultry and the sweat pours off me as I write. I would rather be with Chucha, but, if I go through with this, I shall need perfect coordination of eyes, hands and the rifle. Legs, too. Keyed up now. Better stay so.

I set off on Estrellera early this morning. My dear agriculturalists all disapproved of my absence without leave. Mario is hard at it. Well, it won't do any harm to put off the preparation of seed beds for a day or two until the rains settle down to more regular hours. Back to normal duties, please God, tomorrow!

I was not happy at leaving them. But tilling the soil with rifle in hand like a North American colonist would merely have aroused alarm and agitated questions. In any case everything points to the fact that the mustelids never take to the open in daylight. Never is a strong word. A zoologist from Mars observing my normal habits would conclude that I drink and mate freely after midnight, but never eat. Exceptions have been known.

I found no more tracks leading to or from the water and cantered off to the few stands of palms on the eastern horizon. Nothing there. Shade was possibly sufficient, but cover was not. I do not know what sweat glands the mustelid possesses or where they are situated; but it is certain that no forest dweller can endure the direct blast of the sun for long.

I was half way to Santa Eulalia when I saw two vultures circling down to the llano more than a mile away to the north-east. I hoped that they were only coming to a cow which had wandered off into the no-man's land and died or calved there. I could not persuade myself that it was likely. The ground mists of morning were still confusing the lips of the land, and I heard in the silence the squawking and quarrelling of the birds long before I could distinguish the clear outline of tall, dead grass, never grazed.

A breeze from the east had got up, so I rode round to give Estrellera the scent of the patch. When she showed no excitement we entered the grass. It was thin, and from my height in the saddle I could see far enough ahead to be fairly safe. I was also fairly confident—nothing is ever more than 'fairly' in this amateur pursuit—that the vultures would not have come down unless the mustelid had finished with its kill.

Trailing streaks of excrement they rose heavily, like children's kites with grey and white tails. I approached cautiously, making a circuit round the kill with Estrellera showing strong dislike but no terror. A last vulture took off, and beneath it I got a clear view of red and white. It was long and narrow. I thought the shape was human as I did at the caju tree. When I dismounted and led Estrellera up to it, I saw that it was a mustelid. There was enough left to identify Torn Ear. The ear itself was not in a state to put the matter beyond all doubt, but the right eye was. Since the animal was lying with that side of its head on the ground, the eye had not yet been pecked out. A No 2 shot had pierced it and flattened against the bone of the socket. Damage to mouth and tongue was also cruel. That accounted for the lapping of blood without eating any flesh—if this is not a regular habit. I do not know.

Infinite relief and, of course, pity. I feel it when I shoot to eat. It is odd and illogical that I should feel it even more when I shot to save my life. How can I have more sympathy for a singularly atrocious carnivore than a deer? Does respect come in? Well, this time there will be a clean-picked carcase to be collected at leisure by a cart from Santa Eulalia, if I am here to arrange it.

The track of the beast through the grass was plain enough. I had no difficulty in finding the point where it had entered the patch. Assuming that it would have approached in a straight line —possibly a large assumption for an animal blind on one side and weakened by hunger—I crossed and recrossed the probable trail. I came at last upon tracks in a muddy bottom.

At first they puzzled me. The wounded mustelid seemed to have been progressing by short hops, utterly unlike any of the gaits I knew or any gait for an animal of its size. It took me some time to realize that I was looking at the tracks of a pair loping along in single file. They had been made the previous night. I found a dropping which was not yet dry inside.

So back to the patch of cover where the story was completed. I could have worked it out before if Estrellera's movements and the flattening of the grass by vultures had not muddled the evidence. But I had no reason to suspect it was there.

The two beasts left the long grass side by side with a distance of some six feet between them. I was strangely shocked to find clots of blood on the stems which their heads had pushed aside. There could be no doubt that they had chased and killed their wounded relative. Then, with dawn not far off, they set out in hope of cool shade—thank God, not in the direction of Santa Eulalia!

My theory that the sudden, galloping spate of water could have caught mustelids on the wrong side of the creek proved correct; but I never dreamed of active, hungry beasts besides Torn Ear, assuming that the single pair in my immediate neighbourhood produced over the years the myth of the dancing dwarfs and that they were the only members of the genus I was ever likely to see.

But even rarities breed, and the larger mustelidae such as otter and mink are, I believe, interested and careful parents. The young, like those of the felines, have hunting technique to learn before they are ready to occupy a territory of their own.

The territory of this pair was plainly along the Guaviare between the lower, forested reaches of the creek and the unexplored waterway south-west of the ridge. Pedro confidently expected to find game there. He must have seen open glades, firm ground and game paths while travelling on the Guaviare by canoe.

Why did the pair cross the creek into a forest belt where, according to the llaneros, there was nothing to eat and not a rumour of dwarfs? Failing most unlikely coincidence, I am sure the answer is to be found in the behaviour of the half-blinded Torn Ear. Terrified by her first contact with an animal which stood firm and hit back, she bolted across the creek between pools and was followed at a distance by the interested south pair, perhaps stimulated to form pack and hunt in company. Then at some point, due partly to the absence of game and partly to the deadly attraction of a slow and wounded animal, Torn Ear herself became the hunted.

I rode hard for the marshes, giving a cursory glance to the few palms on the way. If this stranded pair had put the growing light behind them and cantered fast for cover, the only place they could find it was by the water, and I did not think they would find much there.

As usual I was not competent to follow the trail over the open llano. However, after a lot of searching I picked up their tracks again on the border of the marshes. There they had separated, one following the edge of the water, the other farther out near the highest flood mark. Both tracks converged on a thicket of tall brown reeds, canes and a stunted palm or two, where new green shoots were already six inches high.

A lot of this stuff had fallen over in the drought or been battered down by storms. It was waist-high and so tangled that no horse could have penetrated it. A man on foot might have stamped and barged his way through, but he would never have come out alive. The bent reeds formed tents and low lean-to shelters into which the mustelids could slide and from which they could spring without the interruption of any solid growth. The prevailing colour was their own. It would have been perfectly possible to step on one without seeing it.

I dismounted and very nervously smelt the ground where they had entered the reeds. The familiar odour was there, and fresh. Then I rode right round the cover. Estrellera obeyed magnificently. I found no tracks leading out again. If they cannot swim, they are there and will be there till dusk.

I must not let them escape and risk another death on my conscience. I am still arguing with myself, but I propose to go out on pretence of taking the evening flight. There will be a good moon in the first quarter. I am confident that I am fast and accurate enough in semi-darkness to deal with one, but not two. From the little I have seen of their hunting practice I think it likely that I shall be attacked from behind and from a flank simultaneously. What I want, therefore, is to get them chasing in line. If they will oblige, I can then run in the expected half circle and take refuge in the water where my back will be safe. As I see it, they will stop dead but not retire. Two aimed shots should be enough.

If only I had somebody to tell! Since I have not, I must talk to myself, and this is the best way to do it. When I write, I recognize or think I recognize nonsense; but when I surrender to the incomplete, leaping, pointless conversations of the brain, I am no more capable of precision than any other man.

Here and there in this diary I see signs of a tendency to brood. That is, of course, due to lack of male company and is unimportant. I chose this life and I have been well able to handle it.

Multiple indecision. That's the trouble. It would be easier if I had only to consider the evening ahead of me, to dab a spot of white paint on the foresight and get on with it. But Chucha is interwoven with this business. The other question I must face is: how can I be lonely when I have her? That's the heart of the problem. I love her. I will not be separated from her. I demand that I be married to her.

How would this work out, if I am not about to die? In an intolerable paradox. I am nearly twenty years older than Chucha. But all the arguments which are normally used against such a marriage work the wrong way round. In ten years' time or a bit more she will be no longer this firefly, charged with light during the day, regiving it after sunset. She will be a wrinkled, ignorant Indian like Teresa, and I a successful scientist—in the world's sense—at the peak of my career and the prime of life.

What do you say to that, Don Ojen? I say that I do not care. Suppose I had a daughter disfigured in body and stunted in mind by disease, would I stop loving her? But she is not my daughter—she is a pet from the forest. Very well, Indians cherish a pet till it dies. There is no way out.

What vile, selfish arguments in a void! How cynical can I get? Let us imagine that Don Ojen has killed his dragons. In the eyes of whatever blasted society he frequents, he would be a person of interest who could get away with whatever he pleased. His eccentricity and his little Indian wife would be all in character. The bastard could go around wearing silver spurs and a comic hat. For God's sake, what nonsense!

It is Chucha herself I must think of. That little golden organism is compounded of love and nothing else. It is made to love and be loved. Am I to be 'sensible' and hand it over to a Joaquin or an Alvar, or set it up in a Bogotá flat for Valera and his friends?

I will not do it. A vile betrayal! Yet even if I were to spend my life in one of the Andean capitals she would be lost. So imagine her in London, with nothing she understood, nothing that gave her happiness or ever could, her life, me and nothing else.

Now, on a step further! My duty to Santa Eulalia, to Mario and Teresa. I have to go out to-night. Am I afraid? Yes. Am I unwilling? No. Why? Because you refuse to face your responsibilities, Don bloody Ojen. That is not true. What is true is that I refuse to imagine life with her or without her. I therefore offer Death a chance. I say to Death: settle it for me, but, by God, I'll fight you all the way!

Hysterical! High sounding nonsense! I must try to picture Valera trying to suppress a smile. But one thing is certain. Valera wouldn't leave duendes around on the wrong side of the creek. Valera wouldn't muddle his obvious duty with a lot of fifth-rate drivel on whether or not Chucha could make a London hostess. What it all boils down to is that I am prepared to be a little more rash than I would otherwise be. And let us leave the precise meaning of that 'otherwise' to psychologists who have nothing better to do.

10.30 p.m.

That is over, if it is. I cannot eat. I must be alone a little. Chucha, I know, is frightened. Those round, so gentle eyes stared at me, only understanding that there was no crossing the water to so foreign an island. Women—even this firefly—seem able to forget weeks of truth and to read a false significance into two minutes. Perhaps she feels rejected. But I must have time to relax. Let me finish this record, this diary which has become a damned duty to zoology, and I shall be with her again. Nothing but entirety of spirit will comfort her.

I left half an hour before sunset. I carried the rifle in front of me so that she could not distinguish it from the gun. I know very well that she always runs to the wall and looks over it after me. And a lot of use that wall is now after the rains!

It was a clear evening with little chance of rain in the early part of the night. I walked fast up the marshes and checked the tracks before the sun went down. The mustelids were still in the reeds. As the last of the duck were splashing on to the water I moved off some three hundred yards into the open. The wind, such as it was, blew from the llano allowing them to pick up my scent. They were not likely to ignore me. They had eaten very little of their relative, probably finding all but the blood distasteful.

Visibility in the last of the dusk, with a moon in the first quarter, was good. Sure killing range was about thirty yards, but so was charging range. When they started to close in, I hoped they would dance for me to get a better look. If I then missed, as I well might—the target being as narrow as a man—the chase was on.

In the singing silence I thought I heard the canes cracking and shifting. Before I could be sure a last skein of geese came over and swam around with soft, sleepy chatterings. For half an hour I had to endure a soundless, dubiously empty half-circle of silvered peace, continually looking behind me to ensure that the other half was empty.

Half an hour was too much and all wrong. I had believed that the action would begin as soon as they had extricated themselves from the binding, difficult cover along the marshes. It was certain that after sunset hunger and habit would compel them to leave it.

I detected a faint whiff of musk on the wind, so I turned my back on the cover and kept the main watch in the opposite direction. I had expected that one would attack straight up from the water while the other worked round a flank; so long as I knew which flank, I could then run and bring them clearly into sight on my trail. But attack from the llano puzzled me. Although it was more in accordance with their down wind hunting, it seemed to me that they ran a risk of driving their game into the water and safety. I decided that they knew best, that experience must have taught them how to turn me towards the llano.

I write: 'I decided.' But my racing guesswork merely kept half a jump ahead of what their instinctive movements ought to be and decided very little. The only available fact was that one of them, in spite of a natural impatience, had spent a long time working into position out on the open llano. It stood to reason that the other must be on the edge of the dead canes in order to signal me away from the water.

It was therefore essential to pin-point the fellow waiting on the marshes. I tried to do this lying down so as to get a bright background of water through the gaps in the rushes. But the scent of musk had become a little stronger, showing that the other was beginning to close. I was unpleasantly aware that the back of my neck was exposed and that I could not turn round quickly. So I got up and walked slowly towards the cover.

The mustelid's curiosity, its tendency to inspect before committing itself, gave it away. The outline was as vague as a tree stump but bobbed up and down against the stars. I took the outside chance—more to relieve my nerves than with any assurance of killing—lay down, took my time and fired. It paid no attention. The foolhardy courage of the stoat or just utter ignorance of man and his resources? I had ample opportunity for a second shot which either scored an outer in the thick skin or was close enough to convince the mustelid that its prey was being impertinent. The dancing stopped, and I caught a glimpse of it creeping unhurriedly, belly to ground, straight at me before I lost sight of it among the outlying clumps of rushes. This was out of its normal hunting pattern. I had become an enemy, like the jaguar, to be intimidated.

My own pattern was also disturbed. I did not see how I could now line the pair up and bring them after me to the edge of the water. One was in front, meaning business, the other was somewhere out in the llano waiting for the next move of the quarry. I lay down again so that my silhouette could not be seen against the moonlit sky. I was upwind of the fellow I had annoyed, and there was a good chance of my spotting him before he spotted me.

While I was wishing to God that I had never fired those two shots and muddled the natural course of the hunt, a long strip of black cloud. which I had been too busy to notice drifted over the moon. Starlight would have been good enough for close quarters if my eyes had become accustomed to it, but this sudden blotting out of a silver world blinded me. It looked as if I might need the machete again. I had not got it. I was stripped for running.

Nothing happened. No sound. No scent. Loss of contact. My reading of the position then was that I hadn't a hope. My reading now is that the mustelid's night sight, like my own, needed a moment to adjust itself; meanwhile, the compulsion to avenge annoyance faded away and was replaced by the instinct to continue the hunt. It must have changed direction and passed across my right flank to join up with the other.

It was at this point that I probably received the Declaration of Intent, but there was quite enough general panic to be resisted without attending to details of clinical analysis. I prefer to put it this way: the involuntary compulsion to run coincided with my deliberate plan to run. So I ran. All very pretty, but one essential fact was missing. I did not know what lead I had.

I think I would have bolted straight for the water if there had been any quick way of reaching it through the thick stuff where the mustelids had spent the day. As it was, I was forced to stick to my original intention and run more or less parallel to the marsh. When at last I dared to turn my head, I could see nothing; but instinct insisted that they were committed and on my trail.

The moon cleared for a moment and I looked behind again. There they were, both in line and producing the leaping-porpoise effect exactly as when hunting the peccary. The target was impossibly narrow and oscillating as I had foreseen. One, perhaps. Two, no.

I began the curve—the wrong way from their point of view. The distance between us and the distance to the blessed gleaming water were about the same. A man sprinting could hold them over a hundred yards. Horse or deer could leave them standing, if it used its speed and kept straight. But even Tesoro was run down. They do not have the decent doubt of the felines. They know what the end will be.

I charged through the rushes and into the water, went over my knees in mud, stuck fast and could only turn to fire very clumsily. The leader was sitting up and slavering at me. I shot it through the body but missed any immediately vital spot. Water or no, it sprang at me. I finished it with a heart shot almost on the muzzle of the rifle, throwing myself sideways to avoid the falling body.

When I struggled up again, the other had gone. The dead mustelid was floating out of reach in a fan of red water. It had taken up the position of a sinking ship, buttocks and tail above the surface. If that does represent the relative buoyancy of the animal in life, it would certainly find swimming laborious. There will not be much of it left to collect. Alligators should now be working upstream, and what the eels cannot manage they will finish.

I pulled myself out by the reed stems and scraped the mud from my watch. Incredibly, from first contact to finish, only fifty-five minutes. I thought of it then as finish, for the disruption of the hunting pattern was complete, and the lesson surely enough for any animal. In my relief I overlooked the vital stimulus of hunger. This particular individual, whose normal range was far away to the south-west, had no experience of an upright beast of familiar outline which ran, but made a loud noise and was associated with the dangers of water. Its vague picture of an urgent present, lacking cause and effect, only inhibited action without forbidding it.

In any case half of me was ready to welcome a second meeting if the mustelid did not continue its course to the north and the head of the marshes. Now that I had got my breath back and the foresight had stopped wobbling, the odds were acceptable. Conditions were as good as could be expected, though the angle of the moonlight was treacherous, and folds of ground, hardly perceptible in daylight, were in black shadow.

My right flank was protected by the water, my left a target area where nothing within thirty yards could live if I were fast enough. There was of course no protection against attack from behind, but by glancing round after I had passed clear of any possible line of approach I more or less secured myself against surprise. After I had walked a cautious half mile or more I began to curse my sight. The outline of the black dips was fuzzier than it should be. The stars had lost their brilliance. The change was so slight and gradual that I really thought it was the result of intense straining of the eyes. Not until the crescent of the moon was also hazed did I realize that a ground mist was thickening.

In another few minutes I was in almost complete darkness, and the moon only a lighter patch of sky. I could just make out the water and keep direction; otherwise visibility was down to nothing. I stopped to think. Not that it did any good. My position was desperate if the mustelid had not lost interest. I tried my

pocket flashlight, but it was worse than useless. The far end of
the beam showed a mere, blurred oval of llano, leaving me with
even less night sight than I had.

There was no scent to help. In fact all my senses were out of
action except hearing. I would have been thankful to receive
the 'superstitious' fear, which at least would have told me for
certain what I was in for and perhaps turned the rifle in the
right direction. But even that was absent. I was empty of fear and
could understand what Joaquin meant when he said that fear was
over as soon as the prey went down under the teeth and claws.

Always there were little noises from the marsh: the splash of
fish or frog, the rustle of reeds as they parted to let through the
invisible. Under the pall of the mist the faint activity of my
unseen companions was hushed but continuous. Without interruption of the business of living they let my footsteps pass. I
could imagine that they were friendly or that I was no longer
of any importance.

Ten paces behind me two duck rose with a whir and a clatter.
I jumped round and fell on one knee, instinctively meaning to
bring the muzzle of the rifle under the body as it rose for the
final spring. The mustelid, too, was startled by the duck. I heard
a squelch as it slipped on the edge of the mud and then the
unmistakable, soft sound of a leap to firmer ground.

It could kill me when it pleased. Walking backwards was no
use. One fall and it had me. Standing still in the hope of that
last split-second shot was no use either. I tried it. My follower
also stopped still. After we had covered a few hundred yards I
began to learn exactly where it was. My ears picked up the foot-
falls, some real, some no doubt imaginary. There were times when
I knew the beast was far behind, times when it was so close that
I would swing round and cover nothing. I dared not fire. I might
wound. That would infallibly end this state of neutrality. My
only chance of safety seemed to lie in letting it follow me like a
dog at heel for as long as it would.

I strode out more boldly, for there was nothing else I could
do. I remember and repeat that I was emptied of fear—so much
so that I controlled myself by analysing the validity of my
repugnance of what was coming to me. To be eaten—why such
horror of it? Death in war, death in our suicidal transport, we
accept both; or, if we refuse to accept, at least they are not nightmares. Yet this death, quick, clean, a last offering of hospitality
to a fellow hunter, men think the most terrible.

The water tempted me, but I should be floundering in mud before I was out of reach. So we walked on, never hurrying lest one or the other should end this intimacy. When I felt that it was too close and that hunger was overcoming caution, I would turn round gently. Then there was silence. I could never be sure that I had seen it. I think I never did. It can flatten itself to less than the thickness of a man. Even in full daylight one cannot be certain, as I had already discovered, where is the bone and where is skin. The weasel—tiny, but of similar anatomy—can both kill a rabbit and pass through a wedding ring. That should be remembered by the millionaire who thinks he can shoot fast or the proud Brazilian hunter who is not afraid to use a spear as his second line of defence.

We walked in our curious companionship of death until I received a waft of musk. It was not for me; it was for the horses. Much later than the mustelid I picked up the smell of the corral spreading under the mist. That was the first sign that I was nearing home; till then I could not have said whether I had two more miles to go or was already near the outlet of the creek. I knew at once that the beast had broken contact and that I could at last run with safety. It was very necessary. In spite of all the rules, there could be a little gossiping by an open window.

I took the chance that the mustelid was over on the far side investigating the corral, and came in over the rubble of the east wall. Chucha heard me and flung open the kitchen door, staying in the light to welcome me. I shouted to her to shut it, which she did not, and rushed across the courtyard nearly knocking her over in my anxiety.

The three of them drew away and stared at me, for I was plastered with black mud on hair, face and clothes. I must have made a convincing duende straight out of the depths of the marsh. That may have contributed to my escape. Even to the efficient night sight of my follower I was black against black, never clearly distinguishable, smelling of foul water.

Chucha asked me where the duck were. The fire and the spit had long been ready. After all, I never failed. I ignored her. I could not help it. I had no speech. She may have thought that I suspected she was making fun of me. I went straight to the laboratory and the whisky bottle. My clothes slopped off me on to the floor. When I had put on a dressing-gown so as not to shock her blasted peasant prudery, I called to Teresa to take the mess away and rinse it. The woman stammered that the moon was clear again and that she would go out at once and fetch water from the well.

They are all mad, when there is nothing but a closed door between them and death. Just because Mario and Teresa know or think they know that the pitiable dwarfs are as solid as themselves, they are free of anxiety. What curiosities they are! Or perhaps we are all alike. Warn a man that the devil will get him if he doesn't do what he is told, and he obeys trembling. Warn him that his life is in danger, and the effect will wear off in a week.

I made no mistake with Teresa. I told her that there was a duende in the night and that I had seen it. Drastic, for what I say is the word of God. If now there were an accident without obvious cause, I can imagine them seized by such a concentration of twelve years' suppressed terror that they would rather fly hand in hand into the empty llano than stay another moment in the estancia. But it doesn't matter. When they see the dead animal tomorrow and I explain the source of the rumours which have oppressed them ever since the disappearance of Cisneros, I can trust their sound common sense.

The dead animal. Yes. It will not go far from the only food and at first light it will take to the shade of Mario's old house or one of the ruined, overgrown cabins. For such close quarters I shall use the 16-bore—quick, certain, and blast more effective than a single bullet at what is going to be the range.

Chucha came in some ten minutes ago while I was deep in this record. She had the impertinence to ask me why I had frightened the pair just because I had fallen in and bagged no duck. Impertinence? Or a daughter's utter trust in my gentleness? I told her to leave me alone, to go to bed and I would come. She saw that I was shaking with nerves and whisky. Not very tactful after her experience in a dim past. But I have to unwind, God damn it!

Women's lack of steady confidence is so absurd. She looked at me and seemed to wither as if love had suddenly come to an end. What does she think I am up to? Disillusioned with her and looking for another wife among the dwarfs?

Well, of course she cannot know more than I tell her. If it were daylight I should find the child had run outside to talk to her sapling. I lack imagi . . .

EAST OF
DESOLATION

Jack Higgins

*'East of Desolation' is published
by Hodder and Stoughton Ltd.*

The Author

Born too late to fight in the Second World War, Jack Higgins left school at sixteen and was conscripted into the army in 1947. Most of his National Service was spent in Berlin during the airlift: 'the main thing I recall is that Germany in 1947-8 was a sort of privileged nightmare of being able to live well on the proceeds of forty NAAFI fags sold on the Black Market'. Back in England, and out of the army, he tried several jobs—Civil Engineer, Burglary Surveyor for an insurance company, Ministry Clerk, Sales Rep. for a tobacco firm—before deciding to 'cut my losses after discovering how easy it is to pass exams'. With an Honours Degree in Sociology from London University, and a Teaching Certificate from Leeds University, he taught for several years in comprehensive schools, and is now a Lecturer in Liberal Studies at a Polytechnic. He has been writing for some time now, and has had many thrillers published under different pseudonyms and imprints. Several of his books have been translated and sold abroad; *Midnight Never Comes* has been published in eight languages so far. *East of Desolation* was written out of an interest in the Norse voyages produced by a school trip to Iceland. Jack Higgins is married, with two daughters and one son. Besides his writing and lecturing, he finds time to indulge in a new pastime every year; having recently achieved gradings in Judo and Aikido, his present hobby is weight-lifting.

For
ARNOLD SPECTOR
—good friend

CHAPTER ONE

I BROUGHT THE PLANE IN low over the sea and took her up to three thousand as land appeared and beyond, through the harsh white moonlight, the Greenland ice-cap gleamed like a string of pearls.

East from Cape Desolation the Julianehaab Bight was full of smoky mist indicating no wind to speak of and certainly nothing more than five knots, which was something. At least it gave me a chance of dropping into the valley at the head of the fjord. Not much of a one, but better than staying here.

It was cold in the cabin with the night wind streaming in through the splintered windscreen and the lighted dials on the instrument panel were confusing in their multiplicity, occasionally merging together in a meaningless blur.

And then, on the far side of the mist, the waters of the fjord gleamed silvery white in the intense light and the strange twisted moonscape rolled towards the ice-cap, every feature etched razor-sharp.

It was time to go. I reduced speed, put the auto pilot in control and unbuckled my safety belt. When I turned, he was there as he always was, the head disembodied in the light from the instrument panel, eyes fixed, staring into eternity as he lolled back in the co-pilot's seat.

I moved into the darkness of the cabin and stumbled, falling to one knee, my outstretched hand touching the cold, ice-hard face of the other and panic seized me as it always did and it was as if I couldn't breathe as I lurched through the darkness and clawed at the quick release handles on the exit hatch.

It fell away into the night and I stepped into space without hesitation, aware of the intense cold, feeling strangely free. I seemed to somersault in slow motion and for a single moment saw the plane above me in the night drifting steadily eastwards like some dark ghost and then I reached for the ring to open my chute and it wasn't there and I gave one single despairing cry that was swept away into the night as I plunged into darkness.

I usually only got the dream when I was over-tired or depressed, but it always left me in the same state—soaked in sweat and shaking like a leaf. I lay there looking up at the ceiling for a while, then flung aside the bedclothes and padded across to the window. When I rubbed the condensation away a fine morning greeted me.

I was flying out of Frederiksborg that year, Godthaab the capital having got just a little too civilized for comfort. It was a small place about two hundred miles below the Arctic Circle on the south-west coast. The population couldn't have been more than fifteen hundred, but during the short summer season it was artificially inflated by the influx of two or three hundred construction workers from Denmark who were engaged in building rather ugly three-storeyed blocks of concrete flats as part of the government development programme.

But Frederiksborg, like most places on the Greenland coast, still had the look of a raw pioneering town, the mushroom growth of some gold or silver strike. The roads were unsurfaced and most of the town was scattered over a peninsula of solid rock. The houses were made of wood and painted red, yellow and green, and because of the rock foundations everything went overhead and telephone and electric cables festooned the air from a forest of poles.

The harbour was half a mile away at the end of a rocky road beside the new canning factory and contained half a dozen fishing boats, a Catalina flying boat used by East Canada Airways for coastal traffic and my own Otter Amphibian which was parked on dry land at the head of the concrete slipway.

It was almost ten o'clock and I went into the bathroom and turned on the shower. There was a quick knock on the outside door and I wrapped a towel around my waist and returned to the bedroom.

Gudrid Rasmussen looked in. 'You are ready for coffee, Mr. Martin?' she said in Danish.

She was a small, rather hippy girl of twenty-five or so, a Greenlander born and bred, mainly Danish by blood which showed in the fair hair plaited around her head, with just a touch of Eskimo in the high cheekbones and almond shaped eyes. Most of the year she spent housekeeping for her grandfather on his sheep farm at Sandvig about a hundred miles down the coast, but during the summer she worked as a chambermaid at the hotel.

'Make it tea this morning, Gudrid,' I said, 'I'm feeling nostalgic.'

She shook her head in reproof. 'You look awful. Too much work is not good for a man.'

Before I could reply the sound of an aeroplane engine shattered the stillness of the morning and I went to the window in time to see an Aermacchi flip neatly in across the harbour and drop flaps to land on the airstrip beyond the canning factory.

'Here comes your boy friend.'

'Arnie?' There was a touch of colour in her cheeks as she crossed to the window. 'Any girl is Arnie's girl, Mr. Martin. I hold no special rights.'

It would have been pointless to try and pretend otherwise and we stood there together for a moment in silence watching the wheels come down beneath the skis with which the Aermacchi was fitted.

'I thought he was going to take those off and put his floats back on,' I said.

'The skis?' She shrugged. 'He got an extension of his service contract with the American mining company at Malamusk on the edge of the ice-cap. Up there the only place to land is the snow-field.'

His landing was good—not excellent, but then we all have our off-days. The Aermacchi rolled along the airstrip and disappeared from view behind the canning factory.

Gudrid smiled brightly. 'I'll bring your tea while you have a shower, then I'll order breakfast for you. I'll change the bed later.'

The door closed behind her and I went back into the bathroom and got under the shower. It was nice and hot and very relaxing and after a while my headache started to go, which was a good thing considering that I had a two and a half hour flight ahead of me. I pulled on an old silk dressing gown and went back into the bedroom towelling my hair briskly. In my absence, Gudrid had brought in a tray, and the tea, when I poured it, was scalding. I finished the first cup and was pouring another when the door burst open and Arnie Fassberg blew in.

He was about my height, which was a little under six feet, but the resemblance stopped there. My hair was dark, his so fair as to be almost white, his face open, mine closed and saturnine. As yet he had not been used by life or at least had been used kindly and his forehead was as unlined as any child's. By birth an Icelander, he had perhaps the most incredible appetite for women that I have ever encountered, and like all Don Juans he was an incurable romantic, falling in and out of love with astounding frequency.

He presented a slightly theatrical figure in his fur-lined boots and old flying jacket and he tossed a canvas holdall into the corner and moved to the table.

'I though you might have left. I've probably broken all records from Søndre Strømfjord to get here.'

'Any particular reason?'

He helped himself to tea, using my cup. 'You're flying supplies out to that American film actor aren't you?'

He was referring to Jack Desforge who'd arrived unexpectedly in Godthaab early in June in his motor yacht *Stella*. Since then he'd been cruising the coast fishing and hunting and I'd been flying out supplies to wherever he was at regular intervals.

'Why the interest?'

'I've got a passenger for you. She got off the midnight jet from Copenhagen at Søndre. Wanted me to take her straight to Desforge, but I couldn't oblige. Have to be at Malamusk by noon with some spare parts they've had specially flown in from the States. Where is he, by the way?'

'Somewhere north of Disko in the region of Narquassit as I last heard; looking for polar bear.'

There was genuine astonishment on his face. 'At this time of the year. You must be joking.'

'About the only thing outside of a Tibetan yak that he's never laid low. You never know, he could hit lucky. I've seen bear up there myself in August before now.'

'But not often, my friend. I wish him luck.'

'This girl—what's her name?'

'Eytan—Ilana Eytan.'

I raised my eyebrows. 'Israeli?'

'I would have said English.' He grinned. 'Not that it matters—in any language she's a lot of woman.'

'Good looking?'

He shook his head. 'Ugly as sin and it doesn't matter a damn.'

'A rare combination. I look forward to meeting her.'

'She's having breakfast downstairs.'

The door opened and Gudrid entered as I knew she would, her excuse the clean sheets she carried. Arnie swung round and advanced on her.

'Gudrid—sweetheart.'

She side-stepped him neatly and dropped the sheets on the bed. 'You can cut that out for a start.'

He unzipped one of the pockets in his flying jacket and took out a roll of notes. 'I got paid, angel. A thousand dollars on account. Where would we be without our American friends?'

'And how much of that will go across the card table at the Fredericsmut?' she said acidly.

He peeled off two hundred dollar bills and held out the rest of the money. 'Save me from myself, Gudrid. Be my banker like always.'

'What would be the point? You'll want it back again, tomorrow.'

He grinned. 'Put it in the bank then, in your name. Just so I can't get at it. I trust you.'

And as usual, she was putty in his hands. 'If you're sure you want me to.'

'Would I ask if I didn't?' He patted her on the bottom. 'I'd better come and see where you do put it, just in case you get knocked down in the street or anything.'

I didn't need the wink he gave me over his shoulder as they went out to tell me what that meant. Poor Gudrid. Always on hand to keep him occupied in between affairs, never facing up to the hopelessness of the situation from her point of view. And yet in his own selfish way, he had a genuine affection for her and she did act as his banker on occasion, which was probably the only reason he had any money at all.

But I had enough problems of my own without worrying too much about other people's and I finished dressing quickly and went downstairs.

As was only to be expected at that time in the morning, the restaurant was empty except for the girl sitting at a table in the bow window drinking coffee and looking out into the street. I could see at once what Arnie had meant, but he was wrong about one thing—she wasn't beautiful, not in any conventional sense, but she was far from ugly.

She had a strong Jewish face, if one can use that term these days without being called a racialist—a proud face with strong lines that might have been carved from stone. Full red lips, high cheekbones, hooded eyes—a face that was unashamedly sensual and the straight black hair that hung shoulder-length in a dark curtain was perfectly in keeping. No Ruth in any cornfield this, but a fierce, proud little queen. An Esther perhaps or even a Jezebel.

She looked up as I approached, her face calm, the dark eyes giving nothing away. I paused, hands in pockets.

'Miss Eytan? Joe Martin. I understand you want to see Jack Desforge. Mind if I ask why?'

She looked faintly surprised. 'Does it matter?'

'It might to him.'

I sat down opposite her and waved to the waiter in the kitchen entrance who immediately produced a whale steak from the hot-plate and brought it across.

'Are you his keeper or something?' she said without the slightest touch of rancour in her voice.

'Let's put it this way. Jack has a great big sign out that says: *Don't disturb*. I fly supplies to the *Stella* once a week and he not only pays me double—he pays me cash. Now I just love that kind of arrangement and I'd hate to see anything spoil it.'

'Would it make any difference if I told you we were old friends?'

'Not particularly.'

'Somehow I thought you might say that.' She opened her handbag and took out a wallet that was surprisingly masculine in appearance. 'How much do you charge to make the sort of flight you're doing this morning?'

'Five hundred krone.'

'What's that American?'

'Call it a hundred and fifty dollars.'

She extracted three notes and flipped them across the table. 'Three hundred. That means I've paid in advance for the round trip if he doesn't want me to stay—satisfied?'

'Considering that I'll be getting paid twice, how could I be otherwise?' I took out my wallet and put the notes away carefully. 'We leave in forty minutes. The flight should take just over two hours if the wind is right.'

'That's fine by me.'

It was only when she stood up that I realized just how small she was—no more than five feet three or four. She was wearing an expensive tweed suit, nylon stockings and flat-heeled pigskin shoes.

'One more thing,' I said. 'You're dressed just fine for those long country weekends, but you'll need something different for where we're going.'

'Rugged country?' she said. 'Well that should make a change. So far I've found the whole thing just a little disappointing.'

'They don't wear sealskin trousers any more if they can help it,' I said, 'and a whaleboat with a diesel motor is a damned sight handier in rough weather than a kayak, but if it's the rough outdoors you want, I think Disko should satisfy you.'

'I can't wait,' she said dryly. 'Where can I change?'

'Use my room if you like. It's on the first floor—twenty-one.
I'll finish here, then I've a few things to see to. I'll pick you up
in half an hour.'

She went out through the archway and spoke to the porter who
hurried round to pick up the suitcase she selected from the stack
that stood against the wall and she followed him across the hall
to the stairs. At that distance there was something vaguely familiar
about her, but I couldn't pin it down.

She walked well with a sort of general and total movement
of the whole body and in one very quick moment, I wondered
what she would be like in bed. But that would have been Arnie's
reaction. He probably already had his campaign mapped out.

Suddenly angry with myself, I turned back to my steak, but it
was already cold and I pushed it away and helped myself to coffee.

I think it was General Grant who said: War is hell. He should
have added that women are worse. I sipped my coffee and stared
out across the wide street towards the harbour where the Otter
glinted scarlet and silver in the sunlight, but all I kept getting
was a disturbing vision of Ilana Eytan crossing the hall and her
damned skirt tightening as she mounted the stairs. It had been a
long time since a woman bothered me as positively as that.

I borrowed the hotel Landrover and drove down to the harbour,
mainly to get the met report from the harbourmaster's office. I'd
refuelled the Otter on flying in the night before so there was
nothing to do there and at a crate of Scotch per week, Desforge
had become such a valued customer of the Royal Greenland
Trading Company that their local agent had supervised the
loading of his supplies himself.

I drove back to the hotel and went upstairs. When I went into
the bedroom there was no sign of the girl, but I could hear the
shower going full blast so I went into the dressing room and
started to change.

I was as far as my flying boots when the outside door opened
and someone entered. As I got to my feet, Arnie called my name
and I moved to the door. I was too late. By the time I reached
the bedroom, he was already entering the bathroom. He backed
out hurriedly and Ilana Eytan appeared a moment later swathed
in a large, white bath towel.

'I don't know what's supposed to be going on,' she said. 'But
would you kindly send Little Boy Blue here about his business.'

Arnie stood there speechless and she shut the door in his face. I tapped him on the shoulder. 'On your way, Arnie.'

'What a woman,' he whispered. 'My God, Joe, her breasts, her thighs—such perfection. I've never seen anything like it.'

'Yes you have,' I said. 'About three thousand and forty-seven times.' I pushed him out into the corridor and slammed the door.

I returned to the dressing room and pulled on a sweater and an old green kapok-filled parka with a fur-lined hood. When I went back into the bedroom Ilana Eytan was standing in front of the dressing table mirror combing her hair. She was wearing ski pants, cossack boots and a heavy Norwegian sweater.

'Arnie thought it was me in there,' I said. 'He didn't mean any harm.'

'They never do.'

There was a hip-length sheepskin jacket on the bed beside the open suitcase and as she picked it up and pulled it on, I once again had that strange feeling of familiarity.

'Haven't I see you somewhere before?' I said and then the obvious possibility occurred to me. 'In pictures, maybe?'

She buttoned up the jacket, examined herself carefully in the mirror and put the comb to her hair again. 'I've made a couple.'

'With Jack?' And then I remembered. 'Now I've got it. You played the Algerian girl in that last film of his. The film about gun-running.'

'Go to the head of the class,' she said brightly and zipped up her suitcase. 'What did you think of it?'

'Wonderful,' I said. 'I don't know how he keeps it up. After all, he made his first film the year I was born.'

'You make a poor liar,' she said calmly. 'That film was the original bomb. It sank without trace.'

In spite of her apparent calmness there was a harsh, cutting edge to her voice that left me silent, but in any case she gave me no chance to reply and went out into the corridor leaving me to follow with her suitcase feeling strangely foolish.

CHAPTER TWO

As we roared out of the mouth of the fjord and climbed into the sun, I stamped on the right rudder and swung slowly north, flying parallel to the bold mountainous coast.

In the distance the ice-cap glinted in the morning sun and Ilana Eytan said, 'The only thing I ever knew about Greenland before now was a line in a hymn they used to sing at morning assembly when I was a kid at school. From Greenland's icy mountains . . . Looking down on that lot I can see what they meant, but it still isn't quite as back of beyond as I expected. That hotel of yours in Frederiksborg even had central heating.'

'Things are changing fast here now,' I said. 'The population's risen to sixty thousand since the war and the Danish government is putting a lot of money into development.'

'Another thing, it isn't as cold as I thought it would be.'

'It never is in the summer, particularly in the south-west. There's a lot of sheep farming down there, but things are still pretty primitive north of the Arctic Circle. Up around Disko you'll find plenty of Eskimos who still live the way they've always done.'

'And that's where Jack is?'

I nodded. 'Near the village called Narquassit as I last heard. He's been looking for polar bear for the past couple of weeks.'

'That sounds like Jack. How well have you got to know him since he's been up here?'

'Well enough.'

She laughed abruptly, that strange harsh laugh of hers. 'You look like the type he likes to tell his troubles to.'

'And what type would that be?'

'What he fondly believes to be the rugged man of action. He's played bush pilot himself so many times in pictures over the years that he imagines he knows the real thing when he sees it.'

'And I'm not it?'

'Nobody's real—not in Jack's terms. They couldn't be. He can never see beyond a neatly packaged hour and a half script.' She lit a cigarette and leaned back in her seat. 'I used to love the movies when I was a kid and then something happened. I don't know what it was, but one night when the hero and the girl got together for the final clinch I suddenly wondered what they were going to do for the next forty-three years. When you begin thinking like that the whole house of cards comes tumbling down.'

'Not for Jack,' I said. 'He's been living in a fantasy world for so long that reality has ceased to exist.'

She turned, the narrow crease between her eyes a warning sign that I failed to notice. 'And what's that supposed to mean?'

Considering the way she'd been talking I was more than a little surprised at her reaction. I shrugged. 'He's playing a part right now, isn't he? The rugged adventurer cruising the Greenland coast? He'll spend the day in a dory helping to bait and hook a three-thousand-foot line or he'll go seal hunting amongst the pack ice in a kayak, but there's always the *Stella* to return to each night, a hot shower, a six-course dinner and a case of Scotch.'

'A neat script,' she said. 'They could use you at Metro, but what about your own fantasy life?'

'I don't follow you.'

'The tough bush pilot act, the flying boots, the fur-lined parka —the whole bit. Just who are you trying to kid? I wouldn't mind betting you even carry a gun.'

'A .38 Smith and Wesson,' I lied. 'It's in the map compartment, but I haven't had time to shoot anyone lately.'

I'd managed a nice bright reply, but she was hitting a bit too close for comfort and I think she knew it. For a little while I busied myself unnecessarily with a chart on my knee checking our course.

About five minutes later we came down through cloud and she gave a sudden exclamation. 'Look over there.'

A quarter of a mile away, half a dozen three-masted schooners played follow-my-leader, sails full, a sight so lovely that it never failed to catch at the back of my throat.

'Portuguese,' I said. 'They've been crossing the Atlantic since before Columbus. After fishing the Grand Banks off Newfoundland in May and June they come up here to complete their catch. They still fish from dories with handlines.'

'It's like something out of another age,' she said, and there was genuine wonder in her voice.

Any further conversation was prevented by one of those sudden and startling changes in the weather for which the Greenland coast, even in summer, is so notorious. One moment a cloudless sky and crystal clear visibility and then, with astonishing rapidity, a cold front swept in from the ice-cap in a curtain of stinging rain and heavy mist.

It moved towards us in a grey wall and I eased back on the throttle and took the Otter down fast.

'Is it as bad as it looks?' Ilana Eytan asked calmly.

'It isn't good if that's what you mean.'

I didn't need to look at my chart. In this kind of flying anything can happen and usually does. You only survive by knowing your boltholes and I ran for mine as fast as I could.

We skimmed the shoulder of a mountain and plunged into the fjord beyond as the first grey strands of mist curled along the tips of the wings. A final burst of power to level out in the descent and we dropped into the calm water with a splash. Mist closed in around us and I opened the side window and peered out as we taxied forward.

The tip of an old stone pier suddenly pushed out of the mist and I brought the Otter round, keeping well over to the right. A few moments later we saw the other end of the pier and the shore and I dropped the wheels beneath the floats and taxied up on to a narrow shingle beach. I turned off the master switch and silence enveloped us.

'Where are we?' she asked.

'A disused whaling station—Argamask. Like to take a look round?'

'Why not. How long will we be here?'

'Depends on the weather. One hour—two at the most. It'll disappear as unexpectedly as it came.'

When I opened the door and jumped down she followed me so quickly that I didn't get the chance to offer her a hand down. It was colder than Frederiksborg, but still surprisingly mild considering we were twenty miles inside the Arctic Circle and she looked about her with obvious interest.

'Can we explore?'

'If you like.'

We followed the beach and scrambled up an old concrete slipway that brought us to the shore-end of the pier. The mountain lifted above us shrouded in mist and the broken shell of the old whale-oil processing factory and the ruins of forty or fifty cottages crouched together at its foot.

It started to rain slightly as we walked along what had once been the main street and she pushed her hands into her pockets and laughed, a strange excitement in her voice.

'Now this I like—always have done since I was a kid. Walking in the rain with the mist closing in.'

'And keeping out the world,' I said. 'I know the feeling.'

She turned and looked at me in some surprise, then laughed suddenly, but this time it lacked its usual harsh edge. She had changed. It was difficult to decide exactly how—just a general softening up, I suppose, but, for the moment at any rate, she had become a different person.

'Welcome to the club. You said this was once a whaling station?'

I nodded. 'Abandoned towards the end of the last century.'

'What happened?'

'They simply ran out of whale in commercial quantities.' I shrugged. 'Most years there were four or five hundred ships up here. They over-fished, that was the trouble. Just like the buffalo —hunted to extinction.'

There was a small ruined church at the end of the street, a cemetery behind it enclosed by a broken wall and we went inside and paused at the first lichen covered headstone.

'Angus McClaren—died 1830,' she said aloud. 'A Scot.'

I nodded. 'That was a bad year in whaling history. The pack ice didn't break up as early as usual and nineteen British whalers were caught in it out there. They say there were more than a thousand men on the ice at one time.'

She moved on, reading the half-obliterated names aloud as she passed slowly amongst the graves. She paused at one stone, a slight frown on her face, then dropped to one knee and rubbed the green moss away with a gloved hand.

A Star of David appeared, carved with the same loving care that had distinguished the ornate Celtic crosses on the other stones and, like them, the inscription was in English.

'Aaron Isaacs,' she said as if to herself, her voice little more than a whisper. 'Bosun—*Sea Queen* out of Liverpool. Killed by a whale at sea—27th July, 1863.'

She knelt there staring at the inscription, a hand on the stone itself, sadness on her face and, finding me standing over her, rose to her feet looking strangely embarrassed for a girl who normally seemed so cast-iron and for the first time I wondered just how deep that surface toughness went.

She heaved herself up on top of a square stone tomb and sat on the edge, legs dangling. 'I forgot my cigarettes. Can you oblige?'

I produced my old silver cigarette case and passed it up. She helped herself and paused before returning it, a slight frown on her face as she examined the lid.

'What's the crest?'

'Fleet Air Arm.'

'Is that where you learned to fly?' I nodded and she shook her head. 'The worst bit of casting I've seen in years. You're no more a bush pilot than my Uncle Max.'

'Should I be flattered or otherwise?'

'Depends how you look at it. He's something in the City—a partner in one of the merchant banking houses, I think. Some kind of finance anyway.'

I smiled. 'We don't all look like Humphrey Bogart, you know, or Jack Desforge for that matter.'

'All right,' she said. 'Let's do it the hard way. Why Greenland? There must be other places.'

'Simple—I can earn twice as much here in the four months of the summer season as I could in twelve months anywhere else.'

'And that's important?'

'It is to me. I want to buy another couple of planes.'

'That sounds ambitious for a start. To what end?'

'If I could start my own outfit in Newfoundland and Labrador I'd be a rich man inside five or six years.'

'You sound pretty certain about that.'

'I should be—I had eighteen months of it over there working for someone else, then six months free-lancing. The way Canada's expanding she'll be the richest country in the world inside twenty-five years, take my word for it.'

She shook her head. 'It still doesn't fit,' she said and obviously decided to try another tack. 'You look the sort of man who invariably has a good woman somewhere around in his life. What does she think about all this?'

'I haven't heard from that front lately,' I said. 'The last despatch was from her lawyers and distinctly cool.'

'What did she want—money?'

I shook my head. 'She could buy me those two planes and never notice it. No, she just wants her freedom. I'm expecting the good word any day now.'

'You don't sound in any great pain.'

'Dust and ashes a long, long time ago.' I grinned. 'Look, I'll put you out of your misery. Joe Martin, in three easy lessons. I did a degree in business administration at the London School of Economics and learned to fly with the University Air Squadron.

I had to do a couple of years National Service when I finished, so I decided I might as well get something out of it and took a short service commission as a pilot with the old Fleet Air Arm. My wife was an actress when I first met her. Bit parts with the Bristol Old Vic. All very real and earnest.'

'When did you get married?'

'When I came out of the service. Like your Uncle Max I took a job in the City, in my case Public Relations.'

'Didn't it work out?'

'Very well indeed by normal standards.' I frowned, trying to get the facts straight in my mind. It all seemed so unreal when you talked about it like this. 'There were other things that went wrong. Someone discovered that Amy could sing and before we knew where we were she was making records. From then on it was one long programme of one-night stands and tours, personal appearances—that sort of thing.'

'And you saw less and less of each other. An old story in show business.'

'There seems to be a sort of gradual corruption about success —especially that kind. When you find that you can earn a thousand pounds a week, it's a short step to deciding there must be something wrong in a husband who can't make a tenth of that sum.'

'So you decided to cut loose.'

'There was a morning when I walked into my office, took one look at the desk and the pile of mail waiting for me and walked right out again. I spent my last thousand pounds on a conversion course and took a commercial pilot's licence.'

'And here you are. Joe Martin—fly anywhere—do anything. Gun-running our speciality.' She shook her head. 'The dream of every bowler-hatted clerk travelling each day on the City line. When do you move on to Pago Pago?'

'That comes next year,' I said. 'But why should you have all the fun? Let's see what we can find out about Ilana Eytan. A Hebrew name as I remember, so for a start you're Jewish.'

It was like a match to dry grass and she flared up at once. 'Israeli—I'm a *sabra*—Israeli born and bred.'

It was there, of course, the chip the size of a Californian Redwood and explained a great deal. I quickly smoothed her ruffled feathers. 'The most beautiful soldiers in the world, Israeli girls. Were you ever one?'

'Naturally—everyone must serve. My father is a lecturer in

Ancient Languages at the University of Tel Aviv, but he saw
active service in the Sinai campaign in 1956 and he was well into
his fifties.'

'What about this film business?'

'I did some theatre in Israel which led to a small film part,
then someone offered me work in Italy. I played bit parts in
several films there. That's where I met Jack. He was on location
for a war picture. He not only took the lead—he also directed.
Most of the money was his own too.'

'And he gave you a part?'

'A small one, but I was the only woman in the picture so the
critics had to say something.'

'And then Hollywood?'

'Old hat. These days you do better in Europe.'

Suddenly the mist dissolved like a magic curtain and behind
her the mountain reared up into a sky that seemed bluer than
ever.

'Time to go,' I said and held up my hands to catch her as
she jumped down.

She looked up at the mountain. 'Has it got a name?'

'Agsaussat,' I said. 'An Eskimo word. It means big with child.'

She laughed harshly. 'Well, that's Freudian if you like,' she
said and turned and led the way out through the gap in the wall.

Just like that she had changed again, back into the tough,
brittle young woman I had first encountered in the dining room
of the hotel at Frederiksborg, safe behind a hard protective shell
that could only be penetrated if she wished, and I felt strangely
depressed as I followed her.

CHAPTER THREE

OFF THE SOUTHERN TIP of Disko we came across another two
Portuguese schooners moving along nicely in a light breeze,
followed by a fleet of fourteen-foot dories, their yellow and green
sails vivid in the bright sunlight.

We drifted across the rocky spine of the island and dropped
into the channel beyond that separates it from the mainland. I
took the Otter down, losing height rapidly and a few moments
later found what I was looking for.

Narquassit was typical of most Eskimo fishing villages on that
part of the coast. There were perhaps fifteen or sixteen gaily
painted wooden houses strung out along the edge of the shore
and two or three whaleboats and a dozen kayaks had been
beached just above the high water mark.

The *Stella* was anchored about fifty yards off-shore, a slim and
graceful looking ninety-foot diesel motor yacht, her steel hull
painted dazzling white with a scarlet trim. When I banked,
turning into the wind for my landing, someone came out of the
wheelhouse and stood at the bridge rail looking up at us.

'Is that Jack?' she asked as we continued our turn. 'I didn't
get a good look.'

I shook my head. 'Olaf Sørensen—he's a Greenlander from
Godthaab. Knows this coast like the back of his hand. Jack signed
him on as pilot for the duration of the trip.'

'Is he carrying his usual crew?'

'They all came with him if that's what you mean. An engineer,
two deck hands and a cook—they're American. And then there's
the steward—he's a Filipino.'

'Tony Serafino?'

'That's him.'

She was obviously pleased. 'There's an old friend for a start.'

I went in low once just to check the extent of the pack ice, but
there was nothing to get excited about and I banked steeply and
dropped her into the water without wasting any more time. I
taxied towards the shore, let down the wheels and ran up on to
dry land as the first of the village dogs arrived on the run. By
the time I'd switched off the engine and opened the side door,
the rest of them were there, forming a half-circle, stiff-legged and
angry, howling their defiance.

A handful of Eskimo children appeared and drove them away in a hail of sticks and stones. The children clustered together and watched us, the brown Mongolian faces solemn and unsmiling, the heavy fur-lined parkas they wore exaggerating their bulk so that they looked like little old men and women.

'They don't look very friendly,' Ilana Eytan commented.

'Try them with these.' I produced a brown paper bag from my pocket.

She opened it and peered inside. 'What are they?'

'Mint humbugs—never been known to fail.'

But already the children were moving forward, their faces wreathed in smiles and she was swamped in a forest of waving arms as they swarmed around her.

I left her to it and went to the water's edge to meet the whaleboat from the *Stella* which was already half-way between the ship and the shore. One of the deckhands was at the tiller and Sørensen stood in the prow, a line ready in his hands. As the man in the stern cut the engine, the whaleboat started to turn, drifting in on the waves and Sørensen threw the line. I caught it quickly, one foot in the shallows, and started to haul. Sørensen joined me and a moment later we had the whaleboat round and her stern beached.

He spoke good English, a legacy of fifteen years in the Canadian and British merchant marines and he used it on every available opportunity.

'I thought you might run into trouble when the mist came down.'

'I put down at Argamask for an hour.'

He nodded. 'Nothing like knowing the coast. Who's the woman?'

'A friend of Desforge's or so she says.'

'He didn't tell me he was expecting anyone.'

'He isn't,' I said simply.

'Like that, is it?' He frowned. 'Desforge isn't going to like this, Joe.'

I shrugged. 'She's paid me in advance for the round trip. If he doesn't want her here she can come back with me tonight. I could drop her off at Søndre if she wants to make a connection for Europe or the States.'

'That's okay by me as long as you think you can handle it. I've got troubles enough just keeping the *Stella* in one piece.'

I was surprised and showed it. 'What's been going wrong?'

'It's Desforge,' Sørensen said bitterly. 'The man's quite mad. I've never known anyone so hell-bent on self-destruction.'

'What's he been up to now?'

'We were up near Hagamut the other day looking for polar bear, his latest obsession, when we met some Eskimo hunters out after seal in their kayaks. Needless to say Desforge insisted on joining them. On the way back it seems he was out in front on his own when he came across an old bull walrus on the ice.'

'And tried to take it alone?' I said incredulously.

'With a harpoon and on foot.'

'What happened?'

'It knocked him down with its first rush and snapped the harpoon. Luckily one of the hunters from Hagamut came up fast and shot it before it could finish him off.'

'And he wasn't hurt?'

'A few bruises, that's all. He laughed the whole thing off. He can go to hell his own way as far as I'm concerned, but I'm entitled to object when he puts all our lives at risk quite needlessly. There's been a lot of pack ice in the northern fjords this year—it really is dangerous—and yet he ordered me to take the *Stella* into the Kavangar Fjord because Eskimo hunters had reported traces of bear in that region. The ice was moving down so fast from the glacier that we were trapped for four hours. I thought we were never going to get out.'

'Where is he now?'

'He left by kayak about two hours ago with a party of hunters from Narquassit. Apparently one of them sighted a bear yesterday afternoon in an inlet about three miles up the coast. He had to pay them in advance to get them to go with him. They think he's crazy.'

Ilana Eytan managed to disentangle herself and joined us and I made the necessary introductions.

'Jack isn't here at the moment,' I told her. 'I think that under the circumstances I'd better go looking for him. You can wait on the *Stella*.'

'Why can't I come with you?'

'I wouldn't if I were you. Apparently, he's finally caught up with that bear he's been chasing. No place for a woman, believe me.'

'Fair enough,' she said calmly. 'I've never been exactly a devotee of Jack's great outdoors cult.'

The deckhand was already transferring the stores from the

Otter to the whaleboat and I turned to Sørensen. 'I'll go out to the *Stella* with you and I'll take the whaleboat after you've unloaded her.'

He nodded and went to help with the stores. Ilana Eytan chuckled. 'Rather you than me.'

'And what's that supposed to mean?'

'When Jack Desforge starts beating his chest wig it's time to run for cover. I'd remember that if I were you,' she said and went down to the boat.

I thought about that for a while, then climbed inside the Otter, opened a compartment beneath the pilot's seat and pulled out a gun case. It contained a Winchester hunting rifle, a beautiful weapon which Desforge had loaned me the previous week. There was a box of cartridges in the map compartment and I loaded the magazine with infinite care. After all, there's nothing like being prepared for all eventualities and the girl was certainly right about one thing. Around Jack Desforge anything might happen and usually did.

The diesel engine gave the whaleboat a top speed of six or seven knots and I made good time after leaving the *Stella*, but a couple of miles further on the pack ice became more of a problem and every so often I had to cut the engine and stand on the stern seat to sort out a clear route through the maze of channels.

It was hard going for a while and reasonably hazardous because the ice kept lifting with the movement of the water, broken edges snapping together like the jaws of a steel trap. Twice I was almost caught and each time got clear only by boosting power at exactly the right moment. When I finally broke through into comparatively clear water and cut the engine, I was sweating and my hands trembled slightly—and yet I'd enjoyed every minute of it. I lit a cigarette and sat down in the stern for a short rest.

The wind that lifted off the water was cold, but the sun shone brightly in that eternal blue sky and the coastal scenery with the mountains and the ice-cap in the distance was incredibly beautiful —as spectacular as I'd seen anywhere.

Suddenly everything seemed to come together, the sea and the wind, the sun, the sky, the mountains and the ice-cap, fusing into a breathless moment of perfection in which the world seemed to stop. I floated there, hardly daring to breathe, waiting for a sign, if you like, but of what, I hadn't the remotest idea, and then gradually it all came flooding back, the touch of the wind on my face, the pack ice grinding upon itself, the harsh taste of the cigarette as the smoke caught at the back of my throat. One thing at least I had learned, perhaps hadn't faced up to before. There were other reasons for my presence on this wild and lovely coast than those I had given Ilana Eytan.

I started the engine again and moved on, and ten minutes later saw a tracer of blue smoke drifting into the air above a spine of rock that walled off the beach. I found the hunting party on the other side crouched round a fire of blazing driftwood, their kayaks drawn up on the beach. Desforge squatted with his back to me, a tin cup in one hand, a bottle in the other. At the sound of the whaleboat's engine he turned and, recognizing me, let out a great roar of delight.

'Joe, baby, what's the good news?'

He came down the beach as I ran the whaleboat in through the broken ice and, as always when we met, there was a slight edge of unreality to the whole thing for me; a sort of surprise to find that he actually existed in real life. The immense figure, the mane of brown hair and the face—that wonderful, craggy, used-up face that looked as if it had experienced everything life had to offer and had not been defeated. The face known the world over to millions of people even in the present version which included an untidy fringe of iron-grey beard and gave him —perhaps intentionally—an uncanny resemblance to Ernest Hemingway, who I knew had always been a personal idol of his.

But how *was* one supposed to feel when confronted by a living legend? He'd made his first film at the age of sixteen in 1930, the year I was born. By 1939 he was almost rivalling Gable in popularity and a tour as a rear gunner in a B.17 bomber when America entered the second world war made him a bigger draw than ever when he returned to make films during the forties and fifties.

But over the past few years one seemed to hear more and more about his personal life. As his film appearances decreased, he seemed to spend most of his time roaming the world in the *Stella* and the scandals increased by a sort of inverse ratio that still kept his name constantly before the public. A saloon brawl in London, a punch-up with the Italian police in Rome, an unsavoury court case in the States involving a fifteen-year-old whose mother said he'd promised to marry the girl and still wanted him to.

These and a score of similar affairs had given him a sort of legendary notoriety that still made him an object of public veneration wherever he went and yet I knew from the things he had told me—usually after a bout of heavy drinking—that his career was virtually in ruins and that, except for a part in a low budget French film, he hadn't worked in two years.

'You're just in time for the kill,' he said. 'These boys have finally managed to find a bear for me.'

I slung the Winchester over my shoulder and jumped to the sand. 'A small one I hope.'

He frowned and nodded at the Winchester. 'What in the hell do you want with that thing?'

'Protection,' I said. 'With you and your damned bear around I'm going to need all I can get.'

There was a clump of harpoons standing in the wet sand beside the kayaks and he pulled one loose and brandished it fiercely.

'This is all you need; all any man needs. It's the only way—the only way with any truth or meaning.'

Any minute now he was going to tell me just how noble death was and I cut in on him quickly and patted the Winchester.

'Well, this is my way—the Joe Martin way. Any bear who comes within a hundred yards of me gets the whole magazine. I'm allergic to the smell of their fur.'

He roared with laughter and slapped me on the back. 'Joe, baby, you're the greatest thing since air-conditioning. Come and have a drink.'

'Not for me, thanks,' I said.

He had a head start anyway, that much was obvious, but I followed him to the fire and squatted beside him as he uncorked a nearly empty bottle and poured a generous measure into a tin cup. The hunters from Narquassit watched us impassively, a scattering of dogs crouched at their feet. Desforge shook his head in disgust.

'Look at them—what a bloody crew. I had to bribe them to get them this far.' He swallowed some of his whisky. 'But what can you expect? Look at their clothes—all store bought. Not a pair of sealskin pants amongst them.'

He emptied the dregs of the bottle into his cup and I said, 'I've brought a visitor to see you—a girl called Eytan.'

He turned sharply, bewilderment on his face. 'Ilana—here? You're kidding.'

I shook my head. 'She flew into Søndre from Copenhagen last night.'

'Did she say what she wanted?'

I shook my head. 'Maybe she's come to take you home.'

'Not a chance.' He laughed shortly. 'I owe too many people too damned much on the outside. Greenland suits me just fine for the time being.' He leaned across, full of drunken gravity. 'I'll tell you something in confidence—confidence, mind you? There's a lulu coming up that'll put me right back up there on top of the heap and take care of my old age. Milt Gold of Horizon should be in touch with me any day now.'

'Maybe this Eytan girl has a message for you,' I suggested.

His face brightened. 'Heh, you could have a point there.'

There was a faint cry from along the beach and we turned to see an Eskimo trotting towards us waving excitedly. Everything else was forgotten as Desforge got to his feet and picked up a harpoon.

'This is it,' he said. 'Let's get moving.'

He didn't even look to see if he was being followed and I shouldered the Winchester and went after him, the hunters from Narquassit following. You can tell when an Eskimo is happy because sometimes he'll actually smile, but more often than not it's impossible to know how he's feeling at any given moment. Allowing for that I still got a definite impression that the men from Narquassit were something less than enthusiastic about the whole thing and I didn't blame them one little bit.

We reached the end of a long strip of shingle beach and started across a much rougher section that was a jumble of great boulders and broken ice when one of the hunters cried out sharply. They all came to a halt and there was a sudden frenzied outburst of voices as everyone seemed to start talking at once.

And then I saw it—a great shaggy mountain of dirty yellow fur ambling along the shoreline, and as the first dog gave tongue he paused and looked over his shoulder in a sort of amiable curiosity.

You don't need to be a great white hunter to shoot a polar bear. One thousand pounds of bone and muscle makes quite a target and it takes a lot to goad it into action, but when he moves it's at anything up to twenty-five miles an hour, and a sidelong swipe from one of those great paws is guaranteed to remove a man's face.

Desforge saw only the quarry he'd been seeking for so long and he gave a howl of triumph and started to run, harpoon at the trail, showing quite a turn of speed considering his age.

The dogs were well out in front, but the Eskimo hunters from

Narquassit looked considerably more reluctant and I knew why. In their mythology and folklore the polar bear holds roughly the same position as does the wolf for the North American Indian, a creature of mystery and magic with apparently all the cunning of Man: on the other hand they weren't keen on losing their dogs and went after them fast and I brought up the rear.

The bear loped across the strand and skidded on to the pack ice, making for the nearest water, a dark hole that was perhaps ten or twelve feet in diameter. He plunged in and disappeared from view as the dogs went after him closely followed by Desforge, the hunters some little way behind.

I shouted a warning, but Desforge took no notice and started across the ice to where the dogs ringed the hole howling furiously. A moment later it happened—one of the oldest tricks in the book. The bear sounded, striking out furiously with both paws, erupting from the water and falling across the thin ice with his whole weight. A spider's web of cracks appeared that widened into deep channels as he struck again.

The hunters had paused on the shore, calling to the dogs to come back. Most of them managed it safely, yelping like puppies, tails between their legs, but three or four tumbled into the water to be smashed into bloody pulp within seconds as the bear surged forward again.

Desforge was no more than ten or twelve feet away and he hurled the harpoon, losing his balance at the same moment and slipping to one knee. It caught the bear high up in the right side and he gave a roar like distant thunder and reared up out of the broken ice, smashing the haft of the harpoon with a single blow.

Desforge turned and started back, but he was too late. Already a dark line was widening between him and the shore and a moment later he was waist-deep and floundering desperately in the soft slush. The bear went after him like an express train.

Desforge was no more than four or five yards away from the shore as I burst through the line of hunters and raised the Winchester. There was time for just one shot and as the bear reared up above him I squeezed the trigger and the heavy bullet blew off the top of its head. It went down like a tower falling, blood and brains scattering across the ice, and Desforge fell on to his hands and knees on the shore.

He lay there for a moment as the hunters rushed forward to catch the carcass before it went under the ice. When I dropped to one knee beside him he grinned up at me, the teeth very white in the iron-grey beard as he wiped blood away from his forehead with the back of one hand.

'I always did like to do my own stuntwork.'

'A great script,' I said. 'What are you going to call the film—Spawn of the North?'

'We could have got some good footage there,' he said seriously as I pulled him to his feet.

They hauled the bear on to the shore and the headman pulled out the broken shaft of Desforge's harpoon and came towards us. He spoke to me quickly in Eskimo and I translated for Desforge.

'He says that by rights the bear is yours.'

'And how in the hell does he make that out?'

'The harpoon pierced a lung. He'd have died for sure.'

'Well, that's certainly good news. Presumably we'd have gone to the great hereafter together.'

'They want to know if you'd like the skin.'

'What would be the point? Some careless bastard seems to have ruined the head. Tell them they can have it.'

I nodded to the headman who smiled with all the delight of a child and called to his friends. They formed a circle and shuffled round, arms linked, wailing in chorus.

'Now what?' Desforge demanded.

'They're apologizing to the bear for having killed him.'

His head went back and he laughed heartily, the sound of it echoing flatly across the water. 'If that don't beat all. Come on, let's get out of here before I go nuts or freeze to death or something,' and he turned and led the way back along the shore.

When we reached the whaleboat he got in and rummaged for a blanket in the stern locker while I pushed off. By the time I'd clambered in after him and got the engine started, he had the blanket round his shoulders and was extracting the cork from a half-bottle of whisky with his teeth.

'Looks as if they carry this with the iron rations,' he said and held it out. 'What about you?'

I shook my head.

'We've been through all this before, Jack. I never use the stuff, remember?'

I had no way of knowing exactly how much whisky he had put away by then, but it was obvious that he was fast reaching a state where he would have difficulty in remembering where he was and why, never mind make any kind of sense out of past events.

I knew the feeling well. There had been a time when I spent too many mornings in a grey fog wondering where I was—who I was. At that point it's a long fast drop down unless you have enough sense to turn before it's too late and take that first fumbling step in the other direction.

'Sorry, I was forgetting,' he said. 'Now me—I'm lucky. I've always been able to take it or leave it.' He grinned, his teeth chattering slightly. 'Mostly take it, mind you—one of life's great pleasures, like a good woman.'

Just what was his definition of good was anybody's guess. He swallowed deeply, made a face and examined the label on the bottle. 'Glen Fergus malt whisky. Never heard of it and I'm the original expert.'

'Our finest local brew.'

'They must have made it in a very old zinc bath. Last time I tasted anything like it was during Prohibition.'

Not that he was going to let a little thing like that put him off, and as I took the whaleboat out through the pack ice he moved down to the prow. He sat there huddled in his blanket, the bottle clutched against his chest, staring up at the mountains and the ice-cap beyond as we skirted an iceberg that might have been carved from green glass. He spoke without turning round.

'Ilana—she's quite a girl, isn't she?'

'She has her points.'

'And then some. I could tell you things about that baby that would make your hair stand up on end and dance. Miss Casting Couch of 1964.' I was aware of a sudden vague resentment, the first stirrings of an anger that was as irrational as it was unexpected, but he carried straight on. 'I gave her the first big break, you know.'

I nodded. 'She was telling me about that on the flight in. Some war picture you made in Italy.'

He laughed out loud, lolling back against the bulwark as if he had found the whole thing hilariously funny in retrospect. 'The biggest mistake I ever made in my life, produced and directed by Jack Desforge. We live and we learn.'

'Was it that bad?'

He was unable to contain his laughter. 'A crate of last year's eggs couldn't have smelled any higher.'

'What about Ilana?'

'Oh, she was fine.' He shrugged. 'No Bergman or anything like that, but she had other qualities. I knew that the first time I

met her.' He took another pull at the bottle. 'I did everything for
that girl. Clothes, grooming, even a new name—the whole bit.'

I frowned. 'You mean Ilana Eytan isn't her real name?'

'Is it hell,' he said. 'She needed a gimmick like everyone else,
didn't she? I started out myself as Harry Wells of Tilman Falls,
Wisconsin. When I first met Ilana she was plain Myra Grossman.'

'And she isn't Israeli?'

'All part of the build-up. You know how it is. Israeli sounds
better. It did to her anyway and that's the important thing. She's
got a complex a mile wide. Her old man has a tailor's shop in
some place called the Mile End Road in London. You ever
heard of it?'

I nodded, fighting back an impulse to laugh out loud. 'It's a
funny old world, Jack, has that ever occurred to you?'

'Roughly five times a day for the last fifty-three years.' He
grinned. 'I'm only admitting to forty-five of those, remember.'
And then his mood seemed to change completely and he moved
restlessly, pulling the blanket more closely about his shoulders.
'I've been thinking. Did Ilana have anything for me?'

'Such as?'

'A letter maybe—something like that.'

It was there in his voice quite suddenly, an anxiety he was
unable to conceal and I shook my head. 'Not that I know of,
but why should she confide in me?'

He nodded and raised the bottle to his mouth again. It was
cold now in spite of the sun and the perfect blue of the sky. A
small wind lifted across the water and I noticed that the hands
trembled slightly as they clutched the bottle. He sat there brooding for a while, looking his age for the first time since I'd known
him and then, quite unexpectedly, he laughed.

'You know that was really something back there—with the bear,
I mean. What a way to go. Real B picture stuff. We don't want
it good, we want it by next Monday.'

He took another swallow from the bottle which was by now
half-empty, and guffawed harshly. 'I remember Ernie Hemingway saying something once about finishing like a man, standing
up straight on your two hind legs and spitting right into the eye
of the whole lousy universe.' He swung round, half-drunk and
more than a little aggressive. 'And what do you think of that
then, Joe, baby? What's the old world viewpoint on the weighty
matter of life and death, or have you no statement to make at
this time?'

'I've seen death if that's what you mean,' I said. 'It was always painful and usually ugly. Any kind of life is preferable to that.'

'Is that a fact now?' He nodded gravely, a strange glazed expression in his eyes and said softly, 'But what if there's nothing left?'

And then he leaned forward, the eyes starting from his head, saliva streaking his beard, and cried hoarsely, 'What have you got to say to that, eh?'

There was nothing I could say, nothing that would help the terrible despair in those eyes. For a long moment he crouched there in the bottom of the boat staring at me and then he turned and hurled the bottle high into the air and back towards the green iceberg. It bounced on a lower slope, flashed once like fire in the sunlight and was swallowed up.

CHAPTER FOUR

As WE APPROACHED the *Stella,* Sørensen and Ilana Eytan came out of the wheelhouse and stood at the rail waiting for us. Desforge raised his arm in greeting and she waved.

'Ilana, baby, this is wonderful,' he cried as we swung alongside and I tossed the end of the painter to Sørensen.

Desforge was up the ladder and over the rail in a matter of seconds and when I arrived she was tight in his arms looking smaller than ever in contrast to his great bulk.

And she had changed again. Her eyes sparkled and her cheeks were touched with fire. In some extraordinary manner she was alive in a way she simply had not been before. He lifted her in his two hands as easily as if she had been a child and kissed her.

'Angel, you look good enough to eat,' he said as he put her down. 'Let's you and me go below for a drink and you can tell me all the news from back home.'

For the moment I was forgotten as they disappeared down the companionway and Sørensen said, 'So she is staying?'

'Looks like it,' I said.

'When do you want to start back?'

'There's no great rush. I'll refuel, then I'll have a shower and something to eat.'

He nodded. 'I'll get you the evening weather report on the radio from Søndre tower.'

He went into the wheelhouse and I dropped back into the whaleboat, started the engine and turned towards the shore feeling slightly depressed as I remembered the expression in Ilana's eyes when Desforge had kissed her. Perhaps it was because I'd seen it once already that day when Gudrid Rasmussen had looked at Arnie, offering herself completely without saying a word, and I didn't like the implication.

God knows why. At that moment the only thing I could have said with any certainty was that in spite of her habitual aggressiveness, her harshness, I liked her. On the other hand if there was one thing I had learned from life up to and including that precise point in time, it was that nothing is ever quite as simple as it looks.

I thought about that for a while, rather glumly, and then the whaleboat grounded on the shingle and I got out and set to work.

I didn't see any sign of Desforge or the girl when I returned to the *Stella* and I went straight below to the cabin I'd been in the habit of using on previous visits. It had been cold working out there on the exposed beach with the wind coming in off the sea and I soaked the chill from my bones in a hot shower for ten or fifteen minutes, then got dressed again and went along to the main saloon.

Desforge was sitting at the bar alone reading a letter, a slight fixed frown on his face. He still hadn't changed and the blanket he had wrapped around himself in the whaleboat lay at the foot of the high stool as if it had slipped from his shoulder.

I hesitated in the doorway and he glanced up and saw me in the mirror behind the bar and swung round on the stool. 'Come on in, Joe.'

'So you got your letter,' I said

'Letter?' He stared at me blankly for a moment.

'The letter you were expecting from Milt Gold.'

'Oh, this?' He held up the letter, then folded it and replaced it in its envelope. 'Yes, Ilana delivered it by hand.'

'Not bad news I hope.'

'Not really—there's been a further delay in setting things up, that's all.' He put the letter in his pocket and reached over the bar for a bottle. 'Tell me, Joe, how much longer have we got before the winter sets in and pack ice becomes a big problem and so on.'

'You mean up here around Disko?'

'No, I mean on the coast generally.'

'That all depends.' I shrugged. 'Conditions fluctuate from year to year, but on the whole you're clear till the end of September.'

He seemed genuinely astonished. 'But that would give me another six or seven weeks. You're sure about that?'

'I should be—this is my third summer remember. August and September are the best months of the season. Highest mean temperatures, least problem with pack ice and so on.'

'Well, that's great,' he said. 'Milt thinks they should be ready to go by the end of September.'

'Which means you can hang on here and keep your creditors at bay till then,' I said.

'They'll sing a different tune when I'm working and the shekels start pouring in again.' He seemed to have recovered all his old spirits and went behind the bar and poured himself another drink. 'You flying back tonight, Joe?

I nodded. 'No choice, I've got two charter trips arranged for tomorrow already and there could be more when I get back.'

'That's too bad. You'll stay over for dinner?'

'I don't see why not.'

'Good—I'll settle up with you first, then I'll take a shower and change. How much is it this time?'

'Seven-fifty including the supplies.'

He opened a small safe that stood under the bar and took out a plain black cash box. It was one of the strange and rather puzzling things about him, this insistence on paying cash on the barrel for everything. His financial position may have been pretty rotten everywhere else in the world, but on the Greenland coast he didn't owe a cent. He opened the box, took out a wad of notes that obviously contained several thousand dollars and peeled off eight hundred dollar bills.

'That should take care of it.'

I fitted the notes into my wallet carefully and Desforge replaced the cash box in the safe. As he locked the steel door and straightened up again, Ilana Eytan came into the saloon.

I saw her first in the mirror behind the bar framed in the doorway and anywhere in the world from Cannes to Beverly Hills she would have had the heads turning.

She was wearing a slip of a dress in gold thread with tambour beading that must have set someone back a hundred guineas at least. The hemline was a good six inches above the knee, just right for swinging London that year and the black, shoulder-length hair contrasted superbly with the whole ensemble. Perhaps it was something to do with her smallness in spite of the gold high-heeled shoes, but she carried herself with a kind of superb arrogance that seemed to say: Take me or leave me—I couldn't care less. I don't think I've ever met any woman who looked more capable of taking on the whole world if needs be.

Desforge went to meet her, arms outstretched. 'What an entrance. I don't know where you got it, but that dress is a stroke of genius. You look like some great king's whore.'

She smiled faintly. 'That wasn't exactly the intention, but it will do for a start. What about the letter—good news? Milt didn't tell me much when I saw him.'

'More delays I'm afraid.' Desforge shrugged. 'You should know the movie business by now. Milt thinks we'll be ready to go by the end of next month.'

'And what are you going to do till then?'

'I might as well stay on here. It's the perfect solution under the circumstances and I'm having far too good a time to want to leave just yet.' He turned and grinned at me. 'Isn't that a fact, Joe?'

'Oh, he's having a ball all right,' I assured her. 'The only question is will he survive till the end of September.'

Desforge chuckled. 'Don't take any notice of Joe, angel. He's just a natural born pessimist. Give him a drink while I have a shower then we'll have something to eat.'

The door closed behind him and she turned to look at me calmly, hand on hip, the scrap of dress outlining her body so perfectly that she might as well have had nothing on.

'You heard what the man said. Name your poison.'

I helped myself to a cigarette from a box on the bar. 'Jack's memory gets worse almost day-by-day. He knows perfectly well that I never use the stuff.'

'That's a dent in the image for a start,' she said and went behind the bar. 'Sure you won't change your mind?'

I shook my head. 'With a dress like that around I need a clear head.'

'Is that supposed to be a compliment?'

'A statement of fact. On the other hand I've no objection to keeping you company with a stiff tomato juice.'

'Well laced with Worcestershire Sauce?' I nodded.

'We aim to please. Coming right up.'

There was an elaborate stereo record player in one corner and I moved across and selected a couple of old Sinatra LPs, mostly Cole Porter and Rodgers and Hart material, with one or two standards thrown in for good measure.

The maestro started to give out with 'All the things you are' and I turned and went back to the bar. My tomato juice was waiting for me in a tall glass. It was ice-cold, obviously straight from the fridge and tasted fine. I swallowed half and she toasted me with an empty glass, picked up the bottle of vodka that stood at her elbow and poured some in. She added a scoop of crushed ice, something close to amusement in her eyes.

'The perfect drink. Tasteless, odourless, the same results as a shot in the arm and no headache in the morning.'

I think I knew then what she had done and a moment later a sudden terrible spasm in the pit of my stomach confirmed it. I dropped the glass and clutched at the bar and her face seemed to crack wide open, the eyes widening in alarm.

'What is it? What's wrong?'

The taste started to rise into my mouth, foul as sewer water and I turned and ran for the door. I slipped and stumbled half-way up the companionway and was aware of her calling my name and then I was out into the cool evening air. I just managed to make the rail when the final nausea hit me and I dropped to my knees and was violently sick.

I hung there against the rail for a while, retching spasmodically, nothing left to come and finally managed to get some kind of control. When I got to my feet and turned she was standing a yard or two away looking strangely helpless, her face white, frightened. 'What did you put into the tomato juice—vodka?' I said wearily.

'I'm sorry.' Her voice was almost inaudible. 'I didn't mean any harm.'

'What was I supposed to do, make a pass at you on one vodka?' I found a handkerchief, wiped my mouth and tossed it over the rail. 'Something I omitted from the story of my life was the fact that I was once an alcoholic. That was as good a reason for my wife leaving me as all the romantic ones I gave you at Argamask. After I crawled back out of nowhere for the third time, she'd had enough. Her parting gift was to book me into a clinic that specializes in people like me. They did a very thorough job of aversion therapy with the aid of a couple of drugs called apomorphine and antabus. Just a taste of any kind of liquor these days and my guts turn inside out.'

'I'm sorry,' she said. 'You'll never know how much.'

'That's all right, Myra,' I said. 'You weren't to know. Part of that fantasy life of mine that we were discussing earlier today and I'm stuck with it. I suppose we all have things we don't care to discuss in mixed company.'

She had gone very still from the moment that I had used her real name and suddenly I felt bitterly angry and sorry for her, both at the same time.

I grabbed her by the arms and shook her furiously. 'You stupid little bitch—just what are you trying to prove?'

She struck out at me and wrenched herself free with a strength that was surprising. I staggered back, almost missing my footing and she turned and disappeared down the companionway. There was a murmur of voices and a moment later, Desforge appeared.

'What in the hell is going on here?'

'A slight disagreement, that's all.'

'Did you make a pass at her or something?'

I laughed. 'You'll never know just how funny that is.'

'But she was crying, Joe—I've never seen her do that before.'

I frowned, trying to imagine her in tears and failed completely. Perhaps that other girl, the one in the graveyard at Argamask, but not Ilana Eytan.

'Look, Jack, anything she got she asked for.'

He raised a hand quickly. 'Okay, boy, I believe you. All the same, I think I'd better go and see what's wrong.'

He went down the companionway and the door of the wheelhouse opened and Sørensen came out, his face impassive although I realized that he must have seen everything.

'I've got that met report for you from Søndre, Joe. Things look pretty steady for the next couple of hours, but there's a front moving in from the ice-cap. Heavy rain and squalls. You might just about beat it if you leave now.'

It gave me a perfect out and I seized it with both hands. 'I'd better get moving. No need to bother Desforge at the moment, I think he's got his hands full. Tell him I'll see him next week. If he wants me to come for the girl before then you can always radio in.'

He nodded gravely. 'I'll get the whaleboat ready for you.'

I went below for my things and when I returned, one of the crew was waiting to take me ashore. He dropped me on the beach and started back to the *Stella* straight away and I got ready to leave.

I did the usual routine check then started the engine and ran the Otter down into the sea. I took up the wheels and taxied down-wind slowly, leaning out of the side window and checking the water for ice floes before making my run.

When I was about a hundred yards north of the *Stella* I started to turn into the wind and found the whaleboat bearing down on me, Desforge standing up in the prow waving furiously. I cut the engine and opened the side door as the whaleboat pulled in alongside. Desforge tossed me a canvas holdall, stepped on to the nearest float and hauled himself up into the cabin.

'I've got a sudden hankering to see some city life for a change —any objections?'

'You're the boss,' I said. 'But we'll have to get moving. I'm trying to beat some dirty weather into Frederiksborg.'

The whaleboat was already turning away and I pressed down the starter switch and started to make the run. Twenty seconds later we drifted into the air and climbed steeply, banking over the

Stella just as Ilana Eytan appeared from the companionway and stood looking up at us.

'What about her?' I said.

Desforge shrugged. 'She'll be okay. I told Sørensen to make tracks for Frederiksborg tonight. They'll be there by tomorrow afternoon.'

He produced the inevitable hip flask, took a swallow and started to laugh. 'I don't know what you did back there, but she was certainly in one hell of a temper when I went to her cabin.'

'I'd have thought you'd have wanted to stay and console her,' I said sourly.

'What that baby needs is time to cool off. I'm getting too old to have to fight for it. I'll wait till she's in the mood.'

'What's she doing here anyway?' I said. 'Don't tell me she just came to deliver that letter. There is such a thing as a postal service, even in Greenland.'

'Oh, that's an easy one. She's hoping for the female lead in the picture I'm making.' He grinned. 'That's why I'm so sure she'll come round—they always do. She'll be sweetness and light when the *Stella* arrives tomorrow.'

He leaned back in his seat, tilting the peak of his hunting cap down over his eyes and I sat there, hands steady on the wheel, thinking about Ilana Eytan, trying to imagine her selling herself, just for a role in a picture. But why not? After all, people sell themselves into one kind of slavery or another every day of the week.

Rain scattered across the windscreen in a fine spray and I frowned, all other thoughts driven from my mind at the prospect of that front moving in faster than they had realized at Søndre. I pulled back the stick and started to climb.

CHAPTER FIVE

RAIN LASHED against the glass in the hotel door, driven by a sudden flurry of wind and I turned and walked to the desk where Desforge was booking in.

'I'd say we just made it in time.'

He grinned. 'They can keep the great outdoors on a night like this. You'll have dinner with me?'

'I've one or two things to take care of first. I'll see you in about half an hour.'

He went upstairs and I phoned through to the airstrip to see if they had any messages for me. There was one—an extra charter job for the following day. Nothing very exciting—a short hop of forty miles down the coast to Intusk with machine parts for the canning factory. I checked the flight time, made a note of it and turned away.

'Oh, Mr. Martin.' The receptionist came out of her office quickly. 'You've forgotten your mail.'

She held out a couple of letters. One was a bill, I could tell as much without opening it. The other was postmarked London and carried the name and address of a firm of solicitors in Lincoln's Inn. There was a slight, hollow feeling at the pit of my stomach, but I slipped the letter into my pocket and managed a big smile.

'Thanks very much.'

'And there was a message,' the girl said. 'A Mr. Vogel would like you to contact him.'

'Vogel?' I frowned. 'Never heard of him.'

'I believe he booked into the hotel early this afternoon,' she said. 'I didn't see him myself.'

I nodded. 'All right—I'll attend to it.'

Probably a wealthy tourist looking for some good hunting and prepared to pay through the nose for it. Not that I had any objections to that, but for the moment I had other things on my mind.

I think I must have sat on the edge of my bed staring down at that envelope for at least five minutes before I finally decided to open it. The letter inside was beautifully typed, short and very much to the point. It informed me that my wife had been

awarded a decree nisi in the Divorce Court on the grounds of
desertion, that she had decided to waive her right to any main-
tenance and that a sum of two thousand, three hundred and
seventy-five pounds, my share of the proceeds of the sale of a flat
in the Cromwell Road, jointly owned, had been credited to my
account in the City Branch of the Great Western Bank.

It was all very sad, but then the end of something always is
and I sat there for a while remembering things as they had been
once upon a time when the going was good and each day carried
a new promise.

But even in that I was being consciously dishonest, forgetting
quite deliberately the other side of the coin which had also been
present from the beginning. Still, it was over now, the cord finally
cut, and there was no bottle to reach for this time, could never be
again. Let that be an end to it.

I didn't bother to change and simply took off my parka and
flying boots and pulled on a pair of reindeer hide slippers. As I
went out, Arnie Fassberg came up the stairs and turned along
the corridor towards me, a bottle of schnapps in one hand.

'And what might you be up to?' I asked.

He grinned. 'Gudrid's giving me a little supper in her room.'

'What's wrong with your place?'

'She's on duty till one a.m. tonight. I couldn't wait that long.'

He'd had a drink or two already, so much was obvious, and
swung me round like a schoolboy. 'It's a great life, Joe. A wonderful life as long as you learn the big, big secret. Take whatever's
going because you can never count on tomorrow.'

At that moment the door behind him opened and a woman
emerged. Arnie cannoned into her and her handbag went flying.
She was strikingly beautiful and could have been anything
between thirty and thirty-five, with the sad, haunted eyes of a
Renaissance Madonna. He stood there gaping at her, that well-
known expression on his face and she smiled suddenly, the sort
of smile that comes easily to an attractive woman when she realizes
that the man before her is putty in her hands.

'I'm sorry,' he said.

He dropped to one knee, reaching for the handbag at the same
moment that she did and she almost lost her balance so that I
had to catch her.

'Thank you,' she said, glancing over her shoulder and then
took her handbag gently from Arnie's hands as he stood there
staring at her like a lovesick schoolboy. 'Mine I think.'

As she walked along the corridor, her shoulders were shaking with laughter.

'What a woman, Joe,' Arnie breathed. 'What a woman.'

'Aren't they all, Arnie?' I said and left him standing there and went downstairs.

Desforge was already seated at a table in the far corner of the dining room and I moved towards him. The place was pretty full, mostly people I either knew personally or by sight, but there were three who were new to me—the woman from the corridor and two men who were seated together at the table in the bow window that Ilana Eytan had used that morning. I glanced at her briefly on my way across the room and sat on the other side of the table from Desforge.

He smiled. 'You noticed her too?'

'Is there a man in the room who hasn't? Who is she?'

'I haven't had a chance to find out yet.'

'You will, Jack, you will.'

Desforge had a bottle of hock to himself and I shared a fresh salmon with him. We had reached the coffee stage when someone put a hand on my shoulder. I looked up and found one of the two men who had been sitting at the table by the window with the woman. I glanced across and saw that his companions had disappeared.

'Mr. Martin—Mr. Joe Martin?'

He was of medium height and thickset and wore a two-piece suit in thornproof tweed that had been cut by someone who knew what he was doing. His English was excellent with just the trace of an accent that hinted at something Germanic in his background although, as I learned later, he was Austrian.

I disliked him on sight and not for any particular reason. It was simply that I didn't care for solid middle-European-looking gentlemen with bald heads and gold-capped teeth and large diamond rings on the little finger of the left hand.

I didn't bother getting up. 'I'm Joe Martin—what can I do for you?'

'Vogel—Hans Vogel. My card.'

It was an elegant strip of white pasteboard which announced that he was managing director of the London and Universal Insurance Company Ltd., with offices just off Berkeley Square.

'What's it all about, Mr. Vogel?' I said. 'This is Mr. Jack Desforge, by the way, a friend of mine.'

'There is no need to introduce Mr. Desforge.' He reached across to shake hands. 'A very great honour, sir.'

Desforge looked suitably modest and graciously waved him into one of the vacant chairs. Vogel sat down, took out his wallet and produced a scrap of paper which he passed across to me.

'Perhaps you would be good enough to read this.'

It was a clipping from *The Times* only four days old and described an interview with the leaders of an Oxford University expedition which had just arrived back in London after successfully crossing the Greenland ice-cap from west to east. It seemed they had come across the wreckage of an aeroplane, a Heron, with a Canadian registration and a couple of bodies inside or what was left of them. Identification had been difficult, but according to the personal belongings and documentary evidence recovered, one was an Englishman called Gaunt and the other a man named Harrison. The expedition had buried the remains and continued on its way.

Strange, but for the briefest of moments I seemed to see it lying there in the snowfield, the scarlet and blue of the crumpled fuselage vivid in the bright white light of the ice-cap. It was as if it had been biding its time, waiting for the moment when things were going well for me for the first time in years before drifting up from the darkness like some pale ghost to taunt me.

But why hadn't it burned? With the amount of fuel left in the tanks it should have gone up like a torch.

I don't know how I managed to keep my hands still, but I did and read the cutting through again slowly to give myself time.

'What do you think, Mr. Martin?' Vogel's voice cut through to me.

I passed the cutting to Desforge. 'Interesting, but hardly surprising. Earlier this year a similar expedition four hundred miles further north came across an American transport plane that disappeared on a flight from Thule three years ago.'

'That seems incredible. Was no search mounted?'

'As a matter of fact, a highly intensive one, but a million and a quarter square miles of ice and snow is a hell of an area to cover.' I was getting into my stride now, my voice strong and steady as I kept up the flow. 'It happens all the time. It's the uncertain weather conditions on the ice-cap that do it. One moment a clear blue sky, fifteen minutes later the bottom's dropped out of the glass and you're in the centre of a raging storm and in a light aircraft that can be disastrous. What's your interest in this, anyway?'

'A large one, I'm afraid. My firm insured this plane, Mr. Martin. It disappeared more than a year ago on a flight from Grant Bay in Labrador.'

'What was the destination?' Desforge asked.

'Ireland.'

I raised my eyebrows. 'Then they were more than a little off course. Who was flying?'

'Frankly, we don't know. The plane was owned by Marvin Gaunt. Who this man Harrison was I haven't the slightest idea, but that's what it said on the name tab inside his jacket. There was also a wallet containing seven hundred dollars and an American Diner's Club card in the name of Harvey Stein. As a matter of interest, when we checked that through their London office it turned out to be forgery.'

'Curiouser and curiouser,' I said. 'Just like Alice.'

'The most puzzling thing is yet to come, Mr. Martin. The pilot for the flight as logged out of Grant Bay was a Canadian called Jack Kelso and the airport records definitely indicate that the plane only carried Gaunt and the pilot.'

'Sounds like a good storyline,' Desforge put in.

Vogel said: 'But one with little humour in it for my company. After the statutory period had elapsed we paid Gaunt's next of kin—his mother, as it happened—the sum of twenty-five thousand pounds called for under the terms of the insurance policy.'

Desforge whistled softly. 'I'd say that entitles you to some sort of explanation.'

Vogel smiled thinly. 'Exactly how we feel, Mr. Desforge. The whole affair is obviously far too mysterious. As I see it there are three questions which must be answered. Who was this man Harrison? What happened to Kelso? Why was the plane so far off course?'

Desforge grinned and emptied the last of the hock into his glass. 'I said it was a good storyline.'

Vogel ignored him. 'As soon as I read the account of the find I contacted the Danish Embassy in London. They told me that eventually their civil aviation people would be inspecting the wreck, but that for various reasons there would probably be a considerable delay, perhaps even until next summer. Under the circumstances they obtained permission from the Ministry in Copenhagen for me to make a preliminary inspection myself.'

'If you can get there,' I said.

He smiled. 'Which is where you come in, my friend. In Godthaab they told me that Joe Martin was the most experienced pilot on the coast.' He took out his wallet and produced a type-written document which he passed across. 'That's the necessary clearing certificate from the Ministry.'

I examined it briefly and passed it back. 'Have you considered that there might be a logical explanation for this whole thing?'

There was something in his eyes for a moment, a greenish glow that appeared like some warning signal then faded.

'I'm afraid I don't understand,' he said politely.

'That this Marvin Gaunt was up to no good, that Kelso never really existed at all, except for the specific reason of getting that plane out of Grant Bay. That he was really Harrison all along.'

'That's good,' Desforge said. 'That's damned good.'

Vogel sighed. 'Ingenious, but unfortunately it won't wash, Mr. Martin.'

'Why not?'

'Because Jack Kelso was most certainly flesh and blood and the London and Universal Insurance Co. has the best reason for remembering the fact. You see under the terms of Marvin Gaunt's policy, the pilot was also covered for the same death benefit.'

'And you paid out?' Desforge said.

'Twenty-five thousand pounds,' Vogel nodded. 'To Mrs. Sarah Kelso, his widow. She's waiting in the bar now with my associate. Perhaps you gentlemen would like to meet her?'

CHAPTER SIX

THE CROWD in the bar, although exclusively male, was reasonably
well-behaved. There were one or two of the more prosperous
locals, some Danish engineers and surveyors who were on the
coast to work on government building projects during the short
summer season, and a handful of young officers from a Danish
Navy corvette that was doing survey work on the coast that year.

As we pushed our way through, Sarah Kelso was the subject
of more than one conversation and I didn't blame them. Sitting
there at a booth in the corner in the half light of the shaded
lamp that stood on the table, she looked hauntingly beautiful.

Her companion stood up as we approached and Vogel introduced him first. 'This is Ralph Stratton, an aviation expert from
our Claims Department. I thought it might be a good idea to
bring an expert along.'

Stratton was tall and lean with a neatly clipped moustache
and the look of a typical ex-RAF type except for the eyes which
had the same sort of shine that you get when light gleams on
the edge of a cut-throat razor and which contrasted oddly with
the slightly effeminate edge to his public school voice. He placed
a hand as soft and boneless as any woman's briefly in mine and
Vogel turned to Mrs. Kelso.

'I'd like you to meet Mr. Martin, my dear, the young man
we were told about in Godthaab. I'm hoping he's going to help
us.'

'In a way Mr. Martin and I have already met,' she said and held
my hand for a long moment, the dark eyes full of anxiety. When
she carried on, the soft, musical voice was charged with emotion.
'I'm afraid the last three or four days have been something of
a nightmare. None of this seems real at all.'

There was a slight silence and Desforge said quietly, 'Maybe
I'd better see you later, Joe.'

'Not at all,' Vogel cut in quickly. 'Mr. Jack Desforge, my dear.
I'm sure you've no objection if he stays.'

She stared up at Desforge in something close to bewilderment.
'Now I know I'm dreaming.'

He patted her hand gently. 'Anything I can do—anything at
all. You just name it.'

She held his hand for even longer than she'd held mine—long enough to hook him good and hard, which was obvious from his face as we all sat down and Vogel snapped his fingers at a hovering waiter and ordered coffee. Desforge gave Sarah Kelso a cigarette and she leaned back against the padded wall of the booth, her eyes fixed on me.

'Mr. Vogel will have told you what all this is about, I suppose?'

'Except for one thing. I'm still not too clear why you should be here.'

Vogel said: 'I would have thought that was obvious, Mr. Martin. The whole point of our investigation is to determine the identity of the second man found in the wreck beyond reasonable doubt. Is he the mysterious Mr. Harrison, whoever he was—and that has yet to be determined—or Jack Kelso? It seems to me that Mrs. Kelso is the only person who can give an opinion on that point with any certainty.'

'By going out there and viewing the body?' I said, and laughed out loud. 'Considering Mrs. Kelso's vested interest in a positive identification, I must say you show a touching faith in human nature for a businessman, Mr. Vogel.'

Surprisingly it was Desforge who reacted first. 'That's a hell of a thing to say,' he said angrily.

Sarah Kelso put a hand on his arm as if to hold him in check. 'No, Mr. Desforge, your friend has made an obvious point. If that body is not my husband's then I am in a very difficult position. Mr. Vogel is well aware of that.'

He leaned across the table and for a moment they might have been completely alone. 'You know I'll do everything in my power to help you, my dear, but you must know also that my hands are tied.'

She smiled gently and turned to me. 'I have two young sons, Mr. Martin, did you know that?'

'No, I didn't, Mrs. Kelso.'

'Then perhaps you'll realize now that there is more to this than the money—much more. I must know if that man out there is my husband. I must know. Can you understand that?'

The soft eyes were filled with anxiety, one hand reaching out in a kind of desperate appeal to touch mine gently. She was good—more than that. She was brilliant. For a moment she actually had me going along with her and I had to make a real effort to pull myself back to reality.

'Yes, I can understand that, Mrs. Kelso. I'm sorry.'

'I had to inform Mrs. Kelso of what was going on,' Vogel said. 'She asked to come along and we were glad to have her. I should add that as well as a full physical description and photographs, she has also volunteered certain additional information as to identity which can only be confirmed on the spot. Under those circumstances I can't honestly see how she could get away with a deliberately false identification.'

'Have you got a photograph with you?' I said.

He nodded to Stratton who produced a manilla file from a leather briefcase. He passed two photographs across. One was a straight portrait job in half-profile that looked as if it had been taken a year or two back and showed a reasonably handsome man in his late twenties with a strong jaw and a firm mouth. The other was more recent and showed him in flying gear standing beside a Piper Comanche. I think it was the face that had changed most. In the other picture he'd seemed pretty average, in this he looked like a man who'd decided that in the final analysis only the price tag was important.

I laid them down in front of Sarah Kelso. 'So that's what he looked like?'

She stared at me, a slight puzzled frown on her face. 'I don't understand.'

'Let me tell you about the ice-cap, Mrs. Kelso. What it's really like up there. To start with it's so cold that flesh can't putrefy. That means that as soon as life leaves it, a body freezes so quickly that it's preserved indefinitely.'

'But from the expedition report, I got the impression that the bodies were in an advanced state of decomposition,' Vogel said quickly.

'There's only one thing living up there on top, Mr. Vogel,' I said, 'the Arctic Fox, and he's a scavenger as savage as any hyena.' I didn't need to elaborate. Sarah Kelso leaned back, real pain on her face as she closed her eyes for a moment. Now she opened them and there was an astonishing strength in her voice.

'It doesn't matter, Mr. Martin. Nothing matters except the knowing.'

There was another heavy silence broken by Desforge. 'For God's sake, Joe, what's got into you?'

'I just wanted to make sure everyone had got the facts straight, that's all.' I turned to Vogel. 'Now we all know where we are, we can get down to business. First of all I'll have to know where the wreck is.'

Stratton produced a map from the briefcase and spread it across the table. The position had been marked not as a meaningless dot but by two cross-bearings that had been neatly pencilled in by someone who knew his job.

'Can you guarantee this is accurate?" I demanded.

Stratton nodded. 'I drove over to Oxford myself just before we left and had a chat with the two men who led the expedition. They must have known their business or they wouldn't have got across surely?'

Which was fair enough. Only an expert navigator could chart a course with any certainty across that wilderness of snow and ice.

The route of the expedition had been plotted in red ink. It had started from old Olaf Rasmussen's place at Sandvig and had crossed the glacier at the head of Sandvig Fjord by the most direct route, following the high valley through the mountains beyond that led to the ice-cap. They had discovered the plane about a hundred miles inland, not far from Lake Sule.

I studied the map for a while then shook my head.

'You're talking to the wrong man, Mr. Vogel.'

He frowned. 'I don't understand.'

'It's simple. I fly an Otter amphibian, but I also have wheels which means I can put down on land or water, but not on snow.'

'But what about this lake that's marked here,' Stratton said. 'Lake Sule. It can't be more than fifteen miles away from the wreck. Couldn't you put down there?'

'It's usually ice-free for about two weeks during September,' I said. 'Never any earlier than that within my experience.'

'But you could take a look couldn't you? Tomorrow perhaps?' Vogel said. 'I'll pay well. You'd have no worries on that score.'

'I'd be taking your money to no purpose. I can tell you that now and in any case I've already contracted to make three charter flights tomorrow.'

'Whatever you're getting paid, I'll double.'

I shook my head. 'No you won't. I'll still be here trying to make a living after you've gone and I wouldn't last long if I treated people like that.'

'What about getting there by land?' Stratton said. 'I see there's a road from Frederiksborg to Sandvig according to this map.'

'A hundred-mile cart track through the mountain. You could get to Sandvig by Landrover all right in five or six hours depending on weather conditions, but getting to Sandvig isn't the problem. I could fly you there inside an hour. It's what lies beyond that's the trouble. The glacier and the mountains and then the ice-cap. A hundred miles on foot over some of the worst country in the world. At a guess I'd say it took that Oxford expedition the best part of a fortnight.' I shook my head. 'The ideal solution would be a helicopter, but the nearest one of those to my knowledge is at the American base at Thule and that's a thousand miles up the coast from here.'

There was another of those heavy silences and Vogel looked across at Stratton glumly. 'It doesn't look too good, does it?'

Up until then I'd rather enjoyed myself pointing out the difficulties and making the whole thing look impossible, but there had to come a time when I offered the only obvious solution.

'Of course it's just possible that someone could put down in a ski plane up there.'

Vogel was all attention. 'Is there one available?'

I nodded. 'A friend of mine runs an Aermacchi. An Icelander called Arnie Fassberg. You're in luck. He usually take his skis off for the summer, but this year he's left them on because he has a regular charter contract with a mining company on the edge of the ice-cap at Malamusk.'

'And you think he could land in the vicinity of the wreck?' Stratton said.

'He might with luck. It would really depend on whether he could find a snowfield.'

'But not otherwise?'

I shook my head. 'It's a nightmare world up there, a moonscape carved out of ice by the wind, cracked and fissured in a thousand places.'

'This friend of yours, Fassberg I think you said his name was? He is here in Frederiksborg?' Vogel asked.

'He's based at the airstrip here. You could phone him through from the desk and leave a message for him. He'll get it first thing in the morning.'

'Doesn't he live here at the hotel?'

'No, he has his own place on the edge of town.'

'Perhaps we could see him tonight? I would like to get things settled as soon as possible.'

I shook my head. 'Tonight, he's otherwise engaged, Mr. Vogel, believe me.'

'Which means a woman if I know Arnie,' Desforge put in.

Vogel looked at me inquiringly and I nodded. 'Something like that. He takes that side of life very seriously.' I turned to Sarah Kelso. 'You've already met, by the way, just before dinner outside your room.'

Her eyes widened. 'The handsome young man with the white hair? How interesting.' Vogel frowned in puzzlement, but she didn't bother to explain. 'If you don't mind I think I'll go to bed now. I'm very tired.'

'But of course, my dear.' His voice was instantly filled with concern. 'I'll see you to your room.'

'That isn't necessary.'

'Nonsense, I insist. Time we were all in bed anyway. It's been a long day and tomorrow could be even longer.'

We all stood and she held out her hand to me. 'Thank you, Mr. Martin—thank you for all your help.'

Desforge smiled down at her. 'Don't forget now. If there's anything I can do—anything . . .'

'I'll remember.' She smiled up at him warmly, the dark eyes shining for a moment, then walked away on Vogel's arm. Stratton said good night and followed them and Desforge and I sat down.

He sighed and shook his head. 'There goes a real lady, Joe. I thought they'd gone out of style.'

'You think so?'

'I know so.' He frowned. 'I don't know why, but you seem to be doing your level best to give her a hard time.'

'She'll survive,' I said.

Either he hadn't detected the acid in my voice or chose to ignore it, but he carried straight on as if I hadn't spoken. 'She reminds me of someone I used to know a long time ago—Lilian Courtney. You ever heard of her, Joe?'

'I don't think so.'

'She was one of the great original stars of the silent screen. Made her first picture before the first world war. She dropped out when talkies came in. It sounds crazy now, but she thought the whole thing was just a flash in the pan.'

'I think I remember her now,' I said. 'Wasn't there some scandal concerning her death? Drugs or something?'

He flared up instantly. 'That's a damned lie. There were always people who hated her—hated her for what she was—a lady. A real lady in a world of phonies.'

He beckoned to the waiter and ordered whisky. 'Strange, but the older you get, the more you start looking back and the harder you look, the more you realize what a game of chance the whole thing is. The right street corner at the right time.'

'I'm with you there,' I said .'What was yours?'

'The end of the pier in Santa Barbara in 1930—a fine rainy night with the fog rolling in. That's when I met Lilian. She'd gone out for a walk in the rain—one of her weaknesses as I discovered when I got to know her better. Some bum tried to get fresh with her.'

'And you intervened?'

'That's it.' He stared back into the past, a slight smile on his mouth. 'I was just sixteen—a raw kid fresh from Wisconsin who wanted to act. She did everything for me. Clothes, grooming —even sent me to drama school for a while and, most important of all, she got me my first part in pictures.'

'And what did you have to do in return? Sit up and beg?'

It was a cruel and senseless remark that I regretted at once, but I got no chance to apologize. I wasn't even aware of his hand moving, but he had me by the throat with a strength I never knew he possessed and there was a fire in his eyes like hot coals as I started to choke.

'Not a thing—not a solitary damned thing. She treated me like a son. She was a lady, do you hear me? The last time I heard a man say a wrong word about her I broke his jaw.'

He released me suddenly and I sucked in air. 'I get the message. Sarah Kelso's the first lady you've met since?'

'She's got quality, that's for sure and it's a scarce commodity in the world we live in.' He emptied his glass and shook his head. 'What's it all about, Joe? Life, living, the whole bit. Ever ask yourself?'

'At a rough average I'd say around twenty-seven times a day.'

'You can always see the funny side,' he said, 'I wish to hell I could.' He stared sombrely into space. 'I've been living on Stage 6 at Horizon Studios for so long that nothing seems real any more.'

'Except Sarah Kelso?'

There was a cutting edge to my voice that I was unable to conceal and he was immediately aware of it and frowned. 'What do you mean?'

'And the good Mr. Hans Vogel and his associate—the claims surveyor who can afford to wear eighty-guinea Savile Row suits. Salary scales in insurance offices must have risen considerably since I worked in the City.'

'What are you getting at?' he demanded.

'I can smell fish as well as the next man and in this case you don't need to stand too close.' He stared at me blankly. 'It's shot full of holes, Jack, the whole tale. There are so many loose ends I wouldn't know where to start.'

'Are you trying to tell me that Vogel's some kind of crook?'

Is anything ever that simple? I shook my head. 'Maybe you're right, Jack. Perhaps you've been acting one part after another for so long that you've lost all touch with reality. Do you think the villain of the piece always has to look like Sidney Greenstreet or his bully boy like Bogart or Cagney?'

'Stratton?' he said incredulously. 'You're trying to tell me that two-by-four is some kind of tough guy?'

'At a rough guess I'd say he'd slice your throat for a packet of cigarettes in the right circumstances.'

He stared up at me, eyes wide. 'Brother, do you need a good night's sleep.'

'Which is just what I intend to get,' I said sweetly and stood up. 'See you around, Jack.' And I turned and pushed my way through the crowd to the hall.'

I didn't go to bed straight away, there was too much to think about. Outside the wind drove hail like lead bullets against the window and I lit a cigarette and lay on the bed with the radio playing.

When I first heard the knock I thought I was mistaken, it was so gentle, but it came again, a little louder this time and I crossed to the door and opened it.

Sarah Kelso smiled diffidently. 'Could you spare me a minute?'

'My pleasure.'

As I closed the door she moved to the window and looked out into the darkness. 'Is it always as rough as this?'

I crossed to the bed and turned down the radio. 'I don't get the impression you came here to discuss the weather, Mrs. Kelso.'

She turned, a wan smile on her face. 'You're very direct, aren't you, Mr. Martin? In a way that makes it easier. You're quite right, of course. I didn't come here to discuss the weather. To tell you the truth I was hoping you might put me in touch with this pilot you mentioned—Arnie Fassberg I think you said his name was.'

'You mean tonight?' I shook my head. 'I thought I made it clear that he was otherwise engaged.'

'Yes, I know,' she said, a touch of impatience in her voice. 'He's with some girl. Surely that doesn't mean I can't talk to him.'

'What's Vogel think of this?'

'As far as I know he's in bed.' She moved closer and said with a sort of quiet desperation that was very convincing, 'I just want to talk to him, Mr. Martin. I want to know now, tonight, if he can help us. I can't stand much more of this uncertainty.'

I frowned down at her, trying to work out what was going on behind that clear, pure mask she called a face, but she held my gaze unwaveringly.

'All right,' I said. 'Wait here and I'll see what I can do.'

It was quiet at the end of the corridor and there was no sound from inside Gudrid's room. I glanced at my watch. It was just coming up to midnight and according to Arnie she was on duty till one a.m. When I tried the door it was locked, but as I started to turn away, Gudrid came down the service stairs holding a pile of blankets.

There was a glow to her skin and her eyes were shining, giving her the sort of look you find on the face of the cat that's had the cream. Whatever else you could say about him Arnie always seemed to give satisfaction.

'And what can I do for you?' she demanded brightly.

'I thought Arnie might be here.'

'He left about an hour ago. He told me he wanted a good night's sleep for once. He's flying down to Itvak first thing in the morning. Was it something important?'

I shook my head. It can wait. I'll see him tomorrow.'

Sarah Kelso was standing at the window smoking one of my cigarettes when I went in and she turned sharply.

'Too late,' I said. 'He's gone home.'

'Is it far?'

'Five or ten minutes walk.'

'Would you take me?' She moved in close enough to fill my nostrils with her perfume and fixed me with those dark eyes of hers.

'No need to go overboard, Mrs. Kelso,' I said. 'You'll need boots and the warmest coat you've got. I'll meet you in the hall in five minutes.'

She put a hand on my arm and said hesitatingly. 'I was wondering—is there another way out?'

I nodded. 'The service stairs take you right down to the basement. There's a door that opens into the backyard. Would you rather go that way?'

'It's just that Mr. Stratton went back down to the bar. If he saw me going out, he might wonder what was going on.'

'It's certainly a thought,' I said.

Just for a moment I'd caught her off balance and the eager smile slipped fractionally, but she obviously decided to let it go. 'I'll only be a moment,' she said and went out.

There was a force eight gale blowing outside that drove the rain straight into our faces like rusty nails and Sarah Kelso held my arm tightly and huddled against me as we made our way along the main street.

We didn't talk because it took everything we had just to make progress, but when we turned into the narrow street that contained Arnie's place the tall wooden houses on our right broke the force of the wind and the going was a little easier.

Arnie's house was at the far end and backed by rising ground that rose into the foothills, a single-storey wooden building with a veranda at the front. There was a light at the window and a loose shutter swung to and fro in the wind.

I knocked at the door and after a while Arnie opened it and peered out. A scarf was knotted around his neck and he was wearing a dressing gown, but he didn't look as if he'd been roused from his bed.

In that first moment he only saw me and grinned. 'Heh, Joe, you old devil. What can I do for you?'

I pulled Sarah Kelso out of the shadows and pushed her forward. 'Mind if we come in, Arnie? It's damned cold out here.'

His astonishment was plain, but he stood back at once so that we could enter. It was warm and inviting inside with a fire roaring in the stove so that the iron plate on top glowed cherry red.

Sarah Kelso took off her gloves and spread her hands to the warmth. 'This is nice—this is very nice.'

'Arnie Fassberg—Mrs. Sarah Kelso. We'd like to see you on a little matter of business, Arnie, if you can spare five minutes.'

'Business?' he said and dragged his eyes away from her reluctantly. 'I don't understand.'

'Mrs. Kelso can do all the explaining necessary.'

She turned and looked at me coolly. 'You've been very kind, Mr. Martin, but I don't think there's any need for you to stay and go through all this again. I'm sure Mr. Fassberg can see me back to the hotel.'

'Think you can manage that?' I asked Arnie who looked as if he'd been hit by a rather light truck.

'Oh, sure—sure I can, Joe,' he said hurriedly. 'You don't need to worry about Mrs. Kelso. I'll see she gets back to the hotel all right.'

I'd reached the door when she called to me. When I turned, Arnie was helping her off with her coat. It was then that I noticed she'd changed into a peacock-blue dress in jersey wool that buttoned down the front and finished just above the knee. The black leather cossack boots provided just the right final touch.

She crossed to me quickly and put a hand on my sleeve. 'You won't mention this to Mr. Vogel if you see him, will you? I wouldn't like him to get the wrong idea.'

'We must avoid that at all costs,' I assured her solemnly. 'You can rely on me.'

Again that smile of hers slipped, but I turned and went out before she could say anything further.

The wind changed direction, roaring up the funnel of the narrow street, smacking me in the face with the force of a stiff right hand. I was bitterly cold and soaked to the skin as I turned the corner, but it didn't seem to matter one little bit. I wondered how Arnie was doing and laughed out loud. Whether he knew it or not, he was going to have to pay through the nose for whatever he got that night.

CHAPTER SEVEN

IT WAS A FINE bright morning as I walked up to the airstrip to check on the weather. Behind the town the mountains seemed very close in the crystal air like cut-outs pasted on a blue backdrop and sheep drifted across the green foothills in a white cloud pushed by a shepherd and two barking dogs. On such a morning it was easy to understand how the country had got its name and for a moment I thought of those early Viking ships nosing into the fjords in search of the promised land.

Arnie's Aermacchi was already on the runway, a mechanic priming the engine while the young Icelander watched, white hair glinting in the sun. When he saw me he waved and crossed the tarmac, a big smile on his face.

'You looked pleased with yourself,' I said.

His smile widened. 'She's quite a woman, Joe. Not as good as she thinks she is, but I certainly wouldn't kick her out of bed.'

'I couldn't imagine you doing that to a seventy-five-year-old Eskimo woman. I suppose she found time to tell you the tale? Have you met Vogel yet?'

'As a matter of fact I had breakfast with him.'

'Did you mention your night out with Mrs. Kelso?'

He spread his arms wide, an injured look on his face. 'When did I ever open my mouth about a lady?'

'Don't make me answer that,' I said. 'What did she want to see you about anyway?'

He put a hand on my shoulder, his face serious.

'It's love, Joe, from that first wonderful moment when she bumped into me in the corridor outside her room. She just knew she had to come to me.'

'I get the picture,' I said. 'It's bigger than both of you.'

'That's it—that's it exactly.'

'You lying bastard—how about the truth for a change?'

'That's just what I've given you. Oh, she wanted to know if I could help them with this other thing as well. The poor girl's obviously had a very bad time of it lately, but it was me she'd come to see.'

'Then why all the mystery? Why did she ask me to shut up about it to Vogel?'

'I should have thought that was obvious. He's fallen in love with her and like most older men in that position, he's jealous and possessive. She doesn't want to get him stirred up, that's all.'

'He never even loved his mother that one,' I said. 'Still, have it your own way. You're hiring out to Vogel then?'

'I can't afford not to at the prices he's offering. I'll be surprised if I earn my fee though. It's rough country up there. I can't think of anywhere off-hand where I could put down.'

'There's always Lake Sule. Maybe you could land on the ice.'

He nodded. 'I thought of that, but I shouldn't imagine it would be firm enough. At this time of the year it's usually at the half-way stage. I hear you're going to Intusk this morning?'

'That's right.'

'I was wondering whether you'd be interested in taking on an extra trip while you're in that region. I was supposed to fly a supply of drugs to the Portuguese fishing fleet's hospital ship. She's lying off-shore at Itvak. It's only another fifty miles.'

'Suits me,' I said, 'as long as I get paid. What are you going to do?'

'I've got some supplies to deliver to the Royal Greenland Trading Company's store at Sandvig. I thought I could fly on from there and have a look at this plane wreck. It's the only way I can fit it in today. I've got a flight scheduled to Malamusk this afternoon and I can't afford to miss that.'

I could understand how he felt. His connection with the Americans at Malamusk was too important to mess about with just for the sake of squeezing in a charter flight for someone he'd never heard of before. He had a seasonal contract. One trip a week with supplies and technical equipment that paid his expenses for the whole summer. Everything else was gravy.

'Are you taking Vogel and company along?'

He shook his head. 'I'm carrying too much weight on the Sandvig run as it is with those stores. Anyway this is only in the nature of a preliminary survey just to see if there is a snowfield in the vicinity. I don't think I'll have time to land even if I do find somewhere.'

'All right,' I said. 'You'd better arrange for those drugs to be transferred to the Otter. I don't want to be late in getting off. I've a lot on today.'

'They're already on board.' He grinned. 'You're always so reliable, Joe. See you tonight at the Fredericsmut.'

I watched him run across to the Aermacchi and clamber in.

He'd hardly got the door closed before the engine fired and he was away, lifting her far too soon. His nose dropped, but he'd enough sense not to pull back on the stick until he had the power.

He roared across the harbour no more than twenty feet above the water and then his engine note deepened and he started to climb at just the right moment, banking into the sun, all for my benefit of course, nice and fast and showy and one of these days he was going to kill himself doing it.

I had a clear run down to Intusk and Itvak and was back in Frederiksborg before noon to pick up three passengers for Godthaab. From there I flew on to Søndre Strømfjord to meet the afternoon jet from Copenhagen. By four-thirty, I was on my way back with four young Danes who'd come to join the construction crew.

The weather had stayed perfect all day so that there had been no problems to speak of and yet I was tired—really tired. My arms ached and there was a gritty feeling beneath my eyelids as if I hadn't been getting enough sleep. What I really needed was a day off, not that there was any great hope of that.

When we reached Frederiksborg I circled the harbour a couple of times, just to check that I had a clear run, and noticed that the *Stella* had arrived safely. She was tied up at the main jetty and as I came in for my landing someone came out on deck and stood at the rail watching me. I was pretty sure it was Ilana Eytan, but at that distance I couldn't be certain.

I dropped the wheels and ran the Otter up the slipway out of the water. The young Danes gave me a hand to lash her down for the night and as we finished, a Landrover appeared to take them up to the construction camp headquarters. They offered me a lift, but I had business with the harbourmaster and let them go on without me.

When I came out of the harbourmaster's office, Arnie was down at the slipway sitting on a bollard beside the Otter smoking a cigarette and waving vigorously in the direction of the *Stella*. It was Ilana Eytan all right, standing there at the stern rail in her sheepskin coat and a red headscarf.

'I got the impression that your spare time was fully occupied at the moment,' I said.

'I'd toss the whole damned lot of them out of the window for that one. What a woman.'

'I seem to have heard that before somewhere.'

He waved again and she turned and went below. 'The story of my life.'

'Don't give me that,' I said. 'Anyway, how did you get on?'

'At the scene of the crash?' He shook his head. 'Not very well, I'm afraid. To start with I'd some difficulty in locating the plane. From what I could see it's lying at the bottom of a deep gully.'

'And you couldn't land?'

'Out of the question. It's very rough country between there and Sule, Joe. There were one or two places that looked like vague possibilities, but I wouldn't dream of trying them without a ground check and that just isn't practical. I could break a ski or maybe my neck or lose the plane. Even the kind of money Vogel is offering isn't worth that risk.'

'What about Lake Sule?'

He shrugged. 'There was a hell of a lot of mist in that area so I didn't get down very low. From what I could see there was open water, but still plenty of ice about.'

'So neither of us could land?'

'That's certainly the way it looked to me. You could maybe manage it in the Otter later in September, but I wouldn't give much for your chances at the moment.'

'Have you told Vogel yet?'

'This afternoon. He was pretty upset about it, but as I told him, there just isn't anything more I can do.' He glanced at his watch. 'I'll have to go. I've got an evening flight to Malamusk—a special trip with spares for a drilling rig that's broken down. I should be back within a couple of hours. Will you be at the Fredericsmut tonight?'

'Very probably.'

'I'll see you later then.'

I started to refuel the Otter by hand from the stacked jerrycans at the top of the slipway and was still there when he took off ten minutes later. I watched him dwindle into the distance, a hand shading my eyes from the evening sun and when I turned, Ilana Eytan was at the top of the slipway.

'How's the intrepid aviator?'

I emptied the last jerrycan into the tank, screwed the cap home and climbed down. 'Did you have a pleasant trip?'

'I've known better. We hit some ice on the way in this morning.'

'Any damage?'

'The decks aren't awash if that's what you mean. Sørensen's taking her into dry-dock tomorrow.'

'Have you seen Jack?'

She shook her head. 'I think he's keeping out of the way.'

There was a question I'd wanted to put to her, something that had been niggling away at the back of my mind. God knows why. She sat on the bollard Arnie had used and I gave her a cigarette.

'Will you tell me something if I ask it politely enough?'

'Try me.'

'Why did you come. Why did you really come?'

She didn't seem particularly surprised. 'Have you tried asking Jack?'

'As a matter of fact I have.'

'And what was the verdict?'

'He says you're here to make sure of the female lead in his new picture.'

'Well, now, that would seem to make a whole lot of sense to me.' Was there a touch of irony in her voice? It was impossible to be sure and she turned up the collar of her sheepskin coat. 'I can't really think of anything else that would bring me to a God-for-saken hole like this, can you?'

'Not off-hand, but I could give it some thought.'

'You do that and in the meantime you can give me a hand to transfer my stuff from the *Stella*. Sørensen thinks I'd be better off in the hotel at the moment.'

She turned without a word and started across the foreshore to the jetty. I stood there watching her go. She climbed to the con-crete causeway, turned and looked down at me.

'Are you coming?'

'Are you sure you want me?' I said. 'I've a feeling this could easily become a habit.'

I caught her right off guard and for a moment, she was as tongue-tied as any young girl on a first date. Her recovery, when it came, was way below her usual acid standard.

'Don't be an idiot,' she said uncertainly, turned and walked away.

But she knew when I started after her, I could tell by the tilt of her head and the way her shoulders straightened and for some totally inexplicable reason—or at least that's what I tried to tell myself—my stomach went hollow with excitement.

CHAPTER EIGHT

LIKE MOST small communities in out of the way places Frederiksborg had very little crime, but we still had a policeman, Sergeant
Olaf Simonsen, who was responsible for law and order in the town
and an area as great as one of the larger English counties.

He was sitting at the hotel bar when I went in, having a beer
with Jack Desforge, a tall, spare Greenlander, his skin weathered
by forty Arctic winters to the semblance of puckered leather. Just
now he was laughing at something Desforge had said, head thrown
back, a quiet, kindly man, married with five daughters and very
religious—a Moravian like most of the locals. And I had seen this
same man with a look on his face like the wrath of God as he
flushed out a bar full of brawling, drunken fishermen at the
Fredericsmut on a Saturday night with the toe of his boot and an
iron fist.

I sat on the stool next to him. 'Hello, Olaf, what have you been
doing with yourself for the past few days?'

He shook hands. 'I had to go inland—the other side of the
glacier at the head of the Stavanger Fjord.'

'Trouble?'

'The usual thing—reindeer hunters at each other's throats.'

'Anyone hurt?'

'A knifing or two—nothing serious. I think I've quietened them
down. You know Mr. Desforge, of course. He's been making me
laugh.'

I looked across at Jack. 'Anything I should know?'

'I've really hit the big time at last,' he said. 'Some guy turned up
at the hotel earlier wanting an interview for the local press. Naturally I gave him one—I've never turned down free publicity yet.'

'Which paper?'

He started to laugh again. 'That's the whole point.'

I turned to Simonsen. 'The *Atuagagdliutit*?'

He nodded. 'I've just been explaining to Mr. Desforge—he's
now immortalized in the pages of the only newspaper in the world
that's published in Eskimo.'

'And if that isn't worth another drink, I don't know what is,'
Desforge said.

Simonsen shook his head. 'Not for me. I'll have to be off in a moment. I was hoping to catch you tonight, Joe. When I returned there was a memo from headquarters in Godthaab about this plane the Oxford expedition came across. Apparently a Mr. Vogel of the London and Universal Insurance Company approached them with a certificate of search from the Ministry in Copenhagen. I understand they recommended him to see you.'

'That's right.' I gave him the whole story, including the substance of the conversation I'd just had with Arnie Fassberg.

'I can't say I'm surprised Arnie couldn't find a suitable place to land on skis up there, but if that mist had cleared a little allowing him a good look at Lake Sule he'd have seen that there was ample open water for a floatplane landing.'

'Are you certain about that?'

He produced a piece of paper from one of his tunic pockets and passed it across. "See for yourself—that's an extract from the weekly regional met forecast put out by the Americans from Thule. It indicates that mean temperatures have been higher than usual up there for the time of the year.'

I had a look at the report which confirmed what he had said in slightly more technical language and handed it back. 'That seems fair enough to me. They're usually pretty accurate.'

'They have to be.' He put the report back in his pocket. 'So there's no reason now why you can't make the trip. What about tomorrow?'

I stalled for time. 'What are you—Vogel's agent or something?'

He smiled. 'I haven't even met him yet. This is official business now, Joe. The powers-that-be have decided I should go along to keep an eye on things generally and compile a preliminary report for the Ministry people in Copenhagen. It's unlikely they'll be able to get anyone out there till next year. In fact if my report is satisfactory, especially when considered in conjunction with the findings of this aviation expert Vogel has with him, they may decide to take it no further.'

I wondered how Vogel was going to like having a policeman breathing down his neck, but only for a moment. I had my own problems. So I had been right all along. It had been waiting for me out there on the ice-cap for more than a year now and there was no escape. For a brief moment I saw it again in my mind's eyes, silver and blue against the eternal whiteness and a strange fatalism gripped me. I was caught up in a tide of events too strong to fight against and must go with the current and see what happened.

'I suppose I could manage that. It would mean altering my schedules for the next couple of days, but there isn't anything so desperately important that it can't be postponed.

'Good—I think an early start is indicated. Can you be ready for seven a.m.?'

'Any time you like. Will you see Vogel or shall I?'

'I'll handle that—it will give me a chance to meet him.'

'A minor failing of mine.' I said. 'I like to know everything. That wreck is about ten miles east of Sule. How do we get there?'

'On skis of course. We'll do it in two or three hours.'

'That's all right for you and me, but what about the others. Maybe they can't ski.'

'Then they must learn,' he said simply.

'And the woman?'

He shrugged. 'All right, the woman we can haul on a light sledge, but the other two will have to ski or go on foot and they'll find it a rough walk, believe me.'

'All right, you're the boss.'

He adjusted his uniform cap to the regulation angle in the mirror behind the bar. 'If necessary I'll come back to you later. Where will you be?'

'I'd thought of having a meal at the Fredericsmut for a change. It's some time since I've been there."

'The Fredericsmut? You may be in for a lively night, I warn you. There's a Portuguese schooner due.'

I nodded. 'I saw her entering the fjord on my way in. Who is it? Anyone I know?'

'Da Gama.' He chuckled grimly. 'I'd eat here tonight if I were you.'

He went out and Desforge said, 'And who in the hell is this Da Gama—Frankenstein?'

'Something like that. He comes in for supplies about once a month and there's always trouble. One of these days he'll kill somebody—probably has already if the truth's known.'

'Sounds like fun,' Desforge said. 'I think I'll come with you. I could do with a little action and it'll get me out of the way. I don't want to run into Ilana till I'm good and ready.'

'All right,' I said. 'I've one or two things to do. I'll be back in fifteen minutes.'

I left him there at the bar, went to the reception desk and phoned through to the airstrip. I explained that I wouldn't be available for the next couple of days, stressing that I was on government business and asked them to contact the people concerned in Godthaab and Søndre to suggest that they either rearrange their schedules or make other arrangements.

As I had anticipated, there was no particular difficulty and I went up to my room, stripped off my flying gear and had a quick shower. I'd just pulled a heavy Norwegian sweater over my head when there was a knock at the door. I opened it and found Ilana Eytan standing outside.

'I'm looking for Jack. Any idea where he might be?'

I lied cheerfully. 'Not right now,' and then for perverse reason decided to go further. 'I can tell you where he'll be later, though. The Fredericsmut—that's a place at the other end of the main street from here.'

'I'll see him there then.'

I shook my head. 'I wouldn't if I were you. Rough fishermen, hard liquor and a roomful of smoke—not for little girls.'

'In a pig's eye, Joe Martin,' she said and went back along the corridor to her room.

The Fredericsmut was definitely for the lower orders, the sort of place you'll find in any town in the world from Singapore to Jackson Falls, Wyoming. In this case it was a two-storeyed wooden building with a veranda at the front. What went on upstairs was anybody's guess, but through the swing doors that opened from the veranda was a large square room where you could find good plain food in large quantities, any kind of liquor you cared to name and broad-minded women. The one incongruity was a large and shiny juke box that stood by the door and never seemed to stop playing.

We sat at a table at the back of the room close to the bar and I ordered steak and chips for both of us and a lager for Desforge. The juke box was going full blast surrounded by a crowd of youthful Greenlanders, some of them shaking away to the manner born.

Jack groaned as if in pain. 'Is nothing sacred? I come north looking for polar bear, the eternal struggle of man in an alien land, harpoons and sealskin trousers and what do I get?'

'Corduroy trews and the Beatles.'

'Next thing you know one of those outfits in Carnaby Street will be opening up a branch.

I shook my head. 'Just let them try and see what the Royal Greenland Trading Company have to say about it. Maybe they don't have a monopoly any longer, but they still swing a pretty big axe.

The crowd was building up now—construction workers looking for a little fun after a twelve-hour day, inshore fishermen, professional hunters, Danes and Icelanders with a few Norwegians thrown in for good luck, and Greenlanders, some looking pure Scandinavian, others a hundred per cent Eskimo and most of them falling somewhere in between.

'You know when I was a kid my old man was pretty strict with us,' Jack said as we sat there waiting for the food to arrive. 'He died when I was seven and the family had to split up. I went to live with my Aunt Clara in Wisconsin.'

'Did you get on all right with her?'

'Couldn't have been better. She started taking me to the movies, something my father never allowed. This was in the silent days mind you. I can remember one old three-reeler I saw, *The Spoilers*. It's been remade three or four times. The version I saw starred Noah Beery and Milton Sills and they had one hell of a brawl on a set that looked just like this place. Funny how your memory works. I haven't thought of that for years.'

An impudent looking young Eskimo girl in a black silk dress that was a size too small brought the food, leaning so close to Desforge when she put his plate on the table that her breast was crushed against his shoulder.

He asked her to bring him a bottle of whisky from the bar and she ogled him shamelessly, fluttering false eyelashes that somehow looked obscene fringing the slanting, almond-shaped eyes. As she moved through the crowd to the bar someone slapped her backside and there was a sudden burst of laughter. She didn't show the slightest objection when a bearded fisherman in an oilskin jacket pulled her close, kissed her, then passed her on to the man next to him.

'You know there are times when I feel like throwing up,' Desforge said. 'To think of a once proud people reduced to that.'

'It's unfortunate, but primitive races seem to acquire all the vices of our kind of civilization,' I said, 'never its virtues.'

'I've seen the same thing back home on Sioux Indian reservations. A great people reduced to putting on a circus act for tourists.'

'There'll be nowhere left soon.'

'I suppose not.' There was an expression of settled gloom on his face. The girl brought the bottle and a couple of glasses and he poured himself a large whisky.

'I've been thinking of doing a little reindeer hunting. I thought it might be a good opportunity while the *Stella* is in dry-dock.'

'Got any ideas about where to go?'

'The barman at the hotel suggested Sandvig. It seems there are still a few of the old Viking settlements on view in that region or what's left of them. Sounds as if it would be worth the trip even if the hunting doesn't turn out to be a success.'

'You could do worse,' I said. 'There's a man down there I'd love you to meet—Olaf Rasmussen.'

'Rasmussen? Is he anything to do with Gudrid, the chambermaid at the hotel?'

'Her grandfather. He's about seventy-five, a real old Viking. Has a farm near Sandvig with eight hundred head of sheep, but he spends most of his time on excavation work on the old settlements on his land.'

'Do you think he'd put me up for a few days?'

'No question of it—hospitality is his second name. Are you trying to run out on Ilana again by any chance?'

'No, not this time. I'll take her with me if she'll come. How do I get there?'

'That's up to you. You could charter Arnie if he's available or you could even squeeze in with us in the morning if you can be on the slipway at seven. We'll be calling at Sandvig on the way.'

'I'd forgotten such a time existed,' he said. 'Still, it's a thought.'

Just then I noticed Vogel, Ralph Stratton and Sarah Kelso standing just inside the doorway. Vogel saw me in the same moment and said something to the others. He was smiling as they came across.

'I've had a most interesting chat with Sergeant Simonsen, Mr. Martin. It would seem there is a chance for us after all.'

'That still depends on what we find when we get there,' I said as they seated themselves. 'Even if a landing is possible on the lake itself, the weather has to be right. Earlier today for example, when Arnie Fassberg was there, there was such a heavy mist that he didn't get a close look at the lake at all.'

'Is that sort of thing usual?' Stratton asked.

I nodded. 'It happens all the time, even in summer. Hail, rain, mist or perhaps a blizzard that seems to sweep in out of nowhere. An hour later the sky is so blue that you can't believe it's real. How's your ski-ing, by the way?'

'I was born and raised in the Austrian Tyrol,' Vogel said, 'which means I was going to school on skis from the age of five. Mr. Stratton tells me his own experience has been confined to a couple of winter holidays in France, but I'm sure that should prove more than adequate.'

'I'm the odd man out I'm afraid,' Sarah Kelso said, 'but Sergeant Simonsen seems to think that's no problem.'

'From what I've heard you're going to get the de luxe treatment,' Desforge assured her. 'You'll arrive in style without a hair out of place. Now what about a drink?'

By now things had begun to get pretty noisy. People crowded on to the tiny dance floor, there were occasional shrieks from the darker corners and now and then the sound of breaking glass echoed through the haze of tobacco smoke.

'This is hardly the London Hilton.' Desforge leaned across to Sarah Kelso. 'Are you sure you wouldn't rather go some place else?'

'Oh, I should imagine I've got pretty good protection,' she told him. 'To tell you the truth, I'm rather enjoying myself.'

A moment later the doors seemed to burst inwards and Da Gama arrived. He paused inside the door, half a dozen of his crew at his back, a giant of a man in a reefer coat, an old cloth cap pulled down over his dark and greasy hair. He had tiny pig's eyes above flat cheekbones and his skin was so dark that I always suspected he had coloured blood in him.

The juke box kept on playing, but for a moment there was a lull in the general conversation. Da Gama said something over his shoulder to one of his men and laughed harshly. For some reason that seemed to break the tension and people started talking again. He moved to the bar, taking the shortest route, cutting straight through the middle of the crowded dance floor and anyone in his way got out of it quick.

Desforge emptied his glass and filled it again. 'So that's Da Gama? From the look of him I'd say he's probably got a brain the size of a pea.'

'It's his hands you've got to watch,' I said. 'He could break an arm as easily as a rotten stick.'

Strangely enough it was Stratton who reacted most. His face had gone very white and there was a strange glitter in his eyes and then I noticed that his hands were resting lightly on the edge of the table and that he still had his gloves on. They were an expensive-looking pair in soft black leather and somehow deadly. I suddenly knew beyond any doubt that my first estimate of the man had not been far wrong. Effeminate perhaps, but not soft, a mistake people often made about homosexuals. Perhaps it was Da Gama's exaggerated maleness that revolted him.

'He's quite a man, isn't he?' Sarah Kelso said.

'That depends on how you look at it, sweetie.' Stratton lit a Turkish cigarette carefully, still keeping his gloves on. 'Personally, I'm surprised to find he can walk on his hind legs. I thought the human race was supposed to have developed a little over the past half a million years.'

He was certainly right about one thing—Da Gama was an animal; a soulless, mindless brute, savagely cruel and utterly sadistic. Once he got a man down he would stamp him into the ground with as little compunction as any normal individual would crush an ant.

There was a restless gleam in Desforge's eyes that didn't look too healthy and he poured himself another large whisky and laughed shortly. 'You know what they say? The bigger they are the harder they fall.'

'That kind of talk can be dangerous, Jack,' I said. 'Let me give you a few facts. Da Gama never starts a fight, he always leaves that to the other man. That way he keeps out of gaol. But he certainly finishes them. He crippled a sailor in Godthaab in June and half-killed a reindeer hunter in this very bar last month.'

'What do you want me to do?' he demanded. 'Genuflect?'

He didn't get any further. The door opened and Arnie Fassberg came in, Ilana on his arm. She was wearing a rather nice fur coat which looked suspiciously like real mink and she paused at the top of the stairs, her eyes searching the room till she found me. For a long moment she held my gaze, no expression on her face and then she slipped out of the fur coat and handed it to Arnie.

Underneath she was wearing that incredible dress of gold thread and tambour beading and it seemed to catch fire in the hazy light. The effect was all that she could have hoped and about the only thing in the room that didn't stop dead in its tracks was the juke box.

She finally moved, coming down the steps and crossing towards us and voices rose excitedly on every side mingling with laughter —the wrong kind of laughter. I held my breath and waited for the roof to fall in on us.

CHAPTER NINE

DESFORGE lurched to his feet and opened his arms to her. 'And behold, there was a woman of Babylon,' he declaimed.

During the hour or so that we'd already spent at the Fredericsmut he'd consumed about half the bottle of whisky he'd ordered from the bar. I think it was only then that I realized he must have been drinking for most of the day because it was the first time since I'd know him that he actually seemed the worse for liquor. His speech was slurred, his gestures slightly exaggerated and the hair falling untidily over his forehead combined with the iron-grey beard and magnificent physique stamped him as the sort of man to give a wide berth to even in a place like that.

Already people were looking our way and because of Desforge as much as Ilana. For a start just about everyone knew him, which was hardly surprising after a hundred and eleven films, the majority of which had been dubbed into most world languages. Two-fisted Jack Desforge, hero of a thousand bar-room brawls who always came out on top—every man's fantasy figure and constantly having to prove himself like some old time Western gunfighter, to any drunk with inflated ideas or the sailor on a pass who came across him in a bar and fancied his chances.

He introduced Ilana to the others and Arnie brought her a chair. Their reactions were interesting. Vogel gazed at her in frank admiration, the oldest message in the world in his eyes. Stratton was also highly impressed, but in a different way, dazzled, I suspected, as much by the golden image as anything else. Sarah Kelso managed the fixed half smile that most women seem to pull out of nowhere when faced with something they know they're going to have difficulty in competing with. Her eyes did the sort of price job on the dress and accessories that wouldn't have disgraced a computer and reluctantly admitted the final total.

Desforge put an arm round her and squeezed. 'Heh, Arnie,' he said. 'I'm thinking of taking Ilana down to Sandvig tomorrow to do a little reindeer hunting. Can you fly us in?'

'I wish I could,' Arnie told him, 'but I'm flying up to Søndre in the morning.'

Sarah Kelso was just about to light a cigarette and she paused and looked up at him sharply. He ignored her and smiled across at me.

'Olaf Simonsen tells me you're going to have a crack at Sule after all.'

'That's right.'

'I certainly hope that's an accurate met report he showed you. Rather you than me.' He touched Ilana on the shoulder. 'Care to dance?'

She glanced briefly at me, then pushed back her chair. 'I'd love to.'

'That's one hell of a good idea.' Desforge stood up, swaying a little, and held out a hand to Sarah Kelso. 'Let's you and me show them how it's done.'

Although he tried to conceal it, Vogel didn't look too pleased, but she went anyway. The juke box was playing something good and loud and the tiny floor was crowded. I watched them go, then glanced across at the Portuguese. Most of them were watching Ilana, stripping her with their eyes which was only to be expected, but the really noticeable thing about them was that they didn't seem to be talking much. Da Gama leaned back against the bar, hands in pockets, a cigarette hanging from his lips. His face was a stone mask, but his eyes followed Desforge constantly.

When I was thirteen I once found myself out on the wing in a school rugby match, very much a last minute substitution because no one else was available. My one moment of glory came when I brought down the captain of the school team a yard from the touchline, frustrating a win on the part of the other side.

He was a large, beefy individual of eighteen who gave me a thrashing in the shower rooms afterwards with the threat of worse to come if I ever got in his way again. The important thing wasn't that the experience put me off team games for life, but that it gave me a hatred of violence and a loathing for men of Da Gama's stamp, which produced a violence in return that was infinitely more frightening in its implications.

And violence was here now in this room, crackling in the air like electricity, mingling with the smoke, the human sweat, the reek of spilled liquor soaking into my brain as I breathed in so that I felt light-headed and a strange, nervous spasm seemed to pass through me in a cold wave.

And when it came it was from the most unexpected quarter. Another number started on the juke box and Ralph Stratton got to his feet without a word, pushed his way through the crowd and tapped Arnie on the shoulder. Arnie didn't look too pleased and released Ilana reluctantly.

He returned to the table and I nodded toward Stratton and Ilana. 'They dance well together.'

'About all he's good for, I should say,' Arnie commented sourly.

Da Gama spoke to one of his men, a large, dirty-faced individual in a greasy leather jerkin. The man forced his way through the crowd and tapped Stratton on the shoulder. Stratton simply shook his head and kept on dancing. The Portuguese tried again and Stratton shrugged him off. Impatiently this time.

In his Savile Row suit and RAF tie the rather effeminate looking Englishman would have stuck out like a sore thumb in that kind of place even if he hadn't been dancing with the most striking looking girl in the room, and plenty of people were watching. What happened next came as a shock to most of them although I can't say it surprised me particularly.

The Portuguese pulled Stratton round and grabbed him by the lapels. It was difficult to see what happened exactly, but whatever it was, the effect was devastating. I presume Stratton must have kneed him in the groin because the Portuguese cried out sharply, his voice clear above the noise of the juke box. Stratton pushed him away and his right arm swept from behind his left shoulder, the edge of his hand slashing across the neck.

As the man went down, the crowd scattered and all hell broke loose. Stratton just had time to give Ilana a violent shove out of the way and then he had his hands full. The first of the Portuguese was almost on him. Stratton stepped back, raised his knee and flicked his foot forward. He caught the Portuguese about as low as you can go and he went down like a stone.

But the other four were by then too close for any more fancy work and swarmed all over him. Arnie was already on his way as Stratton went under, but Desforge beat him to it, roaring like an angry bull.

He grabbed one man by the neck and the seat of his pants and hurled him across the dance floor to crash headlong into a table which collapsed under his weight, scattering bottles and glasses amongst the crowd. As a woman screamed, Desforge turned his attention to one of the men who was still concentrating on Stratton, and his fist rose and fell like a club at the base of the unprotected neck.

Arnie arrived with a running jump that took him on to the

back of one of the others and they crashed to the floor and rolled over and over, tearing at each other's throats. That left one man who still stood over Stratton doing his best to kick his brains out, but as I watched, Stratton rolled out of the way, grabbed at the descending foot and brought him down.

Desforge moved in to help, but he never got there. Da Gama, who had stayed at the bar watching for the twenty or thirty seconds the whole affair had taken, now intervened. Moving with astonishing speed for such a big man, he burst through the crowd and took Desforge from the rear, clamping an arm across his windpipe like an iron bar.

Both Arnie and Stratton were still fully occupied and quite obviously no one else was going to intervene as Da Gama increased the pressure. Desforge's hands tore vainly at the arm that was choking the life out of him and his face turned purple.

I began to shake, my head swelling like a balloon and the roar of the crowd was as the sea pounding in on some distant shore. I was aware of Ilana screaming at me soundlessly, then turning and hurling herself at Da Gama like a wildcat. He flung her away with his right hand and increased his grip and suddenly the stone mask dissolved into one of the cruellest smiles I've ever seen.

I suppose I must have been trying to destroy every sadistic, mindless lout I'd known in my life when I lifted the chair and smashed it across his head and shoulders. For a moment he became many people. The captain of the school rugby team who'd thrashed me as a boy, the senior cadet who'd supervised the indoctrination of recruits when I first joined the navy, and a certain commander in the Fleet Air Arm who'd pushed several young and inexperienced pilots not only to the limits of endurance, but over the edge. But most of all, he reminded me of one of the male nurses in the home where I'd undergone the cure, a walking animal who'd taken a sadistic pleasure in beating the mentally deficient into insensibility when their hysterical outbursts interfered with his card games on night duty.

The chair splintered on impact. I raised it high and brought it down again and it crumpled as the supports cracked. Da Gama cried out in pain and dropped Desforge to the floor. As he swung round, blood trickled down his face from a scalp wound. I threw what was left of the chair in his face and backed away.

He came in with a rush, hands reaching out to destroy and I dodged to one side and kicked a chair into his path so that he stumbled and fell heavily to the floor. There was a bottle of schnapps on the table at my side and I grabbed it by the neck, smashed it across the edge of the bar and had a knee on his chest before he could move.

The bottle made a fearsome weapon and I shoved the broken end up under his chin, the jagged, splintered edge drawing blood from the taut flesh.

One push and he was finished and he knew it and fear broke through like scum to the surface of a pool.

Whether I would have killed him or not is something I'll never be sure of because a shot echoed through the roaring of the crowd, shocking me back to reality. The silence was like the calm at sea after a storm as Olaf Simonsen moved forward, an automatic pistol in his right hand.

'That's enough, Joe,' he said in English. 'I'll take over now.'

I got to my feet and laid the bottle down very carefully on the bar. I still felt dazed and somehow outside of myself. I was aware of Da Gama lying there, of Desforge being helped to his feet by Arnie and Sarah Kelso. Stratton was still in one piece and stood at the edge of the dance floor calmly wiping blood from his cheek with a handkerchief.

Simonsen lined Da Gama and those of his men who could still stand up against the bar. Two others still sprawled unconscious on the floor and the one Desforge had thrown through the air like a sack of coals sat in a chair clutching what appeared to be a broken arm.

Simonsen came towards me, still holding his automatic and beyond him I was aware of Da Gama glaring at me as he wiped blood from his beard.

'Go home, Joe,' Simonsen said in English. 'And take your friends with you. I'll have a word with you all later.'

I stood glaring at him stupidly and then Ilana appeared, her fur coat draped over her shoulders. She looked white and shaken, but her voice was very calm. 'I think we'd better get out of here, Joe, while we still have the choice.'

She held out her hand and I held on tight and followed her as meekly as a lamb.

Afterwards, nothing made very much sense until I stepped into the shower and shocked myself back to reality under an ice-cold spray. I gave it two full minutes which was all I could stand, then got out and towelled myself dry. As I was dressing there was a knock at the door and Arnie came in. There was a nasty bruise on his right cheek where a fist had grazed him and I noticed that his knuckles were skinned, but he was grinning cheerfully.

'Quite a night, eh? How do you feel?'

'I'll survive. How's Desforge?'

'Ilana's with him now and I'm going home to change. I've got blood all over my shirt; not mine, I'm happy to say. I'll be back in half an hour. I'll meet you in the bar.'

After he'd gone, I finished dressing and went along the corridor to Desforge's room. I knocked on the door and it was opened by Ilana.

'How is he?' I asked.

'See for yourself.'

He was lying on his back covered by an eiderdown, snoring rhythmically, his mouth slightly open. 'The whisky finally got to him,' she said. 'When he wakes up he'll probably think it was all part of some crazy dream.'

'I feel like that right now,' I told her.

She looked up at me, her eyes serious and was obviously about to speak when there was a knock at the door. When she opened it Sarah Kelso was standing there.

'I was wondering how Mr. Desforge is?'

Ilana waved towards the bed. 'If the fans could only see him now.'

Sarah Kelso moved across to the bed and looked down at him. 'Is he often like this?'

'Only four or five times a week.'

Sarah Kelso placed a crocodile-leather wallet on the bedside locker. 'I'll leave this here. I picked it up at the Fredericsmut. He must have dropped it during the fight.'

'Are you sure it's Jack's?'

She nodded. 'I looked inside. Amongst other things there was a letter addressed to him.' She moved to the door and paused. 'That was quite a show you put on back there, Mr. Martin. You're a man of surprises. I wonder what you'd have done if the sergeant hadn't arrived when he did.'

'We'll never know now, will we, Mrs. Kelso?'

'I suppose not.'

The door closed softly behind her and Ilana said, 'We might as well leave him in peace. Shall we go to my room? I'd like to talk.'

She lived right next door which was only to be expected, and yet I was aware of that same irrational anger I'd noticed on other occasions. It was as irritating as it was inexplicable.

She was a highly desirable piece of female flesh, but she was also Jack Desforge's woman even if I did find the idea vaguely unpleasant.

She sat on the window seat and when she crossed her legs the hem of that ridiculous dress rose half-way up her thighs. She asked me for a cigarette and when I struck the match for her, my hands were shaking.

'What's Mrs. Kelso doing here exactly?' she demanded.

It was a good topic of conversation as any and I told her. She listened intently, a slight frown on her brow which was still there when I'd finished.

'Stratton seems to be very expert at taking care of himself for an insurance man,' she commented. 'On the other hand, you didn't do too badly back there yourself.'

'I must have looked pretty crude by Stratton's standards.'

'But effective,' she said. 'Brutally effective. Hardly the sort of thing you could have learned in the City. The trick with the bottle, for instance, wasn't exactly Queensberry Rules.'

'The world I inhabited where I learnt it had only one rule. Do the other bloke before he does you.'

'Will you tell me about it?' she said simply.

'Why not?' I shrugged. 'It doesn't take very long. I told you I was a pilot in the Fleet Air Arm. That was back in 1951 and there was a war on of sorts.'

'Korea?'

I nodded. 'Don't get me wrong. It wasn't exactly the Battle of Britain. We flew coastal patrols from a carrier and the North Korean pilots weren't all that hot. But landing on an aircraft carrier's a tricky business at the best of times—they lose planes and pilots regularly even in peacetime. Most of us got into the habit of priming ourselves up in the most obvious way.'

"Whisky?' she said.

'In my case, rum. But I was special—I turned out to be one of those odd birds you hear about who can't take a drink. Alcoholism is a disease, you know. Something very few people seem to realize. God knows how I survived till my time was up, but I did. The trouble was that afterwards, I found I couldn't stop.'

'And that's what really broke up your marriage?'

'It certainly didn't help. I told you there was a day when I couldn't face the office any longer and simply walked out.'

'And took a conversion course to make you a commercial pilot.'

'I failed to mention the nine months in between. That's when I learned about broken bottles and the right place to sink a boot into a man and how to keep yourself warm and cosy on an Embankment bench with the *Evening Standard* stuffed down your shirt. I must have sampled every doss house in London by the time I was through.'

'What happened?'

'I wound up in a police cell after a punch-up in some dive or another and they got in touch with Amy. She'd been looking for me for months. I might also add that she'd had to do it twice before. She got me into a home or a clinic—call it what you like —where they were doing experimental work on alcoholics. For some strange reason she seemed to think she owed me something. The rest, as they say in the books, you know.'

She nodded. 'But you survived, didn't you? That's the only really important thing.'

'Sometimes I have my doubts.'

I was standing very close to her, staring out of the window, and I looked down at those silken legs and the deep valley between her breasts that was visible through the loose neck of her dress and somehow, my hand was on her shoulder. She was in my arms instantly and I kissed her hard and long so that when she finally broke away she was breathless.

'I was beginning to think I must be slipping.'

It was the sort of remark that was completely in character I should have realized that, and yet it annoyed me and for some perverse reason of my own I wanted to hurt her.

'Are you sure Jack won't be demanding a command performance later on or don't you think he'll be up to it tonight?'

She took a very deliberate step back, but there was no sudden explosion, no slap in the face—nothing so dramatic. She simply shook her head and said calmly, 'You really can be very stupid for such a bright boy. Wait here, I want to show you something.'

She was back in a couple of minutes holding the crocodile-skin wallet that Sarah Kelso had found at the Fredicsmut. She opened it and took out an envelope which she passed across.

'I'd like you to read that.'

It was the letter Desforge had been waiting for—the one from Milt Gold of Horizon. The contents were something of a bombshell. Not only was Gold not ready to proceed with the picture— he'd had to shelve the idea permanently because the backers simply wouldn't take Jack at any price. He was sorry, but the whole thing was out of his hands. He also threw in for good measure the news that all Desforge's California property had been seized by the court order pending the hearing of an action brought by his creditors.

I stood frowning down at the letter and Ilana plucked it from my fingers, folded it neatly and replaced it in its envelope.

'But why did he lie to me?' I said.

She shrugged. 'The Mr. Micawber syndrome, lover—the desperate hope that something might turn up.'

'And you knew about this?'

'That's right.'

'But if there was nothing in it for you, why did you come?'

'Because I chose to—because he needed a friend, something you wouldn't understand.' She stood there, one hand on her hip, very small, very defiant. 'I just wanted to make it clear that I don't give command performances for anybody. Sure, I've slept with Jack Desforge on occasion, but because I felt like it and for no other reason. Now kindly get to hell out of here.'

I didn't argue because something told me that we were at the stage where an attempt at an apology would be about the worst thing I could do, so I did as I was told and left.

When I went into the bar Arnie was sitting on a stool beside Olaf Simonsen. He got to his feet as I approached. "I was just leaving. Where's Ilana?'

'In her room, but I'd take it easy if I were you. She's in a mood to crack heads.'

'Live dangerously, that's my motto,' he said and went out.

I asked for a tomato juice and took the stool next to Simonsen. 'When do you put the cuffs on me, officer?'

He took it half-seriously. 'I don't think there'll be any need for that. How is Mr. Desforge?'

'Sleeping it off. I'll be surprised if he remembers much in the morning. What about the Portuguese?'

'They kept one of them in hospital for the night with a broken arm. Da Gama and the others are back on board their schooner with orders to stay there until it sails again which unfortunately isn't till the day after tomorrow. Still, he's finished on this coast from now on, I'll see to that.' He drank some of his lager and added dryly, 'On the other hand, I'm glad I arrived when I did. A killing is a killing, whoever the victim might be.'

'I know,' I said. 'And I'm grateful.'

He patted me on the shoulder and stood up. 'What you need is a good night's sleep. I'll see you at the slipway in the morning.'

After he'd gone I sat there thinking about a lot of things, but Ilana kept breaking through to the surface and after a while I got up and went back upstairs. It was quiet in the corridor outside my room and I paused at the door, wondering rather bitterly how Arnie was doing. And then I heard her voice raised, sharp and clear and very angry.

I went down the corridor fast and flung open the door of her room. She was half across the bed, Arnie sprawled on top of her, laughing as he pinned her arms. I took him by the collar and yanked him away so hard that he staggered across the room against the wall, almost losing his balance. Ilana sat up, smoothing her skirt and I smiled gently.

'Anything more I can do?'

'Yes, you can bloody well get out of here and take junior with you.'

There were tears in her eyes, humiliation at the thought that it had to be me of all people as much as anything else, I suspected, but as far as I was concerned she'd had enough and I turned to Arnie.

'Let's go, Arnie.'

He glared from Ilana to me furiously. 'So that's the way, is it? I move on and good old Joe here takes over.'

The way he put it made me sound like some sort of faithful hound and I burst out laughing. 'Don't be a clod. Come on, let's get out of here.'

I'd never seen him so angry. 'You've just made the biggest mistake of your life,' he snarled at Ilana. 'Here, I'll leave you something to remember me by. Stick that in your stocking-top and remember Arnie Fassberg.'

He tossed something on to the bed and went out, slamming the door behind him. Whatever it was, it rolled on to the floor and Ilana got down on her hands and knees and looked under the bed. As she stood up, I thought it was just some sort of rough pebble she was holding and then the light caught it and for a moment it glowed with green fire. Her eyes widened and I reached out quickly.

'Here, give it to me.'

I held it up to the light, my throat going dry and Ilana said, 'Is it worth anything?'

I dropped it into the palm of her hand. 'A thousand, maybe two.

It would take an expert to be sure.' The expression on her face was something to be seen. 'It's an emerald,' I said gently. 'That's what they look like before the jewellers get to work on them.'

She looked completely bewildered. 'I didn't know there were any emeralds in Greenland.'

'Neither did I, Ilana,' I said thoughtfully. 'Neither did I.'

CHAPTER TEN

IT WAS ALMOST six-thirty as I walked across to the airstrip on the following morning to get a met report. Not that I needed one—it was going to be a fine day, I could tell. Something to do with the way the ragged tracers of mist lifted off the calm water and the bold clear lines of the mountains against the sky—the sort of feeling, in fact, which can only be the product of experience. But then I was something of an old Greenland hand now which certainly gave me a sense of belonging in a way that I hadn't experienced in a very long time.

On my walk back from the tower I took a short cut past the two concrete hangars the Americans had put up in the war. A jeep stood outside the one Arnie used and as I approached the small judas gate that was set in the great sliding doors opened and the chief mechanic, a Canadian caller Miller, came out with Arnie. They spoke together for a moment, then Miller got into the jeep and drove away.

Arnie turned and saw me. Something was wrong, I could tell that by merely looking at him for, as with most extroverts, ill-luck, when it came, seemed to have a physical effect on him.

'What's up?' I demanded as I approached.

He didn't bother to reply, simply opened the judas gate and went inside the hangar and I followed. The Aermacchi crouched there in the half-light, partially on its belly, partially tilted over on one wing. Both skis were splintered and the undercarriage had been badly damaged. The villain of the piece was still on the scene, an old three-ton Bedford truck kept on the airstrip for general purposes which had obviously been backed into the Aermacchi.

'What happened?' I said.

'I haven't the slightest idea. Found her like this when I came in this morning. You know they don't have anyone down here at night. Miller thinks some drunks have probably been fooling around. Got into the truck for a lark and ended up doing this.'

'Pigs could also fly,' I said.

There was a long pregnant silence in which we simply stared at each other and then a moment when I suddenly felt that he was going to tell me all about it—whatever it was—but it passed.

'Miller's arranged to have the big hoist brought in. We'll soon have her up.'

'What about repairs?'

'He thinks they should be able to manage here. A couple of days, that's all.'

'A hell of a lot can happen in two days, Arnie,' I said.

He laughed happily. 'I wish I knew what you were talking about, Joe.'

'So do I,' I said. 'Anyway, I'll have to be off.' I paused as I opened the judas gate and turned. 'If you find any more pebbles on the beach like the one you gave Ilana last night, save them for me will you? It's time I started thinking about my old age.'

But that sort of sword-play wasn't going to get me anywhere and I left him there in the half-light, a smile on his face and fear in his eyes, and went back to the harbour.

Simonsen and Vogel and his party were at the slipway when I arrived and Stratton and the big policeman were already loading the skis and other items of equipment.

'What's the weather look like?' Simonsen demanded.

'Clear for most of the day. Could be some mist tonight, but if we push hard we should be in and out before it starts.'

He nodded. 'Let's get moving then. I've been in touch with the factor at Sandvig. He'll have a light sledge waiting for us when we touch down.'

There was the sudden roar of an engine on the road behind us and the hotel Landrover approached at speed, braking to a halt a few yards away. Ilana was the first out looking like a St. Moritz tourist in her sheepskin coat, ski pants and sunglasses. The hotel porter slid from behind the wheel and started to unload the baggage as Desforge came round from the other side looking remarkably fit considering the events of the previous night.

'Top of the morning,' he said cheerfully. 'Almost didn't make it.'

Simonsen turned to me, his eyebrows raised. 'Mr. Desforge is coming with us?'

'Only as far as Sandvig,' I explained. 'He and Miss Eytan are going to spend a few days down there looking for reindeer.'

Simonsen seemed dubious. 'Something of a tight squeeze I should have thought.'

He had spoken in Danish, but Desforge seemed to get the picture and said quickly, 'Look, if I'm putting you out at all, let's forget about it. Maybe I can persuade Arnie to take us after all.'

'You'd have a job,' I said. 'He's had a slight accident with the Aermacchi. I'd be surprised to see it flying in less than three days and that's looking on the bright side.'

Simonsen asked me what had happened and I explained briefly. Vogel and Stratton seemed only mildly interested, but Sarah Kelso took in every word, a bright spot of colour glowing in each cheek although the dark eyes gave nothing away. Certainly there seemed no suspicion in Simonsen's mind that the whole thing was anything more than what Miller had suggested and he nodded gravely.

'Poor Arnie—at the height of the season, too.' He turned to Desforge. 'If Joe thinks he can take all of us then I have certainly no objections, Mr. Desforge, but we must leave at once. We have a heavy day in front of us and I don't want to spend a night up there on the ice-cap if it can be avoided.'

'That suits me fine,' Desforge said and he paid off the driver of the Landrover and Stratton and Simonsen started to put his baggage on board.

For the briefest of moments I had a chance to speak to Ilana and moved in close, offering her a cigarette. She took it, bent her head to the match that flared in my cupped hands.

'About last night,' I said quietly. 'I'd be obliged if you'd keep quiet about Arnie's little present for the time being.'

She seemed to gaze through me, curiously remote behind the dark glasses. 'All right—but next time I see you I'll expect some light on the situation.'

It was a statement of fact requiring no answer and I didn't attempt to give one. In any case I'd other things to think about. I climbed into the cabin to check on the baggage, but Stratton obviously knew his business for it had been stacked in the best possible position relative to the passenger load.

I packed them in one-by-one, gave the floats a last careful check, then got in myself, ran her down into the water and took off without any further delay.

Sandvig was fifty miles inland from the sea and protected by a maze of minor islands and fjords that cut deeply into the rocky coast. It was typical of many of the small fishing villages found in the south-west, constructed on the site of one of the old Norse settlements on a narrow shelf at the foot of the mountains, a position which gave it an unrivalled view across the sound. We touched down exactly forty minutes after leaving Frederiksborg and I took the Otter up on to a small beach.

It wasn't much of a place—there were the usual dozen or so painted houses, a small Moravian chapel and a store owned by the Trading Company which bought all the sealskins and shark liver brought in and sold in return everything the inhabitants needed.

Most of the population had already crowded down on to the narrow beach to watch with interest as Desforge and Ilana landed and we passed down the baggage. They were mostly pure Eskimo from the look of them although they all preferred to be called Greenlanders—short, sturdy figures with Mongolian features, brown cheeks touched with crimson and it was interesting to note that although some of them were in store-bought clothes, they all wore sealskin boots.

The factor from the store appeared, two men behind him carrying the light sledge Simonsen had asked for. He spoke no English so I explained briefly about Desforge and Ilana while the sledge was being loaded.

'Everything okay?' Desforge asked.

I nodded. 'I've asked him to run you up to Olaf Rasmussen's place in his jeep.'

'I hope the old guy speaks some English.'

'Better than you do. He'll see you all right.'

'What about the return trip?'

I shrugged. 'You can always get in touch with the airstrip at Frederiksborg on the radio. I'll come in for you whenever you want, always assuming I'm available.'

I looked beyond him to Ilana. I wanted to say goodbye and a little more than that, but I couldn't think of the right way to put it. I believe she knew because she smiled and nodded slightly and I felt unaccountably cheerful as I climbed back into the cabin and started the engine.

It could be pretty tricky taking off from Sandvig when the wind was in the wrong direction because the far side of the fjord consisted of a thousand feet of rock wall that fell straight into green water.

That morning we were lucky, lifting as effortlessly as a bird into the sky, banking across the meadows above the village as I set course and flew on between the great stone walls of the fjord towards the glacier.

It poured over the edge of the ice-cap, white lava spilling outwards like a great fan as it fell into the waters of the fjord. On either side the slopes of the mountains were carpeted by Alder scrub that was nowhere more than three feet in height, but about as impenetrable as an undergrowth of rusting barbed wire. Higher up there was a clearly defined edge where the stuff stopped growing and beyond that, nothing but jagged peaks and razor-edged hogs' backs topped by snow and ice.

We slid over the crest of the glacier and drifted across a sea of ice. At this point it was under tremendous pressure. Checked by the coastal mountains, it lifted in a series of great hummocks, spilling into a thousand crevasses. It was the sort of country that was so difficult that on foot a good day's march might get you six or seven miles. I thought about the Oxford expedition and others before it, inching their way across that barren wilderness and offered up a prayer of thanks to the Wright brothers.

We reached Sule in forty minutes. There wasn't a trace of mist anywhere and I went in low and skimmed across the surface of the blue water. There was plenty of ice about, but mostly thin surface sheets like broken glass.

'What do you think?' Simonsen asked as I took the Otter up.

'Looks fine to me, but let's see if we can find that plane before we land. It could save us some time.'

The ten miles took no more than three or four minutes of flying time, but there was no immediate sign of the Heron. I throttled back, the noise of the engine dying away to a murmur and spoke to them all over my shoulder.

'The plane should be around here somewhere so keep your eyes open. According to Arnie Fassberg it's lying in the bottom of a gully.'

I banked in a wide circle and went down low and Stratton saw it almost at once, crying out excitedly, 'Over there! To the left! To the left!'

I banked steeply and went down again and this time we all saw it lying there at the bottom of a deep gully just as Arnie had described, the silver and blue of the fuselage vivid against the white carpet.

I took the Otter up again and turned back to Sule, my throat dry, a coldness in the pit of my stomach that was compounded half of fear, half of excitement.

Vogel leaned forward. 'How long to get there?'

'That depends on you,' I said, 'or on how good you are on skis. With luck, two or three hours.'

'So barring accidents we should have ample time to get there and back and return to Frederiksborg tonight?'

'If the weather holds,' I said, circled the lake and landed.

It was really something of an anti-climax. The actual touch-down was no trouble at all and the only ice with which we came into contact was the thin crust that lined the shore. It cracked and splintered like treacle toffee as I ran the Otter in to the beach and cut the engine.

The silence was utter and complete and they all felt it. I turned and smiled bravely. 'Let's hope the next leg goes as smoothly. All out.'

I opened the door and dropped to the beach.

CHAPTER ELEVEN

THE LAKE was surrounded by an area of bog and morass, but beyond it the dune-like plain of hummock ice stretched into infinity, the horizon shimmering in the intense white light.

I led the way as navigator, a compass dangling from my neck on a long cord and Simonsen and Vogel followed pulling the sledge by two lines secured to their waists by body harness.

I kept well out in front and paused after half an hour to take another fix and looked back at them. Vogel was obviously as expert as he had suggested and was going well, but Stratton was trailing a hundred yards to the rear. In their hooded parkas and protective goggles they all looked remarkably businesslike, even Sarah Kelso sitting there in the sledge, a blanket wrapped about her legs.

I started forward again, zig-zagging between the hummocks of ice, sweating profusely at the unaccustomed exercise. It was hard work, but I was enjoying it. There was no wind and the sun was warm so that the top surface was slightly damp, sparkling in a thousand places, and I paused on top of a ridge to take my bearings again and gazed across this harsh barren landscape with a conscious pleasure.

I had told Ilana Eytan that I had come to Greenland to make money and like most things in life that was only partly true. Perhaps Desforge romanticized too much, but when I looked out across the ice-cap I knew what he meant when he spoke of the alien land. Here was one of the last places on earth where the challenge was the greatest one of all—survival. Amundsen and Peary and Gino Watkins—they had all felt it, had gone forward eagerly to meet it and in some strange way I felt myself part of the same stream as I went down the other side of the ridge and made my way across the snowfield at the bottom with renewed energy.

It was criss-crossed by a hundred narrow crevasses and half-way to the other side I turned and went back to meet the others.

'Trouble?' Simonsen asked.

'I don't think so if we take it carefully. A few crevasses, that's all, but you'll need me pushing at the back of the sledge to get across.'

'Perhaps I should get out and walk?' Sarah Kelso suggested. I shook my head. 'It isn't necessary, I assure you.'

Stratton appeared at the top of the ridge. He paused, then glided down to join us, losing his balance and rolling in the soft slush. When I helped him to his feet he looked tired and there was sweat on his face.

'Are you all right?' I said.

He smiled brightly. 'A little out of practice, that's all. I'll manage.'

'It's best if we all stick together over the next stretch,' I said, 'It could be tricky. You can help me at the rear of the sledge.'

It took us the best part of an hour to get across, heaving the sledge bodily over crevasses three to four feet wide and any depth you care to speculate. Most of them were fairly sound, but now and then a fringe of soft snow gave an illusion of safety that only Simonsen's instinct and experience saved us from.

On the other side, we took a ten-minute break and then started again, crossing easier ground this time, a rough, sprawling plain, and I made good time, stopping every ten minutes to check my position.

It was just coming up to noon when I paused on top of a rise and looked down to the plain below. What had seemed like a narrow gully from the air was in fact a sizeable ravine and without waiting for the others, I swept down the slope and did a quick stem Christie that brought me to a halt on the rim. There was nothing to be seen and I started forward, following the twisting course.

I turned a bend and the Heron lay below me, crumpled into the snow, one wing two hundred yards further on. The grave was at one side, a cairn of rocks surmounted by a rough cross fashioned from two pieces of the fuselage.

It was quiet and very peaceful and I stood there gazing down at the wreck, so wrapped up in my own thoughts that I failed to hear the approach of the others.

'Strange how it seems to fit into the landscape,' Vogel said.

I turned and found him at my shoulder. Simonsen was helping Sara Kelso from the sledge and Stratton was about a hundred yards in the rear. Simonsen joined us and stood looking down at the Heron, his face serious. After a moment of silence he sighed.

'And now comes the unpleasant bit. Shall we go down?'

We pitched a small tent about fifty yards away from the wreck and left Sarah Kelso there with a primus stove to brew some tea, more to keep her out of the way than anything else. The next bit was going to be pretty unpleasant and there was no reason for her to be involved any more than was strictly necessary.

No digging was necessary, but the stones of the cairn had frozen together and we had to prise them apart with the two steel ice spades we had brought. Simonsen and I handled that part, but Stratton and Vogel helped by pulling each stone out of the way as it came free. I found a leg first, or what was left of one. There was still a shoe on the foot, but the shin bone gleamed through the tattered remnants of a trouser leg. Until that moment there had been a certain amount of conversation, but from then on only the chink of the spades on the cold stone disturbed the silence.

When the last stone was removed the two bodies in their shallow pit looked more pathetic than anything else. For one thing, the emotional highlights were missing. The Gothic horror of the open grave, the shrouded form in the coffin. What was left here was nothing but the framework of what had once been two human beings covered by a few tattered shreds of clothing and here and there, a strip of frozen flesh still clinging to a bone.

We stood there looking down at them for a while and then Simonsen turned to Vogel. 'That photo of yours isn't going to help much here. You said Mrs. Kelso had furnished you with certain other proofs.'

Vogel unzipped his parka, fumbled inside and produced an envelope which he handed to Simonsen. 'Mr. Kelso's dental record.'

Simonsen took out the white card contained in the envelope and got down into the pit. He tried the right-hand body first then turned his attention to the other. He got to his feet and nodded grimly.

'I'm satisfied. This one is Kelso. See for yourself.'

He handed the card to Vogel who got down on his knees and made the necessary examination. When he stood up, his face was grey and sombre and he passed the card to me.

'If you would be so kind, Mr. Martin. The evidence of two completely neutral witnesses should be enough for any court.'

I got down on one knee and peered into the mouth. It didn't take more than a minute to see that its contents matched the card completely. Not only was the number of teeth correct, but three gold fillings and two porcelain crowns were in exactly the right place.

I stood up and passed the card back to Vogel. 'As far as I can see an identical match.'

'That settles it then,' Simonsen said.

'There should also be a gold signet ring on the second finger of the left hand,' Vogel said. 'Inside there is an inscription. *From Sarah with love—22.2.52.*'

The ring was there all right, but the flesh on the finger was still intact and frozen solid. I tried to get it off without success. Simonsen dropped to one knee beside me, took out a spring-blade hunting knife and calmly sliced though the finger. He examined the ring for a moment, then passed it to me. The inscription was perfectly plain and exactly as Vogel had indicated.

There was a short silence and I said brightly, 'I suppose he must just have been wearing someone else's coat.'

Simonsen glanced at me sharply. 'What do you mean?'

'If you look inside the jacket the name on the tab should read Harrison, isn't that right, Mr. Vogel?'

Vogel nodded soberly. 'There was also some identification in his pocket in the name of Harvey Stein.'

'He certainly liked his aliases,' I said.

But Vogel was giving nothing away. 'A riddle to which there can never be an answer now.'

Simonsen looked interested, but obviously decided to let it go for the time being. 'Better get Mrs. Kelso.'

But there was no need for when we turned she was standing no more than ten yards away watching. She still wore her protective goggles so that it was impossible to determine what was going on behind them, but her face was very white as Vogel went forward, the ring in the palm of his hand. She took off her glove and picked the ring up delicately to examine it and then she swayed and would have fallen if Vogel hadn't steadied her.

'Come back to the tent, my dear,' he said. 'There is nothing for you here.'

She shook her head. 'I must see him—I must!'

She pulled herself free and stumbled to the edge of the pit. I don't think she could have looked at what was left of her husband for more than ten seconds because she turned with a sharp cry and ran into Vogel's arms.

Stratton went to help and I watched them return to the tent, something very close to admiration in my heart. She was really very good. On stage at the National Theatre she could have been a household word.

I examined what was left of the Heron with Simonsen who made copious notes on the spot and asked my advice frequently. The wing which had parted company from the body of the plane still carried its two engines and we examined them first. They were in such a state that it was impossible to say what had gone wrong. We didn't fare any better with the other two and the interior of the plane was a shambles, the instrument panel smashed into a thousand pieces.

There was still plenty of blood about, frozen into snails' trails, but when Simonsen asked me to sit in the pilot's seat I managed it with no trace of nervousness although my stomach tightened momentarily.

'Well, what do you think?' he demanded.

I shook my head. 'The instruments or what's left of them, show nothing. The engines don't offer any clues. Frankly I don't think we'll ever know exactly what happened.'

'Then make an intelligent guess.'

'God alone knows. It couldn't have been lack of fuel because she'd been fitted with auxiliary tanks. In fact by all the rules she should have gone up like a torch when she hit the deck.'

'All right, then tell me this? What were they doing up here in the first place when they should have been eight hundred miles south crossing the Atlantic?"

'Some sort of instrument error I should imagine. It's the only feasible explanation.'

He nodded briskly and snapped his notebook shut. 'I'll buy that. Let's go and have a cup of tea. Stratton can have his two cents' worth now.'

He started back and I paused, dropping to one knee to fasten the thong on my left boot. I stayed there for rather longer than I had intended because someone had relieved himself against the side of the plane at that point. One thing was certain. It wasn't a left-over from the Oxford expedition. The yellow stain was much more recent than that. I covered it with a handful of snow and went after Simonsen.

Vogel and Stratton came to meet us. 'Anything of particular interest?' the Austrian asked.

'I think the reports should be completely independent of each other,' Simonsen told him. 'We can compare them later.'

'Certainly.' Vogel nodded. 'Mr. Stratton and I will get started then. The sooner we're finished, the sooner we can get out of here.'

Sarah Kelso gave me tea in an aluminium cup and I drank it gratefully. She looked white and strained and seemed very subdued.

'Can I ask you how it happened?' she said.

I glanced at Simonsen who nodded. 'I don't see why not.'

I told her what I'd found out which wasn't a great deal anyway and volunteered as much of the guesswork as I thought might interest her.

'So it was probably just some sort of stupid error?' she said and shook her head sadly. 'So much of life seems to be like that.'

Simonsen leaned forward and patted her gently on the shoulder, real sympathy on his face and I got up and buckled on my skis.

'Going somewhere, Joe?' he said.

I nodded. 'Just for a quick look round. I shan't be long.'

I went back towards the plane, silent on my skis and paused a yard or two away. Vogel and Stratton were talking together in low tones and the Austrian's voice lifted impatiently.

'But it must be here. Try again.'

I slid forward another yard and stooped so that I could see into the interior of the cabin. They crouched together just behind the pilot's seat. There was a long rent in the padded lining of the cabin and Stratton had his arm well inside.

Vogel glanced sideways and saw me and for a moment the pleasant bland mask slipped and there was murder in his eyes or something very close to it.

I waved and said cheerfully, 'Have fun, I'm just going for a look round.'

I moved along the ravine quickly until I found a place that gave me easy access to the top. I stood on the ridge and took a bearing with my compass. There was something I wanted to see, something I'd noticed from the air, and it couldn't be very far away.

I struck off across the plain threading my way between the hummocks, making quite good time so that I found what I was looking for within a quarter of an hour, a saucer-shaped depression about three hundred yards in diameter, a flat field of virgin snow.

But not quite. The eternal wind soon smoothed the surface

up here on the ice-cap, but a ski plane left pretty distinctive traces. I found one or two on the far side of the depression, already partially obliterated so that only an expert would have known what they were. Much more significant was a large patch of oil and I crouched down and covered it quickly.

As I got up, someone called and as I turned, Vogel came down the slope on the far side of the depression and moved towards me quickly. I rushed to meet him, but he passed me at the half-way mark very fast with a gay cry and kept on going, doing a tremendous stem turn and sliding to a halt in a flurry of snow at the spot where I had found the oil and the ski traces. He paused, removing his goggles to clear the snow from them, glanced about him carelessly, then started towards me.

His face was bland, his eyes sparkled cheerfully, but he'd seen everything he needed to, I couldn't have been more certain.

'I enjoyed that.' He grinned. 'I thought I'd better come after you. Stratton got through it all much more quickly than we'd expected.'

'Did he find anything interesting?'

'Not really—did you?'

There was a nice polite smile on his face as if he really wanted to know, but two could play at that game and I smiled right back at him.

'I'm afraid not, which doesn't help you very much, does it? I suppose this affair must have cost you quite a packet one way and another.'

He chuckled. 'Not to worry. We always adjust to meet changing circumstances. That's the whole basis of the insurance game.'

He pushed off and I watched him go, gliding effortlessly across the snow, a clever dangerous animal. I suppose I should have experienced some kind of fear as I went after him, but I didn't. Instead I was filled with a kind of strange joy and my hands shook excitedly. It was rather like one of those Saturday serials I'd seen as a kid and I couldn't wait to find out what happened in the next instalment.

It was almost six in the evening when we reached Lake Sule again and the strain of the day showed on everyone. The return journey had been uneventful and the weather had held, which had been my chief worry. A sudden blizzard up there on top, even the short-lived summer variety, could have proved fatal.

We loaded up quickly and as I ran the Otter down into the

water a cold wind lifted off the ice, churning the surface in a sudden turbulence. Simonsen glanced over his shoulder at the horizon where grey clouds spread across the sky blotting out the sun.

'Some sort of storm on the way, Joe. We'd better get out of here fast.'

I didn't need any urging. Flying half-blind through a mountain range in rough weather may be some people's version of fun, but it isn't mine. In any case, I'm just not that good a pilot. I turned into the wind, gave her full throttle and got out of there fast.

The real trouble came about forty minutes later when we reached the edge of the ice-cap and flew into the mountains. Heavy rain blew in from the sea in a grey curtain and the Otter rocked in the turbulence.

I found the head of Sandvig fjord and plunged into a cauldron of mist that reduced visibility to three or four hundred yards and was thickening by the minute.

'What do you think?' Simonsen cried above the roar of the engine.

'I think we spend the night at Sandvig,' I said and went down fast while the going was good.

CHAPTER TWELVE

OLAF RASMUSSEN'S farm occupied a commanding position on the crest of a green hill six or seven hundred feet above the village and about a mile further along the fjord. Like most of the homesteads in that part of the country, it was constructed of wood because it was warmer in winter, but in design it was quite unique. The entire length of the house at the front was made up of a hall perhaps seventy feet long and about twenty in height on the old Viking pattern with an enormous stone fireplace.

The kitchen was at the rear of the hall, half a dozen bedrooms on the first floor opening off a railed balcony. Simonsen and I shared the end one for Rasmussen had received us with his customary hospitality, informing me that Desforge and Ilana had gone up into the hills with one of the shepherds as a guide.

I was shaving in the cracked mirror above the wash-stand and Simonsen was lying on the bed waiting his turn for the razor when there was a step on the landing, the door was thrown open and Desforge entered.

There was a cartridge belt round his waist and with the Winchester under his arm and that wild grey beard he looked like some Corsican brigand down from the hills to rape and plunder or rather, what some Corsican brigand thought he ought to look like.

'Heh, Joe, baby, this is great!' he cried. 'How did it go up there on the roof of the world. Is Mrs. Kelso still solvent?'

I nodded. 'So it would appear.'

'No question about it.' Simonsen swung his legs to the floor and sat on the edge of the bed. 'It was Kelso all right. There was a ring on his finger with an inscription as indicated by his wife before we examined him, but most important of all was his dental record. That's one thing that can't lie. In fact it's hung more than one murderer before now.'

'You don't need to tell me,' Desforge said. 'I've played cops on more occasions than I can remember.' He turned to me. 'You'll fly out in the morning I suppose?'

'If the weather clears.'

He grinned. 'It promises to be quite an evening. I'll see you later.'

I dried my face and got dressed again, wondering what Desforge had meant. There had been a kind of affection in his eyes as if he had been genuinely pleased to see me, which was perfectly possible. He was in many ways a desperately lonely man—I'd always sensed that. On the other hand, if it was an evening's drinking he was after, he'd certainly come to the right place. If any man on earth was likely to drink him under the table it was Olaf Rasmussen.

I could hear the old man bellowing at someone in the kitchen when I went out on the balcony—probably some Eskimo woman up from the village to cook for him. A door banged and he passed beneath me, a bottle in each hand, and paused at the table in front of the great fireplace.

Some human beings are different from the day they are born. They have fire in their veins instead of blood and action is the juice of life to them. Olaf Rasmussen was such a man. An Icelander of Danish extraction, he had a master's ticket in both sail and steam and had lived by the sea for the first thirty years of his life, retiring to Sandvig at the age of fifty, ostensibly to raise sheep, but in reality to pursue a lifelong passion for Viking history. Standing there in the firelight he could indeed have been one of those early settlers—Eric the Red himself, perhaps, or Leif the Lucky—an enormous patriarchal figure with hair to his shoulders and a beard that touched his chest.

As I started down the stairs he turned and, seeing me, cried out in Danish, 'Lucky for me the fog came down.'

We hadn't had much of a chance to talk earlier and he lit a cigar and sprawled in one of the chairs by the fire.

I said: 'I don't need to ask how you've been keeping. If anything, you look younger. What's the secret?'

'Women, Joe,' he told me solemnly. 'I've finally given them up.'

His face was very serious and I nodded gravely. 'Is that so? No more Eskimo women up from the village?'

'Not more than two or three times a week. I decided it was time I cut it down.'

He roared with laughter, poured himself half a glass of schnapps and swallowed it down. 'And you, Joe? What about you? You look different.'

'I can't think why I should.'

'A woman perhaps?' I shook my head and he sighed. 'Still the lonely bed. A mistake, boy. Woman was sent to comfort man. It was so ordained by the good Lord.'

I decided to change the subject. 'What do you think of Desforge?'

'An interesting question.' He poured himself some more schnapps. 'When I was twenty I was first mate on a barque out of Hamburg on the Gold Coast run. We touched at Fernando Po at the height of an outbreak of Yellow Jack.' He stared into the fire, lines scoured deeply into his face at the memory of it. 'There were bodies everywhere. In the waters of the harbour, in the streets. But the worst sight of all were the faces of those who knew they had it, who knew there was no hope. It was something in the eyes that told you they were already gone. Walking dead, if you like.' He shook his head. 'It makes me shiver to remember it even now.'

'An interesting story, but what has it got to do with Desforge?'

'He has the same expression in his eyes, the same look of utter despair. Oh, not all the time. Only when he thinks you aren't watching him.'

Which was quite a thought, but we were unable to take it any further because at that moment Ilana Eytan came down the stairs.

'Now this one—this one is a real woman,' Rasmussen whispered, emptied his glass and went to meet her. 'And how was the hunting?' he asked in English.

'Non-existent, but the scenery was magnificent. Well worth the climb.' She smiled as I got to my feet. 'Hello, Joe.'

Rasmussen looked first at her, then at me and laughed suddenly. 'So—now I understand. Good—very good. Entertain yourselves, my children, while I see how the dinner is coming.'

'A remarkable man,' she said when he had gone.

I nodded and gave her a cigarette, more for something to do than anything else. She was wearing her Norwegian sweater and ski pants and looked very small, very attractive and—dare I admit it?—very desirable.

How much of this she read in my eyes I don't know, but she turned away and walked to the end of the hall, staring up at the great oaken beams, at the crossed spears and burnished shields on the wall.

'Is all this stuff real?'

I nodded. 'The hall itself is only a replica of course, but it's built on the foundations of a Viking homestead a thousand years old.'

'I must say Rasmussen certainly looks as if he belongs.'

'He does,' I said.

There was a heavy and rather awkward silence and she seemed strangely ill at ease.

'We found the plane all right,' I said. 'And Kelso. There was a pretty positive identification.'

'Yes, Mrs. Kelso told me that much. We're sharing a room. Did anything else happen?'

'Vogel and Stratton looked very disappointed and I found a spot not too far away where someone had landed in a ski plane recently.'

She was immediately interested. 'Arnie?'

'I don't know anyone else on the coast who runs one.'

'So the emeralds Arnie gave me came from the wreck, is that what you are saying?'

'Something like that. Along with others of course.'

'But how would he know they were there?'

I'd been giving that question some thought on my own account and had decided there was only one plausible answer. 'Sarah Kelso. She paid him a visit the first night she was in Frederiksborg. I wondered what she was up to at the time.'

'Without Vogel's knowledge?'

'That's about the size of it. It certainly raises some intriguing possibilities, doesn't it?'

'What do you intend to do about it?'

I shrugged. 'Why should I do anything? It's all beginning to get far too complicated for a simple soul like me.'

She chuckled. 'Oh, what a liar you are. What a terrible liar. I'm really going to have to do something about you.'

'In which capacity? As Ilana Eytan or Myra Grossman?' I said and regretted it instantly.

The smile faded and there was something very close to pain on her face. 'You won't let it alone, will you?'

I stood there staring at her, filled with self-loathing, trying to find the right words, but I was too late. Behind us Vogel and Stratton came down the stairs with Sarah Kelso and Rasmussen returned from the kitchen a moment later and I started to drown in the sudden outburst of conversation.

The meal which followed was simple but satisfying. Lentil soup, then steamed cod and a side of mutton. Afterwards there was coffee and brandy and we sat round the fire and talked, mainly about Greenland and the early settlers.

Rasmussen stood with his back to the fire, a glass in his hand, and told them the beautiful and tragic story. Of the discovery of the great islands in the tenth century by Eric the Red, of the thousands of Icelanders and Scandinavians who had settled the land until gradually a climatic deterioration set in making life progressively more difficult until 1410 when the last official boat sailed for home.

'But what happened then?' Sarah Kelso demanded. 'What happened to those who stayed?'

Rasmussen shrugged.

'No one really knows. The next three hundred years or so are a blank. When the missionaries came here in the eighteenth century they found only the Eskimo.'

'But that's incredible.'

'True, nevertheless.'

There was a slight silence and Stratton said, 'Do you think the Norsemen really discovered America or is the whole thing simply tales for children?'

He couldn't have chosen a better subject and Rasmussen plunged straight in. 'There can be no doubt whatever that the accounts of the Norse voyages contained in the sagas are substantially true. Men sailed from here, from this very fjord. Leif the Lucky, Eric the Red's son, was the first.' The names rolled from his tongue, echoing from the rafters of the great hall and no one spoke. 'He discovered Vinland—Vinland the Good. Probably the area around Cape Cod in Massachusetts.'

'But only probably,' Vogel said. 'Isn't it true that most discoveries of so-called Norse relics in America and Canada have been discredited?'

'Which does not mean that there is no substance in any of them,' Rasmussen said. 'We read in the sagas that Leif's brother, Thorvald Eiriksson, was killed in a battle with Indians, hit in the armpit by an arrow. The Danish archaeologist, Aage Roussell, excavated the farm at Sandnes up the coast from here which belonged to Thorvald's brother. Amongst other things he discovered an Indian arrowhead, undoubtedly American, and a lump of anthracite coal of the same type that exists in Rhode Island. There is no anthracite in Greenland.'

'Joe was telling me you do a great deal of research into this sort of thing yourself,' Desforge said. 'Ever come up with anything?'

'A great many things. The sagas tell us that Thorfinn Karlsefne and his wife, Gudrid the Fair, settled for a while in America at a place called Straumsey—undoubtedly the Island of Manhattan.

A son was born there—Snorre—the first white man born in America.'

'And you believe that?' Vogel said.

'But of course. In later years he settled here at Sandvig. This very hall is built on the ruins of his homestead. I've been excavating for years.'

There was real enthusiasm in his voice and they were all infected by it. 'Have you anything we can see?' Vogel asked.

'Certainly.' Rasmussen put down his glass, got up and led the way down to the other end of the hall and they all followed him.

It wasn't that I had no interest, but I'd seen the lovingly preserved objects that he kept on display, many times, and in any case I felt like some air. I faded into the shadows, opened the door gently and went out into the yard.

It was about eleven o'clock and at that time of the year it didn't get really dark until somewhere after midnight so that there was a sort of harsh luminosity to the rain and the mist that reminded me strongly of a Yorkshire moor at dawn.

The rain was falling very heavily now, bouncing from the cobbles, and I ran for the shelter of the barn on the far side of the yard. It was a vast, echoing place filled with the pleasant smell of new hay and a ladder led to a loft above.

It was half full of hay and at the far end a door swung to and fro in the wind, a fine spray of rain drifting in. There was a clear drop of thirty feet or so to the cobbles below and a heavy hook and pulley swung from a wooden hoist. Altogether it was a sort of paradise one had loved to play in as a boy and I resisted a strong impulse to slide down the rope to the ground, and lit a cigarette and stood looking out at the rain, filled with a pleasant nostalgia.

The main door creaked below and Ilana called softly, 'Joe?'

I crouched at the edge of the loft and looked down at her. She was dressed as she had been for dinner with the addition of the sheepskin coat which was draped over her shoulders.

She glanced up, saw me and smiled. 'Is there room for one more up there?'

'I think so.'

She climbed the ladder and stood looking about her, hands in pockets. 'This is nice. Why did you cut out? Weren't you interested?'

'Fascinated,' I said. 'Always have been, but Olaf Rasmussen and I are old friends. I've seen it all before. Anyway it was suddenly too crowded in there. Too many people I don't like.

'Does that include me?'

'What do you think?'

We moved along to the open door. She sat on a box and I gave her a cigarette.

'Do you often feel like that? Hemmed in, I mean.'

'Frequently.'

She smiled and shook her head. 'You told me you came to Greenland because you could make more money here than anywere else. That isn't really true, is it?'

I looked out into the rain, trying to get it straight in my own mind.

'In the City I worried about where I was going to park the car. When I found somewhere, I worried about over-parking. Here, each day is a new struggle—people against the wilderness. It keeps a man on his toes. One of the few places left on earth that can give you that feeling.'

'For how much longer?'

I sighed. 'That's the trouble. Icelandair has started running four-day tourist trips from Iceland to Narssarssuaq which isn't all that far from here. There's a good airfield and a reasonable hotel. I've a nasty feeling it's the beginning of the end. It always is once the tourists start coming in.'

'And what will you do then?'

'Move on.'

'With a brand new persona, I suppose?'

I frowned. 'I'm not with you.'

'It's a term Jung used. He argued that most people can't face life in real terms so they invent a persona for themselves—a new identity if you like. We all suffer from the same disease to a greater or lesser degree. You try to present the image of a tough bush pilot, a strong man with steel nerves who can handle anything that comes along.'

'Is that a fact now?'

She carried on: 'Rasmussen sees himself as a latter day Viking. Jack's trouble is that he's had to create and discard so many different identities that he's long since lost any kind of contact with reality.'

'And where in the hell do you get all this stuff from?' I demanded.

'I read psychology and social philosophy for a year at university.'

Which took the wind right out of my sails and I stared at her in astonishment. 'Why didn't you continue?'

She shrugged. 'I just felt that it wasn't for me, that those dons and lecturers with their heads in their books were living the biggest lie of all.'

I shook my head. 'Strange, but I thought I was getting to know you and suddenly I find you're a complete stranger.'

'What did Jack tell you about me?' she said.

'About Myra Grossman,' I corrected her. 'The poor little East End Jewess with a chip on her shoulder and a father with a tailor's shop in the Mile End Road.'

'He must have forgotten to tell you about the other one hundred and sixty-three branches,' she said gently.

I stared at her blankly. 'But why should he do that?'

'Jack's a very complex character. Did he say anything else about me?' I nodded slowly. 'Anything I should know?'

I shook my head. 'Nothing important—nothing I believed.'

'You're a poor liar, Joe.' She smiled gravely. 'Drinkers—real drinkers don't have much interest in sex. I should have thought you would have known that.'

I nodded slowly. 'I seem to have taken rather a lot for granted. I'm sorry about that. Do you believe me?'

'I could give it a try.'

'Then tell me one thing? Why *did* you come out here? That's the one thing I still can't understand.'

She said: 'It's really very simple. I wanted to be an actress and money can't buy you that, only talent. Jack helped me along, got me into pictures. All right, I'm certainly not the greatest thing since Bernhardt, but I can get all the work I want now. They come to me.'

'And you feel guilty about that? You think you owe him something?'

'He was badly in need of financial backing for this picture, the one that's folded. I thought I could interest my father. In fact the truth is that Jack took the whole thing as read.'

'And your father wouldn't play?'

'I felt the least I could do was face him, especially when Milt Gold told me the whole deal was off now.' She shook her head. 'Poor Jack.'

'I find it difficult to cry in my beer over a man who's gone through three or four million dollars in his lifetime, 'I said.

'I don't. I feel personally responsible.'

'That's crazy.' I don't know why, but I grabbed her arm and pulled her to her feet. 'You want to cut that sort of thinking right out for a start.'

Suddenly, she was against my chest and we were kissing, my arms fast around her. She came up for air and smiled, her eyes wide.

'Are you quite sure this is what you want?'

'Ever since I saw you in the saloon on the *Stella* in that ridiculous gold dress.'

'Let's get our terms of reference straight before we go any further,' she said and pushed me away. 'Do you want to make love to me or me in that kinky dress? There's a difference.'

'I'll have to give that at least ten seconds thought,' I said, but as I reached out for her, the door creaked in the barn below and we heard voices.

I put a finger to my lips and tiptoed to the edge of the platform. Desforge was standing with his arms around Sarah Kelso. As I watched, he picked her up in his arms and carried her across to the hay.

I moved back cautiously to Ilana. 'Remember what you were saying about drink and the flesh? Well, Jack's down there in the hay with Sarah Kelso right this minute and it doesn't seem to be bothering him one little bit.'

She held one hand hard against her mouth to contain her laughter and I took her by the arm and led her to the open door and the hoist.

'In case you're interested that's the only way out.'

She shook her head. 'Not for me, I never was the athletic type.'

'So what do we do?' I said.

It was a good hour later, and quite dark, when Desforge and Sarah Kelso left. I helped Ilana down the ladder and we moved through the darkness to the door. It was still raining heavily and we stood there for a moment, my arm around her waist.

'Ready?' I said.

She nodded and we ran across the yard together. We paused on the steps of the porch, laughing, and Desforge said from the shadows, 'That you, Joe? I've been wondering what happened to you.'

For a moment, I thought he was going to make trouble. Instead he said, 'Look, I've decided I've had this place. Any chance of flying out with you in the morning?'

'That's fine by me.'

'See you at breakfast then.'

The door closed softly behind him and I looked down at Ilana. 'What do you make of that or does he think he's in love?'

'He doesn't know what the word means.'

Her face was a pale shadow in the darkness as I held her away from me and looked at her searchingly. 'Do you, Ilana? Do you know what it means?'

'I liked what happened back there in the loft,' she said. 'I like you. That's enough for one night. Step by step, Joe Martin. Step by step.'

She didn't even kiss me good night. Simply left me to think about it, standing there in the darkness listening to the rush of the heavy rain, smelling the earth, and something seemed to melt inside me so that I felt like laughing out loud for the first time in years.

CHAPTER THIRTEEN

WE FLEW OUT of Sandvig just after dawn and landed at Frederiksborg by eight. I got rid of my passengers and started to make up for lost time. I took a couple of miners into Godthaab and carried on to Søndre Strømfjord to pick up some machine parts needed urgently by a deep sea trawler which had come into harbour with engine trouble.

I arrived back in Frederiksborg at one o'clock to find Simonsen clamouring to be taken to a fishing village about a hundred miles up the coast where some Eskimos had been trying to stick harpoons into each other instead of the seals. I dropped him off, promising to return on the following afternoon, and flew back to Frederiksborg.

It was the first opportunity I'd had to look up Arnie and I went to the airstrip. The Aermacchi was there, raised on a couple of chain hoists, and Miller and two mechanics were working on the undercarriage.

'Where's Arnie?' I said.

'Haven't seen him since last night.' Miller grinned and wiped his hands on an oily rag. 'Probably been in bed with some dame all day. A couple of other guys were looking for him. They were back again just after noon. Didn't seem to be having much luck.'

'Who were they?'

'The older one was called Vogel. Sounded like a German or something to me.'

'Austrian,' I said. 'Not that it matters. How's the work coming along?'

'Just fine. He should be able to take her up tomorrow. Tell him that if you see him, will you?'

So the hounds were closing in? I hurried back to town and called at his house but the front door was locked and there was no reply to my knock. That left two possibilities. He was either with Gudrid or drinking at the Fredericsmut which was on my way to the hotel anyway, so I decided to call.

It had been one hell of a day. The kind that needs a couple of double brandies to add zest to it so I ordered black coffee, sat on one of the high stools at the bar and pretended I was a drinking man.

I asked the barman if Arnie had been in and he nodded. 'Earlier this afternoon about one o'clock. He had something to eat here and then two men came in and joined him—the ones who were with you the other night. There was some trouble. I don't know what it was exactly, but he cleared out.'

'What kind of trouble?'

He shrugged. 'I was in the back, but Sigrid was here. Just a minute, I'll get her.'

He went into the kitchen and a couple of minutes later the impudent looking young Eskimo girl who'd served us on my last visit came in. She was obviously in the middle of baking and wiped flour from her hands with a towel.

Her English was about as basic as you could get, so we talked in Danish. Arnie had been half-way through his meal when the two men came in. She couldn't understand what they were saying because they talked in English, but the older man had got very angry and it seemed Arnie had laughed at him. What happened then, she wasn't sure, but there had certainly been some sort of scuffle because a chair had gone over and Arnie had left in a hurry.

I thanked her and she returned to the kitchen. I sat there drinking my coffee and thinking about the whole thing, then went to the telephone, rang the hotel and asked for Gudrid.

She sounded cautious when she came to the phone. 'Who is it?'

'Joe Martin. I'm looking for Arnie.'

She hesitated rather obviously. 'He told me to tell no one where he was this afternoon. Said he wanted some peace and quiet.'

'This is important, Gudrid—really important. Now where is he?'

'All right,' she said. 'He's gone fishing.'

'The usual place?'

'As far as I know.'

'Fine—I'll catch up with him there.'

I put down the receiver and checked the time. It was five-thirty and the usual place was two miles on the other side of the fjord which meant borrowing a boat, not that that would present any difficulty. I left quickly and hurried through the rain towards the harbour.

Fog crouched on the lower reaches of the fjord and the steady drizzle indicated a dirty night to come as I left the harbour. I'd

borrowed an inflatable rubber dinghy powered by a large outboard motor that gave a surprising turn of speed.

Four icebergs moved majestically down towards the sea, strung
out line-astern like battleships, ranging in colour from purest
dazzling white to blue and green. There was a sudden turbulence
in the water to starboard as a piked whale surfaced, white flukes
and belly gleaming as it rolled and went under again.

There was beauty and excitement in just being there with
the prow lifting out of the water and the rain cold on my face,
but none of it really registered. I had to see Arnie, had to have
the whole thing out with him, I knew that now.

I found him drifting in an old whaleboat about a mile
further on, fishing for cod with a hand line. He was wearing an
oilskin coat and sou'wester and I noticed a double-barrelled
shotgun under the seat.

I tossed him a line and he pulled me close. I climbed into the
whaleboat and joined him. 'You're a difficult man to find. I've
just seen Miller, by the way. He says you should be airborne
again by tomorrow.'

'That's nice to know,' he said cheerfully, and passed me a
Thermos. 'Hot coffee—help yourself.'

He returned to his fishing, dropping a spoon-shaped spinner
over the side and I shook my head. 'You never learn, do you?
There's no need for that. Even a bare hook will do. Cod are
bottom feeders. All you have to do is jig it up and down—
like this.'

I took the line from his hand and said casually, 'What have
you done with the emeralds, Arnie?'

'Emeralds?' His face was as innocent as a child's. 'What on
earth are you talking about?'

'The emeralds you found in the wreck of that Heron up there
on the ice-cap, the ones Sarah Kelso told you about. Before you
try denying it I'd better tell you that I found tracks where a ski
plane had landed and a patch of oil about half a mile from
the crash.'

'Am I the only person in the world with a ski plane?'

'The only one in these parts—the only one who makes presents
of uncut emeralds worth forty thousand krone. That was really
very rash of you, Arnie, letting your temper get the better of
you like that.'

His face hardened. 'Why don't you try minding your own
business, Joe?'

I ignored him and carried straight on. 'When we bumped into Sarah Kelso outside of her room that night, I think she got the impression that she'd scored a big hit—that you were so besotted you'd do anything for her, which she saw as a golden opportunity to put one over on Vogel. You could fly in, pick up the emeralds, then return with the tale that any kind of a landing was impossible.'

Most of this was simply intelligent guesswork based on the few facts I did have for certain, but from the expression on his face I was on the right track, so I carried on.

'You even tried to stop me from going in by insisting that a floatplane landing wasn't possible because there was too much ice on Lake Sule. I suppose the plan was for the two of you to fly off into the sunset together, only you weren't quite as sold on her as she'd imagined and came up with a better idea. At a guess I'd say you told her you hadn't been able to land, which, after all, had always been a possibility. She didn't trust you, especially when you let slip the fact that you were flying out the following morning—the day the rest of us were leaving for Sandvig, so she went down to the airstrip, started up that old truck and rammed the Aermacchi just to make sure you wouldn't be leaving.'

He had listened without a murmur, but now he said, 'There was a Catalina in from Søndre yesterday afternoon. I could have flown back there as a passenger and caught a jet to Canada or Europe.'

I shook my head. 'Not with the emeralds on your person—too big a risk with Customs to go through, especially if they're in the quantity they must be to make this whole thing worthwhile. No, you needed the Aermacchi in the air for the scope it gave you. Lots of possible hiding places on board and the freedom to fly anywhere you wanted. That's why you've hung on here and after all, you'd very little to worry about. Sarah Kelso couldn't be certain you were double-crossing her and she couldn't very well tell Vogel. With luck you might have been away today, but now it's too late. Now they're back and after your blood. Vogel knows a ski plane landed up there and from the look of him I shouldn't imagine he has much trouble with simple addition.'

He didn't attempt to deny any of it now. 'I can look after myself,' he said sullenly.

I felt the sort of annoyance you experience with a stubborn child who refuses to see sense. 'For God's sake, Arnie, these men are pros. They've been carving up suckers like you all their lives.'

I suppose it was a mixture of fear and resentment that made him erupt so violently or perhaps it was quite simply that he'd never really liked me.

'Who in the hell do you think you are? Half a man who vomits at the first whiff of a barmaid's apron. Do you think I need you to tell me what to do? Help me, you say? You can't even help yourself.' He pulled the shot gun from under the seat and held it up. 'Let them come, that's all I ask. Just let them come.'

It was grotesque, it was ludicrous and there was nothing I could do, nothing I could say. I suppose I could have turned him in. I could have gone straight to Simonsen, but then he couldn't have done very much, not without some convincing proof and I hadn't any. In any case, I just didn't want to be involved—it could lead to too many complications. I might even have to do some explaining myself and that was the last thing I wanted.

There was a tug as the hook was taken and I hauled in a cod which looked all of three pounds. Instinctively, Arnie clubbed it with the butt of the shotgun.

'At least I've managed to take care of your supper for you,' I said. 'I wouldn't stay out much longer if I were you. This fog is going to get worse before it gets better.'

He didn't reply; just sat there, his face very white under the black sou'wester, clutching the shotgun to his chest, fear in his eyes—real fear. And I left him there, which on looking back on it was the worst thing of all. Instead of trying again, I climbed into the dinghy, pressed the starter button on the outboard and moved away rapidly through the gathering fog.

By the time I had reached the harbour the fog had wrapped itself around me in a damp grey shroud, but I made the anchorage safely, tied up the dinghy and mounted the steps to the jetty.

Somewhere a foghorn sounded as a trawler moved in cautiously, but otherwise it was completely silent as I went along the jetty. I'd left the Otter at the top of the slipway, but I hadn't refuelled her so I set to work, bringing two jerrycans at a time from the stockpile, emptying them and returning for more. It took me all of twenty minutes and by the time I'd finished I was damp with sweat. At one point I heard footsteps approaching and a seaman loomed out of the fog and disappeared again along the jetty without speaking. I might have been the last person alive in a dead world.

I emptied the last can and started to secure the Otter for the night, lashing her down to the ring bolts. At one point I turned suddenly, staring into the fog behind me. I hadn't heard anything and yet I had the feeling that I was being watched, that somewhere just out of sight a presence was waiting for me.

Stupid and illogical perhaps, and yet my flesh crawled and I turned quickly to finish my task. I heard nothing and yet there was the feeling of movement behind me like a turbulence in the air. I started to rise, but I was too late. Someone delivered a stunning blow to the base of my neck and I went down hard. For a moment I lay there, my face against the wet concrete. Something enveloped me, wet and clinging, stinking of fish, and then there was only the darkness.

It was like coming up from deep water, drifting through layer after layer of darkness towards the light seen dimly like the dawn through ragged grey clouds. I finally surfaced, my eyes wide and staring. My head ached and for a little while I couldn't even remember who I was or what I was doing here. Strangely enough the link between this world and the old was the last thing I had remembered, the stink of fish which wasn't surprising as I was lying on a pile of damp nets.

I was in the hold of a ship, probably a trawler from the look of it, although the light was so bad that I could only detect the vague outline of things. There was a hollow drumming as someone moved along the deck above and I sat up.

There was a mild explosion in my head as I closed my eyes involuntarily, clenching my teeth against the pain. Deep breathing was the thing. I tried it for a while and felt a little better.

I got to my feet and stumbled through the gloom, hands outstretched before me until I came to a hatchway above my head, light gleaming faintly through the cracks where it fitted unevenly. It was at least four feet above my head so I did the obvious thing and started to shout.

Footsteps sounded on the deck again, the hatch was pulled back and someone looked down at me. He was just a seaman with a greasy woollen cap on his head, a face like Spanish leather and the sort of long drooping moustache the gunfighters used to wear out west. I recognized him at once as one of the men who'd been with Da Gama at the Fredericsmut on the night we'd had all the trouble.

Which didn't make any kind of sense unless Da Gama was engaged in some sort of private vendetta. The man looking down at me gave no clue. In fact he replaced the hatch and went away again.

I sat down, my head in my hands, and tried some more deep breathing. It didn't work particularly well because suddenly the darkness and the pain and the stench of rotting fish all seemed to come together and I rolled over and vomited.

I felt a little better after that. According to my watch, which still seemed to be working, it was seven o'clock when the sailor went away. It was a good hour later when the hatch was removed and he reappeared.

This time Da Gama was with him. He squatted on his haunches and peered down at me, a cigar clenched between his teeth, the sort of expression on his face that a cat has with a mouse between its paws.

He turned and said something and a moment later a ladder came down. By that time I was too weak to feel anything, even fear, and I scrambled up and collapsed on the deck, sucking in great lungfuls of damp sea air.

He crouched beside me, a look of concern on his face. 'You don't look too good, Mr. Martin. How do you feel?'

'Bloody awful,' I said weakly.

He nodded soberly and then took his cigar from between his teeth and quite deliberately touched the glowing end to my cheek. I yelled like a stuck pig, rolled away from him and scrambled to my feet.

The sailor took a knife from his belt and moved towards me and Da Gama laughed harshly. "Feel better now, Mr. Martin? That's good, eh? That sharpens you up a little?'

I looked around me wildly and the sailor prodded me in the back, the tip of the knife slicing through my clothes and drawing blood. Da Gama tossed off an order in Portuguese, turned and moved along the deck and the sailor pushed me after him.

We went down the schooner's stern companionway and Da Gama opened the door of the cabin at the bottom and stood to one side. He nodded to the sailor, obviously dismissing him, grabbed me by the shoulder and threw me inside so that I lost my balance and went sprawling.

I lay there for a moment, the darkness moving in on me again and then a familiar voice said, 'I say, old chap, you are in a mess, aren't you?'

Ralph Stratton pulled me up from the floor and dumped me in a chair. When I managed to focus I found Vogel sitting on the other side of the table.

CHAPTER FOURTEEN

MY CHEEK was on fire where Da Gama had burned me, but the pain in my head had eased into a kind of dull throbbing. My hands were shaking slightly, but that was reaction, I suppose, and I made a conscious effort to steady them. At least my brain was starting to function and I don't think I'd ever felt so frightened in my life before. If Desforge had been playing the part the scriptwriters would have given him something witty to say, or perhaps he'd have reached for the bottle of cognac and one of the glasses that stood on the table, helping himself with the sort of off-hand bravado with which tough heroes always faced that kind of situation.

But this was me, Joe Martin, weak as a kitten and sick to my stomach because I had a strong suspicion that, whatever happened now, I was going over the side somewhere out to sea with a weight around my feet. I might come up again, or what was left of me, when the ice thawed next spring, but it was more than likely that no one would ever hear of me again.

Or perhaps I was just being melodramatic? I wiped sweat from my face with the back of one hand and said in a cracked voice, 'I wish someone would tell me what this is all about.'

'Don't be stupid,' Vogel said crisply. 'You're well aware why you're here.'

There was a sudden unexpected diversion on deck, a shout of anger, a flurry of blows and drunken voices arguing fiercely. Da Gama went out without a word and I said to Vogel, 'Where does he fit in?'

'A blunt instrument. If the price is right and I asked him to, he would dispose of you without the slightest hesitation. You would do well to remember that.'

The silence hung between us and he left it there for a while, probably for effect. 'When we reached the Heron yesterday I expected to find something which belonged to me—something which had been carefully concealed. It was missing. Do you know what I'm talking about?'

I shook my head. 'I haven't the slightest idea.'

'Then why did you keep quiet about your discovery that a ski plane had landed recently in the area?'

I tried to think of a suitable reply to that one and failed miserably. 'Did I?'

Stratton sighed. 'You're really being very stupid, old chap.'

I noticed that he was still wearing those black leather gloves of his which didn't make me feel any better, especially when he moved around behind me.

Vogel said: 'There is only one ski plane operating on the coast at the moment, you told me that yourself.'

There was no point in denying it and I didn't try. 'That's right.'

'Which would seem to indicate that Fassberg lied to us when he returned from his reconnaissance flight and announced that a landing was out of the question. Why would he do that?'

'Why not ask him?'

'I have done, but he wasn't in the mood for conversation. When I have your contribution to this mystery, we'll try again.' He poured himself a brandy and leaned back in the chair. 'I'll ask you for the second time. Why did you conceal the fact that Fassberg had landed in the vicinity of the crash?'

I decided to try a little improvisation. 'All right, I'll tell you. He's a friend of mine. I didn't know what his game was. On the other hand I didn't want to be the one to land him in any kind of trouble so I decided to keep my mouth shut till I'd seen him.'

'And have you?'

'I haven't had the chance yet. I've been flying all day.'

Vogel sipped a little of his brandy, held up the glass to the light and shook his head. 'No, Martin, it won't do. It won't do at all.' He put down his glass very deliberately and leaned forward. 'You're lying—you're holding something back. Shall I tell you how I know? Because I've looked into your eyes, because I've watched your reactions, listened to what you have said and none of it makes sense—none of it!'

His last few words were shouted into my face and Stratton struck me across the back of the skull with his knuckles so that I cried out in pain. He yanked me back by the hair and clamped an arm across my throat.

'Let's try again,' Vogel said. 'Fassberg landed in his ski plane, went to the Heron and removed what I came to Greenland to recover. Wouldn't you say that was a reasonable assumption?'

'Only if he knew what he was looking for,' I said.

The thought must have occurred to him before, because it just couldn't be avoided and he sat there staring at me. This time you could have sliced the silence with a knife and Stratton said slowly, 'I'd say he's got a point there.'

'Of course he has, you fool.' Vogel leaned forward. 'Who, Martin? Who could have told him?'

'That's something you'll have to work out for yourself, but it would need someone who knew in the first place, wouldn't it? Someone close to you.' I looked up at Stratton. 'What about our friend here? How long has he been around?'

Stratton's hand rose and fell, catching me across the side of the head and I almost lost my senses. I slumped forward, head in hands, fighting the pain, and Vogel said, 'Bring him round, you fool. I haven't finished with him yet.'

There was the chink of the decanter, then Stratton wrenched back my head and poured half a glass of brandy into my mouth. As the nausea hit me there was the usual body-wrenching spasm and I vomited all over his neat grey suit. He gave a cry of disgust, sent me away from him with a tremendous heave and the chair went over. I rolled to the wall and got up as Stratton started to unbutton his jacket. When he had it half off, I sucked in some air, grabbed for the door handle and plunged outside.

He almost had me on the companionway, but I kicked out and caught him full in the face. And then I had the door open and was out on deck. Da Gama was standing no more than three or four feet away talking to a couple of his crew. As he swung round, I kept on going and vaulted the rail. The shock of the icy water was so terrible that for a moment I thought the heart had stopped beating inside me, but then I surfaced and struck out wildly into the fog.

I knew they'd expect me to get out of that freezing water at the earliest possible moment, which meant they'd be strung out along the jetty waiting for me. I took a chance and headed through the fog to the other side of the harbour.

It took me no more than ten minutes, but towards the end I didn't think I was going to make it and then my knee banged against a submerged rock. A few moments later I crawled out of the water and fell face down on a shingle beach.

I was numb with cold, but I forced myself to my feet and stumbled across the beach to a broken line of massive concrete blocks which I recognized as being part of the defensive system laid down at the northern end of the airstrip against winter storms.

I checked my watch. It was almost nine, about three hours since my meeting with Arnie on the other side of the fjord. He would have returned by now, probably not long after me in view of the deterioration in the weather.

I ran across the airstrip, flapping my arms vigorously to try and get some feeling back into them. There was no one about as far as I could see and the hangars were deserted, so I borrowed an old jeep that was kept for general use about the place. Whatever happened now I had to make Arnie realize the kind of people he was dealing with and I drove towards town as fast as the fog would let me.

I parked the jeep at the end of the narrow street and walked towards the house. As I reached the steps leading up to the verandah, the side gate banged and someone ran out of the fog wildly. I had a momentary glimpse of Gudrid Rasmussen's face, eyes wide and staring, and then she was gone.

I hammered on the front door. There was no reply, but the curtain was drawn and a chink of light showed through. I tried again, calling his name with no better success, and went round the side of the house and tried the kitchen door.

I think I knew what I was going to find the moment I stepped inside. For one thing there was a special quality to the silence. It was as if the whole world had stopped breathing and the harsh distinctive odour of gunpowder hung on the air.

The living room was a shambles. The telephone had been ripped from the wall, drawers turned out, cushions torn apart, books scattered across the floor, and blood—fresh blood—splashed across the wall in a crimson curtain.

Arnie lay on his back on the other side of the couch, most of his face missing, his own shotgun lying across his body where the murderer had dropped it. Strange, but at times the face of Death can be so appalling that it freezes the soul, cutting out all emotional response, preventing any normal reaction. I stood staring down at him, trapped in a kind of limbo where nothing was real any more, and all that had happened seemed part of some crazy nightmare.

Somewhere a shutter banged, blown by the wind, bringing me back to reality like a slap in the face and I turned and ran as if all the devils in hell were at my heels.

I parked the jeep in the courtyard at the rear of the hotel and went up the back stairs to my room. When I opened the door

Ilana was sitting by the window reading a book. It seemed as if I was still back there in the fog as her face jumped out to meet me, the smile of welcome fading into a look of astonishment and concern.

I'm not quite sure what happened after that. I only know that I was on my knees and her arms were tight around me. I don't think I've ever been so glad to see anyone in my life before.

I had a hot shower and changed and told her everything. When I'd finished, we did the obvious thing and went along to Gudrid's room. The door was locked, but I knocked several times and called her name and after a while it opened and she gazed out at us fearfully. Her eyes were swollen from weeping and she was shaking as if she had a fever.

She looked at me and then at Ilana and pushed back a tendril of hair that had fallen across her eyes. 'I'm sorry, Mr. Martin, I don't feel very well. I'm going to take the rest of the night off.'

I shoved her back into the room and Ilana followed me. 'I saw you leaving, Gudrid,' I said.

She looked genuinely bewildered. 'Leaving? I don't understand.'

'Outside Arnie Fassberg's place. You ran straight past me. I was on my way in.'

Her face crumpled and she turned and flung herself on the bed, her body racked by great sobs. I sat down and patted her on the shoulder. 'There's no time for that, Gudrid. Have you told the police?'

She turned her tear-stained face to look up at me. 'I didn't kill him, you must believe that. He was dead when I arrived.'

'I believe you,' I said. 'You've nothing to worry about.'

'But you don't understand. Arnie and I often quarrelled—plenty of people knew that. Sergeant Simonsen knows it.'

'He also knows what's possible and what isn't and the idea that you could have let Arnie Fassberg have both barrels in the face at point-blank range is so preposterous that he wouldn't even waste his time considering it.' I took her hands and held them tight. 'Now tell me what happened?'

'I got a phone call from Arnie about forty minutes ago. He asked me to bring round a package I've been looking after for him. He said he knew that I was on duty, but that I must bring it. That it was a matter of life and death.'

'Did you know what was in the package?'

She nodded. 'He told me they were ore specimens that had come into his possession, evidence of mineral deposits somewhere in the mountains that would make him a wealthy man. He told me to keep the package in the safest place I could find. He said our whole future depended on it.'

'What future?'

'We were to be married, Mr. Martin.'

She started to cry again, a handkerchief to her mouth, and Ilana sat down and put an arm round her. I got to my feet and walked to the window. Poor little bitch. So much in love that she'd been willing to believe anything, even a story as shot full of holes as an old skein net.

After a while she seemed to regain some kind of control and I tried again. 'So you took the package round?'

She shook her head. 'I didn't have it to take. I know it's silly, but I was frightened to death—afraid I might lose it or that it might be stolen—there's been a lot of petty theft in the staff quarters lately. Another thing, you know what a terrible gambler Arnie was. He was always giving me money to look after for him one day and asking for it back the next. For the first time I seemed to have him pinned down. I wanted to keep it that way so I posted the package to myself and addressed it to my grandfather's farm at Sandvig. It went with the monthly supply boat first thing this morning.'

'What happened when you told Arnie that?'

'That was the strangest thing of all. He started to laugh and then the phone went dead.'

I nodded to Ilona. 'Whoever was with him must have ripped it out then.'

'I was worried and anxious,' Gudrid carried on. 'So I got my coat and slipped out the back way even though I was supposed to be on duty.'

'And he was dead when you got there.'

She stared into space, horror on her face, and said in a whisper, 'I think I heard the shots as I went down the street, but I can't be sure. The front door was locked so I went round to the back. And then I saw the blood on the wall. Oh, dear God, the blood.'

She broke down completely and I left Ilana to comfort her and went to the window. After a while she joined me. 'So it was all for nothing.'

'All for nothing,' I said. 'It's difficult to think of him as dead. He was so full of life.'

She put a hand on my arm. 'You'll have to go to the police now, Joe.'

'Not yet,' I said. 'There's someone else I want a word with first.'

'Sarah Kelso?'

'That's right. Her reaction to this should be very interesting. I'll see if she's in her room.'

'You'd be wasting your time,' she said. 'She's with Jack. As far as I know they've been together all evening.'

'She'll just have to get out of bed then, won't she?' I said. 'You'd better hang on here.'

'Oh, no you don't.' Ilana brushed past me and opened the door. 'I wouldn't miss this for all the tea in China.'

Desforge's door was locked and I knocked and kept on knocking until I heard sounds of movement inside. When he opened it he was still tying the cord of his dressing gown, his hair was rumpled and he didn't look pleased.

'What in the hell is this?' he demanded.

I forced my way past him and Ilana followed me. 'Get her out here, Jack,' I said.

He stared at me open-mouthed, then slammed the door and moved in belligerently. 'Now look here, Joe . . .'

I crossed to the bedroom door, opened it and said crisply, 'Mrs. Kelso, I thought you might be interested to know that someone just murdered Arnie Fassberg.'

I closed the door again and moved back to the others. Ilana helped herself to a cigarette from a box on the table and Desforge stared at me, his mouth slack.

'You don't sound as if you were kidding, Joe.'

'I wasn't, believe me.'

He moved to the side table where several bottles and glasses stood on a tray, and poured himself a drink mechanically. 'And you're saying she's mixed up in this in some way.'

'That's about the size of it.'

The door opened behind me and, when I turned, Sarah Kelso was standing there, her face very white. She was wearing a button-down jersey dress that had obviously been pulled on in some haste and her hair was all over the place.

'I believe you said something about Arnie Fassberg, Mr. Martin.'

'That's right,' I said. 'He's dead. Somebody used his own shot-gun on him—both barrels in the face at point-blank range.'

She swayed and Desforge hurried to her side and helped her to a chair. 'You're very kind,' she said weakly.

I poured some brandy into a glass and carried it across to her. 'A lot kinder than Vogel and Stratton will be when they get their hands on you. You tried to double-cross them, didn't you? There were emeralds hidden in that plane in the roof of the cabin near the pilot's seat. You told Arnie. You persuaded him to drop in on that first day and recover them, then fly back here and pretend that a landing was impossible.'

'He told me that he hadn't been able to land,' she said, gripping her glass with both hands. 'He lied to me.'

'But you couldn't be sure, could you?' I said. 'Not until the rest of us had reached the Heron, and by that time he might be gone, so you went down to the airstrip at night, started up that old truck and ran it into the Aermacchi.'

She nodded wearily. 'All right—I'll tell you. I'll tell you everything. Vogel is the kind of man who has an interest in many things. Some legal—some a little bit on the shady side.'

'What about the London and Universal Insurance Company?'

'It's a legally constituted company. I know it must be because it paid me out on my husband's death just like Vogel told you.'

'What about your husband? Where did he fit into all this?'

'Jack was flying for a Brazilian internal airline. Just a fill-in job till he got fixed up with one of the big companies. He met this man Marvin Gaunt in a bar in Sao Paulo. He said he'd bought a Heron secondhand from some rich Brazilian, but couldn't get an export licence. He offered Jack five thousand dollars to fly it out illegally to a small field in Mexico. There they would change the registration number and fly the plane to Europe via America and Canada. Gaunt said he had a buyer in Ireland who would pay double what he'd given for it.'

'What went wrong?'

'Gaunt got drunk one night and disclosed that there was better than a half a million in uncut emeralds hidden on board and that Vogel was going to make a fortune.'

'So your husband decided to cut himself in?'

She stared at us tragically. 'I know it was wrong, but we'd had a lot of bad luck. I was working in London while his mother looked after the two boys. Things were very difficult.'

'And Vogel agreed to pay more?'

'He had to. Jack was promised twenty-five thousand pounds and he refused to fly until it was paid over to me in London.'

'He drove a hard bargain.'

She gave a little shrug. 'They didn't have much choice.'

'And you didn't mind where the money came from?' Ilana said.

'There are worse things than smuggling.' She sighed. 'Or at least that's what I tried to tell myself. It was me he was thinking of, remember. Me and the boys.'

They say it only takes one final straw and that was it for me. I clapped her ironically. 'Slow curtain to cheers from the audience.'

'For God's sake, give her a break, Joe,' Desforge said. 'Mrs. Kelso's had just about all she can take for one night.'

'I applaud your sentiments,' I said, 'but just let's get one thing straight, shall we? She isn't Mrs. Kelso.'

There was the kind of silence you get just after one clap of thunder when you're waiting for the next. Desforge stared at me in bewilderment and Sarah Kelso looked like a hunted animal who has just found the last route to freedom closed.

Ilana leaned forward, a slight frown on her face. 'Just what are you getting at?' she demanded softly.

'It's quite simple really.' I opened my arms wide. 'Meet Jack Kelso.'

CHAPTER FIFTEEN

IT HAD ALL STARTED with Jean Latouche, a barrel-chested French-Canadian bush pilot with the loudest laugh I've ever heard and a ragged black beard. He was a sort of twentieth century *voyageur* who used a float-plane instead of a canoe. From what I'd heard, he had the best part of a couple of hundred thousand dollars put away against his old age and a small portion of that had been earned flying in partnership with me on freight contracts to oil survey outfits in up-country Newfoundland.

That year the season had finished in Greenland by the last week in September as far as I was concerned, and I had flown over to Canada to see if I could pick up some extra cash before the snows came. I didn't have much luck, which was a pity, because although I'd managed to save twelve thousand dollars over the season as a whole, I was still on the books of the Silver Shield Finance Company of Toronto for sixteen thousand against the Otter. Not that they were going to cut my throat over it. I'd already paid off more than I needed to according to our agreement, but it was a big disappointment. I'd hoped to start the next season clean with the Otter bought and paid for.

I hung around Goose Bay for three days but nothing seemed to be happening so that I was glad of the work when a couple of geologists chartered me for a one way flight to a small airstrip west of Michikamau Lake called Carson Meadows. It was the sort of trip that netted me more than a couple of hundred dollars after expenses and I was sitting at the bar in the town's one and only hotel drinking black coffee and contemplating the future with foreboding when Jean Latouche came in.

He must have been at least fifty and wore flying boots and a great shaggy sheepskin coat that reached his knees. He dropped his duffle bag against the wall and advanced on me, hand outstretched.

'Eh, Joe, how goes it? You have a good season over there?'

'It could have been worse,' I said. 'It could also have been a damned sight better. How about you?'

'You know me, Joe. A crust, a jug of wine. I don't ask much.'

'Like hell you don't,' I commented sourly. 'Where is it to be this winter? The Bahamas again or are you going to Tahiti this time?'

'You're beginning to sound bitter in your old age,' he said. 'What's wrong?'

'I'm tired, that's all. Tired of running round this God-forsaken country looking for work when there isn't any to be had.'

He swallowed the cognac he'd ordered and asked for another. 'Maybe you ain't been asking in the right places.'

I looked at him hopefully. 'Look, Jean, if you know of something then say the good word for God's sake.'

'Don't get so excited, you probably won't be interested anyway. I know I wasn't. I was in Grant Bay yesterday. I met a fella there called Gaunt—Marvin Gaunt. He had a Heron fitted with auxiliary tanks. He's looking for someone to fly it to Ireland with him.'

'What happened to his pilot?'

'He flew it in from Toronto himself in easy stages. He just isn't good enough to take on the Atlantic on his own, that's all.'

'What's he offering?'

'A thousand dollars plus the return fare.'

'Why didn't you take it?'

'I just didn't like the smell.' He tapped his nose, a wise look on his face. 'I've been around too long, Joe.'

'You think he's up to no good?'

'I don't just think it—I know it.' He got to his feet and clapped me on the shoulder. 'No, it isn't for you, that one, Joe. Anyway, I've got to be on my way. Got a flight to the coast at noon. See you around.'

I didn't, because he was killed a month later trying to land at Gander in a fog so thick you couldn't see your hand in front of your face, but I wasn't to know that as I sat there in that quiet little bar, brooding over my coffee or what was left of it, thinking about Marvin Gaunt and his Heron. A good aircraft, but he'd need those auxiliary tanks fitted to get her across the big pond. Still, with that done, it was a piece of cake and a thousand dollars was a thousand dollars. I paid for my coffee, and hurried back to the airstrip.

Grant Bay was a couple of hundred miles south of Goose and had been constructed to serve the local town and mining interests in the area. As I flew in, it was raining heavily and I wondered what Gaunt was doing there instead of some place like Gander in Newfoundland. It didn't make too much sense, not if he was really looking for a pilot.

There was a small tower, half a dozen hangars and three runways. I got permission to land, put the Otter down and parked beside the first hangar. I had a look inside all of them on the way down, but there was no sign of the Heron.

I found it in the open on the other side of the hangars, standing forlornly in the heavy rain. I walked round it slowly and paused, fascinated. On that side the Canadian registration number painted on the fuselage was crumbling at the edges in the heavy rain. I rubbed some more away with my fingers, just enough to confirm that there had been a previous registration, now painted over, which was very, very interesting and seemed to indicate that Jean's assessment of Gaunt hadn't been too far out.

He was staying at the town's one hotel and I found him in his room, a tall, rather handsome Englishman with the sort of public school voice that was too good to be true. By the time I'd spoken to him for five minutes, I had him pegged as someone who'd climbed rather a long way up the ladder.

'Mr. Gaunt?' I said when he opened the door. 'I heard you were looking for a pilot.'

'Oh, yes,' he said. 'And where did you hear that?'

'Carson Meadows,' I replied promptly. 'Someone was talking in a bar there.'

He stood back and I went in. It wasn't much of a room—the sort you'd expect to find in a place like that. A mahogany wardrobe, an old bed, a thinning carpet. He went to the dresser, took a half bottle of whisky from a drawer and got a glass from the washbasin.

'Join me?'

I shook my head and he poured himself one and looked me over. 'You've got a licence of course?'

I nodded and took out my wallet. Nobody knew me in Grant Bay and in view of the circumstances it might be a good idea to keep it that way. The previous year I'd flown for a Lebanese air freight firm as co-pilot to a Canadian called Jack Kelso. By flying standards he was an old man—fifty-three—and had lived hard all his life, so no one was particularly surprised when he went on a three-day drunk for the last time and died of a heart attack in Basra.

I was with him at the time and had the job of collecting his things together, not that it was really worthwhile because as far as anyone knew he didn't have a relative in the world. I came across his pilot's licence when I was throwing things away and had kept it ever since, more as a souvenir than anything else.

I took it from my wallet and gave it to Gaunt who examined it briefly, then handed it back. 'That all seems to be in order, Mr. Kelso, I've got a Heron down there on the field that I bought cheap in Toronto. I flew her here myself in easy stages, but I'm not up to crossing the Atlantic on my own. I've got a buyer waiting in Ireland who'll double my money if I can get it there by the end of the week. Are you interested?'

'What does it pay?'

'A thousand and your return fare from Shannon.'

'Four thousand,' I said. 'Four thousand and my return fare.' He managed a look of blank amazement, but before he could say anything I added. 'Of course you could wait another couple of days to see if anyone else turns up, but I doubt it. It's the wrong time in the season. Another thing, if that Heron stands out there much longer, the rain will wash the registration right off and then we'll all be able to see what it really is—or wouldn't that bother you?'

He took it right on the chin. 'All right, Mr. Kelso, four thousand. Four thousand plus your return fare. I think we should do very well together.'

'In cash,' I said. 'Before we leave.'

'And when will that be?'

I'd already decided that I'd rather fly back to Goose and leave the Otter there. I could always get a lift back in the mail plane if nothing else was available.

'If the met report is satisfactory we could take-off tomorrow afternoon,' I said. 'Does that suit you?'

'Couldn't be better. I'll have her checked over in the morning.'

'You do that.'

I left him there and went back to the airstrip, already half-regretting my decision, but it was too late for that kind of talk now. I'd said I was going and go I would. The money would solve my personal problems nicely and any stray thoughts about what Gaunt might be up to I pushed firmly into the back of my mind and closed the door. I didn't want to know. As far as I was concerned, it was just another charter or at least, that's what I tried to tell myself.

It was still raining as I prepared for take-off on the following afternoon, but the met report for the crossing was pretty good.

There was no customs control to pass through as it was a passage out and at a field like Grant Bay, formalities were cut to the minimum. Gaunt handled all the documentation and even the two mechanics who tuned the engines for take-off didn't get a clear look at my face, which suited me down to the ground.

Gaunt had my money waiting for me in crisp new hundred dollar bills and I slipped them into an envelope I'd already prepared and posted it to myself, care of General Delivery at Goose Bay. So everything seemed to be taken care of. I'd calculated that we should get about half-way across on the normal tanks before having to switch to the auxiliaries and was sitting in the pilot's seat doing an instrument check when Gaunt joined me.

He was wearing a newish one-piece flying suit and looked extremely cheerful as he strapped himself into the co-pilot's seat.

'Ready to go?' I said.

'Whenever you like. There's just one thing.' He handed me a map that had been neatly clipped to one of the chart boards. 'If you have a look at that you'll see that I've changed our destination.'

The course he'd charted ran north-west from Grant Bay in a dead straight line, cutting across the tip of Greenland and finishing at Reykjavik in Iceland, a flight of about sixteen hundred miles.

'What's the idea?' I said.

He took an enevlope from one of his pockets and passed it across. 'There's another thousand in there—all right?'

They were just as new as the others and just as attractive. I slipped them back into the envelope and put it into the inside pocket of my flying jacket. After all, what did it matter to me? Reykjavik or Shannon. It was all the same.

He smiled contentedly. 'We won't bother informing the tower of our change of destination, old man. I'd much rather they still booked us down as being en route to the old country.'

'You're the boss,' I said and taxied out into the runway.

It was still raining as we took off and the sky was as heavy as lead, but I remembered the forecast and wasn't worried. I didn't alter course until we were well out to sea. The plane handled nicely—very nicely indeed and somewhere on the far horizon, the edge of a cloud was touched with light. I sat back, my hands steady on the controls and started to enjoy myself.

A couple of hours later and five hundred miles out, I'd had my fun. I handed over to Gaunt who hadn't had much to say for himself and went to the lavatory in the tail of the plane. That's when I got my first big shock because when I opened the door there was a man in there dressed like one of the mechanics at Grant Bay. In other circumstances it could have had its funny side, but there was nothing humorous about the Luger automatic pistol he was holding in his right hand.

'Surprise, surprise! Actually I was just about to look you up.' The Luger moved so that the muzzle pointed in the general region of my stomach. 'Shall we see what dear old Marvin has to say for himself?'

The same throwaway public school voice as Gaunt's but this one was for real, I was sure of that and there was a glint in his eye that said he meant business.

'I wouldn't know what all this is about,' I said. 'But I'd be obliged if you'd point that thing somewhere else. Gaunt's doing his best, but I'm the pilot really and we don't want any nasty accidents this far out over the Atlantic.'

'My dear chap, I could fly this crate to China and back with one hand tied behind my back.'

I had the sort of feeling you get in the bar at the Royal Aero Club when some bore with a moustache a yard long takes a deep breath and you know that a second later you're going to get summer 1940, Biggin Hill and what it was really like doing a dozen sorties a day in a Spitfire.

I moved back through the body of the plane and opened the cabin door. Gaunt turned to grin at me and the smile faded.

'Harrison,' he said blankly.

'In person, old man.' Harrison tapped me on the shoulder with the Luger. 'Sit down and take over.'

Gaunt had gone very pale, but he didn't look as if he had lost control. In fact I could almost hear the wheels turning inside as he looked for some way out of this.

'Would someone kindly tell me what all this is about?' I said.

Harrison shook his head. 'Not your affair, old man. All I want from you are a few facts and figures. How long is the course you've plotted from Grant Bay to Shannon?'

I glanced across at Gaunt who nodded. 'We're not going to Shannon.' I said. 'Our destination is Reykjavik in Iceland.'

'Well, bless my soul,' he said. 'That is a turn-up for the book. How far have we come?'

'Just over six hundred.'

He smiled brightly. 'Ah, well, Iceland will suit me just as well as anywhere else.' He looked down at Gaunt. 'You know, Marvin, you were really very stupid. All I wanted was my share.'

'All right, all right!' Gaunt raised a hand quickly as if to shut him up. 'No need to advertise. We can discuss it elsewhere.'

Harrison backed out of the cabin and Gaunt followed him, closing the door. They were out there for a good five minutes and talked all the time, but I wasn't able to catch what they were saying. The shots, when they came, sounded remote and far away. There were two very close together, a short pause and then three more, two of which passed through the door splintering the windscreen.

I put the automatic pilot in control and unstrapped myself quickly. As I got to my feet and turned, the door burst open and Gaunt fell into my arms. I pushed him down into the other seat and he clawed at my jacket as I tried to unfasten his flying suit at the neck. And then blood erupted from his mouth and he lolled back, his head turning sideways, eyes fixed and staring.

Harrison was lying just inside the main cabin, face-down and when I turned him over, he was already dead, shot twice through the body. So there I was, up to my neck in trouble, two dead bodies on my hands, mixed up in something that was obviously far more serious than I'd ever appreciated.

I went down to the galley, poured hot coffee from a Thermos and lit a cigarette. What was I going to do that was the thing? I could always drop them both over the side, but that still meant I had to land somewhere and the plane would take a hell of explaining away because even if I just dumped it there would still be inquiries and that was the last thing I wanted. Of course, the ideal solution would have been to send the damned thing down to the bottom of the Atlantic with both of them inside, but that wouldn't do me much good. There was a variation on that theme, of course. Find a suitable piece of wilderness and bale out leaving the Heron to come down the hard way. With the additional petrol she was carrying in the auxiliary tanks she would go up like a torch.

What I needed sounded like an impossibility. The sort of area so sparsely populated that the crash would pass unnoticed and yet so close to some sort of civilization that I would have a fair chance of walking out.

The solution, when it came, was so simple that I almost

laughed out loud. I hurried back to the pilot's cabin, sat down in my seat again and reached for the chart. I found what I was looking for straight away—the Julianehaab Bight on the south-west coast of Greenland and the little fishing village of Sandvig, the fjord on which it stood cutting inland through the mountains to the ice-cap beyond.

That ice-cap was one of the most desolate places on God's earth. Through the years many planes had disappeared over it without trace. The Heron would be just one more and in any case, the official view when it failed to show at Shannon, would be that it was at the bottom of the Atlantic somewhere.

I calculated the distance to the coast carefully. Four hundred and fifty miles to go and according to the dial, there was enough fuel left in the tanks for approximately another five hundred miles. It couldn't have been more perfect. All I had to do was put it on automatic pilot and jump without switching the auxiliary tanks through. The plane would fly on perhaps another fifty miles, but when the fuel gave out it would nose-dive, exploding like a bomb on impact.

The only tricky bit was going to be the jump, but that was a calculated risk I'd just have to take. I lit a cigarette, reached for the automatic pilot control and found myself looking Gaunt straight in the face. It wasn't very pleasant and I pushed him away to the other side of the seat, switched off the automatic pilot and took control again. All I needed now was a plausibe story for my good friend Olaf Rasmussen when I walked in on him at his farm above Sandvig. But that shouldn't prove too difficult. There was a road of sorts linking Fredericksborg and Sandvig. I could say I'd been on the hunting trip I'd talked about all season, but had been too busy to take. That I'd had some kind of accident and lost all my gear. I had the bare bones of a story. Now I started to concentrate on making it sound convincing.

I brought the plane in low over the sea and took her up to three thousand as land appeared and beyond, through the harsh white moonlight, the Greenland ice-cap gleamed like a string of pearls.

East from Cape Desolation the Julianehaab Bight was full of smoky mist indicating no wind to speak of and certainly nothing more than five knots, which was something. At least it gave me the chance of dropping into the valley at the head of the fjord. Not much of a one, but better than staying here.

It was cold in the cabin with the night wind streaming in

through the splintered windscreen and the lighted dials on the instrument panel were confusing in their multiplicity, occasionally merging into a meaningless blur.

And then, on the far side of the mist the waters of the fjord gleamed silvery white in the intense light and the strange twisted moonscape rolled towards the ice-cap, every feature etched razor-sharp.

It was time to go. I reduced speed, put the auto pilot in control and unbuckled my safety belt. When I turned Gaunt's body had slid round again so that he seemed to be staring at me, mouth slightly parted as if he would speak, head disembodied in the light from the instrument panel.

I moved into the darkness of the main cabin, stumbling across Harrison's body so that I fell to one knee and my outstretched hand touched his ice-cold face. God knows why, but at that moment I suddenly became desperately afraid and lurched through the darkness and clawed at the quick release handles on the exit hatch. It fell away into the night and I stepped into space without hesitation, aware of the intense cold, feeling strangely free. I seemed to somersault in slow motion and for a single moment saw the plane above me in the night drifting steadily eastwards like some dark ghost and then I reached for the ring to open my chute.

For a moment it seemed to stick and my throat went dry. I tugged again with all my strength. I still continued to fall, turning over and then, quite suddenly, I heard what at the right moment is the most reassuring sound in the world—the crack of a chute opening above your head, blossoming like a white flower as the air fills it. I started to drift down into the hills at the head of the fjord.

CHAPTER SIXTEEN

RAIN DRUMMED against the window and I peered out into the gathering darkness.

'What happened after you landed?' Desforge asked.

I turned to face them. 'I had a rather enjoyable twelve-mile hike by moonlight. When I walked in on Olaf Rasmussen I told him I'd been on a hunting trip in the mountains from Frederiksborg. That I'd managed to scramble clear when my jeep had gone over the edge of the road on a washed-out section taking all my gear with it. That sort of thing happens all the time in country like this. He didn't question it for a moment. The following day I got a lift to Frederiksborg in a fishing boat. From there I flew to Newfoundland in one of the Catalina flying boats that East Canada Airways use on the coastal run. They always get out before the ice starts.'

Sarah Kelso sat on the edge of the bed, her handkerchief screwed up into a ball, her face drained of all colour. Desforge turned slowly, looked down at her. 'You certainly fooled me, angel. Who are you, anyway?'

'Does that matter now?' she said.

'No, I suppose it doesn't.'

He poured himself another drink and I pulled a chair forward and sat down in front of her. 'Shall we have the truth now?'

'All right,' she said wearily. 'What do you want to know?'

'Let's start with the emeralds. Who did they belong to originally?'

'The International Investment Company of Brazil. They were a plane shipment to Sao Paulo from somewhere in the interior. Gaunt hi-jacked them with some local help and Harrison was waiting to fly him out.'

'And Vogel was behind the whole deal?'

'That's right.'

'Where did you fit in?'

She shrugged. 'I work for Vogel—have done for years.'

'When the plane went missing what was Vogel's reaction?'

'Oh, he accepted it completely. Said it was just one of those things.'

'Didn't he worry about the mysterious Mr. Kelso?'

She shook her head. 'Not particularly. Harrison frequently used another identity and, in any case, there was nowhere they could have gone—not without Vogel getting some sort of word. Another thing, there was always the insurance which was better than nothing.'

'You mean he actually had the company pay out?'

'Why not? It was a legitimate claim. In any case, you don't seem to realize. He *is* the London and Universal Insurance Company.'

Desforge poured himself another drink. 'From what you say, Joe, it looks as if Gaunt was trying to pull a fast one and Harrison simply caught up with him.'

I nodded and said to Sarah Kelso, 'It was a neat idea to pass you off as Kelso's widow. Tell me something—the dental record and signet ring? Who did they really belong to?'

'Gaunt,' she said.

I glanced up at Desforge. 'Simple when you know how and no one would think to query the cause of death, not with the state those two bodies were in.'

He shook his head in bewilderment. 'One thing I don't understand—what happened to the emeralds?'

I told him about the package Gudrid had addressed to herself at Sandvig and he whistled softly. 'That must be just about the most ironic twist of all. Isn't this about the time when Simonsen should be taking a hand?'

'He's at a fishing village a hundred miles up the coast from here at the moment,' I said. 'Won't be back till tomorrow afternoon. In fact he's expecting me to pick him up.'

'And by that time you'll be long gone I suppose.'

'I expect so.'

I moved to the window and looked outside. The fog was thickening but the rain had slackened off considerably. When I turned, Ilana was standing a couple of feet away. Her eyes were unnaturally large and her skin seemed to have tightened over her cheekbones, ageing her considerably.

'Did you mean that?' she demanded. 'About clearing out before the storm breaks.'

'It would seem the sensible thing to do,' I said. 'If I stay, anything could happen after what I did.'

'Tell me something. If you'd kept quiet would anyone have known that Gaunt and Harrison had been shot to death?'

Desforge cut in quickly. 'She's got a point there, Joe. From what you told us those bodies must have been in a hell of a state.'

'Then why didn't you keep quiet?' she said. 'With any kind of luck you needn't have been involved at all.'

I'd been asking myself the same question for some time now without coming up with an answer that made any kind of sense. 'God knows,' I said. 'Maybe I have a death-wish or something or perhaps I just can't keep out of trouble.'

She smiled gently. 'You won't run, Joe. It's not in your nature—not any more.'

And she was right, I knew that the moment she said it. The days when I turned back on any part of life and simply walked away from it were in the past.

I grinned. 'All right, what do I do now? Sally forth into the night and capture Vogel and Stratton single-handed?'

Desforge went to the window and peered out. 'I wouldn't have thought there was much point. I mean where in the hell can they go in a pea-souper like this.'

He was right, of course. There was simply no way out until the weather cleared and at sea that schooner of Da Gama's wouldn't last half a day with the Danish Navy corvette that had been doing coastal survey work out of Godthaab on its tail. I suddenly realized that the whole thing was as good as over. Vogel and Stratton didn't stand a chance, hadn't from the moment Arnie had been murdered. That had really been a very stupid thing to do. Surprising really, for someone like Vogel, but on the other hand a man was only as good as the people who worked for him.

'What are you going to do about Arnie?' Ilana said.

I shrugged. 'There isn't much we can do, is there? Better to leave things exactly as they are for Simonsen to see tomorrow. I think that's what he'd want.'

There was a knock on the door and when I opened it, Gudrid was standing there.

Her face was blotched and swollen with weeping, but otherwise she seemed to be in control of herself.

'Mr. Martin, I wonder if you'd do me a great favour?'

'If I can.'

'I'd like to charter your plane. Could you fly me down to Sandvig first thing in the morning? I want to get away from here—right away.'

'Olaf Simonsen might not be too happy about that when he gets back tomorrow afternoon,' I said.

'If he wants me, he can come to Sandvig for me.' She clutched my arm. 'Please, Mr. Martin.'

I nodded slowly. 'All right, Gudrid, but it all depends on the weather, remember. You'd better pray for the fog to lift.'

'Thank you, Mr. Martin.' There was real relief on her face as she moved to the door and then she hesitated and turned slowly. 'What was in the package Arnie gave me, Mr. Martin?'

'Emeralds, Gudrid,' I said. 'A fortune in emeralds. He would have been rich beyond his wildest dreams. Enough to go to anyone's head.'

'And that's why he was murdered.' I nodded. 'Do you know who did it?'

'That's for the police to decide. Let's say we have a fair idea. Why do you ask?'

'It doesn't matter,' she said calmly. 'After all, nothing can bring him back now, can it?'

I watched her go and swallowed hard. Another of those times when I could have done with a drink. As I turned, Sarah Kelso got up wearily. Her eyes had sunk into their sockets, her face was pinched and drawn. I remembered the supremely beautiful woman I'd met only three nights ago and could detect not the slightest resemblance.

'If no one has any objection, I think I'd like to go to bed,' she said.

Desforge looked at me, compassion in his eyes. 'Let her go, Joe. After all, where can she run to?'

Which was true enough and I nodded without speaking. She went out, closing the door softly behind her.

'And now what?' Desforge said.

I suddenly realized I was hungry and glanced at my watch. It was just after ten. 'Still time for a late dinner if anyone feels like joining me?'

'And that's the best idea yet,' Desforge said. 'Just give me time to change,' and he went into the bedroom.

I turned to Ilana and held out my hands. She hesitated before taking them. 'What's this for?'

'I just wanted to thank you,' I said, 'for straightening me out.'

'Oh, that!' she smiled faintly. 'I wonder if you'll feel the same way when the court has finished with you.'

'Very civilized people the Danes,' I said. 'Finest prisons in the world, or didn't you know?'

'I always thought that was Sweden.'

'Now you've got me worried.' I pulled her into my arms and kissed her.

In view of the circumstances it may sound macabre to say that I ate a hearty meal, but the truth was that I'd only had a sandwich since flying in from Sandvig that morning. Desforge wasn't far behind me, but Ilana contented herself with coffee and watched us eat.

We sat in the bar for an hour afterwards and I made do with cigarettes and more coffee while Desforge consumed his usual quantity of alcohol. At one stage in the conversation he suddenly pointed out that by flying Gudrid down to Sandvig I'd be able to return with the emeralds, which for some reason hadn't occurred to me before. Beyond that, we didn't really discuss what had happened, but it was there just the same beneath the surface of things and our general conversation was disjointed and without any real pattern to it.

It was half past eleven when we went upstairs. I asked Ilana to check on Sarah Kelso and Desforge and I went on to his room. Ilana joined us within a couple of minutes.

'She's sleeping, which seems the sensible thing to do. It's been a long and interesting day so I think I'll turn in. I'll see you in the morning.'

Desforge was pouring himself a drink, his back to us and she looked up at me very deliberately as if waiting for something. I did the only thing I could think of which was to put an arm around her and walk her to the door. I kissed her briefly. She had expected more, so much was obvious and I couldn't imagine what it might be. There was something close to disappointment in her eyes when she went out.

I turned and found Desforge looking at me gravely. 'You want to watch yourself there, Joe,' he said. 'The hooks are out.'

'You think so?'

'I know so. I've seen it all before. Why waste your time?'

There was a kind of malice underlying what he had said, an edge of viciousness that wasn't really necessary. It was almost as if he hated her now and in view of her father's attitude towards financing the picture, that might well be true. Or perhaps he simply resented her going elsewhere? The old lion still trying to hang on to what was his.

I didn't pursue it and he let it drop and suggested a hand of cards. We played poker, blackjack, a few hands of whist and ended up with a diabolical little game called Slippery Sam that I hadn't played since my navy days. He took a little over two hundred dollars off me and by three-thirty I'd had enough.

I left him and went along to my bedroom. I didn't feel tired and I flung myself on the bed and stared up at the ceiling, thinking about it all.

A moment later Desforge came in. 'She's gone,' he said simply. 'Sarah Kelso?'

He nodded. 'I've just looked in.'

His reasons were pretty obvious, but that didn't concern me now and I swung my feet to the floor and got up. 'Have you checked with Ilana?'

'First place I looked, but there's no sign of her there. Ilana's getting dressed. She'll be here in a minute.'

I left him there and went along the corridor and knocked on Gudrid's door. When she opened it I saw, with some surprise, that she was still dressed.

'Oh, it's you, Mr. Martin.' She nodded towards a couple of suitcases on the bed. 'I couldn't sleep so I've been packing.'

'I want you to do something for me,' I said. 'Mrs. Kelso seems to have disappeared. Check with the rest of the night staff. See what you can find out without making too much of a fuss.'

She nodded breathlessly, her face white and excited, and I left her there, went down the back stairs and let myself out of the yard door. The hotel had two Landrovers which were kept in a garage across the yard. One was obviously in use so I took the other and drove away as quickly as the fog would allow.

The road down to the harbour was deserted and when I reached the canning factory I parked the Landrover and went the rest of the way to the jetty on foot. I was wasting my time, of course. Incredible as it seemed in view of the weather conditions, Da Gama's schooner had disappeared as completely as if it had never existed.

It was just after four as I drove back into the yard at the rear of the hotel and already dawn was seeping through the curtain of fog so that I could see the outlines of buildings clearly.

When I went up to Desforge's room, I found Gudrid and Ilana waiting for me, Desforge pacing up and down restlessly, the inevitable glass in his hand.

He swung round as I walked in. 'Where in the hell have you been?'

'Down to the jetty to check on that schooner of Da Gama's. It's gone, taking them all with it presumably. They must be raving mad. There are icebergs all over the place out there.'

'You've got it all wrong, Joe,' Desforge said. 'You'd better sit down and hear what Gudrid has to say.'

'I had a word with the night clerk,' Gudrid began. 'It seems Mrs. Kelso had a telephone call at eleven o'clock. The girl says it was a man and the conversation was in English. Later, Mrs. Kelso phoned down and asked if there was a map available covering the area of the Frederiksborg-Sandvig road. One was sent up to her.'

'Anything else?'

'Yes, the night porter was putting out kitchen refuse just before midnight when he saw Mr. Vogel and Mr. Stratton come into the yard with a third man he didn't know. They took one of the Landrovers from the garage, but he didn't think anything of that as they are hired out regularly to hotel guests. As he was going back into the kitchen, Mrs. Kelso came out of the back door and joined them. He said that Mr. Vogel kissed her, then they all got into the Landrover and drove away together.'

'She's certainly an expert at changing sides,' Ilana said bitterly.

'Still think they've gone off on the schooner, Joe?' Desforge demanded.

'No, I suppose it's pretty obvious what they're up to,' I said. 'They can reach Sandvig by road in six hours. I know that because I've done it myself. In fact, with luck on their side, they could be there by five or five-thirty.'

'Is there a telephone?' Ilana asked.

Gudrid shook her head. 'There's a radio at the trading post, but the factor doesn't live on the premises. He has a farm up on the hill. He opens the post at eight a.m. We could send a message then.'

'About three hours too late,' Desforge said.

Ilana frowned in bewilderment. 'But the whole thing is so pointless, can't they see that? Where on earth do they go from Sandvig?'

Which was exactly what I'd been thinking myself and there seemed to be only one obvious solution. 'They've probably arranged a rendezvous with the schooner.'

'But what if it doesn't make it?' Desforge said. 'You said yourself they must be insane to take her out in this fog.'

'At this stage in the game they don't have much option. And

there's always another possibility. The airport at Narssarssuaq. That's only a couple of hours from Sandvig by motorboat and plenty of fishermen to take them if the price was right. They could have their pick of flights to Europe via Iceland or the other way to Canada or the States.'

'So—it looks as if nothing can stop them.'

I shook my head and what I said next shocked even me. 'That isn't quite true. I could be at Sandvig in forty minutes in the Otter remember.'

'In this fog?' Desforge laughed abruptly. 'Who are you trying to kid. You can't see more than twenty yards in front of you. You wouldn't even get off the water.'

'Taking off isn't the problem. It's landing at the other end that I don't fancy. I don't know whether you noticed, but one side of Sandvig fjord consists of a thousand-foot wall of rock.'

Desforge shook his head. 'Listen, Joe, I've got a licence—I can fly myself. God knows, I've done enough of it in pictures, but a flight like that is strictly for a nice big studio mock-up with the wind machines howling and the cameras just out there beyond the smoke. People don't do things like that in real life.'

That's all it took. Looking back now, I wonder if he was simply being extremely clever and goading me to do what I'd never seriously intended. If so, he succeeded admirably. I don't know what came over me, but I was suddenly seized by an excitement so intense that it was impossible to handle.

As if he sensed what I was thinking, he said gently, 'You'd never make it Joe.'

'You're probably right,' I said. 'But I know one thing. I'm going to have a damned good try.'

Ilana's face was pale, her eyes burning, but I had the door open and was away before she could say anything.

I went to my room and changed into flying gear. By the time I was ready to go some of my initial enthusiasm had evaporated, that was true, but I hadn't changed my mind, and gripped by a strange fatalism I went down the back stairs and crossed the yard to the garage.

I dropped my bag into the rear of the Landrover and paused. Gudrid's two suitcases were already in and Desforge's Winchester in its worn case. I turned and the three of them stepped out of the shadows.

'Rotten morning,' Desforge said brightly,

'What exactly do you think you're playing at?' I demanded.
Desforge seemed to give the matter due consideration.

'Let's just say we're tired of the tedium of everyday life.'

'You must be raving mad, all of you,' I began and Ilana simply
brushed past me and climbed into the Landrover.

I borrowed a dinghy with an outboard motor and checked my
run from the end of the slipway out there into the fjord. It was
all clear and when I returned, Desforge had the engine warming
up for me.

I strapped myself into the pilot's seat and turned to look at the
two girls.

'Better close your eyes tight. This is going to be pretty hair-
raising.'

That was the understatement of the age. To plunge headlong
into that grey wall was probably the most psychologically terrifying thing I'd ever done in my life, but I held on, giving her full
throttle, lifting her at the earliest possible moment.

Twenty seconds later we climbed out of the fog and turned
south.

It was certainly a spectacular flight. The fog covered the sea
below like smoke in a valley, and to the east the peaks of the
coastal range pushed through it majestically, an unforgettable
sight.

'It doesn't look too good, does it?' Desforge said and strangely
enough there was a smile on his face and his eyes sparkled.

'It's what things are like at Sandvig that matters,' I told him
grimly.

'Worried?' There was a kind of challenge in his voice.

'To be absolutely precise, frightened to death. If conditions are
anything like this at the other end, you'd all better start praying.'

Gudrid turned pale and gripped the arm of her seat tightly.
Ilana offered her a cigarette and said brightly, 'He also likes to
pull the wings off flies.'

'Thanks for the vote of confidence,' I said and concentrated on
my flying.

There was a kind of perverse comfort in having managed to
transfer a little of my own fear on to someone else and for the
next half hour I simply sat there, trimming the controls when
necessary in a sort of reflex action, thinking about the whole
strange business.

From Vogel's point of view, the strength of his plan had been its essential simplicity, but that had also constituted its greatest weakness. A few careful steps across the tightrope and he would have been home and dry. Unfortunately for him there were two things he hadn't reckoned with—my own existence and Sarah Kelso's treachery.

Which made me think of Arnie and for a moment I saw him again, lying there behind the couch, blood on the wall. The most stupid and senseless part of the whole affair. Poor Arnie. What was it he had said? *Take whatever is going because you can never count on tomorrow.* Perhaps he'd had something there after all.

I came back to myself with a start as Desforge gripped my arm and when I looked down, I could see the fog ending abruptly as if someone had sliced it neatly across with a knife and we flew into heavy drenching rain, the sea clear beyond.

From then on the whole thing was a bit of an anti-climax. Certainly visibility in the fjord when we reached it was considerably reduced by the heavy rain, and a tracer of mist obscured Rasmussen's farm up on the hill, but the landing presented no difficulty at all.

I swung in a wide circle, chose a course parallel with the great rock face on the other side of the fjord and two hundred yards away from it, and put the Otter down.

CHAPTER SEVENTEEN

'SO, HERE WE ARE THEN,' I said as we drifted to a halt.

I could have sworn there was an expression of disappointment on Desforge's face, but he forced a grin. 'Rotten third act, Joe. Anti-climax.'

I turned and glanced at the women. 'Okay back there?'

Gudrid had colour in her cheeks again and Ilana smiled, 'As ever was.'

I started to light a cigarette and Desforge held up his hand. 'I thought I heard something.'

I opened the window and rain drifted in and we sat there in silence, the only noise the occasional slap of a small wave against the floats. Desforge told Ilana to pass him the Winchester and he started to unfasten the straps on the gun case as I leaned out of the window.

There was the muffled put-put of a small outboard motor somewhere near at hand and then a voice called in Danish and I relaxed. A small dinghy coasted out of the rain, Bergsson the trading post factor sitting in the stern. He cut the motor and drifted in beside the float.

He grinned up, his beard spangled with tiny beads of moisture. 'Morning, Joe, you're lucky. Half an hour ago the fjord was completely choked with fog, then the rain came in and cleared it all away.'

'It was pretty bad when we left Frederiksborg,' I said.

Gudrid leaned forward. 'Good morning, Mr. Bergsson. How is my grandfather?'

'Fine, Miss Rasmussen. I was with him last on the day before yesterday.'

He was obviously astonished to see her, but before he could carry on I said quickly, 'And not since then? Wasn't there some mail for him on the boat yesterday afternoon?'

'I wouldn't know,' he said. 'The boat was delayed by fog and didn't get in till late last night, so I haven't got around to sorting out the mail yet. It's still in the bag at the store.'

'That's fine,' I said. 'When you open up I think you'll find a package addressed to Gudrid care of her grandfather. We can save you a trip.'

'But I don't understand.' He was by now completely bewildered.

'You don't need to. Just turn the boat round and we'll follow you in.'

He gave up, shrugged and went back to the stern of his dinghy. While he busied himself starting the motor I gave Desforge and Ilana the substance of what had been said.

'What happens when you've got your hands on the sparklers?' Desforge asked.

'We'll borrow Bergsson's old jeep and ride up to Olaf Rasmussen's place and warn him what's in the offing. We should be able to provide some sort of reception committee for Vogel and his friends. Olaf usually has half a dozen Eskimo shepherds around the place and they can revert to the ways of their fore-fathers awfully fast if anyone starts baring his teeth at them.'

Gudrid shook her head. 'But my grandfather will be on his own at the moment, Mr. Martin, surely you haven't forgotten. At this time in the season the shepherds will be away in the hills searching out the sheep, preparing them for the drive down to the valley.' She turned to Ilana. 'Four more weeks—five at the most and winter begins and always so quickly that we are caught unawares.'

'All right, so we go up and get him out of there before they arrive.'

I started the engine and Desforge patted the barrel of the Winchester. 'I could certainly give them one hell of a surprise with this from the loft of that barn. Hell, they'd be sitting ducks when they drove into the farmyard.'

With a cigarette dangling from the corner of his mouth, the Winchester across his knees and the tousled hair falling across his forehead, the reckless gleam in his eyes, he looked too much like a still from one of his own pictures for comfort.

I said shortly, 'Don't be bloody stupid, Jack, we aren't on Stage 6 now. This is for real. People die, they don't just pick themselves up off the floor at the end and take a vacation till the next script comes along.'

He blazed with anger, hands tightening on the gun. 'I wasn't play-acting in the rear turret of that B29, you limey bastard. Thirty-one trips and then I got a slug through the thigh and that was for real. I got medals, baby. What did they ever give you?'

I could have said that I had medals too, whatever that proved, only in my case I'd been only too anxious to forget the whole stupid senseless business as soon as possible, but I didn't. There wouldn't have been any point. I don't even think he'd have understood what I was trying to say. I had a brief glimpse of Ilana's face out of the corner of my eye, shocked and for some inexplicable reason, frightened and I pushed up the throttle slowly and went after the dinghy.

The constraint between Desforge and myself overshadowed everything, diminishing even the excitement of the moment when Bergsson found the package in the mailbag and passed it to Gudrid. She tore off the outer wrapping and disclosed a cardboard shoebox carefully sealed with Scotch tape.

'This is exactly as it was when Arnie gave it to me,' she said.

I took out a clasp knife and cut round the lid quickly. It contained a grey canvas money belt, each separate pouch bulging. I opened one and spilled a couple of the uncut gems into the palm of my hand.

'So that's what they look like?' Desforge said.

I nodded. 'Before the experts get to work on them.' I replaced the stones in their pouch, buckled the belt around my waist and turned to Bergsson. 'Is it all right if we borrow your jeep?'

'Certainly.' He sensed that something unusual was going on, so much was obvious and added awkwardly, 'Look, if there's anything I can do.'

'I don't think so.'

Desforge broke in harshly. 'We're wasting time. Let's get out of here.'

He stalked outside and I paused at the door beside Ilana. 'What's eating him, for God's sake?'

She looked worried. 'I don't know—sometimes he gets like this, nervous and irrational, flaring up into a sudden rage at nothing at all. Perhaps he needs a drink.'

'More likely he's had too many for too long,' I said sourly and went outside.

Desforge was sitting at the wheel of the jeep, the rifle beside him and he glared up at me belligerently. 'Any objections?'

'Suit yourself.'

I climbed into the rear seat. Ilana hesitated, obviously torn between us, but Gudrid solved the problem by getting into the passenger seat beside Desforge.

'Well make your mind up,' he said irritably. 'Are you coming or aren't you?'

She didn't reply—just got into the rear seat beside me and stared straight in front of her, hands tightly clasped as we drove away.

The rain was lifting a little now, not too much, but increasing visibility to fifty yards or so as we followed the winding dirt road up the hill. The slope below us dropped steeply to the fjord and was covered by alder scrub with here and there clumps of willow and birch up to ten feet high. On the right-hand side Iceland poppies showed scarlet amongst lichen covered rocks and there were alpines and saxifrage—even buttercups, so that it might have been the Tyrol on a misty morning after rain.

Desforge was driving too fast considering the conditions, but I was damned if I was going to tell him that. I didn't get much of a chance anyway because when we were about half-way up the hill, the hotel Landrover came round a bend and rushed towards us at what seemed a terrifying speed in those conditions.

There was a moment when everything seemed to stop, the whole scene frozen like a still picture and then Desforge swung the wheel of the old jeep without even attempting to brake and took the left-hand side of the track as the Landrover skidded to a halt. There couldn't have been more than a foot in it as we went by and our off-side rear wheel spun wildly, seeking a grip on thin air.

The jeep dipped sideways, spilling me over the edge and I tucked my head into my shoulder and yelled as I hit the dirt and rolled down the slope through the scrub.

As I scrambled to my feet, the jeep roared like an angry lion and regained the road in a shower of dirt and gravel and Desforge braked to a halt. Behind him the Landrover was already reversing and Stratton stood up and grabbed the edge of the windscreen, an automatic ready in his hand.

He loosed off a wild shot and I shouted. 'For God's sake get moving. Get the women out of here. Make for the farm.'

Desforge had enough sense not to argue and the jeep vanished into the rain as the Landrover braked to a halt above me. Stratton shouted something, but I couldn't catch what it was and then he jumped for the slope, landing thirty or forty feet above me in a shower of stones, the automatic ready in his right hand. As the Landrover took off after the jeep, I turned and ran for my life, ploughing through the alder head-down as he fired twice.

Branches whipped against my face as I scrambled through a

grove of birches and then I stumbled and fell again, turning on my back and going down in the rain, riding a bank of scree in a long breathless slide that ended on a beach right at the edge of the fjord.

I picked myself up and staggered along the shingle, collapsing into the temporary safety of a horseshoe of black rocks. For a moment only as I lay there I might have been a twelve-year-old lying on a Scottish shore on some forgotten morning, my face against the pebbles. And these were the same as they are on most beaches the world over. Typical chalcedony. Translucent red carnelian, brown and red jasper, banded onyx and agate.

My fingers hooked into them and I lay there, hardly daring to breathe, listening for the sound of his pursuit, but there was nothing. Only the rustle of the wind as it moved down from the mountains pushing the rain before it and the quiet lapping of the water.

I waited five minutes and then moved along the shore to a point which was, as far as I could judge, directly beneath the farmhouse. I was pretty certain of my ground because at this point a great granite crag jutted from the hillside and I went up one side of it, making much faster time than I would had I stuck to the scrub.

At this height there was still some fog, but it was thinning rapidly now, swirling around me in strange, menacing shapes. My heart was pounding like a trip-hammer and there was blood in my mouth as I heaved myself over a shelf of rock and crouched on top of the crag. There was a grove of willow trees to the rear, the hillside lifting beyond to the south meadow below Rasmussen's farm.

I took a deep breath, pushed myself to my feet and started forward. At the same moment Stratton stood up from behind a boulder on the edge of the crag and said in a perfectly normal tone as if we were good friends who had somehow missed each other, 'Ah, there you are, old chap.'

As I started to turn he fired and the bullet shattered my wrist, the mark of a real pro who knows that a dying man might still be able to get a shot off at him, whereas a man with a broken wrist can't.

It's true what they say—when a bullet hits you, you don't feel any real pain, not at first. Only a sort of stunning blow delivered with the force of a blunt instrument swung by a rather large man, but the shock effect on the central nervous system is pretty considerable, driving the breath from your body like a kick in the belly.

I fell down, rolling on my face and fought for air. He stayed there at the edge, a slight fixed smile on his face. 'I've been watching you for quite some time actually. Remarkable view from up here, even allowing for the fog.' He shook his head. 'You shouldn't have joined, old chap.'

No shooting from the waist or any of that nonsense. His right hand swung up as he took deliberate aim and I screamed aloud, 'Don't be a fool, Stratton, I know where the emeralds are!'

He hesitated fractionally, lowering the automatic and I scrambled to one knee, my left hand clawing into the dirt. As I came up, I let him have a handful right in the face. He ducked, an arm swinging up instinctively, took a short step backwards and went over the edge.

CHAPTER EIGHTEEN

THE BONES of my wrist had fragmented, I could tell that by the way they grated together when I wound a handkerchief around it in an attempt to stop the bleeding. It still wasn't hurting, not yet. That would come later and I tucked my hand inside my flying jacket and scrambled up the hill.

As I went through the fence at the top and started across the south meadow, a shot echoed flatly through the fog and two more sounded in reply. I put my head down and ran, ducking behind the grey stone wall that was the northern boundary, keeping to its shelter until I came to the farm.

Another shot sounded from the open door of the loft in the barn and two more were fired in reply from the house. I hurried back the way I had come and the moment the farmhouse was out of sight scrambled over the wall and approached from the rear.

The yard by the back door was deserted, but by this time I wasn't caring too much anyway because my wrist was beginning to hurt like hell, the pain crawling up my arm like some living thing.

I ran across the yard, head-down, expecting a bullet in the back at any second, but nothing happened and then I was at the door and it opened to receive me.

I didn't stop running until I cannoned into the wall on the other side of the kitchen. Behind me, the door closed and a bolt was rammed home. When I turned, wiping sweat from my eyes with my left hand, Da Gama was standing facing me.

When I was pushed into the hall, I found Vogel crouched at the shattered window, a revolver in his hand, Sarah Kelso flattened against the wall beside him. Rasmussen lay on the table, eyes closed, blood on his head and Ilana and Gudrid were at his side.

Vogel looked me over calmly. 'What happened to Stratton?'

'He tried to get down to the beach the hard way. I wouldn't count on seeing him again if I were you."

Another bullet shattered the window and everyone hit the floor. I crawled over to Ilana and held out my wrist. 'Do what you can with this, will you? What happened here?'

She pulled a silk scarf from her neck and bound my wrist

tightly. 'When we got here Jack told us to get in the house. He said he was going to ambush them from the loft in the barn.'

'What went wrong?'

'They came in the back way. Stupid, but there it is.'

'This can't be his day for clear thinking,' I said. 'What about Rasmussen?'

'He tried to tackle Vogel and Da Gama hit him over the head with his gun.'

Two more bullets smashed through the window, one of them ploughing into the floor and Gudrid screamed. Vogel turned towards me, his back to the wall as he reloaded his revolver, a smear of blood on his cheek.

'I think we've had enough of this nonsense. Come here, Miss Eytan.' She hesitated and he nodded to Da Gama who flung her forward. Vogel caught her by the hair, wrenched back her head and touched the barrel of his revolver to her temple. 'Mr. Martin,' he said evenly. 'Go outside and tell Desforge I'll blow out his lady friend's brains if he doesn't come out of that barn within the next two minutes.'

I didn't even get a chance to think it over because Da Gama dragged me to my feet, opened the door and shoved me outside. I dropped to one knee and a bullet chipped the wall beside the doorpost. From then on he obviously recognized me and I stumbled across the yard shouting his name.

As I ran into the entrance of the barn, he appeared at the edge of the loft above my head and standing up there in his old parka, the Winchester ready for action, he wasn't Jack Desforge any more. He was that other, legendary figure who had always seemed so much larger than life. As he dropped to the floor and moved towards me, I had the strange illusion that this was somehow a scene we had played many times before.

And when he spoke, it might have been dialogue straight off page fifty-seven of some script that had been specially written for him—the kind of film he had made a score of times.

'You don't look too good, kid. What happened?'

I told him about Stratton. 'But that doesn't matter now. You've got to come in, Jack. Vogel swears he'll kill Ilana if you don't and I got a strong impression that he means it.'

He nodded briefly, a strange remote look in his eyes as if his mind was elsewhere. 'Okay, kid, if that's what you want. How do we know he won't pick us off on our way across the yard?'

'We find that out in next week's episode.'

'I can't wait that long.' He went out through the open door in three or four quick strides and dropped the Winchester on the ground. 'Okay, Vogel, you win.'

For one wild moment I expected to see him go down under a fusillade of bullets. He stood there for a while, hands on hips as if waiting for something, and then the door across the yard opened and Vogel came out pushing Ilana in front of him.

Sarah Kelso followed, Da Gama at her heels, but there was no sign of Gudrid who had presumably stayed with the old man. We all met in the middle of the yard in a kind of awkward silence.

Vogel spoke first. 'The emeralds, please, Mr. Martin.'

I hesitated and Desforge said, and it was as if he was somehow in command, 'Give them to him, Joe.'

I unstrapped the belt and tossed it across. Vogel hefted it in his hand, face quite calm. 'A long wait.'

Ilana moved suddenly to join Desforge and me and swung to face the Austrian, 'And what happens now, Mr. Vogel? Do we get what you gave Arnie Fassberg?'

Vogel smiled gently. 'My dear Miss Eytan, like most determined sinners, I'm quite prepared to carry the burden of my own misdeeds, but I certainly object to being made responsible for someone else's. I don't know who killed the unfortunate Mr. Fassberg, but it certainly wasn't me or any of my associates.'

There was no reason for him to lie, none at all and Ilana turned and stared at me blankly. 'But who, Joe? Who else could it have been?'

'Only one person I can think of,' I said. 'The person who told him about the emeralds in the first place.'

Sarah Kelso seemed to shrink visibly, the skin tightening across her cheeks, a hand going to her mouth involuntarily as she took a hurried step backwards. 'Oh, no—never in a thousand years.'

'But it had to be you,' I said. 'There is no one else.'

For a long moment she seemed to be struck dumb and it was Desforge who spoke, his voice quiet and calm and very, very tired.

'Sure there was, kid, there was me. She found that letter at the Fredericsmut, remember? The one from Milt Gold. She knew I'd reached the end of the line. The night you came back from the ice-cap, the night she was really certain for the first time that Arnie had made a fool of her, she brought me out here to the barn. I though it was just for a tumble in the hay, but there was more to it than that—a lot more. If I could squeeze the emeralds out of Arnie we could split them fifty-fifty and clear out in my boat.'

God knows why, but it was as if I had known all along and my voice when I spoke, seemed to belong to someone else.

'Why did you kill him?'

'I didn't mean to. I knew he couldn't very well go running to the police. I was going to give him something to keep him happy. I was holding him with his own shotgun and he tried to jump me. It was as simple as that.'

Sarah Kelso shook her head.

'But it isn't possible.'

Desforge shrugged. 'What she's trying to tell you is that we were in bed together when it happened.'

'That was certainly my impression,' I said.

He turned to Sarah Kelso. 'Sorry, angel, but I left you for an hour. That's all it took. You were sleeping like a baby.'

'You fool,' I said. 'You stupid bloody fool. Now what happens? What *can* happen?'

'Christ knows, it's a mess.' He shook his head. 'I never thought it would end up like this. In the beginning it seemed like a good idea. I was desperate. There was nothing left, Joe. That letter from Milt was a death sentence. There was a court order out on my property in California against back taxes and the picture deal had fallen through. I was finished. Have you any idea what that meant? There was nothing to come. There was never going to be another picture.'

It was as if he was talking for me alone, as if I was the only person there and in a strange way I understood what he was trying to say. He wasn't making excuses—he was just trying to get me to understand. All his life he'd inhabited the fantasy world, living a series of incredible adventures each contained in its own watertight compartment and as one finished, another began. If you made a mistake the director shouted *Cut* and you tried it again. Nothing was for real—nothing was ever for real and suddenly, I realized what he must have felt like after killing Arnie, standing there with the noise of the shotgun still ringing in his ears, looking down on his handiwork and realizing with horror that this was permanent, this was something that couldn't be adjusted ever.

Ilana stared at him mutely, a kind of dazed incomprehension in her eyes. He ignored her and said to Vogel, 'It seems to me you and I have something in common after all. How were you hoping to get away from here? By rendezvousing with Da Gama's schooner?'

Vogel shook his head. 'You're wasting your time, I've no room for passengers.'

'You're living in cloud-cuckoo land. Tell him, Joe.'

I nodded. 'He's right. Even if the schooner makes it in one piece, there's a Danish corvette doing coastal survey work out of Godthaab that could run you down in half a day.'

Vogel turned back to Desforge, a slight frown on his face. 'You have something else on your mind or you would not have raised the matter.'

Desforge lit a cigarette. 'There's always the Otter down there in the fjord.'

For the first time Vogel's iron composure cracked and he clutched at what was, after all, the only real hope of extricating himself from what was otherwise an impossible situation.

'You can fly?'

'Not like laughing boy here, but good enough for short hauls. Newfoundland, for instance.'

'We could reach Newfoundland?'

'Easily with what's in the tank now. Plenty of remote fishing villages where we could put down and pick up enough gas to continue. We could make somewhere like Maine for our second landing. I'm willing to take my chances after that. America is a big country. Of course I'd expect a cut in the emeralds. Fifty per cent would seem to be about right.'

I could almost see Vogel's brain working as he decided that he could handle that one at the right time and place. 'Agreed. Is there anything else?'

Desforge held out his hand. 'I think I'd like to look after the bank if you don't mind. After all, you and bully boy here seem to be carrying all the artillery.'

Vogel hesitated fractionally and probably decided there was no harm in humouring him. He tossed the belt across. Desforge folded it neatly and stuffed it inside his parka.

'Another thing, no more trouble.' He nodded towards Da Gama. 'I don't want Frankenstein there cutting loose on my friends or anything like that. Now tell him to get the Landrover.'

'Just as you say, Mr. Desforge.'

Ilana turned and hurried away and he had to run to catch her at the door. She started to struggle and he held her very firmly and then she seemed to go limp and sagged against the wall. He had his back to us, hiding her from view and it was impossible to hear what he said, but when Da Gama drove the Landrover into the yard, he turned and came back towards us and I saw that Ilana was crying bitterly.

As Desforge approached, I moved into his path. 'You're kidding yourself,' I said. 'Even if our friend here doesn't put a bullet through your head at the appropriate time, where on this earth can Jack Desforge hope to hide and not be recognized?'

He laughed. 'You've got a point there, kid, but there must be somewhere. I'll have to think about it.'

As Vogel climbed into the Landrover, Sarah Kelso said something to him in a low voice. He pushed her away angrily. 'You've made your bed—now lie on it.'

She turned on Desforge, desperation on her face. 'For God's sake, Jack, if I ever meant anything to you, take me with you. He says I can't go.'

Desforge laughed incredulously. 'You've got your nerve, angel, I'll say that for you. Go on, get in! I'd say we just about deserve each other.'

He turned to me and smiled sombrely.

'Strange how things work out. Have you ever wondered how many changes you'd make in your life if you could do the whole thing over again?'

'Often,' I said.

'Me too.' He nodded. 'But I'd only need to make one. Remember the pier at Santa Barbara in the fog when I met Lilian Courtney for the first time? I should have turned and run like hell.'

It was an interesting thought, but there was no time to take it any further. He got into the passenger seat beside Da Gama and turned and looked at me for the last time. For a second, there was something there, an unspoken message that I couldn't hope to understand and he smiled that famous smile of his, sardonic and bitter, touching something deep inside me, the old indefinable magic that had moved millions of people through the years in exactly the same way.

And then he was gone, the Landrover disappearing into the rain with a roar. When I turned, Ilana had sunk down on her knees beside the door, leaning against the wall, crying steadily.

I went forward and took her by the elbow. Her sheepskin coat was unbuttoned for some reason and as I pulled her up, it opened and the money belt fell to the ground.

I stared down at it in stupefaction, then picked it up awkwardly with my left hand. 'What's this?' I said hoarsely.

'The emeralds,' she said. 'Don't you understand? He slipped them under my coat when he was saying goodbye.'

Perhaps I had lost more blood than I realized or maybe I was moving into shock, but suddenly nothing seemed to make too much sense any more.

I shook my head as if to clear my sight and said carefully, 'But why would he do that? What on earth could he hope to accomplish?'

And then it hit me with the force of a thunderbolt, and I realized what his eyes had been trying to say in those last moments before the Landrover had driven away into the fog. When I looked up, Ilana was staring at me in horror as if she too had suddenly discovered the only possible explanation.

She shook her head dumbly and I pushed the belt inside my flying jacket and grabbed her arm. 'The jeep—where is it?'

'Somewhere behind the barn.'

I turned and ran and heard her call through the rain. 'Don't leave me, Joe! Don't leave me!' There was panic in her voice.

I found the jeep, just as she had said, but with one difference. It was standing in a lake of petrol, a bullet hole in the tank, and I turned, ignoring her desperate cry, scrambled over the wall and ran through the meadow.

I was wasting my time. I suppose I knew that from the start, and yet nothing in this world could have stopped me. I clambered over the fence at the bottom of the meadow and as I went down the slope through the willow trees, the engine of the Otter coughed angrily in the rain below and roared into life.

As I reached the top of the crag, the Otter roared down the fjord, the engine note deepening so that I knew she was lifting off. There was a sudden crashing through the trees behind me as Ilana arrived and at the same moment, a wind coming down from the ice-cap swept the rain to one side like a giant curtain and I saw the Otter for the last time, five hundred feet up and climbing into the morning.

And then she turned, as I knew she would, and came back across the fjord, heading straight for that great wall of stone and going like a bomb.

God knows what happened in that cabin during those last few minutes. I suppose Vogel must have emptied his gun into him, but he held her on the course of his own choosing, straight and true, Jack Desforge, that magnificent, wonderful bastard going out as he had lived in a blaze of glory.

The explosion echoed between the hills as a ball of fire erupted against the side of the mountain and then mercifully the wind died and the curtain of rain dropped back into place.

I think that at that moment I could have sat down and wept for him and for the cruel, senseless waste of it all, but there was no time for that now. Ilana stood staring into the void, then turned and stumbled towards me, tears streaming down her face. I pulled her against my chest and stroked her hair with my one good hand.

'Why did he do it, Joe? Why?' she said brokenly.

I could have given her the obvious answer. That he was tired, that he'd had enough, that he knew, as I had told him, that there was no place on earth for him to hide, but I could do better for him than that.

'To save us,' I said. 'He agreed to fly Vogel out to save us and for no other reason. But somewhere along the line he was going to get a bullet in the head, he knew that. He decided to take them with him, that's all. There isn't a newspaper or magazine in the world that won't swallow that hook line and sinker. They'll believe it because they want to believe it.'

'And Arnie? What about Anie?'

'Vogel and Stratton killed Arnie,' I said patiently. 'I thought you knew that.'

She stood there staring at me, a hand to her mouth and I patted her on the shoulder and said gently, 'Now go back to the farmhouse like a good girl. I'll be along later.' She hesitated and I gave her a push. 'Go on.'

She stared up through the grove and I watched her go. She paused at the edge of the trees and turned. 'You won't leave me, Joe?'

'No, I won't leave you, Ilana.'

I waited till she had gone then scrambled over the edge of the crag and slowly and painfully made my way down to the beach. Whichever way you looked at it, it was ironic. By this time next year somebody would probably be sinking a million or so into a film of it all. I wondered who they'd get to play me and suddenly the whole thing seemed so ludicrous that I started to laugh and the sound of it echoed back across the water as if Desforge was laughing with me.

I found the horseshoe of black rocks on the beach where I had hidden from Stratton earlier, with no difficulty and slumped down wearily. What happened to me now didn't seem to matter. After all, what could they do? Probably a deportation order and maybe I'd lose my licence, but both these things seemed relatively trivial.

One thing was certain. Nothing must be allowed to diminish the magnificence of that final sacrifice. I took the money belt from inside my flying jacket, opened the pouches one by one and emptied them of the pebbles they contained.

The emeralds were where I had left them in a little pile under a flat stone. Slowly and with great difficulty because I could only use my left hand, I started to replace them.